Christmas in Honeywell

ROSEMARY WHITTAKER

Also by Rosemary Whittaker

A Sugarloaf Valentine
A Sugarloaf Mix-Up
A Sugarloaf Surprise
A Sugarloaf Christmas
A Sugarloaf Easter
A Sugarloaf Secret
A Sugarloaf Summer
A Sugarloaf Appeal
A Sugarloaf Adventure
The Cinnamon Snail
Sunshine State
The Wattle Birds
The Feijoa Tree
The Villa Mimosa
Making The Effort

Stopwatch Publications

First printing in this edition, 2025

ISBN-13: 978-1-922651-73-0

Published by Rosemary Whittaker
www.rosemarywhittaker.com

Cover designs by 100 Covers.

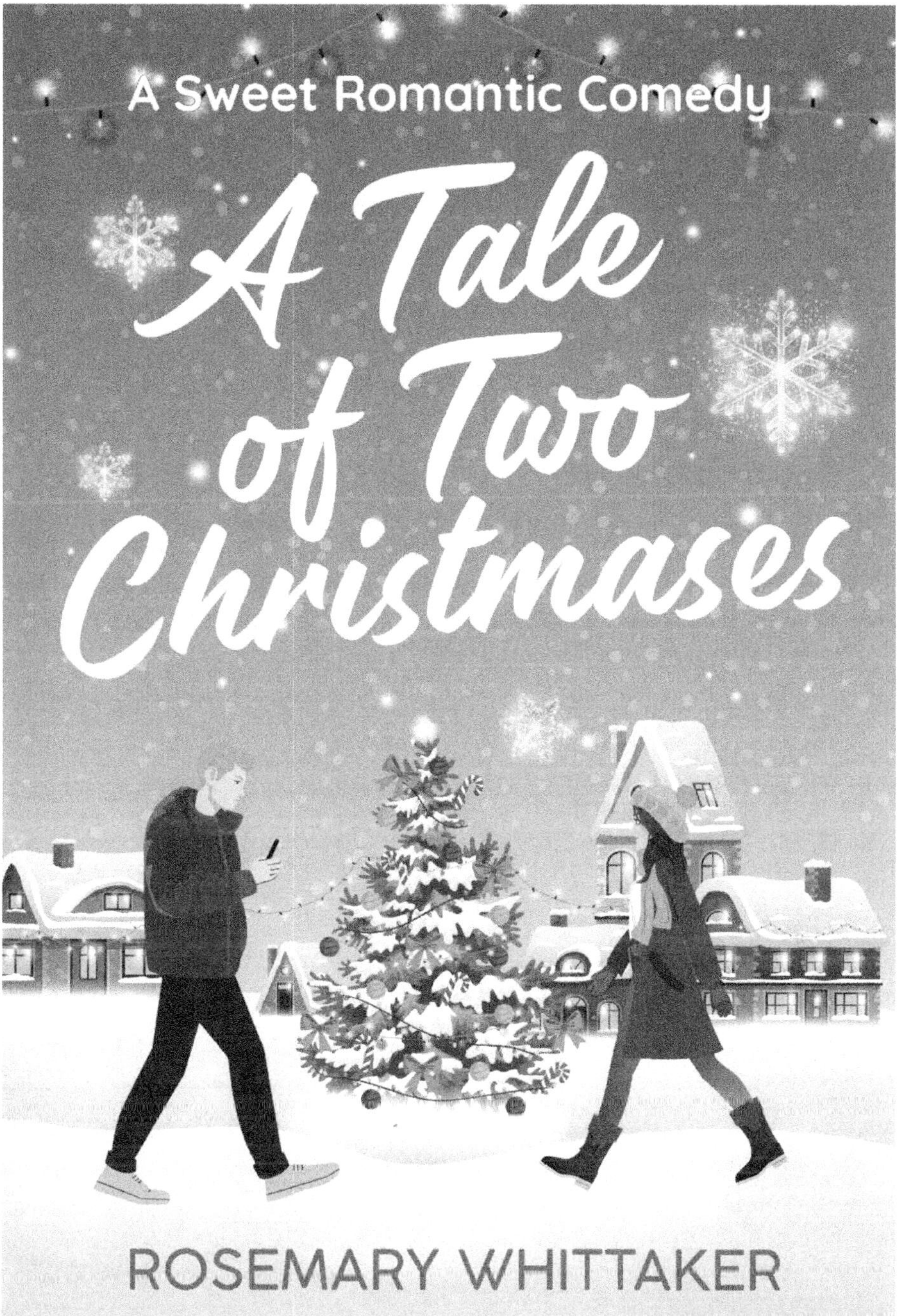
A Sweet Romantic Comedy
A Tale of Two Christmases
ROSEMARY WHITTAKER

Prologue

This Christmas

Prologue

My train is leaving at half past ten, which means I have less than fifteen minutes.

I lean forward to speak to the taxi driver. 'Can you possibly go any faster? I don't want to miss my train.'

He grins at me in the mirror. 'If I go any faster, I'll hit the van in front of me. Relax, love, I'll get you there on time.'

I look out of the window, trying not to think about the traffic jam. Oxford Street is full of Christmas shoppers, clutching brightly coloured bags and battling against the wind. I'm glad I did my shopping early. I usually leave it until the last moment, but I thought I'd better get myself organised this year.

Mum has insisted that I come home for Christmas, despite all my protestations.

'I'm not taking no for an answer,' she said when she called a few weeks ago. 'You're coming home this year if I have to come and get you myself.'

I wanted to argue, but there was no point. She's perfectly capable of arriving on my doorstep and camping out until she gets her way.

'I'm working until Christmas Eve,' I said.

'No, you aren't! I called your office, and the very nice girl on reception said the office is closed for the entire Christmas week.'

'How many times have I told you not to call my office?' I said through gritted teeth.

I was surprised when she gave what sounded suspiciously like a sob. 'Mum, what's wrong?'

She sniffed. 'It's Jamie.'

'What about him?' I said, alarmed. My brother and I don't see each other often, but I'm still very fond of him.

'He's emigrating!'

'Emigrating? That doesn't sound likely. What about Melissa?'

She gave another tragic sniff. 'She's going too. Apparently, it was all her idea. They're moving to America in the new year, and I'll never see him again.'

'Don't be ridiculous. Have you never heard of plane flights?'

'I'm not being ridiculous,' she said in an offended tone. 'This will probably be the last Christmas we ever spend together as a family. You absolutely have to come home.'

I wavered. 'Even if our office is closed, I'll still have a lot of work to do.'

'That's settled,' she said briskly. 'Dad and I will expect you home on the twenty-second.'

I made one final attempt. 'I could just come down for Christmas Day.'

'No, you couldn't. I want us all together for as long as possible.'

She sounded close to tears again. 'You aren't a mother yet, Annie, so you couldn't possibly understand how it feels to be faced with the prospect of never seeing your baby boy again.'

Jamie is twenty-six and left home more than a year ago to move in with Melissa. To hear Mum tell it, you'd think he was eight and going on his first sleepover with a friend.

'Fine,' I said. 'I'll come home if it means so much to you.'

I expected her to give a shriek of delight or at least sound pleased. But she just said, 'That's settled, then. I'll call you nearer the time to finalise the arrangements.' And she rang off, leaving me wondering what had just happened.

Anyway, she's got what she wanted. I'm coming home, and she can have her big schmaltzy Christmas before Jamie disappears into the depths of the United States, never to be seen again. I think Mum imagines her baby boy will be engaging in daily shoot outs with the mafia. Actually, Jamie and Melissa are moving to Florida, so she probably imagines him wrestling alligators.

I hope we aren't going to spend Christmas with her in tears, trying to persuade Jamie to change his mind and find himself a nice new girlfriend who never wants to leave the country. That wouldn't go down too well with Jamie, and I don't blame him. It's an unexpected move, but good for him. Why not do it while he's young and childfree?

But I'd better not say that to Mum. The idea of any future grandchildren being born abroad would just about finish her off. And I don't fancy becoming the focus of her grandmotherly attention. It's bad enough that she asks me every time we speak whether I'm seeing anyone. I don't want her delicately inquiring about my reproductive health and suggesting I find myself a good gynaecologist 'just in case.'

'We're here!' The driver's voice breaks into my reverie.

I jump out and grab my bags. 'Thanks so much! I really thought I was going to miss it.'

'I've been driving this cab for nearly forty years,' he says. 'I've never let anyone miss their train.'

I pay and add a generous tip. 'I'm sorry I doubted you. Happy Christmas!'

'And to you.'

He waves and drives away to pick up another passenger travelling reluctantly home for the holidays. I remember that some people actually want to go home for Christmas. In fact, they've probably been looking forward to it for months.

It isn't that I don't want to see my family. Of course, I do. If Jamie's leaving for America soon, I want to be there to support Mum and Dad. And it will be lovely to see them. It's just that I wish they lived anywhere but Honeywell.

I race across the concourse to my platform. I jump onto the train just as it's about to leave. The guard shakes his head disapprovingly at me, but I can't help that.

I drag my suitcase along the carriages and find my seat just as the train pulls away from the station. I settle back and close my eyes. It's only for a week, I tell myself. I can manage a week back home for Mum's sake. There's no reason for me to go to parties and meet anyone I don't want to.

I've promised myself several long walks in the countryside. That's something I miss in London. We have the parks, but I'm looking forward to taking some of my old walks in the New Forest again.

I open my eyes and watch the buildings slide past and disappear behind us. The sun has come out now, and I enjoy the sparkling frost on the fields as we get further from the city. I take a deep breath and relax. It's Christmas, and I should enjoy it.

The drinks trolley comes by. I buy a hot chocolate and sip it, trying to get myself into a festive mood before I arrive. I'm not sure what state I'll find Mum in, but I need to be prepared for anything. She may be bustling around as usual, doing her Christmas baking and talking nineteen to the dozen about people I've never met. On the other hand, she may be draped in widow's black and sobbing in the corner of the room. There's no real way of guessing.

My phone pings. I almost don't look at it. It's probably someone from the office with a last-minute emergency I won't be able to do anything about. It will only stress me while I'm trying to get myself into a cheerful holiday mood.

But curiosity gets the better of me. I open my phone and look at the screen.

It's from Mum. *Hi, darling. Did you manage to catch the earlier train?*

I text back. *Bit of a rush, but I made it. I should be home around twelve thirty.*

Just in time for lunch! she texts. *Oh, by the way, did I mention that Alex Fielding is home for Christmas?*

I stare at the screen, my mouth dry. How is that possible? I checked before booking my ticket that there was no possibility of running into him this week.

No, you didn't, I type.

It takes her a little while to reply. She isn't terribly quick at texting, and she always insists on full sentences and proper punctuation. Her texts sound just the way she speaks.

Didn't I? I was sure I had. Yes, he came home yesterday. Elaine and Robert are delighted, of course. I'll tell you all about it when you get here. Have a safe trip. See you soon.

I put my phone back in my pocket. I should have gone with my first instinct and ignored it. All my new-found Christmas cheer has disappeared. If I was driving, I'd turn the car around and go straight back home. But I doubt I'll be able to persuade the train driver to switch tracks and go back to London. It looks as though I'm stuck with it.

Why did I allow Mum to talk me into coming home? I should have left her to deal with Jamie all by herself. It's really nothing to do with me.

And now I'll be stuck in Honeywell for an entire week, unless I can think of a plausible excuse to go home early. I wonder whether Mum would accept the bubonic plague as a reason for me to leave. Probably not.

I won't even be able to walk around the village now in case I bump into Alex. It ought to be the other way around. He's the one who should be avoiding me. It's only common courtesy. But I'm sure that wouldn't even occur to him. He'll probably suggest going for a coffee or something if he sees me. I'll just have to make sure he doesn't.

I didn't even want to come home for Christmas. It just felt like the right thing to do. Obviously, no good deed goes unpunished. I close my eyes, trying not to think about the events of two years ago. I usually avoid thinking about Alex. But this time, I can't. Mum's text has put him front and centre. There's no way I'll be able to avoid him entirely this week. At least, not without Mum suspecting the truth. And she's the last person I want interfering in my life and asking questions.

I open my bag and pull out a bar of chocolate. I don't care if I spoil my lunch. I need something to distract me from the week ahead. I break off a piece and cram it into my mouth. But I barely taste it. All I can think about is the fact that after two whole years, I'm about to come face-to-face with Alex Fielding.

Two Years Ago

Chapter One

We're having lunch towards the end of my summer holidays when Mum looks up from her steak. 'The Reverend Martin is looking for volunteers to paint the church hall.'

'Outside or inside?' asks Dad.

'Inside, of course! He'll have to get professionals to do the outside. He won't be insured for people clambering about all over the roof.'

'I can probably help,' I say. 'When does it need to be done? I'm only home for three more days.'

Mum helps herself to more potato. 'He says he'll be making a start this afternoon. I don't think he's too optimistic about getting any helpers.'

'I'll give Suzy a call,' I say. 'It will do her good to do some work for once. Even if she can't come, I'll go along after lunch. I quite enjoy painting.'

'I don't think it's the sort of painting you do at university,' says Mum.

'I don't do any sort of painting,' I remind her. 'I'm studying graphic design.'

'But it's all the same thing,' she says.

'Not unless the vicar is using a computer. Still, I can probably handle a paint roller as well as anyone else.'

Suzy is reluctant when I call. 'Why would we want to be stuck inside on a beautiful afternoon like this? I thought we could go to the pub.'

'We can go afterwards. Come on, Suzy. It'll be fun. What else do you have to do?'

She sighs. 'Lie in the sunshine, thinking what a pity it is that the summer's almost over.'

'You can do that tomorrow,' I promise. 'Shall I call for you on the way there?'

'I suppose so,' she says ungraciously. 'But I'm not staying all afternoon. One hour, maximum.'

The vicar is already there when we arrive, wearing an old pair of jeans and a stained T-shirt. He looks delighted to see us.

'Dare I hope you've come to help me paint the hall?' he asks.

'That's right,' I say, dragging Suzy inside. 'Mum says you'll probably be on your own otherwise.'

He waves around the empty hall. 'As you can see, the crowd of volunteers I've been expecting has been delayed. I'm very grateful you've come along. I thought you might have gone back to university already, Annie.'

'I go on Friday. And I don't have anything planned between now and then. Neither has Suzy,' I add with a grin.

Suzy groans. 'I don't know how much help I'll be, Mr. Martin. I've never done this before.'

'There's nothing to it,' he says. He looks at her rather doubtfully. 'You aren't exactly dressed for it. You'll spoil those lovely clothes. I'll nip home and find you a pair of overalls.'

'Please don't bother,' she says.

I can read her mind exactly. She's never worn a pair of overalls, and she isn't about to start now. She's always perfectly turned out and immaculate.

'If you're sure,' says Mr. Martin. 'You'll be fine, Annie. I don't suppose you'll mind getting your clothes a little messy.'

'Not at all,' I say. 'These are my gardening jeans. At least, that's what I call them to stop Mum throwing them out. As long as I do the occasional bit of weeding in them, she's fine.'

'The paint cans are here,' he says. 'I'm giving the walls a coat of white emulsion.'

'That's easy enough,' I say, seizing a roller and opening a can of paint. 'We'll start at the far end.'

'I'm not using one of those,' says Suzy. 'I'll get spattered with paint.'

She picks up a brush. 'I'll paint around the windowsills.'

I start to roll paint onto the far wall. It's soothing pushing the roller up and down the walls while I listen to the chatter of birdsong floating in through the open windows.

I lay down my roller an hour later. 'I have to take a break, Mr Martin. My back's killing me.'

'You've done a great job,' he says. 'I think we'll get the entire hall finished by this evening.'

'This evening?' squeaks Suzy. 'Annie and I can't stay until this evening. We're going out.'

'Only to the pub,' I say. 'And we can do that any time.'

'But I'm exhausted,' she complains. She looks down at herself disconsolately. 'And I have a splash of paint on my jeans. They're my favourite pair.'

'What did you expect?' I ask, picking up my roller again. 'I need a step ladder so I can reach the top of this wall.'

'There's one on the stage,' says Mr. Martin. 'Would you prefer me to do that part?'

'I'm fine,' I tell him. 'I have a good head for heights – at least, I have a good head for being two feet off the floor.'

I open the ladder and put it next to the trestle table. 'If I put this tray of paint on the table, I can stretch down and just about reach it.'

'Be careful,' he says anxiously.

I dip my roller into the tray of paint and climb up the step ladder. 'This is perfect! I can reach right to the top of the wall. I could probably do the ceiling as well if you want.'

I lean down to dip my roller into the paint again, and the step ladder wobbles.

Mr. Martin looks alarmed. 'Do be careful, Annie. Your mother would never forgive me if you fell off and broke your leg.'

'I'm fine,' I say again.

I lean down a little further and stretch out the roller. The ladder rocks even more perilously, and I shriek, trying to regain my balance. Everything seems to go into slow motion. I make a wild grab for the top of the ladder, miss, lose my footing, and crash onto the trestle table. It collapses under my weight, tipping the paint over my head.

Suzy gives a screech of laughter as I sit up, feeling it running down the back of my neck.

I hear footsteps and look up, expecting to see Mr. Martin. Instead, a complete stranger is looking down at me. I blink up at him, wondering whether the can of paint hit me on the head and knocked me out.

'Are you ok?' he asks. Thankfully, he doesn't seem to be laughing at me.

I wipe my face with my sleeve. 'I think so. But I've spilled the paint.'

'Just a bit.' He holds out his hand to help me up.

'You'll get covered in paint,' I warn him.

'That's the general idea,' he says. 'I'll probably look a whole lot worse than you by the time we've finished.'

Dazed, I allow him to pull me to my feet. He's still holding my hand, which he shakes solemnly. 'Alex Fielding. It's nice to meet you.'

I stare back at him, unable to think what to say. He's tall and blond, with amused hazel eyes and a very nice smile.

'This is the part where you tell me your name,' he prompts me.

'Sorry,' I say, still staring at him. 'I'm Annie.'

Suzy holds out her hand and gives him her most devastating smile. 'And I'm Suzy.'

I groan inwardly. That was short and sweet. When Suzy turns on the full beam of her charm, it's game over. And she's very definitely interested in this man. She doesn't waste that seductive smile on just anyone.

I wonder whether Alex knows what he's letting himself in for. But it's no good warning him. He'll have to find out for himself – just like everyone else.

'It's nice to meet you, Alex,' says Mr Martin. 'I met your parents at the shops this morning. They told me you'd just moved here.'

'They have,' says Alex. 'I'm not quite sure where I'll be living this year. I finished university in June, and I'm looking for a job, but I hope to be here for a few weeks at least. It's a lovely village.'

Mr. Martin looks pleased. 'I'm glad you like it. I hope your parents will be very happy here. I mentioned that we'd be painting the hall this afternoon, and your mother told me you'd be delighted to help.'

'Did she indeed?' says Alex with a laugh in his voice. 'Possibly, she didn't know how dangerous it would turn out to be.'

He smiles at me, and I smile back. It was inevitable that when I finally met the man of my dreams, I would be lying on the floor, covered in paint. And inevitable too that Suzy would be there to provide the perfect contrast.

'I'd better get on with this wall,' I say. 'Do you have a cloth I can use to wipe up the paint, Mr. Martin?'

Alex gives me an odd look. 'Do you intend to carry on?'

'Why not? I can't get any messier than I am now. I may as well finish the job.'

'I'm impressed,' he says. 'I thought you'd want to rush home for a bath.'

'Annie doesn't mind getting messy,' says Suzy with a giggle. 'She isn't interested in how she looks.'

She claps her hand to her mouth. 'Sorry, Annie. I didn't mean it like that. I just meant that you like wearing old jeans.'

'As do I,' says Alex. 'And you obviously don't.'

Suzy looks pleased. 'I like to make an effort.'

'Even when you're painting?' he asks.

She holds up her paint brush. 'I'm going around the windowsills. But the paint's runnier than I expected.'

He raises an eyebrow. 'I think that's how they make it.'

She giggles again. 'I'm not really used to this sort of thing. Perhaps you'd like to help me?'

I mentally roll my eyes as I wipe up the spilled paint. Thank goodness Mr. Martin put down drop cloths or I'd have ruined the wooden floors. It hasn't taken Suzy long to annex the stranger. It never does. He won't know what's hit him.

But Alex doesn't take Suzy up on her offer. Instead, he walks over to me. 'Can I give you a hand with this?'

I hold up the cloth. 'I think I've cleaned up the worst of it. Anyway, most of it went on me rather than the floor.'

'I can see that,' he says. 'What are we doing here?'

'Just giving it a fresh coat of white paint. The rollers are over there.'

'What are we doing after that?' he asks, and my heart skips a beat.

'The pub!' says Suzy. 'Perhaps you'd like to come too, Alex? Annie probably wants to go home and get cleaned up, but you and I could have a drink and get to know each other.'

'I don't mean that,' he says. 'I mean what are we painting on the walls when we've finished emulsioning them?'

'I hadn't envisaged anything else,' says Mr Martin. 'Do you have something in mind?'

'I assumed you'd want some sort of a mural on the walls,' says Alex.

'What a good idea!' Mr. Martin beams at me. 'And we have the perfect person to do it. Annie here is studying art at university.'

'Graphic design,' I say.

Alex looks interested. 'And how are you enjoying it?'

'I love it. It's what I've always wanted to do.'

'I don't suppose you do much actual painting,' he says.

'None at all. But for some reason, everyone seems to think I've spent the past two years sitting with an easel, painting portraits.'

'But you must be able to draw pretty well,' he says.

I shrug. 'I suppose so.'

'You draw beautifully,' says Mr. Martin. 'I saw that painting of the forest you did for your mother last Christmas.'

'Would you like me to paint a mural?' I ask him. 'I don't have time for much, but maybe we could put one on the wall next to the piano.'

'That would be lovely,' he says. 'The hall is mostly used by children's groups. I'm sure they would appreciate it.'

'That's settled,' says Alex. 'What shall we do?'

Suzy looks a little put out at not being part of the conversation.

'Can you draw?' she asks Alex.

'Not a bit!' he says cheerfully. 'But I can fetch paint and run around being a general dogsbody. My mother has trained me very well.'

'How about The Wind in the Willows?' I suggest. 'We could paint a lovely scene with that theme.'

'Along the riverbank?' he says. 'What a great idea. I always loved that book.'

'Me too,' I say. 'My dad used to read it to me when I was little. He says he regretted it once he taught me to drive because I drove like Mr. Toad.'

'It's true,' says Suzy. 'She isn't a very good driver.'

'My favourite part was the Christmas chapter,' says Alex. 'But I was always afraid of the stoats and the weasels.'

'You were not!' I say.

'Yes, I was!' he insists. 'I went camping with my cub scout group when I was about eight, and I was too terrified to leave the tent at night.'

'But a mural will take forever,' objects Suzy. 'The walls will be fine painted white.'

I hardly hear her. 'If someone can find a piece of paper and a pencil, we could sketch something out.'

Mr. Martin pulls a notebook from his pocket. 'I could probably spare you a couple of sheets from this. I use it to remind myself where I ought to be. It rarely works, but it makes me feel better.'

Alex and I sit together on the stage steps.

'Something like this?' I say, sketching rapidly.

'That's great!' he says. 'I'm glad you've left the stoats and weasels in the wild wood where they belong. This is a much nicer scene.'

'And we can have Mr Toad driving past in the background,' I add.

'There's nothing for me to do,' says Suzy. 'I've finished the windowsills, and I'm not using a roller.'

'I can finish painting that last wall by myself,' says Mr. Martin. 'Maybe you can go and fetch the paint if Annie tells you what she needs.'

'I'll go,' offers Alex. 'I have my dad's car today.'

Suzy brightens. 'I'll come with you. You don't know where to buy the paint.'

My heart sinks. If she goes with Alex to buy the paint, it's odds on that the pair of them won't return. Suzy will probably induce him to stop at the pub with her on the way back, and he'll lose all sense of time. I know how Suzy operates.

Rather to my surprise, they're back in less than half an hour. Alex carries the bag of paint pots into the hall.

'You've been quick,' he says, looking admiringly at the stretch of wall where I've sketched out the riverbank and several of the characters.

'It's quite a simple scene,' I say. 'I didn't think we wanted anything too fancy.'

'It's amazing! What can I do to help?'

'Why don't you paint the river and the riverbank?' I suggest. 'Just be careful not to run them into each other.'

'I'll help you,' says Suzy. She picks up a paintbrush and holds it well away from her. 'I don't want to splash these lovely jeans.'

She gives a twirl, obviously expecting Alex to look, but he's engrossed in painting the river and doesn't turn around.

'Not the most sensible outfit to wear for an afternoon's painting,' is all he says.

Suzy looks annoyed. 'We were only supposed to be here for an hour. It wasn't my fault that Annie fell in the paint, then decided to do a mural.'

'That was my idea,' he points out. 'We're lucky to have such a talented artist on the premises. It would be a shame not to make the most of her.'

Mr. Martin finishes the walls while Alex and I paint the mural. Suzy stands well back and contents herself with giving us directions.

Alex straightens up a couple of hours later. 'What do you think, Annie?'

I step back to survey the picture. 'I think it's pretty good. Hopefully, the children will like it.'

Mr. Martin's face lights up when he sees what we've done. 'That's absolutely amazing. Thank you so much, all three of you.'

'I only did the grunt work,' says Alex. 'You should really be thanking Annie.'

'It's fine,' I say, embarrassed. 'I enjoyed doing it.'

'If we've finally finished, says Suzy, 'can we please go to the pub? I'm absolutely starving.'

'Sounds good to me,' says Alex. 'What about you, Annie?'

'I can't go in this state,' I say. 'They'll throw me out.'

'You should go home and have a bath,' says Suzy.

'Nonsense!' says Alex. 'Annie must need something to eat even more than the rest of us. It's a warm evening. We can sit outside in the garden. No one will care that you're covered in paint. You've managed to get some of that green paint on your jeans too. You'll blend in with the scenery.'

I'm sure I see a look of annoyance on Suzy's face, but I don't care. Why should she have everything her own way? I have as much right as she does to get to know Alex. And for a wonder, even with Suzy around, he seems just as keen to get to know me.

We help Mr Martin to stack the remaining paint pots.

'Tell your mother to come and see what you've done, Annie,' he says.

'Most likely, she'll just say that I should have left well alone,' I whisper to Suzy, who gives a snort of laughter.

'Doesn't your mother enjoy great art?' asks Alex.

'I'm sure she does when she gets the chance,' I say. 'But she tends to be quite critical of mine.'

We pull up outside the pub, and I climb out. 'I haven't left any paint on your father's upholstery, thank goodness. I told you I didn't mind walking.'

'You *are* a bit of a mess,' says Suzy. 'Are you sure you don't want to go home and clean up?'

'I'll be fine as long as I don't have to go inside,' I say.

I pull the scrunchie out of my hair and laugh. Instead of the usual movie trope of my hair falling all around my face in soft waves, it stays exactly where it is.

Suzy shrieks with laughter. 'You look like a clown!'

'She looks very nice,' says Alex. 'Like a young Leonardo da Vinci.'

'Do you know what he looked like?' I say.

'Not exactly,' he admits. 'But he was probably covered in paint by the end of the day too.'

'I wouldn't mind being dipped head to toe in paint if it meant I could draw like him,' I say.

He pulls the sheet of notepaper out of his pocket. 'He would never have been able to draw this.'

'That's because The Wind in the Willows wasn't invented back then,' says Suzy.

We find a table at the far end of the pub garden and sit down.

'Alex and I will go inside and order,' says Suzy. 'They'll freak out if they see you looking like that, Annie.'

'What would you like?' Alex asks me.

I give a huge yawn. Now that I've stopped painting, my shoulders are starting to ache. I feel as though I could sleep for a week.

'Surprise me,' I say. 'Suzy knows what I like.'

They reappear a few minutes later carrying three glasses of cider.

'The food will be out in a minute,' says Alex. 'Suzy assures me that I have to try the cider. It's all part of being accepted as a local.'

I take a grateful gulp of the icy drink. 'But you said you weren't going to become a local.'

'I said I may not,' he corrects me. 'It really depends where I manage to get a job.' He gives me a half smile. 'I wouldn't have any serious objection to finding a job around here.'

There's a beat of silence between us. Suzy interrupts before I can answer.

'You should! It's a lovely place to live. Annie wants to get a job in London, but I can't think why.'

I look at her in surprise. Suzy spent our entire childhood grumbling about how much she hated living in the countryside and how she couldn't wait to get away to the city. She's certainly changed her tune. But it's probably all part of her flirting technique. She doesn't really mean it.

'I don't mind cities,' says Alex. 'I went to university in Manchester and had a great time. I'll probably end up living in one again. There isn't a whole lot of call for big engineering projects in places like this.'

'We'll keep our fingers crossed,' says Suzy.

I notice without surprise that she's sitting very close to Alex, and he isn't moving away. To be fair, it's a small bench. If he moved any further down it, he'd fall off onto the grass. And at least he's facing me, which makes it easier to talk to him. On the other hand, I'm not sure I want to give him a clear view of me while I look like this.

How much better it would have been if we'd met in a more normal way. During an evening at the pub, perhaps. I'd have been dressed in something a little more glamorous than my current outfit, and I'd have used something other than Dulux as a hair product. Still, there's nothing I can do about that now.

A server appears carrying a tray.

'Hi Annie,' he says, putting a plate in front of me.

'Hi, Max. I haven't seen you for a while. How are you doing?'

'Can't complain,' he says. He looks at me more closely. 'You look like hell. Did you get caught in an explosion?'

'Yes, at the paint factory,' giggles Suzy.

'Is this your famous steak pie?' I ask.

Suzy selects a chip and bites into it. 'What else? If Alex is going to become a regular here, he needs to know what to order.'

Alex takes a bite of his pie and lets out a low whistle. 'That's it! I'm moving here permanently, job or no job. I'll just become an unemployed twenty-something living in his parents' basement.'

'I don't somehow think you'd enjoy that,' I say.

He takes another bite. 'It would be totally worth it. This pie is amazing.'

By the time we've finished our meal, I'm feeling less exhausted. Alex and I talk about our university courses, and Suzy tells him about her plans to take a childcare qualification.

'Looking after children isn't the most exciting thing in the world,' she says. 'But if you get the right family, it can give you amazing opportunities. Beautiful houses, travel, you name it.'

'Would you like to travel?' Alex asks me.

'I'd love to. Maybe I will once I've graduated. In fact, the university runs an exchange programme with a place in Paris. I've applied, but I don't suppose there's much chance of me getting it. The competition is pretty tough. The course starts in January and finishes at Easter.'

'I'm not sure whether to hope you get it or not,' he says.

His expression is unmistakable. I can't help glancing at Suzy, who looks as though she's bitten on a lemon.

'I find out next week,' I tell him.

'I'd love to hear the outcome,' he says.

'The pub's about to close,' says Suzy. 'I told you we shouldn't have stayed so long at that stupid hall.'

'I should be getting back home anyway,' says Alex. 'It's almost dark, and my parents will worry.'

'Surely, you're old enough to be out by yourself after dark?' I tease him.

He grins. 'They aren't worried about me. Dad's worried about his car. He loves that car, and he's promised to throw me out on my ear if I dare to put a scratch on it.'

He hesitates. 'It's been really nice meeting you. Would you like to do this again sometime?'

'We'd love to,' says Suzy. 'Annie has to go back to university on Friday, but I'm always free.'

He meets my gaze. 'That's a shame. In which case, would you like to meet up tomorrow evening?'

'That's a great idea!' says Suzy. 'Why don't we come here again? We can have a drink, then maybe go on somewhere else.'

'I suppose we could do that,' he says. 'Shall we say around seven o'clock?'

'Great!' says Suzy. 'Come on, Annie. I'll walk you home.'

'I can drive you,' says Alex, but Suzy shakes her head.

'It's just as quick for us to walk.'

I wonder whether she's making sure I'm not left alone with Alex. It isn't likely. The thought wouldn't even cross her mind. I've never been any kind of competition for her, and it's unlikely I am now, especially red-eyed and covered in paint.

I feel a flash of annoyance at the way she's muscled in on tomorrow evening's arrangements. But perhaps Alex intended to ask us both. Even worse, perhaps he intended to invite Suzy, and I got in the way.

But his eyes are warm as he smiles at me. 'I had a great time today. I'm very glad my mother talked me into going along to this painting party.'

'Me too,' I say.

'It was a lucky chance all around,' says Suzy. 'Come on, Annie. Let's get you home. Your mother is going to freak out when she sees you.'

We say goodbye to Alex and walk home together. I'm too tired to talk much, but Suzy keeps up a stream of conversation.

'He's very nice, isn't he?' she says as we cross the playing field. 'He isn't my usual type, but he's very good looking. Don't you think so?'

'I suppose so,' I say.

'You suppose so? Of course, he is. Better than most of the men around here anyway. He seemed very interested in you.'

I fight hard to keep the smile off my face. 'I think he was interested in both of us.'

Suzy tosses her head, and her long, blonde hair ripples out behind her. Mine used to do that. It will probably never do so again. Perhaps the paint is there to stay, and I'll have to go back to university with white splodges all over my head and try to persuade everyone it's the latest fashion.

Hopefully, it will have grown out by Christmas. Surely, Alex will be home again for the holidays, even if he's found a job somewhere else by then.

'What are you thinking about?' asks Suzy as we reach my front gate.

'Nothing,' I lie. 'I'm just a bit tired.'

'Me too,' she says. 'I can't believe you let me in for all that painting. Still, it worked out well. We might not have met Alex so soon if you hadn't.'

Or at all, I think. I'm going back to university in a couple of days, but Alex would have been bound to meet Suzy at some point and be dazzled by her. By the time I met him, he and Suzy might have been a couple.

If Mum hadn't sent me to help out this afternoon, I might never have met him. Maybe fate has taken a hand for once. Perhaps there really is such a thing as 'meant to be'.

I say goodnight to Suzy and go inside to take a long, hot bath.

Chapter Two

Suzy calls for me the following evening. 'I see the paint came out,' she says.

'Thankfully. It was touch and go there for a while. But I got it all out at last.'

'You look very nice,' she says, looking me up and down. 'You don't usually dress up to go to the pub.'

'You said we might go on somewhere else,' I remind her. 'Besides, I'm not exactly dressed up. Unless clean jeans count as dressing up.'

'I haven't seen that top before,' she says. 'Is it new?'

'Fairly. I bought it this term.'

'It suits you.'

'You look very nice too,' I say. 'Then again, you always do.'

She gives a complacent smile. 'I've had this outfit for ages, but I thought I might as well wear it tonight.'

She's wearing jeans so tight they look as though I painted them on when I did the mural. They accentuate her long, slender legs. She's wearing a pale pink top, sleeveless and low cut, and very high heeled sandals.

'Hello, Suzy,' says Mum, appearing in the hallway. 'Where are you two girls off to?'

'We're going for a drink, Mrs. Masters,' says Suzy.

Mum gives her a critical look. 'Won't you be cold in that?'

'It's a lovely warm evening,' I say.

'But it's awfully low cut,' says Mum. 'You don't want all those men at the pub leering at you. Shall I get you a nice wrap to cover up?'

'Bye, Mum!' I say, pushing Suzy out of the door. We walk down the front path, laughing.

'Why are all mothers like that?' asks Suzy, slipping her arm into mine. 'Surely, they were young once?'

'I'm not sure my Mum was. I think she was born wearing Laura Ashley.'

'And Boden,' adds Suzy.

We arrive at the pub a few minutes later. I'd expected Alex to be there before us, but there's no sign of him.

'Perhaps he's in the garden,' says Suzy.

But there's no sign of him there either.

I sit at the nearest table. 'It's a lovely evening. Why don't we order a couple of drinks and wait for him out here?'

'I'm not waiting for long,' says Suzy. 'I never wait long for any man. It's bad for their vanity.'

'He's only five minutes late. And we said around seven.'

'I'll give him fifteen minutes exactly,' she says. 'I'll have a spritzer while I wait.'

I order the drinks. There's still no sign of Alex inside the pub. He doesn't seem the type to be late, especially as he's the one who suggested us all meeting up. Or him and me meeting up. Or him and Suzy meeting up. I'm still not quite sure.

I carry the drinks outside. Suzy looks annoyed. 'If he isn't here by the time I've finished this, we're leaving.'

'I'm quite happy to wait,' I say, but she shakes her head.

'You have a lot to learn about men. If you don't start as you mean to go on, they'll walk all over you.'

I can't imagine anyone walking all over Suzy. The boot is always firmly on the other foot. I wonder what it would feel like to be so beautiful that heads turn whenever you walk into a room. I once saw Suzy actually stop traffic. I'd always assumed this was just another trope, but we were crossing the road last year when a van passing on the other side suddenly slammed on its brakes and nearly hit the kerb. The driver looked embarrassed as he drove away. Suzy of course thought it was a great joke.

Still, very few people can look like that. And if Alex wanted to see me again, even when I was wearing my oldest jeans and had my hair full of paint, hopefully he'll like how I look now I've had a chance to clean up.

Suzy drains her glass. 'We're going!' she announces.

'Let's have another drink first,' I say. I have no intention of leaving yet, but I don't want to betray how keen I am to see Alex again. Especially not until I know for sure which of us he intended to meet.

Suzy wavers. 'Maybe one more.'

'I'm looking for someone called Annie,' says a voice behind us.

'That's me,' I say. 'At least, that's my name. There may be several Annies here tonight, for all I know.'

The man doesn't smile. 'Are you Annie Masters?'

'Yes.' I wonder what this man could possibly want with me.

'I'm Max,' he says. 'I'm the relief bartender.'

'Ok,' I say cautiously. Maybe I'm the thousandth customer today, and he's come to offer me free drinks for the rest of the night.

'Someone called Alex phoned earlier,' he says. 'He isn't able to come tonight, so he asked me to let you know if I saw you. He says he forgot to get your phone number yesterday.'

'He isn't coming?' says Suzy, her face darkening.

'Is he alright?' I ask.

Max pulls out a piece of paper and studies it. 'He's been offered a job interview in Edinburgh tomorrow. He had to go off to London to catch the night train. He asked me to apologise.'

'When's he coming back?' asks Suzy.

Max looks at the paper again. 'He'll be home on Saturday morning.'

'Isn't that a shame?' says Suzy, brightening. 'Annie's leaving on Friday. But I'm sure I'll bump into him when he's back.'

I feel a sick swoop of disappointment. Perhaps I was too quick to assume that fate had taken a hand. At least, if it has, it appears to have changed its mind.

'I hope you're not too disappointed,' says Suzy when Max has left. 'I know how much you liked him.'

'Of course not,' I say. 'We've only met him once. How about you? Are you disappointed?'

'Hardly!' she says. 'He isn't really my type. I prefer men who work out. Well, at least he had the decency to send us a message. And it sounds as though he'll be moving to Edinburgh. So, that's that.'

'Yes,' I say quietly. 'I suppose that's that.'

Chapter Three

I arrive home for the Christmas holidays in a state of great excitement. Not only have I been away from home for the past few months, but I know from Mum that Alex is home for Christmas.

She told me he arrived a few days ago. I would have liked to have been there when he arrived, but I promised to stay for a few extra days while a friend resat an exam. I surprised myself by passing with high marks, but Evie has struggled with the course, so I stayed for moral support.

But now I'm heading back home for ten days. I'm staying until New Year's Day. There will be the usual whirl of excitement – meeting friends, seeing my parents, wrapping presents, and making the Christmas cake. But most of all there will be Alex.

I tell myself it's ridiculous to get so excited. For all I know, he may have met someone in Scotland. Or he may not be interested in me. But even while I'm telling myself to keep my hopes in check, I'm fizzing with excitement. It somehow feels right. There was such an instant connection when we met in the summer. Everything felt so easy and natural. So, while my head tells me to be cautious, my heart is bursting with excitement.

Dad meets me at the station and gives me a huge hug. 'Welcome home, Annie! We've missed you.'

'And I've missed you,' I say sincerely.

He picks up my cases. 'It's out of sight, out of mind for young people when they go off to university. You'll have been too busy partying to spare us a thought.'

'Not true,' I say, following him towards the car. 'I've been counting the days.'

'Your mother will be pleased to see you. She's been holding off making the pudding until you were home. She says it's not right to make it without you.'

'She's quite right,' I say. 'I've been helping her make the Christmas pudding for as long as I can remember. I love putting the sixpence, the thimble, and the ring in it. Do you remember the time you broke a tooth on the thimble?'

'I do indeed,' he says. 'I had to ring around to find an emergency dentist on Christmas day of all days! I'm not going to tell you how much that cost.'

I give a choke of laughter. 'I remember how cross Mum was – not because you had to find a dentist but because you'd chipped the thimble.'

'We got a metal one after that,' he says, slinging my case into the boot. We'd better hurry or your mother will be thinking we've had an accident.'

Mum is waiting for us at the front door, wearing an apron with a picture of the Eiffel Tower on it. Her hands are covered in flour. She bends forward to kiss me. 'Careful! I don't want to get flour all over your –'

She breaks off, looking disapprovingly at my old duffle coat. 'Are you still wearing that? I thought you'd have got rid of it ages ago.'

'I'm a student, remember? But that's lucky because it means I can hug you properly.'

'Lunch is ready,' she says, giving me a quick hug. 'Your father can take your case to your room while I serve up. I'm afraid there's no time for you to change. I've made a cheese souffle, and they don't wait for man nor beast.'

I follow Dad upstairs. 'I wasn't going to change anyway. This is the smartest outfit I've brought with me. Except for a party dress.'

'You'll be needing one of those,' he says. 'Your mother seems to have something planned for every day you're here.'

'Of course, she has! She'll probably grumble about me wearing the same thing each time, but that's too bad. And it's a lovely dress.'

It's a short, black dress, woven with shimmering sparkles. I spent an entire Saturday shopping for it. I ended up spending far more than I could afford and had to borrow my train fare home. But I don't care. It's absolutely perfect.

Mum monopolises the conversation during lunch. I have to hear the full history of the harvest festival, the fruit and produce show, and last week's Christmas Bazaar.

Dad leans back in his chair when lunch is over. 'I think she's all caught up now. It probably feels as though you've never been away, Annie.'

'My head's certainly spinning,' I agree, pushing away my plate. 'That was delicious, thanks, but I can't eat another bite.'

'But it's apple pie!' says Mum, shocked. 'You love my apple pie!'

'I'm not used to eating so much at lunch time,' I say.

'Because you don't take care of yourself properly,' she says. 'Look at you – you're thinner than ever. Don't you find time to eat at university?'

'I'm studying too hard,' I say.

Dad looks anxious. 'You aren't short of money, are you? I don't like to think of you skipping meals because you can't afford them.'

'I'm absolutely fine,' I reassure him. 'I tend to eat my main meal in the evening, that's all. I seem to be so busy during the days that time gets away from me.'

Mum gives me a suspicious look. 'You aren't on drugs, are you?'

I stare at her in bemusement. 'What put that into your mind?'

'I know what it's like at those places,' she says. 'Half the students are smoking marijuana cigarettes all day, and the other half have eating disorders.'

'I can promise that I neither smoke pot all day nor have an eating disorder,' I say gravely.

'I'm glad to hear it,' she says. 'In which case, I can't understand why you aren't eating your apple pie.'

A look of shock flashes over her face. 'You aren't –?'

'I'm not suffering from morning sickness either, if that's what you're implying,' I say.

'The thought never crossed my mind,' she says, but she looks more cheerful.

She gives me a sidelong look. 'Are you seeing anyone at the moment?'

'Isn't that a tactful segue?' I say. 'As it happens, I'm not.'

She nods. 'There's plenty of time for that. You're at university to study, not to chase after boys.'

'Very true,' I say. 'In fact, I've brought so much work home with me that I probably won't see you very much at all these holidays. I certainly won't have time for any parties.'

She looks so horrified that I burst out laughing. 'I'm only teasing you. You seem to have a very odd idea of student life. It's all quite normal, really. It isn't much different to being at school, except that no one cares whether or not you attend lectures.'

'You don't need to worry about Annie,' says Dad. 'She did very well in her exams, remember?' He smiles at me. 'We're very proud of you, love.'

'Thanks, Dad. I'm glad I've got them out of the way. I'm in Paris next term, but I have my finals in the summer, so I definitely won't be spending all my time partying.'

I've arranged to meet Suzy that afternoon to catch up. Mum is annoyed when she hears this.

'I'd hoped we could go shopping together this afternoon,' she says. 'I'm sure you need something nice to wear for all these parties. Being a student isn't an excuse to look as though you've dressed from a jumble sale.'

I'm too excited to be annoyed. 'I've already bought a new dress for tomorrow night.'

'Wonders will never cease!' She puts the last of the plates into the dishwasher. 'Where did you get it?'

'Selfridges.'

'How did you afford that?'

'I'm the campus drug dealer,' I say without thinking. 'Oh, don't look like that, Mum! I saved up for it all term.'

'Can I see it?' she asks.

'You'll see it tomorrow. I'm wearing it to Mira's Christmas party.'

'But I need to look at it first,' she says. 'It might not fit.'

'Seriously, how do you think I've coped with living away from home the past two years? I've managed to get dressed perfectly well each morning without my mother there to sew on buttons and check me for creases.'

She sniffs. 'Judging by the way you're dressed today, you haven't done a very good job of it. Those old jeans have a rip in one knee. Go and put something else on, and I'll have them darned for you in a trice.'

I drop a kiss on the top of her head. 'They're supposed to be like that. I paid extra for that rip.'

Disregarding her shocked exclamations, I pick up my bag. 'I have to go. I'm meeting Suzy in ten minutes.'

Suzy jumps to her feet when I open the cafe door. 'Sweetie! I've missed you so much!'

I hug her delightedly. 'Me too! How have you been?'

She waves to the server for another cup of coffee. 'I've been really busy with my course. Only two more terms to go, thank goodness.'

I settle myself comfortably and pull off my hat and gloves. 'How's it going?'

'It's not too bad,' she says. 'It's better than my job at the supermarket.'

'When do you start applying for nannying jobs?' I ask.

'Around Easter, I expect. There's quite a lot of competition for the best jobs, so they advertise them well beforehand. That way, they can get the best nannies for their little darlings.'

'I'm sure you'll have no trouble,' I say. 'Any family would be lucky to have you.'

She blows me a kiss. 'You're so sweet. What about you? What are you going to do when you graduate?'

'I'm not quite sure. I'd like to get a job in London for a while, but the competition's pretty stiff. I've decided not to worry about it for the next few months.'

'Quite right,' she says. 'We should forget about all that and enjoy Christmas. Are you going to Mira's party tomorrow?'

I nod. 'I've been really looking forward to it.'

I don't add that I've mostly been looking forward to seeing Alex. I know from Mira that he's been invited, but I don't want to jinx things. For all I know, he already has a girlfriend in Edinburgh.

'What are you going to wear?' she asks. 'I bought the most amazing dress last week. It's very low cut, and very short. It wasn't so short on the model, but …'

'That's what comes of being so tall,' I say. 'I wish I had legs like yours.'

'But nothing's ever long enough.' She eyes her long, slender legs complacently. 'My mum almost had a fit when she saw the dress. She wanted me to take it back, but I told her it was on sale, and they don't refund sale items. I'm not sure she believed me, but I don't care. There's no way I'm returning it. If she had her way, I'd be wearing some frumpy old full-length dress with a high neck and long sleeves.'

'My mum's exactly the same,' I say, giggling at the remembrance of Mum offering to lend me one of her own dresses. 'I wish you could come tomorrow. It won't be the same without you.'

She pouts. 'I know! I was so upset when Mum and Dad insisted that I go to visit Aunty Zara with them. At first, I absolutely refused. But Mum reminded me that Aunty Zara always gives me a cheque for Christmas. So, in the end I gave in. She's absolutely loaded, and she's never married or had children, so it's definitely worth staying in her good books.'

I give her an uncertain smile. I'm fairly sure she's joking, but it doesn't seem in great taste.

She notices my expression. 'Don't look so serious. Anyway, there's still the Fieldings' New Year's Eve party. You're going to that, aren't you?'

'Mum says we've all been invited. It will be my last night here. I'm off to Paris on New Year's Day.'

She doesn't look too enthusiastic. 'Oh, that's right. How very glamorous.'

'I'm sure they'll work us pretty hard while we're there,' I say. 'It won't all be sightseeing and partying.'

'Maybe you'll meet some gorgeous French guy,' she says. 'Then you'll move over there permanently and never give the rest of us a thought.'

'I'm more likely to meet someone who looks like Quasimodo. And I'd never move there permanently. I'm only going until Easter.'

I don't add that I have no intention of meeting any Frenchman, handsome or not. As far as I'm concerned, there's only one man I'm interested in, and he's very much not French.

We spend the afternoon chatting about our Christmas plans. Suzy gets up to leave at last.

'I promised Mum I'd help her with the tree, and we have some awful people coming over for lunch tomorrow. I have to go to Aunty Zara's in the evening, so

I won't be able to see you before the party. I hope you have a wonderful time. I'm so jealous.'

She gives me a quick hug and picks up her parcels. 'I probably won't see you until after Christmas. So, here's your present.'

I reach into my own bag. 'I almost forgot. Here's yours. I hope you like it. We're busy on Boxing Day, but maybe we can meet the day after and do something then.'

'Sounds lovely.' She blows me another kiss and heads for the door. She turns in the doorway. 'Have an amazing time at the party. Don't do anything I wouldn't do!'

Just one thing, I think hopefully as I wave her a cheerful goodbye.

Chapter Four

I spend the whole of the following afternoon getting ready for the party. Mum tries several times to get me to eat something, but I refuse.

'Honestly, Mum, I'm fine. Please don't fuss. There'll be plenty of food at the party.'

'But there won't be a proper meal,' she argues.

'I ate an enormous lunch.'

She still isn't convinced. 'I don't think you eat enough. I wouldn't get through half an hour if I ate like you. If you're worried about your weight, you shouldn't be. You have a lovely figure.'

I'm too excited to feel annoyed. 'I'm not worried about my weight. I had a big lunch, that's all.'

'Perhaps I'll pop something in your bag for later,' she says.

'Leave the girl alone!' says Dad. 'She's twenty-one and quite capable of deciding whether or not she's hungry.'

'Thanks, Dad,' I say. 'Stop worrying about me, Mum, and go and get ready yourself. You have your own party to go to. What are you wearing?'

I knew this would distract her. 'I'm wearing my new wrap dress,' she says. 'You haven't seen it yet.'

'No, but you wrote and told me about it. It sounds lovely.'

'It really is! Pure silk, and thirty percent off. I couldn't believe my luck when I saw it.'

She heads towards the stairs, still burbling enthusiastically about her find.

Dad smiles at me. 'She doesn't change.'

'I wouldn't want her to. It's lovely coming home for Christmas and knowing that everything will be the same.'

They drop me off at Mira's on their way to their own party.

'Call if you need a ride,' says Dad. 'We're going to midnight mass, but we can collect you on our way home.'

'And make sure you eat something!' shouts Mum as they drive off.

I'm still laughing as I ring the doorbell. Mira answers, wearing a gold jumpsuit and a tinsel crown. 'Come in! Lovely to see you. Sorry about the noise.'

The house is already crowded, but I can't see anyone I know. I follow Mira into the main room. There are paper chains everywhere, and fake snow has been sprayed onto every available surface. In the corner is a huge Christmas tree with flashing lights. There's a table at the far end, covered with every type of beverage imaginable. It might not be Mum's idea of a finger buffet, but it would look pretty good to most people.

I put my bottle of Chardonnay next to a six-pack of lager and help myself to a glass of wine. I turn to find myself facing Alex. I'm so surprised that I almost drop my glass. 'Hi, Alex!'

'Hi,' he says. 'Did I startle you?'

'Yes, no, I mean … I wasn't startled!' I stammer. What's wrong with me? Why couldn't I have said hello like a normal person?

In my place, Suzy would have flicked him an indifferent look and walked away. I've seen her do it a thousand times, leaving her poor victim staring after her, mesmerised. But I'm not Suzy and never will be. If Alex likes me, it will have to be for who I am, not for who I'm not. Even in my besotted state, I know that would never work.

He gestures to my glass. 'What are you having?'

'Erm …' I stare helplessly at my glass, my brain numb. What am I drinking? It could be rubbing alcohol as far as my brain is concerned.

He grins. 'Never mind. I'll have a beer. It's lovely to see you again, Annie. How have you been?'

'Fine, thanks,' I manage. 'You?'

'Not too bad. I've been hoping to see you again.'

I feel a thrill of pleasure. The words are simple enough, but his tone is unmistakeable. I search frantically for something to say. I want to say something witty, but my mind remains obstinately blank. I stare at him in silence, and he grins again.

'That's ok. You're probably trying to find a polite way to tell me you don't even remember me.'

I manage to find my voice at last. He must think me an absolute idiot. 'Of course I remember you!' I say, annoyed to hear my voice come out in a strangled squeak.

'Glad to hear it,' he says. 'How's the course going?'

'Fine, thanks. How's the new job?'

'Also fine, thanks,' he says with a slight smile.

Are we going to spend the entire evening discussing our jobs and studies? What happened to the easy camaraderie we enjoyed during that halcyon afternoon in the summer?

He seems to sense some of what I'm thinking. 'Now that we have that out of the way, would you like to dance?'

I give a sigh of relief. 'I'd love to.'

I put down my drink and take his outstretched hand. He leads me into the other room where several couples are dancing energetically.

My heart sinks. *Grandma Got Run Over by a Reindeer* isn't the most romantic start to the evening.

Alex doesn't let go of my hand. 'Shall we come back and try a bit later?'

The noise has reached such a crescendo that I can't make my voice heard, so I just nod. He points towards the room we came from, and we walk back together. He hasn't let go of my hand. I try not to read too much into it. The hallway is packed, and it makes sense for us to stay together. But I can't help a thrill of excitement at the feel of his touch. His hand is warm and his clasp firm. I just about manage to restrain myself from twining my fingers between his. If he only means to guide me, it would be beyond embarrassing to attempt such an intimate gesture.

He draws me inside the room. 'That's better. I'm starting to feel my age.'

'All the noise?' I ask, amused.

'It's depressing, isn't it? I went to parties far noisier than this while I was at university and never thought anything of it. You're still at university, aren't you? Perhaps you haven't yet reached that stage.'

'I'm not much of a one for loud parties,' I say. I don't add that I'd have gone to any party, however noisy, if there had been a chance of seeing him there.

'Mira and I are old friends,' I say. 'This party seemed a good opportunity to catch up with everyone.'

'What would you like to drink?' he asks.

'Not the wine I tried earlier. It was like paint stripper.'

'I paid a lot for that bottle,' he says with a hurt expression.

I clap my hand to my mouth. 'I'm so sorry. I didn't mean to be rude. I don't know much about wine.'

I look at him in consternation and see the corners of his mouth twitch. 'You're teasing me.'

'I am indeed.' He picks up the bottle of wine and inspects the label. 'Chateau Duck Pond, I see. What some people will bring to a party. No doubt they hid this bottle at the back and are busy drinking buckets of the good stuff.'

'What did you bring?' I ask.

'That bottle of Merlot. I stole it from my father's wine cellar. Hopefully, he won't notice. He has plenty down there.'

'Are you a wine connoisseur too?' I say.

'Not a bit of it. I class wine into five groups – red, white, an odd mixture of the two, drinkable, and undrinkable.'

'I don't even go that far,' I say. 'I don't really like it at all.'

'Not even champagne?'

'Champagne isn't wine,' I say and see his mouth twitch again. 'Is it really?'

'I'm afraid so. What did you think it was – some sort of liqueur?'

'We don't all have parents with a well-stocked wine cellar,' I say.

'What do your parents drink?' he asks.

'I think Mum mostly drinks gin and tonic. She says she used to drink something called snowballs when she was a girl, but they've apparently gone out of fashion. Mum likes to keep up with the times.'

He nods. 'My mum's generally a port and lemon sort of woman.'

'I like port,' I say, pleased to be able to join in.

He laughs. 'Also wine.'

'No!' I say, embarrassed.

'I'm afraid so. But it's fortified, so we can agree not to count it. What about your dad?'

'I think he mostly drinks beer in the summer. He probably drinks whisky in the winter.'

I look at him in sudden consternation. 'That isn't a wine too, is it?'

'I really want to tell you it is. I'm almost convinced you'd believe me. But no, you're safe there.'

I laugh. 'Fine, I'm not sophisticated about alcohol. Perhaps if I tried some of the better stuff, I'd change my mind. But most of the wine at the parties I go to comes out of boxes, and I've never really seen the point.'

'What do you drink instead?' he asks.

'Alcopops,' I confess. 'They take away the bitter taste of the alcohol. Otherwise, I stick to soft drinks. I actually prefer them.'

He nods gravely. 'You're naturally high on life.'

'Something like that. What about you?'

'Ever since I moved to Scotland, I've drunk nothing but Irn Bru and whisky.'

'Not seriously?' I say, startled.

'Not seriously. But that seems to be the general assumption. Mum was delighted to see me looking so healthy when I arrived home. She was convinced I'd been living on deep-fried Mars bars for the past few months.'

'I'd love to try one of those,' I say without thinking.

'Come and visit me, and I'll buy you as many as you can eat.'

I can't tell whether he's serious. I'm hopeless at this. If Suzy was here, she'd have been ready with some light retort, and the conversation would have flowed easily instead of flowing like mud.

He doesn't seem to notice my hesitation. He gestures towards the array of bottles. 'What's it to be? There's certainly some vodka here. I could mix it with blackcurrant squash for you.'

He peers more closely at the label. 'At least, that's what it claims, but I'm not sure I'd trust it.'

'I'll have an orange juice,' I say.

He reaches for the carton. 'Just as I said – high on life!'

He hands me the glass of orange juice. 'Would you like me to go and look for some ice?'

'No, thanks.' If he goes to the kitchen, he might get waylaid, and I won't see him again.

'Or we could take it outside,' he says. 'It's certainly cold enough out there.'

He gives me his trademark grin. 'How about it? I could give you a tour of the gardens if you like. They're absolutely magnificent.'

'But this is a two-bedroom terrace,' I say.

He nods. 'Which makes it all the more surprising. It's one of Honeywell's hidden treasures. In fact, I believe it was featured in last month's Homes and Gardens.'

Before I can speak, a group of my schoolfriends bursts into the room. They descend on me with hugs and squeals of greeting. 'Annie! We've missed you. How long are you home?'

'A week,' I say, glancing at Alex.

'Only a week?' says Emma. 'That isn't very long. I thought they had long holidays at university.'

'Usually, we do. But I'm leaving for Paris on New Year's Day.'

Out of the corner of my eye, I see Alex make a slight movement. 'Paris?' he asks.

I give him a nervous smile. 'Yes, I got that exchange place. I won't be back until Easter.'

'Lucky thing,' says Emma enviously. 'I'd love to go to Paris. All those gorgeous men!'

'That isn't why I'm going,' I say. 'It's a really great opportunity for my design course, and I couldn't turn it down.'

Emma looks curiously at Alex. 'This is Alex Fielding,' I say.

'Nice to meet you,' she says. 'Do you live around here?'

'I live in Scotland,' he says. 'I'm home to see my parents for Christmas.'

I'm sure I don't imagine his eyes flicker towards me and away again.

'Goodness!' says Emma. 'So many exotic places. First Paris, and now Scotland.'

'Scotland isn't exotic,' says her boyfriend Matt.

'It's more exotic than here,' she says. 'I can't wait to move away from this place.'

'Don't you like it?' asks Alex. 'I think it's rather nice. I haven't seen much of it yet because my parents only moved here the week before I went to Scotland. But it seems a lovely village.'

'That's because you didn't grow up here,' she says. 'It was awful. There's never anything going on, and there are only two buses a day into town. Everyone raves about how pretty it is, but they should try living here.'

'Is that how you felt?' Alex asks me.

'Not particularly. I've always enjoyed living in the country.'

'That's because you were such a swot!' says Emma. She turns to Alex. 'She always had her head in a book, and she enjoyed things like long country walks. But I can't stand them. Give me a city every time.'

'London's great,' I agree. 'There's always something going on. Too much, sometimes. It can be a relief to come home to visit my parents.'

'But you aren't planning to move back here permanently?' asks Matt.

'Probably not,' I say, trying not to look at Alex. 'There isn't much work here, for one thing. And I haven't got London out of my system yet. I'll probably try to find a job there when I graduate.'

'I somehow imagined you'd move back here,' says Alex.

'I don't see why. Are you planning on moving here just because your parents live here?'

'There wouldn't be any work for Alex either,' Emma points out. 'You're far better off where you are, Alex. Edinburgh sounds like fun.'

'It's great,' he says. 'But I'd like to set up on my own one day. That way, it won't matter so much where I'm based.'

'I think Annie has the right idea,' she says. 'Who wants to be buried alive in a place like this? Anyway, this is a party. Would you like to dance?'

Alex puts down his glass. 'Good idea.'

I stiffen. Has he forgotten he offered to show me the garden? And now he's going off to dance with Emma.

He holds out his hand to me. 'Shall we risk it again?'

With a feeling of relief, I take his hand. I see Emma wink at Matt, but I don't care.

Thankfully, the music has quietened down since our last visit, and there are far fewer couples. Most people seem to have headed to the kitchen to find something to eat. I feel as though I never want to eat again. All I want is to spend the entire evening in here dancing with Alex.

Last Christmas starts to play. He puts his hands on my shoulders, and I slip my arms around his neck.

He's the first to break the silence. 'Paris! So, they accepted you.'

'I'd have mentioned it earlier, but I wasn't sure you'd be interested,' I say.

'I'm interested in anything to do with you, Annie.'

My heart skips a beat. 'What do you want to know?'

'Are you really leaving on New Year's Day?'

'I am. But I'll be back at Easter.'

He thinks about this. 'So, you're only home for a week? We'll just have to make the most of it.'

Does he mean what I hope he means? I look at him questioningly, and he smiles. 'What do you have planned for this week? Are you booked solid with family things?'

I feel fully capable of making sure my entire family goes down with food poisoning if they try to stop me leaving the house. But I keep my tone light. 'Tomorrow is Christmas Day, and Dad's brother always brings his family down to spend Boxing Day with us. Apart from that, I'm pretty much free. How about you?'

'Same,' he says. 'Well, perhaps not quite the same. I don't remember your father's brother bringing his family to visit us on Boxing Day. But Aunty Em always comes to us on Christmas Day and stays for a couple of days. She insists on cooking the turkey every year, even though my mum tries to stop her.'

'Is it that bad?' I ask.

'Worse! None of us is quite sure what she does to it, but it comes out of the oven like baked cardboard. Our entire family has to arrange a visit to the dentist early in the new year.'

'My mum's a really good cook,' I say. 'But she doesn't let any of us help her on Christmas Day. She's worried we'll spoil it.'

'What about the twenty-seventh?' he says.

I try not to appear too eager. 'What would you like to do?'

'I'll leave that up to you,' he says. 'You pick this one, and I'll choose next time.'

'You might not like what I choose,' I warn him.

'I just want to spend some time with you, Annie. I don't mind what we do.'

'But what if I decide we're going to have a picnic with turkey sandwiches made by your aunt?'

He pulls a face. 'I'd still give it a try.'

There's a sudden shriek from the hallway. 'It's almost midnight, everyone! Come and fill your glasses.'

'I had no idea it was that late,' I say.

'Shall I get you another orange juice to drink a Christmas toast?' he asks.

We go back to the front room and survey the table.

'There doesn't seem to be a whole lot left,' says Alex.

He picks up the carton of orange juice and shakes it. 'Oddly enough, this is still nearly full.' He pours us both a glass.

'Don't you want something stronger?' I ask.

'Not at all. What better than a nice, cold glass of orange juice to drink a Christmas toast?'

'It won't be cold,' I say. 'It was warm when I drank it before, and this room is stifling.'

He hands me the glass. 'Have you forgotten we were going to take them outside to chill them?'

We go into the kitchen and slip out of the back door without anyone noticing us. I give an involuntary shiver.

'Would you like my sweater?' he asks.

'Bad idea,' I say. 'You'd die of hypothermia in about three minutes flat.'

I look down the garden. 'It's cloudy, so I can't see too well, but this garden looks pretty small. When you promised me the tour, you made it sound as though it was several acres.'

'It used to be,' he says without missing a beat, 'but they sold it for development. If we come here again next Christmas, there'll be nothing but high rises and a huge supermarket.'

'My mum would have something to say about that,' I say. 'She's on the parish council, and she'd have a fit if anyone suggested it.'

'Perhaps it was some other garden I was thinking of,' he says, unperturbed.

'Versailles, perhaps?'

He frowns. 'Let's not talk about France until we have to.'

I put down my glass next to his. 'We'd better not leave these too long or they'll be frozen solid.'

He looks at his watch. 'Only one minute to go. I promised myself when I met you in September that I wouldn't leave it until Christmas Day to kiss you, so we don't have much time.'

He turns to face me. 'If that's ok?'

My brain seems to have frozen. I can't think of any words to say. Instead, I smile up at him, and he puts his arms around me.

'It was a near thing,' he says, 'but we still have about twenty seconds.'

I hardly hear him. I point to an upstairs window where someone has forgotten to close the curtains. The first few flakes of snow are starting to fall through the beam of light.

Alex looks pleased. 'Right on time. I ordered that last week, but I wasn't sure whether the delivery van would make it. It was very important to me that it should be snowing the first time I kissed you.'

We stand for a few seconds, locked in each other's gaze. From somewhere inside the house comes a roar of sound, 'Three, two, one ...'

'Zero,' whispers Alex and pulls me towards him.

Chapter Five

I barely sleep when I get home. I don't feel tired. I lie in bed and stare up at the glow-in-the-dark stars my father stuck on my ceiling when I was a child, thinking of how Alex and I looked up at the stars together. We stayed there after he kissed me, his arm wrapped around my shoulders, watching the snowflakes drift down through the bars of light. I didn't want to speak, fearful of breaking the spell.

Mira broke it for us a few minutes later when she burst outside, clutching a plate. 'I'll throw these out for the birds. They'll be gone by morning.'

She saw us and stopped. 'What are you two doing out here? It's freezing!'

Her eyes widened, and she disappeared as abruptly as she'd come. But the spell was broken. I shivered, suddenly aware of how cold I was.

'We'd better go inside,' said Alex. 'I don't want you freezing to death just when I've found you.'

Those words stay with me half the night as I watch the stars on my bedroom ceiling. I could almost swear they move and change positions as the night goes on, just like the real constellations they're mimicking.

Just when I've found you! That's exactly how I feel too, as though I've been looking for something I wasn't even conscious of, and last night I finally found it. I smile as I remember kissing Alex. It felt so right. Nothing like the boys I kissed in my teens, or even the English student with whom I briefly imagined I was in love during my first year at university. Those kisses felt artificial, as though I was observing myself and commenting in my head on what I was doing. Kissing Alex was nothing like that. It felt so natural and right.

The constellations move faster and faster, and I finally fall asleep. I doze on and off all night, swimming through a tangle of dreams about Alex, which makes it all the more annoying when Mum comes thundering down the landing, shouting, 'Hurry up, darling! Don't you want to see whether Santa's been?'

I push my feet into my slippers and emerge onto the landing.

'Happy Christmas!' shrieks Mum.

'Happy Christmas,' I say. 'Can you turn down the volume a little?'

She gives me a suspicious look. 'Don't tell me you have a hangover! Did you spend all night drinking on an empty stomach? I knew you should have had something to eat. Didn't I tell her, Graham?' she says as Dad appears behind her, tying the belt of his dressing gown.

'Happy Christmas, Annie,' he says, kissing me. 'Tell her what?'

'That she should have had something to eat!' says Mum impatiently.

'You tell me a lot of things. But if Annie wants something to eat, there's no reason why she shouldn't. I can make her some pancakes while she opens her presents.'

'Not now. I'm talking about last night,' she says even more impatiently. 'Do you never listen to a word I say?'

She stomps off down the stairs, leaving us to follow at a safe distance.

'She has a terrible head this morning,' whispers Dad. 'She and Brenda Dawkins got through the best part of three bottles of wine last night.'

I stifle a giggle. 'And she has the cheek to accuse me of having a hangover.'

'Good party?' he enquires.

I beam at him. 'The best!'

'That's good.' He shoots me a quick look. 'You're allowed to have a hangover if you like. You're over twenty-one, and it isn't your mother's sole prerogative.'

We find Mum busily adjusting the stockings hanging from the mantlepiece.

'See?' she says. 'I told you Santa would come. Oh, here's Jamie. Happy Christmas, darling. Don't make too much noise. Your sister has a hangover.'

Jamie raises an eyebrow. 'Good for Annie. I didn't think she had it in her.'

'Don't encourage her!' says Mum. 'You should take some Alka-Seltzer, Annie, or you'll be in no fit state to enjoy Christmas. And pancakes won't help. You'd better have a full English breakfast.'

I laugh. 'You can make one if you like. Better still, I'll make you one. Come and sit down.'

'I am a little tired,' she says, allowing me to lead her to an armchair next to the fire. 'But nothing like you. Do as I tell you next time and line your stomach first.'

'I will,' I promise.

'I'll cook the breakfast,' says Dad. 'You stay and watch the children open their presents, Liz.'

'Good idea,' says Jamie. 'Otherwise, Mum will have no idea at all what's in our stockings.'

Mum darts a shocked look at me and makes a frantic gesture to Jamie.

He rolls his eyes. 'I think she has it figured out by now. She's twenty-one and, as she never tires of telling us, an adult.'

He gives me a sideways glance. 'Which is probably a good thing if the reports of what you got up to last night are true.'

'What are you talking about?' says Mum. 'What did she get up to last night?'

'Absolutely nothing!' I say. 'Jamie's being an idiot, as usual.'

She isn't satisfied. 'What did she get up to last night?'

'I thought we were going to open our presents,' I say.

She ignores me. 'You'd better tell me at once, Jamie. And don't look at me like that, Annie. Judging by the state of you this morning, you won't remember a thing about it.'

'I drank nothing but orange juice last night,' I say.

'Then someone must have spiked your drink. I hear that happens at parties nowadays. You aren't supposed to leave your drink unattended. I should have warned you.'

'I didn't leave my drink unattended,' I say. 'It was in my hand at all times.'

'Well, something obviously happened or your brother wouldn't be so concerned.'

'Not concerned,' I say, giving him a filthy look. 'He's just trying to make trouble.'

'She's right,' says Jamie. 'Nothing happened last night at the party. I didn't stop Sara Matthews choking on a sausage roll, and Mira didn't see Annie kissing Alex Fielding.'

Mum looks stunned. 'Is that true, Annie?'

'No!' I say, glaring at Jamie.

'I suppose Mira could have been wrong,' he says. 'She was pretty far gone by the end of the night. Maybe it was someone else Annie was kissing.'

'Alex Fielding,' says Mum thoughtfully. 'You could do a lot worse, Annie. Elaine tells me he has a very good job in Scotland. Engineering, apparently.'

I can't resist. 'He told me last night that he lives on deep-fried Mars bars.'

She gives an indulgent smile. 'All young men live like that when they first leave home. He needs someone to look after him.'

'And it sounds as though Annie is volunteering,' says Jamie, dodging the slap I aim at him.

'I don't plan to look after anyone,' I say. 'And certainly not Alex Fielding.'

'If that's your attitude, you'll never meet someone,' says Mum, but thankfully she drops the subject.

It isn't until we're finishing our Christmas pudding that Alex's name comes up again.

Jamie takes a huge bite and winces. 'Ouch!'

He spits something onto his plate and pokes it dubiously with his finger. 'What's this? It's the ring. That means marriage. Wasn't Annie supposed to get that?'

He rinses it carefully in his glass of water and hands it to me. I throw it back at him.

'What's all this?' asks Dad.

'Nothing!' I say.

'Your daughter hooked up with Alex Fielding at the party last night,' says Jamie with an innocent look.

'Don't say hooked up. It's a horribly vulgar expression,' says Mum.

'Sorry,' he says. 'I mean she's courting.'

'Alex Fielding?' says Dad. 'He's a nice lad. Are you going to see him again, Annie?'

I slam down my spoon. 'I didn't hook up with anyone last night. And neither did I get drunk. Leave me alone, please.'

Dad glances at me. 'That's enough, Jamie. Don't spoil a perfectly good meal. Anyway, I want to hear about your new girlfriend. You've hardly told us anything. Her name's Melissa, I think?'

Jamie launches into an enthusiastic recital about the absent Melissa and all her virtues, making her sound like a cross between Mother Teresa and The Archbishop of Canterbury.

Jamie and I clear up after lunch. He gives me a shamefaced look as he opens the dishwasher. 'Sorry about that, Sis. I went a bit far.'

I'm not yet ready to forgive him. 'More than a bit.'

'A lot far,' he says. 'Come on, Annie. It's Christmas. Peace?'

'I suppose so,' I grudgingly agree. 'But if you bring up that subject again, I'll tell Mum about the time you set fire to the boxes in the garage when you were smoking and blamed it on Paul Fisher.'

He laughs. 'I didn't know you knew about that.'

There are a lot of things I know about you,' I warn him. 'Just drop it, ok?'

He keeps his word, and the subject of Alex Fielding doesn't come up again either today or Boxing Day. It's always nice to see our uncle and cousins, but this year I hardly have patience to listen to their news and play all our usual Christmas games.

I keep looking at the clock, thinking how slowly the time is passing. And I still haven't decided where to take Alex tomorrow.

I'm thankful when they finally leave, and I'm able to go to bed, pleading exhaustion after all the festivities.

Chapter Six

I wake early the following morning. I know exactly where I'm going to take Alex. I open my phone and text. *Are you free at eleven?*

He texts straight back. *As a bird. Where are you taking me?*

I smile to myself as I answer. *That's a secret!*

His answer appears a minute later. *Fine, but you'll have to give me some clues. What's the dress code - ball gown, wetsuit, or ice hockey gear?*

I quickly type. *None of the above. Although now I'm worried about what you'll choose when it's your turn. Jeans and a warm sweater. Thick shoes too if you have them. Meet you at the spinney near the bus stop?*

I don't want to suggest meeting at either of our houses. I haven't met his mother, but if she's anything like mine, the whole thing could be excruciatingly embarrassing. For the time being, I'd prefer to meet him well away from both of them.

My phone pings. *I'll be there.*

I stare at it, wondering if he's still looking at his screen, waiting for me to message back. Of course, he isn't. We've said everything we need to. He'd probably gone to put away his wet suit for a later occasion.

Texting is odd, I reflect as I open my wardrobe. For the brief time you're messaging someone, it almost feels as though they're right there inside your phone, looking up at you. Then you say goodbye, and they disappear, and you realise they've been miles away from you all the time. Still, it isn't for long. I'm meeting him in a couple of hours.

I go downstairs to find Mum in the kitchen making coffee.

'Would you like one?' she asks.

'Just a quick one,' I say without thinking.

Her eyes narrow. 'Why? Are you going somewhere?'

'I thought I'd take a walk this morning. It's been so full on here for the last couple of days that some exercise might be nice.'

She looks thoughtful. 'Perhaps I'll come with you. Some fresh air would be nice after all that cooking.'

I almost let out a strangled squeak. I hadn't imagined that anyone would offer to come with me. None of my family are great walkers.

I think quickly. 'That would be lovely, but I'm planning on taking a long walk. I'll probably take some sandwiches with me and make a day of it.'

She considers this. 'Perhaps I'll sit this one out. If that's alright with you?'

I breathe a sigh of relief. 'Of course. Some other time.'

'But you aren't going without breakfast,' she says. 'Not on a day like this. Go and sit down, and I'll bring you something.'

'I'd love some toast,' I say. 'And while you're doing that, I'll make some sandwiches in case I stay out all afternoon.'

Mum bustles around making toast while I quickly cut a pile of sandwiches. I add a packet of biscuits and some chocolate.

'You won't be hungry if you get through that lot,' she says. 'You seem to go from one extreme to the other.'

'I'm being prepared,' I tell her. 'Wasn't that what they told us when I was a brownie?'

'I think that was Jamie in the cub scouts,' she says. 'Still, it's a very good motto to live by.'

I find an old backpack and put the picnic in it. Brownies can be just as well prepared as cub scouts. It may not be exactly what Brown Owl had in mind, but there's no reason not to apply her principles to a date with Alex.

It feels odd to think of this as a date. I've thought about him every day since September, but I didn't really expect anything to happen between us. It was like the time I had a crush on Justin Bieber when I was fifteen. Fun to think about and dream about, but something that even in my besotted state I never expected to happen.

Still, here I am, about to meet Alex for what is very definitely a date. You can't kiss someone as he kissed me on Chrismas Eve and then claim to be meeting up as friends.

I say goodbye to Mum, hoping I don't have a goofy smile on my face to give me away. Her eagle eye rarely misses anything. Luckily, she's up to her elbows in bread dough and barely looks up.

'Have a good time, love. Don't stay out after dark. I worry.'

'I won't,' I say. 'But you'll have to let me stay out after dark someday.'

'What you do when you're at university is your own business,' she says. 'When you're at home, under my roof, you can show a little consideration.'

'Got it,' I say. 'No boys, no drinking, and no smoking behind the bike sheds.'

She stops kneading. 'Don't be so ridiculous. I didn't say anything about boys. You're old enough to go out with a nice boy if you like. I've been meaning to ask you. Are there any …?'

'Not even a nice one,' I say hastily, wishing I'd never started this subject. 'I must get going if I plan to be back before dark. I don't want to turn into a pumpkin and freeze out there all night.'

'It's apple, not pumpkin,' Mum says absently. 'Although I'm not sure why I've bothered. I'm only making it because it's your brother's favourite, and now he's announced that he's going out with Melissa tonight.'

'Dad likes apple pie too,' I say. 'I'm sure it will all get eaten.'

'Yes, well!' she says in a tone that leaves me in no doubt what she thinks about having to cook a pie just for Dad.

I wonder whether all married couples end up like this – keen to find out about each other's favourite food, then thirty years later not considering it worthwhile to make it. Will Alex and I ever be like that? I stop this thought in its tracks. This is our first date. For all I know, it will go terribly, leaving us both hoping never to see the other one again.

The snow that started to fall on Christmas Eve continued throughout most of Christmas Day and Boxing Day. It stopped last night, but it shows no sign of thawing. The air is bitterly cold and would normally keep me indoors. But today I barely notice it. I walk as quickly as possible to our meeting place, feeling the snow crunch and squeak under my boots, almost skipping as I go.

Alex is waiting for me, stamping his feet. 'You made it!'

'Did you think I wouldn't?'

'For all I knew, it could have been an elaborate prank on your behalf,' he says. 'Setting me up to wait in the snow for hours, then sending one of your friends instead.'

'Suzy?' I say without thinking.

He looks surprised. 'I didn't have anyone specific in mind.'

I relax. Why did I mention Suzy?

'In fact, I rarely manage to persuade beautiful women to meet me,' he adds.

An image of Suzy flashes through my mind again, but I squash it. 'Now that we've ascertained it wasn't a prank, are you ready to go?'

'Absolutely!' he says. 'I took you at your word and left my wet suit and ice hockey stick at home.'

'Do you play ice hockey?' I ask as we walk towards the bus stop.

'Not only do I not play ice hockey,' he says, 'but I've never even been to an ice rink.'

'I wish I'd known that. I could have taken you ice skating today.'

'I'm glad you didn't,' he says. 'Personally, I've never seen the appeal. Sliding around the ice at dangerous speeds balanced on ridiculously thin pieces of metal and periodically crashing into other people has always seemed a strange way to spend an afternoon. And they have the cheek to charge you on top of it.'

'It's actually great fun,' I say. 'You don't know what you're missing.'

'I'll try it one day if you really want me to,' he promises. 'But now that we've established where we aren't going, where are we going?'

The bus slides to a halt beside us. 'You'll see,' I say, jumping onto the step and paying for both our tickets before he can object.

The journey into town feels a little awkward. We sit together on the back seat, and I'm reminded of taking the same bus into town for my first date when I was fifteen. Mason Carter asked me rather awkwardly whether I liked Star Wars because there was a back-to-back showing at the Odeon that weekend.

There were few films I disliked more, but I was flattered to be asked. I was even more flattered that he'd asked me and not Suzy. I spent an excruciatingly boring five hours sitting in the cinema, wondering why I'd come.

Alex seems to read my mind. 'It makes you feel like a teenager again, doesn't it?'

'How did you know what I was thinking?'

'I always know what you're thinking,' he says in a syrupy voice.

I grin. 'I bet you don't know what I'm thinking right now!'

'Thankfully not,' he says. 'I was remembering taking the bus into town with friends.'

'Didn't you say you grew up in London? It must have been an awful lot easier for you to take the bus than it was for us. There are only two a day. If you miss this one, you have to wait for three hours or give up and go home.'

'I'm very glad we didn't miss it,' he says, squeezing my hand.

He doesn't let go, and we spend the last five minutes of the journey with his hand firmly gripping mine. It makes me feel even more like a teenager, but it's nice. I've almost come to think of our Christmas Eve kiss as something magical, completely separate from real life. But the feeling of his hand in mine makes me feel comfortably connected again.

'Did you tell your parents where you were going today?' he asks.

'As a matter of fact, I didn't,' I say guiltily. 'Did you tell yours?'

'Also not. My parents are great, but …'

'Mine too,' I say. 'My mother is the village telegraph. If we had a massive nationwide power outage, and all other forms of communication were down, Honeywell would be absolutely fine. She'd make sure the lines of communication were kept open somehow.'

'My mum's a bit like that too,' he says. 'Although she isn't as terrifyingly efficient as yours, by the sound of it. Her saving grace is that she's easily distracted. She has lots of mad enthusiasms, but they don't last terribly long before she's on to the next thing. So, if she doesn't get to pass on a piece of news at once, there's a good chance she'll forget it.'

'This is our stop,' I say.

He drops my hand and picks up my backpack. 'What have you got in here – rocks? We aren't going to a rock-throwing contest, are we?'

'Not today,' I say. 'But I'll bear it in mind for another time.'

'Rock climbing?' he says.

'How many rocks do you think I have in here?'

He shrugs. 'Rock climbing for beginners, or for those who don't like heights.'

The bus stops and the driver opens the doors.

'You have a very odd impression of me,' I say, jumping out into the snow.

I lead the way down the high street and turn into a small shopping arcade. 'Here it is.'

He peers at the shop front. '*Paint Your World*'?

'That's right. They opened over the summer, and I've been dying to come here. But it felt weird to come by myself.'

He follows me inside. 'I don't see why. If you want to do something, there's no reason not to do it.'

'Is that the Alex Fielding philosophy of life?' I ask.

'Not always, but it seems a pretty good one.'

A boy who doesn't look a day over fourteen comes over to greet us. 'Good afternoon. Welcome to *Paint Your World*.'

He leads us towards a nearby table. 'Do you know the rules?'

'Perhaps you'd better explain them,' I say, not wanting to interfere with his evident desire to show off his knowledge of his job.

He points to the rows of shelves. 'You each choose one of those clay figures and paint them any way you like. The paints are here on the table. When you finish, bring them to me. I'll glaze them and put them into the kiln to fire. You can pick them up two days from now.'

'It seems to me that you have an unfair advantage,' Alex tells me.

'Meaning?'

He gestures to the pots of paint. 'Meaning that you can draw, and I can't.'

'There's no drawing involved,' I say. 'And I've seen you with a paintbrush. You're pretty good.'

'That was because you put me on river and grass duty. You didn't trust me to do any of the detailed stuff.'

'Not true,' I say. 'You were too chicken to try.'

'I didn't want to spoil the beautiful picture.'

I smile. 'You're the only one who has to live with this one. What are you going to paint?'

He considers the rows of figures. 'I think I'll paint this little guy.'

He picks up a puppy wearing a scarf and inspects it. 'I'll do my best to make sure the other dogs don't laugh at you,' he promises.

'Seriously – a puppy? I expected you to choose something far more ...'

'There's no good end to that sentence,' he says. 'Far more what?'

'I don't know. Macho, perhaps?'

'You told me I could choose,' he says. 'And I choose Cuthbert. How about you? I don't see any toads or water rats on display. A distressing omission. I'll have to talk to the management.'

'I think I'll paint this castle,' I say, picking it up and bringing it back to the table.

'I expected you to choose something a little more challenging,' he says.

'What do you mean?'

'Everything's marked out for you. It's symmetrical, and the bricks are already stamped on it. It doesn't seem particularly challenging for someone with your artistic talent.'

I pick up a paintbrush. 'That's what you think. This is the bare bones of the structure. I can add as little or as much as I want. That's the beauty of creativity.'

'Interesting.' He selects a pot of lilac paint. 'I'm going to start with the collar. Don't talk, or you'll distract me, and Cuthbert will be the laughingstock of the dog population of Honeywell.'

We paint in silence for a while. At last, Alex lays down the puppy and scrutinises my handiwork. 'That's beautiful. Is it any particular castle?'

'Not intentionally,' I say. 'I just liked the shape.'

'Square?' he says with a teasing glint in his eye.

I flush. Is that what he thinks of me? 'I don't mean the shape of the castle. And most castles are square, aren't they?'

He reaches out to pick it up, but I stop him. 'It isn't dry yet. You'll smudge it.'

'Is it the symmetry you like or the feeling of being safe?' he asks.

'I don't know. It's exactly the right proportions. It feels right.'

I pick up a tiny paint brush and dip it into the green paint. 'Don't distract me or the rose leaves will go everywhere.'

'Roses?' he says. 'You're being very thorough.'

'Of course. You didn't think I was going to paint the entire thing grey and brown?'

'It seems appropriate for a castle,' he says.

I squeeze a little pink paint onto the pallet. 'But that's only the beginning. You have to get the foundations right or none of it will work. Once you've done that, it's up to you what you want to do next. Everyone who paints these castles will do something different.'

'Like these puppies,' he says, picking up Cuthbert and inspecting him.

'I can safely say he's one of a kind,' I say, laughing at the orange and pink checked scarf.'

'So is your castle. I like the ivy.'

I don't look up from my rosebud. 'Castles have to have ivy.'

'But not all castles have roses.'

'Climbing roses are my favourite,' I say. 'I'm having them anyway.'

'Your rules,' he says. 'You can paint a zombie looking out of one of the turrets if you like.'

'That sounds like your kind of castle.'

He laughs. 'Not really. But I'm glad you're painting lots of plants. Cuthbert will love playing in them.'

'He isn't coming anywhere near my castle,' I say, shielding it from him with my arm as he zooms the puppy towards it. 'And put him down before you break him.'

'You sound like my mum,' he says.

I can't help smiling. 'I sound like my mum too. What a terrible thought. Fly him around the castle as much as you like.'

He swoops the puppy in circles. 'Who needs Godzilla when you have Cuthbert? But perhaps he'd better not fly over the castle anymore. I'd hate for him to forget himself at that height.'

I put down my paint brush and look at the finished castle.

'It's lovely,' he says. 'I can see why you went into art.'

'Graphic design,' I say.

'But it must take a lot of the same skills. I think I'd know who had painted that castle even if no one told me. It's neat and delicate and thoughtful and original and very pretty, just like you.'

'Thank you,' I say, embarrassed.

He waves the puppy at me. 'Cuthbert is waiting for a similar compliment.'

'He's definitely an Alex Fielding creation,' I say. 'Messy and unpredictable, but oddly lovable.'

He gives me a smug look. 'That's the nicest thing you've ever said to me.'

I pick up the castle. 'I think it's dry enough to take it to the counter. Come on, Cuthbert.'

The young boy takes our models. He looks appreciatively at mine. 'You're very talented.'

'And?' Alex prompts him.

The boy looks at the puppy. 'It's a good effort. Practice makes perfect. Maybe you can come again and try painting a different model?'

'That put me in my place, didn't it?' says Alex when we get outside. 'It reminds me of my old school reports. *Tries hard, could do better.* I bet you never got comments like that.'

'Probably not,' I say. 'I was always terrified of my teachers being upset with me, so I worked really hard.'

'Whereas I wasn't particularly bothered,' he says. 'Where did you get that from?'

'Get what from?'

'Caring what people thought about you.'

I'm about to brush this off with a light comment, but he's looking unusually serious.

'I'm not sure,' I say slowly. 'Perhaps from my mother. It's always been important to her what people think of her. She lives in dread of not having a perfectly clean house and an immaculate garden. And she likes to be appropriately dressed for every occasion.'

'Some people are like that,' he says. 'But I can't imagine you being obsessed with a house and garden and fancy clothes.'

I look down at my faded jeans. 'I'm not sure what leads you to that conclusion! I don't know why school made me so nervous. It just did. It felt important for my teachers to have a good opinion of me.'

'I'm sure they did,' he says. 'How could they not? So, that's what led to you being such a perfectionist?'

'Am I a perfectionist?'

'Surely you've realised that by now? I noticed it the first time we met when you were so insistent on getting every tiny little detail of that mural right. It didn't seem hugely important to me that Mr Toad had a checked waistcoat instead of a striped one. But it was obviously important to you, and I respected that.'

'A lot of children use that hall,' I say defensively. 'I wanted to make it perfect for them.'

He takes my hand. 'I'm not criticising you, Annie. It's a great thing to care so much about other people and making them happy. But don't be too hard on yourself in the process. And don't be too hard on other people when they don't live up to your standards.'

'I don't care what other people do,' I say. 'We all make our own choices.'

'And I'm sure yours will always be good ones. It's one of the things I really like about you – how much you care.'

He smiles at me, and my heart skips a beat. For whatever reason, he's someone whose good opinion of me matters desperately. But that doesn't seem to be an issue. He seems to like me just as I am. Which is a good thing because I know I'm falling for him very quickly.

He breaks the silence. 'Have we finished? Would you like to find something to eat?'

I point to my backpack. 'You don't get off that lightly. This was only the beginning. You can eat when we get there.'

And, ignoring all his questions and increasingly ridiculous speculations, I lead him back towards the bus stop.

Chapter Seven

I refuse to tell him where we're headed, despite his repeated questions. He attacks me in various ingenious ways during the journey, but I don't answer.

'You're like a toddler,' I complain at last. 'Can't you wait for ten more minutes to find out?'

'Sorry,' he says with a contrite expression. He waits another thirty seconds before asking plaintively, 'Are we there yet?'

'No wonder your teachers didn't like you,' I say.

'I never said that.'

'Yes, you did. You said it earlier on when we were talking about our reports.'

He shakes his head. 'I said I didn't get great reports, not that my teachers didn't like me.'

'There doesn't seem much difference to me.'

'Maybe that's because you equate success and approval.'

I consider this. 'I don't think so. I like to do my best. What's wrong with that?'

'Nothing,' he says. 'What would our society do without perfectionists and high achievers?'

I don't answer. I've always taken it for granted that doing my absolute best is a good thing, whereas Alex seems to regard it as a bit of a joke.

'Have I upset you?' he asks gently.

'Not really. But I always have the feeling you're laughing at me.'

'I laugh at everything.'

'There must be some things you take seriously,' I say.

'I take you very seriously,' he says.

'Not noticeably.'

He squeezes my hand. 'I'm sorry. I always make jokes when I'm nervous.'

I look at him in surprise. 'Nervous? About me?'

'Of course! Do you realise how nerve racking these past few months have been for me? First of all, I meet the girl of my dreams. Then she's whisked away and refuses to give me her number –'

'That's not right,' I say. 'You never asked for my number.'

'Yes, I did. I gave Suzy my number when I met her again and asked her to pass it on to you. I didn't like to ask her for your number directly. It might have put her in a difficult position. Besides, it wouldn't have been fair to you. But I hoped very much that you might make some sort of contact between then and now.'

He sees my stunned face and adds quickly, 'I realise there was absolutely no reason for you to do so. But I still hoped that by some miracle you would. I must have checked my phone fifty times a day over the past few months.'

'But I didn't have your number,' I insist. 'Suzy never mentioned it to me. I suppose she must have forgotten.'

'Maybe, but I know she still has it because she's texted me a few times.'

I feel a spurt of anger, which I quickly suppress. It isn't Suzy's fault. She probably forgot.

'Maybe you didn't make it clear that you wanted me to have it,' I say at last.

'I don't see how I could have made it any more clear,' he says. 'She must have known that I was interested in you.'

'What did she text you about?' I ask in as neutral tone as I can manage.

'This and that,' he says casually. 'She suggested visiting me one weekend, but I had a work thing, so it wasn't convenient.'

I swallow hard. 'Would you have said yes otherwise?'

'It's a free country,' he says. 'At least, for now.'

Which wasn't quite what I asked. But I don't want to press the subject.

'If she'd remembered to give me you my number, would you have texted me?' he asks.

I'm not sure how to answer. I'm still smarting over his casual revelation that he and Suzy have been in contact for months without me knowing anything about it. Suzy didn't mention it when we met at the cafe. Hopefully, that was because it was too unimportant for her to remember. But if she was planning to go and visit him, she must have liked him.

'We're getting off at the next stop,' I say. 'Can you press the button?'

He gives me an odd look but does so. 'Are you ok?'

'I'm fine.' I look at his feet. 'I'm glad you wore thick boots. You're going to need them.'

'And to think I nearly wore my flippers,' he says.

The bus pulls away, and Alex looks around him. 'Where are we?'

'You haven't been here before?' I ask.

'I don't think so, although everything looks different in the snow. I was only here for a week in the summer. I haven't had time to explore the area yet.'

'That's what I thought. I hope you're ok with walking?'

'I'm familiar with the general concept,' he says. 'I have been since my first birthday.'

I pick up my backpack and lead him across the lane towards the base of a small hill. 'How about climbing?'

'We aren't going up there?' he says.

'Why not?'

'The other way of putting that is *why*?' he says, following me.

'You know what Mallory said about Everest?'

He groans. 'Because it's there? I've always thought that was a ridiculous answer. It's a combination of snarky self-satisfaction and completely evading the question.'

I quicken my pace. 'I thought your philosophy of life was to try everything once?'

'To try some things once,' he says. 'And then to repeat the best of them as often as possible.'

'Which is what we're doing,' I say. 'You've never been up to the top of St Michael's Hill. By the time you have, you'll probably add it to your list of things you want to do repeatedly.'

He bends down to re-tie his shoelace. 'I have snow coming in over the top of my boots. I somehow doubt that climbing a hill in the middle of nowhere on a freezing cold winter's day will end up on my list of annual must dos. But you never know. I could be wrong.'

'That's the spirit,' I encourage him. 'Are your boots really not thick enough?'

He straightens up. 'They're fine. I'm being a wuss. My parents tell me that as a child I never walked anywhere without first ascertaining whether there was an alternative means of transport.'

'Like the bus?'

'Like being carried or sitting in my push chair,' he says. 'Mum says she was terrified I would insist on riding in that to my first day at school.'

'I'd love to have seen that.'

'I spared her that,' he says. 'My manly pride would never have coped with it. I got her to take me in the car instead.'

'We don't have a car or a pushchair,' I say. 'And I don't have the faintest intention of carrying you. So, you're on your own.'

'The story of my life,' he complains, quickening his pace to catch up with me.

We turn off the path and strike off across an expanse of snow.

'The snow isn't as thick as it looks,' I say. 'Can you see those tufts of grass peeping through? Follow those.'

'I may not be country raised like you,' he says, 'but I've read plenty of books about this sort of thing. I think it's all a trick, and you're luring me off the path and into a swamp.'

'Wouldn't I get sucked into the swamp too?' I ask.

'You were raised in the countryside,' he says. 'You probably know all the secret routes, like in The Hound of the Baskervilles.'

'With Cuthbert playing the part of the hound? I can't quite see it.'

'We can't collect him for another two days,' he says. 'I'm not sure what he'll do without me.'

'If he's anything like his master, he'll probably be busy trashing my castle.'

He pokes a tuft of grass with his boot. 'Seriously, are you sure this will take my weight?'

'Perfectly sure. I've been coming up here all year round since I was a little girl.'

He moves closer to me. 'Nevertheless, I'd feel an awful lot safer holding on to you.'

I hold out my hand. 'Come on then. It's less effort than carrying you.'

We pick our way across the patch of snow towards the path on the other side. At one point, I put my foot on a deceptively solid patch of snow, which gives way, and I disappear almost up to my thigh.

Alex reaches down and pulls me out. 'I thought you knew every inch of this mountain?'

'Every other inch,' I say. 'And it isn't a mountain. It's barely even a hill.'

'A pretty big hill. Are you ok? You must be soaked.'

I brush the snow off my jeans. 'Nothing to worry about. Unlike you, I laced my boots tightly enough that the snow didn't go down them.'

He doesn't take my hand again but instead slips his arm around my shoulders. I feel the warmth of his body against mine as I put my arm around his waist.

'That's better,' he says. 'Now we're like proper mountaineers.'

'They use ropes,' I say.

'I know. And crampons, whatever they are. But we'll have to do the best with what we have.'

He turns and looks back the way we've come. 'It's a good thing your mum didn't know we were coming here today.'

I follow his gaze. 'What do you mean?'

'She'd find it pretty easy to track us.'

'She is a bit like a bloodhound,' I agree.

'Like Cuthbert.'

'Not yet,' I say. 'First, he has to go into the kiln.'

'True. He has a busy couple of days ahead of him. I only hope he'll survive the baking process.'

'He'll be fine,' I say. 'Unless he has a bubble in him.'

'A bubble?'

'Yes, it's important to work the clay to get all the air out of it before it goes into the kiln. Otherwise, it might explode.'

He stops dead. 'That's it! I'm going back to rescue him.'

I tug at his arm. 'I was only teasing. He'll be fine. He'll be ready for his bloodhound duties in no time. Not that it would take a trained bloodhound. Those tracks are as clear as day.'

'True,' he says. 'You can see where we came off the path over there. Your footprints are the smaller ones going in a completely straight line. The footprints of a woman who knows exactly where she's going.'

I squint against the rays of the setting sun. 'They didn't go in a straight line for long. Look at that messy patch of snow. That's where I disappeared down the hole.'

'And where I carried out my daring rescue,' he adds. 'If it hadn't been for me, you'd have been stranded here all night.'

'We're on the main path now,' I say. 'So, you can stop worrying.'

'I'm still not letting go,' he says. 'It doesn't feel safe. There could be wild animals around.'

'Such as?'

'I don't know. I've already told you I wasn't raised in the countryside. Wolves, probably. And badgers.'

'Badgers?'

'I thought you'd read The Wind in the Willows,' he says. 'As soon as it goes dark, there'll be stoats and weasels and goodness knows what appearing and planning to attack us. We'll have to light a fire.'

I point towards a snow-covered pile of rocks. 'That's exactly what I intend to do.'

He gives me a suspicious look. 'I can't tell whether you're joking.'

'I'm not. My dad keeps a pile of single-use barbeques in the garage. I swiped one this morning when he wasn't looking.'

'You're a marvel,' he says. 'But what are we going to cook? Don't say that it's my job to fashion a makeshift bow and arrow and stalk some innocent squirrel or pigeon?'

'Of course not.' I open my backpack and pull out the barbecue. 'It won't be terribly traditional. Mum would have had asked questions if I'd tried to take a steak or sausages. She always knows exactly what she has in the fridge.'

He brushes the snow off the flattest rock and perches on it. 'Now I really am intrigued. What did you manage to bring?'

I hand him a box of matches. 'You light the barbecue, and I'll unpack the food.'

'I'm glad you've given me the manly job,' he says, taking the matches from me. 'You can't think how it boosts my confidence.'

I look up from unpacking my bag. 'Manly job?'

'Making the fire,' he says. 'Men have been doing that since the dawn of time.'

'You'd better hope those matches didn't get wet when I fell in that hole,' I say. 'Otherwise, you'll have to demonstrate those manly skills with a couple of twigs.'

He strikes a match and carefully lights the barbecue. 'Thank goodness for that. I might have had to buy you a pub dinner instead. Now it's your turn.'

'Are you sure you don't want to cook?' I say. 'Men always seem to insist on cooking at barbecues. I'd hate to damage your fragile masculinity.'

He settles back onto the rock. 'Not at all. My work is done. I'll sit here and tell you what you're doing wrong. I don't suppose you thought to bring a beer?'

I open the packet of sandwiches. 'Only a flask of coffee, I'm afraid.'

He looks disappointed. 'You didn't have the forethought to make it Irish?'

'My dad would notice if any of his whisky disappeared.'

He sighs. 'Never mind. If we get into trouble on the way back down, I expect they'll send us one of those St. Bernard's with the little kegs around their necks.'

I lay the cheese sandwiches carefully on the grill and wait until they're cooked on one side. I forgot to bring a fork, so I pick up a twig and use it to flip the sandwiches over.

'That smells good,' he says appreciatively. 'Cheese sandwiches aren't the first thing that comes to mind when you think about planning a barbecue. But you never know, it could catch on.'

I perch next to him on the rock while we finish the grilled cheese sandwiches.

'What's next?' he asks when the last one has disappeared. 'Baked Alaska?'

'Maybe next time.' I reach into my backpack and pull out a packet of digestive biscuits, a bag of marshmallows, and a bar of chocolate.

'S'mores?' he says. 'Fantastic! We used to make those when we went camping.'

I give the barbecue a dubious look. 'It's nearly gone out. But there should be enough heat left to make them.'

'Of course, there is!' He picks up two long sticks and hands me one. 'Put some marshmallows on the end of that and hold them over the heat.'

We manage to melt our marshmallows, only dropping one of them into the flames. Alex hooks it out with his twig and eats it anyway.

We break the chocolate into pieces and sandwich the biscuits together with the chocolate and marshmallows.

'Next time MasterChef is recruiting, you and I are definitely going to enter,' Alex says through a mouthful of biscuit. 'The judges won't know what's hit them.'

'It must make a change from deep-fried mars bars,' I say. 'What's it really like in Scotland?'

He swallows the last few crumbs. 'It's absolutely lovely. I was in two minds about taking that job, but I'm glad I did. Edinburgh's a great town to live in, and the countryside around it is stunning.'

I put down my stick and brush biscuit crumbs off my jeans. 'Why were you in two minds about the job?'

He doesn't answer for a moment. When I glance at him, I'm surprised to see his face has turned pink.

He meets my eyes at last. 'I'm embarrassed to say it was because of you.'

'Because of me?' I echo, astonished.

He nods. 'If you remember, we met the day before I was offered that interview. I almost turned it down. I know I'd only just met you, but I didn't want to move so far away. It seemed like a miracle that we'd met at all. If my parents hadn't decided out of the blue to move to Honeywell, we'd never have met. But they did, and we did, and I fell for you at once. Meeting you felt like, oh, I don't know, coming home. Does that sound ridiculous?'

'No,' I say quietly. 'That's exactly how I felt too. Did you really consider not taking that job because of me?'

He puts his arm around me. 'I really did. I thought about looking for jobs in London instead. But I told myself not to be ridiculous. For all I knew, you wouldn't want to see me again after you'd gone back to university. So, I went for the interview and decided to take the job when they offered it to me. It's a great firm, and I'm getting good experience there. But I don't necessarily plan to be there forever –'

He breaks off, and I rest my head on his shoulder. 'I'm glad. I mean, I'm glad that it's a good place for you to work and that you're enjoying it.'

I feel his shoulders shake as he laughs. 'That's it?'

I move closer to him. 'I'm also pleased that it might not be forever.'

We sit in silence watching the sun slip closer towards the horizon.

'We'd better pack up soon,' I say at last. 'We don't want to be climbing back down the hill in the dark.'

'Let's watch a bit more of the sunset,' he says.

I sigh. 'It's absolutely gorgeous, isn't it? That's why I decided to bring you up here. You get the best view for miles around. It's lovely in the summer, but I think that sunset on a snowy day is the most beautiful thing I've ever seen. But it gets dark very quickly once the sun reaches the horizon.'

He turns to face me. 'In which case, I'd better not try to count down like I did on Christmas Eve.'

'Not unless you want a broken ankle.'

He looks at the sky. 'I reckon we have about fifteen minutes before the sun sets. Ten minutes to walk down the hill …'

'And five for …?' I ask.

'This,' he says, bending his head to kiss me.

Chapter Eight

I wake on Friday with a pleasurable feeling of anticipation. I switch on my phone. There's always a text waiting for me from Alex. He's obviously an earlier riser than I am, at least during the holidays.

As I'd hoped, there's a new notification on my screen. *Ten o'clock - usual place?*

I like that we've already fallen into a shorthand together. There's no need for formal greetings and preliminaries. Besides, it will give nothing away to Mum if she manages to get a look at my phone. I've changed the passcode as a precaution, but there's no real need. Mum is completely technologically challenged. Still, I feel safer with an entirely new code.

I was tempted to make it out of the letters of Alex's name. But even if Mum would have been baffled, Jamie wouldn't. And from the hints he's been dropping all week, he has a fair idea of what's going on.

There's nothing I can do about that. Alex and I have agreed that we'll let our families know we're seeing each other at the New Year's Eve party. Hopefully, we can find a private place at midnight. I can't imagine the embarrassment of kissing him as the clock strikes, watched by so many curious pairs of eyes.

I wouldn't put it past Mum to criticise our technique. I can hear her voice. 'Not like that, Annie! Why are you so awkward? Go on, Alex, try again. Don't take any notice of her. She's just being difficult.'

I text him a quick thumbs up and jump out of bed.

There's just enough time for a quick shower and breakfast before I have to leave. I hum to myself as I shower, careful to keep the volume low. Mum's keen ears are quick to detect any unwonted cheerfulness in any of us.

No one is downstairs. I wonder where everyone is. Jamie stayed over at Melissa's last night and won't be back until this evening. Perhaps Mum and Dad have gone to the supermarket. Mum's been complaining that her Christmas Eve food delivery has almost disappeared.

I switch on the kettle and pour myself a bowl of cereal, adding a generous splash of the full fat milk I find hidden at the back of the fridge. Mum has insisted that Dad drinks skimmed milk ever since the doctor told him his cholesterol was slightly raised.

I dump my bowl into the dishwasher and go upstairs to pack my bag. I have no idea what to take with me. Alex has been annoyingly vague.

You wouldn't tell me where we were going. Now it's your turn to sweat, he texted yesterday.

All he would tell me was that I should wear old clothes, which seems to rule out lunch at a Michelin starred restaurant. I'm thankful for that. I'm never comfortable in overly formal surroundings.

I leave the house, remembering to double lock the front door. Mum is convinced that Honeywell is a hotbed of crime. She suspects all new inhabitants and visitors of being possible burglars. She only relaxes her vigilance when they've lived there for five years without displaying any obvious criminal tendencies.

I reach the spinney before Alex and walk up and down, stamping my feet to keep warm. The snow still hasn't melted, although the temperature has at least climbed above zero during the past couple of days.

Alex arrives a few minutes later. He smiles as he sees me glance quickly around. 'It's far too cold for the village busybodies to be out.'

'My parents are out today,' I tell him. 'I have no idea why. It would be just like them to be walking past at the exact moment you arrived.'

'We'd better get out of here,' he says, looking amused. 'Hurry up. The bus arrives in five minutes. We don't have three hours to spare if we miss it.'

The bus is pulling up as we get to the stop. We run the last few steps and jump on board.

'It's my turn to pay today,' he says. 'That's why we're doing something free.'

He laughs at my startled expression. 'I'm kidding. You're incredibly easy to wind up, aren't you?'

The bus ride into town feels far more comfortable than the last one. We chat easily as the bus jolts and rattles along the country lanes.

We get off at the final stop and walk along the high street hand in hand. I don't bother to check whether there's anyone I know. We'll only be jumping the gun by a couple of days. It's worth the risk.

'We're taking that shuttle bus,' says Alex.

I stare at it suspiciously. 'I can't read the logo on the side.'

'It was the only one I could get at such short notice,' he says. 'I hired it especially.'

'You didn't?'

'Of course, I did. It's the Alex Fielding version of a limousine.'

We cross the road, and I stop dead. 'Seriously, Alex – paintball?'

'I'm afraid so,' he says. 'It looked too good to resist.'

A group of teenagers approaches from the opposite direction and climbs on board the bus.

Alex sighs. 'I knew this would happen. I told them I wanted to hire the whole thing. But you know how it is with the youth of today …'

I can't help laughing. 'If it's absolutely inevitable, let's go.'

We climb onto the bus and sit near the front. A man in a camouflage suit speaks to the driver, the doors close, and the bus pulls away from the kerb.

The man nods to us and goes to sit with the teenage boys.

'What made you choose this?' I ask.

'I've always wanted to try it. You're my convenient excuse.'

'I'm flattered,' I say politely.

Half an hour later, the bus pulls into a car park by the side of the road. The man in camouflage walks to the front of the bus.

'Right, everyone, listen up! This is a fun day out, as long as you follow the rules. Any mucking about, and you're out. No ifs, no buts, no excuses, and absolutely no refunds, so don't even ask.'

'I think he's talking to you,' whispers Alex.

'I do have a criminal face,' I whisper back.

The leader gives us a sharp look. 'That goes for you two as well.'

'Yes, sir,' says Alex.

I nudge him. 'I thought you'd arranged this bus just for us. I suggest you don't bring him next time.'

The instructor explains the rules and hands out the protective clothing. 'You'll see from your map the area in which you need to stay. I've marked each person's starting point. The rules are simple. Once you've been shot, return to base, where lunch will be provided.'

'Do you think he's brought a barbecue?' I say.

'I doubt it,' says Alex. 'This isn't a romantic date like yours. But you and I will always have s'mores.'

'You'd better get going,' I warn him. 'You need to get to your starting point before those teenagers see you. At your height, you'd be a sitting duck.'

He shoots me a challenging look. 'May the best man win.'

'Thank you. I intend to,' I say and run off down the path.

I reach my starting point and listen for the whistle. Did Alex really find our previous date romantic? Painting models and getting soaked hiking up a hill is hardly a candlelit dinner for two, but I'm glad he enjoyed it. It's rare to find someone who enjoys the same sorts of things as I do. I hope he wasn't being polite.

The whistle shrills through the frozen air, making me jump. I'd almost forgotten where I was. I look around me nervously. There's no one in sight. I haven't decided whether to take cover and wait for my opponents to arrive or start stalking them.

I hide behind a bush while I consider my options. My feet are already frozen, so I decide on the second one. There's no point staying here, only to be discovered an hour later, unpainted but frozen to the spot.

I set off cautiously through the undergrowth, keeping hidden as far as possible. This isn't the best time of year to hide behind foliage, but there's enough cover for me to make a fair bit of progress without fear of being shot.

I reach a clearing and see to my surprise that Alex is standing there, studying his map. My first instinct is to shout to him to hide, but that isn't the point of the game. I consider whether I could hit him from here and decide I probably couldn't.

There's very little cover between us. If I make any noise or sudden movements, he'll turn at once and see me. I have no idea whether he's a good shot, but I don't want to take the risk.

I stand behind a holly bush, thinking hard. I've just decided to break cover and race towards him, taking my chances on being able to hit him before he turns around, when a movement catches my eye. One of the teenage boys has emerged from behind a tree and is walking stealthily towards Alex, his gun raised to his shoulder. Without stopping to think, I step out from behind the holly bush, aim at him and fire.

To my amazement, he lets out a gasp and staggers. He spins around and sees me standing there. He gives me a furious look, and I shrug. 'Sorry.'

He glares at me and stalks off towards the main path. I turn to look for Alex, but he's disappeared. I barely have time to wonder where he's gone when I hear a branch break behind me.

'Don't even think about it,' says an amused voice.

'Are you going to shoot me in the back?' I wait for the clatter of his gun and the splatter of paint, but it doesn't come.

I turn at last to see him grinning at me. 'Any last requests – a cigarette, perhaps, or a final s'more?'

'I should have shot you when I had the chance,' I say resignedly.

He looks surprised. 'When was that?'

'Just now! That boy I shot was about to shoot you. You were standing right in the middle of the clearing, looking at your map and not even watching. You were a sitting duck.'

He lowers his gun. 'Seriously, you shot him to save me?'

'It was instinct. It won't happen again. Anyway, that's what we're meant to be doing – shooting all our opponents. So, go ahead. I should have kept my eye on you.'

He doesn't move. 'It feels a bit unsportsmanlike. You saved me, and now I haven't shot you, so we're quits. Why don't we team up and beat those kids together?'

'We aren't supposed to be working in teams.'

'No one will court martial us if we don't follow the rules exactly,' he says. 'Besides, it's only until we've taken them all out. After that, it's you and me. No mercy shown.'

'What's the plan?'

He waves his map. 'Everyone's starting positions are marked on here. I think we should check those out first. Not everyone will have left them. Some of them will have decided to stay and snipe at the people looking for them. But if we're working together, that should make it easier. One of us can cause a diversion and catch their attention, and the other one can shoot them.'

'Talk about unsportsmanlike!' But I follow him as he sets off down the path.

We hear shouts and yells nearby.

'It's hard to tell where the sounds are coming from on a day like this,' says Alex.

'It's the snow,' I say. 'It makes the sound travel further, but it's a bit echoey.'

He points. 'I'm pretty sure it was coming from over there. Shall we check it out?'

We step off the path and make our way carefully towards where the sound is coming from. As we get nearer, we hear yells and laughs and the noise of paintball guns firing.

Alex leans down to whisper in my ear. 'You go that way and hide in that clump of trees, and I'll go in the other direction. That way, we'll have them surrounded, and we can pick them off before they even know we're here.'

I stifle a giggle. He looks so serious. 'Good luck!' I whisper.

'There's no need for luck when you have strategy and cunning,' he whispers back.

He makes a choking sound, and I turn in alarm. 'Are you ok?'

He's doubled over. When he straightens up, holding out his hand, I see it's covered in red liquid.

'They got me!' he gasps. 'Run for it, Annie!'

I hesitate a moment too long, not sure whether to stay and check he's alright.

'That's the one who got Matt!' says a voice behind me.

I turn around to see two boys standing with their guns pointed at me.

'You aren't supposed to be working in teams,' I say without thinking.

'Neither are you,' says the taller one.

I clench my teeth and wait for them to shoot me.

'Stop!' shouts Alex. 'How much?'

'How much for what?' says the red-headed boy.

Alex pulls his wallet out of his pocket. 'How much not to shoot her?'

'Alex!' I say, trying not to laugh.

'Are you serious?' says the boy.

'Perfectly serious,' says Alex. He takes a few steps towards them. 'I have … let me see … twenty-five pounds. I also have a few first-class postage stamps, if they're any good to you.'

'We could get you banned for life if we told Ted you tried to buy us off,' says the first boy.

'Yeah,' chimes in the other. 'Where's your sense of fair play?'

Alex shrugs. 'I tried,' he tells me.

'This is for Matt!' the boys say in unison and shoot me. The paint capsules hit me in the stomach and chest, and I gasp, temporarily winded. 'That hurt!'

'It would have hurt a whole lot more without the protective clothing,' says Alex. 'What are you waiting for?' he asks the boys. 'Go and finish the game. And I hope you both trip over your guns and break your legs.'

The boys laugh. 'See you!'

'What was that you were saying about strategy and cunning?' I ask.

Alex takes my hand. 'We'll get them next time.'

'You think I'm playing this again?'

'Of course. Don't tell me you didn't have a good time?'

'I suppose I did,' I admit. 'Shall we go and get some lunch?'

Ted is waiting for us at the meeting place. He looks at me in surprise. 'How many people shot you?'

'Only two,' I say, helping myself to a sandwich. 'But it was at pretty close range.'

'Ah, well,' he says philosophically. 'I hope you enjoy your lunch. There's a flask of hot coffee over there.'

An hour later, everyone is back in the car park. A fair-haired girl of about sixteen is the only one not to have been shot. She's awarded a small trophy while everyone whoops and cheers.

'That's the third time you've won, isn't it?' asks Ted.

'It's good practise,' says the girl. 'I do archery in the summer, so this is a way to keep my hand in.'

'I'm glad we were only doing paintball,' whispers Alex. 'I wouldn't want to be around her when she has a bow and arrow. It would be like taking part in the Hunger Games.'

We all pile onto the bus, talking and laughing.

'I'm sorry I can't spend the rest of the afternoon with you,' says Alex as the bus sets off. 'I told Mum when I came home that I'd go to see my great uncle with her. And this is the only afternoon he's free. Maybe we could meet up this evening?'

'I can't,' I say. 'I'm going out to dinner with my family.'

'And I'm at my grandparents' house all day tomorrow. So, it looks as though I won't see you until our New Year's Eve party.'

'I'm looking forward to it,' I say.

'So am I. But I'm not looking forward to New Year's Day.'

I sigh. 'I know, but let's not think about that now. At least I'll see you on New Year's Day, even if it's only for a few minutes after midnight.'

'What time do you leave for Paris?' he asks.

'Dad's taking me to catch the seven o'clock train. I'm really not looking forward to that. Everyone else will be tucked up safely in bed when I leave.'

'Can I come and see you off?' he asks.

'Do you really want to get up at six thirty on New Year's Day and come to the train station?'

'If it means seeing you.'

I feel a rush of pleasure. He doesn't seem to regard this as nothing more than a holiday romance, to be forgotten the moment I leave the country.

'You'd be very welcome to come,' I say at last. 'But don't forget that Dad will be there.'

'Not if I pick you up and take you,' he says.

'I'd love that. But then everyone would know about you and me.'

He put his arm around me. 'They have to know sometime or other. I thought we'd agreed to tell them at the party if things were going well.'

'We did,' I say. 'So, things are going well?'

He draws me closer. 'I think so. Don't you?'

'I do.' I rest my head on his shoulder.

'We've even bought a puppy together,' he reminds me. 'It takes most couples a lot longer to make that kind of a commitment.'

'You don't even know whether he's survived the kiln,' I say.

'True, but I'll find out this afternoon. Mum's bound to spend ages with my great uncle. I'll slip out for a breath of air and pick up the castle and Cuthbert. I'll bring them to the party with me.'

'And we'll tell our parents then,' I say.

'Or we can wait until I kiss you at midnight. That ought to give them a clue.'

'Everyone kisses everyone at midnight on New Year's Eve,' I say and feel his arm tighten around me.

'Not the way I plan to kiss you. Would you like a demonstration now?'

'In front of those boys who shot us? I don't think so.'

He sighs. 'You're probably right. But they won't be at the party, so all bets are off.'

We reach the bus stop all too quickly. We thank Ted and watch the teenagers walk down the high street, chattering and laughing.

Alex and I take the bus back to Honeywell. Neither of us talks much on the journey. I'm trying not to think about New Year's Day, and I'm pretty sure he is too.

'I'll see you tomorrow night,' he says when we arrive at our stop.

I look along the street, but there's no one there I know. I tiptoe up to kiss him. 'I can't wait.'

Chapter Nine

New Year's Eve doesn't start too auspiciously. First, Mum runs out of asparagus.

'Someone will have to go to the supermarket,' she says. 'I promised to take a quiche tonight, and I can't make it without the asparagus. How can a bunch of asparagus disappear? It can't have grown legs and walked out of the fridge all by itself.'

'Don't look at me,' I say. 'I don't even like asparagus. Can't you substitute spinach or something?'

'No, I can't! Everyone loves my asparagus quiche. I really want to take one to the party tonight.'

As soon as I get back from the supermarket, she discovers she's run out of eggs. I turn around and get back in the car. There's no point in arguing with Mum when she's in this sort of mood.

She cheers up a little after lunch. 'Now that's out of the way, I can spend the afternoon helping you with your packing.'

'I've done it,' I say.

'But you're bound to have forgotten something. And you've probably thrown everything in there any old how. By the time you get to Paris, it will be all crumpled and grubby. You know how important it is to make a good first impression. Those Parisian women are always perfectly turned out. I don't know how they do it.'

'They'll be too busy sorting out their own outfits to care what I look like,' I say.

But Mum is having none of it. 'You're an ambassador for your country. We can't have their first impression of British women spoiled by crumpled clothes.'

'I think they've probably met British women before,' I say. 'It's the twenty-first century. I'm sure at least a few of them have ventured through the channel tunnel.'

But there's no point in arguing. She ushers me upstairs, where she inspects my suitcase. 'Just as I thought! Nothing gets done around here without me. You haven't folded those shirts properly. It will take you hours to iron them all when you arrive.'

I sit on the bed. 'It's a good thing I never iron anything.'

She gives a gasp of horror. 'Of course, you must iron your clothes! Have you packed your travel iron?'

'Not only have I not packed one, but I barely even know what one is. I'm sure the family I'm staying with will have an iron if I really want one.'

'Do you know the French word for iron?' she asks.

'Not a clue. But I know how to point at things and grunt.'

Mum sighs. 'If it isn't like you to have done no preparation at all. Have you learned any of the language?'

'Only what we did at school. I'm sure I'll pick it up when I'm there. And the course is in English.'

'Maybe you'll meet a nice French man while you're out there,' she says hopefully. 'They're very handsome, aren't they?'

'All of them?' I ask.

'You know what I mean! All the French presidents are very good looking.'

'Maybe that's how they got to be president,' I say. 'All the other French men are so hideously ugly that there was no competition.'

She pulls out a pile of sweaters. 'I think we'd better start again from the beginning. You've put your boots on top of everything. They should have gone in first.'

'Feel free, if it makes you feel better,' I say resignedly.

She sits back on her heels, looking anxious. 'I'm worried about you, going so far away all by yourself.'

It's barely further than university,' I say. 'And you don't worry about me there.'

'Of course, I do!' she says. 'But we could get to you in a couple of hours in an emergency. It would take us much longer to get to Paris. There's the Channel, for one thing.'

'You could always swim.' I see her anxious look and relent. 'I'll be perfectly ok. I'm staying with a family, and several of my friends are going too. It's only until Easter. I'll be back before you know it.'

'Maybe we could come and visit you,' she says, brightening.

I quail. 'I don't think there'll be time. I'll be extremely busy with my studies. The exchange program has arranged several trips for us, and my host family says they'll take me down to their ski lodge one weekend.'

'It doesn't leave you much time for meeting anyone,' she says, returning to the subject like a dog with a bone.

'Who says I want to meet someone?' I ask, trying not to smile as I think about Alex.

Mum eyes me keenly. 'You never tell me anything about your personal life. Are you seeing anyone at university?'

'Not at the moment.'

She pauses. 'What about down here?'

My first instinct is to deny that too. But she's going to find out at the party tonight anyway. I give her an enigmatic smile. 'You never know.'

'I won't say I haven't had my suspicions,' she says.

'I've never known you not to have suspicions. But they're rarely correct.'

She locks the suitcase. 'Come downstairs and have a cup of tea. You can tell me all about it.'

'I didn't actually say there was anything to tell,' I say, following her. But this seems as good a time as any, and I'm sure Alex won't mind. For all I know, he's already told his parents.

As I close my door, there's a loud crash and a scream, followed by a series of muffled thumps.

I run to the head of the stairs and look down in horror. Mum is lying at the foot of the stairs, crumpled up in a heap.

'Mum!' I shriek, racing down the stairs and kneeling next to her.

She doesn't move. Horrible visions chase each other through my head as I kneel there, panic stricken. I should check whether she's still breathing. I put a hand on her back.

She groans and rolls over. 'What happened?'

I let out a gasp of relief. 'Are you ok? For a moment, I thought …'

She tries to sit up and gives a gasp of pain. 'My ankle!'

'Don't try to stand,' I say. 'Can you straighten your leg?'

She winces. 'I don't think so.'

'Where's Dad?' I ask.

'He's playing golf,' she says. 'He won't be back for hours. You can try ringing him, but he never hears his phone when he's at the club.'

'I'm going to call an ambulance.'

'Don't be ridiculous,' she says. 'I don't need an ambulance.'

'Mum, you can't move, and you've fallen down the stairs. You can't stay here.'

'Of course not,' she says. 'You'll have to take me to the hospital. Give me a minute. I'm sure I'll be able to walk if you help me.'

She props herself up against the bottom stair. 'It's feeling better already. Perhaps I don't …'

'Yes, you do,' I say firmly. 'The only question is how we get you there.'

I try Dad's number. As Mum predicted, there's no answer.

'I think I can get to the car alright,' she says. 'I'm feeling a lot better now.'

I help her to stand, and she puts her arm around my shoulders. It takes us a while to walk down the hall and out to the car, but we make it at last. I recline her seat and help her in, and she lies back, her face white and strained.

Even driving as carefully as possible, I can tell she's in considerable pain. I pull up outside emergency and run in. Three nurses come out and manage to manoeuvre Mum out of the car and onto a trolley. I follow them inside.

'I suspect she's broken her leg,' says one of the nurses. 'We'll take her straight down for an x-ray. Would you like to wait here?'

I sit in the waiting room, my thoughts in a whirl. How could everything change so suddenly? One moment, Mum is laughing and joking, and the next she's in a hospital bed, having sustained goodness knows what injuries. Thank goodness it wasn't any worse.

I'll put off going to Paris for a while. If need be, I can cancel it altogether. They can find someone else to take my place. Plenty of people applied for the course. I can't possibly go and leave Mum if she's in any danger.

It seems an age before a nurse comes to get me. 'Your mother's had an x-ray, and they've taken her to pre-op.'

'An operation?' I say, startled.

'She's broken her leg,' says the nurse. 'But it isn't a straightforward break. She has a compound fracture, and she'll probably need the bone pinned.'

'Can I go and see her?'

'Of course,' she says reassuringly. 'We've got her a little more comfortable and given her something for the pain. She's been very brave about it. Is she always like that?'

I haven't thought about this before. Now that I do, I realise Mum very rarely complains about anything major. She's quick to fuss and complain about small things, but she's surprisingly stoical about the bigger ones.

I find her propped up in a hospital bed. She's still pale, but she looks more cheerful. 'I'm so sorry, love.'

I bend down to kiss her. 'Don't be ridiculous. You couldn't help what happened. I'm so glad you're ok.'

'They're going to operate this evening,' she says, looking anxious.

'So they told me. Don't worry, Mum. You'll be absolutely fine.'

Her face crumples. 'Did you manage to find your father?'

'Not yet. He didn't answer his phone. But he should be back from golf very soon. Would you like me to drive home and bring him back here?'

She looks relieved. 'If you wouldn't mind. It doesn't feel right him not being here.'

I leave her lying with her eyes closed and walk as quickly as I can to the car park.

Chapter Ten

Dad's car is in the drive when I pull up. I run into the house and find him sitting at the kitchen table.

He sees my face. 'Annie? What's wrong?'

My legs give way, and I grab the back of a chair to steady myself.

'Annie?' he says again. 'Sit down, love, and tell me all about it.'

I clear my throat. 'I'm sorry. I didn't mean to worry you. Mum's going to be fine, but she had an accident this afternoon. She fell down the stairs, and she's broken her leg. It's quite a complicated break, and she's having surgery this evening.'

He reaches for his coat. 'Where are my car keys?'

I follow him to the door. 'Are you ok to drive?'

He looks at my pale face. 'I'm probably in a better state than you. Did you call an ambulance?'

'Mum wouldn't hear of it,' I say. 'We managed to get her into the car, and I drove her there.'

'And I was at the golf club.' He closes his eyes. 'The one time she needed me, and I wasn't there.'

'But I was,' I say. 'You can't live your life expecting something awful to happen. But she wants to see you.'

He wipes his eyes. 'Of course, she does. I'm never playing another game of golf!'

I give a shaky laugh. 'She won't like that. She says it's the only thing that gets you out from under her feet.'

We find Mum lying in bed with her eyes closed.

'Don't worry. She's had her pre-op meds,' whispers the nurse. 'She's doing fine.'

I look at Dad, who's staring down at Mum with such an expression of tenderness in his face that it makes me catch my breath. I've always thought of my parents as gently fond of each other, having been married long enough to have grown accustomed to each other's ways and learned to accommodate themselves to all the little rubs and irritations of everyday life. But seeing his face as he looks down at Mum, I realise it's far more than that. He really loves her, just as she is. I blink back the tears. I hope I find that sort of love one day. Maybe I already have.

This thought brings me back to reality. Alex! I'm supposed to be meeting him tonight at the party. I should let him know what's going on.

I pull out my phone, and Dad comes out of his reverie. 'I don't think you're supposed to use those in here.'

'I'll go outside. I'll be back in a couple of minutes. Will you be ok?'

'Of course,' he says. 'You should take some time to yourself. You look a little battered.'

'I'm fine. It was all a bit of a shock.'

He squeezes my hand. 'You did marvellously. I'm so grateful you were there.'

I leave him sitting next to Mum, holding her hand.

I step outside into the cold dusk. It isn't even five o'clock, and it's already dark. I shiver in the cold night air. When I open my phone, I see a text from Alex. The sight of his name on the screen makes me smile, as it has all week. I'd better get used to it. I'm not going to see him for the next three months, so texting is all we have.

I try not to wonder whether he'll visit me in Paris. Of course, he won't. He has his new job. From the sound of it, his firm is keeping him pretty busy. And we've only been together a week. It would be ridiculous to expect him to drop everything and fly to a different country to see a girl he's only known for a few days.

But I can't help secretly imagining us walking hand in hand along the Seine on Valentine's Day and having dinner at the top of the Eiffel Tower while he tells me how much he's missed me.

I look at the text. *All ready for tonight? Do you think our parents will have a collective heart attack and end up at the hospital?*

I blink in shock before remembering that he has no idea what's happened today.

I text back. *Not funny. I'm at the hospital right now with my mum.*

His reply comes back almost instantly. *I'm so sorry! What happened?*

I'm typing a reply when the phone rings.

'Annie?' he says, and I promptly burst into tears. He waits patiently while I get myself together.

'Sorry,' I say at last. 'I'm fine.'

His voice is sharp with anxiety. 'What's happened?'

'Mum's broken her leg. I'm sorry if I panicked you. She fell down the stairs this afternoon. Dad isn't there, so I had to get her to the hospital by myself.'

'Why didn't you ask me?' he asks.

'It didn't occur to me. I was so busy getting her out to the car. She'll be fine, but she has a multiple fracture, and she's going to need surgery. I think she's going in around seven. I was about to text you and let you know.'

'Should I come to the hospital?'

'I don't think so. I'd love to see you, but now probably isn't the time. Let's get this operation over with, and we can tell them then.'

'I wasn't planning to tell them anything,' he says. 'I just wanted to offer you some support.'

'I know, and I'm very grateful. But Dad and I are here, and it would probably be easier to keep it that way.'

'I'll let my parents know,' he says. 'I'm sure they'll be concerned. I suppose that means you won't be at the party tonight.'

I bite my lip. 'I may be able to get there later. I want to stay here until Mum's through the operation. But I can probably come for an hour or two after that.'

'The party ends at eleven,' he says.

'Really?'

'No, not really,' he says with a hint of a laugh in his voice. 'It's a New Year's Eve party, remember? I was trying to lighten the mood. Sorry, it's probably not the best time.'

'Not really,' I say. 'But I appreciate the thought.'

'What a thing to happen right before you go to Paris,' he says.

'If I go to Paris. I have no idea what I'm going to do tomorrow.'

'Of course. But if your mum's anything like mine, she'll insist you go regardless.'

'She won't be able to do much about it,' I say. 'She'll be in bed with a broken leg.'

He laughs. 'Don't you believe it. She'll still be running the show from hospital. Just you see. Please let me know how it goes. And don't feel you have to come to the party if you don't feel like it. I'll see you before you go, even if I have to get up at three in the morning and camp outside your house.'

I give a reluctant smile. 'Let's hope it doesn't come to that. I should probably go now.'

'Of course,' he says. 'Take care of yourself. I hope it all goes well. I … I'll see you soon.'

He rings off, and I stare at the screen, wondering what he meant to say. Surely not, 'I love you'? Of course not! I must be more tired than I realised.

I find Dad standing outside the ward.

'They've taken her down to theatre,' he tells me. 'The doctor says it could take a while, depending on how complicated the operation is. He suggests that we get something to eat at the cafeteria. It looks as though this could be a long night, and on New Year's Eve of all times! I expect the hospital is extra busy today.'

'It will probably be worse tomorrow,' I say. 'Mum's timing is impeccable, as always.'

We sit in the cafeteria for an hour. I allow him to buy me a sandwich, although I'm not hungry. But it gives him something to do and hopefully keeps his mind off what's happening to Mum.

'We're supposed to be going to Elaine and Robert Fielding's party tonight,' he says at one point. 'I know how much your mother was looking forward to it. She's been making her famous asparagus quiche.'

'I know,' I say. 'I've been to the supermarket twice today.'

'You should go to the party,' he says. 'I'll stay at the hospital tonight, but it's your last night here. You'll want to say goodbye to everyone.'

'It isn't important. I'd rather be here with Mum.'

'That's my job,' he says. 'You've more than done your part today. Your mother would hate to think she'd spoiled your last night at home.'

'It may not be my last night. I'm not going to Paris until I know she's ok.'

'You can get that out of your head at once,' he says. 'Even if I agreed with you, which I don't, your mother would never allow it.'

We haven't heard anything by nine o'clock. Dad paces up and down the corridor, his face tight.

'I'm sure they've almost finished,' I reassure him.

He seems to remember where he is. 'Of course, they have. You're not to worry, Annie.'

It's odd to think that our positions are so entirely reversed. When I was a child, it was his job to comfort me. Now he needs me to offer support.

A nurse appears a few minutes later and smiles when he sees us. Dad lets out a gasp of relief. His eyes ask a question.

The nurse nods. 'Everything went very well. She's in the recovery room right now. They'll be bringing her up to the ward in about half an hour. Why don't you go and wait for her there?'

'I told you it would be alright,' I say in a choked voice.

Dad wipes his eyes. 'I never doubted it for a second. It's a perfectly simple operation. There's no need for you to stay. You get off to the party now. You can give them all an update.'

I shake my head. 'I want to see Mum before I go. I'll pop out and send a couple of texts, and then I'll be back.'

It's still icy cold outside, but I hardly notice it in my relief. It's a shame that Mum will have to be in bed for a while. She'll absolutely hate it. But it could have been so much worse.

I pull out my phone to text Alex and see to my surprise that I have several texts from Suzy. Maybe Alex has mentioned Mum's accident to her, and she wants to know how Mum is getting on.

I open the first text and freeze. It's a selfie of Alex and Suzy. She's snuggled up very close to him, her head on his shoulder. She's captioned it, *Guess what?!!!*

I open the next text. I can almost hear Suzy's voice as I read it. *You'll never guess who I've been making out with! Remember Alex – the guy who stood us up at the pub? The party tonight is at his parents' house. Anyway, we got chatting, and one thing led to another … you know how it is. He's a really good kisser!*

I open the third text. Suzy has sent a shocked emoji. *I forgot to tell you – he has a tattoo! You know I'm a complete sucker for tattoos. It's a dolphin on his lower back. Well, a bit lower than that! Don't ask me how I know* 😊 *You should hurry up. This is a great party. Lots of gorgeous men here. S x*

I lean back against the wall, trying to get my thoughts in order. This is ridiculous. Suzy must have got him confused with someone else. But that doesn't seem possible. How many people have stood us up at the pub?

I try to get my breathing under control. There's a simple explanation for this. There must be. I start to write a text to Alex, then stop. What if it's true? It can't be – but what if it is? I won't be able to bear it.

What do I really know about him? I've had two dates with him and built everything up in my mind into something far more than it is.

A thought strikes me. Suzy always posts party photos on Facebook. Possibly, she's done that tonight.

I open my page and look at my feed. As I thought, Suzy has been active tonight. I run my eyes down the string of pictures. They're almost all selfies, and they almost all include Suzy and Alex sitting very close together. There's one of her ruffling his hair and him laughing. The last one is of her kissing his cheek and doing a thumbs up gesture. She's captioned this one. *Hot hot hot!!!*

I feel as though someone has wrapped their hands around my heart and is squeezing hard. I'm too shocked even for tears. Suzy and Alex? It isn't possible. But it's also entirely possible. Even if he's been drinking, there's no excuse for him making out with Suzy. But then, most men don't need an excuse to make out with Suzy. They're just grateful she's noticed them.

Another text flashes onto the screen. *Alex has told me you're not coming tonight. I hope your mum's ok. I probably won't see you before you go to Paris, so have a wonderful time. Got to go. Alex is getting impatient, if you know what I mean … I'll tell you all about it when I see you S x*

I take a deep breath and text Alex with shaking fingers.

Suzy says you and she are having a great time together. I won't be able to make it tonight, so I'll say goodbye now.

I wait for five agonising minutes before he replies. I don't want to imagine what he might have been doing during that time.

I'm so sorry, Annie. I wish you'd been able to make it. Who am I going to kiss at midnight now?

How dare he? Does he find this funny?

I'm sure you'll find someone, I text back. *Men like you usually do. By the way, do you have any tattoos?*

There's a pause before he texts back. *Just one – a dolphin. But absolutely no one knows about it, and I'd really like to keep it that way. Do you want me to send you a picture of it?*

I blink back the tears. So, it's true.

No thanks, I type back. *I can't think of anything I'd like less. But I'm sure you'll find someone to admire it.*

There's another agonising pause before he texts back.

Are you sure I shouldn't come over to the hospital?

I flinch when I read this. I don't want him within one hundred miles of me right now. With any luck, by tomorrow night he won't be.

I type back with surprisingly steady fingers.

I wanted to talk to you in person, but that's obviously not going to happen now. This week has been fun, but I don't think it's working out between us. I'm off to Paris tomorrow, and I'd really like to go as a single person. I'm sure you understand. Anyway, whether you do or not, that's my decision. I'd appreciate it if you would respect it and not contact me again

Annie

I hit send before I have time for second thoughts. I hesitate before deleting his number and blocking it. I switch off my phone, shove it deep inside my pocket, and go back inside.

This Christmas

Chapter Eleven

The train pulls into the station, and I jump into a taxi. Everything here looks just the same as I remember. Mum greets me at the door as usual. She's wearing the same Eiffel Tower apron she always does, and she's covered with flour. I wonder whether she and Dad have shares in a wheat company.

The tree is already decorated, and the house is festooned with tinsel. Carols are playing in the kitchen. Clearly, we're going to have a traditional family Christmas if it kills her. I take my bag upstairs to my old bedroom, which smells of furniture polish and Windolene.

I stare out of the window into the front garden, checking for anyone lurking in the bushes. I wouldn't put it past Alex to have heard the news I'm home and popped around to tell me about his latest girlfriend.

It's only when we're eating lunch that Mum mentions his name again. 'So, what do you think about Alex Fielding coming home for Christmas?'

'Not much.' I can't think of anything else to say.

'You aren't eating,' she says. 'What's wrong? Aren't you hungry?'

I take a forkful of shepherd's pie, barely tasting it. 'I'm not terribly hungry, but it's very good.'

'So it should be at that price! I couldn't believe it when I went to the supermarket yesterday. Mince has gone up yet again.'

I hardy hear her. It's nothing to me that Alex has come home for Christmas. His parents live here. He has a perfect right to spend Christmas, Easter, or any other time of the year here. I simply hadn't expected it.

His Facebook page said he was going to Thailand this year – probably with one of the many girlfriends I used to hear about from Suzy. Either he's changed his mind or his girlfriend has discovered his true character and refused to go with him. Good for her. It's far better to find out these things early rather than have years of your life wasted.

The kitchen door opens, and Dad comes in. His face lights up when he sees me. 'Annie! I didn't expect you so early!'

I rub my cheek on the collar of his coat. He's worn the same aftershave for as long as I can remember. Hugging him feels warm and safe and comforting, and I'm suddenly glad I came home.

'Your lunch is in the oven,' says Mum, reaching for a pair of oven gloves.

He gives her a guilty smile. 'That's very kind of you, but I had lunch at the club.'

'But you knew Annie was arriving this morning! You could have come home for lunch this once.'

He kisses the top of her head. I'm sorry. I thought she was arriving on the three o'clock train.'

'That was the original plan,' I say. 'But Maggie told me not to bother coming into the office just for the morning. I was already packed, so I decided to take the earlier train.'

'You can have some crumble and custard,' says Mum. 'I've never known you to turn that down, however full you were.'

'Well, perhaps a little bit,' says Dad.

He sits down next to me. 'You're looking very well, my dear. They aren't working you too hard at that place of yours?'

'Work's fine,' I say. 'It's been quite busy. One of our senior managers is leaving next month, and I'm hoping I might get promoted. It's a bit of a longshot, but I think it's worth going for.'

'Of course, it is!' says Mum. 'There's no point in being a shrinking violet. If you don't blow your own trumpet, no one else will do it for you. That's what I always say.'

'That isn't generally your problem,' says Dad, helping himself to custard.

'Why hide your light under a bushel?' says Mum.

I'm surprised to find I'm enjoying the crumble. 'Are these your plums?' I ask Dad.

'Yes, they're the last of this year's crop. Your mother took most of them. She made quite a bit of jam for the village fête.'

'I took second place for my plum and apple this year,' says Mum. 'But I didn't even place in the most symmetrical vegetable category. I've always says that category's fixed, haven't I, Graham?'

'You have, indeed. To hear you tell it, the entire organising committee has come straight out of a Dan Brown novel.'

'You may laugh,' she says, 'but I'm convinced we don't know the half of it. People go home with rosettes each year who don't know compost from caviar. Anyway, how's Robert? Did you beat him?'

He nods. 'It was a close thing, but I got a fluke birdie on the ninth hole and finished well under par. So, Robert had to buy lunch.'

'Is that Robert Fielding?' I ask in what I hope is a casual tone.

'That's right,' says Mum. 'He and your father play golf every Saturday. It's got to be quite a thing.'

I force myself to speak again. 'I had no idea you were so friendly with the Fieldings.'

'Oh, they're super people!' she says. 'Elaine and I were on the Christmas Bazaar committee together last year, and we got to know each other very well. She's an absolute hoot! And your father and Robert have hit it off together. It makes such a difference having friends in the village who enjoy the same sorts of things as we do.'

I decide not to ask anything more. Any further discussion is bound to lead to mention of Alex. Even, heaven forbid, suggestions that he and I should get together while we're here. Mum is convinced that whenever I come home I must be desperate to look up anyone I've ever known, however vaguely, and however long ago.

'Come and sit with me by the fire,' says Dad, 'and tell me everything you've been doing since we last saw you. Your mother will only unpack and repack the dishwasher all over again if you try to help.'

'That's because you don't have the faintest smidge of spatial awareness,' she says. 'Do you know, Annie, I caught him trying to put the fish knives into the dishwasher last week – with their handles up! Did you ever hear of such a thing?'

I settle into an armchair next to the fire. 'Does she ever sit down?'

'Hardly ever,' says Dad. 'I married a whirlwind.'

'When is Jamie coming home?' I ask.

He darts a quick look towards the kitchen. 'Not until Christmas morning.'

'I thought this was supposed to be a huge family Christmas?'

He lowers his voice. 'Best not to talk about it unless your mother brings up the subject. She gets a little emotional. So, we've agreed not to discuss it before he gets here.'

'That suits me,' I say. 'I don't want to have to cope with tears and dramatic scenes before I have to.'

I stretch out my toes luxuriously towards the blaze. 'It must have been cold out there on the course today.'

'Not too bad,' he says. 'Has your mother told you that Alex is home for Christmas.'

'She mentioned it. Somehow or other, I'd picked up the idea that he was going elsewhere this year.'

Somehow or other? I may have glanced at Alex's Facebook page once or twice over the past couple of years, but that's nothing. Everyone checks social media occasionally to see what people from their past are up to.

'He was supposed to be going away,' says Dad. 'But he agreed to come home at the last minute because –'

The door flies open, and Mum comes in carrying a tray. She arranges the coffee cups on a side table. 'Have you told her the news about Alex?'

My heart plummets into my stomach in one sickening swoop. So, that's the reason he's here. He's getting married, and he's brought his new fiancée home to spend Christmas with his parents.

Well, good for him! Not so good for his fiancée, of course. Anything involving Alex Fielding is bound to end in tears sooner or later. But there's no point in anyone telling her that. She'll have to work it out for herself. Just as Suzy did. Just as I did.

I force my voice to remain steady. 'News? About Alex?'

Mum pours me a cup of coffee. 'Not about Alex, silly. About Robert and Elaine. It's all terribly exciting. They're getting married!'

'I thought they were already married,' I say. 'They both have the same surname.'

'Remarried, then!' she says impatiently.

'Do you mean they got divorced?'

She clicks her tongue in exasperation. 'Don't be so silly! Of course, they didn't get divorced. They're renewing their vows. Isn't that romantic?'

'Renewing their vows?' I say blankly. 'But why?'

'That's exactly what I asked when it was first mentioned,' says Dad. 'I thought that people only renewed their vows after one of them had an affair. But your mother assures me that isn't the case.'

'Of course, it isn't!' says Mum. 'I don't know where you get these daft ideas from.'

'Why are they renewing their vows?' I ask again.

'It's their silver wedding anniversary in June,' says Mum.

'So, why aren't they doing it then?'

'They're going out to Hong Kong to see Caitlin,' she says. 'But they wanted Alex to be there for the vow renewal, and apparently he's busy over the summer.'

'Is Caitlin back for Christmas too?'

Mum shakes her head. 'She couldn't make it. But they're seeing her over the summer,' she adds as if that makes everything clear.

'When is it happening?' I ask without much interest.

She looks even more pleased. 'Christmas Eve.'

'Christmas Eve?' I say, startled.

'Yes, it's in two days' time. And we're all going.'

My mouth falls open in shock. 'What do you mean by all? Do the Fieldings even know I'm home?'

'Of course, they do. They said we must be sure to bring you along. It's an afternoon event, with a buffet in the hall afterwards. And they're putting on an evening do for all the young people.'

'What young people?' I ask.

'Well, youngish,' she amends. 'I don't suppose any of us old fogeys will stay late, but they've booked the hall until midnight for anyone who wants to stay. Elaine has arranged a hot supper about nine and a lovely disco for all you youngsters.'

I went to plenty of discos in the church hall when I was a teenager. But there aren't very many young people living in the village nowadays. Most of them have moved away for work. It isn't the sort of place where most people can afford to buy a house. The thought of the middle-aged members of the village jigging around happily to the Bee Gees and the best of Abba makes me smile.

'I'm sure the Fieldings have only asked me out of politeness,' I say. 'There's no reason for me to go. I don't even know them. Please thank them for being kind enough to think of me, but I'd prefer to stay at home in the warm.'

'You can't do that!' says Mum. 'They're absolutely counting on you coming. It would be terribly rude if you didn't turn up. And, as I say, Alex will be there.'

Of course, he will. He's apparently the sole reason his parents are having their vow renewal now instead of waiting until the summer. But that's no reason for me to go along. Of all the people in the world I have absolutely no wish ever to meet again, Alex Fielding is right at the top of the list.

Still, I can surely find some excuse between now and then. I can make some arrangements with one of the old school friends Mum's always so anxious for me to meet. She can hardly object to that. I'll call Brandon after lunch.

She's still talking excitedly, although I haven't heard a word of it. '… and the most gorgeous purple silk!' she finishes triumphantly.

I give a murmur of assent, hoping she won't ask me what she's just said. But she's still burbling on about what is apparently shaping up to be the social event of the year in Honeywell.

'Would you believe that Robert was all for ordering sparkling wine? Elaine wasn't having any of that. "If you want me to marry you all over again, the least you can do is spring for some Cristal!" she told him. And she was quite right. It isn't as though they can't afford it. Look at that lovely big house of theirs. They have a gardener three times a week, even in the winter, and Mrs Bailey has just upped her cleaning hours. A couple of bottles of good champagne won't bankrupt them.'

'It all sounds quite elaborate,' I say. 'Couldn't they have held the party at their house? It's certainly big enough.'

'That was the original plan,' she says. 'But they thought that as they were having the vow renewal in the church, it would be easier to have the reception in the church hall afterwards.'

Even more reason not to go. That place holds very mixed memories for me.

I go upstairs to unpack after lunch, wondering how I'm going to get out of this vow renewal. If Mum insists, I'll go to the ceremony and say hello to the happy couple afterwards. But there's no way I'm attending the evening party. Even if I have to fake appendicitis, I'll find a reason to come home early.

I look out of my bedroom window at the leaden sky. If it starts snowing quickly enough, we might all be snowed in, and the vow renewal will have to be cancelled.

I stop myself. Elaine and Robert have probably put a lot of effort into the preparations. I decide that the snow can hold off until after the ceremony. But it can be quickly followed by a blizzard that cuts the buffet short and entirely prevents the evening party.

Chapter Twelve

The cold morning light wakes me far earlier than I'd planned. I didn't close my curtains properly. I roll over, pulling the quilt over my head and trying to recapture the dream I was having. What was it about? Something about Alex, which is annoying.

The more I try to remember, the more it slips away. I keep my eyes tightly shut. I can still manage another hour's sleep. It's one of nicest things about coming home. In London, I have to be up at six every morning to reach the office by eight. But here, there's nothing to do and nowhere to be. I can sleep all morning if I like.

I'm just starting to drift off again when my bedroom door flies open with a crash.

'Are you going to lie here all day?' demands Mum. 'It's nearly eight o'clock!'

I groan and burrow even more deeply under my quilt. As a small child, I believed that if I couldn't see Mum, neither could she see me. Perhaps this is still true.

I wait for the door to close and her footsteps to retreat along the landing. Instead, the light snaps on, and the room is flooded with light.

I push back the quilt and sit up. 'Is there a fire?'

'A fire?' she says. 'Of course not! At least, I don't think so. Can you smell something? Is your father trying to make toast again?'

I push my hair away from my face and rub my eyes. 'Don't worry. I can't smell any smoke. What's the emergency?'

She marches over to the corner of the room and opens the wardrobe doors. 'I hope you've hung up your things properly. I don't have time to iron anything for you this morning.'

'Hung up what things? I'm only here for a few days.'

She wheels around to face me. 'Haven't you unpacked yet? You had all yesterday afternoon to do it. I suppose I'll have to do it, just like I have to do everything around here.' She bends to unzip the suitcase.

'Don't do that!' I say. 'All your presents are in there, and I haven't had time to wrap them yet.'

'I don't know what you've been doing since you got here,' she says. 'Hurry up and take a shower and unpack your case. All your clothes will be getting crumpled.'

'Jeans don't tend to crumple,' I say.

She looks horrified. 'Please don't tell me that's all you've brought with you? You must have packed a couple of nice dresses.'

'I didn't think I'd need any. No one warned me that I'd be arriving home in the middle of the wedding of the year.'

'But what about Christmas Day?' she says. 'We always dress up on Christmas Day.'

'*You* always dress up on Christmas Day,' I correct her. 'I have to dress smartly every day for work. I'm not doing it on holiday as well.'

'It isn't only Christmas Day,' she grumbles. 'It's all the other things too. Vera and Mark always have a drinks party on Boxing Day. You know that.'

'I don't, actually. But what does that have to do with me?'

'Don't be so silly. Of course, you're invited. Everyone's dying to see you. Some of our newer friends haven't even met you.'

I pick up a towel. 'They've managed to get along fine until now. I'm sure they'll cope. I don't want to spend all my time going to drinks parties and making small talk with people I don't know. I came home for a break.'

'We'll see,' she says ominously. 'Now you need to get a move on.'

'I don't mind cold toast,' I say. 'It sounds as though Dad's burned it anyway.'

She sighs. 'I'll go down and see what he's up to. Then we'd better get going. The shops were a zoo at the weekend. Goodness knows what they'll be like today.'

'What shops?' I ask, but it's too late. She's already bustling down the stairs, calling to Dad to switch off the grill.

I roll my eyes and go to have a shower. I find my parents sitting at the kitchen table eating bowls of cereal.

'What happened to the toast?' I ask.

'What toast?' says Mum, handing me the milk. 'Your father and I always have muesli for breakfast. You know that. It keeps us regular.'

Without waiting for an answer, she resumes her conversation with Dad.

'So, Ursula said to me, "Why not take the park and ride?" I told her I wasn't sitting for half an hour on some smelly old bus trying to balance a pile of carrier bags on my knee. From what Alison says, it's very unreliable, anyway. She and

Diane had to wait half an hour in the pouring rain last week. Annie and I will take the car and park in Church Lane.'

She turns to me. 'That's why we need to get going as quickly as possible. The shops open at nine. Even the overflow car parks will be full by ten.'

I pour myself some cereal. 'I'm not going to the shops. I've brought all my Christmas presents with me.'

Dad puts his bowl into the sink. 'I wouldn't waste your energy arguing, if I were you. Your mother's decided that you're going to the shops, and that's that.'

I make one last feeble protest. 'I'm sure Mum can do her shopping without me.'

'Of course, I can't!' says Mum. 'I don't know what size you are. Even if you told me, it probably wouldn't fit. Sizing is all over the place these days. I do wish they wouldn't keep changing everything.'

'Why do you need to know my size?' I ask.

She snatches away my bowl and puts it on the counter. 'I'm not having my daughter going to the wedding dressed like one of those punk rocker people.'

'Vow renewal,' I say, making an ineffectual grab for my bowl. 'I haven't finished that.'

She ignores me. 'Go and brush your teeth. I want you downstairs in exactly five minutes. And put on some nice underwear – if you own any.'

I throw up my hands. 'I'm not even going to ask. I don't think I'd like the answer.'

Half an hour later, we're threading our way through the traffic at the edge of town.

'It gets worse every year,' says Mum, narrowly avoiding a delivery truck. 'Honestly, doesn't that man know he's supposed to park in the pickup bay? Why do people have to leave their Christmas shopping so late? It makes it most unpleasant for everyone.'

'We've left it just as late,' I say. 'Watch that man!'

She slams on the brakes. 'What was he thinking? He stepped out without looking. It would have served him right if I'd hit him.'

'That's the Christmas spirit!' I say encouragingly.

Thankfully, there are a few spaces left in the Church Lane carpark. Otherwise, I wouldn't have put it past her to have shunted one of the parked cars out of the way.

She switches off the engine and looks at me. 'Do you have a comb?'

'Unsurprisingly, no. Why?'

She rummages in her bag and pulls out a comb. 'Why do I have to think of everything? Your hair is all over the place. Tidy it up, for goodness' sake!'

She produces a gold lipstick tube and a small powder compact. 'While you're at it, why don't you pop a bit of this on?'

'My hair's fine, thank you,' I say. 'I brushed it before I left the house. And why are you trying to make me wear' – I unscrew the lipstick and grimace – 'peach coloured lipstick?'

'It's actually sea coral,' she says, putting it back into her bag. 'And it cost the earth.'

'They saw you coming,' I mutter under my breath.

She leads the way towards the main shopping street, talking all the way. 'I wonder if we have time to start at the chemist. I promised your father I'd get him some corn plasters.' She looks at her watch. 'Probably not.'

'I still don't know what we're here for,' I complain, following her as she bustles through the crowds, flexing her elbows menacingly to clear a path.

'I've already told you,' she says. 'We need to buy you some smart clothes.'

I sigh. 'I suppose I'll have to get something for this stupid wedding, seeing that you've accepted the invitation without consulting me. But I don't need anything else.'

She isn't listening. We've reached the department store. 'Just in time,' she says.

She darts inside, and I follow her. There's no point in arguing with her when she's in this mood. Hopefully, we'll find something quickly and be able to leave.

I catch sight of her halfway up the first escalator. I'm tempted to claim that she disappeared entirely, and I wasn't able to find her. I could go to the bookshop down the high street, switch off my phone, get myself a cappuccino, and sit there reading until she arrives.

I reluctantly decide it isn't worth it. Not only would Mum be incandescent with rage, but she would still drag me back to the department store to choose an outfit.

Besides, I don't want to upset her. It's been too long since I came home, and I know how much she's been looking forward to it. So, I follow her up the escalator to the first floor.

'There she is!' says Mum when we reach the top.

My heart sinks. A woman is sitting in the coffee shop, waving at us madly. 'You made it! And here's little Annie. My goodness, don't you look grown up?'

'It's Elaine Fielding!' Mum hisses in my ear.

I give the woman an awkward smile. 'Hello, Mrs Fielding. It's nice to meet you.'

'Not Mrs Fielding,' she says. 'Call me Elaine! Come and sit down. What will you both have?'

'I don't think we have time to stop,' I say. 'We're here to buy something for me to wear to your vow renewal. Congratulations, by the way.'

'But we agreed to meet here first,' says Elaine. 'Liz said we'd need a coffee before we got started.'

Mum doesn't meet my eye. 'A cappuccino would be lovely.'

'Three cappuccinos coming up,' says Elaine. 'Decaf for you, Liz? How about you, Annie?'

'I'll have caffeine,' I say. I'm tempted to ask for a shot of whisky in it. If an Irish cappuccino isn't yet a thing, I'll make it one.

'Did she say you'd arranged to meet here?' I ask Mum.

She pushes the pile of carrier bags to one side and sits down. 'I thought it would be nice for us to have some company today.'

'I'm not sure how to take that.'

'Don't be so silly,' she says. 'It's always good to have a fresh pair of eyes. And Elaine has super taste. She's the one who persuaded me to buy that gorgeous leaf-green two-piece last spring. Remind me to show it to you when we get home. If you'd bothered to unpack your things last night, you'd have seen it in the wardrobe.'

'I'm sure it's very nice,' I say.

'It is, actually.' She brightens. 'It came from Xander's. Perhaps we'll start there today. I wouldn't mind having a quick browse.'

I sip my coffee in silence while Mum and Elaine talk about the vow renewal. Apparently, there's still a lot to do.

'I never expected it to be so much work,' says Elaine. 'It started out as quite a simple affair, but it seemed to grow and grow. Your mother is a terrible influence on me.'

'Nonsense!' says Mum. 'If a thing's worth doing, it's worth doing properly. I always say that, don't I, Annie?'

'You do always say that,' I agree. I catch Elaine's eye and detect a flash of amusement.

'That's enough talk about our wedding arrangements,' she says. 'I'm very glad you're able to come, Annie, but all these silly details must be boring you senseless. I'm far more interested to hear what you do in London. Tell me everything!'

'There'll be plenty of time for that over lunch,' says Mum. 'We ought to get going. It could take us quite a while to find exactly the right thing.'

My heart sinks. I've been planning on buying the first decent outfit I see and leaving. Evidently, Mum has other plans.

Elaine picks up her bag. 'Good idea. If we can't find anything we like here, I thought we might try Plum's. They had some lovely evening dresses when I was in there last week.'

'I'm sure we'll be able to find something here,' I say. 'And it's still only ten o'clock. We'll be home well before lunch. You must be very busy with all the last-minute arrangements.'

She shrugs. 'It's all under control. I've given Robert a list and told him I want it all done before I get home. It's about time he started pulling his weight with this vow renewal. If not, Liz has promised to stand up and object when the vicar gets to that part.'

'I have indeed,' says Mum. 'Our husbands need to learn that we modern women have options.'

She sees my expression. 'Don't look like that, young lady! Your generation doesn't have the monopoly on feminism.'

'Absolutely not,' agrees Elaine. 'Now, if you're both ready, let's make a start. We have plenty to do if we're going to give Annie a complete makeover by closing time.'

She takes Mum's arm, and the two of them set off towards the escalator. Is it my imagination or is Mum actually humming *Pretty Woman*? I follow them reluctantly, wondering what on earth I've let myself in for.

Chapter Thirteen

If the first floor was crowded, the second floor is even more so. Half the town seems to be here, pushing their way through the crowds, banging fellow shoppers with bulging carrier bags, and above all, shouting. It feels as though every single shopper has been separated from their companions and is yelling at the top of their voice in an effort to attract their attention.

Mum and Elaine seem unperturbed. They happily join in the shouting, and Elaine uses her shopping bags to carve a path through the crowds towards the evening wear.

Judging by the shocked gasps and glares as she passes, the packages are doing their work very effectively. Maybe she gift wrapped a set of bricks for the occasion.

'Keep up, Annie!' shouts Mum.

'What?' I shout back.

'Keep up!' she booms, making a nearby shopper jump.

'I'm right here,' I say. 'Where do you want to start?'

She sweeps a look around the racks of clothes. 'Not those, for a start. Who would be daft enough to wear something like that?'

She points to one of the dresses. A woman emerging from the changing rooms wearing the same dress gives her an affronted look and storms back inside.

'Don't shout so loud,' I say. 'That woman looked really upset.'

'I can't hear you!' she snaps, but her cheeks are pinker than usual.

She brightens as she catches sight of a rail of dresses. 'This is more like it. What lovely frocks.'

I groan inwardly. Any item to which she refers as a 'frock' will inevitably be hideous.

'There you are!' Elaine appears, an armful of clothes resting on her carrier bags.

'I nearly dropped these,' she goes on, pushing the tangle of fabric into Mum's arms.

Mum looks horrified. 'Oh, no, Elaine! These aren't the sort of thing at all!'

She holds up an indigo jumpsuit, covered with sequins. 'What would Annie want with something like this?'

'To wear it, of course!' says Elaine cheerfully. 'She's young. She doesn't want to look like her mother.'

'And what's wrong with the way I look?' says Mum.

'Oh, you know what I mean.' Elaine hands me a bright green bodycon dress. 'This would be perfect for you. You could wear a shrug during the ceremony. But you could take it off afterwards, and you'd be all ready to party.'

'I really don't think so,' I say, trying not to laugh. 'Thanks, anyway.'

'I should think not!' says Mum. 'You'd need a lamp post to accessorise that outfit.'

'Don't be so narrow minded,' says Elaine. 'Annie's far too pretty to –'

'I don't see what pretty has to do with it,' objects Mum. 'Besides, they probably are pretty, or no one would –'

'This is a most inappropriate conversation for someone of my tender years,' I tell them. 'Anyway, I'd prefer something a little more sedate.'

'I knew it!' says Mum triumphantly. 'I told you we should have started with Country Casuals.'

'I wouldn't go that far,' I say. 'But I'd rather look for a compromise. How smart is this vow renewal?'

'Not at all!' says Elaine.

'Very!' says Mum.

'Perhaps we should start by settling the degree of formality,' I say. 'It would save us a good deal of time.'

'It isn't formal at all,' says Elaine. 'You should feel free to wear something young and form-fitting. You're only young once.'

'But not too form-fitting,' says Mum.

'Shall I go and wait in the coffee shop while you settle the issue?' I ask.

'You'll do nothing of the sort,' says Mum. 'We'd never get you back up here. She's terrible at shopping,' she tells Elaine. 'It was the exactly the same when she was young. She never liked anything I suggested. If she'd had her way, she'd have lived in jeans.'

'I still would,' I say, releasing my arm from Mum's grasp. 'But I'm perfectly happy to buy something appropriate for tomorrow's ceremony, as it's a special occasion.'

'Which is exactly what I've been saying,' says Mum. 'If you hadn't spent so much time arguing, we could be done and home by now.'

'Nonsense!' says Elaine. 'You can't hurry these things. Half the fun is in looking at everything and trying it all on.'

I groan inwardly, but I try not to allow my feelings to show. 'I still don't know how formal it is. Let's start there.'

'You should wear exactly what you like,' says Elaine.

'Except jeans,' adds Mum.

'Perhaps not,' says Elaine. 'The vicar might not like it. Although I saw a beautiful pair earlier. They had flowers embroidered up the sides, and a lovely rhinestone belt.'

'Perhaps a dress?' I say, seeing Mum's face turn from pink to puce.

'A dress would be lovely,' she says.

'As long as it's not too frumpy,' adds Elaine, following us over to a rack of dresses near the window.

'What about this red one?' I say, selecting one at random.

'It isn't very ...' begins Mum.

'Festive,' agrees Elaine.

'I was going to say warm,' says Mum.

'It doesn't need to be warm,' says Elaine. 'The vicar says the heating will be on ready for midnight mass. If Annie's chilly, she can wear –'

'Thermal underwear,' nods Mum. 'I have a spare set I can lend you, love. I'm afraid it's ankle length, but you'll be wearing boots.'

Elaine looks amused. 'I was going to say I have a lovely fur stole I could lend her. You know the one? Robert brought it back from Norway when he went fishing.'

'Oh, that's a lovely piece,' agrees Mum. 'But you don't want to risk it getting spoiled.'

'Spoiled?' says Elaine. 'What could she possibly do to it in church?'

Mum purses her lips. 'Annie's never been careful with her things. You're having those lovely candles at the end of each pew. She might easily –'

'Go up in flames?' I say.

She looks annoyed. 'I was going to say you could easily get wax on one of the sleeves. I doubt that would ever come out. You'll be far better off with my thermals.'

'You're both very kind,' I say, 'but I'm sure I'll be fine.'

I rub the fabric between my fingers. 'This is pure wool. I imagine it's surprisingly warm.'

'Especially with a nice pair of thermals underneath,' says Mum. 'I'm not talking about the kind you used to wear when you were a little girl. The newer ones are lovely and stylish. Your father and I bought matching sets last year. They have the loveliest little bow at the neck. Mine, not his, I mean.'

'I'll think about it,' I say, laughing. 'In the meantime, I'm going to try on this dress if I can find a spare changing room.'

They follow me, arguing as they go.

'I'll drop my fur stole around this afternoon so she can try it,' says Elaine. 'It would look lovely with that dress.'

'I'd never forgive myself if anything happened to it!' says Mum. 'No, really, Elaine. I wouldn't enjoy the service at all, worrying about it.'

I slip inside a cubicle to try on the dress. I don't really expect it to be suitable. I just wanted to get away from the squabbling. Looking at myself in the mirror, I'm surprised how well the dress suits me. It's a deep cherry red with a roll neck. It's a pity I'm not buying it after Christmas when it will probably be on sale. But even at full price, it's a beautiful dress.

I emerge from the changing rooms to find Mum and Elaine still squabbling.

'It's lovely,' I say. 'I think I'll buy it.'

'We haven't seen it on,' says Mum.

'But I have. And you'll see it on Christmas Eve.'

Elaine looks horrified. 'You can't buy the first thing you see! I mean, who does that?'

'I do,' I say. 'I came to buy something for your vow renewal, and I've found it. But don't let me stop you. I can easily go and wait in the coffee shop until you're both ready.'

'Don't be silly,' says Mum. 'I don't want you filling yourself up with cake and not being able to eat your lunch.'

'She used to do that when she was little,' she tells Elaine. 'I'd spend all day cooking, then Graham would give the pair of them a bag of crisps to keep them going, and Annie wouldn't eat her dinner. I told him time and time again that she had a tiny appetite, but would he listen?'

'It must be why she has such a lovely figure,' says Elaine.

'She gets that from me,' says Mum complacently. 'I've always been able to eat what I like.'

'What are you wearing to the ceremony?' I ask her.

She immediately forgets about my childhood snack habits. 'I have the most beautiful dress. Elaine and I chose it together so we wouldn't clash. You can't have the matron of honour and the bride dressed the same.'

'You're the matron of honour?' I ask.

'Of course, she is!' says Elaine. 'There wouldn't be much point otherwise.'

'Point in what?' I say, confused.

She turns pink. 'I mean there's no point in having a vow renewal if you can't have your best friend at your side.'

'Exactly,' says Mum.

'And what are you wearing?' I ask Elaine.

'Oh, it's lovely!' says Mum. 'It's the most beautiful –'

Elaine pokes her. 'It's supposed to be a secret.'

'I'm sorry I asked,' I say.

'It isn't important,' she says. 'It's just a silly tradition.'

I look at my watch. 'We don't need to stay for lunch after all. I mean, we have what we came for, and it's only eleven o'clock.'

Elaine looks disappointed. 'But I was looking forward to getting to know you and hearing all your news.'

'I don't really have any,' I say. 'And I know that Mum wants me to help her with the mince pies.'

Mum wavers. 'That's true. And you haven't wrapped any of your presents yet. It might be better if we got going, after all.'

'That's a shame,' says Elaine. 'It was lovely to meet you, Annie. Perhaps we'll have a chance for a really good catch up after the ceremony.'

'That would be nice,' I say, privately resolving to avoid her if at all possible. She seems very nice, but she's Alex's mother, and anything I tell her is bound to get back to him.

I toy with the idea of telling her all about my new rocket scientist boyfriend, who models on the side, but reluctantly decide against it. Mum would inevitably demand to meet this paragon, and I don't know anyone who could conceivably fit the description. Brandon would be delighted to take part in such a scheme. But unfortunately, Mum already knows him.

I'll stick to my original plan and keep my head down and my life as private as possible. There are only five more days to go. I should be able to get through those without too much difficulty. After that, I can make my escape back to London, leaving Alex and his entire family behind me.

Chapter Fourteen

I wake abruptly from another dream about Alex. There's nothing surprising about that. I'm in the place I most associate with him. If that wasn't enough by itself, I've heard his name more often over the past couple of days than at any time during the past two years. Mum seems obsessed with the subject. She seems to know more about him than his own family, and certainly more than I do.

Probably Elaine, who appears to be an exceptionally proud mother, talks about him non-stop. It's only surprising that Mum should have retained such a wealth of detail about someone so wholly unconnected with her. I love her dearly, but her biggest fan couldn't say she isn't the teeniest bit self-centred.

It also appears that she talks about me quite as much as Elaine does about Alex. I'd always assumed that with Mum, out of sight was out of mind. Perhaps I've misjudged her.

In any case, it's no wonder that, having spent the afternoon with our two mothers, I should have Alex more than usually on my mind. Alex, with his hazel eyes and ready smile.

I can't quite remember what I was dreaming of when I woke so abruptly. Possibly something to do with the time we painted the village hall together. With Suzy, I remind myself. But it was such a magical day that I scarcely noticed Suzy, although Alex clearly did.

It will feel strange walking back into that hall tomorrow. My water rat and Alex's riverbank may have chipped and faded or given way to whatever is currently in fashion. It's probably covered in pictures of Spiderman now.

I'm thinking about getting up when Mum bustles in, already talking at top speed. '… so, you see, there's very little time!'

She gives me a disapproving look. 'Are you still in bed? Hurry up or half the day will be gone!'

I eye her suspiciously. 'I missed most of that. Are you talking about something specific? You aren't planning another makeover?'

'Don't be so silly,' she says. 'You've already bought a dress. Why would you need another one? Unless you mean for tonight? Why didn't you say something sooner? We could have got you something while we were shopping. You really are the most disorganised girl. And I can't spare any time this afternoon.'

I hold up my hand. 'And breathe! I have no idea what you're talking about. Why would I need another dress?'

She clicks her tongue. 'For tonight! Honestly, I sometimes think that no one in this family listens to a word I say.'

'What's happening tonight?' I ask.

'The party, of course!'

'I thought that was tomorrow?'

She almost stamps her foot. 'You're being deliberately obtuse. I'm in no mood for that today. You're perfectly aware that I'm talking about the drinks party.'

'Whose drinks party?' I say despairingly.

'Robert and Elaine's! I forgot you'd need something nice to wear for that too. There's nothing for it. You'll have to wear something of mine. We can look through my wardrobe after breakfast.'

Without waiting for me to reply, she disappears.

I shower and dress. Perhaps Dad can help me navigate the shoals of Mum's thought processes.

I find him downstairs eating his usual muesli and reading the paper. Mum is nowhere to be seen.

He lays down his paper when I walk in. 'How did you sleep?'

I pour myself some coffee. 'Fine, thanks. Is it my imagination or did Mum appear in my bedroom this morning talking about a party?'

'That sounds quite likely,' he says. 'She and Elaine are in quite a tizz about tonight.'

'I thought the vow renewal was tomorrow.'

'It is. Tonight's the rehearsal dinner.'

He has such a wry expression on his face that I can't help laughing. 'They're doing this in style, aren't they? I thought only Americans had rehearsal dinners.'

'Apparently, they're quite a thing over here now too,' he says, pouring himself some more muesli. 'Don't tell your mother about this, by the way. I'm only supposed to be having one small portion.'

He pulls a face as he holds up the milk jug. 'She's convinced I won't fit into my suit tomorrow. She wanted me to go for a jog this morning. A jog – I ask you!'

He picks up his spoon. 'I suppose I should count myself lucky. Elaine has had Robert on a low carb diet for the past couple of months. She calls it a bootcamp. Goodness knows why.'

'Poor Robert,' I say. 'Has he lost much weight?'

'Not a pound,' he says cheerfully. 'Why do you think he and I spend so much time at the golf club? Lunch in the clubhouse is all that keeps the poor chap going. He says he sees Mary's pie and chips floating above his head as he falls asleep each night. He's also taken to reading recipe books for fun.'

'But doesn't the golf work off most of the calories?'

'We haven't actually been playing!' he says, shocked. 'It's far too cold to be wandering around the greens at this time of year. We're much better off in the clubhouse. There's usually someone there to talk to, and I've picked up lots of tips for when we start again in the spring.'

'I don't blame you,' I say. 'If I didn't have a job and bills to pay, I'd be hibernating at this time of year.'

'It's one of the benefits of retirement,' he says. 'And what your mother and Elaine don't know can't harm them. Robert got his tailor to let out his suit trousers and move his jacket buttons. Elaine was delighted when he tried it on last week. She and your mother are so impressed that they're planning to try this bootcamp diet thing for themselves in the new year.'

'You're a disgrace,' I tell him affectionately. 'But you still haven't told me about tonight. They can't have invited me to the rehearsal dinner. That's for members of the wedding party.'

'It isn't exactly a dinner,' he says. 'They thought about having one, but most of their friends are busy this week. And everyone's already giving up their Christmas Eve for the vow renewal. So, they decided on a drinks party instead. It starts about seven. I do hope you're coming. I'll never hear the last of it from your mother if you don't.'

'So, that's why Mum is fussing about outfits. She wants to lend me something to wear. But I refuse to appear in public wearing a darling little rayon two-piece. I'm afraid I won't be there, anyway. I'm meeting a friend tonight.'

'Are you?' he says. 'I didn't think you knew many people around here these days. Who is it? Not Alex?'

'Of course, not Alex! I barely know him. Anyway, he's bound to be at this drinks thing, isn't he? I'm meeting Brandon.'

He wrinkles his brow. 'Do I know him?'

'Of course, you know him! He and I were at school together. He moved down here when I was fifteen. He was over here all the time when we were in the sixth form.'

'Oh, that Brandon!' he says with an air of having finally placed him, although I'm reasonably sure he's only ever met one Brandon.

'Nice boy,' he says after a moment's thought. 'Your mother always thought there was something going on between the pair of you, but I thought she was barking up the wrong tree. In fact –' He breaks off, looking embarrassed.

I laugh. 'And you were quite right. Brandon's never made any secret of the fact he's gay. Mum would have known that if she'd ever let him get a word in edgeways.'

'So, you've kept in touch?' he asks.

'Pretty much. I see him occasionally when he comes up to London, and we chat between times.'

'Do you keep in touch with anyone else?' he asks. 'Suzy, for instance.'

'Not as much as I should have. We didn't have much contact after she went to Northampton. You know how it is. You get busy, and the gaps grow longer and longer until you suddenly realise it's been a couple of years.'

'So, the pair of you didn't fall out?' His tone is light, but his eyes are keen.

'Not at all. We just drifted apart.'

I don't add that we've barely spoken since she started dating Alex. She sent me regular updates while I was in Paris, but they broke up just before I came home. Apparently, he cheated on her with someone in Edinburgh and she didn't want to talk about it. I didn't blame her.

'And how about Alex?' he asks. 'Do you and he stay in touch?'

'There's nothing to stay in touch about. I barely knew him. In fact, I hadn't given him a thought until I came home this year. Since then, he seems to be everyone's sole topic of conversation. That, and the wedding. But Alex and I have absolutely nothing in common, so there's no reason we should have stayed in contact.'

'Fair enough,' he says placidly. 'Your mother will be very disappointed about tonight. She's counting on you being there.'

'In our matching outfits? Maybe another year. Give me your bowl, and I'll take it through to the kitchen. I'd better go and break the sad news to Mum without delay before she chooses me a twinset and pearls.'

Chapter Fifteen

I pick up Brandon at seven o'clock.

'You haven't changed a bit!' he says when he sees me. 'You barely look a year older.'

'I last saw you six months ago,' I say.

He flicks my cheek. 'Only teasing. It's lovely to see you so soon. I usually have to wait until I come up to London.'

'I don't get down here very often,' I agree.

'That's an understatement. Still, you're here now. Where shall we go?'

'You choose,' I say. 'But first, I want to see your flat. I haven't been here before.'

'I invited you to the housewarming,' he says.

I feel a pang of guilt. 'So you did. But I was busy at work that week.'

He doesn't look convinced. 'It seems to me that you're busy at work every time you don't want to do something.'

'I always want to see you,' I say.

'Flattery will get you everywhere. Come in then, if you'd like the tour. It won't take long. It's very small.'

Small is an understatement. It's barely even a studio flat. The room into which he leads me obviously serves as both living room and bedroom. There's a quilt and two pillows lying on what seems to be a sofa bed at one side of the room, and a tiny kitchenette in the far corner.

He smiles. 'You're trying to work out the politest way to ask where the rest of it is. Don't worry. Everyone has the same expression when they see it. The answer is that there is no rest of it. There's a tiny bathroom through that door, and that's it. It's all I could afford, and it's perfect for someone as lazy as me. I never have to take more than ten steps in any direction.'

'That isn't what I was thinking,' I say. 'At least, not exactly. You've seen my flat in London. It's pretty small. I was just surprised to hear that you'd bought a place. You never seem to settle anywhere for long.'

'I can always rent it out if I want to go travelling again,' he says. 'Oddly enough, that urge seems to have subsided. I rather enjoy having my own place. And I like my current job – which is a miracle in itself – so I'll be here for a while.'

'Old age catches up with us all,' I say.

'At least one of us still looks about nineteen,' he says. 'What's your secret, Annie?'

'I don't have a man in my life,' I say teasingly.

He sighs. 'Neither do I, but it doesn't seem to have such a good effect on me. Never mind. I'll let you buy me several drinks while I tell you all about it.'

'I knew there was a reason you wanted me to be the designated driver,' I say. 'Come on, then. You can give me directions to wherever it is we're going.'

I drive him into town, and he directs me to a wine bar behind the main row of shops.

'This place only opened a few months ago, but I think it will do well,' he says as he opens the door and ushers me inside.

'I don't care as long as it's warm,' I gasp. Even the short walk from the car has made my eyes stream and my fingers go numb.

'It's horribly cold this evening,' he says, guiding me over to a table near the fireplace, where I'm thankful to see a fire blazing merrily in the grate.

'You order for me,' I say, slipping off my coat and holding out my hands towards the warmth. 'I'll have whatever you're having.'

He waves to the server. 'Two chimichangas, and a bottle of Merlot, please.'

'I'm driving,' I remind him.

'Who says this is for you? I'll let you have one small glass if you insist. But the rest is for me.'

I look at him more closely. 'Are you ok, Brandon? You don't seem your usual bubbly self.'

He sighs. 'I'm fine. I've just run out of holiday spirit.'

'I'll buy you a brandy, if you like.'

'Seriously, Annie, don't you ever wish you could wake up one morning and find that Christmas has been cancelled?'

'Every year!' I say without thinking.

He raises an eyebrow. 'You too? Well, aren't we a pair of old Grinches?'

'Not that old,' I say.

'Too young to feel like that, at any rate. You go first. Tell me why someone who has a wonderful job in her favourite city and has come home to spend time in the bosom of her loving family should feel so down.'

I take a sip of my wine. 'It's awful, isn't it? Christmas used to be my favourite time of year.'

'Mine too,' he says. 'What went wrong?'

The wine hits my stomach, and I feel a warm glow. 'It feels strange to be spending Christmas with Mum and Dad. Everything's exactly the same – the house, the traditions. And my parents are exactly the same too. It ought to be perfect. But somehow, it feels all wrong.'

'Perhaps that's because you've changed,' he says. 'Ah, here's our food. I'm ravenous!'

I take a bite. 'Good choice. This is delicious. Do you really think I've changed?'

'Yes, I do. I can't quite put my finger on it. You used to be more relaxed, more comfortable in your own skin. But over these past couple of years, you've seemed a bit on edge.'

He takes a bite of his chimichanga. 'I'm probably completely off base. Everyone changes as they get older. But you don't seem as happy as you used to be. Maybe that's it. Are you happy, Annie?'

I open my mouth to tell him I'm perfectly happy, but I stop. This is Brandon – one of my oldest friends. If anyone will understand, it's him.

I take another gulp of wine. 'For the most part, I am. I love my job and my flat, and London's a really exciting place to live.'

'But ...?' he encourages me.

'I'm saying that I have the life I always dreamed of.'

'Which is lovely,' he says, pouring himself another glass of wine. 'But plenty of people achieve their dreams, only to find they aren't what they wanted after all. There's no shame in that.'

'I know. But that isn't me. I love what I do. If I had a chance to do it all over again, I'd make all the same choices.'

'That's good,' he says, still watching me carefully. 'But I can't shake the idea that something's missing. You can tell me. I won't tell anyone.'

'Silent as the grave?' I say, and he laughs.

'It's more that I don't know any of the same people as you do. I haven't even seen your parents for years, so there's no one I could gossip to.'

'And there's nothing to gossip about anyway,' I say. 'Why don't you tell me about your life? What's going on with you?'

He seems to accept my change of subject. 'Nothing much. Marcus and I broke up a few months ago.'

'I'm sorry. Was it a joint decision?'

'It was very much not a joint decision,' he says. 'It was a Marcus decision.'

He looks so dejected that I lean over to give him a hug. 'I'm sorry, Brandon. For what it's worth, I think he made a huge mistake.'

'You never met him,' he points out.

'I didn't need to. Anyone who dumps you needs their head tested.'

He looks a little more cheerful. 'Who wouldn't want to be with me, right? I'm a catch.'

I stop laughing. 'Yes, you are. And don't you dare forget it!'

He squeezes my hand. 'Thanks, Annie. I've really missed you. We should make an effort to see each other more often.'

'We should. I keep promising myself to visit Mum and Dad more often. Knowing that you're settled here will be a great incentive.'

'Why is that?' he asks. 'I mean, why don't you come to see them more often? Have you had a falling out?'

'Not at all. It's just that –' I break off. I don't want to explain to Brandon that I avoid coming home whenever Alex is likely to be there, and he seems to be home for every single holiday.

'It's just that you what?' he presses me.

I stare back at him helplessly. I'm too tired to come up with any more excuses of the kind I use to fob off my parents. It would be a relief to talk to someone.

He picks up the wine bottle and waves it threateningly. 'If you don't tell me, I'm ordering another one of these. And you'll be joining me, even if I have to pay for your taxi home.'

I put my hand over my glass. 'Fine – you win! But I'm switching to orange juice now. I don't want to come out in the cold tomorrow to fetch Dad's car.'

'I knew that would do it,' he says. 'So, what's the big secret? Why don't you come home anymore?'

I take a deep breath. 'Partly, it's because I'm really busy. I'm going for a promotion at work and putting in lots of extra hours. But if I'm being honest, I don't come home very much because there's someone here I don't want to see.'

His expression changes. 'That isn't good.'

'It's nothing to worry about. It's just this man –'

'Or woman,' he says.

'What do you mean?'

He looks smug. 'Let's not be thoughtlessly heteronormative.'

'But I've already told you it's a man!'

'True,' he says. 'My mistake. Carry on.'

I roll my eyes at him. 'I met him right before my third year at university and ... well, I suppose I fell for him.'

'You never mentioned this to me. What's his name?'

'His name doesn't matter. The feeling wasn't mutual. In fact, he ended up going out with Suzy for a few months.'

'Suzy Madison? Then he isn't worth a second of your time. Any man who would choose Suzy Madison over you needs a lobotomy.'

'How do you know?' I say. 'You would never have fallen for either of us.'

'I'm gay, darling, not blind! Seriously, Annie, you're better off out of it.'

'So I told myself. Not the part about Suzy. She couldn't help being so beautiful. But I was determined to get over it and not allow it to get in the way of my friendship with her. It might have taken me some time, but I would have managed it, if not for –'

I break off, my voice wobbling treacherously. I feel an unaccustomed rush of tears.

It's ok,' he says, taking my hand. 'If it wasn't for what?'

I stare into the fire. 'If he hadn't started seeing her while he was supposed to be with me.'

'But why are you still upset with him?' he asks. 'That was two years ago.'

'It's hard to say. He and I only went on a couple of dates before he cheated on me with Suzy. And then a few months later, he cheated on her with someone else. But I really thought he could be the one. I know how ridiculous that sounds, but we got on so well together. I could have accepted him deciding he didn't want to see me again. But cheating on me with my friend was something else.'

He nods. 'What did he have to say for himself?'

'Nothing. What could he have said? Anyway, I was leaving for Paris the following day. That was good timing, as it turned out.'

He gives me an odd look. 'You didn't talk to him about it at all?'

'What was there to say? I sent him a text before I left saying that it wasn't working out for me, and I'd prefer to go to Paris as a single woman.'

'Hang on!' he says. 'I seem to remember you dating some guy in Paris.'

'André,' I say, not quite meeting his eye.

'I know that look,' he says. 'Don't think you can hide anything from me.'

'I'm not!' I protest.

He lifts the wine bottle. 'Tell me everything or I'll pour you another glass of this.'

I move my glass out of his reach. 'Perhaps I may not have been entirely honest about André.'

He looks delighted. 'You made him up?'

'Oh, he existed, all right. He was the son of my host family. I got to know him and his girlfriend pretty well while I was over there.'

'I'm impressed!' says Brandon. 'A ménage à trois? That's very French.'

'Don't be ridiculous. André and Francine took me to see all the sights, and we usually took some selfies.'

He gives me a mock stern look. 'I don't remember seeing three people in all those pictures you posted on Facebook.'

'They must have been the ones Francine took,' I say.

'I'll check.' He opens his phone and starts scrolling through it.

I reach out and take it from him. 'Fine – I may have cropped them a little.'

'You sneaky thing! I take it that was for this guy's benefit?'

'For mine, really. It felt easier and cleaner if he thought I'd started seeing someone else. I didn't want him messaging me and stirring it at all up again.'

'I understand,' he says gently. 'Your pride was hurt.'

He's right. I was utterly humiliated when Alex went off with Suzy. But I'd have died rather than let him know that. All I wanted was to show him that I'd moved on too and wasn't giving him a second thought.

'You're sure you don't need that wine, after all?' asks Brandon.

'I'm fine. Honestly, I am. I haven't thought about my time in Paris for years.'

'Poor André,' he says with such a comical look that I burst out laughing.

'You think he's still pining for me? He sent me an invitation to his wedding last year, so I imagine he's got over me by now.'

He considers me carefully. 'Aren't you a dark horse? Are there any other fake French fiancés I need to know about?'

'Not fiancé,' I say. 'That would have been far too complicated. It was a brief holiday romance – beautiful while it lasted.'

'That was wise,' he says. 'Your mother would have been planning the wedding before you'd even got back from Paris. Did she know about it?'

'She did. I wasn't going to tell her, and she doesn't use Facebook. But she kept going on about Alex and wanting to know what was going on with us. So, I told her about André. She was quite cut up when it all came to nothing.'

'The bar's about to close,' he says. 'We'd better get going. All I can say is that you're a terrible daughter.'

He sees my face. 'I'm only joking. It was a wonderful idea, and no one got hurt.'

No one but me, I think as I reach for the bill. 'This one's on me. It's been so lovely to see you again.'

'Fine,' he says. 'But the next one's on me. And let's not make it so long this time.'

Chapter Sixteen

We walk quickly back to the car. I push my hands deep inside my pockets. Even with my thick gloves, my fingers are still numb by the time we reach the car.

My phone beeps as I open the car door. I flip it open and peer at the screen. 'I can't make head nor tail of this. Can you read it?'

Brandon takes the phone and squints at it. 'It's certainly not in any language I recognise. Unless it's French? Maybe it's from André saying that he's left his marriage of convenience and is on his way over here at this very moment. Hang on! I think there are some words among the gibberish. Yes, I'm sure there are. I can make out *Dad*, *immediately*, and *trunk*. Do you think your father's going on holiday?'

I snatch the phone from him. 'I don't recognise the number, but I think the text is from Mum.'

I scrutinise it more carefully. 'I think it's supposed to say they need me to pick them up. I don't think that's *trunk*. I think she's trying to say *drunk*.'

'That makes more sense,' he says. 'Where are they tonight?'

'At a drinks party. But it's local, so they were supposed to be walking home. That's why Dad let me have the car this evening.'

'Perhaps he's too drunk to walk,' he says. 'Or too cold.'

'I suppose I'll find out when I get there. I'll drop you home en route.'

'I can come with you, if you like,' he says.

'There's no need. I'm sure I'll be fine.'

He grins. 'Let's hope your dad is too.'

'Don't get out,' he tells me when I drop him home. 'You'd better go and find out what's wrong. Text me later and let me know.'

'I will,' I promise. 'But there's something I forgot to ask you tonight. Are you doing anything tomorrow?'

'The usual. Watching *White Christmas* and drowning my sorrows in a bottle of absinthe.'

'Any other year, I'd offer to join you,' I say. 'But do you think you could tear yourself away from Bing Crosby and alcohol poisoning and come to a party with me instead?'

'At your parents' house?'

'No. It's a long story, and I haven't got time to go into it now. I have to go to a wedding vow renewal, and there's a party in the church hall afterwards. I don't really want to go by myself. Will you come?'

'How could I refuse such a flattering invitation?' he says drily. 'I suppose I could come for an hour or two if it would help you out.'

'It really would,' I say gratefully. 'I'll text you the details. Thanks, Brandon.'

I wave and drive off, wondering what I'm going to find when I reach the Fielding's house.

Judging by the noise streaming out, it seems to be quite a large party. I park outside the house and pull out my phone. I have no intention of knocking on the door. I'll only be swept inside and forced to join the festivities. I'm just here to pick up my parents. The wheel has turned full circle since Dad used to pick me up from parties when I was a teenager.

I quickly text the number Mum used to message me. *I'm here as soon as you're ready.*

A text flashes up on my screen. *Who's this?*

I sigh. Perhaps Mum is drunk too. *It's Annie. Who do you think?*

There's a longer pause before a text comes back. *Annie? This is Alex.*

I stare at the screen, uncomprehending. I must have got the wrong number somehow. But how likely was it that I accidentally reached Alex Fielding?

Fingers trembling slightly, I text back. *I'm here to pick up my parents.*

I know you are, comes the immediate reply. *Your mum borrowed my phone to text you.*

I don't want to get into a back-and-forth text conversation with Alex Fielding. *Can you let them know I'm here?*

I wait for an acknowledgement, but it doesn't come. Instead, I see the front door open and a silhouetted figure peer out. I slump down in my seat, wishing I hadn't parked right outside the house. Still, it's too late to do anything about that. I can hardly switch on the car and drive away. Besides, it's very bright in the house and pitch dark out here. He probably won't be able to see me.

I will the front door to close again and the figure to disappear. But it steps outside onto the snowy path and walks towards the gate.

I slump even lower, trying not to breathe. A tap on my window makes me jump. I didn't see the garden gate open.

'Annie?' says a well-remembered voice.

I sit up and roll down the window. 'Hi, Alex!' I say with fake enthusiasm. 'How are you?'

'I'm fine, thanks. Why are you hiding out here?'

'I'm not hiding. I'm waiting.' I hear my voice slide half an octave higher than usual and force myself to bring it down again. I overcompensate, and my next words come out as a deep growl. 'I'm here to pick up my parents.'

His lips twitch. 'I can see that. But I don't think they're ready yet. The last time I saw her, your mother was leading a conga around the upstairs landing, and your father was showing the vicar how to make a fifty-pence piece disappear.'

'But Mum texted me to pick them up immediately.'

'So, that's why she wanted to use my phone! She wasn't too clear. She told me she had to make an urgent phone call. As soon as I handed it to her, she disappeared with it. I've only just got it back.'

'She told me to come at once,' I say. 'Can you tell her I'm here?'

'I think you'd better come and tell her yourself.'

'I'm in a hurry.'

He looks surprised. 'Are you going out somewhere?'

'No, I'm coming home from somewhere.' I don't give any further details. It's none of his business where I've been tonight or with whom.

'I hope you had a nice time,' he says.

I climb out of the car and follow him up the path. 'Yes, thanks. I was catching up with an old friend.'

'And now you're catching up with another,' he says as he ushers me inside the house.

I bite back an acid retort. I don't want to get into a conversation with him. I just want to collect my parents and go home.

'Can I get you a drink?' he asks, holding out a hand for my coat.

I don't take it off. 'No, thanks. As I say, I'm here to collect my parents.'

'Not even a small one?' he says. 'Come on, Annie, it's Christmas!'

'I'm perfectly aware of that!' I snap. I see the look of surprise on his face. 'I'm sorry. I'm quite tired.'

'Why don't you find somewhere to sit while I look for your parents?' he says.

I make my way through the crowd of people in the hall and into the conservatory, where I find Elaine lying on what looks like a garden lounger, holding an empty glass.

'Annie! How lovely!' she exclaims. 'I was so disappointed when your parents said you weren't coming tonight.'

I sit down on the matching lounger. 'I'm not really here. I've been out this evening. I wouldn't be here at all if Mum hadn't asked me to pick them up.'

'Now, why did she do that?' she says. 'She knows perfectly well that she and your father are getting a lift home with the vicar.'

'But she texted me and told me to come at once because Dad is drunk.'

'He's not the only one! But I have no idea why your mother should have dragged you into it.'

She squints over my shoulder. 'There you are, Liz! We were just talking about you.'

I turn to see Mum standing in the doorway, looking flushed and unsteady.

She waves to me. 'Hello, darling. What a time you've been!'

'I came as quickly as I could. I thought there was some emergency.'

'Emergency?' she says vaguely. 'Oh, yes! Your father can hardly stand.'

'But why did you have to call Annie?' asks Elaine. 'You know that David has offered to take you both home.'

Mum waves a hand, splashing a little of her wine as she does so. 'Oops! Sorry about that. These wine glasses are awfully small, aren't they?'

'They look the usual size to me,' I say coldly.

She ignores me. 'Now that you're here, you can stay and enjoy the party.'

'No, I can't. I'm absolutely exhausted, and I'm going home. Can you make up your mind whether you and Dad need a lift?'

She looks at Elaine, who jumps up. 'One drink before you go! It's Christmas!'

'So everyone keeps telling me,' I say. 'Fine, I'll stay for one drink.'

'I'll go and find Alex,' says Elaine.

'There's no need,' I say hurriedly. 'I can get my own drink.'

'I wouldn't dream of it. You're our guest. Alex! Alex!!!!'

He appears in the doorway a moment later. 'Did I hear my mother's dulcet tones?' He catches my eye and grins.

'There you are!' says Elaine. 'What a time you've been. I'll go and get Annie a drink. Is champagne alright for you?'

'You were calling for Alex to go and fetch the drinks,' I remind her.

She looks at me blearily. 'I don't think so. I'll go and …'

'So will I,' says Mum, and the pair of them disappear.

'It's been like this all evening,' says Alex. 'You don't know what you've missed.'

'Are parties at your house always like this?'

'Always,' he says, sitting next to me. 'Surely, you remember?'

'I never came to a party at your house.'

'You must have done.'

'There's no must about it. I think I'd remember.' Fearing that this might be open to misconstruction, I add, 'I'd remember a party like this.'

'That's the point of this sort of party,' he says. 'No one ever remembers them. Perhaps that's what happened with you. You came to hundreds of them, but you can't remember.'

I don't laugh. 'I think you're probably confusing me with someone else.'

'What do you mean?'

I stare out of the window, not wanting to meet his eye. 'You're probably thinking of Suzy.'

'Suzy?' he says blankly. 'Oh, you mean that Suzy?'

'Yes, I mean that Suzy.'

'I'd forgotten all about her,' he says. 'We hung out with her a couple of times, didn't we?'

For a moment, I'm speechless. Forgotten all about her? Forgotten the girl with whom he had a fling while he was supposed to be with me? I don't know which is worse – him lying and pretending not to remember Suzy or him having actually forgotten the whole incident.

I'm about to give him a piece of my mind when the door opens and Elaine comes in, carrying two glasses of champagne.

'There you are!' she says as though she'd expected us to have disappeared in her absence.

'Where else would we be?' says Alex. His tone is light, but I can't quite read his expression.

She plonks down the glasses of champagne on an upturned wine box. 'Oh, you know. I thought maybe you'd gone out into the garden or something.'

'I'd be more than happy to show Annie the garden,' says Alex.

I stand abruptly. 'I really must be going. It's been lovely to see you again, Elaine.'

'But you haven't drunk your champagne,' says Alex.

I give him a cold look. 'You can drink them both. You've always been good at having your cake and eating it too.'

My eyes fill with tears. I quickly turn and leave the room before he can see them.

Chapter Seventeen

I wake with a sinking feeling on Christmas Eve. Ever since childhood, this has been my favourite day of the year – even more special than my birthday. I love the delightful anticipation of knowing that Christmas Day is on its way, yet I still have to wait. In some ways, it's even more special than Christmas Day itself, which always carries with it the sense of time ticking away.

When Christmas Day is over, it's gone for a whole year. But Christmas Eve is special. It has no weight of expectation. It's the magic doorway into the day for which everyone is waiting.

I hear a door slam, followed by Mum's voice. 'Graham! Where are you? I've been calling and calling!'

I pull the pillow over my head and groan. I hadn't intended to get up this early. The vow renewal isn't until two o'clock. I'd planned to sleep in, have an early lunch, and take my time getting ready. Not that I care what anyone thinks about the way I look, but it seems a shame to have bought a new dress and not make an effort with the rest of my appearance.

Obviously, that plan isn't going to work now. Mum's voice floats up the stairs, sounding increasingly hysterical. 'Drat that man! He's never there when you want him.'

I open my bedroom door. 'What's wrong?'

She gives me a tragic look. 'It's the cream!'

I take a beat to consider what cream this might be. Knowing Mum, it could be anything from Elizabeth Arden's newest age-defying serum to hair-removal lotion for her legs.

'What about the cream?' I say. 'Have you broken the jar?'

Mum flaps her hands. 'It isn't in a jar, silly! It's in pint pots or gallons or something. I don't know.'

How much face cream does she need? I speak in a soothing voice. 'I'm sure we can get you some more. And people won't be looking at you. All eyes will be on the bride.'

She looks annoyed. 'What do you mean? Of course, they'll be looking at me. Elaine and I spent ages choosing my dress.'

'I have some face cream you could use,' I offer, not wanting to get into an argument while she's in this mood.

'Face cream?' she says. 'If it isn't like you to go off at a tangent just when I need some help.'

'So, what cream are we talking about?'

She flaps her hands again. 'The cream for the trifles, of course. What did you think I meant?'

There's never any real way to tell what she's talking about when she's in this mood, so I give her an encouraging nod. 'You've lost the cream for the trifles?'

'Of course, I haven't lost it!' she says. 'Elaine's rung to say their fridge went out last night, and all the cream was in it. She doesn't know what time the power went out, so she doesn't dare use it. Imagine poisoning an entire wedding reception!'

'She could have put it out in the snow,' I say. 'That would have kept it cold.'

Mum gives me an annoyed look. 'It's easy to be wise after the event, isn't it? There's nothing for it. You'll have to drive out to the farm shop and pick up some more.'

'Can't they deliver it?' I ask. I'm still barely half awake, and Mum is making even less sense than usual.

'Apparently not,' she says. 'Go and get dressed. You can take your father's car. I have no idea where he is. Typical man!'

I know from long experience that it's pointless engaging with Mum when she's in this sort of state.

I yawn. 'I'll have a shower and get dressed.'

'Don't dawdle!' she says. 'Elaine needs it as quickly as possible. The caterers will be there soon to start work. She says that Robert's nowhere to be found either.'

'Maybe he and Dad are having a quick round of golf before the ceremony,' I say, immediately regretting it when Mum's face turns almost purple.

'If I find out that's where he is, I'll murder him! I told him I needed him here this morning in case there were any last-minute hiccups.'

Twenty minutes later, I pull up outside the farm shop. There's only one other car outside. I run into the shop, clutching the piece of paper Mum has given me. There's no one serving, but there's a man waiting by the counter. I'd recognise the back of that head anywhere.

I take an instinctive step back towards the door, but the jangle of the bell makes him look around.

His face lights up when he sees me. 'Annie! What are you doing here?'

I stare at him, confused. What am I doing here? For a moment, I can't remember. Something about trifles and food poisoning.

'Cream!' I manage at last in a slight croak.

His face crinkles into that familiar smile. 'Quite a coincidence. Both of us here on the same errand.'

'You're here for cream too?' Realisation dawns. 'For the trifles?'

'What else? Apparently, our fridge went out last night. The trifles themselves were ok, but Mum doesn't dare risk the cream. So, she sent me on a dairy run.'

'It's a pity she didn't call my mum first. She sent me on exactly the same errand.'

'Liz was the first person she called,' he says. 'I suppose they must have got their wires crossed somehow.'

He takes a step towards me. 'It's good to see you, Annie. I was really happy when Mum told me you were coming to the wedding. Are you coming to the party too? Maybe we can catch up there.'

'I'll probably come for a little while,' I say.

He's looking at me with all the old warmth in his eyes. 'I'm glad to hear that. I really want to talk to you.'

'I may not be able to make it,' I say. 'I'm supposed to be meeting a friend.'

'Bring them too,' he says. 'There'll be plenty of food. And someone will have to eat all the leftover trifles.'

'I'll tell him.'

He hesitates for a fraction of a second. 'Him?'

'Yes, he's a friend from school.'

'I look forward to meeting him.'

'If I'm not needed to fetch the cream, I'd better get going,' I say. 'Mum's already in quite a state.'

One corner of his mouth tilts upwards. 'I expect mine could give her a run for her money. We're swarming with hairdressers, makeup artists, the works. It's like being in a spa. No wonder Dad's gone out.'

'Mine's gone out too,' I say. 'Do you think they're together?'

'I know they are. They were heading to the Red Lion for a pre-wedding get together.'

I giggle in spite of myself. 'Like a stag night?'

'No, they had one of those last week. Mum and Liz didn't want them to, but Dad said that if he had to go through all the palaver of getting married again, he was jolly well going to have the fun parts too.'

'I bet that went down well,' I say.

'He nearly had to sleep on the sofa that night. I don't think the evening was too bad. They just went out for dinner and a few drinks. It's a good thing really. Dad told me that his first stag night was in London, and it all got a bit out of hand. He woke up the next morning in Birmingham, handcuffed to a lamppost. It's probably one of those experiences that's enjoyable the first time, but you don't want to repeat it.'

'I thought your motto was try anything once,' I say without thinking.

He looks pleased. 'You remember. And yours is to do everything properly.'

'Not anymore. People change. I've changed.'

He studies me carefully. You don't seem any different to me.'

'Well, that was all a long time ago,' I say.

He looks even more amused. 'You don't show your extreme age.'

'You know what I mean.'

'I used to,' he says gently. 'At least, I thought so.'

The blood rushes to my face as I stare at him, unable to speak. If I didn't know how he was capable of behaving, I would almost have thought he was sincere. My heart twists. If only things had worked out the way I'd hoped. I thought I'd found the perfect man. Not really the perfect one, of course. Everyone has faults. But the perfect man for me – the person whose strengths compliment my weaknesses and vice versa.

But that wasn't the real Alex, I remind myself. The real Alex would never have behaved as this one did. If he'd cared for me as he pretended to, he could never have hurt me like that.

'I guess you thought wrong,' I say in a choked voice. 'I have to get going.'

I don't wait for him to speak but leave the shop and jump into my car. I pull away without looking over my shoulder.

I feel a bit calmer by the time I reach home. It was a shock to see him there. But I survived it, and now I can face the vow renewal with more confidence. I know that the Alex I've kept in my mind, against my better judgement, isn't the real Alex. So, the sooner I put that part of my life behind me, the better.

I find Mum in her bedroom, backcombing her hair.

'Did you get the cream?' she asks.

'There was no need,' I say in as casual a tone as I can manage. 'There must have been some mix up in communication between you and Elaine. When I got to the shop, Alex was already there.'

Mum swings around in her chair, one side of her hair sticking out at an absurd angle. 'Alex Fielding?'

'Do you know any others?'

She frowns. 'As a matter of fact, there's an Alex at the gardening club.'

'Let's assume it wasn't that one.'

She turns back to the mirror. 'Did you have a nice chat?'

'About the cream?' I ask.

'Of course not! I meant a chat with Alex. You haven't seen him for a while, have you?'

'I saw him at his parents' party last night.'

'Not really,' she says. 'There were far too many people there for you to talk properly.'

'I talked as much as I wanted to. I haven't seen him for years, which suits me fine.'

I bend to pick up a tube of mascara. 'I hope this is waterproof. You're going to need it. Elaine told me she and Robert have written their own vows.'

'I know. I helped her,' says Mum smugly. 'And of course I'm not going to cry. But I was talking about Alex. You and he used to be such friends.'

'No, we didn't. We barely knew each other.'

'Elaine says you went out a couple of times,' she says, watching me closely.

I'm not sure how to answer this. Alex and I agreed not to tell anyone about that until the New Year's Eve party. And I didn't go to the party. I broke up with him by text. It's yet another demonstration of his complete lack of trustworthiness.

I meet Mum's eyes in the mirror. 'Maybe we did. It's all so long ago. But I haven't spoken to him in years. We're very different people.' And without waiting for an answer, I leave the room.

I hear the back door slam and go downstairs to find Dad in the kitchen, looking flushed.

He starts when he sees me. 'I didn't think you'd be up yet.'

'It was a little difficult to sleep through Mum yelling for you at the top of her voice,' I tell him.

He takes off his coat. 'Does she know I've been out?'

'Of course, I know!' Mum is standing in the doorway, her hair swept up into what looks suspiciously like a beehive.

Dad gives her a sheepish smile. 'Hello, love. You look very nice.'

'Where have you been?' she demands. 'I needed someone to fetch the cream, and as usual you were nowhere to be found. I had to send Annie instead.'

She sniffs. 'I knew it! You've been out drinking. And now you'll be too drunk to go to the wedding.'

'I've had two pints,' he tells her. 'And the wedding isn't for another couple of hours. You don't seriously think I'd get drunk on the morning of my best friend's wedding?'

Her eyes narrow. 'And was Robert with you?'

He drops two slices of bread into the toaster. 'As a matter of fact, he was. I was helping him to steady his nerves.'

'Did you give him a talk about the facts of life?' I ask.

Mum frowns. 'Don't be so coarse, Annie!' After a moment's thought, she adds, 'If he doesn't know them after twenty-five years of marriage, he never will. Where do you think Alex and Caitlin came from?'

'I always imagined the stork brought them,' I say.

I quickly make my escape, but not before Mum has snatched the bread from the toaster. 'This won't soak up the alcohol, Graham! I'll cook you a proper breakfast. Hopefully, you'll be able to walk down the aisle in a straight line.'

I slip upstairs, smiling to myself. Despite everything, it's nice to be home. My parents don't change, but I wouldn't really want them to. However infuriating they can be at times, I love them both dearly. Perhaps Christmas won't be so bad after all.

Chapter Eighteen

We leave the house soon after one o'clock, with Mum fussing and worrying until the very last moment.

Dad takes her hand and leads her towards the car. 'Stop it, love. If you carry on like this, you won't enjoy the wedding. And you know how much you've been looking forward to it and how hard you've worked.'

'Vow renewal!' snaps Mum, but she gets into the car.

I've been so busy making sure I look presentable that I haven't noticed what Mum is wearing. 'You aren't walking up the aisle in your gardening trousers?' I ask.

She pulls down the visor to inspect her face in the mirror. 'Don't be so daft. Elaine and I are getting changed in the vestry. I'll have to walk across the car park to the church, and it's very muddy.'

'I could have dropped you at the side door,' says Dad.

She gives an impatient sigh. 'Please don't interfere. Elaine and I have it all planned out. For all we knew, it might have been pouring with rain today, and we'd have been bound to get splashed. You just worry about yourself.'

'Do you need any help getting dressed?' I ask.

'I'll be fine, thank you, darling. Mandy and Jean will be there to help us with the fiddly bits.'

I wonder yet again what Elaine and Mum are planning to wear. Mum has been unusually reticent and evaded all my questions, telling me that it's unlucky to talk about outfits. It didn't stop her inspecting my dress very critically and making sure my boots were clean and polished. Fiddly bits could mean anything from a mini dress to full biking gear. I wouldn't put anything past Mum. Having spent a morning with Elaine at the shops, I wouldn't put anything past her either.

We pull up outside the church, and Mum disappears down the side path towards the vestry.

'I expect you'll be glad when this is all over,' I say as we watch her go.

'It's been quite fun,' says Dad. 'Robert and I thought it was a ridiculous idea when Elaine and Mum suggested it. But it's quite sweet really. And he and I have got to know each other much better over the last few months. He's a very decent fellow.'

'I'm sure he is,' I say. 'Elaine seems nice too.'

He looks at me in the mirror. 'I don't know Caitlin very well, but Alex seems like a good man.'

I pick up my bag and open the car door. 'So everyone keeps telling me, although I can't imagine why. I'll see you after the ceremony.'

I'm greeted at the back of the church by someone I barely recognise, although he seems to know me.

'Annie? I don't suppose you remember me. We were in primary school together. David Paxton.'

'I thought you looked familiar,' I say. 'How are you?'

'Great, thanks.' He waves towards the altar. 'This will be me in a few weeks' time.'

'You're being ordained?' I ask, confused.

'Not quite. I'm getting married. Lisa Parry. She was in our class too.'

'I remember Lisa. Congratulations! Maybe you'll be renewing your vows in twenty-five years' time.'

He pulls a face. 'I doubt it. I never knew that planning a wedding was such an undertaking. I've told Lisa that I only plan to do it once. She quite agrees. If we'd known how much trouble and expense it was, we'd have eloped months ago.'

'Why didn't you?' I say.

He stops smiling. 'The families, really. They'd have been terribly upset. Lisa and I realised that family is more important than anything. Still, we'll both be glad when it's all over.'

I walk towards the pew he indicates, which is nearer to the front than I'd like. I'd have preferred to hide at the back. But perhaps there won't be many people here, and they want to keep us all together.

I sit for a few minutes, turning over the order of service in my hands without reading it. David is right. Family is important – if you have a good one, which I have. I haven't seen mine as much as I'd have liked over the past couple of years. I've told myself that's all Alex's fault. But I have to let that go now. If I'm really over him, I can no longer use him as an excuse. My life is my own, and it's up to me to choose how I live it.

Listening to the gentle hum of the organ music and the chatter around me as the pews fill up, I feel strangely peaceful for the first time in a long while. I thought that taking a job in London would give me time to think about the future. But it hasn't worked out that way. Maybe the noise and bustle have stopped me from thinking clearly. Coming back to my childhood home, where there's very little noise and nothing ever happens, was exactly what I needed to sort out my head.

Even when I see Alex walk up the aisle and take his place next to Robert on the steps, I feel no more than a slight pang. I've spent so long trying to put him into my past, where he belongs. It's taken me coming home and facing him again to finally achieve it.

The organ music stops, and there's a cold rush of air up the aisle as the doors are flung open. The ancient organ makes a great gasping sound, as though filling its lungs with air, and Mrs. Bantry crashes into the familiar sound of the wedding march.

Everyone stands as the bridal procession begins. I crane my head around, but there are so many people that I can't see anything. There are gasps and whispers around the church. When Elaine comes level with my pew, I have to stifle a laugh. Robert is in a traditional morning suit, as is Alex. I'd expected Elaine to wear something suitable for her age and the fact that she's been married for twenty-five years.

Instead, she's wearing a full-length white bridal gown with huge puffy sleeves and a train. She also has a heavily embroidered veil. She's obviously going for the full bridal experience. Well, good for her. Why not?

Elaine's train is surprisingly long, and it takes Mum a few seconds to catch up. When I see her, I give a snort of laughter which I quickly turn into a cough.

Mum is wearing a full-length bridesmaid's dress in a shocking shade of violet. Unlike Elaine's dress, hers is strapless and very tight fitting. I'd expected her to be wearing flowers in her hair. Instead, she's opted for a tiara of amethysts and diamonds. It perches on her upswept hair like a bird of paradise.

As we take our seats again, I look at Robert and Alex. Did either of them have any idea of the splendour in store for them? Robert doesn't look surprised, so probably Elaine showed him the dress in advance. But Alex looks stunned. His mouth has fallen slightly open, and he's staring at his mother with such an expression of bemusement that I almost burst out laughing.

As if sensing my presence, he turns his head and looks at me. For a moment, we stare at each other, caught in each other's gaze. I recognise the familiar glint of amusement in his hazel eyes and can't help responding. My heart begins to thud in the annoying way it does whenever he's around. I want to look away, but I can't.

The vicar clears his throat, breaking the spell. 'Dearly beloved, he begins. 'We are gathered here …'

I look down at my order of service, no longer wanting to laugh. I'm completely over Alex Fielding. So, what am I doing staring at him like a lovestruck teenager? I need to get myself under control.

I look at the back of Elaine and Robert's heads, trying to compose myself and determined not to meet Alex's eyes as I listen to the familiar words of the service. I've always loved weddings, with their hope and optimism and promise of the future. It's nice that Robert and Elaine have spent twenty-five years together and are still enough in love to want to celebrate it all over again. I wonder whether I'll ever find that for myself. Maybe not, but I know I could never settle for anything less.

The vicar raises his eyes from the prayer book at last. 'And now, I believe that the bride and groom have written their own vows. I'm very much looking forward to hearing them.'

He nods to Robert, who pulls a piece of paper from his pocket and unfolds it. He looks pink but determined.

'Elaine, I knew the moment I saw you that you were the person with whom I wished to spend the rest of my life.'

He pauses and straightens the paper. 'I didn't think it was very likely that I'd succeed. You seemed to have every young man in the area buzzing around you, and I didn't think you would ever notice me –'

'I probably wouldn't have,' interrupts Elaine, 'if it hadn't been for –'

He holds up a hand. 'I believe it's still my turn.'

There's a ripple of laughter. Elaine doesn't look remotely abashed. 'Go on, then.'

He smiles at her. 'Thankfully, you hit that lamppost with your father's car one evening. I've never seen anyone look so scared. I couldn't understand it until I met your father.'

A fresh wave of laughter runs around the church. I chance a look at Alex and see he's laughing too.

Robert folds up the paper and puts it back in his pocket. 'I would have taken the blame for you, no matter what. I couldn't bear to think of you being so upset. But luckily for me, you agreed to go to dinner with me afterwards. And the rest, as they say, is history.'

He looks down at his wife with such love in his eyes that I feel my own eyes fill with tears. 'Elaine, we've spent twenty-five very happy years together. We've had two beautiful children, and we've been blessed with a lovely home and wonderful friends. But if we'd had none of those things, I still wouldn't have a moment's regret about marrying the woman I'm very sure I couldn't live without.'

The woman sitting next to me gives an audible sob and pulls out a handkerchief. 'That's what I want,' she whispers to me, and I nod.

The vicar clears his throat. 'Thank you, Robert. I'm not sure you'll be able to beat that, Elaine. But I'm very sure you're going to try!'

Elaine beams around at the congregation. She turns back to Robert. 'I've written you a poem. But I know how much my poems embarrass you, so I'll give it to you later. When I first suggested we do this, you weren't too thrilled. But I'm very glad you agreed. It gives me the chance to say in front of everyone how much I love you. Thank you for twenty-five happy years. Thank you for loving me and supporting me, and thank you for our children.'

She looks over at Alex. 'There's something I want to say to you too. When you meet the person you're supposed to be with, you have to have the courage to tell them how you feel. It took a lot of courage for your father to tell mine that he'd backed his car into a lamppost. But if he hadn't, he and I might never have got together, and you wouldn't be standing here today. That's all I have to say.'

'I think that's about it,' she says to the vicar. 'So, why don't you hurry up and declare us man and wife again so we can get on with the next twenty-five years?'

The vicar raises an eyebrow. 'If you've quite finished telling me how to do my job, Elaine?'

He looks around the congregation. 'I seem to have missed out the part about objecting. It also seems a little late for that. May I assume that no one here has any objection to raise? Good. Then I now declare Robert and Elaine man and wife. You may kiss … oh, I see you're a little ahead of me.'

The congregation bursts into applause as Robert and Elaine break apart and walk back down the aisle, hand in hand. Mum seems unsure whether to follow them. Dad takes her hand, and she beams up at him. I watch them walk down the aisle together, feeling a lump in my throat.

I glance at Alex, who's talking to the vicar. I feel a momentary impulse to go and talk to him, but I squash it. I have nothing to say to him. Perhaps if I'd found the courage to contact him while I was in Paris, we could have talked and worked things out.

But I know that isn't true. I need someone I can trust with my life. I thought I'd found that with Alex, but he turned out to be someone I barely knew. There's no point in living in the past. I fell so madly in love with him that I attributed all sorts of qualities to him that he didn't possess. That was probably as much my fault as his. And there's nothing either of us can do about it. We'll both have to get on with our lives in our own separate ways.

Chapter Nineteen

Alex lifts his glass and taps it with his knife. The ringing sound makes everyone turn to face him. I keep my eyes fixed on my plate. I hate speeches at the best of times, and this one promises to be especially painful. Boring, I correct myself. It promises to be especially boring. I hope he'll get through it quickly and let everyone get on with their evening.

It's surprising how many people have turned out on Christmas Eve. It isn't the most convenient time to hold an event like this. Still, almost everyone here knows each other, so possibly the entire village is treating it as a giant Christmas party.

Mum and her friends have always been keen on parties, usually involving Tupperware or candles. Maybe Santa will walk in at any moment, clutching a sackful of Ann Summers products, and solemnly hand them out to everyone. Then again, perhaps not. The vicar and both the churchwardens are present, and Mum would have a heart attack.

I look across at her. She's flushed and laughing as she talks animatedly to Elaine, whose veil is now slightly askew.

My attention is recalled by Alex clearing his throat. People around me shush each other and point towards him. I chance a look at him and look quickly away again. Most unluckily, he's chosen the exact same moment to look in my direction.

I fix my gaze on a spot about four feet behind his right shoulder. That should give everyone the impression I'm listening closely to his speech. Meanwhile, I'll be at liberty to allow my thoughts to wander.

'Ladies and gentlemen,' he says, his voice a little higher pitched than usual. 'It is my very great pleasure to be giving this toast today.'

He looks at his father, who gives his son an affectionate smile. Alex seems to gain confidence from this. I wonder why he seems so nervous. Surely, he has to give presentations at work, and probably to a far larger audience than is now gathered in Honeywell parish hall.

'I was a little taken aback when I arrived home for Christmas and found myself in the middle of wedding preparations,' he goes on. 'At first, I had a horrible feeling they were for me.'

There's a burst of laughter. Everyone looks at Elaine, who takes another gulp of champagne and waves around to all her friends. I'm not sure she's even listening. My own mother is just as bad. She's sitting sideways on her chair as though it's a horse and she's one of the young ladies of the house, riding side-saddle and waving to the adoring villagers.

Alex goes on. 'Mum has been on at me for years to find a nice girl to settle down with and provide her with a few grandchildren to spoil. I thought for a moment that she'd finally taken matters into her own hands.'

He pauses as the ripple of laughter becomes a roar. Everyone turns towards Elaine, who returns their gaze with a gracious wave of her champagne glass, spilling a little of it onto the snowy tablecloth.

Robert is laughing as hard as anyone. It's a shame that such nice parents as these should have produced a son like Alex. They deserve so much better. If he does eventually settle down and marry someone, which is perfectly possible – he is after all very nice looking and quite personable if you don't notice the duplicitous soul beneath the pleasant exterior – he'll only get bored and chase after some other woman.

He clears his throat again. 'Thankfully, that isn't the case. But it is my very great honour and privilege to be present at my parents' second wedding –'

This catches Elaine's attention. She turns her eyes from her champagne glass, into which she's been gazing as though it contains the answer to the mysteries of the universe.

'You were at our first one too, darling, although I don't suppose you remember much of it.'

Everyone looks from Elaine to Robert, then at Alex's stunned face. She seems to sense some of this discomfort.

She waves her fork at him. 'Don't look like that! Your father did the right thing in the end, which is all that matters.'

I look at Robert, whose expression, I'm glad to see, has switched from frozen immobility to outright amusement.

For a moment, no one speaks, then Alex taps his knife again on his glass. 'It looks as though the Fielding family will have plenty to talk about over Christmas dinner this year. It should be more interesting than our usual discussion about Aunty Em's top secret method of making the turkey too tough to chew.'

There's a fresh gale of laughter. I join in without thinking until I remember I'm not listening to the speech. I look out of the window. It's almost dark now, and I see a few flakes of snow tumbling softly down through the light cast by the lamp posts. I'm glad I wore my warmest tights and boots, even though I drew the line at borrowing Mum's thermals. The village hall isn't exactly known for its amenities, and the temperature threatens to fall below freezing tonight.

I keep my eyes focused on the snow, which is now falling more thickly – huge flakes tumbling and scrambling over each other in an attempt to reach the pavement first.

The last time I was here was during that ill-fated painting party. I've often felt as though my life has been sliced into two parts – the part before I fell in love with Alex and indulged in so many ridiculous dreams about him, and the part after Suzy texted me the news that she and not I had been his choice.

Nothing has been the same since then. I've carried on with my plans for my life and succeeded with them. I've partied and had fun, exactly as students are supposed to. I've got the job of my dreams. Yet none of it has been even faintly like my imaginings.

Perhaps this is true for everyone. People spend their teenage years creating impossibly detailed rose-tinted dreams, only to be faced with inevitable disappointment when none of them turns out as they planned. It is, as adults repeatedly told us throughout our younger years, life.

But to me it feels different. My dreams, even before I met Alex, nevertheless contained him, or at least the promise of him. And when he disappeared from my life completely, he left an Alex shaped hole.

If he had simply left to take up the threads of his own life, it might have been different. After all, people come and go. They disappear and occasionally reappear, and that's the way things are.

Maybe it's only when they reject you first that the pain is so prolonged – when they go out of their way to let you know how little you mattered to them and that they preferred someone else. It's better to be a ghost, a shadow they barely even notice, than to be someone they've spent time with, have clearly seen standing in front of them, and have still rejected.

Another burst of laughter brings me out of my musings and back to reality. I have no idea what Alex has said. Judging by the looks on her fellow guests' faces, Elaine has interrupted his speech again.

He smiles at her and looks around at the assembled guests. 'I really shouldn't be the one giving this speech. My mother is far more entertaining. Dad, you should get Mum to propose the toast at your next wedding.'

Elaine gives him an owlish look. 'I don't know what you're talking about. Your father and I won't be doing this again. One vow renewal is quite enough for anyone. Let someone else have a turn next. And it will take us a very long time to pay for all this champagne.'

'Even longer if you keep drinking it at this speed,' Robert interposes drily.

Alex raises his glass. 'But, as I've undertaken the task, let me see it through. I always like to finish what I've started – even when it's Aunt Em's turkey!'

I clench my fingers until the nails bite into my palms. He likes to finish what he's started, does he? Obviously, that doesn't include relationships. He'd barely begun seeing me when he hit on Suzy. And from what Suzy told me, it didn't take him long to cheat on her with someone else. It's hardly the mark of someone to whom the word commitment actually means something.

Still, I can hardly bounce out of my seat and denounce him in front of all the guests. He's free to tell whatever story about himself he likes. It's absolutely nothing to me.

I reach over and refill my glass. If this wedding is bankrupting his parents, it will come out of Alex's inheritance – and serve him right.

I doubt it will set them back too much. The house is huge, and I remember Mum mentioning they went on a month-long cruise only last year. They won't miss a couple of glasses of champagne, and I can certainly do with it.

I take a deep gulp, catch Mum's eye, and give her a defiant smile. I remember to leave enough for the toast. I'm toasting Elaine and Robert, not acknowledging the quality of Alex's speech, most of which I haven't heard anyway.

People are raising their glasses expectantly. Alex nods to his parents.

'In conclusion, all I can say is that I hope one day to be as lucky as you two have been.'

Perhaps try being faithful to one woman at a time first, I think, wondering whether anyone would notice if I quickly refilled my glass. Perhaps not. I have an evening party ahead of me, and I want to keep a clear head so I can avoid Alex as far as humanly possible. Throwing up or bursting into tears in front of him may not make the best impression.

His eyes grow more serious. 'I've often thought that it's something of a miracle when someone finds the person who makes them smile, makes their heart dance, and makes them laugh. Someone with whom you want to grow old, dance your first and last dance with, and all the dances in between.'

He stares down at the table. 'It's even more of a miracle if that person feels the same way about you. Mostly, they don't. And that's something you have to come to terms with and learn to accept while you build a different life to the one you dreamed about and hoped for. Everyone has to find a way around the disappointments of life and build new dreams on the wreck of the old ones.'

He looks up again. 'But very occasionally, the stars align. And when they do, you get the sort of enduring marriage we see before us today. In fact, it was so good they wanted to do it twice. And why not? Love like that deserves to be celebrated. So, Mum and Dad, if you decide to do this again in twenty-five more years, please invite me to be a part of it for the third time. Ladies and gentlemen, please raise your glasses to my parents!'

There's a roar of voices making the toast. In spite of myself, I feel moved. Elaine and Robert are evidently popular, and the look of affection he gives her as he leans across to kiss her is unmistakable.

True love is out there – at least for some people. I hate to admit that Alex could be right about anything, but I have to agree with him that the odds are very long indeed.

Maybe it's easier if you're prepared to compromise. There's nothing wrong with looking for something less than perfection. Life isn't all made up of perfect solutions and Hollywood endings. For many people, a warm companionship is preferable to nothing. Someone with whom to share the details of the day and help carry the burdens of life, a way to prevent the echoing loneliness I know so well.

But loneliness is still infinitely preferable to that. Pleasant companionship isn't for me. I want the real thing. And if I can't have that, I'd prefer to march through life alone.

Chapter Twenty

Walking into the hall again feels like walking into a school reunion – something I've carefully avoided since leaving Honeywell. I received an invitation to my school reunion last year, accompanied by a form inviting me to list my many achievements and triumphs since leaving its hallowed portals for the final time. It seemed an imposition on so many levels. Who's to say I've achieved anything at all? And if I have, who knows whether I'm eager to share it?

I suppressed the urge to fill in the form saying I'd become either a brain surgeon or a rocket scientist and refrained from adding that disclosing personal information would be in direct violation of my parole conditions. Instead, I contented myself with saying that I'm currently working in graphic design and ticking the box marked *I am unfortunately unable to attend.* But people must enjoy them, or no one would go. Suzy, I know, went to it and thoroughly enjoyed herself.

I pause for a moment in the vestibule with its stacks of leaflets about village activities, local businesses and neighbourhood attractions. There's a mirror above the table, and I can't help noticing how well this red dress suits me. It isn't a colour I normally wear, but it brings out the colour in my cheeks and complements my dark hair.

I catch sight of Brandon at the far end of the hall, talking to a very good-looking dark-haired man. He waves to me to join them.

'This is Annie,' he says to the man. 'She and I are fellow survivors of St Michael's sixth-form college for local delinquents. Annie, this is Stephen. He's here to visit his family over Christmas. They're friends of Robert and Elaine. He's going back to Somerset on the twenty-eighth.'

Trust Brandon to have elicited all this information before he's been here for five minutes. He probably already knows the details of Stephen's childhood, whether he owns a pet, and how much he earns. But that's Brandon. He isn't unduly nosey. He just loves people. He doesn't care who they are or what they do. He always finds some way of connecting with them. It's one of the many reasons I love him.

'Can I get either of you a drink?' I say. 'Anything you like. It's an open bar.'

'Really?' says Stephen. 'That's very generous of Robert and Elaine.'

'They're too much in love to think of practicalities,' says Brandon soulfully.

'How do you know?' I say. 'You weren't even at the church. But they really do seem like a very happy couple. It was a lovely ceremony.'

'Do they have children?' asks Stephen.

I hope he doesn't notice the tell-tale flush stealing up my cheeks. 'A boy and a girl.'

'Perfect!' says Brandon. 'A ready-made page boy and flower girl.'

'They're a bit old for that,' I say. 'Alex is about twenty-five, and Caitlin's a couple of years younger.'

'That's a shame,' he says. 'Plenty of people seem to have their children at their weddings nowadays. I always assume they've put off getting married until the children were old enough to save them some money by doing those jobs for free.'

'Do you live locally too?' Stephen asks me.

'Annie shook the dust of this place off her feet long ago,' says Brandon. 'She traded us in for the delights of the big city. But I still live in the area,' he adds, and I almost laugh at the blatant look he directs towards Stephen.

'So, what brings you back here?' says Stephen. 'Have you come to visit Brandon?'

'I'm back to see my parents for Christmas,' I say. 'Not that it isn't nice to see Brandon too.'

'Naturally,' says Brandon.

'Don't let me interrupt you,' I say. 'I'll go and find myself a drink.'

I wander off towards the bar and ask for a Baileys. The afternoon's champagne has worn off, and I need something to get me through this evening. I won't stay for long. Mum said she'd pop in and collect me just before midnight and take me next door for the Midnight Mass, but I have no intention of staying at this party until midnight.

I'll show my face, chat to the few people I remember, and make good my escape, preferably without coming into contact with Alex more than is strictly necessary. I'll go back home and go to church with my parents from there. The red dress is beautiful, but not as warm as I expected, and I can make the excuse that I want to change into something warmer first.

I look into the small room off the main hall, where a few people are dancing. A couple I vaguely recognise from drinks parties at my parents are energetically if inexpertly doing the twist.

'Annie?'

The voice makes me jump, and I almost spill my drink. Where did he come from? He wasn't here when I arrived, and I felt a flicker of hope that he wasn't coming at all. Elaine was distinctly the worse for wear after the reception, and he might conceivably have decided to stay home and keep an eye on her.

The silence lengthens between us. He breaks it at last. 'How are you, Annie? I wanted to talk to you this afternoon, but you disappeared very quickly. I'm glad you came back tonight.'

I take a hasty swig of my drink before answering. 'Hello, Alex. I'm fine, thanks.'

He gives me a quizzical look, and I stare back, determined not to be tricked into further speech.

'How's life been treating you up in London?' he says at last. 'I hear great things of you from Mum and Dad.'

If he wants to prod me into asking what he's heard about me, he isn't going to succeed. I'm determined to give him only the barest minimum of information. My life is absolutely none of his business and never has been.

I force myself to speak lightly. 'Everything's fine, thank you. I enjoy my work very much. It's what I've always wanted to do.'

'I know it is, I remember how keen you were on design. I've followed your career with interest,' he adds teasingly.

I'm furious to feel myself blushing. 'I'm amazed you don't have anything better to do. Well, it's been nice to see you, but I'm sure you have plenty of other people you want to catch up with.'

I'm surprised to see what looks like a hurt expression on his face. I don't allow myself to think about it but wave to Brandon, who's still talking to Stephen.

'Coming!' I call and add to the bartender. 'Another one of these, please.'

I take the drinks and join Brandon and Stephen, feeling Alex's eyes boring into my back.

'What was that all about?' asks Brandon, taking the glass I hand him. 'Oh, sweetie, you know I don't drink these.'

'Take it!' I say. 'And stop staring over my shoulder like that.'

'Is someone bothering you?' asks Stephen, turning his head to look.

'Not really,' I say.

I don't want either of them going over and telling Alex to leave me alone. That would only make me look ridiculous.

I take a sip of my drink, keeping my back to Alex. 'It's just hard to shake off people from your past.'

Brandon takes a sip and pulls a face. 'Good grief! Don't tell me you seriously enjoy these. We need to educate your palate.'

'What do you usually drink?' Stephen asks him.

'Whisky, for choice. Single malt when I can get it.'

'I'll see what the bartender can do,' says Stephen.

Brandon waits until he's disappeared. 'Not the best time, darling.'

'It's like that, is it? Far be it from me to be the third wheel. I'll go and turn into a pumpkin all by myself.'

'I knew you'd understand,' he says. 'That man isn't really bothering you, is he?' He nods towards the bar, where Alex is still standing, looking around the room.

'No, but I'm not in the mood for one of those, "Do you remember?" conversations. That's the worst of coming to something like this. Everyone thinks you want to spend the entire evening reminiscing about all the stupid things you did when you were young.'

'I don't remember you doing too many stupid things,' he says.

'Just the one,' I say without thinking.

There's a pause, and I sense him looking at me.

'I see,' he says at last, a note of sympathy in his voice. 'Is that the reason you don't come home very often?'

'No! I mean, I don't know what you mean,' I say.

He puts an arm around my shoulders and gives me a squeeze. 'You don't need to talk about if you don't want to. Let me know if you need any help. I'll pretend to be your outraged boyfriend if need be.'

I laugh in spite of myself. 'What about Stephen?'

He shrugs. 'It might complicate things slightly. But I know the code – sisters before misters. The offer's there if you need it. Here he comes.'

Stephen re-joins us, holding two glasses of whisky. 'They've really pushed the boat out for this, haven't they?'

'They have indeed,' agrees Brandon. 'And it should take the taste away.' He looks disdainfully at the glass he's still holding. 'Do you want this, Annie? You look as though you need it.'

I shake my head, and he pours it into a pot plant. 'The poor thing looks as though it's on its last legs. This ought to revive it.'

'I'd better circulate,' I say. 'Nice to meet you, Stephen.'

I make my way around the edge of the room, carefully staying on the opposite side to Alex. I catch his glance once or twice, but I look away immediately.

I bump into a small group I know from primary school and chat to them for ten minutes. I'm surprised to find that two of them are now married to each other. It shouldn't be that surprising. It's what people do, I think, making admiring noises as they pull out their phones to show me pictures of their six-month-old baby.

It's probably something about coming back to the place where you grew up that makes it seem as though time has stood still. If I'd stayed here, it wouldn't feel so surreal. Looking around the hall, which, apart from the lavish party decorations, hasn't changed at all, I feel like my gauche eighteen-year-old self again. It's difficult to imagine that person doing anything as grown-up as getting married and having children.

Still, I have grown up. I've moved away, gone to university, graduated, and am now working at a job I love. It was only coming back here that made me feel so awkward and indecisive. Once I'm on the train and pulling away from Honeywell station, I'll be fine.

Whoever said you could never go home is wrong. You absolutely can. Whether you should is an entirely different matter. If you're expecting home to be waiting for you completely unchanged, you're setting yourself up for disappointment. Perhaps the best thing is to treat the place as somewhere familiar yet unreal, like Disneyland. A place you know from childhood even if you've never visited it. A place that's different enough to give you a delightful break from your everyday life, yet familiar enough for you to feel comfortable. You can't stay there forever, and neither would you want to.

Lost in these musings, I don't notice Alex making his way across to join us until I hear his voice. 'Nice to meet you all. Thanks for coming.'

I try to extricate myself from the group, but it's no good. I'm hemmed in on both sides by the married couple, who are now showing me pictures of their dog.

'Are you all catching up with Annie?' he asks. 'Hopefully, you've been able to get more out of her than I have.'

Everyone's eyes turn to me. 'There's no huge mystery about my life,' I say. 'But I don't care to share it with people I scarcely know.'

Alex looks at me, his expression unreadable.

'Annie's bought a flat,' says Lily. 'It all sounds terribly exciting. I didn't think anyone could afford a flat in London nowadays.'

'It's a studio,' I say. 'And it isn't in central London. You talk as though I've bought a mansion in Park Lane.'

'I hope it comes with free parking,' says Alex, and I'm annoyed to hear myself laugh.

'Don't all flats come with a parking space?' asks Lily, puzzled.

'If you park in the wrong place in London, you go directly to jail,' says Alex.

I ignore him. 'Your little boy is gorgeous, Lily. And your puppy,' I add, seeing Tom still scrolling through pictures of their cavoodle tearing up their flowerbeds. 'I'm so pleased that things are going well for you both.'

I look over at Brandon, wondering whether to signal to him. But I can't think of a subtle way of indicating that I need rescuing, and I've agreed to leave him alone with Stephen.

'What about the rest of your life?' says Alex. 'You've told us that you're enjoying your job, and we've heard about your flat. How about your personal life? Are you seeing anyone special?'

I consider telling him to mind his own business. But this is his party, in a manner of speaking, and I have no desire to create an atmosphere or make anyone else feel uncomfortable.

I'm about to brush off the question when Brandon looks over and catches my eye. I have no idea what possesses me. Before I have time to think, I've waved to him and blown him a kiss.

'Is that your boyfriend?' asks Lily staring over at him. 'He's very good looking, isn't he? Did you meet in London?'

'No, he lives locally,' I say. Why didn't I just say I'm single?

Brandon says something to Stephen and walks over to the group. 'Hello, darling,' he says in a faintly mocking tone. 'Aren't you going to introduce me?'

I try not to glare at him. 'This is Lily and Tom, and Maggie and Josh,' I say curtly. 'Oh, and Alex,' I say as an afterthought.

Alex holds out his hand to Brandon. 'Nice to meet you.'

Brandon put his arm around my shoulders. 'Lovely to meet you all.'

Lily is eyeing him with frank curiosity. 'How long have you two known each other?'

All eyes turn towards us. I open my mouth to answer, but Brandon is quicker. 'Not very long,' he says easily. 'But when you know, you know. Am I right?'

He runs his fingers through my hair, brushing a stray wisp off my face. I itch to slap his hand, but there's nothing I can do right now. I'll have plenty to say to him later.

Alex is watching us both. 'Congratulations. If you'll excuse me, there are some people over there I really must talk to.'

He walks away, and I feel a mixture of relief and disappointment. I ought to feel pleased that Brandon reacted so quickly. Now that he's staked his claim, so to speak, I'll be free from any further questions from Alex.

I leave the group and walk to the far side of the hall. The mural is still there, partially hidden by loudspeakers. I peer around a speaker and see Mole's nose twitching as he inhales the spring air.

A flood of emotion washes over me. I remember that day so vividly. It was the day I first met Alex and tumbled head over heels into love with him. It turned out to be a stupid crush on someone who wasn't the person I thought he was. But it was still the most painful thing I've ever experienced.

I study the scene, completely forgetting my surroundings. If I turned my head towards the window, I'd be surprised to see the snow falling outside.

All I remember is that warm September afternoon and the first scent of autumn in the air. I remember falling into the can of paint and collapsing at Alex's feet. I spent one of the happiest afternoons of my life painting these murals. They're slightly faded but otherwise exactly the same.

I'd give anything to be able to go back to that afternoon and do things differently. I'd never have agreed to go out with Alex and would have avoided all the pain that followed.

I wonder whether this is strictly true. Would I really have missed out on that Christmas week? Maybe you can't entirely protect yourself from being hurt. Without the lows, there would be no highs. I've spent the past two years insulating myself from everything that might hurt me – avoiding coming home and only dating people with whom I have no real expectation of becoming serious. And what good has it done me? Am I any happier as a result? Would I have been better taking risks and having fun and letting the future take care of itself?

It's a lot to think about. And now definitely isn't the time. But I'm determined to make some changes in the new year.

I take one last look at Mr. Toad's beautiful motorcar, remembering how Alex insisted on mixing up the exact shade of red for it. I remember too how impatient Suzy was. She said that no one would notice.

Alex disagreed. 'Annie would know. She obviously loves The Wind in the Willows. Every time she looked at it, she'd regret not taking the time to get it right.'

Suzy rolled her eyes. 'It's a stupid children's story. It isn't real life.'

'What's the difference?' I said, then blushed as Suzy laughed. 'I mean, books are real life too. A real person makes them up and creates new worlds for us to enjoy.'

'Talking rats and toads!' scoffed Suzy. 'I think I'll stick to the real world if you don't mind.'

I was too annoyed to speak, but Alex answered for me. 'There's no harm in making sure you get something just right. Especially if it's really important to you. And this is important to Annie.'

Suzy tossed back her hair and gave him a dazzling smile. 'Perfectionism is boring. I prefer to take a few risks and see what happens.'

A touch on my shoulder makes me jump. I turn to see Alex standing there, smiling at me. I shake my head to clear away the mists of two years ago.

'I thought I might find you here,' he says. 'I came to see these yesterday. I was worried someone might have painted over them, but I'm glad they haven't.'

'Me too,' I say without thinking.

'It's a shame to paint over memories,' he says. His tone is light, but his eyes are serious.

'It's certainly a waste of paint,' I say.

'From a practical point of view, yes. But I've never thought of you as practical.'

'What's that supposed to mean?'

'I don't mean that you're disorganised,' he says. 'Quite the opposite, in fact. But I always had you down as a bit of a dreamer. It's one of the things I most liked about you.'

I meet his eyes squarely. 'People change. I'm not the same person I was back then.'

He gives me a half smile. 'You seem pretty much the same to me.'

'Well, I'm not. Don't pretend to know anything about me, Alex, because you don't. You probably never did.'

His eyes are hurt. 'I think I did. And people don't change, not really.'

'Perhaps not,' I say more calmly. 'But our perceptions of people change. We think we know them, and we imbue them with all sorts of characteristics and virtues. But that's not necessarily who they are. And we blame them for that when actually we should be blaming ourselves for wanting them to be someone they aren't.'

'Is that for me?' he asks. 'Are you saying that I disappointed you?'

I'm caught off guard. How can he even ask that when he must know full well that he disappointed me? If not, he really isn't the person I imagined.

I shrug. 'I'm talking about people in general. Anyway, now isn't the time. It's all in the past, and that's where it should stay. We should –'

'What's in the past?' he says. 'You and me? Are you talking about what happened between us?'

'Alex, there is no you and me,' I say calmly. 'There barely ever was. We had a couple of dates, and it didn't work out. That's perfectly normal. Why bring it up now?'

'But it was more than that,' he says. 'We only went out a couple of times, but we were really good together. You know we were. And then you threw it all away.'

A surge of welcome anger floods over me. For a moment, I was in danger of succumbing to the seductive influence of our shared memories. Thankfully, he's reminded me of who he is and what he did.

I turn away from the pictures. They're firmly in the past. There's no sense in continuing to look back at them.

'This is pointless, Alex. You and I had a week together years ago, and it didn't work out. It happens all the time, especially at that age. No bones were broken. Let's leave it at that, ok?'

He nods. 'If that's how you see it, there's nothing else to say. But for the record, it wasn't as easy for me as it seemed to be for you.'

I gasp. How dare he? I've given him a polite and civilised way out, an adult perspective on the situation. Why did he have to ruin it?

He sees my expression, and his own face snaps in shock. 'I'm sorry. What did I say?'

'Nothing,' I say. 'I'm a bit tired. I think I'll find Brandon and see if he wants to leave.'

'This Brandon guy,' he says. 'Have you known him for long?'

'Since I was fifteen,' I say coolly. 'He and I hit it off right from the start, and we've been friends ever since. You know how it is when you meet someone who just gets you?'

'I thought I did,' he says quietly. He holds out his hand. 'Friends?'

'Of course.' I feel the tears sting the back of my eyes.

He stares at me, and I stare back, not knowing what to say. I want to stand here with him forever. I want to turn on my heel and walk away. More than anything, I want to turn the clock back to that week when I was sure he loved me.

'Annie?' he says, taking a step towards me. I don't move away. 'Couldn't we …?'

He doesn't finish his sentence. The hall door bangs open with a crash, making the people standing nearby jump. I turn to look, with a feeling of inevitability. There, standing in the doorway, wearing a microscopic red mini dress, is Suzy.

Chapter Twenty-One

Brandon is the first to break the stunned silence.

'Nice entrance!' he says with enthusiasm. 'Hello, Suzy. Long time, no see.'

She gives him an indifferent look, then her eyes flicker with recognition. 'Oh. Hi, Brandon. How are you?'

Her eyes fall on me, and her face lights up. 'Annie – you're here! I hoped you would be. That's why I came. How are you, Angel?' She launches herself at me enthusiastically, kissing my cheek.

'I'm great, thanks,' I say, hugging her back. 'It's so good to see you. Sorry I haven't been in touch for a while. Life's been …'

'Oh, I know! Same here!' She gives a trill of laughter. 'I mean, obviously not as busy as yours, what with your glamorous, fast-paced life in London and everything.'

I'm taken aback by the tone in her voice. Is it bitterness or amusement? I can't quite tell. It's gone in an instant, and I realise I must have imagined it.

'Hello, Suzy.' Alex has walked up behind us, and I feel the same stab of pain as when I first heard that he'd picked her over me.

'I'm leaving,' I tell Suzy. 'But I'm home for a few more days. I'd have called you if I'd known you were in the area. You have my number, don't you? Let's catch up before I go back to London.'

'That would be heaven!' she exclaims, although with less enthusiasm in her tone than I would have expected.

'You're leaving, Annie?' says Alex, his eyes flicking from me to Brandon.

'Yes,' I say curtly.

If anything could have strengthened my resolve not to stay, it's Suzy's arrival. I have no intention of watching Alex make another play for her right under my nose. I don't think Suzy is stupid enough to fall for his particular line again, but who knows? They're both adults, and it's none of my business what other people do or don't choose to do. I'm also an adult, and it's my prerogative not to hang around and watch for a second and, if anything, more humiliating time.

'Can I speak to you before you go?' Alex says quietly to me.

'You are speaking to me!' I say in what I hope is a jocular tone.

'I mean alone,' he persists, and I see a few curious eyes turn towards us.

'Can you make it quick?' I say. 'I'm really tired, and I'd like to get home before it starts snowing in earnest.'

'It will only take a moment,' he says.

Brandon, whom I thought I could count on to protect me, doesn't move. Alex opens the door to let me pass through into the little vestibule beyond. I turn to face him, shivering a little. After the warmth of the hall, it's chilly out here. Not as cold as it will be outside. It's a sort of no man's land between the warmth of the inside and the cold of the outside. It feels curiously familiar. It's the same space I've occupied in regards to Alex for years.

I turn to face him. 'What do you want to say?'

He looks taken aback. 'Nothing in particular. I mean, quite a lot of things. I've been wanting to talk to you for a long time,' he adds with a smile.

I don't trust my voice to speak. For some bizarre reason, I feel perilously close to tears, which is ridiculous. I find him annoying and persistent, and I have absolutely no interest in him or his stupid life. Which is hardly a reason to suddenly feel I want to burst into tears and howl on his shoulder.

'If you've wanted to talk for me for so long,' I say, swallowing hard, 'you must surely know what you want to say. Can you move it along a bit, please? I'm getting cold.'

'Are you sure about going home with this guy?' he says abruptly.

'If it were any of your business –' I say curtly.

'I'm perfectly aware that your life has nothing to do with me,' he says. 'If I didn't know it before, you've made it very clear again today.'

He looks down at me, and his voice softens. 'I'm trying to look out for you, Annie. You've had quite a bit to drink, and so has he. He isn't driving, is he?'

I feel a wave of cold anger, which helps me to keep my voice steady. 'How much I have to drink is absolutely none of your business, Alex Fielding. What are you planning to do – call my parents and tell on me? In case you haven't noticed, I'm over eighteen and perfectly able to make my own choices.'

He looks as though I've hit him. 'I'm not saying you aren't.'

I carry on, using my anger as fuel. 'Let's get this straight, shall we? I'll drink as much as I choose, and I'll go home with anyone I want to. Are we clear on that?'

'Crystal clear,' he says, his face closing.

I feel a wave of compunction. 'I don't mean –'

Before I can finish this sentence, the door bangs open, catching me on the elbow. I turn to see Suzy standing there.

'I'm not interrupting anything, am I?' she says, giving us both a keen look.

Alex doesn't speak. I rub my elbow. 'Nothing in the world. Is Brandon ready? He and I were about to leave.'

'I think I saw him getting his coat,' says Suzy. She holds out a hand to Alex. 'What I really came out for was to fetch this man. I want to dance with him. As soon as I heard what they were playing, I couldn't resist. Do you remember this one, Alex?'

Alex doesn't seem to have heard her. He's still staring at me as though he wants to say something but can't quite find the words.

The door opens again, and Brandon appears, pulling on his coat. Above the noise and chatter of the crowd inside the hall, I hear the faint strains of *Last Christmas*. So what? It's just a stupid song.

Suzy grabs Alex's hand. 'Come on, you, for old times' sake!'

'Do you fancy a dance before we go?' Brandon asks me.

'No, let's get going. Lovely to see you again, Suzy. Give me a call. Have fun!'

I turn abruptly, feeling Brandon's arm slide protectively around my shoulders, and we're out into the cold night air.

Chapter Twenty-Two

We arrive home just as my parents are setting out for midnight mass. I say goodnight to Brandon and walk up the path in the dark, wondering why it isn't snowing properly. It's certainly cold enough.

Mum gives me a sharp look. 'Why have you left the party so early? Are you on your own?'

'Brandon walked me home. He's leaving his car here tonight and taking a taxi home.'

She looks annoyed. 'There was no reason for you to leave just because he did. You should have stayed and talked to … everyone.'

'I have a headache,' I say shortly. 'I'm going to bed.'

Mum looks unconvinced, but Dad takes her arm. 'We'll be late if you don't stop talking. Will you be alright, Annie?'

'I'll be fine,' I say wearily. 'I just need some sleep.'

'Don't forget to hang up your stocking before you go,' says Mum. 'Dad and I have already hung ours up, but there's plenty of room. They're in the Christmas box under the stairs. Santa won't know you're home if he doesn't see it. Goodness knows, he's probably forgotten you ever used to live here!'

Dad drags her off still talking loudly about the scarcity of my visits home and the turkey and the oven timer. I pull myself wearily up the stairs, only just finding the energy to carefully hang up my red dress. Mum will be terribly upset if she comes in tomorrow morning to find it in what she likes to refer to as my 'floordrobe'.

I fall into bed, utterly exhausted and longing for the entire Christmas charade to be over so I can go back to London and resume the life I have so carefully constructed for myself – the life that makes me happy.

Despite my exhaustion, I don't sleep until the early hours. I stare at the ceiling, wondering what happened to my life. How often have I lain in this very room on Christmas Eve, desperately trying to sleep on the one night of the year when sleep eludes all but the very young and the very old?

I try to count the stars on the ceiling. As a testament to his careful and methodical nature, Dad arranged them into accurate constellations for me. As a child, I fell asleep each night staring at Ursa Major or Orion's belt. It was nice to have the actual night sky inside my house. It made me feel connected with the great world outside while still feeling safe and protected.

By the time I left for university, Ursa Major had lost several stars, and Orion no longer had a belt, but it still comforted me to look at them.

I hear Mum and Dad return in the early hours. Even if I'd been asleep, I would have been woken by Mum's exaggerated shushing and heavy tiptoeing up the stairs. Either she's still running on fumes from the wedding reception or she's taken an extra generous gulp of the communion wine. Maybe she and Dad stopped in at someone's house for a nightcap on the way home.

She finally goes to bed, after innumerable trips up and down the stairs for unspecified reasons. But I'm still unable to sleep. I'm more than ever convinced it's a mistake to go home. What is there waiting for everyone but some form of disappointment? Places change, people change, making it more difficult to hold onto treasured childhood memories. If you can't come back permanently and build a proper life, it's better to avoid the past as far as possible.

Lost in these dreary thoughts, I drift into an uneasy doze, waking in the chill, grey dawn for absolutely no reason at all. I'd have preferred to sleep for as many hours as possible and avoid most of Christmas Day and all its festivities.

But it's no good. I'm too wide awake to sleep again. My head throbs painfully as I slide out of bed, feeling a momentary dizziness as my feet hit the floor. I pad silently along the landing to see whether Mum still keeps the aspirin in the same cupboard. She'll probably need some herself. She doesn't usually drink this much, even at weddings. At least, she never used to. But what do I really know about my parents' lives nowadays, or they about mine? It's a depressing thought.

I find the aspirin and gulp down a couple with a glass of water. I feel a little better. It will be hours before Mum and Dad wake up, so I decide to go for a walk. Hopefully, it's raining. It will match my mood and reinforce my sense of dramatic despair.

I ease open the front door, careful not to let it click and risk waking Mum and Dad. I catch my breath in delight. Rain might be more poetic and match my mood, but I love white Christmases.

When I was about ten, Dad woke me and Jamie very early one Christmas morning and took us outside to throw snowballs before breakfast to give Mum a chance to wake up slowly. Maybe that was after another Christmas party.

Well, good for her. Parents should be allowed a life of their own, despite having children. Everyone thinks it's natural for children to reach for independence, so why not their parents?

It's right that Mum and Dad should have their own life and plenty of friends. It would be selfish to expect them to exist in some sort of limbo between their offspring's visits. And it would be a dull enough life for Mum and Dad if all they lived for was my infrequent visits. I resolve to come home more often from now on. I've faced my worst fear and found it to be, if not nothing, then at least entirely manageable.

It might even be helpful if Alex starts going out with Suzy again. I could think less of them both and cease to regret what I've lost – which is absolutely nothing. I can see that now. It's time to stop running away from something that doesn't exist and start walking towards what I want – my life in London, my career, my friends and colleagues.

Resisting an urge to pick up a stick and scrawl *Girl Power* in the snow as Suzy used to when we were young, I scrunch down the snowy path and set off towards the old mill. It becomes increasingly difficult to sustain my mood of exaltation. Its Christmas Day and there's plenty of snow. But that will soon melt, and I'll be left with the grey emptiness of winter stretching ahead of me.

I pick up my pace. It's bitterly cold, and a few more flakes are starting to fall. I push my hands deeper into my pockets, trying to enjoy the morning. If I was ten years younger, I could make a snowman.

But I don't want to stop for too long and risk hypothermia. I press on, looping around the mill and back across the field as quickly as my chilled limbs allow. There's no one out except for a few dog walkers in the distance. They all look as hunched and miserable as I feel. I hope they have warm firesides and good Christmas dinners to return to.

At least, my appetite won't be a problem after this walk. I feel ready to face Mum's turkey with Dad's special cranberry stuffing. I can probably even manage a portion of Christmas pudding. The last thing I want is to make my parents anxious about me. Why should I spoil their day when they worked so hard to make all my childhood Christmases so special?

Filled with the glow of good intentions, I swing into the lane that leads to our house and stop abruptly. Standing at the end of our driveway, huddled in a thick, winter coat and holding an envelope in his hand, is Alex.

Chapter Twenty-Three

For a moment, we just stare at each other. He's clearly as shocked to see me as I am to see him. Recovering himself, he holds out the envelope.

'What's this?' I ask, pleased to hear how steady my voice is.

He hesitates. 'I was … delivering this card.'

My momentary flicker of elation dies. It's a card from his parents. What else would it be? I wish I'd stayed in bed this morning. He would have put the card through our door, and I would never have seen him.

I take the envelope. 'I'll see that my parents get this, thanks. Happy Christmas,' I add lightly, determined not to show that I see him as anything more than a casual acquaintance.

His hazel eyes flicker with what looks like amusement, which annoys me. What does he have to be so pleased about? With a sickening thud of my heart, I remember Suzy. Of course! The best man is supposed to get together with the bridesmaid, so he's only following tradition. Not that Suzy was a bridesmaid exactly, or even present at the vow renewal. But someone like Alex would never allow a minor detail like that to get in his way.

'I have to go,' I say. 'My parents are waiting for me, and I've been much longer than I expected.'

'You weren't here last night?' he asks, his expression unreadable.

'Yes, I was. That's Brandon's car.'

'I see,' he says quietly. 'Well, say hello to Brandon for me, and I hope you have a lovely day.'

He turns and starts to walk away. I watch him go, my thoughts in a whirl. 'Alex!' I hear my voice say.

He turns to face me, his hands still stuffed into his pockets, his face asking a question.

'This has my name on it,' I say.

He smiles slightly. 'Yes.'

'Then why did you tell me to give it to my parents?'

'You said that, not me.'

'So, this is for me?' I feel immediately embarrassed at the question. I can read, can't I?

'For you,' he confirms at last.

I tear open the envelope and pull out a card. My eyes fill with tears when I see the picture. 'How did you …?'

'You gave it to me the first day we met.'

I look at the motor car and the riverbank. 'It was only a sketch. I didn't expect you to keep it, much less have it made into a card.'

'It was the only thing of you I had left,' he says quietly. 'Of course, I kept it. When I heard you were coming home this year, I decided it was time I found the courage to talk to you. I know it's too late for us now, but I still wanted you to have it.'

He gestures towards Brandon's car. 'I wasn't sure last night. He said you'd only just met, then you said you'd known him for years. I thought you might be pretending he was your boyfriend to get rid of me, despite what Suzy said last night about you two being on the verge of getting engaged. So, I decided to take a chance today. But he brought you home, and I see he's still here.'

I ought to feel angry. If I was the heroine of an old melodrama, I'd have slapped his face for making such crass assumptions, then stormed off. Instead, I'm surprised to feel a bubble of laughter rising inside me.

'It isn't a secret, is it?' he says. 'If so, I'm sorry I said anything.'

'Actually, it is,' I tell him. 'It's such a huge secret that Brandon will be extremely surprised to hear the news when he comes back later today to collect his car.'

He looks so astonished that I start to laugh again. I stop abruptly when I remember Suzy. No doubt they're back together again, and he's rushing off to spend Christmas Day with her.

'You and he aren't together?' he says slowly

I shake my head, biting my lip. 'But it looks as though you and Suzy are.'

I don't meet his eyes but stare at my footprints in the snow. I stamp my feet, suddenly aware of how cold they are.

When I raise my eyes again, I see him looking at me with an expression that makes my heart thud. I look away. This isn't a road I'm ever going down again.

When he speaks, his voice sounds far away. I'm not sure whether it's because he's speaking quietly or because the blood is rushing through my ears at what seems like a hundred miles per hour.

'Suzy?' he says. 'What do you mean?'

I scuff my toe in the snow, trying to make a mini snow angel but only succeeding at making something that looks like a buffalo.

'When you and she went off to dance together last night, I assumed you might get back together.'

I force myself to look at him directly, a bright smile on my face. I might feel as though my heart is breaking all over again, but there's no reason why he should guess that. Pity is the last thing I need from Alex Fielding.

He frowns. 'You've lost me. I understand what you mean by together, but "back together" seems to indicate that she and I were once together. And nothing could be further from the truth.'

I feel a flash of anger at his duplicity, quickly followed by an emotion I can't quite define.

'Your memory can't be that bad,' I say. 'Or have there been so many other girls that you've lost track? I'm talking about that New Year's Eve party. You and Suzy were certainly together back then. I remember it clearly because I was stuck at the hospital watching it all on Facebook.'

He looks thunderstruck. 'So, that was why –'

He stops. 'I mean, there was absolutely no reason why you should have wanted to continue dating me. But me and Suzy? How could you have got that idea?'

'Are you seriously denying that you and she got together that night, and that it only ended when you cheated on her with someone else?' I say hotly. 'Maybe you thought she'd be too embarrassed to tell me about that, but she wasn't. Why should she be? She hadn't done anything wrong.'

He takes a step towards me then stops. 'That's exactly what I'm saying! I don't how you got your wires crossed, but crossed they most certainly were. It would never have entered my mind to ask Suzy out. In fact, the boot was entirely on the other foot –'

He stops abruptly. 'But that's neither here nor there. As for us dancing last night, I can assure you that she and I were never an item and never could be. As soon as I heard what was playing, I made an excuse and left. You probably don't remember, but –'

'But you did!' I insist. 'You started seeing Suzy that night. You were all over her on Facebook.'

'She was all over me,' he says. 'But you didn't see me reciprocating.'

I try to remember. 'Maybe not, but she texted me to say you'd been making out, and she told me she'd seen your tattoo.'

'My tattoo?' he says, thunderstruck. 'Do you mean that stupid dolphin sticker Caitlin gave me for Christmas? I only stuck it on to horrify Mum.'

'So, how did Suzy see it?' I say.

'She didn't! It isn't anywhere I'd have shown anyone –'

He stops abruptly and rolls his eyes. 'Caitlin! It must have been. She and Suzy were talking together at the party and giggling about something. But I had no idea what they were saying.'

I stare at my feet. 'So, you and she weren't together until the Easter holidays when you told her you were seeing someone else and dumped her?'

'I think I'd remember something like that,' he says.

'It was a long time ago,' I mumble.

'Not that long! But even if it were twice as long, I would still remember.'

He turns to face me, and the look in his eyes makes my heart thump even harder. 'Not only was I not dating Suzy, but I was also head over heels in love with someone else.'

The silence stretches between us, no longer separating but connecting us. I become aware that the street is absolutely silent, all sounds muffled by the thick covering of snow. It's so silent that I'm sure he must be able to hear the beating of my heart.

I raise my eyes to meet his. 'I didn't know that.'

'Don't you want to know who it was?' he says, a sudden glint of his old, teasing smile in his eyes.

I nod, unable to tear my gaze from his.

He takes another step towards me and stops, as though unsure whether I'm going to turn and run. When I don't move, he puts his hands on my shoulders.

'Annie, there was no one for me but you back then, and there's no one else for me now. Whatever happens, that isn't going to change. So, what I need to know is whether there's any chance you could ever feel the same way about me?'

Without stopping to think, I fling my arms around his neck and kiss him. For one stunned second, he seems to freeze, then his arms go around me too. We stand locked together for what seems like hours.

When at last I pull away to breathe, he still doesn't release me. He looks down at me with a smile in his eyes. 'So, is that a yes?'

'I think it must be,' I say breathlessly.

He looks over my shoulder and laughs. 'Which is lucky because your mother is watching us out of your living room window.'

Chapter Twenty-Four

I turn to see the living room curtains flicker then quickly close again. I don't move. The feel of Alex's arms around me is too precious to lose. I've waited so long for this, even when I've told myself there was nothing to wait for. I feel as though I could stand in the snow for hours and never feel the cold as long as Alex is with me.

'We should go inside,' he says. 'I didn't mean to stand out here for so long. I don't want you to freeze to death now that I've finally found you.'

I smile up at him, remembering him saying this once before. 'I'm not sure what my mother will have to say about this. But I can promise she'll have something to say. And it won't be brief.'

'She'll be delighted,' he says, tucking my hand into his pocket and holding it in a firm, warm clasp.

'Don't be so arrogant! You have no idea what my mother has planned for my future. It may not include you at all.'

'I'm not being arrogant,' he says. 'Haven't you realised yet that none of this is our doing?'

'What do you mean?'

He gestures towards the house. 'All of this. I mean, none of this. We can't take any credit for it. The whole thing has been a put-up job between our parents.'

'I expect you'll get to the point in your own time,' I say resignedly. 'And preferably before I freeze into a solid lump of ice.'

'I didn't get it at first,' he says, 'but Mum let the cat out of the bag last night. She had rather a lot to drink at the wedding reception, and apparently your parents dropped in on their way home from church and the four of them drank quite a bit more.'

'What did she say?' I ask, now totally bewildered.

He tucks a strand of hair behind my ear. 'To cut a long story short, apparently she and Dad were in despair about you and me. I have no idea how they figured out how I felt about you. Possibly they saw Cuthbert sitting sadly on my chest of drawers. Or maybe it was the fact that I carefully engineered all my visits home around the times I thought you'd be here.'

'But that's exactly what I did!' I say. 'At least, the other way around. There were so many times when I planned to come home. Then I saw a Facebook post saying you were coming, and I changed my plans.'

'So, there we were,' he says, 'both of us watching the other on social media. Me trying to meet you, and you –'

'Trying to avoid you,' I say, feeling my cheeks turn pink.

'What a lot of time we've wasted,' he says gently, pulling me into his arms again and looking down into my eyes. My arms go around his neck, and he bends to kiss me again. We're interrupted by a snort of laughter behind us.

I whirl around to see Brandon standing there, a huge grin spreading across his face. 'Well, this is a surprise!'

'It isn't what it –' I begin, hardly aware what I'm saying.

'It's exactly what it looks like!' says Alex.

'And to what do we owe this turnaround?' asks Brandon. 'If I'm allowed to ask, that is.'

He smiles more gently at my flushed face. 'I'm kidding. You know that. I'm very pleased for you. It's a Christmas miracle!'

He looks at his windscreen. 'What's all this? It can hardly be a parking ticket on Christmas Day. His Majesty's traffic wardens can't be that dedicated to their endless pursuit of justice. Besides, I'm allowed to park outside your house. I've been doing it for years.'

He reaches for the paper and unfolds it. 'Another Christmas miracle! This is from Stephen. It's his phone number and the address of the place where he's staying. So, as much as I'd love to stay and hear all about it, I must be off. But I want all the details later. Happy Christmas, Annie.'

He kisses my cheek before raising an ironic eyebrow at Alex. 'Happy Christmas to you too. I have the strangest feeling we'll be meeting again quite soon.'

Alex grins. 'You can count on that.'

'You aren't planning to gate-crash a complete stranger's Christmas Day?' I say.

'That's entirely up to him,' says Brandon. 'But it would be only polite to return his message in person, seeing as he's gone to all this trouble to track me down.'

He unlocks his car and waves to us as he drives off.

I reach up to put my arms around Alex's neck. 'Now, where were we when Brandon so inconsiderately interrupted us?'

'Hard to remember,' he says. 'Talking about the weather, perhaps? Or your mother.'

I jump. 'I knew there was something I wanted to ask you!'

'Annie, I was joking,' he says, reaching for me again.

I hold him away from me. 'What were you saying about our parents?'

'Haven't you figured that out yet?' he says. 'It appears that both sets of parents had far more idea about our feelings for each other than we did. My mother was a bit standoffish with yours for a while after they first moved here because she had the impression that Liz's horrid daughter had hurt her baby boy. And your mother was convinced that Elaine's awful son had played fast and loose with her daughter's affections.

But they got together last year over some cake stall or other, and they got along much better than they expected. That turned into lunches and days out. Before you know it, the pair of them were comparing notes and figuring out the real situation.

They put two and two together and came up with, if not exactly four, then at least some approximation of it. After that, it was child's play to a pair of schemers like them. But first, our fathers had to be dragged away from the golf course and drafted in as co-conspirators. Mum was the first to come up with the idea of this vow renewal. Dad wasn't too keen on the idea, but then your mother got involved. In the end, he decided it was easier to give in.'

'What about my dad?' I say.

'He was just relieved not to be the one standing up there in front of everyone. Mind you, from what my mother says, he may not be off the hook yet. According to her, Liz is very keen on this whole vow renewal idea. Your dad may find himself marching up the aisle much sooner than he imagines.'

'As long as she doesn't get any ideas about needing a bridesmaid,' I say.

His lips twitch. 'Apparently, that was Plan B. If you weren't completely blown away by my James Bond-like appearance in a tux, and my stellar performance during my wedding speech, they were going to try again. This time with you in a low-cut bridesmaid's dress designed to catch my attention and finally galvanise me into action.'

'If they pick a day like today,' I say, 'I'll be wearing jeans and three sweaters and a woolly hat and gloves.'

'And Cuthbert and I will be watching you, thinking you're the most beautiful woman we've ever laid eyes on,' he says gently.

I feel the tears sting my eyes. 'And to think this wonderful plan might all have gone wrong. I almost didn't come home this year. In fact, I only agreed because Mum is so upset about Jamie emigrating –' I break off.

'– to America?' he says.

I sigh. 'Don't tell me that was all made up too?'

'Don't be so suspicious!' he says. 'It doesn't become you. Your mother got it almost right. Jamie and his girlfriend are going to Florida for a fortnight next month. Apparently, she wants to visit Disney World.'

'My mother really is a piece of work,' I say.

'Very true,' he agrees. 'But mine gives her a run for her money. So, the only thing left to decide is in which house we'll be eating our Christmas dinner.'

'What time do your parents eat?' I ask.

'We always have our Christmas dinner in the evening.'

'And we always have ours at lunchtime,' I say. 'You know what that means?'

'I hope you have a good appetite,' he says. 'We could try and book somewhere else today if you'd prefer to be alone. I could call The Red Lion and see whether they have any vacancies.'

'We'd probably end up sharing a table with Brandon and Stephen. Anyway, our parents seem to have gone to rather a lot of trouble for us. The least we can do to thank them is eat two Christmas dinners.'

'You won't say that after you've tasted Aunt Em's turkey,' he warns me. 'But I agree. They had no business meddling like this, but I'm very glad they did. And we may not have to eat two dinners every year. We may be able to invite them all to ours one day.'

'Don't get ahead of yourself,' I warn him. 'If you start talking like that, Mum will be decorating nurseries and registering for preschools before the Christmas pudding has been eaten.'

'I won't,' he promises. 'Anyway, she'll be quite busy for a while. She has a wedding of her own to plan. Now that our mothers have the bit between their teeth, I don't think your father will get away with just the one case of Cristal. None of them will have time to notice what you and I are up to.'

'Don't you believe it,' I say, glancing back at the house where the corner of the curtain has been stealthily pulled back again.

I look up at Alex, a wave of happiness washing over me once more. 'But I don't care! She's worked hard enough for her Christmas miracle. We should let her enjoy it.'

'I agree,' he says. 'By the way, if I know anything about your mother, the moment Christmas is over, this will be all around the village.'

He pulls me even closer and smiles down at me. 'So, why don't you and I really give her something to gossip about?'

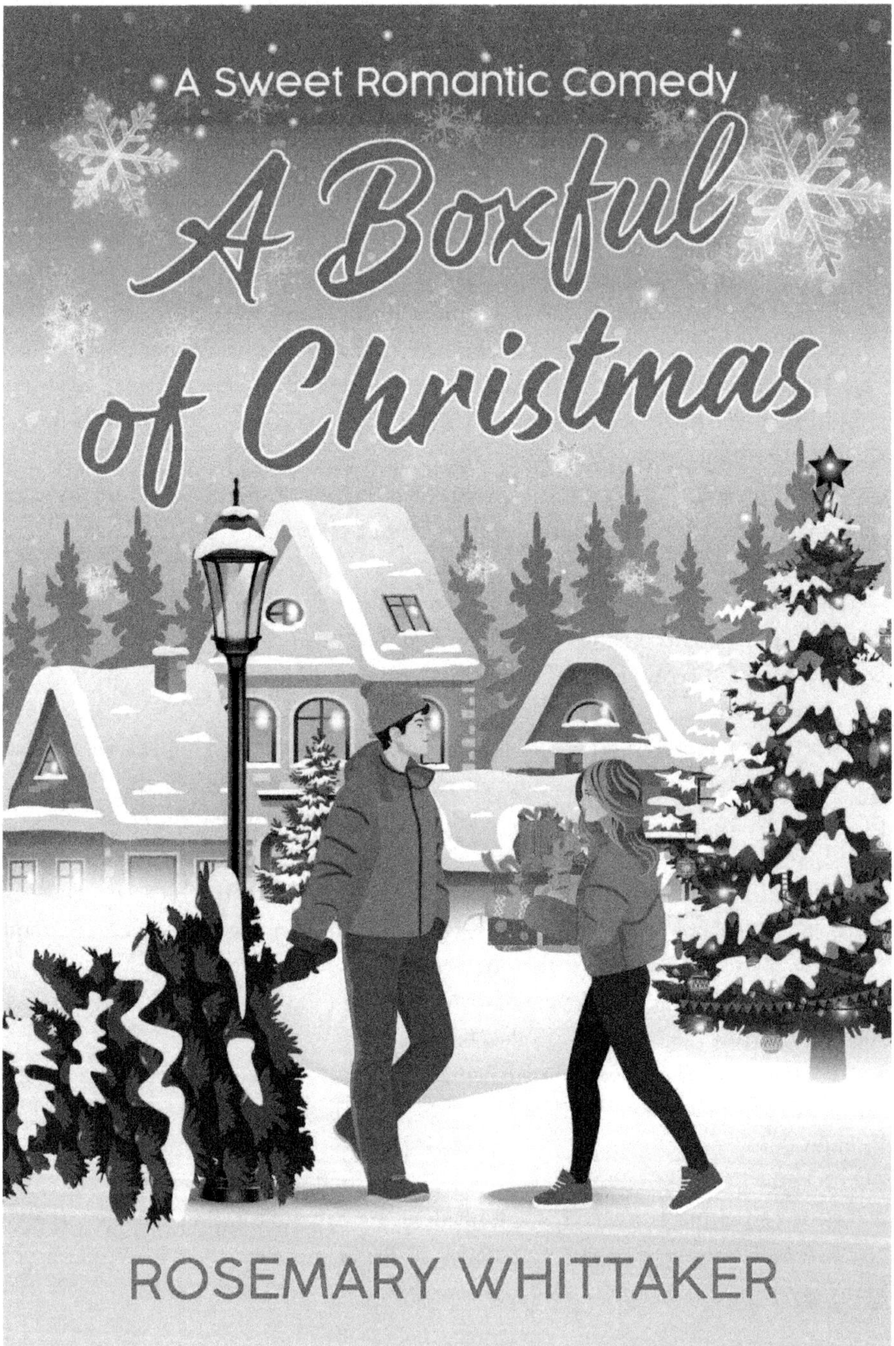
A Sweet Romantic Comedy
A Boxful of Christmas
ROSEMARY WHITTAKER

Chapter One

The scent of roasted chestnuts mingles with cinnamon and fresh pine as I follow the market director across the village green.

'That's your stall over there,' she says. 'The one between the Snowball Saloon and Kingsley's Christmas Trees.'

She waves towards an empty wooden hut before rushing away to talk to a group of men struggling to assemble a reindeer carousel.

I drop the boxes I'm holding onto the grass. Neither of my neighbours has arrived yet. I'm not sure why I arrived so early. But I've been dreaming of this day for almost a year now, and I can't wait to make a start.

'Emma!' shouts a voice, and I turn to see Ollie waving at me from the far side of the village green.

'What is it?' I shout back.

'I forgot the trolley!' He lopes over to my stall and gives me an apologetic smile.

'How can you have forgotten it? I put it on the pavement right next to your van before we left.'

He sighs. 'It must still be there. I was so exhausted from loading all those boxes that I didn't notice it. Shall I go home and get it?'

'No, that would take too long. We'll have to carry the boxes ourselves.'

'Or you could carry them while I supervise?' he suggests.

'Not a hope. You volunteered for this, and you can see it through. There aren't too many of them.'

He groans. 'I know exactly how many there are. My back still aches from lifting them into my van.'

'I'll buy you something from the Snowball Saloon when we've finished,' I promise.

Ollie looks up at the sign saying *Honeywell's Finest Eggnog*. 'Fine, I'll help you. But it had better be good eggnog.'

He follows me to his van and opens the back door. I look at the boxes stacked neatly on top of one another and feel a surge of excitement.

'It's really happening!' I say.

'It really is. You've done an amazing job, Em.'

'Not yet. We don't know whether any of this will sell. What if everyone thinks it's a ridiculous idea? I've spent all of my savings on it.'

He hefts the largest box out of the van. 'People will be lining up to buy them. Especially after a few glasses of eggnog.'

'As long as the customers aren't too drunk to pay.'

'They'll think they're getting more value if they're seeing double,' he says.

We spend the next twenty minutes carrying boxes from his van to the stall.

'One more trip should do it,' he says at last, dumping a bag of decorations onto the counter.

We walk back to collect the last few boxes. Ollie locks the van and looks around the fair. 'It's larger than I expected. You should have plenty of customers.'

'Drunk customers,' I remind him, and he laughs.

'Drunk or sober, it's a great idea. I have every confidence in you, Em. When you're running an international chain of Christmas shops, I'd like you to remember who was there for its humble beginnings.'

'You shall be my Managing Director,' I promise. 'I'll pay you a seven-figure salary, and you can go home early whenever you like.'

'And drink as much free eggnog as I want?' he says.

'That goes without saying. We'll have a nog fountain in the lobby of my headquarters in New York.'

'New York?' he says. 'I like the sound of that. I keep hinting to Ed I'd love to go there for my thirtieth birthday, but he's always overtaken by his trademark selective deafness.'

'I'll go with you,' I say.

'Will you really?'

'Of course. Or I will if you lend me the money. Every penny I have is tied up in this stall.'

'How about you visit me there as soon as I get my first executive bonus?' he asks. 'I'll be living in a penthouse on Fifth Avenue. I'll have plenty of room.'

'What about Ed?'

'Ed has to move there too,' he says. 'I can't figure out how to work our new coffee machine.'

We walk over the frozen grass and stop dead. My stack of boxes has disappeared under a pile of Christmas trees.

I let out a shriek of horror. 'Who put those stupid trees there?'

I give the nearest one an ineffectual kick. 'Ouch!'

A man emerges from behind the hut. 'What are you doing to my trees?'

I glare at him. 'Don't you mean what have you done to my boxes? They'll be ruined.'

'I moved them behind your stall,' he says. 'There's no need to make such a fuss about it.'

I'm temporarily lost for words, which may be a good thing. The words rushing through my brain are enough to get me banned from any Christmas fair.

'You had no right to move them,' I say at last.

He shrugs. 'Would you prefer me to have left them where they were? These trees are heavy.'

'I know they are. I think that one has broken my toe. Why couldn't you have waited to unload them? You could see my things were here first.'

'But I didn't know where you were,' he says. 'Or even who you were.'

'You do now,' I say, annoyed by the look of amusement on his face.

'Not really,' he says. 'You could be a random woman who visits Christmas fairs each year to shout at people.'

'Well, I'm not! I'm working here too. Or I will be if you stop hiding my boxes.'

'Not hiding,' he says. 'I've already told you I put them behind your hut.'

'But I put them exactly where I wanted them to be,' I say stubbornly. 'Ollie and I carried them all the way from his van, and they were extremely heavy.'

'I don't know what to tell you,' he says. 'I was in a hurry, so I did what I thought was best. I'll help you move them back once I have these trees on their stands.'

'I don't need you to help,' I say. 'I need you to stop blocking my stall with your stu … Christmas trees.'

He laughs. 'I'll have them out of the way in a few minutes. They're actually Norway Spruces, not stu … Christmas trees. I considered planting those this year, but the spruce is a hardier variety and doesn't shed its needles as quickly.'

He holds out his hand. 'I'm Tom Kingsley, by the way.'

I shake it reluctantly. 'Emma Hartley. And this is –'

'Oliver Johnson,' says Ollie, shaking Tom's hand. 'Emma's carer.'

'My what?' I say.

Ollie grins at Tom. 'I follow her around the Christmas markets, trying to stop her yelling at random stall holders. Not always successfully, as you can see.'

'Ah!' says Tom. 'A seasonal job, I assume?'

'The extra money comes in handy over the holidays,' says Ollie. 'I'm hoping to pick up some more work at Easter when Emma likes to run amok around the local egg hunts.'

'Hilarious,' I say. 'And Tom isn't a random stall holder. He's a stall holder who's blocking access to the space I've booked and paid for. I could report him to the market director.'

'You could try,' says Tom. 'But the last time I saw Frances, she was shouting at the men putting up the carousel. You'll have to wait in line if you want to complain to her. By which time, I'll have sorted my trees and replaced your boxes exactly where you put them.'

He picks up the nearest tree and nails it onto a couple of pieces of crossed wood.

'Can I help you with that?' says Ollie.

'I'm sure he's fine,' I say. 'Why don't we take a look at what the other stalls are selling?'

'I'd love some help,' Tom tells Ollie. 'I'd hate to inconvenience Emma any more than I need to.'

He gives me a mocking smile, which I ignore.

'Can you be as quick as possible?' I ask Ollie. 'It's almost four o'clock, and the fair opens at six.'

'I'll do my best,' he says. 'Go and find yourself something to eat. You didn't have any lunch.'

'We'll be ready in about half an hour,' says Tom. 'I'll move your boxes back after that. What's in them?'

'My Christmas goods,' I say.

'I mean specifically.'

I feel my cheeks turn pink. I've barely told anyone what I plan to sell at this market. It seemed such a good idea when I first came up with it, but I'm losing confidence by the minute. I can't keep it a secret forever. The first customers will be arriving in a couple of hours. My stall won't be much of a success if everything stays hidden under a blanket.

'It's called A Boxful of Christmas,' I say. 'It's exactly what it sounds like. It's Christmas in a box. I've organised the holiday into various themes, so there's something to suit everyone. A box for someone living on their own, one for families, one for baking enthusiasts, that sort of thing.'

I stop and watch his face for a reaction. Not that I really care what he thinks. All I care about is that he gets his trees away from my stall as quickly as possible.

Tom nods. 'Right.'

I can't help myself. 'Right? Is that all you have to say?'

He looks surprised. 'What did you want me to say?'

'That it's a wonderful concept, and you're sure it will do well?'

'I have no idea how well it will do,' he says. 'You must have studied the market, or you wouldn't be selling these boxes.'

'I have studied it! I've done loads of customer research, and I'm sure people will be excited to buy them.'

'Great,' he says, picking up a second Christmas tree and fixing it to a stand.

I should let this go, but I can't. Tom is one of the first people I've told about my idea, and it's annoying he doesn't seem interested.

'It *is* great!' I say. 'It's a lot more original than what you're selling.'

'I agree,' he says.

'Thank you.'

'I mean I agree that Christmas trees are boring,' he says. 'Then again, so is Christmas.'

It takes me a moment to catch his meaning. 'What do you mean? Christmas is the most wonderful time of the year!'

He unties another tree and shakes out its branches. 'I'll take your word for it. I've never much enjoyed Christmas. I'll be glad when it's over.'

He turns away, leaving me standing there with my mouth open in shock.

Chapter Two

I'd like to continue the argument, but Oliver touches my arm. 'Now is not the time, Em! Go and find something to eat.'

'Fine!' I pick up my bag and walk towards the nearest food stall, still in shock.

How can someone say they don't like Christmas? It's like saying they don't like breathing air. Maybe Tom isn't a carbon-based life form at all and doesn't need oxygen and whatever else it is we breathe. Helium? Ethanol?

It makes no sense. Why would someone who hates Christmas sell Christmas trees at a Christmas market when there are a million other things he could do? This must be his idea of a joke. In which case, it's a good thing Ollie encouraged me to leave. I don't want anyone ruining my first night here.

I stop to inspect the rows of gingerbread people. They're golden and shiny and make my mouth water. If there's one smell that's the absolute essence of Christmas for me, it's ginger. And nutmeg, and cinnamon, and citrus zest, and peppermint, and pine. Fine – there are a thousand smells which make up my idea of a perfect Christmas. But ginger is definitely one of them.

'Do you bake these yourself?' I ask the woman behind the stall.

'I'm afraid not,' she says. 'I order them from the local bakery. But I decorate them myself. I'd like to bake my own cookies, but I can't afford to hire a commercial unit yet. And I live in a house share where it's difficult enough to get anyone to wash up, let alone keep the kitchen clean enough to pass a health and safety inspection.'

'That's a shame,' I say. 'I love the smell of freshly baked gingerbread.'

'Me too. Maybe next year. Which one would you like?'

I select a Christmas elf for me, with striped leggings and a pointy hat. It takes me a little longer to choose one for Ollie. I finally decide on a Superman. Tom can buy his own gingerbread person if he wants one. Maybe I'll drop one of my heaviest boxes onto it and see how he likes that.

'I'm Emma,' I say to the woman. 'I have a stall here too. It's my first year.'

'That's exciting,' she says. 'Which one?'

I point in the general direction. 'The one next to the Christmas trees. I haven't been able to unpack any of my things yet because someone's dumped a load of trees in front of my stall without asking.'

'That's Tom Kingsley,' she says. 'His family owns that Christmas tree farm over in Fryston. Do you know it?'

'I don't live locally,' I say. 'My home is in Oxford.'

'We always get our Christmas trees from Kingsley's Farm,' she says. 'Most people around here do. What are you selling?'

I'm reluctant to launch into my spiel after Tom's lukewarm reaction. I don't want to see her polite smile as she tries to find something nice to say. I couldn't bear for someone else to think it's a terrible idea. Worse still, a ridiculous one.

'Christmas decorations,' I say briefly. 'And a few candles. Things like that.'

'That must be why they've put you next to the Kingsley stall,' she says. 'You can do some cross-marketing with Tom.'

I somehow doubt this. I have no wish to team up with someone whose entire demeanour reeks of Bah, Humbug!

'Maybe,' I say. 'I'd better be getting back to prepare for the opening. Lovely to meet you.'

'You too,' she says. 'I'm Lucy. Come over and see me any time you need a gingerbread hit. I'll give you a discount.'

'Likewise,' I say. 'My stall is called A Boxful of Christmas.'

'That sounds fun,' she says, and she appears to mean it. 'I'll pop over this evening when my friend comes to take over here.'

I buy two cappuccinos from the stall next to hers and carry them over to where Ollie is nailing the last Christmas tree to its stand.

Tom's getting your boxes now,' he says. 'I'll help you unpack them.'

'Drink this first,' I tell him.

He takes the cup I hand him and unwraps his gingerbread man.

'It reminds me of you,' I say. 'Heroes don't always wear capes. Sometimes, they wear frosting underpants over their clothes.'

'I love it!' he says. 'What did you choose for yourself?'

I hold out the elf, and he laughs. 'I might have known. Did you get one for Tom too?'

'They didn't have any Grinches.'

'Are you still annoyed with him?' he asks. 'It isn't mandatory to love Christmas as much as you do.'

'But it isn't mandatory to hate it as much as he does.'

Ollie takes a bite of his cookie. 'He said he didn't particularly enjoy it, not that he hated it. Plenty of people find Christmas stressful.'

'I know they do. Which means they don't choose to visit Christmas fairs, let alone sell at them.'

'That's nonsense,' he objects. 'No one expects every single fishmonger to love eating fish. Or people who work in stationery stores to write all their letters by hand.'

'But this is different. We aren't just selling products here. We're selling something far more important.'

'Such as?' he says.

I wave my hands in explanation. 'A dream, a vision, the spirit of Christmas. And you can't put a price on that.'

'Apparently, you can,' he says, showing me the tag on the nearest Christmas tree.

'You know what I mean. I hope Tom doesn't spoil people's experience with his attitude. Buying your tree is one of the most magical parts of Christmas. It's all about the promise and the expectation. It's where Christmas really begins.'

'Not for me,' he says. 'Drinking seasonal beer and opening my Whiskies of the World advent calendar is when Christmas really starts for me.'

Tom appears holding my last few boxes. 'Where shall I put these?'

'With the rest of them,' I say.

He places them carefully on the grass, and I look at my watch. 'I should get these organised. I'm way behind, thanks to this delay.'

'Do you need any help?' asks Tom.

'No, thanks. I have all the help I need. Are you ready, Ollie?'

Ollie drops his cup into a nearby bin. 'I suppose so. It's a far cry from my executive corner office looking out over Central Park, but I'm willing to slum it here with you for the next few weeks.'

I unpack the glossy gift boxes and line them up along the red and green cloth-covered counter while Ollie hangs the holly garlands from the roof. I locate the glass snowmen with their hand-painted scarves, my felt gingerbread men, and my ceramic robins, and arrange them around the boxes to give a festive feel. I finish off with a miniature Christmas tree at each end of the display. I've already decorated them with tiny ornaments which shimmer in the light from the streetlamp behind us.

Tom has been watching me. 'I don't recognise that particular species of pine. Is it a bonsai variety of the well-known stu … Christmas tree?'

I try not to laugh. 'No, and neither are they Norway Spruces.'

'I have a spray I can sell you to stop them dropping their needles,' he says.

'I'm sure you do. But these trees don't need your chemical-laced sprays.'

'Because they're magical?' he asks.

'You can poke fun at me all you like,' I say. 'Christmas *is* a magical time of year, and people love it. I want to do my part to make it even more special for them.'

'And I want to turn a profit and go home,' he says. 'You'll be sitting out here in the cold almost every night until Christmas. Wouldn't you like to make some money from it?'

'Of course, I would. All I'm saying is that it isn't only about the money.'

'It is for me,' he says. 'I'm doing this to help my mother. My family have been running the farm for decades. But I can't help wishing they'd decided to run a coconut farm in the Caribbean. I wouldn't mind spending Christmas on a beach, drinking rum cocktails and selling coconuts.'

'Me too,' says Ollie. He catches my eye. 'Although it's far more fun being here with you in the freezing cold.'

'I should think so,' I say. 'Don't forget we're having eggnog. That ought to warm you up.'

'You should take it easy with those,' says Tom. 'They're surprisingly potent.'

'I have a strong head,' I tell him.

Ollie gives a snort of laughter. 'Says the woman who collapsed into a paddling pool and nearly drowned after two glasses of Pimms last summer. Ed and I thought we might have to call an ambulance.'

'That's not how I remember it,' I say defensively. 'I'm sure I won't pass out after a single glass of eggnog.'

'If you do, I can strap you to one of my Christmas trees and carry you home,' says Tom. 'Depending on where home may be for you two.'

'We'll be fine,' I say. 'But thanks for the offer. Are you trying to sabotage my stall by getting me too drunk to work? What's wrong, Tom? Afraid of the competition?'

'Not at all,' he says. 'And you aren't my competition. In case you hadn't noticed, I'm selling Christmas trees.'

'But no one puts up a Christmas tree and leaves it bare,' I say. 'They decorate it. And I'm selling decorations.'

'That's not competition,' he says. 'At most, it's symbiosis.'

'That's a good word for it,' says Ollie. 'You two should team up together to sell more products.'

'I'm fine,' I say. 'I don't need any help selling my products. Especially not –'

I break off, and Tom laughs. 'Not from a Christmas hater like myself?'

'Your words, not mine.' I fasten a final string of lights to the edge of the stall and step back to admire the effect.

'That looks great,' says Ollie. 'You've done an amazing job, Em!'

'It does look good,' I say in relief. 'Thanks so much. I couldn't have done any of this without you.'

'Of course, you could. All I did was fetch and carry.'

'And provide meals when I was too tired to eat,' I add. 'Your support has made all the difference. Yours and Ed's. I'm so grateful to you both.'

'That's what friends are for,' he says, slipping an arm around me and giving me a hug. 'How could such well-known Christmas lovers as me and Ed refuse to be a part of this?'

I hug him back. 'I knew you wouldn't prefer to be in the Caribbean, lassoing the coconuts. It looks wonderful, doesn't it?'

'It does,' he agrees. 'The Snowball Saloon seems to be open. I'll get us all a glass and we can drink a toast to following our dreams.'

'Or nightmares,' I say with a glance at Tom, who laughs.

'I don't want to squash anyone else's dreams. I just don't have any of my own. Your stall looks great, Emma. I hope you do a roaring trade.'

'Thank you,' I say, ashamed of my earlier ungraciousness.

Ollie hands us both a glass of eggnog. I take a sip and try not to cough. It's incredibly strong, but I refuse to admit Tom was right.

Ollie raises his glass and clinks it against mine and Tom's.

'In my capacity as Managing Director, chief box-carrier, and general all-round dogsbody,' he says, 'I would like to declare A Boxful of Christmas officially open for business!'

Chapter Three

Tom looks at his watch at around five thirty. 'I'll be back in a bit,' he tells us.

'What about your trees?' I say.

'What about them?'

'Are you leaving them here all by themselves?'

His lips twitch. 'That's the general idea. Why? Do they need a babysitter?'

'Of course not. But who will look after them?'

'They'll be fine,' he says. 'What do you think will happen to them while I'm gone? They're too big to steal. And you and Oliver will be here if anyone decides to make the attempt.'

'We're working,' I say. 'Neither of us has any intention of putting ourselves at risk to protect your Christmas trees.'

'You mean my stupid Christmas trees?' he says.

'Those too.'

'I wouldn't expect you to,' he says. 'But perhaps you could note down a physical description of the criminals, car registration details, that sort of thing. It would be useful information for the police.'

'They won't come all the way out here for something so minor,' I say. 'They have better things to do than scour the countryside looking for lost Christmas trees.'

'I'm afraid she's right,' says Ollie. 'Even if the police could afford the manpower, how would they tell which trees had been stolen and which had simply run away? They all look the same to the untrained eye – branches, trunks, needles. Can you imagine trying to organise an identity parade to identify the stolen trees? Number three, step forward! No, I mean number five! Are you sure of your identification, madam? No? Then I'm afraid we'll have to let the thieves go. We can only hold them for twenty-four hours without charging them.'

'It wouldn't even get that far,' I say. 'The Christmas tree thieves would have taken them to the chop shop long before then and altered their appearance.'

'What a horrible image,' says Tom. 'Are you saying the criminals would strip my trees for parts? Turn them into wood chips and sawdust?'

I pull a face. 'You've been watching too many horror films. All anyone would have to do is decorate them. By the time those trees were covered in strings of tinsel and coloured baubles, even their own mothers wouldn't know them. Let alone someone like you, who doesn't seem to care about them at all.'

'I'm callous enough to take the risk,' he says. 'In the meantime, I'd be most grateful if you two could keep an eye on my trees and make sure they don't escape. I'll do the same for you sometime.'

'No, you won't,' I say. 'I don't plan to leave my stall unattended even for a moment. I've worked too hard to make this business a success.'

'Fair enough,' he says. 'See you later.'

We watch him stride over to his truck and drive away.

'I wouldn't blame those trees if they did try to escape,' I say. 'Imagine being a Christmas tree sold by someone who hates everything you stand for. The poor things have spent the entire year growing on a farm, trying to become the most perfect versions of themselves, all ready to bring some family joy. Then a horrible man comes along, cuts them down, throws them into a van and takes them to a market, where he tells everyone they're stupid and pointless.'

Ollie finishes the hot dog he's been eating and wipes the ketchup from his chin.

'It's a tragic story, Em. That Tom guy is the absolute worst. Do you think he's planning to abolish Christmas entirely?'

'I wouldn't be surprised if he stands for parliament just so he can change the law,' I say.

He grins. 'I can see it now. First, he'll introduce a backbench bill and blackmail everyone in his party into voting for it. The country will wake the following morning to the announcement that Christmas has been banned, and all mentions of it have been struck from the history books.'

'You may mock,' I say, 'but Tom would love that. He'll introduce a second bill to make sure all the most famous Christmas books are only taught in context, and none of the best-known Christmas films can be shown when anyone is awake.'

'Will they all be re-titled to teach us their proper lessons?' he asks. 'The Grinch who Saved Christmas from Consumerism or Rudolph Would Have Done Better to Conform.'

'Exactly!' I say. 'Schoolchildren all over the country will be learning about The Thrifty Triumph of Ebeneezer Scrooge and Frosty's Complete Meltdown.'

'What will you be doing while this anti-Christmas revolution is taking place?' he asks. 'Leading protests in the streets, I suppose. Carrying banners saying *Hands off our Christmas* and *It's a Cinch – Don't be a Grinch!*'

'I'll be heading up the resistance,' I say.

'Parachuting onto village greens with your guerrilla carol singers?' he says. 'I can see it now. You'll bring Christmas back into everyone's lives, and they'll hold a parade for you. After that, Christmas will no longer be celebrated once a year. Under your benign dictatorship, it will be – what – every month?'

'Still only once a year,' I say. 'Otherwise, it would lose its magic. But I'll give the entire country the whole of December off work to celebrate.'

'Will you visit Tom in prison?' he asks.

'He won't be in prison. I'll sentence him to fifty years of community service. He'll have to spend the whole of December playing Santa in a shopping centre. He can spend the rest of the year making Christmas decorations for people to sell at markets like this one.'

'I can't wait to watch the movie they make about it when it's all over,' says Ollie. 'The Great Christmas Escape. Who will be playing you?'

'Someone extremely talented and beautiful. How about you?'

'Am I in it too?' he asks. 'What an honour.'

'Of course. You and Ed will play a pivotal part by cracking the codes and infiltrating Tom's secret meetings.'

He looks impressed. 'I had no idea I was so brave.'

'And handsome,' I say.

'That too,' he agrees. 'I'd like to be played by Ryan Reynolds if he's available. And Ed can be played by Cary Grant. I've always had a thing for tall, dark, impossibly suave men.'

'I hate to burst your bubble,' I say apologetically. 'But those two men are from different eras.'

'That's the magic of cinema,' he says. 'One of us can be CGI. Maybe both of us. It would keep the production costs down.'

'We can set it in New York if you like,' I offer. 'You and Ed can climb the Statue of Liberty and go skydiving off the Empire State Building.'

'Sounds perfect,' he says. 'In the meantime, I see the first few customers heading our way. And here comes Mr Grumpy, right on time. It looks as though his Christmas trees have missed their chance to stage that jail break and spend the rest of their lives living as outlaws in the local woods.'

Chapter Four

Ollie drives me over to the fair again the following evening.

'I'm glad I left your unsold boxes in my van last night,' he says. 'I don't like the idea of loading and unloading every single one each day.'

'Have you been driving around with them all day?' I ask.

'I have. I don't even intend to charge you for the extra petrol. Call it an early Christmas present.'

'I wasn't thinking about the additional weight,' I say. 'What if they'd been stolen?'

'I have an alarm. And I park right behind the bookshop.'

'But someone could smash it open and grab the boxes before you arrived.'

'Trust me,' he says. 'If anyone tried that, I'd run out to find them lying in the carpark, shrieking about their collapsed vertebrae.'

'But you manage to carry them to and from my stall.'

'That's because I'm exceptionally strong,' he says. 'Like Superman.'

I laugh. 'That's not why I chose that cookie for you. It was because you've saved me so many times.'

'And because of my rippling muscles,' he says. 'The boxes will be perfectly safe in my van. The alternative is to lock them inside the stall each night, and you don't seem keen on that idea.'

'I'm not. The stalls are left unattended overnight, and there's no security guard. It wouldn't take long for someone to crowbar even the strongest padlock and make off with the stock.'

'I don't want to be rude,' he says. 'But I'm not convinced the local gangs are looking for cute boxes of Christmas decorations to fence down at the pub.'

'I'm not taking the risk,' I say.

'Then they're staying in my van each night. My back is precious.'

I don't say any more as we drive along the high street towards the village green. Tom isn't there when we arrive. Neither are his trees.

'Do you think he'll come back tonight?' I ask Ollie.

'Why wouldn't he?'

'It seems a lot of effort to go to each evening for a festival he doesn't approve of.'

'He's doing it to make money,' Ollie reminds me. 'Like most of the people here. I doubt many of them see it as their mission in life to make everyone's Christmas perfect. Most of them will have identified a marketing opportunity and decided to cash in on it.'

'You're so cynical,' I grumble. 'Why can't they do both?'

'Because this is real life,' he says. 'Most people don't love Christmas the way you do. And Tom is obviously one of them.'

'Fine, but he doesn't have to say it's boring and overrated.'

Ollie points to the edge of the green. 'His truck has just pulled up. Do you plan to spend the evening arguing with him about the true meaning of Christmas?'

'No. I have far better things to do with my time.'

'I'm glad to hear it. It's obvious neither of you will change the other's mind. Find something to talk about that you both agree on.'

'I doubt we agree on anything much at all,' I say. 'But I promise not to pick a fight with him. Thank you for bringing my things over. I wish my car boot wasn't so small. It would take me several trips each night. But you don't need to stay here all evening. I'm sure you have something better lined up.'

'Not better,' he says. 'Different. Ed and I are going to the theatre tonight. Our friend Jacob is starring in The Music Man, and he's given us free tickets.'

'Lucky you. Think of me freezing here as you sit in the nice warm bar sipping Chardonnay during the interval.'

'There's a stall selling mulled wine at the fair,' he says. 'Six glasses of that, and you won't even feel the cold.'

'Six glasses of that, and I'll be dancing on my stall. But I'll bear it in mind.'

Tom appears, carrying two large Christmas trees. 'I'm glad to see you back, Emma.'

'Why wouldn't I be here?' I ask. 'The fair runs until Christmas Eve.'

'I thought I might have put you off,' he says.

'It would take more than that to destroy the magic of Christmas. And I sold lots of boxes last night. So, not everyone thinks my idea is a disaster.'

'I told my mum about your business,' he says. 'She thinks it's a wonderful idea. You'll be glad to know she's not a Christmas-hater like me.'

'I suppose she can't be if she works on a Christmas tree farm. How long have your parents been running it?'

'Since they were married. But Dad died last year, so it's just Mum running it now.'

'I'm sorry,' I say. 'I didn't realise.'

'There's no reason why you should. You hadn't even heard of our farm until last night. I'd better get the rest of my trees.'

He disappears back to his truck.

'Do you think that's why Tom doesn't like Christmas?' I ask Ollie. 'Because he associates it with his parents' business, and his father is no longer there?'

'I have no idea,' he says. 'It isn't something you can easily ask someone.'

Tom reappears, carrying several more trees.

'Would you like us to put them onto their stands for you?' I offer.

He looks surprised. 'That's kind of you, but it won't take me a minute.'

'I should be going,' says Ollie. 'The curtain goes up at seven thirty, and I have to feed Ed first. He isn't a big fan of the theatre, but he'll tolerate it if he gets an enjoyable meal beforehand. I'll swing by here at ten to collect you.'

'Will the play be over by then?' I ask. 'Don't leave early on my account. I'm happy to wait for you here. I can add up the evening's takings. If tonight's sales are as good as last night's, it will take me a while.'

'I can give you a ride home if you like,' says Tom. 'It would be a shame to cut Ollie's evening short.'

'You?' I say, and he grins.

'Don't sound so surprised. I may not live up to your superior standards for appreciating Christmas, but I'm always happy to help a friend in need.'

'But what about the boxes?' says Ollie.

'I can dump them in the back of my truck, under a pile of Christmas trees,' says Tom, laughing at my horrified face.

'Sounds great,' says Ollie. 'Got to fly! See you later, Em.'

I arrange my sample boxes neatly along the front of my stall and add the decorations.

'I'm glad you did so well last night,' says Tom.

'Thanks. And it looks as though you sold out of trees.'

'We usually do,' he says. 'Our farm is several miles away. Some people drive over for lunch and choose their own tree, but it's a lot simpler for the people who live in Honeywell to buy them here.'

'What's your farm like?' I ask.

'You should come and see it for yourself,' he says. 'It would be an excellent research project.'

'Or you could tell me about it and save me the trip. How many Christmas trees do you have?'

'About ten thousand.'

'How long do they take to grow?'

'Several years,' he says. 'It depends on how large we want them to get.'

'I'm always hearing about rural crime,' I say. 'Farmers having their tractors stolen or their crops trashed. Could someone drive out to your farm in the middle of the night, dump a load of trees into their truck, then sell them at a market like this one?'

'They wouldn't get near the place,' he says. 'We're locked down like Fort Knox. Our entire farm is covered by CCTV. Even if someone got past all that, the rottweilers would take care of them. They don't mess around.'

'I'm surprised you have any visitors,' I say. 'I wouldn't want to spend an afternoon having to watch out for savage dogs.'

'We only let them out at night,' he says. 'And we give our customers a code word in case they're attacked.'

'Really?'

'Absolutely,' he says. 'It wouldn't be responsible to do anything else. If you're ever at our farm and see a pack of dogs charging towards you, just shout, "Candy Cane!" at the top of your voice. They'll slink back to the house at once.'

'What else do you have?' I ask. 'Cows and sheep?'

'We don't keep livestock,' he says. 'Unless you count my mother's hens. She mainly keeps them for herself, but she sells the spare eggs when the hens are laying well.'

'What about bees?' I ask.

'What about them?'

'I thought all farmers kept bees.'

'We don't,' he says. 'We sell honey in the farm shop, but we get it from a neighbour who has about twenty hives.'

'Don't you need bees to pollinate your fruit trees?' I ask.

'I suppose we might – if we had fruit trees.'

'You must have fruit trees!' I exclaim. 'All farms have orchards.'

'My parents can't have read the manual,' he says.

'Fine,' I say. 'I know nothing at all about farming, and you know everything. But I don't understand how you can make a living when you only sell one thing. A seasonal thing, too.'

'We don't only sell one thing,' he says. 'We have a pick-your-own soft fruit business that's always done very well. And my parents grew a variety of vegetables and ran a veg-box business before my father died.'

'Does your mum still do that?'

'No, she's cut down on a lot of those extras this year. And now she's decided to sell up and retire. It's obvious her heart isn't in it any longer.'

'How about you?' I say. 'Did you never consider working on the farm full time?'

'I used to think I would,' he says. 'But things change. I have an older sister, Katie, who lives in Newcastle with her partner and children. She comes home when she can, but it's quite a drive, and her youngest hasn't started school yet. So, I was the obvious choice to come back and help Mum with the trees this year.'

'It must feel sad to see the place sold,' I say.

'Not really,' he says. 'I haven't lived there for almost seven years.'

He looks at the gate. 'Here they come, right on time. Are you ready, Emma? The more boxes you sell tonight, the fewer I'll have to carry back to my truck!'

Chapter Five

Lucy comes over to visit my stall the following evening.

'I haven't had time to look at what you're selling,' she says. 'Hi, Tom. How are you?'

Tom has been leaning against his hut, watching the people walk around the fair, all chattering and laughing.

'Hi, Lucy,' he says. 'I haven't seen you for a while.'

'They've moved your pitch,' she says. 'Aren't you usually over there?'

She points to the far side of the green where Santa is sitting on a rickety sleigh, spray painted with silver.

'That's right,' he says. 'But Mum asked for a larger pitch this year. Dad ended up taking a lot of orders last year and having to deliver them. It wasted a lot of time.'

'How's your mum?' she says. 'This must be a tough time of year for her.'

'It's a busy few weeks on the farm,' he says. 'That seems to be taking her mind off things.'

'What if your crop failed?' I ask Tom. 'How would you cope?'

'Failed in what way?' he says.

'I don't know. I'm not a farmer. Some tropical disease that only attacks Christmas trees?'

'I haven't come across any so far,' he says. 'The farm has remained remarkably free from plagues and pestilence since I was born.'

'No frogs or swarms of locusts?' I say.

He shakes his head. 'As I say, we've been lucky.'

'What about fires?' I persist.

He laughs. 'Fire isn't a big problem this time of year. Try coming over to the farm and lighting one. You'll find it more difficult than you might think.'

'Not if I bring a can of firelighter fluid,' I say.

'I wouldn't advise you to try it. You have to get through several padlocked gates and a lot of barbed wire to access our farm. You'd be stopped long before you'd opened the can. And don't forget our large and extremely aggressive dogs. I doubt you'd manage to burn even one of our trees.'

'Why would I want to burn Christmas trees?' I protest. 'They're my favourite kind of tree.'

'I might have guessed,' he says.

'Do you remember climbing that enormous oak tree during our class picnic?' Lucy asks Tom.

She turns to me. 'It was our final year of primary school, and we went to Compton Woods for a picnic on the last day of term. We were all going to different high schools the following year, so it was a chance for us to be together for one last time. Tom and I decided it would be fun to climb the highest tree we could find when Mr Channing wasn't looking. But we got stuck halfway up and couldn't get down. We didn't dare shout because we'd have got into terrible trouble. So, we stayed up there for the entire afternoon and missed all the fun.'

'What happened?' I say. 'You obviously got down somehow, or you'd still be up there.'

'One of our classmates spotted us and told Mr Channing,' she says. 'He called the school caretaker, who came over with a ladder and got us down. It was lucky it was the last day of term, or we'd have been in detention for a month. Tom and I were always getting into trouble. Who was it that ratted us out, Tom? Wasn't it Ruby Archer? She never liked me.'

'I have no idea,' he says.

'I'm sure it was,' says Lucy, with a gurgle of laughter. 'It was exactly the sort of thing she'd do. I wonder what happened to her.'

'No idea,' says Tom. 'I think I'll get myself a glass of mulled wine. Would either of you like one?'

'That sounds great,' says Lucy.

'It does,' I agree. 'Hang on a moment while I find my purse.'

'No need,' he says. 'This one's on me.'

He disappears towards the stall at the far end of the market.

'I've barely seen Tom since he left for university,' says Lucy. 'I was surprised to see him back this year, but I suppose he's standing in for his dad.'

I wonder what Tom studied at university. Mistletoe Management, perhaps, or Festive Forestry, with a minor in the art of tinsel management.

'Tell me about yourself, Emma,' she says. 'Do you have a partner?'

'Not at the moment. I was seeing someone for a few months last year, but it fizzled out.'

'I saw a good-looking guy helping you set up your stall,' she says.

'You did. He's one of my oldest friends. And he has a partner. I'm staying with them for a few weeks while I do this stall.'

She pulls a face of mock disappointment. 'Isn't it always the case? All the good ones are snapped up early. What about Tom?'

'What about him?'

'He's good-looking too. And he's lovely and muscular. It must be from lugging those Christmas trees around all his life.'

'Are you planning your move?' I say, laughing.

'Not a hope! I've known him far too long. You can't date someone you saw throwing up at your year three Christmas party. Anyway, I have a boyfriend. Max is the manager at our local supermarket. That's where we met. I was returning an out-of-date yogurt, and the customer service woman called him over to approve the refund. Have you ever heard anything so romantic?'

She asks me more about myself, and I give her the bare bones of my life history. It doesn't even interest me, so it's difficult to imagine why it might interest anyone else. I tell her about my uneventful childhood just outside Oxford and my three years in Coventry studying business and psychology.

'I wasn't sure what I wanted to do when I graduated,' I say. 'I took a temporary job at a florist's in Oxford, and I'm still there. Once I decided to start this Christmas-box business, I needed to save up as much money as possible.'

'I'm a dental assistant,' she says. 'I work in Compton. It's not far from here.'

'Is that fun?' I say. 'Or is it a step towards something else, like becoming a dentist?'

'Not a hope,' she says. 'I don't mind peering into people's mouths all day, but you wouldn't catch me operating a drill. It's such a huge responsibility. So much could go wrong. I don't know how dentists do it.'

'Maybe we should swap jobs,' I say. 'I never use the drill on any of our flowers. We don't even offer them anaesthetic when we trim their stalks.'

'I'll bear it in mind,' she says. 'But I really enjoy my job, despite all the fearsome implements.'

'I don't mind working in the flower shop,' I say. 'But I really want to run my own business.'

'I'm sure you will,' she says. 'Here comes Tom with our mulled wine. I've drunk so much of it this week that I could light Santa's sleigh home all by myself.'

'Three glasses of mulled wine,' says Tom. 'What are you two talking about?'

'Lighting Santa's sleigh on Christmas Eve,' I say.

'Speaking of Santa, our resident one doesn't look too happy,' he says. 'I'm not a Christmas authority like Emma, but I didn't think a surly demeanour was the main hiring criterion.'

I look over at Santa, who's slumped down in his sleigh, staring into the distance.

'He looks as though he has the weight of the world on his shoulders,' I say. 'Maybe he's having trouble at home.'

'With Mrs Claus?' asks Tom. 'I hadn't thought of that. Do you think she's running around with one of the elves behind Santa's back?'

'Perhaps she's put him on a diet,' suggests Lucy. 'She may be sick of letting out his red suit every year.'

'Santa's supposed to be well covered!' I say. 'Mrs Claus should be ashamed of herself.'

'Maybe she wants to move to Florida,' says Tom. 'I wouldn't blame her. It can't be the most exciting existence living at the North Pole all year around with no one to talk to except a mince pie addict who randomly shouts, "Ho, Ho, Ho!" The modern woman must want more than that.'

'Mrs Claus is fine,' I say. 'She loves Santa, and she loves Christmas. That's not why he's under the weather tonight. He probably has a cold.'

'I'm not convinced,' says Tom. 'It seems to me Santa is having second thoughts about this whole Christmas lark. You'd better watch out, Emma, or you'll wake up on Christmas morning to find your stocking is completely empty.'

Chapter Six

I wake late on Saturday morning to the delicious scent of fresh coffee. Ed must be up, seeing as he's the only one who can operate the coffee machine.

I open the curtains, then climb back into bed, enjoying the warmth and the weight of the thick quilt on my legs. A few stray snowflakes swirl lazily past my window. They fall more thickly, like tiny ballerinas pirouetting to the street below. It's going to be another cold day.

There's a knock on the door, and Ollie opens it. 'You're awake! We didn't expect to see you yet.'

I yawn and sit up. 'What time is it?'

'Ten o'clock. I only knocked because I heard you open your curtains. Otherwise, I'd have left you alone. Coffee?'

'I'd love one. I'll be down in two minutes.'

'I'd offer to bring it to you in bed,' he says. 'But Ed and I always have fresh pastries on Saturday mornings, and you'd be bound to get crumbs everywhere.'

'I would not!' I protest, and he laughs.

'Yes, you would. Then you'd spend the rest of the week complaining about them. Like the Princess and the Pea.'

'She didn't make crumbs in her bed,' I say. 'Someone put a dried pea under her mattress. The clue is in the title of the story. It isn't the Princess and the Enormous Stack of Croissant Crumbs.'

'I've always thought that was one of the more ridiculous fairy tales,' he says. 'Who wants to sleep on a giant pile of mattresses? You'd lie awake for the entire night terrified of falling off and crashing to the floor. That would do far more damage than lying on a tiny dried pea.'

I reach for my dressing gown. 'That princess was a rubbish house guest. Who goes to stay in someone else's castle uninvited and spends all their time grumbling about how uncomfortable their bed is? When your host asks how you've slept, the only polite answer is, "Very well, thanks." Not to whine about how sore your back is. I bet she didn't even offer to help load the dishwasher.'

'Exactly!' he says. 'How did you sleep last night, Em?'

'Terribly. You need to buy a new guest mattress. I'm bruised from head to toe.'

I take a quick shower, then join Ollie and Ed in the kitchen where Ed is starting on his second pastry.

'Hey, Emma!' he says when he sees me. 'How's it going? Did you sleep ok?'

'Covered in bruises, apparently,' says Ollie. 'But you know Em. She never complains.'

He holds out the box of pastries. 'Apricot or raspberry? Ed seems to have eaten both of the pain au chocolat.'

'Apricot, please. But I should have bought these. I'll get up early and buy some tomorrow. It's the least I can do to thank you for letting me stay here. You'll have to tell me which bakery you like best.'

'Chez Michelle,' he says. 'But I'll come with you. I'd hate for you to be intercepted by the big, bad wolf on your way back home with your basket of goodies.'

'You're getting your fairy tales muddled up,' I say, taking the mug of coffee Ed hands me.

'I'll still come with you,' says Ollie. 'It's tricky to find, and you're terrible with maps. To be fair, it's a little off the beaten track. Ed and I had been living here for almost a year before we discovered it. Now we're some of their best customers.'

'Do you have plans for today?' Ed asks me.

'Not really. I have to make up some more boxes for tonight. I imagine Saturday is a busy night at the market.'

'I can help you with that,' says Ollie. 'Which boxes have been your best sellers this week?'

'The movie marathon box has been selling well. I'm almost out of those embroidered red blankets I put in them. And I've sold out of my festive pet boxes and taken orders for several more.'

'I'm not surprised,' he says. 'I wouldn't mind being a dog if my owner bought me a box full of pet treats and puzzles and warm winter booties. By the way, I told Tom we might drive over to visit his farm today. Ed's working in the bookshop this afternoon, but you and I can go.'

'Why would we want to do that?' I ask.

'I thought you'd be pleased. Have you forgotten it's a Christmas tree farm? Your favourite kind of tree.'

'They are when they're decorated,' I say. 'Not so much when they're growing in a muddy field.'

'Take some tinsel with you,' he says. 'I'm sure Tom won't mind.'

'I'm sure he will. Or the vicious dogs will. Tom has probably trained them to take people's legs off at the knee if they go anywhere near his precious stock.'

'The mangled leg will match your bruised back,' he says. 'Come on, Em. Some country air will do us both good. Ed and I are stuck in that bookshop day in, day out. Never a glimpse of daylight or a breath of fresh air. We'll be turning into vampires soon.'

'Do vampires run bookshops?' I ask. 'It doesn't seem likely.'

'That's why it makes such an excellent cover. Once you've finished eating all our pastries, we'll drive over there.'

'Only after I've made up my stock,' I say. 'That's what I'm here for, not running about the countryside sightseeing.'

By one o'clock, we're driving out of Christchurch towards the New Forest. I try to navigate using the map on Ollie's phone but get myself hopelessly confused.

'The map's upside down,' I say, turning the phone over. 'But each time I try to get it the right way up, it turns around again.'

Ollie pulls over to the side of the road and takes the phone from me. 'That's because you've switched it to auto rotate, you ridiculous woman. Not that the map was upside down in the first place. We aren't in Australia. The farm is right here – next to the label saying *Kingsley Christmas Tree Farm*.'

'It's further away than I expected. Do you really want to drive all the way out there?'

'It's only six miles past Honeywell,' he says. 'Their website says they have a cafe where you can buy me lunch.'

'I'll be happy to, if we ever reach it. The map has turned upside down again!'

We turn off up a small track twenty minutes later, and I point in the general direction of where I hope the farm is.

'I hope you're guiding us in the right direction,' says Ollie. 'I only have half a tank of petrol left. If we end up stranded miles from nowhere in this weather, I'll never forgive you.'

'Relax,' I tell him. 'Winters in New York will be far colder than this.'

'But I'll have my lovely, warm penthouse and office,' he says. 'I'll shuttle between them in my private, chauffeur driven limo. I won't notice the weather as I drive along Fifth Avenue, ignoring the admiring crowds lining the route. "There goes Ollie Johnson," they'll say. "He made seven million dollars before breakfast."'

'And he still can't work his coffee machine,' I add. 'I'm sure you'll be a tremendous success in New York. Until then, you're stuck driving this van. Are your tyres up to this rough track?'

'They've encountered far worse,' he says. 'Ed and I drove to Italy last year. Some of those rural roads would have defeated an expensive Mazda or a Ferrari, but my van was quite happy with them.'

'Mind out for the rottweilers,' I warn him. 'They'll drag me out the moment they catch sight of the van. And I'm not convinced shouting, "Candy Cane!" will have much effect.'

'The hellhounds seem to be at the dog sitter's today,' says Ollie, pulling up outside a small stone building with a sloping slate roof. A wooden sign above the door reads *Kingsley's Farm Shop*.

Ivy scrambles up the walls and around the windows. The building looks as though it's been growing here for centuries. Several baskets of apples stand next to the door.

'Is the shop open?' I ask.

Ollie climbs out of the van. 'Tom said it would be, and he ought to know.'

I walk around to join him. 'In which case, his pack of wild dogs must have eaten him. They'll be hiding somewhere, watching us, like the Hound of the Baskervilles.'

'Did that hound hang around farm shops waiting for his next victim?' he asks.

'Conan Doyle wasn't explicit about that. But it's likely.'

'If there are savage dogs in the vicinity,' he says, 'why don't they eat these apples or go into the shop? It would be much simpler than waiting outside hoping for someone to turn up.'

'Maybe they can't turn the handle,' I say. 'Or else they broke in earlier and ate Tom. They checked his texts and saw he'd sent you directions to this place, so now they're lurking behind the till waiting for us to arrive.'

Ollie opens the door and motions for me to go inside. 'I'm happy to take the risk. It's been a long time since we ate those pastries, and I want my lunch.'

Chapter Seven

I step inside and look around with interest. The shop is well laid out, with shelves of local jams and jars of honey. Dried herbs and flowers hang from the beams above my head. There's a sturdy table in the centre of the shop, filled with baskets of eggs and bundles of vegetables. A hand-painted sign over the archway says *Cafe This Way*.

'That looks hopeful,' says Ollie. 'Is anyone here?'

A woman emerges from the room behind the till. 'How can I help you today?'

'We're here for lunch,' says Ollie. 'If the cafe is still open?'

'It's open until five o'clock,' she says. 'Come on through.'

We follow her through the archway into the small cafe. An assortment of mismatched tables and chairs are arranged on the deep grey flagstones. Each table has a candle in the centre and a small arrangement of silk flowers.

'Sit wherever you like,' says the woman. 'As you can see, we aren't too busy.'

Not busy is an understatement. Ollie and I are the only ones here. Maybe there were lots of other customers earlier in the day. I hope so. It's sad to see a place like this empty.

The shop door opens, and the woman waves. 'In here, Tom!'

'Coming!' says a voice, and a moment later, Tom walks into the cafe.

'I'd given up hope of seeing you here today,' he says when he sees us.

'That's Emma's fault,' says Ollie. 'She can't learn to read a map to save her life.'

'I also didn't know we were coming until just before we left,' I say. 'I had no time to consult my globe and prepare.'

'This is Ollie and Emma,' Tom says to the woman. 'Emma and I work together at the markets each evening. This is my mother, Helen.'

Helen beams at me. 'Tom's told me all about you. I was so interested to hear what you're selling. Such an original idea. And is this your … partner?'

'Only in crime,' Ollie tells her. 'I have a much better partner than this at home. He can even read maps. Ed and I have been together for about five years. We also run a bookshop.'

'A bookshop?' she says. 'Would I know it?'

'The Rabbit Hole. Near Christchurch Quay.'

'I've been in there!' she says. 'You have those lovely stained glass windows.'

'We do,' says Ollie. 'We also make the best hot chocolate in Hampshire. But only for very special customers.'

'I forgot to mention to Mum you might be coming over today,' says Tom.

'That was wise,' says Ollie. 'The chances of us arriving were less than fifty-fifty once I'd let Emma loose with the map. We could have ended up axle deep in a snowdrift on some desolate moor.'

'We don't have a lot of desolate moors around here,' says Tom. 'But we do have the odd rickety bridge and abandoned barn.'

'I'll be careful driving back,' promises Ollie. 'That van is the most expensive thing I own. Sad, but true. I can't afford to replace it in the near future. The bookshop is barely breaking even at the moment.'

'What a shame,' says Helen. 'It's the same for us. Business isn't what it used to be. This time last year, the cafe was full on Saturdays. Now we're lucky if we have ten customers during the entire day.'

'We'll try to make up for that,' says Ollie. 'Bring out your largest lobster and a bottle of your finest champagne. Emma's paying.'

'I'm afraid we aren't licenced,' says Helen.

'I'm glad to hear it,' I say. 'Not only can I not afford champagne, but Ollie's driving. I want to arrive back at the fair in one piece tonight.'

Helen points to a board near the window. 'We don't have an extensive menu. The lunch specials are on that blackboard.'

'It all looks great,' I say. 'I'd love some of your Harvest Soup.'

'It comes with crusty homemade rolls,' she says.

'Even better,' I say. 'How about you, Ollie?'

He studies the board. 'I'm torn between your chicken and mushroom pie and your Ploughman's Platter.'

'I suggest the Ploughman's,' says Tom. 'We get our cheese from a local dairy farm, and it comes with Mum's homemade pickles.'

Helen disappears, and Tom pulls out a chair and sits down. 'Do you mind if I join you?'

'Not at all,' I say. 'But you should know Ollie doesn't share food. You'll have to buy your own.'

'I had my lunch an hour ago,' he says. 'I've been cutting the trees for tonight, and I was starving.'

'Am I correct in assuming the fair is busier at the weekends?' I ask.

'Pretty much. It starts off fairly quietly at the beginning of December, then numbers build up once people realise Christmas is only a week away. That's when we get our best Christmas tree sales.'

'I can't imagine leaving it so late,' I say. 'Why would anyone want to miss out on any of the magic? It seems such a waste.'

'People used to wait to put up their trees until after they'd finished work on Christmas Eve,' says Tom. 'You'd have hated that.'

'I would,' I agree. 'I know Christmas only comes once a year, but that's all the more reason to make sure it lasts for as long as possible.'

Helen returns with my soup, which smells delicious.

Ollie surveys his enormous plate of bread and cheese with satisfaction. 'This should do the trick. These pickles look great. Did you really make them yourself, Helen?'

'I did,' she says. 'We sell them in the shop too.'

'That's your Christmas present for me and Ed sorted,' Ollie tells me. 'A couple of crates of pickles would hit the spot perfectly.'

'I'm afraid we've almost sold out,' says Helen. 'But we have some strawberry and ginger jam if you like that sort of thing.'

'He does,' I say. 'But I've already bought his present, so he's out of luck. I'll buy myself a jar, though. I love homemade jam.'

'It's one of our best sellers,' she says. 'We grow the fruit here, so it seems a pity not to do something with it. We used to do well with the pick-your-own soft fruit, but business has tailed off over the past few years. I suppose it's easier for people to go to the supermarket.'

'My dad took me to pick strawberries every year when I was young,' I say. 'It's one of my favourite memories. The man running the farm threatened to weigh me before and after we'd picked our strawberries and bill Dad for the difference.'

'We always priced that in for families with young children,' she says. 'It was such a pleasure to watch them running around and competing to find the biggest strawberries.'

I finish my soup. 'That was delicious, Helen. Like summer in a bowl.'

'It's a winter vegetable soup,' says Tom.

'I don't care,' I say. 'That's what it tasted like to me. My dad grew tomatoes each summer, and Mum made tomato soup. This reminds me of that.'

'City girl,' he teases me. 'I can tell you didn't grow up on a farm.'

'You're a city boy too,' I say. 'So, you have no room to talk.'

'I haven't forgotten my roots,' he says. 'I can identify kale and pumpkin in a soup when I need to.'

'Emma's right about tasting tomato,' says Helen. 'We had a glut this year, so I canned several kilos.'

'I told you so!' I tell Tom triumphantly. 'I'm not so stupid after all.'

'When you two have finished bickering,' says Ollie, 'I would like to say this is the best Ploughman's lunch I have ever eaten. I'm bringing Ed here for lunch next weekend.'

'Tom and I weren't bickering,' I say. 'We were trading culinary expertise.'

'You were bickering,' he insists. 'Just like you do every evening at the fair.'

'That's not true!' I say. 'Is it, Tom?'

'Do you want me to answer honestly?'

'Of course!' I say. 'Well, maybe. It depends with whom you're planning to agree.'

Tom looks from me to Ollie. 'I'd like to agree with you both.'

'You can't,' says Ollie. 'Don't be such a wimp. Pick a side!'

Tom smiles at me. 'I would say you and I have … robust discussions.'

'What do you disagree about?' asks Helen. 'Politics or the environment or musical tastes?'

'Nothing like that,' I say. 'We mostly disagree about Christmas.'

She looks surprised. 'What about it?'

'How important it is.' I'm aware of how ridiculous I sound.

'Important in what way?' she asks.

'To people in general,' I say. 'It's a wonderful time of year and an opportunity for people to come together and enjoy the magic of the season. Whereas Tom seems to think it's all about the bottom line.'

She darts a quick look at Tom. 'I see.'

'That's rather a one-sided view of things,' says Tom. 'I'd say Emma is too focussed on making Christmas perfect, while I'm more about letting it happen and seeing how it goes.'

'You can't let Christmas happen!' I protest. 'Someone has to think about it and plan for it. Otherwise, it ends up being just another day.'

'Which suits some people fine,' he says. 'I have no objection as to how you want to organise your own Christmas. And your sales are going well, so there's clearly a market for what you're doing. As long as you make room for the idea that not everyone sees the holiday the same way as you do.'

His tone is gentle, but I feel stung by the implied criticism. 'Of course, I understand that. But you don't have to make me feel as though what I'm trying to do isn't worthwhile, because it is.'

'Fair enough,' he says. 'I admit you're fun to tease because you take it so seriously, but I take your point. And in return, maybe you could avoid giving the impression you see me as someone whose dearest wish is to track down Santa as he flies over the UK on Christmas Eve and take him out with an air rifle.'

'What was Tom like as a little boy?' I ask Helen. 'Did he hate Christmas as much in those days?'

Tom snorts. 'What did I just tell you?'

'Sorry,' I say. 'I meant to ask whether Tom's attitude towards Christmas was always one of studied neutrality?'

'It's such a long time ago,' says Helen. 'I remember Tom and Katie baking cookies to leave out for Santa each year. And Tom loved to go out to the vegetable patch and choose the best carrot for Rudolph. But Christmas was a busy time of year for our family. We were working flat out until Christmas Eve, so we didn't enjoy the magic run up to it that your family obviously did.'

'That's understandable,' I say. 'Have you always run the market stall too?'

'We did when Michael was alive,' she says. 'I didn't plan to do it this year, but Tom insisted on coming back to run it for me.'

'That was nice of him,' I say.

'What did I tell you?' says Tom. 'I'm a living saint.'

'If you've finished trading compliments,' says Ollie, 'I'm afraid we need to get going. I promised Ed I'd be back by four o'clock. We have to finish our stocktake before Monday. We can't all sit around at Christmas fairs every night discussing the role Christmas plays in our modern culture. Some of us have actual work to do.'

I look around the cafe. 'I'm glad you don't allow the rottweilers in here. I'm not a fan of large dogs.'

'Rottweilers?' says Helen, and Tom laughs.

'I believe Emma is referring to Bonnie.'

'I thought you had a pack of fierce dogs,' I say.

Helen looks even more puzzled. 'Bonnie is a border collie. We adopted her after she had an accident on the sheep farm where she worked. She's a little lame, but she trots around pretty well, and she's wonderful company for me.'

'Tom definitely referred to rottweilers,' I say. 'Are you sure you don't have a pack hiding somewhere around?'

'Quite sure,' says Helen. 'It isn't the sort of thing you could overlook.'

'We didn't see any barbed wire either when we drove up the track,' I say. 'Or mined trenches. Maybe we came up the wrong road.'

'There's only one road up here,' says Helen. 'What on earth has Tom been telling you?'

'He implied your whole operation was protected by a local infantry battalion,' I say. 'We were surprised to make it all the way to the shop without coming under sniper fire.'

'I may have exaggerated slightly,' admits Tom. 'But Emma seemed extremely anxious about our security, so I wanted to put her mind at rest.'

'We should get going,' says Ollie. 'Lovely to meet you, Helen. I'll definitely bring Ed here next weekend.'

'I may see you at the markets,' Helen says to me. 'I like to visit them each year, and I'm most intrigued to see your stall. With any luck, I can get all my Christmas shopping done in one go this year.'

Chapter Eight

Saturday evening is as busy as Tom predicted. Either the crowds are building up as Christmas grows closer or there isn't anything good on TV tonight.

Business is brisk. I sell out of several family craft boxes and have to take orders for more. I'm starting to believe this could become a successful business.

I gradually become aware of a commotion opposite my stall. Santa is no longer sitting in his spray painted sleigh, punctuating the crisp night air with his loud Ho, Ho, Hos. He's standing next to one of the reindeer, shouting and waving a bottle. Several upset looking parents are ushering their children away from the queue.

'What's going on?' I ask Tom.

'Santa may have been indulging in a little something to keep out the cold,' he says.

Lucy comes running over. 'Someone said there was a problem with Santa.'

'You could say that,' says Tom.

'Do we need to call an ambulance?' she asks.

'I doubt it,' he says. 'But I wouldn't advise going near him with any naked flames.'

She looks startled. 'You don't mean …?'

'I'm afraid so,' he says. 'Santas are human too.'

'They aren't supposed to be!' I say. 'They're supposed to be magical.'

Tom gives me a mocking smile. 'I'm sorry, Emma. I didn't realise you still believed.'

'You know what I mean! He's a magical figure to human children. Anyone lucky enough to play him should respect that.'

'I don't think he got the memo,' he says.

Several people have rushed across to the reindeer enclosure, headed by Frances, the market director. Santa turns to meet them, whirling his fists. A group of men encircles him at a safe distance, trying to corral him. To my annoyance, I hear Tom laugh.

One man makes a dart towards Santa, who leaps backwards, colliding with a fibreglass reindeer and sending it flying.

'Don't worry, Emma. It wasn't Rudolph,' says Tom.

'Very funny. But someone might get hurt. Can't you do anything?'

He nods and strides over to the enclosure, where Santa is taking another swig from his bottle. He offers it to Tom, who laughs and shakes his head.

'Come on, mate. You need to put that down and go home. There are children here. You're upsetting them.'

Santa gives him a bleary look. 'I'm upsetting *them*? What about me? I sit here every night in the freezing cold, listening to spoiled kids whining about all the things they want me to bring them. It's no life for a man of my talents.'

'I'm sure it isn't,' says Tom. 'Let me run you home, and you can sleep it off in your lovely warm bed.'

'But what about my naughty and nice list?' demands Santa.

'You can leave that with me,' says Tom. 'I'll make sure it gets filled out properly.'

'I hope so,' says Santa. 'It's a grave responsibility. I'm not allowed to delegate it, even to the elves.'

'I promise I won't let the elves get their hands on it,' says Tom. 'I'll keep it safely under lock and key until Christmas Eve.'

'If you're sure,' says Santa. 'Perhaps a lie down might be a good idea. I'm feeling unaccountably dizzy.'

'That's nothing to the headache you'll have tomorrow morning,' says Tom. 'Make sure Mrs Claus gives you plenty of water to drink before you go to bed.'

Santa hiccups. 'I'll remind her. Wonderful woman. Never forgets anything she's told. But she may not be there. Said she had some meeting or other tonight. Women's book club or something. Can't think why she bothers, but she seems to like it.'

'Tell the elves then,' says Tom. 'Unless they're too busy in their workshop?'

Santa frowns in an effort to remember. 'I live in the North Pole, you know. About ten miles from here.'

The market organiser steps forward and takes his bottle from him. 'You live in Inkbridge. Jason has volunteered to give you a ride home.'

'In my sleigh?' says Santa, whose belligerent demeanour has been replaced by an air of polite curiosity.

'You'll have to leave that here,' says Tom. 'Air traffic control has strict rules about pilot blood alcohol levels.'

'Quite right,' says Santa. 'Great responsibility. Can't be drinking before setting off. The reindeer wouldn't like it. Apparently, people think Rudolph has a red nose because he drinks too much, but that isn't the case. I don't remember what his deal is. Maybe he has a cold.'

Lucy is shaking with laughter. 'Who thinks Rudolph has a drink problem?' she whispers to me.

'I have no idea,' I say. 'But do you want to argue the toss with him?'

'I most definitely do not! Tom's doing a great job, isn't he?'

'He is. I'm surprised he's bothered about Christmas being ruined for anyone. But he may have been thinking about the children.'

'He was thinking about you,' she says. 'You looked so upset when it kicked off.'

'I was upset,' I say. 'But only because I saw a young girl crying. Poor thing. I hope she doesn't remember this.'

'I expect she was more upset by the shouting,' says Lucy. 'But Tom has that under control. He and Santa appear to have developed quite a rapport.'

We watch as Tom shepherds Santa towards a small hut at the side of the reindeer enclosure. They emerge a few minutes later, Santa now wearing jeans and a parka. His hair is standing on end, and there are traces of shiny glue around his chin.

'That's great,' says Tom. 'Jason's taking you home now, and this will all seem like a bad dream in the morning.'

Santa throws his arm around Jason's shoulders. 'Stout fellow! Maybe we could stop at The Red Lion on the way home.'

We watch them weave across the grass towards the car park. Tom comes back to his stall, and Frances follows him.

'I appreciate you stepping in,' she tells Tom. 'What a disgraceful scene.'

'It could have been worse,' he says.

'I don't see how. The first I heard of it was when a parent came to tell me Santa had offered his son a cigarette.'

Lucy gives a snort of laughter. 'He didn't?'

'Yes, he did,' says Frances. 'When Edward told him he didn't smoke, Santa said he shouldn't either. He's trying to give up, and would Edward like a shot of bourbon instead?'

'And what did Edward say to that?' asks Tom.

'He didn't,' says Frances grimly. 'His father stepped in and threatened to knock Santa's block off. At which point, Santa pulled the bottle of whisky out of his pocket and offered to smash it over the father's head. That's when the mother came to look for me. They're threatening to sue the fair for damages.'

'That seems rather extreme,' says Tom.

'That's what I said, but people think they can sue everyone these days.'

'Where are they now?' I ask.

'Waiting for me over by the main entrance,' says Frances. 'The father wants to know what I'm prepared to offer them to make up for their ruined experience.'

'Do you have someone else to play Santa?' says Lucy.

Frances looks even more harassed. 'I can't ask just anyone. They have to be registered. I'll try to find someone tomorrow. This one came from an agency. I'll be telling them exactly what I think of their due diligence.'

'Why don't you take the family to my stall?' says Lucy. 'Tell Edward he can choose anything he likes.'

'That's kind of you,' says Frances. 'I doubt they'll fall for it, but it's worth a try.'

'Tell him he can choose a children's Christmas box from my stall too,' I say.

Frances hurries off, and Lucy and I turn to look at Tom.

'What?' he says. 'I'm not giving them one of my Christmas trees. Edward would only spike his hand on a branch, and the parents would add me to the lawsuit. He'd far prefer what you two are offering.'

'What he wanted was to see Santa,' I say. 'But there's nothing we can do about that.'

Tom sighs. 'There may be. I'm certified to work with children because of the children's events we used to hold at our farm. I don't know whether it would cover me for such a demanding role as this, but we could ask Frances.'

'You'd be prepared to step in?' I say, hardly able to believe my ears. 'But you hate Christmas!'

'Still not true,' he says. 'I can take it or leave it, but so can many people. What do you say – shall I volunteer my services for tonight?'

I give him an impulsive hug. 'That would be wonderful. Thank you so much.'

'I doubt I'll do such a good job as my illustrious predecessor,' he warns me. 'Those are large shoes to fill. All I can do is my best. But if things get sticky, I can always offer the brats the odd cigar or nip of whisky.'

'Frances is taking those people over to my stall,' says Lucy. 'See you in a minute.'

She runs over and starts talking to the small boy and his parents.

'Has Santa left his costume here?' I ask Tom. 'We'll be stuck if he hasn't.'

'He wasn't carrying anything when he left,' he says. 'So, I assume he has. I expect it reeks of whisky.'

'It will air out,' I say. 'Put it on while we wait for Frances.'

'Not a hope,' he says. 'She hasn't agreed to it yet. Hopefully, she won't. I'm regretting having offered to do this.'

'No, you aren't. You aren't half as Grinchy as you like to pretend. You don't want to disappoint the children any more than I do.'

He blows out his cheeks. 'If you say so. You and Lucy can watch my stall for me. And I know exactly how much is in my cash box, so no funny business.'

'The Christmas elves are bound to notice your sacrifice and make you a pair of shoes tonight,' I tell him. 'Make sure you do your job properly. I can't afford to give away any more of my stock to placate angry parents.'

Frances trots over to us. 'Lucy has told me about your kind offer, Tom. I can't tell you how grateful I am. Are you able to start at once? There are plenty of children here tonight, and we don't want to let them down.'

Tom gives me a half smile and walks towards the reindeer enclosure.

'I only hope he can erase the unfortunate impression,' says Frances. 'Little Edward is clutching a bag of gingerbread trains and seems quite happy. And his mother says she's seen your stall and would love one of your Christmas craft boxes. If Tom can complete the triple and give Edward the perfect Santa experience, we may avoid that lawsuit after all.'

Chapter Nine

Tom appears ten minutes later, dressed in Santa's red robes and wearing a long, white beard. At least, I assume it's him. He's the correct height, but that's all. I couldn't in good conscience swear in a court of law to its being Tom. Maybe that's why so many books and films use the idea of someone dressing up as Santa to commit a crime or make their escape unnoticed. A Christmas fair would be the perfect environment for criminal enterprises. The Case of the Kidnapped Reindeer or the Missing Mince Pies.

The man in the Santa suit sees me watching and waves. It isn't a positive proof of his identity, but it's a good sign. I wave back as he climbs into the rickety sleigh and gestures to the first child to join him. I notice without surprise that the little boy's mother stays close. Word of Santa's erratic behaviour must have spread.

I can't hear what Tom says to the child, but their interaction seems to go well. The mother doesn't drag him away and storm off, so Tom must have remembered enough Santa-adjacent things to say to him.

The boy jumps down, and the next parent leads his children over to the sleigh. He has twin girls of about five. They both jump onto Tom's lap and start talking to him earnestly. They're clearly used to doing everything together. Tom chats with them for a minute, poses for a photo, then hands them back to their father.

I can't watch every single child while I'm busy selling my stock and keeping an eye on Tom's stall. I take the money for three of his trees and hope to goodness I haven't charged the wrong amount.

Lucy comes over an hour later, carrying two paper cups.

'Hot chocolate for you both,' she says. 'How's Santa doing? Does he have time for a break?'

'There's only one more child in the queue,' I say. 'We could line up behind him and sneak Tom his drink under the pretext of handing him our Christmas lists.'

'I don't dare leave my stall any longer,' she says. 'The guy from the hot dog stand is watching it for me. Can you do it?'

I carry the drinks over to the reindeer enclosure, where I hear Tom telling a small boy that his sleigh runs on magic, so he doesn't have to keep stopping for petrol.

'My dad's getting an electric car,' says the boy. 'Maybe you could get one of those too.'

'It's kind of you to worry about me,' says Tom. 'But Santa doesn't need electricity. He powers himself. Off you go now, and don't forget what I told you about making your bed each morning.'

The boy slides off his lap and turns to face him. 'I'm not sure I believe in you, but I thought I'd visit you anyway in case you forgot about my Lego castle.'

'The important thing is not that you believe in me, but that I believe in you,' says Tom solemnly. 'Make sure you go to sleep early on Christmas Eve or I won't be able to deliver your presents.'

The boy gives him a dubious look and nods. 'See you, Santa!'

He runs over to his parents, and Tom laughs. 'It's hard work being a possibly fictional figure. I'm not quite sure whether to believe in myself.'

'You should,' I say. 'You're as real as anyone, and a lot nicer than most. Thank you for doing this. Lucy brought you a cup of hot chocolate and a reindeer cookie.'

'Great,' he says. 'Santa left half a bottle of whisky in his hut. He must have overlooked it when he left in such a hurry. Maybe I could add a shot while no one's looking.'

'Don't you dare!' I say. 'You know what happened when your predecessor tried that. Control yourself and eat your cookie instead. I wonder whether Santa will remember the whisky when he wakes up tomorrow. You'd better hide it.'

'That's not the only thing he left behind,' says Tom. He pulls a piece of paper from his pocket and hands it to me.

'What's this?' I say.

'It's his naughty and nice list. It appears Santa took his job seriously. Or he did until the point at which his blood alcohol level threatened to overtake his actual blood volume.'

I scan the list. 'I don't think much of the calibre of the children who've visited this fair tonight. Not a single one has made it onto Santa's nice list.'

'It's a sad commentary on our times,' says Tom, taking a bite of his cookie.

'Susie Green ought to be ashamed of herself,' I say. 'Santa writes here that she asked him for a unicorn, and he doesn't have time to take spoiled children to petting zoos.'

'I'd have put her on the naughty list too,' agrees Tom. 'But she's nowhere near as badly behaved as Harrison Turner. Imagine asking for a robot butler! Santa is quite right to note he's not a tech-support worker. What else has he scribbled next to Harrison's name?'

I squint at the paper. 'Cola? I'd have thought Santa would want Harrison on bread and water for the foreseeable future.'

'Coal?' suggests Tom.

'That makes more sense. Do people still do that when their children are naughty?'

'Archie Smith's parents don't,' he says. 'They're getting an electric car. I'm afraid you'll have to stop distracting me now. I see a family coming this way with several small children in tow. I hope none of them asks me for a playhouse. Santa isn't a real estate agent!'

I spend the rest of the evening alternating between my stall and Tom's. I'm delighted when I sell his last Christmas tree as the fair closes.

Tom joins me in his Santa outfit. 'How was business?'

'Brisk,' I say. 'I've sold all your trees. I couldn't remember the exact prices, so I charged everyone a pound. I hope that was ok.'

He looks at his cash box. 'Santa's elves appear to have made up the difference, so that's fine.'

'You must be in their good books,' I say, and he smiles.

'Don't sound so surprised. Look how nobly I stepped into the breach and played Santa tonight. If that doesn't prove what a Christmas lover I am, I don't know what does.'

'You win,' I say. 'The Christmas halo belongs to you. Will there be a presentation on the final day of the fair?'

'I wouldn't be surprised,' he says. 'And a statue too. But I hope they find someone else to play him tomorrow night. I'm not cut out for too much Christmas cheer.'

'Is there nothing about Christmas you enjoy?' I say.

'Plenty of things! Who doesn't look forward to frantic last-minute shopping, accompanied by relentless muzak? Or spending hours looking for the one bulb that's blown in your string of lights? Or pretending your grandmother's top secret fruit cake recipe is delicious, and you'd love another slice, when it would be far more useful as a doorstop?'

'Those things aren't what Christmas is about!' I protest. 'They're incidentals.'

'Incidentals that happen every single Christmas without fail,' he says. 'What beats me is what you find so exciting about it. I can understand why Christmas is magical for children. But don't most adults grow out of it?'

I gesture to the groups of people walking back across the village green, talking and laughing. 'Apparently not. Otherwise, this fair would be out of business.'

'I've given you my list of Christmas marvels,' says Tom. 'Why don't you give me yours?'

'Because Christmas isn't a list,' I say in frustration.

'Santa begs to differ,' he says, waving the piece of paper. 'I'm taking this home and framing it. I have a feeling Santa and I have a lot in common.'

'That wasn't the real Santa,' I say without thinking.

He laughs. 'Why would you tell me that just as I was getting into the spirit of things?'

'Sorry to burst your bubble,' I say. 'But I can't make you a list. It's impossible to put it into words.'

'Show me!' he surprises me.

'Show you what?'

'What Christmas means to you. I'm serious. Put your money where your mouth is, Emma Hartley. This fair is closed on Wednesdays, doubtless to give Santa a chance to sleep it off. I'm free this Wednesday. You can take me wherever you like, and we can do whatever you want. If by the end of the day, you've managed to show me the magic of Christmas, I promise never to say a bad word about the season again.'

'Are you serious?' I ask.

'Deadly,' he says. 'I'd offer to do the same in return and take you out for a Christmassy day, Tom Kingsley style, but I suspect you wouldn't enjoy it. It would start with us being unable to find a parking space at the shops. And it would only get worse, culminating in a visit to drunk Santa and ending up on his naughty list. I vote we give that a miss. But you ought to do better than that. According to you, the magic of Christmas is everywhere. The difficulty will be how to fit everything into one day. What do you say?'

I study his face. He appears to be serious. I don't like the thought of messing things up and making him even more cynical about Christmas. But that would be difficult. And it's hard to resist the temptation to prove him wrong while enjoying some of my own favourite things.

'Alright,' I say at last. 'Challenge accepted. Meet me at Ollie's flat at nine o'clock sharp on Wednesday morning. We'll enjoy a magical day of Christmas, Emma style.'

Chapter Ten

I walk over to The Rabbit Hole after lunch the following day. Ed is nowhere to be seen, but Ollie is sorting through a stack of children's books.

'I didn't expect to see you here,' he says when I walk in. 'Aren't you supposed to be making up some more boxes?'

'Yes, but I need some help, and you're the only person I knew how to find.'

'I'm flattered,' he says. 'What sort of help?'

'I was talking to Tom about Christmas last night.'

Ollie rolls his eyes. 'For a change. There are a million other subjects the pair of you could talk about. Why constantly revert to the one you'll never agree on?'

'That's the point,' I say. 'I may persuade him to agree on this one. He suggested we go out on Wednesday so I can show him the magic of Christmas. Only I don't have the faintest idea of how to go about it.'

'The Magic of Christmas sounds like a cruise liner,' he says. 'Are you taking him to the Caribbean?'

'I couldn't afford that if I wanted to. I'm thinking of something more local, but I don't know what.'

'You're the expert,' he says. 'If you don't know the answer, how should I?'

'I'm simply looking for some suggestions. What's your favourite part of Christmas?'

'I've told you,' he says. 'Seasonal beer and spirits. That's when Christmas really starts for me.'

Ed wanders in carrying a pile of books. 'Hi, Em! What are you doing here?'

'Not what one might hope,' says Ollie. 'Most people who enter our hallowed portals do so with the vague intention of purchasing some form of reading material. But not Emma. All she wants is to find out what I like best about Christmas.'

'Did you tell her?' says Ed.

'I mentioned something about beer.'

Ed shakes his head. 'Rookie mistake. You should have withheld the information until she bought something.'

'Fine!' I say. 'What would you like me to buy?'

'How about Crime and Punishment?' says Ollie. 'For some unknown reason, copies of that book don't seem to be flying off the shelves as fast as you might imagine. Maybe it's not Christmassy enough.'

'Do you have something lighter?' I ask.

'Physically or metaphorically?' says Ed. 'How about a comic? We've just got the new Simpsons annual in.'

'Something in between,' I say. 'Do you have any good Christmassy novels? They might give me some ideas for Wednesday.'

Ed frowns. 'Christmassy novels? Why didn't that occur to you while you were doing the orders, Ollie? I hear seasonal literature is all the rage these days.'

'Never mind,' I say. 'I can see a stack of Christmas romances on that display. I'll choose one of those.'

'I didn't realise you were looking for romance,' says Ollie. 'Have you mentioned that to Tom?'

'Don't be ridiculous,' I say, annoyed to feel my cheeks redden. 'This is research so I can show him what Christmas is about. You're no help, so maybe – ' I turn over the nearest book and inspect its front cover – 'Snowflakes over Broadway will be.'

'That's a New York Times bestseller,' says Ed. 'What the author doesn't know about romantic Christmases isn't worth knowing. Danielle someone or other, isn't it?'

'She's quite a well-known writer,' adds Ollie. 'I believe she's the daughter of Charlie Someone-or-Other, youngest son of the Shropshire Someone-or-Others.'

'I'm not looking for a romantic Christmas,' I say. 'All I need is some ideas for a magical one.'

'Remind me what the book is about?' says Ed.

I turn it over and look at the blurb.

In the bustling heart of Manhattan, two hearts are about to collide in a winter romance. Sophie is a talented pastry chef who dreams of opening her own bakery. Alex is a workaholic executive who's lost sight of what really matters.

As the Christmas season approaches, Sophie is determined to make her pop-up bakery a success, while Alex is desperate to meet his deadline for his year-end bonus. When a chance encounter brings them together, both their worlds are turned upside down.

Will the enchantment of Christmas in the city help Sophie and Alex find love and rediscover the joy of the season? Love and holiday magic dance through the pages of this charming winter romance.

'Disappointing,' says Ollie. 'Don't we sell any books about Christmas tree salesmen and florists? Or a bookshop owner and his gorgeous partner?'

'I could keep looking,' I say.

'Don't bother,' he says. 'I expect I'd have noticed it in the catalogue.'

I hand the book to Ed. 'This is the sort of thing I want. All about the magic of Christmas. I'll buy it.'

'Ring it up before she changes her mind,' says Ollie. 'Getting Emma to open her purse is a rare event.'

'Not true,' I say. 'I'm happy to open my purse. It's just that there's never much in it.'

'I'll give you the friends and family discount,' says Ed, putting the book into a bag.

'No, you won't!' I say. 'You're already giving me a place to stay for several weeks. I can pay full price for this book.'

'Too late.' He reaches over and takes my card, tapping it on the reader. 'You can buy another one when you've finished reading that.'

'She won't need to,' says Ollie. 'It sounds exactly like every Christmas rom com ever written.'

'Thanks for the recommendation,' I say. 'Do you talk like that to all your customers?'

'Only the ones who've already paid. We don't offer refunds unless our stock is damaged, and that book was pristine when Ed handed it to you. You're stuck with it.'

'Can I read it in here?' I ask.

'Be our guest,' he says. 'There are plenty of chairs, and it adds to the ambience for our customers to see a beautiful woman engrossed in a book. Or you.'

I spend the afternoon curled up in an armchair reading, hardly noticing when Ollie brings me a hot chocolate. I finish the book just before closing time.

'How was it?' asks Ollie. 'Did it give you lots of amazing ideas for your date?'

I close the book. 'Alex and Sophie had a wonderful Christmas season. They took a carriage ride through Central Park and drank cocktails at the top of the Empire State Building. They bought roasted chestnuts from a street vendor and went to see a Broadway show. And they had dinner at the Rainbow Room and saw the Christmas tree in Times Square.'

'It sounds terribly cliched to me,' says Ed. 'Did they also take a helicopter ride over the city?'

'A hot air balloon,' I say. 'Alex thought it would be quieter and more romantic.'

Ollie sits on the sofa next to me. 'You and Tom can't get over to New York and back in a day, but there must be something in there you could use. Which date was their best one?'

'Ice skating at the Rockefeller Centre,' I say. 'Sophie took Alex one evening to show him you don't need to spend lots of money to get into the Christmas spirit.'

'There's an outdoor skating rink in Marsham,' he says. 'Why not take Tom there?'

'I can't skate,' I say.

'So what?' he asks. 'I doubt Alex and Sophie were doing triple lutzes all over the place.'

'They weren't,' I say. 'She sprained her ankle after half an hour. He sat up all night with her in the hospital, even though he had a huge work presentation the following morning.'

'There you go,' he says. 'Sprain one of your ankles, or preferably both, and Tom will realise the true meaning of Christmas.'

'That's not what Alex realised,' I say. 'It was the moment he understood Sophie was more important to him than earning his bonus.'

'Is that what you want Tom to realise?' he asks, and I flush.

'Absolutely not! I'm only trying to show him Christmas can be fun.'

'Then I wouldn't advise you to sprain your ankle,' he says. 'I don't want to carry your boxes all by myself if I can help it. But skating is a good idea. It's very Christmassy. What else did the characters get up to?'

'He helped her out at the soup kitchen where she volunteered,' I say. 'It showed him not everyone was as fortunate as he was, which was another excellent lesson for him.'

'Tom volunteered to play Santa Claus,' says Ollie. 'Which means he's already less selfish than this Alex character. I have to say I don't much like the sound of him. I don't believe he deserved Sophie. It sounds as though she settled.'

'You haven't read it,' I say. 'Alex was a changed man by the end of the book.'

'I'm not sure anyone really changes,' he says. 'Which is why I don't hold out much hope for what you're trying to do. Tom doesn't like Christmas very much. So, what?'

'It was his idea, not mine,' I say. 'If I'm doing this, I'm doing it properly.'

'Fine,' he says. 'So, we have ice skating and soup kitchens. What else?'

'Sophie took him to see her bakery, and he helped her ice the Christmas cookies because her assistant was sick. Sophie wouldn't have been able to fulfil her orders otherwise.'

'A touching story,' he comments. 'I can see why you enjoyed it.'

'It's better than your suggestion,' I say. 'If I'd read Crime and Punishment this afternoon, I'd be taking Tom to visit a pawnbroker, followed by a quick trip to Siberia. I'm going back to the flat to start dinner now. Maybe I'll put the book next to your bed for some light night time reading. It should give you some wonderful ideas for when you and Ed move to New York.'

Chapter Eleven

I'm surprised to see Helen climb out of the Kingsley truck the following evening. She carries a couple of small Christmas trees over to Tom's stall.

'Hello, Emma,' she says when she sees me.

'Can I help you with those?' I ask.

'I'm only carrying the small ones,' she says. 'I leave the actual work to Tom. So, this is your stall – A Boxful of Christmas. It looks lovely. No wonder you're doing so well. How did you come up with such an original idea?'

'I'm not sure it's that original,' I say. 'I'm only grouping things together by theme. People have been selling Christmas hampers forever, and they're just foodstuffs arranged by theme. My boxes are a collection of Christmas items, that's all.'

'They're a lot more than that,' she says. 'They're such a thoughtful idea.'

She opens the lid of the nearest box. 'Christmas for One. What's inside this? Oh, it's lovely, Emma! A tiny tree with a string of lights, a gingerbread scented candle, a Christmas bubble bath, a Christmas music CD, a book, and a box of chocolates. Do you sell many of these?'

'A fair few,' I say. 'But my best seller has been the children's Night Before Christmas activity box.'

'I like the fact so many of these contain books,' she says, opening more of the boxes. 'So few people seem to have the time to read these days.'

'I'm lucky to be friends with a bookshop owner,' I say.

'Ollie?' she asks.

'That's right. He and Ed agreed to provide the books on a sale-or-return basis. It benefits both of our businesses. They've been amazing. They offered me a place to stay while I was here, and they've helped me make up these boxes. I couldn't have done any of this without them.'

'I'd like to meet Ed,' says Helen. 'I hope he and Ollie do come over to visit us before Christmas.'

'You can count on it,' I say. 'Ed is a total foodie. As soon as he heard Ollie describe the cheese your neighbour makes, he checked your location and threatened to drive over by himself if Ollie wouldn't take him. Unlike me, Ed is excellent at reading maps!'

'I'll let our neighbours know how much Ollie enjoyed their cheese,' she says. 'Dairy farms are having a tough time of it, and they're trying to diversify as much as possible. Meadowbrook Farm moved into cheese making about ten years ago, and they're making quite a success of it.'

Tom arrives carrying the largest Christmas tree I've ever seen. It must be almost eight feet tall.

'Who's going to buy that?' I say. 'It's too big for most people's houses.'

He dumps the tree onto the grass. 'You'd be surprised. Some people go all out for Christmas. Much like you, Emma. I imagine you have a tree at home that takes up your entire living area.'

'My living area is also my sleeping area,' I say. 'I rent a studio flat in Oxford.'

'Does that mean you sleep outside in a tent each December to make room for the tree?' he asks.

'I do not. I sleep in my bed as usual. I have a small, tasteful Christmas tree, and I decorate it with a different theme each year.'

'We've always supplied the Manor House at Compton,' says Tom. 'They have a much larger tree than this.'

'I imagine a manor house has plenty of room,' I say. 'You could never fit that tree into a three-bedroom, semi-detached house.'

'Which is why we sell smaller ones as well,' he says. 'That way, people can put them into different sized spaces.'

'Thanks for the maths lesson,' I say.

'Have Ollie and Ed got their tree yet?' Helen asks me.

'They have a beautiful one in their bookshop,' I say. 'I helped them to decorate it with miniature books and bookmarks. We made a star for the top out of the pages of a damaged book.'

'What was it about?' asks Tom.

'Something about carbon dating,' I say. 'But that's irrelevant because no one will check the words. We had a lot of fun making that star. I love origami. And Ollie made two reindeer to go under the tree. They look more like dalmatians, but he and I know what they are. He and Ed don't have a Christmas tree at home because they're expecting to spend most of their time between now and Christmas at work. They open again on Boxing Day. How about you, Helen? I expect you have an amazing tree each year.'

'We did when the children were small,' she says. 'It feels like a lot of work nowadays. I always put one up in the shop, but I'm not terribly good at decorating it. I sometimes look at the Christmas trees in magazines, with their themes of silver and white, or purple and gold, and wonder whether any of the trees we sell end up looking like that. I hope so.'

'I expect the one at the Manor house does,' I say.

'I saw a picture of it in the local newspaper once,' she says. 'They hold a charity event each year to raise money for the hospice. They must have used a professional tree decorator. It looked stunning.'

'You don't need a professional to decorate a tree,' I say. 'It just takes practise.'

'Not for me,' she says. 'I could practise for years and never produce anything half as beautiful.'

'How about you?' I ask Tom. 'I assume your flat in London is a proudly Christmas tree free zone?'

'You assume a lot of things,' he says. 'I didn't buy one this year because I was coming home for Christmas. A real tree would have been dead by the time I got back to my flat, and I know you wouldn't approve of that.'

'Even with your magical spray?' I ask, and he laughs.

'It's not that magical. I could have an artificial tree, but I don't like them. I used to love the smell of our freshly cut Christmas tree after we cut it down on a snowy day and brought it indoors. The entire house smelled of pine and resin. That's when I knew it was time for Mum to start making the mincemeat.'

'Tom Kingsley!' I exclaim. 'Did you say something nice about Christmas?'

'Possibly, but there are very few witnesses around, and I intend to deny it if challenged.'

'I still don't understand why Tom is supposed to dislike Christmas,' says Helen.

'Neither do I,' he says, giving me a challenging look.

'Maybe not dislike,' I say. 'But the first time we met, he told me he only saw Christmas as an opportunity to make money.'

'Before threatening Tiny Tim with an axe,' adds Tom.

'You always liked it as a child,' says Helen.

'It was fine,' says Tom. 'I need to get the other trees from the truck. The fair will be opening soon.'

He strides away to fetch the next lot of trees.

'Did Tom ever consider coming back to work at the farm?' I ask Helen.

'He seems quite happy in London,' she says. 'I don't imagine he's given it a thought. That's why I put it up for sale.'

Tom comes back carrying a stack of Christmas trees. 'What are you two talking about?'

'Christmas,' says Helen. 'Emma, I've been thinking some more about tree decorating. Would you be prepared to come over and help me with the one in the shop? I'd give you lunch, of course.'

'I'd love to,' I say. 'Trimming trees is one of my favourite things about Christmas. I'm free tomorrow if you are.'

'Wonderful!' she says. 'Tom can come over to pick you up and make sure you don't get lost.'

I look over at Tom, who's busy nailing the largest tree to its stand.

'That's a kind offer,' I say. 'And if he behaves himself properly, we'll let him dress up in his Santa costume and hang the star.'

Chapter Twelve

Tom picks me up mid-morning the following day.

'I may as well put your stock into my truck,' he says when he arrives. 'It will save Ollie having to drop it off at the market tonight. Thanks for doing this, Emma. I know anxious Mum is to get our tree done.'

'I'm free all afternoon,' I say. 'I'm happy to help her with anything she likes. I didn't see much of the farm when I was there last week. Maybe you can show me the rest.'

'I should warn you Bonnie will be there,' he says. 'Have you brought your protective gear?'

'I like Border Collies,' I say. 'Is she a good guard dog?'

He laughs. 'Not at all. She's delighted to see everyone who comes to the farm. She'd welcome any burglars with open arms and show them how to open the cash register.'

'How long have you had her?' I ask, climbing into the van next to him.

'About three years. She loves it here, and she's great company for Mum, especially now.'

'It must be lonely living on the farm by herself,' I say.

'I imagine so. But she'll be able to retire once she's found a buyer.'

'Have you considered taking it over?' I say, and he shakes his head.

'It would need a lot of work to make it a going concern, and Mum would feel she ought to stay and help me get it back on its feet. She needs to go and do the things she and Dad planned to do together.'

'Such as?'

'I know Dad was keen to visit Greece,' he says. 'He had a friend who used to live on one of the islands and loved it. And Dad always wanted to visit America.'

'Any particular part?' I ask.

'He planned to start on the east coast and drive all the way to California, stopping wherever the fancy took him.'

'Do you think your mum wants to do that without him?'

He shrugs. 'I don't know. She doesn't talk much about her plans. What about your parents? Where do they live?'

'I grew up in a village outside Oxford,' I say. 'We had a huge old house that was always in need of repair. It had an orchard, and a stream in the garden, and we kept chickens and a goat.'

'But you live in the city now?' he says.

'That's right. I rent a flat near to my work. It would be too far to drive in from Kinsden each day.'

He nods. 'Will you stay in Oxford when you start your own business?'

'If I start my own business,' I correct him. 'I don't know. I always thought I'd stay in that area forever, but lately I've been thinking about a change.'

'Ollie mentioned something about New York,' he says, and I laugh.

'That's the plan. He wants me to open a multi-million-pound empire there and employ him as CEO.'

'What would Ed do?' he asks.

'Open New York's largest bookstore and drink inordinate amounts of coffee.'

'It's good to have dreams,' he says.

He swings the truck off the road and starts along the rough track towards the farmhouse. 'Let's see whether Bonnie is around. You have to meet her sometime, and you'll be quite safe if you're with me.'

Helen meets us at the farmhouse door.

'Thank you so much for coming,' she says when I climb out of the truck.

'Thank you for inviting me. And for sending a taxi for me.'

'I hope it wasn't too uncomfortable?' she says.

'Not at all. My ride here had two things going for it. It was free, and I didn't have to read the map.'

'You may have to on the way back to the market,' says Tom. 'I dropped my phone this morning and broke the screen. It's still working, but only just.'

'I'll take her myself if you keep talking nonsense,' says Helen. 'Come on in, Emma. Lunch is almost ready.'

'Aren't we eating at the cafe?' I ask.

'Carolyn's working in the shop this afternoon,' she says. 'So, it seemed a good time for me to take a break and eat here.'

'I'll go and check what Bonnie's up to,' says Tom. 'I'll see you in a minute.'

I follow Helen into the kitchen and she motions to me to sit down at the large wooden table.

'This is lovely,' I say. 'I've always liked rustic décor, but only when it's appropriate. I'm not keen on using it in a modern house.'

'I know what you mean,' she says. 'I have a friend who lives on a housing estate outside Honeywell. None of the houses was built later than the eighties, but the builders went with a Georgian theme. The houses have pillars outside their front doors, and sash windows. The developers even designed the garage doors in the same style.'

'I went to school with a girl whose parents were obsessed with Greek architecture,' I say. 'They lived in a beautiful thatched cottage miles from anywhere. From the outside, it looked like a picture on a chocolate box. But when you went inside, the entire place was decorated with gold pillars and fluted chair legs. It made you feel as though you ought to be wearing a toga.'

'What a shame,' says Helen. 'I always feel sorry for houses like that. They deserve better. What's your flat in Oxford like? Gothic, colonial, rustic?'

'Nothing so interesting,' I say. 'It's about as bland as you can get. My landlord owns several of the flats in our building. He's painted them cream and laid oatmeal carpet throughout. It must make it easier to rent them out if you keep everything neutral. I asked him last year whether I could paint the kitchen blue, but he refused. He said if I didn't like it, he had twenty other tenants lined up who would love the place as it was. I suspected he was telling the truth, so I didn't raise the subject again.'

'This kitchen could do with a coat of paint,' says Helen. 'But it hardly seems worth it now I'm selling up.'

'How would you paint it if you knew you'd be here forever?' I ask.

She considers. 'I can promise there wouldn't be any gold leaf or Grecian pillars. I'm not very good at visualising that sort of thing. What would you advise?'

'If it were me,' I say, 'I'd strip back those painted beams and expose the natural wood. I'd keep everything as original as possible, like your Aga. I'd paint the walls in earth tones, with touches of cream and sage green, and I'd find some Shaker style cabinets. But everyone's taste is different.'

'That sounds lovely,' she says. 'I promise I'll call you in as a consultant if I ever need one.'

'Are you looking forward to retirement?' I ask.

'I haven't given it much thought,' she says. 'Michael had all sorts of plans. He wanted to retire as soon as possible and travel the world.'

'Will you enjoy that?'

She looks embarrassed. 'I feel as though I ought to. But I don't know. I love this place, and it will be a real wrench to leave it. It's difficult to imagine what I'll do next. I'd like to take some holidays and see different places, but that wasn't what Michael had in mind. He wanted to see the entire world before we were too old and tired.'

'Running this farm must have been hard work,' I say.

'A place like this always is,' she says. 'Tom had lots of plans for its future while he lived at home. But after he went to London, he seemed to forget about the farm. That's natural enough. He grew up here, and he hadn't experienced anything else. Once he'd given city life a try, he found he preferred it.'

'How about his sister?' I say. 'Did she never think about taking over the family business?'

Helen laughs. 'Katie couldn't shake the dust off her feet quickly enough. She hated living in the countryside as a teenager. She said there was nothing to do. She had no interest in the farm. She never helped out during her holidays as Tom did. She stayed with school friends once she was old enough and worked at supermarkets and cafes.'

'You have a cafe here,' I say.

'That was Tom's idea,' she says. 'He rebuilt the shop and cafe from scratch the year before he left. It was an unused outbuilding, but he saw its potential. He came up with lots of ideas. The soft fruit business was his suggestion too. He wanted to build it up into something big at one time, but Michael wasn't keen to be tied down.'

'What would you like to do during your retirement?' I ask.

'I don't have a clue,' she admits. 'My whole life has been spent running this farm. I'll feel utterly lost without it. I wish I were creative like you. Maybe then I could run a home business to supplement my pension.'

'You don't need to be creative for that,' I say. 'All you need is an idea.'

Helen sighs. 'That's the difficult part. Anyway, I could be living here for a while yet. Finding a buyer for this sort of place is a huge undertaking. We may have to sell it to a developer. Five years from now, this could be a new housing development, although hopefully not Georgian.'

'Definitely not!' I say. 'Or Tudor either. It would be a shame for a beautiful place like this to disappear. How long has your family lived here?'

'More than a hundred years,' she says. 'Michael's great-grandfather bought it before the first world war. It wasn't a Christmas tree farm back then. He kept sheep and goats. But Michael's grandfather preferred agriculture. He experimented with various crops over the years and ended up specialising in Christmas trees.'

'You can't let that history be destroyed!' I say impulsively.

'It may not be my choice,' she says. 'Nothing lasts forever.'

The timer pings, and she reaches for a pair of oven gloves. 'I hope you can eat lasagna.'

'It's one of my favourite dishes,' I say.

'Wonderful!' she says. 'Would you mind going into the yard and calling Tom to tell him lunch is ready?'

Chapter Thirteen

We don't discuss the future of the farm over lunch. I hope I haven't overstepped any boundaries in what I said about selling the place. It's none of my business. The farm belongs to Helen, and it's up to her what she does with it.

'Have you decided how we should decorate our Christmas tree?' Helen asks me while we're eating our apple crumble and custard.

'That's up to you,' I say. 'It's your tree and your shop. I've brought a selection of decorations for you to choose from.'

'I'll need some help,' she says. 'Do you apply the same rules to decorating Christmas trees as you do to houses?'

'Rules?' I say.

'You told me you don't like it when people decorate their homes unsympathetically. Is it the same with Christmas decorations? Should we be decorating the tree in a rustic style because we're on a farm?'

'That's entirely your choice,' I say. 'I don't think the same rules hold true for Christmas trees. I decorate my tree at home in a different style each year. You should choose what you like.'

'What themes have you used?' she asks.

'Hundreds, although some have been more successful than others. My Hollywood glamour theme is one I prefer to forget. I used a feather boa instead of tinsel. The landlord's cat used to visit me in the afternoons, and I came into the living room one day to find he'd mistaken the boa for a strange and exotic bird. Somehow, he'd managed to get up the trunk in search of his prey. From the looks of things, the feather boa put up a good fight, but Mr Whiskers was eventually triumphant. I was picking feathers out of the carpet and chairs for weeks.'

'What did you do?' says Tom, looking amused.

'Kicked Mr Whiskers out of the flat,' I say. 'He was banned until after New Year's Day.'

'Did you redecorate the tree?' he asks.

'I don't remember too clearly. I think I left most of the feathers where they were, sprayed the tips of the branches silver, and hung lots of snowflakes for a winter wonderland feel.'

'And was Mr Whiskers banned every year after that?' he asks.

'Only at Christmas. I love cats but, ironically enough, my landlord refuses to allow his tenants to keep pets. Mr Whiskers is as close as I'll ever come. Speaking of pets, I haven't met Bonnie yet. I'm beginning to think she's mythical, like your barbed wire and landmines.'

'You'd be wrong,' he says. 'I think she must be down at the shop with Carolyn. She doesn't like to be too far from there when it's lunchtime. But she's certainly not mythical. She was helping me cut the trees this morning.'

'A dog of many talents,' I say. 'Have you taught her to use a chainsaw?'

'No, but she runs around while I put the trees into the truck. She thinks she's herding them.'

'It's a pity you don't keep sheep,' I say.

'Bonnie's too lame to herd sheep,' says Helen. 'But she did a sterling job last summer when the hens got out. She had them rounded up and back in their cage before they'd got further than the boundary fence.'

'You should bring Bonnie to the fair one night,' I tell Tom. 'She could keep the children in order while they're lining up in the reindeer enclosure. It would be a shame if any more of them ended up on Santa's naughty list.'

'I didn't show that list to the new Santa,' he says. 'It didn't seem fair on the children.'

'The new Santa is an improvement on the last one,' I say. 'Frances seems pleased with him.'

'She is,' says Tom. 'Not that it's a high bar to clear. She only needed him to stay sober and not offer tobacco products to the children. But this new guy seems to be a hit.'

'Tom told me what happened,' says Helen. 'I felt guilty for laughing, but I couldn't help it. I hope the children weren't too upset.'

'Children nowadays are a lot tougher than we were,' says Tom. 'Archie Smith had the cheek to tell me to my face he didn't believe in me.'

'It was kind of you to stand in at short notice,' says Helen.

'It was,' I agree. 'If Tom's career in advertising doesn't work out, he has a bright future in the Kris Kringle business.'

'Only in December,' says Tom. 'How would I make my living for the rest of the year?'

'I don't know,' I say. 'I wonder what Santas do in the off-season?'

'Go to Australia?' suggests Helen. 'Don't they celebrate Christmas at a different time of year to us?'

'I'm afraid not,' says Tom. 'Same date, different weather.'

'Maybe Santas enter professional pie-eating competitions,' I suggest. 'It would get them into shape for the upcoming festive season.'

'Or run karaoke bars,' says Tom. 'So many possibilities.'

Helen stacks the plates. 'If we've finished eating, we should go over to the shop and look at this Christmas tree.'

'We haven't decided on a theme yet,' I say.

'We always decorated our family Christmas tree the same way when I was young,' says Tom. 'Mum and Dad started by hanging the decorations Katie and I had made at school while she and I did the tinsel and the baubles. Then Katie and I fought over whose turn it was to put the angel on top. And we finished with the switching-on of the lights. But that doesn't help us here. I doubt our customers will be too excited to see the glitter covered fabric conditioner lid I made in year one.'

'I bet they would,' I say. 'But Helen may want to save that for the family Christmas tree. I've made a list of suggestions. Here it is.'

I hand Helen a piece of paper, and she looks at it with interest.

'I love these ideas,' she says. 'I'm not sure which to choose.'

'What are they?' says Tom.

'Nordic charm,' she reads. 'Old-time glamour, Santa's workshop, Victorian Christmas, rustic Christmas, traditional Christmas, winter wonderland, and fairytale forest.'

'I don't have the faintest clue what any of those would look like,' says Tom. 'I'll leave it to you and Emma.'

'Nordic charm,' decides Helen. 'That sounds intriguing.'

'Could you get the boxes of decorations out of the truck?' I ask Tom, who nods and disappears.

We meet him in the shop a few minutes later. He sets down the boxes next to the Christmas tree. 'Hi, Carolyn.'

'Hello, Tom,' says a middle-aged woman who's busy sorting the jams by flavour.

'This is Emma,' says Helen. 'Emma, this is Carolyn. She works in the shop three days a week. I don't know what we'd do without her.'

'I hear you're decorating our Christmas tree for us,' says Carolyn, and I feel embarrassed in case she thinks she should have been asked to do it.

'Helen asked me,' I say. 'I'm not an expert, but it's something I enjoy doing.'

'I'm glad someone does,' says Carolyn. 'Helen and I decorated the one in here last year. It looked as though the tree had been to a wild party the previous night and hadn't recovered from its hangover. Not the greatest advertisement for a business like this.'

'I'm sure it was great,' I say. 'I was wondering why you don't have a brightly decorated tree down by the entrance to the farm. It would catch people's eyes as they drive past.'

'It's a good idea,' says Helen. 'Maybe the people who buy the place will do that next year.'

'If they don't decide to use the land for something else,' says Tom.

'That would be such a shame,' I say. 'Your mum says your family has been living here for more than a century. That's quite a heritage.'

'Or a habit,' says Tom. 'Would you like me to unpack the box?'

We watch as he lays out the contents on the floor.

'These are interesting,' says Helen. 'There isn't a lot of colour.'

'Except for the Christmas hearts,' I agree. 'But it will be beautiful when we've finished. We're going for a minimalist look, but not too sparse.'

I pick up the string of white fairy lights and thread it through the branches.

'We'd better test these before we go any further,' I say.

I plug in the cable, and the lights spring to life. Their soft, warm light illuminates the branches, and I feel the usual thrill of excitement when I see it.

'They're beautiful,' says Helen. 'What comes next?'

'These wooden ornaments,' I say. 'You can help me. Put them wherever you like.'

I hand Tom a birchwood star and gesture to the tree.

'I'd prefer to watch,' he says. 'I'm no expert.'

'You don't need to be an expert. How do you think most people manage? Hang it wherever you like. There's no wrong answer.'

'There might be,' he says. 'I know nothing about Scandinavian Christmas rules. They have some fearsome creatures in those parts, and some extremely vengeful gods. I don't want to incur the wrath of a mountain troll if I put the ornaments in the wrong places.'

'Don't be such a wuss,' I say.

'I'll start,' says Helen. 'I'm not afraid of trolls or Odin's ravens.'

She hangs several wooden animals on the tree, while I add red and white paper hearts.

'I like those,' she says. 'Did you make them yourself, Emma?'

'I did. I've always enjoyed paper weaving. They don't take long once you get used to making them. I put some in the craft kits for my family boxes. They've sold well, so these hearts may even now be adorning trees all over Honeywell.'

Tom hangs his star on one of the lower branches. 'What comes next?'

'Not a lot,' I say. 'Can you hand me that string of orange slices?'

I arrange the garland among the branches and add a string of wooden beads.

'We could leave it here,' I say. 'But I like to add some sparkle. Helen, can you hang some of those frosted snowflakes while I add the finishing touch?'

I tiptoe up to attach the woven straw star to the top of the tree, then step back to admire the effect.

'It's gorgeous,' says Helen. 'Who would have thought something so simple could be so stunning?'

'The Scandinavian people?' says Tom.

'I love this style,' I say. 'It shows off the beauty of the Christmas tree instead of overwhelming it with a mass of colour and sparkle. You could almost imagine yourself in the middle of a Norwegian pine forest on a snowy night.'

'I love it too,' says Helen. 'It gives me such a feeling of tradition.'

'That's why I like it,' I say. 'It makes me think of close-knit communities handing down their customs to each new generation. There's something comforting in that idea.'

'I agree,' she says. 'But it isn't always possible to avoid change. Things move on, whether we like it or not, and we have to move on with them.'

'That's right,' says Tom. 'Otherwise, we'd still be using carrier pigeons and sending smoke signals.'

'There's no need to be so literal,' I tell him. 'I'm only talking about Christmas. I'm not trying to ban printing presses or prevent the invention of the steam train.'

'I'm with Emma,' says Helen. 'This may well be my last Christmas on the farm. I plan to enjoy a bit of tradition while I can.'

Chapter Fourteen

Helen helps me pack the rest of the ornaments into the box and tape it shut. 'What are you two doing this afternoon?' she asks.

'I'd love a tour of the farm,' I say. 'Unless Tom has other things to do.'

'I don't,' he says. 'I've cut down tonight's trees. I'm free until the market this evening.'

We finish our drinks, and I fetch my coat and gloves from the house. Tom and I set off towards the Christmas tree plantation. Bonnie appears from nowhere and joins us before we've gone more than ten steps. She seems delighted to meet me, and I realise Tom was right when he said she was unlikely to challenge intruders. She politely holds out her paw for me to shake, then trots happily along between us as though she's known me forever.

We walk between the rows of trees, their branches glistening with the residue of this morning's frost. I reach out to touch one, allowing the silky-smooth needles to slide through my fingers.

'Did you say there are ten thousand trees?' I ask Tom.

'Yes, but it's more complicated than that. Each tree takes up to twelve years to grow. We cut most of them well before then, but the largest ones can take that long. We maintain a schedule of continuous planting, so we always have trees ready to go.'

'That must take a lot of planning,' I say.

'I wanted to expand that number,' he says. 'But Dad wasn't keen.'

'Why not? Did he think you'd run out of customers?'

'It wasn't that,' he says. 'We always sold out by Christmas Eve. But he didn't like the idea of expanding the farm. He said it would be too much of a risk. He and Mum barely made it pay as it was. He didn't want to take out a loan and end up in debt trying to expand something that was destined to fail.'

'Why did he think it would fail?' I ask. 'You have plenty of land here, and you've told me you have more customers than you can supply.'

'Dad said scaling up is never as simple as you might think,' he says. 'Every business has its natural size, and Dad felt we'd reached ours.'

'That makes sense,' I say.

'I used to have all sorts of plans for this place,' he says. 'I wanted to expand the vegetable plots, add an orchard, keep our own bees, and sell the honey. I thought we could brew our own cider and mead too. But Dad wasn't interested. We had some spectacular rows about it. In the end, I gave up and took a job in London. It seemed better than staying at home and upsetting Mum with endless arguments when it was obvious Dad would never change his mind.'

'I'd have thought he might have wanted his children to carry on the family business,' I say.

'Apparently not. He kept telling me I'd be far better off seeing some of the world before tying myself down in a place like this.'

'He didn't see the world,' I say.

Tom frowns. 'That was the problem. I didn't realise until it was too late how much Dad disliked it here. His family always expected him to take over the business when my grandfather died, and he accepted that. He worked hard to provide for his family. He and Mum both did. But it wasn't until after I'd left home that I realised it had never been his own choice. It was something he'd been forced into.'

'Did he tell you that?' I ask.

He shakes his head. 'Dad never talked about how he felt about the farm. But I went home for his birthday a couple of years ago, and he showed me the plans he'd made for his and Mum's retirement. It was a detailed list of all the places he wanted to see before he got too old. He planned to take the train across Europe and maybe go on one of those river cruises through Germany. He wanted to see the cherry blossom in Japan and visit the Great Wall of China and drive right across America and go on a whale watching tour in Canada. Most of all, he wanted to visit Greece and see the Acropolis and the Parthenon and sail around the Greek islands.'

'Was your mum keen to travel too?' I ask.

'I believe so. She seemed pretty excited about the whole thing. That's when I realised he'd been waiting all those years to escape. It wasn't until I finally left the farm that he felt able to plan his life the way he wanted, not the way someone else wanted it to be. When I discovered that, it felt as though someone had hit me with a sledgehammer. I wish he'd talked to me about it sooner. I wouldn't have stayed here as long as I did if I'd known what he was thinking.'

'Did you consider buying them out?' I ask.

'I doubt I could have raised the money, even if they'd agreed to sell it to me. But the main reason I didn't consider it was that I knew they wouldn't have left if I'd done that. Mum would have insisted they stay on to help me. It would have been a huge undertaking by myself, and I couldn't afford much help to start with. I couldn't do that to Dad, not when he was about to retire.'

'I understand that,' I say. 'And then he died?'

'And then he died, just as he was about to follow his dreams.'

There's a bitter note in his voice. I don't dare ask any more questions. It seems too painful a subject.

Tom breaks the silence. 'I'm not sure I'll ever get over the guilt. If only I'd realised sooner and got out of their hair, they might have sold the farm and done all the things they planned to do. But I was too obtuse to see it. By the time I did, it was too late.'

'I can see why you feel like that,' I say. 'But it was just as much his responsibility to tell you how he felt. You can't carry the blame for it your entire life.'

'Maybe,' he says. 'But it still hurts. Losing him was bad enough without feeling I'd made things worse.'

'You're taking it too personally,' I say. 'If your dad hated the farm so much, he could have sold up and done something else decades ago. There must have been something that kept him here all those years.'

'I don't think he knew what else to do,' he says. 'He grew up here as I did. It was what he knew. His family couldn't afford for him to go to university. It was one of the reasons he was so insistent Katie and I did. He said he wanted us to see the world and take advantage of the opportunities it had to offer.'

'I take it he didn't expect you to come back afterwards?'

'I'm sure he didn't. He seemed almost disappointed when I graduated and talked about coming home and expanding the business. That's when he started digging in his heels and refusing to try any of the things I suggested. Eventually, it seemed easier to leave him to it. It made sense when I realised what his retirement plans were. But at the time, I was frustrated and upset with him, and I told him so. That's another one of my regrets. I would never have talked to him like that if I'd known he wouldn't be around for much longer.'

'You can't think like that,' I say. 'No one knows what the future holds. Did the pair of you get on alright after you'd left?'

'We did,' he says. 'It seemed at one time as though he wanted to discuss the whole thing with me, but I avoided the conversation. I didn't see the point in opening old wounds. Then Mum called me one day to say he'd gone. He'd had a heart attack while he was planting trees. He was dead before the ambulance arrived.'

'I'm so sorry,' I tell him. 'I can't imagine how awful that must have been for you.'

He nods. 'It was almost a year ago, but I still can't quite believe it. I'm not sure I ever will.'

'It was kind of you to come home to help your mum this Christmas,' I venture.

'It was the least I could do. I wanted to talk to her about the farm and what she planned to do next. But there was a For Sale sign at the entrance when I arrived, so I didn't need to. I'm glad she isn't staying here without him. It must remind her too much of their life together. It's time she escaped and made a life for herself after working so hard at something she didn't enjoy.'

'I'm sure she has happy memories too,' I say. 'She and your dad raised a family here and spent their married life here. It must be difficult to walk away from all that.'

'But she has plenty to look forward to,' he says. 'She should get a good price for this place, and she can start the retirement they planned. It's a shame Dad isn't here to do it with her, but Mum's always been pretty independent. She was talking about going to Paris the other day. And she seemed quite keen on that tree you decorated for us today. Maybe she'll go to Norway next year and see the Northern lights and the minimalist Christmas trees and meet a reindeer.'

'That sounds like fun,' I say. 'She could take a side trip to Lapland and meet the real Santa, not the one from the Christmas fair.'

'There are so many wonderful things she could experience,' he says. 'And the sooner the farm sells, the sooner she can go off and do them.'

Chapter Fifteen

Tom arrives at Ollie's flat at exactly nine o'clock on Wednesday morning.

'Are you sure you want to do this?' I ask him.

'Not in the slightest,' he says. 'But I've come all the way out here now, so I may as well make the most of it.'

He sees my face and laughs. 'I'm kidding, Emma. I can't wait to find out what you have lined up for me. Are we starting with a sleigh ride through the Honeywell woods? You'll have to remind me of the words to Jingle Bells.'

'That sounds wonderful,' I say. 'But I couldn't afford to hire a sleigh. I'm taking you ice skating instead.'

He looks alarmed. 'Are you serious?'

'Why not? It's a Christmassy thing to do.'

'It sounds like a dangerous thing to do,' he says. 'But I'd hate to dampen your enthusiasm. Lead on!'

We walk to my car, and I hand him my phone. 'Can you look up a place called Marsham?'

He hands it back. 'I don't need to. I know where it is. But I didn't realise they had an ice rink.'

'It says on their website it's a pop-up.'

'Does that mean if we fall, we'll bounce up?' he asks.

'If I say yes, will you stop complaining?'

'I'm not complaining,' he says. 'I'm ascertaining the facts.'

'Have you never been ice skating?' I ask.

'Not since I was at primary school. Don't tell me – you go every week, and you're an expert.'

'Not even close! The last time I visited the Oxford ice rink, I hit my head and had to be carried off the ice by the Saint John's Ambulance volunteers.'

'And yet you're voluntarily planning to go back on the ice?' he says.

'Of course. It's like getting back on a horse after you've had a fall.'

He gives me a look of mock alarm. 'Are you taking me horse riding too?'

'Don't worry. It's far too expensive. Although you must be able to ride a horse.'

'Why do you say that?' he asks.

'I thought everyone who grew up on a farm rode them.'

'It was a Christmas tree farm,' he says. 'Not a dude ranch. How many horses do you imagine we kept?'

'I have no idea. You may have kept a few for hauling the Christmas trees to the truck.'

'You mean the covered wagon?' he says. 'Pa saved up the money he got from gold prospecting to buy that wagon. It was his pride and joy. We used to drive into Honeywell for provisions every six months. Those trips were the highlight of my year.'

'Fine,' I say. 'You didn't keep horses, and you don't know how to skate. We'll be in Marsham soon. Do you want to stay in the car telling stories of your pioneer days, or would you prefer to get out and enjoy gliding over the ice on this beautiful winter's day?'

'As long as it doesn't pop up while I'm on it,' he says.

We arrive at the rink, where we hire two pairs of skates and sit on a bench to lace them up.

'I notice we're the first ones here,' says Tom. 'Or did you pay extra to ensure we had the rink to ourselves?'

'I can't afford that sort of extravagance,' I say, pulling my laces tight and finishing with a double bow.

'I'd be disappointed if you had,' he says. 'Keeping things to yourself isn't what Christmas is about.'

'What do you think it's about?' I say, levering myself to my feet and hoping I don't look as nervous as I feel.

'That's what I'm about to find out,' he says.

I follow him onto the rink and watch him lose his balance and sit down hard on the ice.

I hold out my hand to help him up. 'Are you alright?'

He doesn't take it. 'I'd pull you over too. Give me a minute, and I'll figure out a way to stand up. Why don't you entertain me by demonstrating the waltz while I do so?'

'Because I have no wish to break my neck,' I say.

I push myself away from the edge and strike out cautiously for the centre of the rink, trying not to think about the last time I went skating. I relax as I remember the feel of the ice slipping past beneath my skates. I circle the ice once and return to find Tom holding onto the wooden rail looking anxious.

'If I break any bones, I won't be able to carry my Christmas trees from the truck to my stall,' he says as I skid to an ungraceful stop beside him.

'Relax when you fall,' I say. 'That's the secret.'

'I don't somehow think it is. I think the secret is not to fall.'

'Even better,' I agree. 'Are you ready to give it another try?'

We set off together. The terrified look gradually leaves his face, and I remember Alex and Sophie skimming gracefully around the ice rink at Rockefeller Plaza. Tom and I aren't quite up to their standard, but we may be in an hour or two, assuming either or both of us haven't sprained our ankles by then.

Alex took Sophie to the emergency room when she had her fall. I'm not sure how far the hospital was located from Rockefeller Plaza, but Alex could afford a taxi to pretty much anywhere in the city. I only have half a tank of petrol, and it needs to last for the entire day. And I don't know where the nearest hospital is. I almost ask Tom but decide against it. He looks worried enough without me talking about ambulances and compound fractures.

'I could get used to this,' he says a while later. 'It isn't as scary as I thought. And I feel less conspicuous now more people are arriving.'

'Me too,' I say. 'When I saw we were the only ones here, I half expected the attendant to put on Ravel's bolero and start holding up score cards.'

'We have a way to go before we rival Torvill and Dean,' he says. 'But that was an impressive turn you executed just now.'

'Entirely unintentional,' I admit. 'But I'm glad you liked it.'

'I'm enjoying the whole thing,' he says. 'I was wondering, and I'd hate to spoil the Christmas spirit in any way, but is it possible the ice is slightly damper than when we first arrived?'

'Damper?' I look down at my feet. 'Oh, I see what you mean.'

'Please don't think I'm criticising,' he says. 'I didn't like to say anything earlier in case this was a part of the whole Christmas experience. But there appears to be half an inch of water on this rink, and it's growing deeper by the minute.'

'The ice can't be melting,' I say. 'There was a heavy frost this morning, and the air is pretty chilly.'

'But not below freezing. It must be at least six degrees now the sun's come out.'

'But they have a freezer thing,' I object. 'Isn't that supposed to keep the ice cold?'

'Maybe it's stopped working,' he says. 'Would you like me to ask the owner what's happening? Or shall we see whether he can rent us some water skis so we can make the best of it?'

People are leaving the ice. Several people have converged on the man who sold us our tickets. He's pointing towards the generator and shrugging.

We skate unsteadily to the edge of the rink, and Tom helps me off the slushy ice.

'If you'd warned me in advance this might happen, I'd have worn shorts,' he says. 'Never mind. I'll know for next time.'

I unlace my skates and pull on my boots.

'What's going on?' I ask the person sitting next to me on the bench.

'The generator's packed up,' she says. 'But they're refusing refunds to anyone who's been here for more than half an hour.'

'Have we been here for that long?' I ask Tom, who looks at his watch.

'We've been here for more than an hour. Doesn't time fly when you're enjoying yourself?'

'No refund for us,' I say, picking up my skates and lacing them together.

'It's hugely unfair after we entertained that man for at least twenty minutes by ourselves,' he says. 'And I believe it was watching our virtuoso performance that encouraged so many other people to have a go. He should have paid us, rather than the other way around.'

'You're welcome to tell him so,' I say, indicating the angry crowd gathered around the rink operator. 'But I doubt you'd get far.'

'And it may not be in the genuine spirit of Christmas,' says Tom. 'I doubt that haranguing that poor man falls under the category of peace and goodwill towards all men.'

'Probably not,' I agree. 'I'm sorry about this. But I have several other things planned for today, and at least neither of us has broken or sprained anything.'

'It's a Christmas miracle,' he says. 'Let's return these skates before he decides we've been using them as surfboards and tries to charge us a premium. After that, I'm all yours.'

Chapter Sixteen

We drive into Christchurch and park near the river.

'Ollie says Merton's department store is the best place for toys,' I say as we walk along the high street.

'You're buying me a toy?' asks Tom. 'Shouldn't I wait until Christmas morning to see whether I've made it onto Santa's nice list?'

'We aren't here to buy things for ourselves,' I tell him.

The automatic doors open, and a blast of warm air hits us as we go inside. Bing Crosby is singing White Christmas as we make our way through the perfume section, which is decorated with glittering garlands and smells like a tropical forest.

'Bing had the right idea,' says Tom, following me towards the lifts. 'If Hampshire had the forethought to order a white Christmas, we wouldn't have had to swim for safety an hour ago.'

'It was a miniscule amount of water,' I say. 'You're talking as though we had to wear our life jackets and set off flares to alert our rescuers.'

He ducks to avoid a stray garland of tinsel hanging above an arrangement of scented candles. 'Fair enough, but I'm almost sure I saw a shark. I didn't like to worry you while you were busy making your escape, and it only looked like a basking shark.'

We find the lifts and ride up to the top floor.

'We've established you aren't buying me toys,' says Tom. 'And it would be unkind of you to buy any for yourself while I'm here. So, who are we buying them for? Santa?'

'He has an entire workshop,' I say. 'What would he want with department store toys?'

'The elves may be on strike,' suggests Tom. 'I hear they've finally unionised.'

'No, they haven't! There's no need. They have the best pay and conditions imaginable.'

'You can't be sure of that,' he objects. 'Santa may keep them ten to a room and deduct their food and lodging from their pay.'

'You don't seem to have the faintest understanding of who Santa is,' I tell him.

'I know who he is,' he insists. 'He's a grumpy old man who drinks and smokes too much and makes arbitrary decisions about who should and shouldn't go on his list.'

'That wasn't the real Santa, and neither is that one over there.' I point to the far end of the department, where a line of children is waiting outside Santa's Crystal Grotto.

'I'm glad you told me,' says Tom. 'I was planning to join the queue and ask him for a PlayStation. So, who are we buying for today?'

'We're choosing gifts for the Wishing Tree,' I say. 'It's over there. Come and choose a card.'

We walk over to the large Christmas tree in the middle of the floor.

Tom inspects it. 'This isn't one of ours.'

'How do you know?' I ask.

'The first clue is that it's made of plastic. It's also the wrong colour.'

'They could have sprayed it silver after it arrived here,' I say.

'You may also notice it doesn't have a watering system,' he says. 'And it's on a metal stand. A real tree would have shrivelled up and dropped its needles ages ago.'

'It doesn't matter,' I say. 'The important thing is the gifts underneath it.'

I reach out and pull a tag off the tree. 'Girl aged six. I'll take this one.'

Tom examines the tags before selecting one for a ten-year-old boy. 'I should be able to do something with this.'

'Can you remember back so many decades?' I tease him.

'Eighteen years,' he says. 'I doubt that toys have changed that much since then.'

We walk between the stands, inspecting the toys. Tom picks one up and studies it. 'What's a LaserGig 2000?'

'I have no idea,' I say. 'Why don't you ask one of the staff?'

'Where's the fun in that? It appears to have a button underneath. Let's see what happens.'

'I don't think you're supposed to do that,' I say, but it's too late. The laser is already flashing.

'I'm not sure what it's meant to do,' says Tom. 'But it's going on the list of possibilities. I'd have loved something like this when I was ten years old.'

'In your pre-Ebenezer Scrooge incarnation,' I say. 'Can you remember what you were given for Christmas that year?'

'No,' he says. 'Can you? On second thoughts, don't bother answering that. I'm sure you remember every single Christmas in vivid detail. It wouldn't surprise me to hear you keep a stack of folders under your bed, listing every gift you've ever given or received.'

'Prepare to be surprised,' I say. 'I do nothing of the sort. I keep telling you, Christmas isn't about the gifts. It's about the spirit of the season.'

'I'd agree with you,' he says, 'if I weren't so sure that whatever this thing is would have made my childhood Christmas perfect. I'm putting it in my basket, anyway, along with this model aircraft kit.'

'It's one present per card,' I say.

'Then I'll get another card,' he says. 'Several more if need be.'

'I've only budgeted enough for one gift for each of us,' I say.

He looks surprised. 'I'm not expecting you to pay.'

'But this is my day to show you the true meaning of Christmas. Of course, I'm paying!'

'Not a hope,' he says. 'Now you can get yourself another card too.'

I look at the tree and select a card for a four-year-old girl.

'It's very kind of you,' I say. 'I know exactly what I'm getting for this little girl. I was desperate for a tea set when I was four. I couldn't believe it when Santa forgot to bring it.'

'Did you at least get one for your birthday?' he asks.

'Not that I remember. It's in September, so I may have forgotten about it by then. When's your birthday?'

'Christmas Day,' he says.

'No!' I gasp.

'Not really,' he says. 'But wouldn't it be fun if it was?'

'I don't think so. You'd have had to celebrate on a different day. Everyone deserves their own special birthday.'

'It's July 28th,' he says. 'At the start of the summer holidays. I enjoyed not having to go to school on my birthday.'

'I didn't mind,' I say. 'I got to see my friends. And I celebrated my birthday again when I had my party.'

'Are you as mad keen on birthdays as you are on Christmas?' he asks. 'Do you plan to add birthday boxes to your repertoire?'

'It's funny you should say that. I have thought about it. Valentine's boxes too. And Easter boxes if the business takes off.'

'You could put a real bunny inside those,' he suggests.

'No, I couldn't. They'd eat the chocolate, and everyone knows rabbits can't eat chocolate.'

'Not everyone,' he says. 'I've never considered the subject before. We were usually too busy trying to stop them eating our vegetables to worry about their favourite confectionery.'

He picks up a toy octopus. 'I like this little fellow, but I don't expect a ten-year-old would.'

'They might,' I say. 'I had a red panda when I was that age. He got lost when I took him with me on holiday. I missed him terribly.'

'Let's put Mr Octopus into the basket and decide who gets him later,' he says.

We walk around a stand of wooden construction toys, and Tom's face lights up when he sees what's on the other side.

'Musical instruments! Just the thing to wake everyone up on Christmas morning. My aunt bought me a toy drum kit one year. Dad didn't speak to her for the next six months.'

'I don't blame him,' I say.

'Spoilsport! How about this xylophone? I'm sure one of our recipients would love that. And we could add a set of handbells.'

'Fine,' I say. 'I don't suppose their parents will track us down later.'

'Not if you go back to Oxford,' he says. 'Are you set on that?'

'I may not have any choice. At least I have a proper job there.'

'One you enjoy?' he asks.

'I like the creative part of it – making up the bouquets and flower arrangements. I'm not so keen on the paperwork.'

'Would you consider staying in this area if your Christmas venture was successful?' he asks.

'I might. I'd love to be nearer to Ollie and Ed, and the area itself is gorgeous. I've been thinking for a while I'd like a change. I've never lived anywhere except Oxfordshire, and I'd like to see more of the world.'

'Before leaving for New York,' he agrees. 'It's a good idea.'

'New York may take a while,' I say. 'And to be honest, that's Ollie's dream, not mine. I'm happy staying in this country building up my business. I don't mind too much where I'm based.'

'I love the New Forest,' he says. 'When I was a child, I could never imagine wanting to live anywhere else.'

'Yet you moved to London?' I say.

'That was different. I'd discovered Dad's retirement plans by that time. I felt bad enough about not realising what he wanted and getting out earlier. And I was fine in London. I have a marketing degree, so it was easy enough to find work.'

I don't want to bring up painful memories while we're having so much fun, so I decide to change the subject.

'How about a board game?' I suggest. 'There's an entire section over there. Did you play board games at Christmas?'

'Not as far as I remember,' he says. 'But I'm willing to bet your family did. All of you wearing Christmas hats, I have no doubt.'

'I loved playing Monopoly,' I admit. 'I was always the dog, and my brother used to give me a ride around the board in his racing car.'

'You must have had a different set of rules in your game,' he says. 'Maybe you bought the seasonal edition.'

'It was only at Christmas. We stuck to the regular rules at other times. But Christmas Day was special.'

'I can't imagine Katie giving me a ride around the board at any time of the year,' he says. 'She's the most competitive woman in the world. She used to hide the Community Chest cards if she thought there was any danger of me winning. Her children are the same. The last time I visited, they managed to turn a simple game of hide-and-seek into a tactical operation. Not only did I lose each time, but I got into trouble with Katie for messing up her linen cupboard.'

'Perhaps we should rule out board games,' I say. 'We have no idea who will get them, and we don't want to be responsible for family carnage, especially not on Christmas Day.'

'I agree. But I'm not ruling that out!' Tom points to a stand near the checkout. 'I'd have loved one of those when I was small.'

He picks up the sleek black and silver racing car and sets it down on the carpet. 'How does this remote-control work? Ah, yes, I see.'

The car hums to life, and Tom sends it zooming down the aisle towards a rocking horse.

'I'm impressed,' he says. 'It handled that bend like a pro. Let's see how it accelerates. A model like that ought to go from zero to one hundred in under five seconds. Especially at this price.'

He slides the lever, and the car shoots forward at a surprising speed, its wheels sending up sparks on the nylon carpeted floor.

'Careful!' I say in alarm as it hurtles towards a small boy who's busy inspecting a toy giraffe.

The child sees the car and lets out a shriek. He dodges out of its path and crashes into the shelf of board games. The box at the end tips over and, in a display which would delight a domino player, knocks the next one down. I can only watch helplessly as the entire display collapses in slow motion.

I bend down and start picking up packs of Uno cards. Several boxes of Connect Four and a variety of Monopoly sets have skidded across the floor and under the stands. Tom switches off the car and runs over to join me.

'Sorry about that,' he says. 'I don't believe the driver checked his mirror before making that last turn.'

'Put it down, for goodness' sake!' I say. 'And help me pick these up before someone notices us.'

'Too late!' says Tom as a woman darts out from behind the cash desk and rushes over.

'What do you think you're doing?' she snaps.

Tom looks up and gives her a disarming smile. 'Some of these board games fell off the shelf, and we're picking them up.'

Her face relaxes. 'I see. For a moment there, I thought –'

The little boy comes running towards us, the giraffe tucked under one arm.

'Vroom!' he shouts excitedly.

'What did he say?' asks the shop assistant.

'Zoom?' says Tom with an innocent smile. 'Maybe he thinks giraffes rush around the savannah. I believe they're more the type to roam gracefully.'

'Vroom!' shouts the boy again. He spots the car and darts towards it with a gleeful look. 'Vroom!'

'Goodness!' says the assistant. 'What's that doing there? It's supposed to be on the stand. We'll have to put a lock on it if people are going to allow their children to play with it.'

She beckons to the boy's mother. 'Could you please keep an eye on your child? He could have damaged this very expensive toy.'

'Charlie!' says the woman. 'I told you not to touch anything! Honestly, I take my eye off you for a second, and you get up to all sorts.'

She sees the giraffe and snatches it away from him. 'I told you we aren't buying this.'

The boy sets up a wail, and Tom steps forward at once. 'It wasn't Charlie. It was me.'

The shop assistant frowns. 'What was you?'

'The car,' says Tom. 'I took it off the stand. I wanted to see how fast it would go.'

'So, those boxes didn't fall off by themselves?' says the assistant, annoyed.

'Not entirely,' I admit. 'But we'll put them back. None of them is damaged.'

'I'm afraid I must ask you to leave,' she says.

'That seems rather extreme,' I say. 'It was an accident.'

She points to the stand where Tom found the car. 'Didn't you read the sign?'

We look at the stand and see a sign saying, 'Please ask the assistant if you wish to inspect this car more closely.'

Tom gives her an apologetic smile. 'I'm afraid I didn't notice that. But no harm done. We'll clear up these boxes while you put the car away.'

The assistant doesn't move. 'I believe I asked you both to leave. Would you like me to call security?'

'But we're buying presents for the wishing tree!' I protest.

She glances down at my basket. 'If you accompany me to the register, I'll ring these up for you.'

'Thank you,' I say, relieved.

'And then I would like you to leave,' she says.

Tom holds out his hand to Charlie's mother. 'Please allow me to pay for the giraffe. Charlie seems to have taken a great liking to him.'

'You don't have to do that,' she says.

'I want to,' says Tom. He bends down to talk to Charlie. 'I believe his name is Gerald. Shall we ask the assistant to put him in a bag so you can take him home with you?'

Charlie stops crying and beams up at him. 'Yeth!'

'Yes, please,' says his mother. She smiles at Tom. 'I can't refuse now you've named him. I'd never hear the last of it.'

Tom joins me at the register, and we each pay for our toys.

I hand the gift cards to the assistant. 'I assume you can work out which gift goes with each card.'

'It isn't rocket science,' she says. 'And now I must ask you to leave before you cause any more … accidents.'

Tom hands Gerald to Charlie. 'Happy Christmas.'

'Come on!' I say, my cheeks scarlet, as I hurry towards the lift to avoid the security guard walking towards us.

'What's wrong?' says Tom as I press the button. 'Have you never been thrown out of a toy shop before?'

'No!'

'What a sheltered life you appear to have led,' he says. 'It's time you broadened your horizons.'

'I expect you've been thrown out of hundreds,' I say.

'At least,' he agrees. 'It was a Christmas tradition in our household.'

'I don't believe you.'

'Maybe not toy shops,' he says. 'But I was once asked to leave an all-you-can-eat buffet for interpreting their offer too literally. It's almost the same thing.'

The lift arrives, and I step inside. 'That's the last time I visit Merton's department store.'

'Stop worrying so much,' says Tom. 'It will be something to tell your grandchildren around the fire each Christmas. "Children, you may think Grandma Emma is staid and boring. But have you heard about the time she destroyed half a department store and they had to call several burly security guards to throw her out?" You'll go up in their estimation when you tell that story, I guarantee.'

'That's not quite how I'll tell it,' I say. 'I'll say I was trying and failing to babysit an overgrown child, who ought to have known better.'

'Suit yourself,' he says. 'I prefer my version. It makes you sound edgy and mysterious. Here we are at the ground floor. Where are you taking me next – to the Christmas china factory? I'll try not to trip over a flower arrangement and send an entire display of Royal Doulton flying. Not unless there's another innocent looking child there on whom I can pin the whole thing.'

'I wouldn't trust you within ten miles of any crockery,' I say. 'We're having lunch, then going to The Rabbit Hole. Even you can't do more than a hundred pounds worth of damage in a bookshop.'

Chapter Seventeen

We stop for lunch at Il Piatto, a small restaurant down a side street near the river. Ollie and I ate here when I visited him this summer. It was the first time I told him about A Boxful of Christmas. I half expected him to laugh, but he was immediately enthusiastic about the whole idea. He started expanding on it, his ideas growing increasingly wild, until at last I had to tell him to stop and let me approach the project at my own pace.

I tell Tom about this as we sit in a booth and the server hands us our menus.

'What else did Ollie want you to do?' he asks.

'I can't remember more than half of it. He mentioned me opening a chain of stores across the UK before expanding into Europe. Ollie was never one to think small.'

'Do he and Ed plan to open more bookstores?' he asks.

'I don't believe so. They seem perfectly happy running this one. They both like this area, and they managed to buy their flat last year. I think they're settled here for the foreseeable future. Ollie's trying to live vicariously through me.'

'Don't you like the idea of running your own chain of shops?' he asks.

'Maybe not a chain, but a shop of my own would be wonderful. But that would take years. Even then, everything would have to go right for me first.'

'I'm sure it will,' he says. 'I've never seen anyone with such a passion for what they do. It's inspiring.'

'You mean ridiculous?' I say, waving to the server.

'No, I don't,' he says. 'There's nothing ridiculous about following your dreams.'

'I agree,' I say. 'But you think the dream itself is ridiculous. Selling the magic of Christmas to the world.'

'Disney and Hallmark have already done that,' he says.

'But that's only one kind of Christmas. The kind where extended families live in enormous houses that look as though they've employed Martha Stewart to do their Christmas decorations. It's totally unrealistic and fake.'

'It's the kitchens that get me,' he says. 'Have you ever seen a film or a TV series where the house doesn't have an immaculate kitchen at all times? There's never anything left out on the worktops, no washing up in the sink, no spilled ketchup. It makes no sense.'

'You're right,' I say. 'I grew up watching re-runs of the Brady Bunch, and their house was always perfect. Mind you, they had Alice, who seemed to work seventy-hour weeks without complaining. Unpaid housekeepers may be the key to a successful life.'

'What would your ideal Christmas look like if it weren't a Hallmark one?' he asks.

'There'd be lots of mess and clutter, but everyone would have a good time.'

'Is that the kind of Christmas you grew up with?'

I'm saved from having to answer by the arrival of the server.

'I'll have the gnocchi, please,' I say. 'How about you, Tom?'

'Sounds good,' he says.

'What were we talking about?' he asks as the server picks up our menus and leaves.

'Hallmark Christmases,' I say, sidestepping the question. 'What about you? Do you come home for Christmas each year, spreading your very own brand of cheer and goodwill around the farm?'

'This is my first Christmas back home for a few years,' he says. 'And my last one, I suppose. I went skiing with some friends last year. I wish I hadn't. If I'd know it would be Dad's last Christmas, I'd have come home instead.'

'I know,' I say sympathetically. 'But you can't think like that. We have to live our lives, not structure them around what may or may not happen, especially those things which are entirely out of our hands.'

'I still wish I'd come home,' he says.

'Your mum will be pleased you're here this year,' I say. 'It won't be easy for either of you, but at least you'll be together. How about your sister? Will she be coming too?'

'They're planning to drive down on Christmas Eve,' he says. 'Mark is working until the 23rd. I'm glad they'll be here. The children will take Mum's mind off things. How about you? How long are you staying with Ollie and Ed?'

'Until the day after Boxing Day.'

'Will you come back to Honeywell next Christmas?' he asks.

'I'd like to. It's been a lot of fun working at the fair. But I don't want to impose on Ollie and Ed too much. They've done enough for me as it is. It will be strange seeing someone else selling Christmas trees at the fair next year. Will you miss it?'

'Miss sitting in the freezing cold every night, explaining to ungrateful customers why a locally grown Christmas tree costs more than an imported plastic one?' he says. 'What do you think?'

'You always look as though you're having fun.'

'It's the mask I wear to hide my existential despair,' he says. 'Much like Santa's beard. Why do you think he never takes it off, even though everyone knows it's only glued on? He doesn't want us to see the empty, hollow shell of a man that lies underneath.'

'You need something to eat,' I say. 'Ollie gets like this whenever his blood sugar is low. Which, to be fair, hardly ever happens. Ed makes sure there are always snacks available. Ollie has a special cupboard in the bookshop, filled with his favourite mint cream cookies. Speaking of food, here's ours. That should fill your metaphysical void as well as the physical one.'

'How about my sense of nihilistic absurdity?' he asks, picking up his knife and fork.

'They do a wonderful blackberry cheesecake here,' I say, taking a bite of my gnocchi. 'Guaranteed to induce a state of almost transcendent euphoria.'

'I look forward to it,' he says. 'This gnocchi is excellent. I was hungrier than I realised.'

I hand him the basket of bread. 'I'm not surprised. First, you went skating –
'

'Swimming,' he corrects me. 'Water skiing, at best.'

I ignore this. 'Then you spent an hour playing in the toy store, culminating in being thrown out on your ear and being banned for life.'

'I wasn't banned!' he protests.

'Banned!' I say inexorably. 'They'll have located us on the store's CCTV by now and fed our images into the computer. If either of us goes within ten feet of the front entrance, hundreds of sirens will go off, and the police will automatically be called.'

Tom raises an eyebrow. 'You appear to have some experience in this sort of thing. I take it this has happened to you before?'

'I've watched Minority Report,' I say. 'By now, our names and descriptions will have been circulated to all the toy stores in Hampshire. We'll be detected and arrested before we get near any of them.'

'They don't know our names,' he objects.

'Of course, they do. They've seen our credit cards. They'll know our addresses, our spending history, and very likely our mothers' maiden names and our favourite flavours of ice cream.'

'You should have warned me that spending the day with you would turn into a dystopian nightmare,' he grumbles. 'I'd have stayed safely at home on the farm with the rottweilers.'

'You're the one who started it all,' I remind him. 'No one asked you to touch that car. In fact, they put up a sign specifically asking you not to. What did you expect? Actions have consequences.'

'But what about my niece and nephews?' he asks. 'I haven't bought their Christmas presents yet. How can I do that if I'm banned from every toy store in the country?'

'Only in Hampshire. You'll have to drive to another county or shop online. As long as you use a false name and credit card number, you should be fine.'

He finishes his gnocchi and regards me with amusement. 'It's been an education getting to know you, Emma Hartley.'

'Likewise,' I say. 'Are you ready for that cheesecake now? We have to be at the bookshop in half an hour, but it would be a shame not to try it.'

'Are you sure you're only taking me to a bookshop?' he says suspiciously. 'Not to rob the post office?'

'Nothing so exciting,' I assure him. 'I promise the next stage of our Christmas programme will be entirely uneventful.'

We finish our lunch and walk as quickly as possible to The Rabbit Hole. It's only a few streets away, but my hands are numb by the time we reach it. I tore a hole in my woollen gloves when I was taking off my skates, and the wind whistles through the gap, feeling as though it's coming directly off the Arctic tundra.

'We should have gone skating this afternoon instead of this morning,' says Tom, shoving his hands deep into his pockets. 'They won't need a generator if this keeps up. The forecast said snow was on the way. It didn't say it was coming directly from Norway.'

'It would have been lovely to skate in the falling snow,' I say dreamily, thinking of Alex and Sophie and the way the flakes rested on her shining blonde hair while Alex thought he'd never seen anything so beautiful.

'No, it wouldn't,' says Tom. 'It was bad enough having to swim several miles to safety. We'd never have survived if we'd been caught in a blizzard in the middle of the ice.'

'That rink was about ten metres across,' I say. 'All we needed to do was skate in a straight line.'

'It doesn't work like that,' he says. 'Haven't you read what happens to people when they're caught in snowstorms? They entirely lose their sense of direction and go around and around in circles. That's what would have happened to us. We'd have spent several hours going in the wrong direction, then collapsed onto the ice. With any luck, the rescue services would have arrived with hot drinks and flashlights before the worst happened.'

'Don't you have a torch on your phone?' I ask.

'The battery is flat.'

'And whose fault is that?'

He grins. 'How was I to know a simple day out with you required flashlights and emergency provisions? You might have warned me in advance.'

'If it comes to that,' I retort, 'how was I to know a day out with you would involve barely escaping a six-month sentence for criminal damage? Anyway, we're here now, so stop complaining.'

Chapter Eighteen

The door of The Rabbit Hole chimes merrily as we enter. There are fairy lights strung everywhere, and the artificial log fire is glowing in the corner.

'You made it!' says Ollie, rushing over and giving me a hug. 'Ed and I were about to send out a search party.'

'You said three o'clock,' I remind him. 'We're five minutes early.'

Ed waves to us. 'Hi, Em. And this must be Tom. I've heard so much about you.'

Tom gives him a wary look. 'Why do I suspect not all of it was good?'

'Paranoia,' I say.

Ollie points to a couple of armchairs. 'You should bag the best chairs before the reading begins.'

'Reading?' says Tom warily. 'Who's doing that?'

'You are, of course!' I say and laugh at his horrified expression.

'I am,' Ed reassures him. 'Unless you decide to volunteer once you've got into the spirit of the thing.'

'I don't expect I shall,' says Tom, sitting down in the nearest armchair. 'No doubt, Emma has told you about my appalling attitude to Christmas.'

'It has been mentioned,' says Ed. 'But when you've known Emma for as long as I have, you'll realise she's slightly prone to exaggeration.'

'I am not!' I say indignantly. 'I have literally never exaggerated a single thing in my entire life.'

'I stand corrected,' says Ed. 'Shall we make a start?'

Several customers have arrived with their children and settled into the various chairs and sofas by the fire. I sneak a glance at Tom, who's looking around the shop with interest. There can't be anything here to which he can take exception. If I'd set out to imagine the archetypal Christmas scene, I need have looked no further. Disney would pay good money to be allowed to send one of their consultants to The Rabbit Hole to take notes about their steaming mugs of hot chocolate, plates of cookies, and towers of Christmas books.

'Welcome!' says Ed, picking up a book. 'We're delighted to have so many of our regular customers with us this afternoon. And a few new faces too.'

He nods to Tom, whose face flickers in alarm as though he thinks Ed is a stage hypnotist who will pull him out of the audience and force him to cluck like a chicken.

'I thought we'd start with The Night Before Christmas,' says Ed. 'And then we can move on to The Wind in the Willows.'

He clears his throat and opens the book. I close my eyes as I listen, remembering all the times Dad read this to me on Christmas Eve when I was a child.

'And to all, a good night!' finishes Ed, and I open my eyes again to find Tom watching me. I give him an embarrassed smile, and he smiles back.

'That was lovely,' says Ollie. 'Thank you, Ed. And now it's my turn to read about the mole and the rat.'

He and Ed swap chairs, and Ollie starts the familiar story of the mole going home for Christmas. I've heard it a thousand times, but I love it. It's one thing that never changes. I wish that were true of everything. Maybe not everything, but the really important things in life. I suddenly remember Dad saying to me when I was small and crying about losing something. 'If nothing ever changed, there would be no butterflies.'

Ollie reads beautifully. He always has. I first met him in the student union bar at university when he was holding forth about Proust. He caught my eye halfway through and collapsed into laughter, and I realised he was nowhere near as pompous as he was trying to appear.

He told me later he was trying to impress the barman, who was a fellow student on his course. I don't remember whether they got together. If they did, it wasn't for long, because Ollie graduated the following summer and met Ed, and the rest is history. It's nice to know some people make relationships work. I hope Ollie and Ed find a way to stay together. I'd miss this annual book reading.

Ollie finishes the chapter to rapturous applause.

'I always said I could make a living treading the boards,' he remarks complacently.

'You still can,' says Ed. 'If you don't get those invoices done before we close, the pair of us will be out in the snow and searching for other careers.'

The customers mill about, looking at the displays of Christmas books Ollie has helpfully arranged into tempting piles.

'That was great,' says Tom. 'I'm tempted to buy some for myself.'

'You should,' I say. 'Didn't you say your nephews and niece were coming for Christmas?'

'Great idea! Especially as you've made it impossible for me to buy them any toys.'

'That was entirely your own doing,' I say. 'I have absolutely no sympathy for you.'

'Help me choose,' he says, picking up the nearest book. 'Would they like this one?'

'How should I know? I have no idea how old they are.'

He frowns in concentration. 'Edward is seven, Charlotte is five, and Jakey is three and a half.'

Ollie hands him a copy of The Train to Impossible Places. 'You should start with this one. I love it. And for the younger ones, I'd recommend Mog's Christmas and Dear Santa.'

'You're the expert,' says Tom, pulling out his wallet.

Ed rings up the books while Ollie joins me on the sofa. 'What have you two been up to today?'

I catch Tom's eye and look away. 'This and that. We skated, and we did some toy shopping. And now we're buying books. The usual Christmas stuff.'

Tom sinks into an armchair opposite us. 'If what we got up to today is Emma's definition of normal, I'd hate to be on the receiving end of one of her more unusual days.'

'I'm all agog,' says Ollie, looking from Tom to me. 'I hope you're going to fill in the details before I die of curiosity.'

'There's nothing to tell,' I say. 'One or two small hiccups, but nothing worth boring you with. Just typical Christmas fun. And now we're here, and nothing could be more Christmassy than your shop. The readings went well. You seem to have sold plenty of books.'

'We usually do,' he says. 'But that isn't the only reason we do it. Ed and I always love our Christmas story afternoon. It feels as though Christmas has properly begun once I've heard Ed reading The Night Before Christmas.'

'I thought Christmas began when you drank your first Christmas whisky or beer,' I say.

'It does,' he says. 'We're closing in ten minutes, and I have four bottles of Christmas beer in my snack cupboard. I hope you and Tom mean to stay and enjoy them with us.'

'I'd love to,' says Tom. 'Unless Emma has something else planned for us. It's almost dark now, so it may be time for night manoeuvres around the local countryside.'

'I thought about that,' I say, 'but I couldn't find my compass. Christmas beer sounds great. We can sit by the fire and tell ghost stories.'

'Ed won't sleep if we do that,' says Ollie. 'He had nightmares for weeks after I showed him Alien.'

Ed turns the shop sign to Closed. 'It's a few minutes early, but there aren't many people on the high street. It's too cold.'

Ollie fetches the beers. 'Is this the last stop on your tour of Hampshire's winter wonderland?' he asks me.

I look at my watch. 'We have one more stop, but not for half an hour. I set the timer before I left the flat like you showed me.'

Tom looks alarmed. 'I don't like the sound of that. Anything that needs a timer can't be good.'

'This is,' I say.

He doesn't look convinced. 'Timers make me think of those awful fitness tests we had to do at school. We had a sadistic PE teacher who used to be in the army. Are you setting me a Christmas running challenge through the streets of Christchurch while you three watch in disbelief, then tell me to drop and give you twenty push-ups?'

'That wasn't on my original list,' I say. 'But I'm always open to new ideas.'

'Then it's something to do with a bomb,' he says. 'You're forcing me to defuse an enormous Christmas cracker in two minutes before it explodes glitter all over me.'

'It's neither of those things,' I reassure him. 'Enjoy your beer and stop fretting.'

'I'll turn the lights down,' says Ollie. 'We'll feel more Christmassy by candlelight.'

He dims the shop lights and produces an enormous candle in the shape of a gingerbread house.

'This is guaranteed to fill the room with the delicate scent of cinnamon,' he says. 'With the faintest hint of spruce and citrus.'

I settle back in my chair and sip my beer. 'This isn't bad. I'm not usually keen on beer, but this one is lovely and spicy.'

'What did I tell you?' says Ollie. 'You've wasted your entire day trying to get Tom into a Christmassy mood, when all you had to do was open a couple of these. What do you say, Tom? Are you a convert to the wonder of Christmas yet?'

'A few more of these, and I might be,' says Tom, smiling at me.

'This is absolutely perfect,' I tell Ollie. 'If being here doesn't change Tom's mind, nothing will. It –'

There's a loud wailing noise, and it starts to rain. We stare at each other, stunned, for a split second before Ed leaps to his feet.

'You've set off the smoke alarm!' he yells at Ollie, who makes a lunge for the candle and snuffs it out.

'It's too late for that!' shouts Ed. 'The sprinkler is on an automatic circuit.'

Tom wrenches the shop door open, and an icy draft blasts through the shop.

I pull off my coat and start waving it near the smoke alarm.

'The books!' shouts Ollie.

I stop waving my coat, leap onto the sofa and hold it underneath the sprinkler while the others race around, moving piles of books out of the way of the water.

The shrieking stops abruptly, and the sprinkler eventually follows suit. I climb down from the sofa, clutching my sopping wet coat.

'Are the books alright?' I gasp.

'Most of them,' says Ed. 'But that pile of magazines is ruined. Also those bookmarks.'

'At least it wasn't our first edition Dickens,' says Ollie.

'And now we know the sprinkler system works,' says Ed. 'That's important in a bookshop.'

'I'm so sorry,' I say. 'This was all my fault for asking you to make it Christmassy for Tom.'

'Nonsense,' says Ed. 'Ollie's been dying to burn that candle ever since he got it. I refused to let him burn it at home because it would clash with our "scent of the ocean" room diffuser. So, if anyone's to blame, it's me.'

'You two should get going,' Ollie says to me. 'We can clean up in here. Don't look so distraught, Emma. These things happen. At least there were no customers in the store. And the disaster didn't occur before I'd had the opportunity to enchant everyone with my reading. We'll see you both later.'

Chapter Nineteen

It starts to snow as Tom and I leave the bookshop and head back along the high street towards Ollie and Ed's flat.

'That was unexpected,' says Tom as we reach the lobby.

'Everything that's happened today has been unexpected,' I say, and he laughs.

'Don't say that! I've been impressed with how well you've kept it all under control until now.'

I pull my keys out of my pocket. 'Of course, you have. We skated on slush and got soaked, got ourselves thrown out of a toy department, then got soaked all over again in a bookshop.'

'It seems to be a bit of a theme,' he agrees. 'Are you planning to order a pizza, then spray me with the shower while I eat it?'

'That could be arranged,' I say darkly.

He follows me up the stairs to the flat. 'I should have packed a towel. I used to be a boy scout, and we were supposed to be prepared at all times. I'm not sure for what, but preparation was definitely a theme. Akela was always asking us to light fires and tie knots and decode strange messages in Morse Code.'

'I can't imagine you as a boy scout,' I say.

Tom looks hurt. 'Are you saying you don't see me as an outdoorsy, macho type?'

'You're quite outdoorsy,' I say. 'At least, you are at the fair. But we all are. We don't have any choice. I'm not sure about the macho part. You made enough fuss at the ice rink.'

'I merely commented on the dampness of my jeans,' he says. 'There's nothing unmanly about that. James Bond would have had plenty to say if his dinner suit got soaked while he was escaping piranhas or laser-wielding sharks.'

'You're obsessed with the idea of sharks,' I say, opening the front door and stepping inside. 'There were none at the ice rink, and there are none here. Or there weren't when I left this morning.'

'How about squid?' he says, hanging up his coat and taking mine from me.

'Maybe in the fridge,' I say. 'Ed is quite fond of calamari. What are you doing with my coat?'

'Taking it to the bathroom and wringing it out,' he says. 'What possessed you to wear it after we left the shop? If I'd realised how wet it was, I'd have given you mine.'

'Is that what James Bond would have done?'

'Indubitably,' he says. 'He'd have handed you his dinner jacket without a second thought. I expect he'd have made some dreadful pun too.'

I leave him to deal with my coat while I go to the kitchen and check the oven timer. It beeps five minutes later, and I open the oven to inspect the cookies. I made the dough last night and rolled it out and cut it into shapes this morning. They're cooked to perfection.

'Something smells good,' says Tom, appearing in the kitchen doorway.

I point to the cookies. 'They're cardamom and ginger.'

'What are we doing with these?' he says. 'Having a festive cookie fight? Taking them to the poor? Opening a cookie museum?'

'Decorating them,' I say, handing him an apron. 'It's an important part of Christmas.'

'Decorating them how?' he says.

'That's up to you. I've filled several icing bags with different coloured frosting. We have sprinkles and sugar shapes and edible glitter. This is your chance to be creative.'

'Not my strong suit,' he says. 'I'm more of a cookie connoisseur than a designer.'

'This is the time to explore another side of yourself,' I say. 'Why not start with a snowflake? The white icing is over there.'

'I'll try anything once,' he says, picking up a cookie. 'I hope you don't plan to sell these at the fair. Your customers will demand refunds, and I'll have to pretend I've never seen them before in my life.'

'I'm not planning to sell them,' I say. 'They haven't been made under approved conditions. These are for private consumption only.'

'Now, there's a plan I can get on board with,' he says. 'If you want a taste tester, I'm all yours.'

'That comes later,' I say. 'For now, we decorate them.'

I put on a CD of Christmas music and start icing a beard onto one of the Santa cookies. Tom watches me, amused, then picks up an icing bag and begins to decorate his snowflake.

'I'm rather pleased with this,' he announces after a couple of minutes. 'The silver glitter adds a classy touch. Can I take it home with me? My mum doesn't usually think much of my cooking skills, but she'll have to eat her words when she sees this.'

'Of course,' I say, putting the final button onto Santa's suit. 'I'll write you a report if you like. "Tom has been very well-behaved today. He has played in the snow, stopped a little boy from crying, eaten all his lunch, listened to a story, and taken part in our craft afternoon."'

'I sound quite impressive, don't I?' he says. 'If we leave out the fact I was the one who made the little boy cry in the first place.'

'But you did something about it,' I say. 'That's the main thing. Life isn't about trying not to make any mistakes. It's about recognising them and putting them right.'

'Except when it's too late,' he says.

'It's almost never too late.'

'I wish that were true,' he says. 'But some things can't be fixed.'

I know exactly what he's talking about, but there's nothing I can say, so I hand him a reindeer cookie.

'Try this one. Don't forget his red nose.'

'Why does it have to be red?' he asks.

'Because that's what the song says.'

'So what? Anyway, how do we know this one is Rudolph? It could be Smasher or Chancer or Stupid or Vomit.'

I give a choke of laughter. 'Which children's books did you read?'

'It was a long time ago,' he says. 'I seem to remember the reindeer had strange names. Santa seems quite avant garde.'

'No one is more traditional than Santa!' I say severely. 'What colour are you going to make his nose?'

'Or her nose,' he says. 'I could make it blue. It's cold enough up at the North Pole.'

'You do you!' I say. 'I'm about to ice one of these stockings. You should try a Christmas tree next. It's your area of expertise.'

It takes us another hour to finish the cookies. I lay them out on the tray to admire them. 'Ollie and Ed will be impressed with these. Speaking of whom …'

There's the sound of a key in the lock, and Ollie pokes his head around the kitchen door. 'How's it going?'

'Great timing, as always,' I say. 'You're just in time for the taste testing.'

'How are the books?' asks Tom.

'All safe,' says Ed, appearing behind Ollie. 'Thanks to your prompt action with your coat, Em. Do you need us to buy you a new one?'

'It was water, not paint,' I say. 'At least, I assume it was. If not, you should have a word with your security company. And my coat gets much wetter than that when I walk home in the rain.'

'Or wear it to go skating,' adds Tom.

'What did happen today?' says Ollie. 'You keep dropping hints, but neither of you will tell me anything about it.'

'There's nothing to tell!' I say. 'Take off your coats and let's taste these cookies.'

We sit at the kitchen table and Ollie picks up a miniature sleigh. 'Did Sophie and Alex make this kind of cookie?'

'Who?' says Tom.

'Friends of Ollie,' I say. 'Don't worry about it.'

'Ok,' he says. 'I'm going to try one of these Christmas stockings. I love the way you've iced the stripes, Emma. You must have a steadier hand than me. It was as much as I could do to ice a snowflake smoothly.'

'All it takes is practise,' I say.

Tom lifts the cookie to his mouth and takes a bite. An odd expression passes across his face. For a moment, I think he's choking. I start to my feet, all ready to do whatever that manoeuvre is which involves throwing your arms around someone from behind and squeezing as hard as you can.

I'm interrupted by Ollie, who has bitten into a snowflake and promptly spat it out again.

'Ollie!' protests Ed before coughing and grabbing for a napkin. He claps it to his mouth, obviously spitting out his cookie too.

I look at Tom, whose face wears a mixture of shock and amusement.

'What?' I say.

'Nothing!' he says.

'There's clearly something.' I grab a gingerbread person and lift it to my lips.

'Stop!' Ollie and Ed yell in unison.

Tom leans over and takes the cookie from me. 'There may have been something wrong with the recipe.'

'No, there wasn't,' I say. 'Unless you mean the spices? I used a teaspoon of cardamom. The recipe says it gives it a warm and Christmassy flavour.'

'I expect that's it,' says Tom.

'No, it isn't,' says Ollie. 'I know what cardamom tastes like. Ed always puts it in his rice pudding.'

He looks at the counter top, and his eyes crinkle in amusement. 'How much sugar did the recipe call for?'

'I don't remember,' I say. 'About 100 grams, I think. Why?'

'And you used the sugar from that jar there?' He points at the jar standing next to the vanilla pods.

'Yes. Why?'

'It's salt, you nincompoop!'

He fills a glass of water and hands it to Tom. 'You should drink that before your electrolytes end up dangerously out of balance.'

'It can't be salt!' I say. 'The jar's too big.'

'We buy it in bulk,' he says. 'Didn't you look at it as you poured it in? The crystals are the wrong size.'

'I thought it was caster sugar,' I say, my face flaming as I watch Tom drink his water in one gulp.

'Pure sodium chloride,' says Ollie. 'Only you, Em!'

I stare at the cookies, dismayed. 'Are they all ruined?'

'Unless the salt magically gathered itself into one section of the dough and left the rest salt-free,' he says. 'Even then, you'd be left with the problem that there's no sugar in them.'

'It looks like snow tonight,' says Ed. 'Maybe we could use these cookies to salt the driveway instead?'

'That way, we can be sure of getting out to the emergency room for a blood pressure check,' agrees Ollie, laughing.

Tom seems equally amused. 'Mum's always complaining about the slugs in her vegetable patch. I'll take some of these home for her. She can crush them up and put them around the cabbages.'

I try to laugh, but to my horror, I realise my eyes are full of tears.

'Em?' says Ollie, reaching for my hand.

I pull it away. 'That's great! Let's all laugh at Emma for messing things up yet again!'

Tom looks concerned. 'That isn't what we're –'

'Yes, it is!' I shout. 'You all think I'm a joke. Well, maybe I am. But I was trying my best to plan a perfect day for you and show you that Christmas can be fun. And I couldn't even manage that. Fine, I give up! You're right, and I'm wrong. Christmas is for children and losers, and it's much more fun to stand on the sidelines and mock. I'll leave you all to it!'

I turn and storm out of the kitchen. I almost head to my bedroom, but the door doesn't lock, and Ollie would be bound to come and look for me. I can't face anyone while I'm in this state. I don't understand why I'm so upset, but I am. I feel small and stupid and insignificant.

I wrench open the front door and run down the path to the street. The snow is falling more thickly, and the world is silent. I reach the high street and set off along it, with no idea where I'm headed. All the shops seem to be closed. I look around for a cafe where I can hide in the warm until I'm sure Tom has left. I haven't brought my phone with me, so I can't even text Ollie to find out.

Hopefully, Tom won't stay for long. Even now, he may be packing a bag of slug repellent cookies and setting off back to his cabbage patch.

Chapter Twenty

It's much colder than I expected. Maybe I'll die on the street like the little match girl, and they'll find me tomorrow morning lying on someone's doorstep with a peaceful expression on my face. Then they'll be sorry. I realise that won't work because I don't have any matches. I'll have to find somewhere soon or I really will freeze.

'Emma!' The voice comes faintly through the frosty night air.

I don't turn around but stride on more quickly, realising I'm almost at Merton's department store. My heart leaps when I see it's still open. I hesitate outside the door. No alarms have gone off, so maybe I'm not banned for life, after all.

'Emma!' shouts the voice again, and I turn to see Tom running up the street towards me.

I duck into the store, hoping he'll run past without noticing.

He doesn't. He bursts in after me. 'Emma! Stop!'

I pretend to study the new range of Ralph Lauren perfumes. With any luck, he'll go up to the toy department and get himself thrown out again. It would serve him right.

'There you are!' he gasps.

I turn to face him. 'What do you want?'

'I've been trying to catch up with you for the past five minutes,' he says. 'I took the wrong turning when I left the flat. I started following some other poor woman until I realised she was wearing a coat. I raced back to the high street and saw you ahead of me. But I couldn't make you hear me.'

'I thought you'd been a boy scout,' I say. 'You can't have been a very good one.'

'I never said I was.' He hands me a thick sweater. 'Ollie said to give you this.'

'And now you have. Please tell him I'll be home in a while. I have a few things to do first.'

'I also brought your phone,' he says. 'So, you can tell him yourself. And then I want to talk to you.'

'There's nothing to say. I've made a complete idiot of myself, and I'd like to be alone for a while.'

'Excuse me, sir, but we're about to close,' says a voice behind us, and I realise it's the same security guard we met this morning in the toy department. He doesn't appear to recognise us. It's a good thing I'm not wearing my coat.

'If you could make your purchases, we're about to close,' he repeats.

Tom looks at me with a quizzical expression. 'How about it, Emma? Have you selected your favourite perfume?'

'I'm still thinking about it,' I tell him.

'In which case,' he says, 'maybe we should allow the staff to go home. You should put on that sweater before you leave. It's cold out there.'

I drag the sweater over my head. 'I'm aware, thank you.'

'Would you like my coat as well?' he asks.

'Then you'd be the one who freezes to death,' I point out.

'I'll be fine,' he says. 'I've been running. Don't worry about me.'

'I wasn't,' I say. 'I was thinking of it as a positive.'

'Is there anywhere open around here?' Tom asks the security guard.

'There's a cafe on Catherine Street,' says the man, pointing.

'Fantastic,' says Tom.

I follow him out of the store and towards the cafe. I don't have to speak to him if I don't want to, but I could use a hot drink.

Tom seems to read my thoughts. 'We can sit at separate tables if you like.'

He opens the door to the cafe, which is small but brightly lit and smells of cinnamon and ground coffee. There are only six tables, and five of them are occupied.

'I could stand,' offers Tom, and I suddenly laugh.

'Don't be ridiculous. Order us some coffee before I freeze to death.'

It's beautifully warm in here, and I'm already thawing out. By the time our drinks arrive, I'm feeling a lot better.

'They've stopped serving meals,' apologises Tom. 'They offered me their last two cookies, but I thought …'

'It's far too soon,' I agree. 'I'm sorry I yelled at you back there. I suppose you want an explanation.'

'No, I don't,' he says, his face uncharacteristically serious. 'I'm sorry you were so upset. All I wanted was to make sure you were ok and not buried up to your neck in a snowdrift.'

'It wouldn't have made any difference if I had been,' I say. 'You'd never have found me. You'd have spent the entire evening digging some other woman out of a snowdrift instead.'

'Probably,' he agrees. 'What a waste of time! Luckily, I saw you as you reached Merton's. I admired your courage in going back there.'

'It was that or turning into a lump of ice,' I say. 'And I knew it was you they'd be keeping an eye out for, not me. If the worst came to the worst, I was planning to tell that security guard who you were.'

'Quite right, too,' he says. 'By the way, it might be a good idea to tell Ollie and Ed you're ok before they organise a search party of their own. It will save us all spending the evening tracking each other around the town and missing each other by inches.'

I quickly text Ollie. *Sorry about running out. I needed some space. Thanks for the sweater!*

A text pings back at once.

All good. See you when we see you. Love ya! Ollie x

I take a sip of my coffee, avoiding Tom's eye. That's the trouble with dramatic gestures. They feel satisfying at the time, but eventually you have to face everyone. Either you pretend nothing has happened, and hope they do the same, or you have to explain yourself. Which is almost impossible because you have no idea what caused you to react like that in the first place. All you know is that you've revealed a secret piece of yourself to other people, leaving them free to interpret it in any way they choose.

'Feeling better?' asks Tom when I've finished my drink.

I give him a non-committal smile, hoping to convey an impression of complete normality. With any luck, I can persuade him he's imagining things and I always go for a brisk walk in the snow after baking cookies.

'You don't have to talk about it,' he says, 'but I'm sorry about what happened back there. I had an amazing day, and I hate to see you so upset.'

I roll my eyes. 'Of course you had an amazing day! It couldn't have gone any better if I'd been planning it for months. First, the skating rink melts. Then they call security and throw us out. Nothing daunted, I take you to a magical Christmas reading at a quaint old bookstore and end up almost destroying their entire stock. And I complete the day by doing my best to kill you all with salt poisoning.'

'Is that what you were doing?' says Tom. 'And there was me thinking you'd made a mistake with the recipe.'

'No, it was that other thing.'

'Fair enough,' he says philosophically. 'Well, no harm done. Your evil plot failed, so you won't end up spending the night in a jail cell.'

'I'd plead extreme provocation. No judge would dare convict me.'

His lips twitch. 'It's as well to have your defence prepared well in advance.'

He takes my hand. I almost pull it free, but it's nice to feel I'm not completely alone, that someone cares about me. Tom may not understand why this Christmas is so important to me, but that doesn't matter. He can see I'm upset, and he's trying to make me feel better.

'Emma,' he says gently. 'I mean it when I say I had a wonderful day. It was funny when the ice melted and when we got thrown out of Merton's. And I loved spending the afternoon in the bookshop. Ok, it had a somewhat dramatic ending, but there was no real damage done. As for the cookies, it wouldn't have bothered me if they'd been made of Play-Doh. I didn't mind what we did today. All I cared about was being with you. Why do you think I asked you to spend the day with me?'

'To show you the true spirit of Christmas,' I say.

'I wouldn't have cared if you'd taken me to a petting zoo and we'd been chased by emus,' he says. 'And I understand the spirit of Christmas as well as the next person. I just wanted some time with you. You and I didn't get off to the best start, or I'd have asked you out ages ago. I almost worked up the courage several times, but I thought it might be awkward for you if you turned me down, then had to keep working with me each night. This felt like the perfect excuse. I knew you couldn't resist the opportunity of converting me once and for all to the magic of Christmas, and I'd get to spend the day with you. It seemed like a win-win situation.'

'They don't keep emus at petting zoos,' I say.

'Tigers, then. Do you understand what I'm saying?'

I feel suddenly shy. 'I think so.'

'Is there any chance of us doing this again?' he asks. 'Maybe not the skating and criminal activity but spending the day together.'

I smile back at him. 'I'd like that.'

'I'm afraid we're about to close,' says the woman behind the counter.

Tom looks amused. 'Are we setting the record for being thrown out of the most places in one day?'

'They're closing,' I say. 'The only place we were actually thrown out of was the toy department.'

He doesn't look convinced. 'We had to leave the skating rink, then the toy store, then The Rabbit Hole, then Merton's again, and now this place. It all counts.'

'You need to get out more,' I say.

'I'm happy to, especially if you'll join me.'

He pushes back his chair and holds out his hand to me. 'Are you warm enough to walk home? It's only a few minutes.'

'What would you do if I said no?'

'Throw you over my shoulder and carry you,' he says.

I take a step backwards. 'That won't be necessary. I'm perfectly warm now, thanks.'

We leave the cafe and set off together down the high street. The snow is falling more thickly, muffling the usual street sounds. All I can hear is the soft crunch of our footsteps as we walk quickly towards the flat. The snowflakes brush my face like tiny, frozen feathers as we walk.

Tom stops on the corner of Jason Street.

'This is the right direction,' I say. 'Ollie's place is just down there.'

'I know,' he says. 'But before we go back to the flat, there's something I …'

He studies my face for a moment before leaning down and kissing me. I close my eyes, allowing myself to get lost in the moment. His hands find my waist, and he pulls me closer to him. His lips are surprisingly warm in the frosty air. Time seems to pause as we stand there, locked together.

'Oy, mate! You're blocking the pavement!' says a jogger, almost crashing into us.

Tom turns his head to look at him. 'And you're ruining a perfect moment.'

'Stand in the road and have your perfect moment there,' the jogger advises him. 'This pavement is for people who are moving.'

He pushes past and jogs off down the street.

'I hope he gets jogger's elbow,' says Tom, watching him go.

'Is that a thing?' I say, slightly breathless from our kiss.

'It would be if I had my way,' he says. 'Do you remember where we were when he so rudely interrupted us?'

An uncontrollable shiver shakes me. I'd forgotten for the past few minutes how cold it was.

'I'd better get you home,' says Tom. 'It wouldn't be romantic to dump your lifeless body on Ollie's doorstep.'

'It would be rather thoughtless,' I agree. 'Bin day isn't until Friday.'

He tucks my hand into his pocket and slips his arm around my shoulders.

'Perhaps we should run back to Ollie's?' he suggests. 'With any luck, we may be able to catch up with that jogger and trip him up.'

Chapter Twenty-One

Ollie and Ed are going out for dinner at a friend's house on Thursday evening. I offer to drive over to the fair myself, but Ollie refuses.

'I'm fine taking you if you don't mind arriving half an hour early.'

'That works for me,' I say. 'I'm sure I can find something to do.'

'Or someone to talk to,' he says, and I blush.

'What's that supposed to mean?'

He gives me a sidelong glance. 'I was referring to that purveyor of fine arboreal products – Mr Christmas himself.'

'You mean Tom?'

'Sharp as a tack, as always,' he says. 'What happened after you rushed out of here yesterday evening? You didn't look too upset when you came back. Can I assume all was not lost, and Tom didn't turn his back on Christmas because you failed to show him the magic of the season?'

'You can assume what you like,' I say.

I have no intention of discussing last night with Ollie or anyone else. Not until I know where this is going. Tom may have been secretly drinking throughout yesterday to alleviate the tedium of our Christmas activities. In which case, he may retain absolutely no memory of kissing me.

Ollie parks the car next to the green and carries my boxes over to my stall as usual.

'No sign of Mr Christmas,' he says when he sees Tom's stall is still locked up. 'Maybe he's hiding somewhere to surprise you.'

'Like where?'

'How should I know?' he says. 'We know he has a propensity for dressing up and pretending to be someone he isn't. I hear he promised to deliver completely unrealistic gifts to several children.'

'That's not true,' I say. 'In fact, he went to considerable trouble to remove some of those children from Santa's naughty list. He did a great job as Santa. The new guy is ok, but he isn't a patch on Tom.'

'Speaking of whom,' he says, pointing to the car park. 'I believe I recognise that truck. Time for me to leave.'

'Have a lovely time tonight,' I say.

'See you at ten o'clock,' he says.

'You can't come out to collect me,' I object. 'You're having dinner with your friends. I'll get a taxi.'

'I was planning to slip out for half an hour,' he says. 'But it occurs to me you might prefer someone else to take you home. Shall I ask him?'

He waves to Tom as he walks over to us, carrying a Christmas tree on each shoulder. 'Hi, Tom. Are you rushing off tonight, or do you have time to take Emma home?'

'I'd be delighted,' says Tom.

'Wonderful,' says Ollie. 'I have to fly. See you whenever, Emma. Don't feel you have to rush back.'

He waves again and walks back to his car.

'That wasn't my idea,' I say to Tom.

'What wasn't?'

'Asking you for a ride home. Ollie and Ed are going out tonight. I was happy to leave my boxes here overnight and take a taxi. I still am. I'm the only person still bringing my things to and from the fair each night. Maybe it's time I started leaving them locked in the hut.'

Tom's eyes are alight with laughter. 'Is my truck not good enough for you?'

'Of course, it is. I didn't want to take out of your way, that's all.'

'Has it occurred to you I might like to be taken out of my way?' he says. 'I had a great time yesterday. The least I can do is give you a ride home, with or without your boxes.'

'Yesterday was a failure,' I say. 'You don't have to be polite.'

'The end part wasn't,' he says, and I flush.

'Oh, that.'

'Yes, that,' he says. 'I'm hoping to repeat it in the near future. Would you like to have lunch with me tomorrow? I was thinking of Allegro's. It's quite near to Ollie's flat. My sister was raving about it the last time she was home.'

'Sounds great,' I say. 'Let someone else mess up the cooking for once.'

Lucy wanders over a few minutes later. 'Hi, Emma. I haven't seen much of you lately. I wondered whether you fancied getting a coffee sometime? I'm free tomorrow around noon if you are.'

'Any time except tomorrow,' I say. 'I'm having lunch with someone.'

'I might be free for coffee,' Tom tells her, and she looks surprised.

'Oh … er …'

'He's winding you up,' I say. 'Ignore him.'

'I'm afraid I am,' says Tom. 'Not that I wouldn't enjoy a caffeinated beverage with you, Lucy, but I'm busy tomorrow. I have a lunch date with a beautiful woman.'

Lucy looks from me to Tom and smiles. 'I see. We can have coffee some other time.'

'I wouldn't miss it,' says Tom.

'She's still talking to me,' I say. 'I'll call you, Lucy. How's the gingerbread business?'

'It's great,' she says. 'I'm selling out most nights. I'll be hiring a unit next year and making my own.'

'Maybe I could use them in my Christmas boxes if I come back next year,' I say.

'You should move here permanently,' she says. 'One of my housemates is moving out in the new year. I could put in a good word for you.'

'I can't think much beyond this fair right now,' I say. 'Sales are going well, but there's still a while to go. I may already have exhausted the entire customer pool from the greater Honeywell area.'

'I doubt it,' she says. 'I heard someone talking about your stall when I was in the bakery today picking up my cookies. She said she'd bought one of your relaxation boxes and was feeling far less stressed about Christmas than usual. The woman she was talking to said she'd make a note to visit you when she comes to the fair. Word of mouth is the best kind of marketing.'

'I hope so,' I say. 'But I don't dare jinx it. I intend to keep working until the last possible moment and not take anything for granted.'

'You appear to have a customer,' Tom tells Lucy.

'So I do. I'd better run. Enjoy your separate lunches tomorrow, both of you.'

'I'll pass on your good wishes to my date,' promises Tom.

The evening passes more quickly than usual. Lucy is right that word seems to have spread. I sell out of my family boxes before eight o'clock and sell my last Christmas for One box a few minutes before the fair closes.

'There won't be much for me to carry to my truck,' says Tom. 'It's a good job because my back is aching from this afternoon's delivery. I had to drive Mr Campbell's tree over to Compton and help him set it up. It was a nine-footer, and it weighed a ton. But it looked lovely once it was in place. I almost suggested he used your services to decorate it.'

'I'm glad you didn't,' I say. 'I can decorate regular Christmas trees, but I wouldn't want the responsibility for something like that. If he lives in a manor house, he'll have lots of people coming in and out over Christmas, like the mayor or the local squire. They'll expect to see a professionally decorated tree.'

'Don't underestimate yourself,' he says. 'You have a real talent for it. If you start this business of yours, I was going to suggest you expand it to offer a tree decorating service. If you come back here next year, you could team up with whoever's selling the Christmas trees. It's a shame we didn't think of it this year.'

'That's a good idea,' I say. 'It's just a pity they won't be Kingsley Christmas trees.'

'There's nothing special about our trees,' he says. 'And maybe the person who buys our farm will decide to continue growing them.'

'I hope so. I think I'll leave the rest of my boxes here tonight. I don't want you dislocating a vertebra on my behalf.'

'I'm fine,' he says. 'I've sold all my trees, so I'm ready when you are. Will Ollie and Ed be home by the time we get there?'

'I doubt it,' I say. 'Ollie's a talker. He won't leave until he's kicked out.'

'Even better,' says Tom. 'I've been very much hoping you'll invite me in for some of those leftover cookies.'

Chapter Twenty-Two

I arrange to meet Tom outside Allegro's the following day. He's already waiting when I arrive.

'I'm glad you found the place,' he says.

'It's a two-minute walk from Ed and Ollie's flat.'

'I know,' he says. 'But I'm aware of your orientation problems.'

'My what?'

'Your sense of direction,' he says. 'I was worried that if I chose anywhere further afield, you wouldn't turn up, and I'd discover later you'd spent the afternoon wandering around the wilds of Hampshire getting yourself lost in snowdrifts.'

'I wouldn't do anything so stupid. I'd have given up and gone straight home.'

'Which would have been disappointing for me,' he says. 'Shall we go inside before we freeze to death out here?'

It's warm inside the restaurant, and I'm delighted when the server sits us in a booth next to a huge log fire.

'We could do with one of these at the fair,' I say. 'It gets cold standing behind that stall every evening.'

'I doubt Frances would want to risk it,' he says. 'Can you imagine letting our original Santa loose near an open flame of any kind?'

'Our new Santa doesn't seem to drink,' I say. 'And he's the jolliest one I've ever seen. I don't know how he does it.'

'Me neither,' says Tom. 'It was bad enough having to stand in for him for one night. I couldn't keep up that level of cheerfulness for long.'

'Maybe it's his vocation,' I suggest.

He raises an eyebrow. 'I doubt any little boy decides the only thing he wants to be when he grows up is a Santa impersonator.'

'I don't see why not. People train to be clowns and mimes trapeze artists. That must be a deliberate decision on their part. You don't wake up one morning and decide to work in a circus. There has to be planning and forethought.'

'That's different,' he says. 'There's a surprising amount of skill involved in that sort of thing. How much skill does it take to play Santa for a few weeks?'

'Quite a bit. You saw what happened when someone completely unqualified got the job.'

'That was the demon drink,' he says. 'If it hadn't been for that, he would have been fine. He was ok to start with.'

'He wasn't as cheerful as he might have been,' I say.

'That was because Mrs Claus was running around with one of the elves,' he reminds me, and I laugh.

'All I'm saying is that playing Santa takes skill.'

'But not training,' he says. 'Otherwise, I wouldn't have done such a superb job.'

'An adequate job,' I say. 'I can't go further than that.'

He looks hurt. 'That's the last time I do a favour for you. And please don't suggest I enrol in Santa school to learn my craft. It would be a waste of an entire half day. I can imagine the timetable. Nine a.m. – how to shout Ho Ho Ho! Ten a.m. – how to ask children what they want for Christmas in a way that looks as though you care. Eleven a.m. – how to pose for pictures. Noon – graduation.'

'I'd argue with you some more,' I say. 'But my recent attempt to get you into the Christmas spirit was a complete disaster, and I'm afraid of making things worse.'

He reaches for my hand. 'No, it wasn't. I had a wonderful day. I'd been wondering ever since we first met how I could persuade you to go out with me. I made such a bad first impression, and I couldn't think how to improve your opinion of me.'

'I may have slightly rushed to judgement,' I say. 'I took it too personally when you said you weren't a fan of Christmas. It felt as though you were looking down on something that was incredibly important to me.'

'I didn't mean to make you feel that way,' he says.

'I know you didn't, but I'm finding this Christmas rather a strain.'

The server appears, and I order the risotto. Tom opts for chicken cacciatore.

'I thought you might go for the roast turkey,' he says.

'That's for Christmas Day,' I tell him. 'It makes it far less special if you eat several Christmas dinners in the run up to the day itself.'

'Do you have rules for everything to do with Christmas?' he asks.

'Not rules. But I'm keen on traditions. There's nothing wrong with that.'

'I suppose not. Does your family have hundreds of Christmas traditions?'

I stare at the tablecloth. I don't want to talk about my family, but it's a reasonable question.

'We used to,' I say. 'Not any longer.'

'What changed?' he asks.

'My parents got divorced last year.'

I expect him to nod and move on. It's quite common for people's marriages to break up, especially once their children have grown up and moved out. There's nothing anyone can usefully say.

'I'm sorry to hear that,' he says. 'Any particular reason?'

I almost tell him to mind his own business. He doesn't know my parents, so there's no reason I should discuss them with him. But he looks genuinely interested, and it would be a relief to stop pretending I don't care about what's happened.

'Apparently, they hadn't been happy for a while,' I say. 'My brother and I went home for Christmas last year, and my parents told us over lunch they were selling the house. We couldn't believe it. They'd lived there since before we were born. I thought maybe it was becoming too much for them as they were getting older and they were planning to buy something more manageable for when they retired. But it wasn't that at all. They said they'd decided to go their separate ways, so this was our last Christmas together in the family home.'

Tom pulls a face. 'It doesn't sound the most tactful way to go about things.'

'It wasn't. I was angry with them both when they told us. But I came to realise it can't have been easy for them either. Christmas was the only time they could guarantee James and I would both be there, and they wanted us to have the chance to take our childhood things from the attic. That was thoughtful of them, I suppose.'

Tom doesn't look convinced. 'They must have known how special Christmas was to you. They could have chosen some other time.'

'I'm not sure they did know that,' I say. 'I've always loved Christmas. Most children do. But a lot of that was to do with going back to my childhood home each year, with all its memories. It was such a shock to realise that was over. I wasn't sure how I'd ever come to terms with it, especially with the divorce on top. But then I came up with the idea of this Christmas business, which took my mind off things a bit.'

'Have they sold the house?' asks Tom.

'It sold within a few weeks. They moved out in February, and they both bought themselves a flat. Mum went to Bath, where most of her family are, but Dad stayed in Oxford.'

'Do you still get to see them both?' he says.

'I do, but it's awkward. I'm not sure how to relate to them separately. I've only ever known them as a unit.'

'It will take time,' he says. 'Is that why you decided to come here for Christmas?'

'Mostly,' I admit. 'There are several fairs around Oxford, but I didn't want to stay there over the holidays. Not for this first year, at least. Mum and Dad both invited my brother and me for Christmas, and they were upset when they heard the other one had asked us, which was pretty unreasonable of them. I suggested going to Dad in the morning and driving to Mum's after lunch, but she said I wouldn't get there early enough to make it worthwhile, and I should spend the whole day with Dad and leave her by herself.'

Tom raises an eyebrow. 'And what did you say to that?'

'I told her not to be so ridiculous. I was still trying to decide what to do when I heard she was going to the South of France for Christmas and New Year. She said I was welcome to go along, but I told her I had to go straight back to work after Christmas. It wasn't strictly true, but by then I was fed up with the pair of them trying to get us onside and treating us as some sort of trophies. When Ollie suggested I do the Honeywell fair, I jumped at the chance. It meant I didn't upset Mum by choosing to spend Christmas with Dad, but I didn't have to spend Christmas with her in France. She says she isn't celebrating the day at all. She plans to lie on the beach with a good book and be thankful she doesn't have to sweep snow off the drive each morning. I'm hoping things will have settled down by next year, and my parents will behave more reasonably.'

'I'm sorry,' he says. 'I hope spending Christmas with Ollie and Ed will take your mind off everything you're missing.'

'I expect it will. At any rate, it won't be dull. Things never are with Ollie around. But it won't be the same. Dad and I have hung up our stockings together for as long as I can remember. We left cookies for Santa and a carrot for the reindeer and sprinkled talcum powder in front of the fireplace so we could tell whether Santa had been. There was always a boot print when I went downstairs on Christmas morning. And tiny hoof prints.'

'I'm so sorry,' he says again.

'Don't be,' I tell him. 'Plenty of people don't make a big deal of Christmas. It was difficult for me because I've never coped well with change. It's time I learned to do so. Anyway, my brother is spending Christmas with his girlfriend's family, Dad is going to Cornwall with his sister and her husband, and Mum will be topping up her suntan in Biarritz. I suppose that's their way of avoiding it all.'

'And what's your way?' he says. 'Making sure everyone has the perfect Christmas?'

'That's not what I'm doing!' I protest. 'No one has to celebrate it if they don't want to. All I'm doing is giving people the opportunity to have a perfect Christmas, if that's what they want. And lots of people do. I've sold almost two hundred Christmas boxes since I arrived.'

'You've done really well,' he says.

The server appears with our food.

'That risotto looks good,' says Tom. 'I wanted you to eat something you enjoyed on our first date.'

'Is that what this is?'

'Absolutely!' he says. 'To be fair, I thought of our day out together as our first date. But it doesn't really count because you knew nothing about it.'

'I was there,' I say.

'But you didn't know it was a date.'

'That's because it wasn't,' I say. 'Do you go on many dates where the woman doesn't realise that's what they are?'

'I can't think of any,' he says. 'Anyway, this lunch counts because I invited you and you said yes, which makes it an official date. Do you think we should order champagne?'

'Don't jump the gun,' I say as the server returns with our drinks. 'A glass of house red is enough for me. And if you keep up the pressure, this will be an extremely short date.'

'That would be a shame,' says Tom. 'I've been looking forward to trying the chocolate souffle.'

'I'm afraid that needs to be preordered,' says the server. 'It's a dessert for two. Should I let the chef know?'

Tom smiles at me. 'What do you say, Emma? Will you be here in an hour's time? It's our first date,' he tells the server. 'I'm not sure how well it's going.'

'Why not order it anyway?' says the server. 'If your companion leaves, you may be glad to have something to take your mind off it.'

'If I decide to leave,' I tell him, 'you'll be boxing it up for me to take with me. And Tom will be paying.'

'It's a deal,' says Tom. 'Chocolate souffle for two, please. I'll let you know nearer the time in what kind of packaging and how many spoons.'

He looks at his watch as the server moves away. 'I hope you'll still be here by the time it's cooked.'

'Not unless you stop telling everyone it's our first date,' I say.

'Why? I'm happy you've agreed to have lunch with me. You'll notice I didn't mention our last date to him, which was tactful of me.'

'I appreciate your discretion,' I say. 'I don't imagine you can order salt cookies in a place like this.'

'I could call him back and ask.'

'Don't bother,' I say. 'I'm quite happy with my risotto.'

Tom picks up his wine glass and taps it with his knife. 'I would like to propose a toast. To Christmas!'

'Christmas?' I say, bemused.

'That's right,' he says. 'It's the holiday that falls between Halloween and Valentine's Day.'

'I'm familiar with it. But I didn't expect you to drink to it.'

'Why not?' he says in a more serious tone. 'If it weren't for the Honeywell Christmas fair, I would never have met you.'

'And if it weren't for you selling your Christmas trees, I would never have met you,' I say. 'I'm glad you're changing your mind about the holiday season.'

'I wouldn't go that far,' he says. 'But it may not be as bad as I used to think. Now hurry up and eat your risotto or the chocolate souffle will be here. First date or no first date, I intend to fight you for every last mouthful.'

Chapter Twenty-Three

The rest of the week passes quickly. I go to the fair as usual each evening and try to concentrate on selling my stock. But it's difficult to keep my mind on it with Tom running his stall right next to me.

We spend as much time together as possible during the days. I make up my boxes each morning, while he cuts his trees and packs the truck ready for the fair. But we're usually free in the afternoons, and we go for long walks in the New Forest, stopping at village pubs. One day, Tom persuades me to go sledging with him near the farm, but we give up after overturning the sledge for the eighth time and return to the cafe, where Carolyn makes us toasted sandwiches and Bonnie sits under the table while I surreptitiously feed her my crusts.

Neither of us has mentioned what might happen after Christmas. For now, we seem content to live in the moment and enjoy our time together.

We go back to Allegro's for lunch on Friday. The server recognises us and smiles when we walk in.

'Shall I request the chef to put on a chocolate souffle?' he asks Tom.

'What do you say, Emma?' says Tom. 'Do you plan to stay for the entire meal?'

'I expect so. I'm pretty hungry. That chocolate souffle sounds good to me. What will you be having, Tom?'

'It's a dessert for two,' says the server.

'She's well aware of that,' says Tom, shepherding me to the booth where we sat last time.

'Should I order two souffles?' says the server with a puzzled frown, and I shake my head.

'One will be fine for now. Tom can order himself something else if I finish the entire thing.'

'I preferred you on our first date,' grumbles Tom.

'Likewise,' I say. 'Now we're on our sixth date, or maybe our seventh, you no longer offer me your coat.'

We order linguine con capesante, and the server disappears.

'If we're not careful, this will be another place we get ourselves banned from,' I warn Tom. 'Christchurch isn't that large. We don't want to run out of places to eat before Christmas.'

'We should be alright,' he says. 'This guy was here at the start of our romance. He won't want to risk missing out on watching it develop.'

'I'm sure all he wants to do is get through lunch and go home,' I say. 'I doubt he's even faintly interested in the lives of his customers.'

'I think you're wrong,' he says. 'But the way to prevent us being thrown out is for you to share nicely. That shouldn't be beyond your capabilities.'

The server arrives with our food, and we spend the next few minutes eating in silence. Tom looks up from his plate at last.

'Speaking of numbers of dates, it won't be so easy seeing each other after Christmas. You're going back to Oxford, and I'll be in London.'

'I'm trying not to think about that,' I say. 'But the cities aren't too far apart. We can meet at the weekends if we want to.'

'I know,' he says. 'But it won't be the same.'

'That's because we're on holiday,' I say. 'We're working while we're here, but it isn't the same as everyday life.'

'You're right,' he says. 'But I wish you weren't.'

I lay down my knife and fork and study his face, wondering whether now is a good time to talk to him about something that's been on my mind all week.

Tom smiles back at me. 'What is it?'

'Nothing,' I say.

'That's clearly not true,' he says. 'If there's something on your mind, tell me. I'd like to know what it is.'

'Ok,' I say cautiously. 'It's something I've been wondering about for a while. It's about the future of the farm.'

A flicker of annoyance crosses his face. 'I'm not sure what there is to talk about. There's already been some interest in it. I expect it will have sold by the new year.'

'That was quick,' I say.

'Not really. It's an attractive set-up for the right buyer. Mum won't have any trouble in getting a good price for it.'

'That's the thing,' I say. 'Are you sure that's what she wants?'

He frowns. 'Of course I'm sure. You aren't suggesting she lets it go for less than it's worth?'

'That's not what I'm saying. I'm asking whether she wants to sell at all?'

'I don't understand the question,' he says. 'Mum's the one who put it up for sale. The sign was already up when I arrived home.'

'I know it was.' I press on, trying to ignore the resentment in his voice. 'But I don't know why she did that. You've told me she wants to retire, and maybe she does. But I'm not convinced. From the few things she's said to me, I get the feeling she's selling the farm because she doesn't want you to feel pressured to come back home.'

'That's ridiculous!' he bursts out. 'She's selling it so she can travel the world, just as she always planned to.'

'Just as your father always planned to,' I say. 'Are you sure that was her dream too?'

He doesn't answer for a moment. When he does, it's in a sharper tone. 'I know you mean well, Emma, but you don't know what you're talking about. My mum has a mind of her own. She isn't the sort to be pushed into things by someone else.'

Everything is warning me to drop the subject and find something less contentious to talk about. But I can't. It's possible I'm wrong about this, but it feels too important to leave it unsaid. I struggle to find the right words. I have no wish to upset Tom, and I know this is a difficult subject for him.

'I was wondering about you too,' I say. 'You keep talking about all the things you'll do when you go back to London. But is that what you want, or is it what you think everyone else wants you to do?'

'It's what I want,' he says at once. 'I've told you I enjoy my job in London, and I like the place I rent. I don't know why you're trying to make my visit home into more than it is.'

'I'm not,' I say. 'And you're the only one who knows what you want. I've only known you for a few weeks, so I can't tell what that is. But you've often talked to me about the farm and all the plans you used to have for it. And you sound so enthusiastic when you do. I can't help wondering whether you're happy never to see them come to fruition.'

'Perfectly happy,' he says. 'Did you never have dreams when you were a child that you look back on and laugh at? I was going to be an astronaut when I was six. Do you think I sit and cry whenever I hear about a rocket launch because it should have been me?'

This makes me smile. 'I don't know what you do when you watch space programmes. I haven't known you long enough to guess.'

'Exactly!' he interrupts. 'You haven't. You and I only met a few weeks ago, so neither of us is in a position to tell the other what they do and don't want.'

'I'm not trying to do that!' I protest. 'I know I'm putting this badly. All I'm saying is that from where I'm standing, your mother seems not to want to leave the farm, and you appear to have missed it.'

His face is tense as he looks down at the table. He lifts his head and meets my eyes at last. 'And from where I'm standing, you don't have a leg to stand on when it comes to talking about families and communication.'

I'm too shocked to answer. I've never heard that tone in his voice before.

'It's pretty arrogant of you to sit there telling me what the members of my family do and don't want,' he continues more calmly. 'When did you last talk properly to your own family?'

I start to speak, but he lifts his hand. 'I know your parents got divorced, and that's never easy for anyone. But they didn't die. They're still around, and you're lucky enough to have the chance to speak to them. Instead, you came down here to avoid having to face the situation head on. I don't entirely blame you, but maybe you should think about your own family a little more and mine a little less.'

I try to answer, but the tears have sprung to my eyes, and I know I won't be able to keep my voice steady.

His expression softens as he looks at me. 'I'm sorry, Emma. I didn't mean to sound harsh. Maybe we should each deal with our own family situation and allow the other one to do the same.'

I swallow hard, trying to choke back the tears. I'm not sure whether they're heartbroken or angry tears. I think back over the past year, to the shock of Mum and Dad's announcement, swiftly followed by the sale of their house. I've done my best to cope with it all in an adult and mature way. I didn't try to talk them out of the divorce or tell them how upset I felt at the loss of my childhood home. I've visited them both and talked as positively as I could about their new lives and all the opportunities they can enjoy.

And now Tom is sitting across the table from me, telling me that wasn't enough, and I should have acted differently. He thinks I should have done more to support my family instead of feeling sorry for myself and running away. I feel a sudden blaze of anger at the way he's happy to judge my situation without knowing the first thing about it.

'Emma?' he says more gently, taking my hand.

I wrench it away. 'Don't!'

'Why are you so upset?' he says. 'I'm only pointing out the similarities in our situations. You've told me I don't communicate with my family, and I'm saying neither do you. What's more –'

'What?' I say suspiciously.

'Nothing,' he says. 'Shall I tell him we're ready for that souffle?'

'No! What were you about to say?'

He shrugs. 'Only that there's something more than a little ironic about this business you're running. You're determined to make sure everyone has a magical Christmas now that your own holidays aren't going so well. You talk a lot about the spirit of Christmas, but some of that has to do with family and loved ones. I'm wondering where that fits in with your current situation.'

'You have no idea what you're talking about!' I say. 'I see my family all the time! I've made an enormous effort with them this year, even when I didn't feel like it.'

'I know,' he says. 'But you seem to be angry with them because they aren't doing everything exactly as they've always done. Life isn't like that. Things change, people change, traditions change. All we can do is try to change with them. That's what I'm doing. Things have changed for Mum this year in ways I can't imagine. I'm trying to be sensitive to that and support her as she tries to make a new future for herself.'

'No, you aren't,' I say. 'You're sticking your head in the sand because you're frightened of having a difficult conversation with her. You're avoiding talking to her and being honest with her. And that's equally as cowardly as whatever it is you think I'm doing.'

His face turns white with anger. 'You don't have the faintest idea about my relationship with my mother.'

'I know a little about your relationship with your father,' I say. 'You've told me he didn't tell you what he wanted, and you avoided telling him what you wanted. It seems to me you're making exactly the same mistake with your mother.'

His jaw is tight as he stares at me. I stare back defiantly, too angry to care what he thinks of me.

'Maybe it's a good thing we had this conversation sooner rather than later,' he says at last.

'Maybe it is,' I say.

The server arrives carrying a silver dish with our chocolate souffle.

'Are you ready for dessert?' he says, smiling, as he lays it on the table between us.

'As a matter of fact, I'm not,' I say.

I pick up my bag and shrug on my coat. 'You can take that second spoon back to the kitchen.'

Tom looks startled. 'You aren't leaving?'

'Yes, I am.'

'Will you be taking the souffle to go?' the server asks me, bewildered.

'No, thanks,' I say. 'I'll leave it for Tom. I'm sure it's delicious. The last one was.'

He nods and moves away.

Tom stands to face me. 'Don't you want to talk about this?'

'I'm not sure there's much to talk about,' I say. 'At least, not with each other.'

'You're probably right,' he says after a long pause. 'Will you be ok getting home?'

'It's just around the corner,' I say, giving him an awkward smile. 'Bye, Tom.'

His eyes are full of pain, but he doesn't try to prevent me from leaving.

'See you around, Emma,' he says.

I walk home as slowly as possible, hardly able to believe what's just happened. One moment, everything was fine, and we were making plans to travel from Oxford to London to see each other each weekend. The next, we were telling each other all the things we've been doing wrong with our lives and possibly breaking up.

Luckily, Ed and Ollie are out when I get home, so I don't have to talk to anyone. I make myself a cup of coffee and sink into an armchair, trying not to think about our fight. My phone beeps, making me jump, and I see it's from Tom. For one second, I think he's texting to ask me to meet him and talk things through properly. But my heart sinks as I read the words on the screen.

Won't be there tonight. Going away for a few days. I have some things to sort out. Tom

I have no idea what to make of this. Is this a ruse to avoid me until I've returned to Oxford? Surely not. He knows I'm here until after Christmas. But if he stays away until the end of the Christmas fair, he'll be able to avoid me entirely. And avoidance seems to be his modus operandi.

I stare blankly out of the window, hardly noticing it's started to snow again. So, that's it. Instead of giving himself time to cool down before looking for an opportunity to talk with me about what's happened, Tom has decided to run away.

Chapter Twenty-Four

I wake three days later with the feeling that something has changed. It isn't anything to do with Tom. It's the light in my room. It feels oddly unfamiliar.

Ollie taps at my bedroom door. 'Have you looked outside?'

'Not yet.'

He walks over to the window and opens my curtains. 'It's been snowing all night. You can barely see where the road ends, and the pavement begins.'

I stare out at the sky, which is a pearlescent white. I look down at the street, which looks as though someone came along with a giant sieve during the night and dredged it with icing sugar.

I squint at the bright light. 'Is it still snowing?'

'Not as hard as it was, but it doesn't look as though it will melt any time soon. Hurry up and get ready. Ed always makes pancakes when it snows. It's the thing I'm most looking forward to when he and I move to New York. They eat pancakes every single day over there, rain or shine.'

'Are you sure?' I ask. 'I thought they ate eggs, sunny side up.'

He laughs. 'Is that what you read in that dreadful book? Did Alex live off nothing but fried eggs? I'll bet he did. He sounds the type.'

'They also had freshly squeezed orange juice and bagels.'

'We'll have those as well,' he says. 'But pancakes are the law. With maple syrup and bacon. We'll need to eat them every day if we don't want to fall foul of immigration laws.'

'I'd like mine without bacon,' I say. 'And I'm fine with lemon and sugar.'

'That's good to hear because I used the last of the maple syrup on mine. I planned to boil up some sugar and water and hope you couldn't tell the difference.'

I find Ed in the kitchen finishing his plate of pancakes.

He looks up as I come in. 'Yours are in the oven keeping warm. I didn't dare tell Ollie where I'd put them or you'd have been stuck with toast and jam.'

I carry my plate to the table and sit down. 'Thanks for this. Ollie says you always make pancakes when it snows. I thought most people only made them on pancake Tuesdays.'

'I don't cook them that day,' he says. 'It's a matter of principle. I don't approve of man-made holidays.'

I roll my eyes and pour lemon juice over my pancakes, finishing with a sprinkle of sugar. 'I'm glad you have this tradition, anyway. How deep is the snow? Will you two get to work alright?'

'I'm about to send Ollie out to clear the path,' he says.

'Why can't you send Emma?' complains Ollie.

'Because she's our guest,' says Ed. 'And you have to go because I made the breakfast. It's the law.'

'So many laws,' I say. 'You two must live in a permanent state of legal angst. First, Ollie has to eat a ten-course breakfast each day when he moves to New York. And now you're laying down the law about household tasks.'

'Ollie's moving to New York?' he says. 'When was he planning to mention that fact to me?'

'You're coming too,' says Ollie. 'Emma is going to pay me a salary beyond my wildest dreams to become the face of the internationally renowned Boxful of Christmas franchise.'

'I see,' says Ed. 'This is the first I'm hearing about it. What am I supposed to do while you're doing that?'

'Whatever you like,' says Ollie. 'I'll be earning enough for both of us. You could set up a yoga studio overlooking Central Park, or maybe a sock shop.'

'That's delightfully random,' I say. 'Why would Ed want to open a sock shop?'

'Exactly what I was wondering myself,' says Ed.

'I'm making the point that the world will be your oyster,' says Ollie. 'Speaking of which, you could set up a seafood emporium on Fifth Avenue. You could call it Ed's Nautical Nosh.'

'I could,' says Ed. 'But I doubt I will. In the meantime, and in the absence of the munificent salary Emma plans to pay us, you and I need to make a living. The shovel is in the cupboard in the hall.'

They leave for work half an hour later. I wonder if this weather will affect the Christmas fair. I hope not. There's only one week to go, and I haven't yet hit my sales target. I should be ok as long as the fair stays as busy as it has been. But there are no guarantees.

I clean the kitchen, wondering for the hundredth time what Tom's doing. It's pointless, but I can't help it. It's clear that whatever he and I had is over. To be honest, it had barely begun, so there's no reason for me to feel upset. We have almost nothing in common. If it hadn't been for Frances placing our stalls next to each other, we wouldn't have met, let alone got to know each other.

It was a stupid holiday thing that was over before it had started. Tom will go back to London after Christmas, Helen will sell the farm and retire, and I will … I have no idea how to finish that sentence. What I do next depends on how well I do with sales over the next few days. And how well I do over the next few days depends on me getting over to Honeywell each evening.

I'm glad to think I've started leaving my boxes locked in my hut each night. It will make things much easier today. Hopefully the roads will be clear tonight, and I can drive over to the fair. If not, I'll walk. It's only seven miles, and I know the way. It feels rather drastic, but I don't care. I need to get to there, one way or another, and I don't intend for anything to stop me. Certainly not a few flakes of snow.

I look out of the window at the deep drifts. Fine, a few tons of snow. Either way, I won't allow it to get between me and my dream. I wonder whether Tom has given up on his stall entirely, but it's nothing to do with me. He's been gone for the past three days, and I haven't heard from him. I need to stop thinking about what might have been and work out what I'm going to do next. I can't rely on other people for ever. Ollie and Ed have been fantastic in allowing me to stay here, giving me rides, and helping me to prepare my boxes. But this is a one off. If I want to make a success of this business, I can't keep leaning on other people. I have to make my own plans and see them through. Which is why I'll walk over to Honeywell tonight if I have to.

It stops snowing around ten a.m. I hear the gritters driving along the high street late morning, and they arrive outside our flat after lunch. I should be able to drive over to Honeywell tonight if I'm careful. I consider whether to take a sleeping bag and a flask but decide that's going a bit too far. I'd freeze to death if I tried sleeping in that tiny hut all night.

Ollie and Ed arrive home at four o'clock.

'We closed early,' says Ollie. 'We had three customers all day, and one of them didn't even buy anything. It's enough to make you despair of the book reading public.'

'I'm sorry,' I say. 'Did you offer them a fine selection of Russian misery lit?'

'I reserve that for our more discriminating customers,' he says. 'I tried to get one woman to buy Snowflakes over Broadway. I told her one of our recent customers had been raving about it. But she said she didn't read trashy rom coms.'

'What a cheek!' I say. 'I hope Danielle Someone-or-Other doesn't hear about that. It sounds as though this woman could benefit from reading a story about the holiday spirit.'

'Ollie hinted to her very strongly that independent book shops are going out of business in droves,' says Ed. 'She told him it was because their staff are so pushy and don't take the trouble to find out what their customers have come in for.'

'What had she come in for?' I ask.

'To ask where the nearest chemist was,' says Ollie. 'Not one of our more successful days. You need to hurry and go global if Ed and I aren't to starve.'

'First, I have to get to the fair,' I say. 'They've cleared the roads now. I should be alright if I set off early.'

'You can't go on your own,' says Ollie. 'You'll get stuck in a snowdrift, and Ed and I won't see you until spring.'

'If you come with me, we'll both be stuck in the snowdrift,' I point out. 'Which means our rations will only last for half as long.'

'But we can keep each other warm,' he says. 'I don't think you should drive there on your own. My van is heavier than your car, which means it won't skid around so much in the snow.'

'You're welcome to come,' I say. 'But you'll have to stay all evening. It isn't worth you driving back and forth in this weather.'

'No problem,' he says. 'I expect I'll find someone to talk to. I usually do. Will Tom be there?'

'I have no idea,' I say curtly, and he and Ed exchange looks.

'He hasn't been there for the past few nights,' I say more calmly. 'Maybe he's decided it isn't worth it. Sales have been pretty good at the farm this year. He may have decided running that stall each night is more trouble than it's worth.'

'Maybe,' says Ollie. 'But there's a simple way to find out. Why don't you call him?'

'Because I don't want to. Tom made it clear he didn't want me sticking my nose into his family's business. And I don't intend to. I have my own life to worry about.'

'Fair enough,' he says. 'I didn't mean to pry. Your private life is your own business. Just make sure you don't throw away something you might wish later you'd hung onto.'

Chapter Twenty-Five

Ollie and I set off at five o'clock. There are very few cars on the road, which makes it easier to drive. The main road out of town is easy enough to navigate, but it gets trickier as we turn into the smaller roads that lead towards Honeywell.

Ollie switches to full beam and pulls a face. 'The snow ploughs haven't been along here.'

'Can we make it?' I ask.

'If we take it slowly.'

If I weren't so anxious to arrive at the fair, I would enjoy this journey. The beams of our headlights cut through the darkness, revealing a winter wonderland around us. The trees on each side of the road form an archway of glistening white, and we pass several cottages whose thatched roofs are hidden under a thick blanket of snow.

'It's like a fairy tale,' I say. 'That cottage we passed a minute ago could be made of gingerbread.'

'Don't say that,' warns Ollie. 'Now I'm expecting an enormous wolf to jump out of the bushes and attack us at any moment. This van isn't built to withstand that.'

'There's no wolf in Hansel and Gretel,' I say. 'Just lots and lots of gingerbread. I should tell Lucy about that cottage. It would save her a fortune.'

'There's Honeywell up ahead,' he says. 'I can see the lights of the Red Lion. I'm glad they haven't capitulated to a few flakes of snow and closed for the week.'

'Hopefully, that means the fair will be open too,' I say. 'I doubt many people will be driving in, but maybe some of the locals will stop in for half an hour on their way to the pub.'

We drive into the village with care, and he pulls up next to the village green.

'There won't be many parking inspectors out on a night like this,' he says. 'And it isn't too far to walk. Are you ready?'

I climb out of the car and immediately sink up to my knees in a snowdrift. I pick my way through the snow to the main entrance. Several people are already here, setting up their stalls and laughing and joking.

Ollie catches up with me. 'It looks as though it's going ahead.'

'Thank goodness.'

I quicken my pace as I head towards my stall. Someone has swept a path between the stalls to make them easier to access. A group of people is clustered together at the far end of the fair, pointing and gesturing. When we get closer, I see Lucy is one of them.

'Hi, Lucy. What's going on?' I ask, then stop dead as I realise what they're pointing at.

My stall is still there, but only just. The roof has collapsed. One piece is sticking out of the empty space below.

I stare at it in shock. 'What happened?'

'Oh, Emma, I'm so sorry,' says Lucy. 'I only arrived a few minutes ago. It looks like your roof gave way under the weight of the snow.'

'When?' I say, my mouth dry.

'Sometime during the night, they think.

'What about my stock?' I say, and she pulls a face.

'It doesn't look good.'

I push past her and lean over the counter.

'Careful!' someone says. 'It doesn't look too stable.'

My boxes are lying in a tumbled heap at the back of what's left of the stall. Most of them have been crushed or torn.

'The ones underneath may be fine,' says Lucy.

I reach over and pick up the nearest box. The cardboard falls apart the moment I touch it, and the contents fall out. It's obvious they're ruined. The mindfulness book is soaked through, and the aromatherapy diffuser has been crushed. Only the bottles of oil are salvageable. I pick up a craft box, whose contents aren't remotely saleable. None of my other boxes is in any better condition.

'I'm so sorry,' says Lucy again. 'I can't believe this has happened.'

Ollie takes my arm. 'Let me get you something to drink. Then we'll see what can be done with the rest of your stock. It can't all be gone.'

I don't trust my voice to answer. I'll only burst into tears or start yelling at him. And he doesn't deserve that. He's been nothing but helpful, and I owe him a huge debt of gratitude for everything he's done.

He sees my face. 'Back in a second.'

Lucy slips an arm around me. 'It may not be as bad as you think. We may save some of it. I'll help you make new boxes, and Frances will give you another stall. With any luck, you'll be back in business by tomorrow evening.'

'I don't think so,' I say, struggling to keep my voice steady. 'I don't have time to replace the things that are ruined. And I had to order those boxes three months in advance. That's it for me this Christmas.'

Ollie returns with a glass of mulled wine. 'Drink this, then I'll take you to the pub.'

I take the glass. 'I'll drink this, but then I'd like to go home. We can take anything that isn't ruined with us, but there won't be much.'

'Don't you want to check with Frances whether she can give you another stall?' he asks. 'Tom's stall is free, and you told me he may not be back.'

'I don't want Tom's stall,' I say. 'And I don't care whether he's coming back. The only thing I care about is that my stall has been destroyed, and my plans have been ruined. Can we please go home?'

'I'll help Ollie clear up,' says Lucy. 'There's no need for you to do anything.'

I try to argue with her, but thc tears are too close. I don't want to break down in front of the group of interested onlookers, so I allow Ollie to walk me back to the van and settle me into the passenger seat. I stare out of the window, fighting back the tears. This isn't the end of the world. It isn't even the end of my business if I don't want it to be. I may not go full time this year, but I don't have to give up entirely.

Ollie opens the back doors and puts a couple of bin bags inside. 'This is all we've been able to salvage. Frances says she'll arrange to have the rest of your stuff disposed of when someone comes to remove the stall.'

He climbs in and starts the engine. 'I'm so sorry, Em. I know how much this meant to you.'

He drives carefully back towards the Red Lion, crosses the junction and retraces our journey here. We pass the cottage I thought was made of gingerbread. It no longer looks twinkly and shiny and idyllic. It looks as though it has a damp problem. As for the big, bad wolf emerging from the woods and attacking us, he's welcome. I won't even put up a fight.

Chapter Twenty-Six

We don't talk much when we get home. Ollie tells Ed what's happened, and Ed immediately pours me a whisky. It seems to be his go-to remedy for everything.

'I'd prefer a cup of tea,' I say. 'I don't like whisky.'

'Are you sure?' he says. 'It's the best thing I know for shock. And colds and flu. And feeling perfectly healthy.'

'Perfectly sure,' I say. 'I don't like the taste of spirits at all.'

In the end, Ollie drinks it while Ed makes me a cup of tea.

'This doesn't have to be over,' he says when he hands me the mug. 'You can save up and start again. You know you're always welcome here.'

'There's no point,' I say gloomily. 'I'm terrible at this.'

'What happened to your stall was an act of God,' says Ed. 'Not a poor business decision on your part.'

'I ought to have taken out insurance,' I say. 'But it was so expensive, and I never envisaged anything like this happening. Why did it have to be my stall?'

'Whose stall would you prefer it to have been?' he says. 'Tom's?'

I flush. 'I didn't want it to be anyone's stall. But it wouldn't have damaged Tom's business half as much as it has mine. He can sell his Christmas trees at the farm if he wants to. And they're selling the business anyway, so what do they care?'

'Do you have enough stock left to put together more boxes?' he asks.

'I could only manage a few. And it's too late to get any more boxes printed. It's over for this year.'

'What a shame,' he says. 'I hope this doesn't entirely spoil Christmas for you. I know how much you love it.'

'Loved it,' I say. 'I'm not sure I still do.'

'Nonsense!' says Ollie. 'You can't let one setback spoil Christmas forever. You still have a job. You can save up and try again next year. Ed and I would love to have you.'

'Maybe.' I finish my tea. 'I think I'll have an early night. Thanks for everything.'

I climb into bed, trying not to think about what's happened. But it's no good. The moment I close my eyes, I see my shattered stall and the crushed boxes. I open them again and stare at the ceiling. This entire month has been a disaster. I thought I'd met someone special, but that turned out to be an illusion. My business has been a spectacular failure. And now I'm facing the prospect of returning to a life I don't enjoy for at least another year. For the first time in my life, I wish I could go to sleep before Christmas and not wake up until the new year.

I drift off to sleep in the early hours and don't wake until ten o'clock. Judging by the silence in the flat, Ed and Ollie have left to persuade the unsuspecting public to buy some books. I make myself some breakfast and consider going for a walk. But it snowed again during the night, and the pavement hasn't been cleared. I don't want to spend Christmas in hospital with a broken leg. Even spending it alone in my flat with Mr Whiskers would be better than that.

I sort through the bin bags we brought home with us from the fair. It's worse than I thought. I can use barely any of this. I'll clean up what I can and take it to a charity shop. Someone ought to enjoy it.

Ollie and Ed arrive home around six o'clock.

'What's this?' says Ollie, looking around the hall. 'Don't tell me you're going to the fair tonight, after all?'

'I don't have enough stock left to make any boxes,' I say. 'I'm taking this lot to the charity shop tomorrow morning. Someone ought to benefit from my general uselessness.'

I try to smile as I say this, but my voice cracks.

Ed gives me a hug. 'You aren't useless. You've done an amazing job. You should have seen some of the mistakes Ollie and I made when we took over the bookshop.'

'I don't remember making any,' says Ollie. 'But these aren't all binbags. Why are your suitcases here too?'

'I put them here ready for tomorrow morning,' I say. 'I'm going home.'

'You can't!' he says. 'What about Christmas?'

'I wouldn't be very good company.'

'But you can't spend Christmas alone in your flat with only that psychopathic cat for company!' he objects.

'Mr Whiskers isn't a psychopath,' I say. 'At worst, he's a sociopath. And I won't be in my flat alone. I'm going to call Dad and see whether he'd like me to go down to Cornwall with him. And I'm taking Mum up on her invitation to spend New Year with her. It's time we reconnected.'

'I wouldn't mind going to the South of France for New Year,' says Ed.

'Usually, I'd hate it,' I say. 'I like snow and twinkly lights and mulled wine. But this year, I want to ignore the holidays until they're over. And where better to do that than the South of France?'

'If anyone asks you what you do for a living,' says Ollie, 'you'll have to tell them you're a *vendeuse* of *les boîtes de Noel.*'

'I'm actually a *fleuriste*,' I say. 'But I doubt anyone will ask me what I do. Mum says she's looking forward to a quiet fortnight enjoying the sun. I can't stay for long, but I should spend some proper time with her. We can't recreate the past, but maybe we can make some new traditions together.'

'New York would be better,' says Ollie. 'But you have to cut your coat to suit your cloth.'

'She won't need a coat in the South of France,' says Ed. 'I'm tempted to stow away in your suitcase, Em. But that would mean leaving Ollie in sole charge of the stocktake, and I dread to think what might happen.'

'I'm sorry I can't offer you a job in New York,' I tell Ollie. 'But this business is going nowhere. I doubt it ever will.'

'Don't give up hope,' he says. 'I never wanted to go to the States, anyway. I didn't like to tell you while you so obviously needed me over there, but I'd take Christchurch over New York any day of the week. We have a Priory. And a quay! How could the Americans compete with that?'

'New York has a few famous buildings,' I tell him.

'Overrated,' he says. 'And there's the strong possibility I might run into this Alex bloke. He sounds like a pill.'

'And I was never all that committed to the idea of a seafood shop on Fifth Avenue,' says Ed. 'Don't worry about us, Em. We'll be fine.'

'I vote we have pizza tonight,' says Ollie. 'It's on me.'

'To celebrate me leaving?' I say.

'Not even close. We'd love you to stay for Christmas, but that's your call. Maybe next year.'

I somehow doubt it, but I don't say so. It's nice to know my friends are there for me when I need them. Lucy texted this morning to say the offer of a room in her share house is still open, and she'd love to have me as a housemate. That would have been great if things had worked out with my business, but now it's another reminder of how close I came to achieving my dream and how I failed because of a lack of preparation and care.

The pizza arrives at seven o'clock, and we eat it while watching It's a Wonderful Life. I protest when Ollie starts streaming it, but he insists on watching one final Christmas movie before I give up on the holiday forever.

'We've watched this every year since we met,' he says. 'I doubt we ever will again. In the future, I imagine you'll look down on those of us who celebrate Christmas. You'll try to persuade us it's a commercial holiday, and our minds should be on higher things. Let me have this one last time.'

'You're a ridiculous man!' I tell him. 'I have no intention of giving up Christmas forever. Only for this year. It's been a bit much, and I need a few days to lick my wounds and get over myself.'

'Won't your mother be celebrating the holidays at all?' he says.

'I have no idea. But she won't be doing the usual things.'

'She'll be missing out on the Christmas spirit,' he says. 'And now you plan to do the same.'

'Only for this year. I'll be back to full jollity next year. You and Ed can come to stay with me if you like. I'll introduce you to Mr Whiskers.'

'I like cats,' he says. 'But Ed is allergic, so I'd have to leave him at home.'

'That's a shame. Maybe I'll come to you instead.'

'To do the fair again?' he asks.

'Probably not.'

He looks sympathetic. 'Because of Tom?'

'No!' I say. 'My plans for the future have nothing to do with him. Besides, the Kingsley farm will have been sold by then. Helen will be travelling the world, and Tom will be back in London. I'll never see either of them again.'

'That seems a shame,' he says. 'But it's none of my business.'

'You have enough on your plate without worrying about me,' I say. 'Will the bookshop be alright?'

Ed helps himself to another slice of pizza. 'Of course, it will. It's been a tough year for everyone, but things are picking up. Now that Ollie has given up his plan of moving to New York, he'll be able to put all his energies into marketing. We'll be fine.'

'I'm glad,' I say. 'I love that bookshop. There should be more places like it.'

Ollie opens the fridge and pulls out a bottle of champagne. 'We were saving this for Christmas Day. But you won't be here, so we should drink it now.'

I start to protest, but Ed stops me. 'I agree with Ollie. Life is for living, not for putting off until some vague magical future when everything is perfect. That day never comes, and all you're left with is a bottle of oxidised champagne which ought to have been drunk three years ago.'

'Champagne should last for longer than three years,' I say.

'Not the kind we buy,' says Ollie. 'We'd be lucky if this stuff reached the two-year mark without going off. Not that we've ever made the experiment.'

'Six months is about our limit,' agrees Ed. 'And this bottle won't make it that long.'

He pulls out the cork before I can protest further and pours three glasses.

'What shall we drink to?' he says.

'The bookshop,' I suggest. 'May it make you both rich beyond your wildest dreams!'

'That's a little ambitious,' says Ollie. 'You need a premier Krug for that sort of toast. I'll settle for making an honest living.'

'Fine,' I say, raising my glass. 'To The Rabbit Hole – may it remain in profit until you retire. And may anyone who comes in to ask directions to a different establishment slip on a patch of ice and break their leg.'

Ollie clinks his glass against mine. 'This vintage should be up to that.'

Ed takes a deep gulp of his champagne. 'Thank you for that, Emma. Now it's our turn to make a toast to you. What should it be?'

'I can't think of anything,' I say. 'To my train to France being on time?'

'That's not a toast!' says Ollie. 'That's a ridiculous expectation. At least, it is on this side of the channel. You need a better dream than that.'

'I tried that,' I say. 'And look how it turned out. In the future, I'll keep my plans smaller and not rely on any one day of the year to bring me happiness.'

'What about your plan to bring the spirit of Christmas to the whole of Hampshire?' asks Ed.

'It was an overly ambitious idea,' I say. 'From now on, I'll concentrate on something more achievable – like making sure Mr Whiskers has a good time.'

'I refuse to be a guest at such a pity party,' says Ollie. 'Anyone would think you'd lost the family fortune and ancestral home in a game of poker.'

'Why don't we drink to me finding my way?' I say. 'It's a vague enough plan for this champagne to cope with. And it gives me a fair amount of leeway.'

'It's slightly better,' he says. 'But I don't like to see you giving up like this. It isn't like you.'

'I'm not giving up,' I say. 'I'm reevaluating a few things, that's all. It's confusing when things don't turn out the way you planned.'

'It is,' says Ed. 'But my grandmother always used to say that when a window closes …'

'A trapdoor opens?' I say. 'I believe she was right.'

'This is getting too philosophical,' complains Ollie. 'And my champagne is going flat. I need to drink to something. I don't care what. Someone suggest a toast, for goodness' sake.'

Ed picks up his glass and turns to me. 'To the true spirit of Christmas, whatever it means to you.'

I hesitate, then lift my glass. 'I can live with that. To the true spirit of Christmas, whatever that may be.'

Chapter Twenty-Seven

Ollie helps me pack my car the following morning. I'm taking far fewer boxes home than I brought with me. Can it really be only four weeks ago that I watched the men load up the delivery van in Oxford before following it down to Christchurch? I was so full of excited plans for the future that I couldn't allow myself to contemplate the possibility of failure.

And here I am, returning home less than a month later with my dreams in tatters. It's a depressing thought.

Ollie and Ed have reiterated their offer to stay with them over Christmas, but I've refused. I'm sure it's the right thing to do. I told them it was because I would be such poor company, which is partly true. But I'm perfectly aware the real reason is because I don't want to be anywhere that reminds me of Tom.

No matter how many times I tell myself that he and I barely knew each other, it doesn't feel true. It feels as though I came to know him better in the few short weeks we spent together than almost anyone other than Ollie, who probably knows me as well as anyone except my family. And I'm no longer sure they know me as well as I thought.

I can't know them very well either or I'd have seen the signs of trouble long ago instead of being blindsided by my parents' divorce. I may even have been able to help, although I can't think how. Children don't usually act as marriage counsellors to their parents. Even if I couldn't have done that, I could have prepared myself in advance for the announcement that my family had totally imploded. That way it might not have taken me so much by surprise or hurt so much. And I may not have behaved so idiotically during my time in Honeywell.

I hug Ollie and Ed goodbye, promise to send them a postcard from the South of France, and set off. I've memorised the route as far as Winchester. I'll stop and consult the map when I get there.

The snow has been cleared along all but the smallest side streets, but the roads are icy, and it takes me a while to get out of the town and onto the dual carriageway.

I glance at the Christmas card on the seat beside me, wondering whether I would have done better to have posted it to the Kingsley farm. But there's no guarantee it would have arrived before Christmas if I had. And I'd like to say goodbye to Helen in person. With any luck, she has no idea there was ever anything between me and Tom, so she won't think it's strange I've decided to go home a little earlier than planned.

I haven't decided what I'll do if Tom is there. I'm not sure whether I want to see him again or not, but I'm leaning towards the latter. There's no point in rehashing last week's row. We both made our positions clear, and we're unlikely to change our minds by talking about it. If anything, we're more likely to have another argument, and I don't think I could bear that at the moment. I'm still too upset by the failure of my Christmas venture.

Was Tom right that I was using the Christmas fair as a reason not to face up to what's happened with my family? I hated him for saying it, but I have an uneasy suspicion there's some truth in it. I have to come to terms with it all at some point, but I can't do that over Christmas. My memories of family Christmases feel fragile enough already. I can't bear for them to be entirely destroyed, which might very well happen if I try to talk to my parents too soon about how I feel.

All I can do for now is go home, try to see Dad at some point over Christmas, then travel to see Mum and celebrate the new year with her. I can't think about any other family memories right now. I'll keep those for another time and concentrate on staying connected to the individual people who made up that family unit.

They haven't changed. They're the same people they were while I was growing up. It's just that the way they were combined has changed, and I need to find a way to see them differently. Maybe families are like snowflakes. Each one is made up of the same substance as all the others, but they grow in unique ways so that none of them looks exactly the same as any of the others.

This is a cheering thought, and I consider it further as I navigate the snowy lanes between Honeywell and the Kingsley farm. If families are like snowflakes, if you group enough of them together, you'll get an entire community, like a snowball. On the other hand, if the snowflakes are the individuals within a family, then the family is the snowball. Which makes the community – what – a snowman? An entire family of snowmen? Perhaps I should rethink this analogy on the way back to Oxford. It will give me something to think about apart from the fact my time in Honeywell has been such a spectacular failure.

I turn off the main road and drive up the track to the farmhouse, keeping an eye out for Bonnie. There's no sign of her, and when I climb out of the car and nervously knock at the farmhouse door, no one answers. There are no lights in any of the windows either, so I drive back down the hill and park outside the shop.

Carolyn is arranging a display of Christmas cards and smiles when she sees me.

'Hi, Emma. How are you doing?'

I'm not sure how to answer this. I could tell her the truth, which is that I've never been worse. I've failed spectacularly at the one thing I wanted to do. I've lost my stock and most of my savings. I'm going back home to a family which has spectacularly collapsed over the past year and which I'm not sure will ever form a coherent whole again. To crown it all, I've met and fallen for a man who thinks I'm ridiculous and immature and who never wants to see me again.

But that isn't what people mean when they ask how you are, so I settle for the conventional answer.

'Good, thanks. You seem busy in here.'

'I'm rushed off my feet,' she says. 'I'm dealing with the shop and the cafe by myself today. Were you looking for Tom?'

'No!' I say a little too quickly. 'I dropped in to say goodbye to Helen. I'm driving back to Oxford this afternoon, and I wanted to wish her a happy Christmas before I left.'

'What a shame,' she says. 'You've just missed her. She took the Land Rover out about an hour ago and said she didn't know how long she'd be. You could wait if you like?'

'I'm afraid I can't,' I say. 'I want to get home before dark if possible. I don't know what the roads will be like once I get past Winchester. The snow was bad enough coming here from Christchurch.'

'I skidded a few times on my way to work this morning,' she says. 'I don't remember such a cold December.'

I hand her the envelope I brought with me. 'Could you give that to … Helen when you see her?'

'Will do,' she says cheerfully. 'Or Tom, if I see him first.'

I hesitate. 'Is he back home, then?'

She shakes her head. 'Not that I know of. Helen hasn't mentioned it if he is. She said he'd gone away for a few days. I thought you might know where was.'

There's a definite note of curiosity in her voice. But I'm not getting into a discussion about Tom with her or anyone else.

'Not a clue,' I say as cheerfully as I can. 'He disappeared without a word, and no one seems to know where he is. Anyway, I must be going. Thanks for delivering the card. Happy Christmas, Carolyn!'

'You, too,' she says. 'I hope we see you again, Emma.'

'It isn't likely,' I say. 'I was only in this area because of the Christmas market.'

She nods. 'Maybe you'll do it again next year.'

'Maybe,' I say.

I climb into the car and drive carefully down the track towards the main road. So, that's that. My last piece of business in this area has been transacted, and I no longer have any reason to be here.

I swing the car out onto the snowy highway and set off in the direction of Oxford.

Chapter Twenty-Eight

Felicity insists on us both working in the shop on Christmas Eve.

'It's one of our busiest days,' she says, 'although not as busy as Valentine's Day. We'll be rushed off our feet that day. I can never understand it. It isn't as though Valentine's Day is a movable holiday. It's on February 14th every year, yet plenty of people forget all about it until the actual day. It's amazing the number of people pleading with us to tell them we haven't run out of red roses because their relationship may not make it if we have. It means I can charge them extra when I finally locate our "last" few roses. They're so relieved they don't seem to care what they pay.'

'That seems unfair on the people who haven't been able to get to the shop earlier,' I say.

She shrugs. 'No, it doesn't. If their relationship is so important to them, they should plan ahead.'

'I suppose so. But Valentine's Day isn't important to everyone.'

'I'm not forcing anyone to buy flowers,' says Felicity. 'But the people who want them ought to think about it in good time. It's like Christmas Eve. We'll have all sorts of people coming in today who haven't bothered to buy Christmas presents for their loved ones and imagine a bunch of flowers will get them off the hook.'

'Some people like receiving flowers for Christmas,' I say. 'I'd be delighted if someone gave me a poinsettia or an amaryllis.'

'But you put a lot of thought into your Christmas presents,' she says. 'You started your shopping in September this year.'

'Only because I expected to be too busy selling at the Christmas fair to have time to think about anything else.'

'I'm sorry about that,' she says. 'It's great to have you back today. I'd be rushed off my feet otherwise. But I wish it had been under different circumstances.'

'Me too.' I pick up a bunch of roses and carefully trim their stems. 'But it isn't the end of the world. I can try again next year.'

'That's the spirit,' she says. 'When you've finished doing those roses, can you add some holly berries to those wreaths?'

I don't have time to think about anything other than flowers all morning. Felicity is right. We have a steady stream of customers until lunchtime. Most of them seem stressed and harassed, and there's little evidence of Christmas spirit.

I don't mind. It matches my mood. This is the first Christmas I haven't looked forward to. I'm usually beside myself with excitement on Christmas Eve, thinking about the gifts I've bought for my family and friends, and looking forward to waking up in my old bedroom at Mum and Dad's and finding a stocking at the foot of my bed.

Not this year. It isn't just the failure of my business. It's something else. It feels as though Tom's lack of enthusiasm about the holiday rubbed off on me without me realising. And his comment about me needing to grow up stung all the more because I suspected he was right. Christmas is for children, not for adults. At least, not in the same way.

I wonder where Tom is spending Christmas this year. Is he even back from wherever it is he went? I tear my thoughts away from the subject. I'll never hear from him again, which is fine. I hope things work out for him, but that doesn't mean I want to hear about his life in excruciating detail.

'I'll take my lunch break now,' Felicity tells me at noon. 'You can have yours when I get back.'

'No problem,' I say. 'The rush seems to have died down now. Even the last-minute shoppers won't dare leave it much later.'

'It looks that way,' she agrees. 'In which case, we'll close early. I'm sure you're keen to start your preparations.'

I'm saved from having to answer as a young couple come into the shop. They look tired and tense.

'I've told you already,' the man says. 'I'm not staying for more than a couple of hours. And if she brings up the subject of my hair again, I'm not letting it go.'

'Don't say that!' says the woman. 'I've told you a hundred times my parents love you. My mum wishes you had a better job, that's all.'

'There's nothing wrong with working in construction,' he says. 'And she can talk! She spends four hours a week volunteering at that charity shop of hers and thinks that gives her a right to tell everyone else what they should be doing with their lives.'

'How can we help you?' says Felicity brightly.

The man shrugs. The young woman looks close to tears.

'We're looking for a flower arrangement to take to my parents tomorrow,' she says. 'We're spending our first Christmas with them, and we want it to be perfect.'

The man gives an almost imperceptible snort but doesn't say anything.

'How about this one?' says Felicity. 'Mixed evergreen and berries with white roses. It would look lovely as a centrepiece on the dinner table.'

'That's a good idea,' says the woman. 'Are there any lilies in it? My mother's allergic to those.'

'None at all,' Felicity reassures her. 'Otherwise, I could make you up something specially.'

'I think this arrangement looks lovely,' says the woman. 'What do you think, Steve?'

'Do you have anything with barbed wire and poison ivy?' he asks.

'I'm afraid not,' says Felicity.

'You aren't making the slightest bit of effort!' says the woman. 'I don't even think you want to come tomorrow.'

I catch the man's eye and frown. He has the grace to look contrite. 'Of course, I do, Miranda. That flower arrangement looks exactly the right sort of thing.'

'That's what I think,' she says, mollified. 'And we can get a bottle of port for my dad. He loves that.'

I pick up the flower arrangement and wrap it in Christmas paper.

'Christmas can sometimes be difficult when it comes to families,' I say, adding a twist of ribbon and surveying the effect. 'But it's worth making the effort, even if you don't feel like it. You may even find you enjoy the day more than you expect.'

We watch them leave, and Felicity gives me an odd look. 'That sounded heartfelt. I thought you loved Christmas.'

'I wasn't talking about me,' I say. 'I was talking about them. It sounds as though their Christmas may be a little sticky.'

'Her mother sounds like a bit of a battle-axe,' she says. 'But if they love each other, they'll work it out.'

'I expect so,' I say.

She buttons up her coat. 'I'll get going before someone comes in demanding a bouquet of foxgloves and deadly nightshade for their ex-boyfriend.'

'We don't have any of those left,' I say. 'I'd have to make it from scratch.'

'The deadly nightshade is in the fridge,' she says, pulling on her scarf. 'We may be out of foxgloves, but you could substitute some hemlock. Don't forget to add a few sprigs of baby's breath. I ordered too much last week, and I've been putting it in as many things as possible.'

'Will do,' I say. 'Enjoy your lunch.'

I watch her walk briskly down the street towards The Grub Hub. She goes there almost every day and always orders the same thing – a turkey and Swiss cheese on rye. I'm never sure whether this shows a lack of imagination or proves she's a woman who knows what she wants.

I tidy up the counter and am about to refresh the water in our last few festive arrangements when the door opens behind me. I resist the urge to tell whoever it is we're closed until the new year.

A familiar voice speaks. 'Hi, I'm looking for something extremely Christmassy.'

I swing around to see Tom standing there. He's wearing a thick coat and scarf, and there are snowflakes in his wavy brown hair. I stare at him, unable to speak.

He puts down the bag he's carrying and smiles at me. 'Hi, Emma. This is the seventh florist shop I've visited today. I'm glad I've finally found you.'

Chapter Twenty-Nine

Neither of us speaks for a moment. I can still hardly believe he's here.

'I'm sorry I didn't call you before you left,' he says.

'It's fine,' I say.

'No, it isn't,' he says quietly. 'It's the very opposite of fine. You have every right to be angry with me.'

'I'm not angry,' I begin, then catch his eye. 'Maybe I was a bit. But there was no reason for you to contact me. You made things perfectly clear the last time I saw you. You didn't want me commenting on your life or being involved with it in any way.'

'Is that what you thought?' he asks.

'Of course. When someone tells you their life is nothing to do with you, and you should concentrate on sorting out your own life, it isn't a huge stretch to believe them.'

He reaches for my hand, but I pull it away. 'It's fine, Tom. You were right when you said we barely know each other. We both have separate lives, and neither of us wants the same things as each other. Let's not make it anything more than it was.'

'Is that how you really feel?' he says in a low voice.

Everything in me is screaming that it isn't, but there's no point in starting this again. He's made his position very clear.

'I went to see my sister in Newcastle,' he says when I don't answer. 'I wanted to ask her about what you said to me when we had our … disagreement.'

I give an involuntary snort. 'That's putting it mildly. You told me to stay out of your life and not to think I knew anything about you and your family.'

I'm pleased to see his face turn pink. 'I wasn't as coherent as I might have been.'

'You seemed perfectly coherent to me.'

'You gave me a shock,' he says. 'I'd been thinking I knew my parents and what they wanted and didn't want. Then you came along and announced I didn't know the first thing about them.'

It's my turn to feel defensive. 'I didn't say that. I said you should talk to your mum and ask her to tell you what she wanted instead of assuming you already knew.'

'I know,' he says. 'But you hit a nerve. What I heard was that I'd failed miserably to communicate with my father before he died, and now I was repeating the same thing with my mother.'

'I had no idea you'd take it like that,' I say. 'I had a feeling Helen didn't want to sell up and retire, and I thought you should talk to her about it. I didn't mean to imply you weren't a good son. I'm sorry, Tom. I didn't realise it would upset you so much. I wouldn't have said anything if I had.'

'I'm the one who should apologise,' he says. 'I had no business storming off like that and not contacting you for days. In my defence, my phone finally packed up while I was there, and your number was in it. I called Mum and asked her to go over to the market and find you, but she said you weren't there. They told her what had happened to your stall, but she didn't want to tell me about that until I got home.'

'When did you get back?' I ask.

'Midnight last night. Katie told me exactly what you told me. She said I should stop moping around feeling sorry for myself and go back home. After which, I should stop being such a coward and tell Mum what I wanted.'

'And did you?' I ask.

'I did. Mum and I had a long talk this morning. She told me Dad didn't want to stay on the farm for the rest of his life because it had never been his dream. He wanted me to have the freedom to follow my own dreams, not to feel trapped in the same way he had. Which is why she put the farm up for sale without consulting me. She assumed I was as happy with my life as Katie is with hers. She said she was terrified of putting pressure on me and making me feel I had to come back and help her run the place because that was what she wanted.'

'I'm sorry your father wasn't happy with the way his life turned out,' I say.

'He wasn't as unhappy as you might think,' says Tom. 'It wasn't his choice to take over the farm, but he enjoyed the outdoor lifestyle. Mum told me she offered several times to help him find something else to do, but he didn't want that. She said she was never convinced they would travel as much as Dad thought they would after they retired. They took the ferry to Calais one weekend, and he was sick both ways. He told her he was never going on a boat again. And apparently, he wasn't too good on airplanes either. But it kept him going until retirement, so she didn't argue.'

'Did your mum never want to travel?' I ask.

'She'd have liked to see some of the places on his list. She still would. But she hated the thought of leaving the farm for good, and she always hoped Dad would change his mind.'

'Do I take it she isn't selling up, after all?'

'That's right,' he says. 'She and I have been drawing up all kinds of plans.'

He pulls a sheet of paper out of his pocket and hands it to me.

I look at the heading. 'Kingsley's Christmas Village?'

'We plan to expand the Christmas tree plantation,' he says. 'We sold all our trees this year, and we could easily have sold more. With a bit of work, we could eventually double the number we grow. But we want to do far more than that. If we grew more of our own produce, we could start up the veggie-box business again and use the rest of the vegetables in the cafe. We could make a real feature of everything being home grown. And Mum would like to make more jams and pickles for the shop. They're always popular.'

'That makes sense,' I say. 'But I don't understand what Kingsley's Christmas Village is about.'

'We're already known as a Christmas tree farm,' he says. 'I thought we should lean into that and make it more of a thing. We want to make the place a one stop place for Christmas. We're thinking of building an outdoor ice rink and renovating one of the barns as a workspace for local artists.'

'That's a great idea,' I say, forgetting for a moment I'm upset with him. 'You could run a monthly craft fair. It would bring people to the farm, and they'd be bound to stay for lunch and look around the shop while they were there. But it would mean a huge amount of work. I imagine it would cost quite a lot too.'

He nods. 'The biggest hurdle will be raising the money for the improvements, but it's not impossible. We've decided to sell some of the land to fund it. We own more than we're currently able to use, and we think several of our neighbours might be interested in expanding. If not, we'll have to look for someone else. Land is at a premium around there. It shouldn't be too difficult to find a buyer.'

'I'm sure a property developer would be happy to take it off your hands,' I say.

'We'd prefer to sell it to local businesses like ours,' he says. 'Anyway, that should give us enough money to invest in some of the things we'd like to do. With any luck, we can have it up and running by next Christmas.'

'Sounds great,' I say, my enthusiasm disappearing as I remember my own Christmas business catastrophe.

Tom seems to read my mind. 'I'm so sorry, Emma. If I'd had any idea what had happened to your stall, I'd have left Newcastle and come straight back to see you.'

'There wasn't anything you could have done,' I say. 'The roof fell in during the night. I didn't find out until I arrived at the fair the following evening.'

'I still wish I'd been there.'

'You had your own stuff going on,' I say. 'We both did. I'm glad you've sorted it out now. And I'm glad you'll be staying on the farm and following your dreams. I hope it's a tremendous success for you both.'

'Thanks,' he says. 'But that's not why I'm here.'

'Why are you here?' I ask.

He smiles. 'I've come to offer you a job.'

Chapter Thirty

Whatever else I was expecting, it wasn't this.

'I have a job,' I say at last, waving towards the vases of flowers on the shelves.

'I know you do,' he says. 'And this florist shop seems a nice place, now I've finally tracked it down. But I'm hoping it isn't your dream place to work forever.'

I don't answer. I'm not sure what he's saying, and I have no intention of making myself look like a fool yet again. I've done enough of that over this past month.

'Aren't you going to ask what the job is?' he says at last.

'You're the one who came to find me.'

'True,' he says. 'And I'm very glad I managed it. I would like to offer you the position of Director of Christmas Operations at Kingsley's Christmas Village.'

I blink. 'Is that an actual job title?'

'It will be if you say yes,' he says. 'You're the obvious candidate for the post. You're a fan of Christmas, you have a proven track record of selling Christmas products –'

'Although not for insuring them,' I interrupt.

'We'll take care of that side of things,' he says. 'Leaving you to manage the creative side of the business. As I was saying, you're the best person for the job.'

'How many applicants have you had for the position?'

'None as yet,' he admits. 'If you turn us down, we'll have to start looking, but I doubt we'll ever find a better qualified candidate.'

'Don't you have to advertise the job more widely?' I ask.

'Maybe once the business is established. But so far, it's only an idea, which means we're entitled to headhunt anyone we like.'

'I've never been headhunted before,' I say, pleased.

'I'm surprised,' he says. 'I would have thought your current employer would have searched you out and made you an offer you couldn't refuse to become one of their dynamic sales team.'

'She did make me an offer I couldn't refuse,' I admit. 'But that was because my rent was due, and I couldn't find anything else.'

Tom looks shocked. 'She didn't offer you renumeration beyond your wildest dreams? Then you don't owe her any loyalty. You should feel free to change employers at a moment's notice.'

'Are you offering me renumeration beyond my wildest dreams?' I ask.

'I'm afraid not,' he says. 'At least, not to start with. But we can revisit that when the business makes a profit. I wish I could offer you a New York salary if it meant you'd say yes. As it is, all I can tell you is that I don't want to do this without you. If it hadn't been for you, our farm would have been sold, and we wouldn't have thought of the Christmas village. That was all you, Emma.'

'No, it wasn't,' I say. 'I would never have come up with that idea in a million years. That was you and Helen.'

'I'm not talking about the details,' he says. 'But you were the inspiration for it. You, and your love of Christmas. All I could think about while Mum and I were discussing it this morning was how much I wanted you to be a part of it all. We're thinking of adding a tree-decorating service next year. Customers can select from a list of themes, and we can deliver them ready decorated. We'd also like to sell your Christmas boxes in the shop.'

'You don't need me for that,' I say. 'Helen can make her own boxes to sell. I haven't copyrighted the idea.'

'I may not need you,' he says gently. 'But I want you. I've known that since the day we first met.'

'You had a funny way of showing it,' I say. 'You allowed me to think you'd put your trees down on top of my boxes.'

'I'm sorry,' he says. 'In my defence, they were quite small stu…Christmas trees.'

'Not true. But I'll let it pass.'

'I didn't have much hope you'd ever give me a chance,' he says. 'Not after you'd discovered my shameful secret.'

'That you hate Christmas?'

'I never hated it,' he says. 'As you very well know. But it took meeting you to make me realise how much I enjoy it. I love how much you love Christmas, Emma. And I love how hard you work to make sure other people enjoy it too. I quickly realised how much I was looking forward to going to the fair each evening. And it didn't take me long to realise why. Even when you forced me into that ridiculous Santa costume, I didn't care, not if it meant I could be with you.'

I feel the tears start to my eyes. 'I don't know what to say. I'm not even celebrating Christmas this year.'

'Aren't you spending it with family?' he asks.

I shake my head. 'I thought I might drive down to Cornwall with Dad, but he and my aunt and uncle decided to drive down early. They'd gone by the time I got back here. I'm planning to visit Mum after Christmas, but Paris has had worse snowfall than we have, so I'm not even sure I'll make that. I don't want to risk spending New Year's Eve trapped in a snowdrift with hundreds of strangers. I've seen Murder on the Orient Express.'

'So, you're spending tomorrow by yourself?' Tom says incredulously.

'Yes.'

'Christmas?' he pursues. 'The season of the year you love more than any other?'

'Loved,' I say. 'I'm not sure I feel the same way about it any longer.'

His lips twitch as he unbuttons his coat and pulls it off. He's wearing the most garish Christmas sweater I've ever seen, covered with reindeer and glittery snow.

'Where did you get that?' I say.

'A gift shop in Newcastle,' he says. 'It's battery controlled.'

He reaches inside the neck and presses a switch. Immediately, the reindeers' noses start flashing.

'But why?' I say, bemused.

He switches off the battery. 'I wanted to show you how much I love Christmas. I've bought one for you too. It's in that bag if you want to see it. I didn't anticipate arriving in Oxford to find you'd given up on Christmas forever. I could send it back and buy you one with the Grinch on it.'

'I'm not the Grinch!' I say between tears and laughter. 'I'm just taking a break.'

'That's fine,' he says. 'You should do that for as long as you like. But I hope it won't be forever. Not when you've finally persuaded me of the magic of Christmas.'

'That sweater isn't the magic of Christmas,' I say. 'It's a migraine in knitted form.'

'I still plan to wear it,' he says. 'And I haven't given up hope of persuading you to wear yours too. I was going to put it under the tree for you tomorrow, but we could wear them on the drive back to the farm if you prefer.'

'I haven't said I'll take the job,' I remind him.

'True, but I very much hope you will. Also that you'll come back home with me for Christmas. Mr Whiskers will miss you, but Bonnie would be delighted to see you.'

'Mr Whiskers spends Christmas Day with my landlord,' I say. 'He likes to be close at hand to supervise the cooking of the turkey. I was planning a vegetable curry, and he doesn't like that.'

Tom takes both my hands in his and looks into my eyes. 'In which case, it seems to me you're out of excuses. Please say yes, Emma. Kingsley Christmas Village won't be nearly as much fun without you. We need an official Director of Christmas Operations. I'm willing to learn, but I'm a complete novice at this sort of thing, and Mum wants to concentrate her energies on expanding the cafe and the shop.'

'I want a proper contract,' I say. 'And full creative control over all decorations. And an annual trip to New York to study the Bloomingdales' Christmas display.'

'Make a success of the business and you can have anything you like,' he promises. 'Is that a yes?'

I look into his deep brown eyes, stunned by the speed at which things are moving.

'Do you really want me?' I whisper.

'More than anything in the world,' he says, pulling me into his arms and kissing me as though he never wants to let me go.

I draw back at last. 'I don't think your HR would approve of you behaving like this with your staff members.'

'I haven't written your contract yet,' he says.

'And when you do?'

He traces my cheek with his finger. 'I'll have it put into the company bylaws that the Director of Christmas Operations can kiss whoever she likes.'

'That should cover it,' I say.

'I'll have the contract drawn up the moment we get back home,' he promises. 'Until I do, could you please let me know who I'm about to kiss again – my new Director of Christmas Operations or Emma, the woman I'm very sure I can't live without?'

I wrap my arms around his neck, hardly able to believe what's just happened, and smile up at him. 'How about both?'

A Sweet Romantic Comedy
The Christmas Cookie Club
ROSEMARY WHITTAKER

Chapter One

My laptop pings, and my heart sinks as I see yet another message from my manager, Caroline.

Hi, Lucy, could you run your eyes over this again and make the translation sound a little more … charming?

I open the attachment. There's nothing like starting a Monday morning with a deep dive into a brochure on skin blemishes. I roll my eyes as I scroll through the endless jargon, wishing the coffee machine hadn't chosen today of all days to break down.

Does Caroline seriously expect me to give this a sprinkle of fairy dust and throw in a happily ever after? Because if there's one thing the German language is known for, it's charm.

I start typing, smoothing out the edges of phrases like *enlarged pores* and *unsightly blemishes.* I hate wasting my time turning a facial cream update into the equivalent of a romance novel. And all for a boss who will no doubt change her mind by this afternoon and demand I rewrite the entire thing in a more professional tone.

I'm barely onto the second page when my screen pings again. *Urgent: Quick Turnaround Required.*

I know what's coming. Yet another badly written piece of copy for me to transform into the sort of German that won't make the recipient fall asleep before the end of the first paragraph. This job was supposed to launch me into the cutting-edge, dynamic forefront of modern language translation. Instead, I'm trapped in a cycle of endless revisions and last-minute requests for product descriptions I don't care about.

'Lucy, have you finished that brochure for Berlin?' asks Mark, appearing next to my desk.

'Almost. I'm busy making it gripping yet easy to read.'

He raises an eyebrow. 'Do I detect a note of cynicism? Everything you write needs to be "easy to read". That's pretty much our whole brand. We make contemporary and accessible beauty products for the modern European. All our ad copy has to be clear and accessible. That's why we hired you.'

'I know. I'll finish this face cream copy as quickly as possible. Then I have to make a start on Caroline's thing about non-paraben deodorants. She says the marketing team is expecting a final version by the end of the day.'

He nods and disappears. With a sigh, I click on the document again.

'Easy to read!' I mutter to myself. If only I could translate my way out of here. I used to love language – the way it can bridge gaps and create connections. Now it feels like a tedious puzzle I'm being paid to solve, with absolutely no reward at the end.

It's almost noon, and I've barely made a dent in my work. I won't have time for lunch today. Panic creeps in, tightening its grip around my chest. I push myself harder, typing furiously, and then the screen freezes.

'No, no, no!' I mutter, jabbing at the escape key. But it's no use. My computer, in a masterstroke of timing, has decided it's done for the day. If only I could join it.

I pick up my desk phone and call IT, praying someone is available. A voice answers after a few rings.

'This is Dave,' says the world's least enthusiastic tech support agent.

'It's Lucy,' I say. 'My computer's frozen. I can't access anything.'

'Have you tried restarting it?'

'I didn't want to lose what I was doing.'

Dave sighs deeply, as if my request has wounded him personally. 'Someone will be along shortly,' he says and hangs up.

I pull out my mobile phone so I can answer emails while I wait. I open my inbox and see a follow-up message from Caroline.

Lucy, are you anywhere close to finishing that deodorant copy? The Berlin team is asking.

I resist the urge to hurl my phone across the room and instead politely reply that I'm waiting for the IT department – whose spirit animal is the sloth – to fix my computer. With any luck, she'll call Dave and tell him to get a move on. He may listen to her.

I skim through the rest of my emails and decide they aren't important. The Germans will just have to wait for my computer to be fixed before they get their brochure. Although I can't imagine they're really looking forward to receiving such a dull document.

I haven't eaten anything since early this morning, and I have a long afternoon ahead of me. It annoys me to think my colleagues in Germany are probably eating their lunch right now. I was accidentally copied on a document explaining that our European offices have strict rules about working hours and proper time off. I've never dared tell Caroline I saw it. She believes longer hours equal greater productivity, and lunch breaks are only for the weak.

I fish a granola bar out of my bag and eat it as quickly as I can in case she walks past and sees what I'm doing. I could tell her I'm eating lunch at my desk, but she'd be sure to see my screen is off and make some sarcastic remark I could really do without today.

Not for the first time, I wonder why I took this job. It looked great on paper, but it was never the sort of translation work I'd been dreaming of. Mum and Dad told me it would look good on my CV, and I suppose they were right. But they don't have to work here. Yet again, I calculate the minimum time I can spend at this company without looking like I'm a quitter.

My phone rings. I swallow my last bite rather too quickly and start coughing.

'Hello?' I manage, wondering whether it's someone from the Berlin office, in which case I ought to have said, '*Guten Tag!*'

'Lucy?' says Caroline's irritated voice. 'Have you finished that document yet?'

'Almost. But my computer – '

'I can't think what's taking you so long. I sent it this morning.'

I don't tell her it was two pages of the most badly written ad copy I've ever had the misfortune to read, and that I had to rewrite the entire thing before I could even think about translating it into German. Knowing my luck, it will turn out she wrote it herself. She's annoyed enough already without me insulting what she probably considers to be shimmering prose.

'It's my computer,' I explain. 'I was in the middle of writing a sentence when –'

'Don't bother,' she interrupts me. 'I've heard it all before. Sort it out, and get that document to me within the next hour, ok?'

She rings off, leaving me staring at my phone and wondering where she's sitting today. I don't have the best aim in the world, but if she's in one of the nearby cubicles, I should be able to lob my phone and hit her with a carefully planned throw. I'd have to pretend it wasn't my phone, but it's password-protected, so she'd probably never know.

I look at my phone again and change my mind. Anonymity isn't possible when you've been stupid enough to choose a bright pink case decorated with giraffes. It seemed a good idea at the time – something to cheer myself up on a dull winter's morning. If only I'd had the forethought to buy a plain blue one like everyone else. But there's nothing I can do about that now. My phone will have to remain unlobbed for the present.

It rings again, and I give a squeak of frustration. What does she want to tell me now – she has a twenty-thousand-word novella for me to translate about the importance of choosing the correct foundation?

I pick it up and jam it to my ear. 'What now?'

There's a pause before anyone speaks. Have I just signed my own letter of dismissal? I scrabble around for something to soften my answer, but my brain has given up for the day. Caroline will just have to deal with it.

'Lucy?' says a voice. It's pleasant and low-toned – nothing like Caroline's high-pitched, cut-glass shriek.

'That's right,' I say.

'It's Mum.'

My shoulders sag in relief before tightening again. There can only be one reason for her to call me in the middle of a busy workday.

'What's wrong?' I ask. 'Has something happened with Dad?'

'Dad's fine,' she says in a reassuring tone. 'I'm sorry. I didn't mean to worry you.'

'Are you sure he's ok?'

'Perfectly sure. I've just spoken to him, and he sends his love.'

'Just spoken to him? Where is he?'

'He's at home,' she says. 'But I'm not.'

A fresh wave of panic surges over me. 'Is there something wrong with you?'

'I'm fine too,' she says. 'If I could just –'

'You can't be fine!' I say. 'You're calling me during the day, and you aren't with Dad. Tell me what's going on!'

'I'm doing my best,' she says. 'But you keep interrupting me. I promise that Dad and I are both well. It's Gran.'

My heart sinks. 'What about her?'

'She's had a fall, and they've taken her to the hospital. They say she's broken her hip, and they're operating this afternoon.'

I let out a breath. 'That doesn't sound too bad. Will she be alright?'

'As far as I know. They don't seem too worried.'

'That's good.' I hesitate. 'I'm glad you told me, but couldn't it have waited until I got home this evening?'

'Not really. You see, it's Humphrey.'

I consider this for a moment. 'That is a problem.'

'I know,' she says. 'I'm looking after him at the moment. I drove down to Honeywell as soon as I heard. I can stay with him tonight, but I have to get back home to Dad by tomorrow evening. One of the neighbours is kindly sleeping over at our house, but she can't stay a second night.'

'How about Gran's neighbours?' I ask. 'Couldn't one of them look after Humphrey?'

'I'm trying to find someone, but I haven't had any success so far. Most people in the street are a similar age to her, and I don't know anyone else who lives in the village these days.'

There's a long silence. She doesn't break it, but I know what she wants to ask. I want to help. I really do. But there's no way I can. I'm up to my eyes in work, and it's only going to get worse in the run-up to Christmas.

'I'm sorry, Mum –' I stop, staring around the office. Am I about to tell her that what's going on here is more important than making sure Gran isn't desperately worried about her beloved dog? Am I about to tell myself the same thing? Not a hope.

'Don't worry,' she says. 'I knew it wasn't likely. I'll sort something out.'

'I was about to say I'm sorry I can't get there this evening,' I say. 'But I can catch a train tomorrow morning. I could be with you around lunchtime.'

Her voice is thin with relief. 'Oh, Lucy, that would be wonderful! Are you sure?'

'Perfectly sure. It's about time I took a few days off.'

'But what will your manager say? You told us she can be rather difficult at times.'

'I don't remember saying that. I guess I must have been having a bad week. Caroline will understand.'

'That's wonderful!' she exclaims again. 'I'm so grateful, Lucy. Please thank her for me and tell her it shouldn't be for too long.'

I look at my blank computer screen, then at the double doors at the far end of the office. There's no sign of Dave or any of his IT minions. If previous experience is anything to go by, no one will turn up for hours. In the meantime, Caroline will stop by my desk every five minutes or bombard my phone with messages asking why I haven't anticipated all her unreasonable requests and produced these documents by sometime last week. If I'm not here, and my phone mysteriously runs out of battery, she can't do any of that.

I push back my chair, pick up my bag, and sling my jacket over my shoulder.

'I'd better get going,' I tell Mum. 'I have a lot to do before tomorrow morning.'

I ring off and, without looking at anyone, I walk towards the door.

Chapter Two

There's no direct train the following morning, and I have to change twice. I settle into my seat on the final train and stare out at the frosty countryside. When did I last take this trip? I remember passing fields with golden haystacks and helping Gran pick apples from her Bramley tree. It must have been sometime in September. Three months ago.

I should visit her more often. I know how lonely she's been since Grandpa Ed died. But there's always so much going on at work that I lose track of time. I resolve to do better in the future. I hate to think of Gran having to move out of her cottage due to lack of proper support. She's lived there since she was married, and it would break her heart if she had to leave. But I mustn't get ahead of myself. The important thing is for her to recover from her operation. We can worry about everything else later.

Mum is waiting for me when the train pulls into the station. She's the only person on the tiny platform.

Her face lights up when she sees me. 'Lucy! I'm so grateful to you for coming at such short notice!'

She enfolds me in an enormous hug. It's familiar and comforting, but I feel the usual wash of guilt when I realise I haven't seen her recently either.

'How's Gran?' I ask.

'She came through the surgery well. I stopped in at the hospital before coming to meet you. She's been in a fair amount of pain, and she's woozy from whatever they've been giving her for it. I told her you were coming to look after Humphrey. She seemed pleased about that. You can pop in and see her this afternoon.'

'How will I get there? Do taxis venture out as far as Honeywell, or is there a bus?'

'There's no need for that,' she says. 'You can drive her car. It's insured for the whole family.'

Gran sold Grandpa's station wagon after he died, saying it was far too big for her and that she hated driving it. She recently bought herself a brand-new hatchback. Apparently, she's very pleased with it, although I understand Humphrey was less impressed. He's never liked cars, but I hope he's got used to this one by now. If so, he and I can take some walks in the New Forest. Otherwise, we'll have to stick to the lanes around Honeywell.

I ask about Dad as we drive to Gran's cottage.

'He's doing well, all things considered,' Mum says in the cheerful tone she always uses when she talks about him. 'The insurance company has finally settled, so we can get the house properly adapted for him, which will make all the difference. And don't forget it's still early days. His physiotherapist is doing wonders. Dad won't be in a wheelchair forever.'

She tells me this every time she sees me. I'm never sure which of us she's trying to persuade.

'What about the other driver?' I ask.

'As far as I know, he's fine now, which is something to be thankful for. There's no point in two lives being ruined.'

I'm not sure I'd be so forgiving in her place. The driver whose car hit Dad's a year ago was uninsured, and he'd lost his licence several months previously after being caught drunk driving. Personally, I'd like to see him in prison for the rest of his life rather than only two years. But Mum is a far nicer person than me. She and Dad get on with things without discernible bitterness. It's the best way, but I don't think I could ever be like them.

I put all this out of my mind as we turn into Bramble Close. It's a small cul-de-sac with just nine houses.

Mum pulls up outside the cottage at the furthest end and switches off the engine. 'Here we are, love. Let me help you with your bags.'

'I'm fine, thanks. I didn't bring much with me. I didn't think I'd need it. Mostly jeans and thick boots so I can take Humphrey for lots of muddy walks.'

Mum unlocks the front door, and we're greeted by loud barking.

'That's enough, Humphrey!' she says as he comes pelting down the hallway to greet us. He skids to a halt and looks up at me with suspicion.

I bend down to scratch his ears. 'Don't be so ridiculous! You know perfectly well who I am. We played tug-of-war with Gran's cardigan last time I was here, remember?'

'With Gran's cardigan?' asks Mum, puzzled. 'Why would you do a thing like that?'

I set down my bags at the foot of the stairs. 'It wasn't my idea. Humphrey was trying to bury it under the apple tree. He wasn't happy when I tried to take it off him, and it turned into quite a tussle. By the time I got it away from him, it had no buttons, and one sleeve was torn right off.'

I smile at the memory. 'Gran came out and found us. She said a magpie must have pulled the cardigan off the washing line and pecked holes in it and that Humphrey had wandered outside and found it. He looked up at her with those big, innocent eyes as though he'd never been near a washing line in his life and was shocked to think his fellow creatures could be capable of such a terrible thing. I didn't argue. You know how Gran refuses to hear a word against him. She could find him standing in the kitchen eating tonight's steak, and she would claim the butcher had dropped by with some samples and asked Humphrey to do a taste test.'

'I hope he won't be too much of a handful for you,' says Mum.

'We'll be fine. Won't we, Humphrey? Just leave my clothes alone, and we won't have a problem.'

I look around the hallway. 'This cottage is always so neat. I have no idea how Gran does it, especially with him around.'

'Your grandmother has always been very house-proud,' says Mum. 'She taught me from an early age that there's a place for everything, and everything should be in its place.'

'I hope I can maintain her exacting standards. Tidiness isn't my strong suit. But it should only be for a few days. And I can lock Humphrey out in the garden while I'm cleaning.'

I catch his eye and laugh. 'I'm only joking. I'll need you to scrub the bathroom for me each morning.'

Mum follows me upstairs. 'I thought you could sleep in the spare room while you're here. I've made up the bed for you. I slept in Gran's bed last night, but I've stripped it and washed everything this morning. Perhaps you could make it up again once the bedding is dry?'

'No problem,' I say. 'Or Humphrey can if I'm too tired.'

We go back down to the kitchen, and Mum shows me where she's put the coffee.

'Gran only drinks tea,' she says. 'But I know you're a coffee fiend.'

'Guilty as charged. Especially today. I've already drunk about five cups. My job is giving me a serious caffeine addiction.'

'How are you enjoying your work?' she asks. 'I hope it wasn't too inconvenient for you to take time off.'

'Not at all,' I assure her. 'It's about time I took a proper break. The last time I had a week off was when I came to stay with you and Dad in July.'

She frowns. 'You need to take better care of yourself than that. No job is worth putting your physical and mental health on the line.'

'It isn't that bad. And Caroline has said she wants us to use up our annual leave rather than rolling it over to next year. I'll use that as a bargaining chip if I have to stay here for longer.'

Mum still looks worried. 'Don't jeopardise your chances of a promotion.'

'Make up your mind,' I say. 'Either I should take my holiday allowance or I shouldn't.'

'I'm sorry,' she says. 'I worry too much.'

'Yes, you do. But that's understandable. First, there was Dad's accident, and now there's Gran. You have a lot on your plate. Please don't add me to your worries. I can look after myself. I'm looking forward to spending some time in the countryside with plenty of fresh air and exercise. Humphrey will see to that.'

She looks at her watch. 'It's almost one o'clock. Why don't I make us something to eat before I leave?'

'Even better,' I say. 'Why don't I make us something to eat while you take a break? Knowing Gran, the larder will be full of delicious things. And if I can't find what I need, I'm sure Humphrey will be only too delighted to show me.'

Chapter Three

Mum leaves after lunch. I'm going straight to the hospital once I've seen her off, so we have to leave a disconsolate Humphrey behind in the house. The overstretched NHS might take a dim view of him accompanying me. I could pretend he was my emotional support dog, but I doubt anyone would believe me. I can't think of any physical or mental condition that would be improved by the addition of a giant, over-active canine of indeterminate heritage.

'He'll be fine by himself for a little while,' Mum assures me. 'He's been as good as gold each time I've had to pop out for a few minutes.'

She hesitates. 'He chewed one of the sheets in the laundry basket, but I'm sure he didn't mean to.'

'You sound like Gran,' I tell her. 'There's nothing Humphrey could ever do that she wouldn't excuse.'

'He'll be fine,' she says. 'He'll quickly get used to having you around.'

'I hope so. But I can't stay here forever. We need to make some plans.'

Her face is anxious. 'I know. I felt terrible asking you to drop everything and come down here at a moment's notice, but I couldn't think what else to do.'

'You did the right thing,' I say. 'I wasn't complaining. But if Gran ends up staying in the hospital for longer than we expect, either I'll have to stay here or we'll have to find someone else to look after Humphrey. I can't imagine my landlord would let him stay with me in London, and the poor love would hate it. He needs to be in his own home and see all his usual people.'

I hand Mum her overnight bag. 'Is this all you brought with you?'

'It's all I had time to pack. Give Gran my love when you see her, and let her know we have everything under control. There's no reason for her to worry. She needs to concentrate all her energies on getting better.'

'I'll tell her,' I promise. 'And please give Dad my love too and tell him I'll come and see you both as soon as I can. I'll be there for Christmas if not before. With or without Humphrey.'

Her face creases with worry. 'I don't think …'

'I was joking,' I reassure her. 'Gran says Humphrey gets carsick after just a couple of miles. And I'll be facing a lifetime rail ban if I try to smuggle him on the train and he chews all the seats. Anyway, I'm sure Gran will be home long before Christmas.'

I feel a slight sense of panic as I watch her pull away. While Mum was here, I had someone to turn to – someone who would answer my questions with her usual calm good sense. Now I'm all on my own, and I'm not sure how I'll cope.

I tell myself to stop being so defeatist. If Mum can cope with everything life has thrown at her, I should be able to manage a small thing like this. I have no idea how our family would have survived if she hadn't been there to hold everything together last year. Christmas was a nightmare, with Dad in hospital after the crash, and no one knowing whether he would wake up at all, let alone recover enough to walk again and lead a normal life.

We still don't know how things will end up, but he's doing far better than any of us imagined possible. He's back home now, which was his first goal. He's still in a wheelchair, which he finds hard to accept. But, considering how bleak things looked last year, we have a lot to be grateful for. It's a shame everything has fallen on Mum. I feel the familiar pang of guilt that I haven't been there for her as much as I'd have liked to be. I originally suggested giving up my job and going home until Dad recovered, but she wouldn't hear of it.

'That's the last thing we need,' she told me rather more firmly than usual. 'Your father and I are so proud of everything you've done. We couldn't bear to see you throw it all away. What would make us both the happiest would be for you to stay where you are and keep following your dreams.'

But I'm not sure I am following my dreams. After I graduated, I was too busy looking for work in an overcrowded field to think much about the future. When I got my current job, I was so determined to hang onto it at all costs that I didn't stop to consider what those costs might be. I don't have time to think about all of that now, but it's something I need to consider when this crisis is over.

I arrive at the hospital twenty-five minutes later, thankful not to have been caught in the rush-hour traffic. I ask the way to Gran's ward and take the lift to the third floor.

A nurse coming out of the ward sees me and stops. 'Were you looking for someone in particular?'

'Lavender Hollis.' I say. 'She's my grandmother. She was admitted yesterday after a fall, and she had surgery on her hip. Is it possible for me to visit her?'

She holds open the door for me. 'Of course. She's in that bay over by the window. I'm sure she'll be delighted to see you.'

Gran is lying in bed, looking paler than usual. Her eyes are closed, so I sit in the chair next to her until she wakes up. I wait in silence for ten minutes, wondering how long I should leave her to sleep.

A nurse appears with a tray of medicines. 'Lavender Hollis?' she says, and Gran opens her eyes.

The nurse hands her a plastic cup containing three tablets and a glass of water. 'Time for your pain killers.'

She gestures towards me. 'And it looks as though you have a visitor.'

Gran's face lights up. 'Lucy! How long have you been here?'

'Only a few minutes,' I say, leaning over and kissing her cheek. 'I didn't want to wake you.'

I take her hand. 'What have you been getting up to?'

'I don't remember,' she says. 'Your mother tells me I fell down the stairs, but I have no memory of it. All I know is that I woke up in the hospital. They told me they'd put a pin in my hip, and I'd be here for a few days.'

Her face is pinched with anxiety. 'I'm so worried about Humphrey.'

'There's no need to worry,' I reassure her. 'Mum looked after him last night, and I'm here now. I got to Honeywell at lunchtime, and he and I are getting along fine. I won't go back home until we've sorted something out for him.'

She still looks worried. 'He's an enormous responsibility.'

I laugh. 'In every sense of the word.'

'You won't put him in the kennels?' she asks. 'You know his history.'

None of us likes talking about it, but we all know about Humphrey's early life. He was poorly treated as a puppy and ended up in a shelter. Gran adopted him soon after Grandpa Ed died, and the pair of them have never looked back. It's a match made in heaven, but Gran has to be extremely calm and gentle with him at all times, no matter what he gets up to. She's always said she has no difficulty with that, and I can see why. Humphrey is one of the most charming and lovable dogs I've ever met, despite his many quirks.

'I promise we won't put him in the kennels,' I say. 'Mum told me he didn't settle there the one time you tried. He needs to stay at home in familiar surroundings, and we'll make sure he does. Humphrey and I will be quite comfortable together in your lovely cottage. He's promised to show me all the local walks.'

Her face relaxes. 'You're a good girl, Lucy. I'm so sorry about all this.'

'Don't be silly. Which of us has not, at one time or another, fallen down the stairs and ended up in hospital? Perhaps not in hospital exactly, but I fell down the stairs at home on my eighteenth birthday. I may or may not have drunk more than was wise at my party. The jury's still out on that.'

'I remember that,' she says. 'Your mother was terribly upset, but your father thought it was funny.'

'I'll bet he did. Mum takes things so seriously. I can't think how she and Dad ended up together, but I'm glad they did. They balance each other out.'

'They do,' Gran agrees. 'And your mother hasn't had much to laugh about this past year.'

'I know. She's been amazing. She's held everything together and never once complained.'

'And now I've added to her worries,' she says. 'That's the last thing I ever wanted to do.'

'No, you haven't. I've told her to leave everything to me and not to worry about a thing.'

'But you'll have to go back to work soon,' she says. 'Who will look after Humphrey then?'

I give her a reassuring smile. 'Mum always says the way to solve even the biggest problem is one step at a time. And Humphrey's living situation is my first step. Do you have any friends or neighbours who could stay with him for a week or two?'

'I don't think so. He likes to sleep in his own bed. He doesn't adapt well to unfamiliar places.'

'Then we can look for someone to care for him in your cottage,' I say. 'That shouldn't be too difficult. There must be dog sitters in the area who could help out.'

'I've tried that once or twice,' she says. 'But it hasn't worked out. Humphrey is rather territorial about people he doesn't know sleeping in his house. I had a friend visit me last year. He prowled up and down the landing all night, barking outside her room every few minutes. We had to book her into a bed-and-breakfast the next day so we could all get some sleep.'

'That makes it more difficult,' I admit. 'But Mum says he was fine with her last night, and I'm not expecting any problems while I'm here. Humphrey and I have always got along very well together. Try not to worry about him. I'm sure I can find a solution that works for all of us.'

Gran doesn't look convinced, but she doesn't say anything more. Her eyelids have started to droop. I expect the painkillers are kicking in, which is a good thing. Time for me to leave and let her rest.

'I should get back to Humphrey,' I say. 'I've been gone for a while, and he'll be ready for a walk. Hopefully, we'll meet some other dog owners, and I can ask them if they have any suggestions.'

She nods sleepily, and I lean over to kiss her goodbye.

'Is there anything else I should know about before I go?' I ask. 'Quirks with the hot water or the central heating?'

She shakes her head. 'It's all quite straightforward. Call your mother if you have any questions. She knows the cottage like the back of her hand.'

'Then I'll leave you to have a lovely sleep. I'll come in to visit again tomorrow afternoon.'

Her grip on my hand tightens. 'Don't forget about the cookie club.'

Have the painkillers done their work too well and caused her to hallucinate?

'The cookie club?' I ask cautiously. 'Is that something Humphrey likes to eat? Where do you keep them?'

'The club,' she repeats. 'Don't forget about it.'

I'm about to agree that I won't and tiptoe away before she can become more agitated, but something stops me.

'I'm not sure what you're talking about, Gran. Did you say I shouldn't forget about a cookie club?'

Her eyes are almost closed now, but she speaks clearly enough for me to hear. 'That's right, dear. The Honeywell Christmas Cookie Club. You'll be in charge of running it this year.'

Chapter Four

Humphrey is delighted to see me when I arrive back from the hospital. I'm not sure what he got up to in my absence, and I don't have the energy to enquire too closely. The important thing is that he hasn't broken into the larder, so I should be able to feed us both this evening.

I find his harness and lead and take him out for a walk. We head in the direction of the water meadows but turn off well before we reach the boggiest parts. I don't want to have to rescue him from a marsh in the middle of winter.

It was bad enough when I brought him here last summer. He came home plastered in mud, and I had to help Gran give him a bath. It took the two of us almost an hour, and the bathroom was a swamp by the time we'd finished.

It isn't as though Humphrey dislikes baths. His eyes light up at the sound of running water. It's more that he hasn't grasped their purpose. As far as he's concerned, a bath is just an opportunity to displace enormous volumes of water. Getting himself clean is an alien concept to him, one I doubt he'll ever understand.

I may have to face that challenge before Gran comes home, but it's a treat I'm happy to put off for as long as possible. I know she gives him regular baths, but I'm not sure how. Perhaps she calls in reinforcements. I must remember to ask her when I visit tomorrow. And I need some clarification on that cookie club thing too.

Humphrey has a lovely time running around the field and chasing the local crows, although actually catching anything seems to be another idea he doesn't quite grasp. I really don't want him to catch birds, but it would be nice to think he had the ability if he ever needed to survive in the wild.

Humphrey's idea of being a hunting dog is to let out a volley of barks loud enough to alert even the deafest wildlife before running around in excited circles for several seconds. Only then does he take off in the general direction of the birds, which are of course long gone. He returns to me each time with a puzzled expression that seems to say he senses there's something wrong with his technique, but he can't quite figure out what it is. After which, he sees another bird, and the entire process starts again. Still, it keeps him happy. I hope he runs off enough excess energy to sleep well tonight, even without Gran in the house.

We don't meet any other dogs, so I can't ask their owners for dog-sitting suggestions. Maybe it's too cold for dog-walking. The temperature has dropped sharply since this morning. I wonder whether we might have snow tonight, and if so, what Humphrey will think of that. He and I could build a snowman together tomorrow. He may prefer us to make a snowbird, although he stands as little chance of catching that as he does the real thing.

I'm glad Mum left clear instructions about his meals. Tonight's menu is steamed chicken and rice. I locate a chicken breast in the fridge and carefully poach it while the rice steams. Cooking is not my forte, and I don't want to give him food poisoning on my first evening here.

Humphrey wanders around the kitchen while I work, looking at me hopefully. I tip the rice into a bowl and chop the chicken on top. He places his paws on my chest, and I have to use my free hand to push him away.

'You can't eat it yet. You'll burn your tongue.'

He gives me a blank look, and I sigh. 'Do you have even a shred of common sense? On second thoughts, don't bother. I already know the answer.'

He waits until I think his meal is cool enough, then polishes it off in three swift bites, licks the bowl, and grins up at me.

'I spent ages making that,' I say. 'The least you could have done was to take your time eating it.'

I remember Mum saying this to us when I was small. I finally understand where she was coming from. It must be frustrating to spend all afternoon preparing something that disappears in seconds, knowing you'll have to do the same thing only a few hours later.

My appreciation for her patience is growing by the minute. I resolve again not to make her shoulder the burden of this situation. I'm a grown woman, and I can sort everything out by myself. She has enough on her plate. Unlike Humphrey, who's now looking at me as if he can't remember when he last ate but is reasonably certain it was several days ago.

'Too bad,' I say. 'I'm not having you throwing up in the middle of the night while I'm the only one around to clean it up. Despite what I said to Mum, I have no faith at all in your housekeeping abilities.'

He gives a deep sigh and retires to his basket at the other end of the kitchen to brood over my refusal. He watches with offended eyes as I make myself a grilled cheese sandwich, pour myself a glass of milk and sit at the table.

'We need to set some ground rules so you and I both know where we stand,' I say. 'And rule number one is that I get to eat my meals in peace without being made to feel as though I'm snatching food from the mouths of starving dogs.'

His shoulders slump, and I relent. 'You can have my crusts when I've finished. But not if you sulk.'

He tips his head on one side and surveys me placidly. I'll bet Gran gives him her crusts too. She's besotted with him and thinks nothing is too good for him. I can kind of see why, but there's no way I'm telling him that. He needs to know who's boss right from the start.

I toss him the crusts, then go to the living room to watch something before bed. Humphrey accompanies me and flops down beside the wood burner.

'I'm not sure whether Gran has any wood,' I say. 'And it's too cold to go poking around outside right now. We can check tomorrow morning.'

He pads over to the sofa, climbs up and collapses next to me.

I give him an ineffectual push. 'I don't expect you're allowed up here.'

He closes his eyes and ignores me. There's no point worrying about it tonight.

'You can stay here this evening,' I say. 'But if Gran tells me tomorrow that she never lets you sit up here and you didn't inform me of that fact, you'll be sorrier than a very sorry thing.'

Humphrey shifts himself so he's taking up most of the sofa. I push back, but it's like trying to move the Forth Bridge. I tuck my legs into the tiny space remaining and switch on the television.

I switch it off an hour later. There was nothing good on, and my legs are going to sleep. Humphrey looks perfectly comfortable, sprawled in an untidy heap next to me, his legs twitching occasionally. I hope he's making a better job of catching birds in his dreams than he does in real life. I'm glad there were no other dog-walkers around to witness his ineptitude.

It's been a long day, and I'm exhausted. My main priority should be to get a good night's sleep so I start my stay here rested and refreshed. There's a lot to do if I want to get everything organised and return to London with a clear conscience.

Humphrey appears to be sound asleep. I decide to leave him where he is. He can sleep in the kitchen if he wakes up later. Or he can sleep in Gran's room. Mum said he has a basket by her bed.

I tiptoe out of the room and set off down the hall as quietly as possible. I've only made it as far as the bottom stair when he appears in the doorway.

'I didn't want to wake you,' I tell him.

He trots into the kitchen and waits by the back door.

'Do you need to go outside and do your business?' I ask. 'Better now than in the early hours.'

I open the door, and he shoots out into the night. I hope the garden is secure. I don't fancy the idea of chasing down the street after him in this weather.

He reappears a few minutes later, looking pleased with himself.

'Whatever you've done will have to wait until tomorrow,' I say. 'I'm going to bed. Are you staying down here or sleeping upstairs in your basket?'

He rushes down the hall and takes off up the stairs. I follow as he hurls himself through the guest room door and launches himself onto my bed.

'Wrong room,' I say. 'Your bedroom is down there.'

He rolls over onto his back and starts snoring.

I poke him. 'That has to be fake. No one could snore like that without waking themselves up. Come on, Humphrey. Let me take you to your basket.'

He flops over onto his side, but the snoring continues. I debate whether to pick him up and carry him to Gran's room. But it's no good. He must weigh almost as much as I do. I collect his basket from her bedroom and dump it next to my bed.

'There you go,' I tell Humphrey. 'You can sleep in here if you must, but you'll have to turn down the volume.'

He doesn't move. I lean against him, hoping to push him to the edge of the bed. Nothing happens. I consider sleeping in Gran's room tonight, but I haven't made up the bed, and I'm too exhausted to think about finding clean sheets and wrestling with the quilt cover. I glance over at the basket, wondering how comfortable it is. I could curl up in it, pull a blanket over me and pretend I was camping. I look more closely at the dog hairs and traces of slobber and decide against it.

'You are the most annoying dog I've ever met,' I tell him crossly, but he doesn't stir.

'Last night, I had a lovely double bed all to myself,' I say, climbing in and searching for a space in which to curl up. 'And now here I am, sharing a bed with the world's largest and most ridiculous dog.'

Humphrey shifts enough for me to wedge my legs down beside him. I give him my scariest frown, but without effect. Either he really is asleep or he's very good at pretending to be.

I settle down for the night, thinking about how quickly things have changed. Yesterday, I was battling to make cosmetic products sound new and exciting for all our European customers, and today I'm acting as an unpaid servant for a giant, untrained dog. How the mighty have fallen.

Chapter Five

Humphrey wakes me the next morning by the simple expedient of rolling over and lying on my chest.

I push him as hard as I can. 'Stop it! I'm still asleep.'

He doesn't move. I open my eyes to find him staring at me.

'What?' I say.

He licks my face and sighs deeply.

I sit up. 'That's something that needs to stop right now. I have a perfectly good flannel for when I want to wash my face. Your services won't be required, thank you.'

He sighs again and rolls off the bed, landing with a heavy crash on the floorboards. This house is over one hundred years old and probably has woodworm, dry rot, and goodness knows what else. I close my eyes, half expecting the bed to disappear through the floor and for us both to end up in the living room. When nothing happens, I open them again.

'These pre-war houses were built to last,' I say. 'It stands to reason they must have been if you've been living here for three years, and this one is still standing.'

I swing my legs out of bed and shiver. 'I can't think why you wanted to get up. It's lovely and cosy under the duvet.'

Humphrey ignores me and leads the way downstairs to the kitchen, where he trots over and looks hopefully at the fridge.

'You'll have to move if you want me to find whatever you believe is in there,' I tell him. 'Let's check the instructions Mum left for us.'

I pull the piece of paper off the fridge and study it. 'You're out of luck. You have dried food for breakfast. Did you think you could trick me? That won't work, I'm afraid. I'm not a junior supply teacher.'

Humphrey thumps his tail and watches intently as I reach into the cupboard and measure out his food.

I put the bowl in front of him. 'I should inform you in advance that I intend to do everything by the book while I'm here. Gran will have my guts for garters if I don't. So, if you have any ideas of talking me into doing anything she wouldn't like, forget it.'

Humphrey isn't listening. He demolishes his breakfast in a few quick bites before looking up at me like a Charles Dickens orphan.

I pick up the bowl and dump it in the sink. 'No, you may not have any more! And if you keep asking, I'll send you up the chimney to clean it out.'

I consider his frame. 'Perhaps not. You'd get stuck within the first few feet. Whatever possessed you to grow to this size? Any normal dog would have had the sense to stop long ago. I hope you've finished now. You barely fit in this cottage as it is. If you keep going, Gran will have to extend into next door's garden, and the neighbours are sure to complain.'

I pour myself a bowl of cereal. Ignoring his wistful look, I open the fridge to get myself some milk before realising I ran out last night.

I sigh. 'We'll have to go to the shops before we do anything else this morning. Do they let you go inside, or do I have to tie you to a lamp post?'

He gives me a look that says he would have no difficulty in uprooting any lamp post to which he was tied.

'Perhaps I should go to the shops by myself,' I say. 'I'll have to ask Gran what she does when she has to take you out.'

The letterbox rattles, and Humphrey barks loudly and leaps to his feet. Before I can stop him, he races to the front door and returns a moment later with a mouthful of envelopes, which he drops at my feet. He looks up at me like a dog who knows he's done something clever and hopes for a treat.

I pick up the envelopes and wipe off the slobber as best I can. 'Maybe let me fetch them next time?'

His shoulders sag, and I reach down to pat him. 'Sorry, Humphrey. You did a great job. I'll take you out for a nice, long walk in a minute to say thank you. But first, I need my breakfast.'

Cereal is out, so I make myself a couple of slices of toast and spread them thickly with butter. I ignore his pleading eyes and eat it as I look through the envelopes. None of them seem important – a flyer for a local business, something about local planning permission, and what appears to be a utility bill.

I lay the last one on the counter for later, toss the others into the recycling bin, and run upstairs to prepare for what I suspect will be a busy day. I have a long list of things to do, all arranged in order of importance.

Most pressing is to find someone who can look after Humphrey while Gran is in hospital. Next is to arrange someone to help her at home when she's released. She won't be able to walk Humphrey for a while, and she'll need help with personal care too.

I shower quickly and pull on a pair of jeans and my thickest sweater. It's a chilly morning. A quick look outside tells me it didn't snow in the night, but the sky is thick with greyish-white clouds. I remember being snowed in here one winter as a child. We woke in the morning to find the garden had disappeared under a thick blanket of snow. Most of Bramble Close was invisible too. We'd come down by train, and there was no way to get to the nearest station until the roads were cleared.

Honeywell isn't a huge priority for the local council at the best of times, and Bramble Close is even less so. We couldn't get out for four days, which I found wildly exciting, but Mum told me afterwards she'd been concerned we would run out of food. I make a mental note to check the contents of the larder and the fridge before we go shopping. I could manage on restricted rations for a few days, but Humphrey definitely wouldn't enjoy it.

I put his harness on and make sure I have the front door key before setting off. He joyfully drags me along the lane. Ten minutes later, we arrive at the high street. We would have got here more quickly if Humphrey hadn't insisted on exploring every single hedge and testing the thickness of the ice on every puddle.

'Anyone would think this was the first time you'd been along this street,' I say. 'But I'm sure you and Gran walk along here all the time.'

I march him along to the corner shop. He shows a strong desire to stop at the bakery, but I drag him away.

'You won't be allowed in there. Come on! I want to get us some groceries in case there's a blizzard tonight and the whole village is snowed in until the new year.'

Humphrey doesn't look convinced, but he allows himself to be shepherded to the corner shop. I'm pleased to find he's allowed inside so long as he stays on his lead. That's not a problem as far as I'm concerned. The only time Humphrey is going to come off his lead is in the fields next to the water meadows.

I buy as many groceries as I can carry and load them into my backpack.

'When do you close?' I ask the woman behind the counter. 'I may need to make another run later today. Humphrey here eats as much as a small army.'

She smiles at him. 'We all know Humphrey. He's a lovely boy, aren't you, Humphrey? Are you staying with Mrs Hollis?'

I lift my backpack onto my shoulders. 'She's in hospital with a broken hip. I've come down to look after Humphrey for a few days. I'm her granddaughter, Lucy.'

She looks shocked. 'I'm sorry to hear that. I had no idea. Please give her my love when you see her and tell her I hope she gets better soon. I'm Shirley, by the way.'

'Nice to meet you,' I say. 'I'll pass on your message when I visit this afternoon. You don't know of anyone who could look after Humphrey until Gran gets home, do you?'

'Not off the top of my head. But I'll ask around. Meanwhile, let me know if you need anything. There are plenty of people in the village who would be happy to do whatever they can to help your grandmother.'

Humphrey gives his lead an insistent tug, and I almost overbalance.

'I'm coming,' I tell him. 'I expect you want to go to the bakery, but I've already told you that's not happening.'

'They don't mind,' says Shirley. 'The owners allow dogs to go in as long as they're well behaved.'

I give Humphrey a dubious look. 'I'm not sure I'd go as far as to say he's well behaved.'

She laughs. 'Take him in and say hello. They make excellent coffee, and they may have some suggestions about a dog sitter. Those girls know everyone in the village, and they can be extremely persuasive when they want to be.'

I waver. I could do with a cup of coffee. Mum only got me instant, and I didn't bring a cafetière with me.

'They sell dog biscuits too,' says Shirley. 'I'm sure Humphrey wouldn't say no to a nice biscuit, would you, darling?'

Humphrey gives her a look that says quite clearly he would never say no to a nice anything. He also manages to convey the impression his current caregiver hasn't remembered to feed him since she arrived.

A look outside tells me it's starting to sleet. That does it. There are few things I hate more than sleet. It can't decide whether to be good, honest rain or a magical snowfall, so it compromises on cold, damp sogginess.

'Come on, Humphrey!' I say, tugging on his leash to distract him from the shelf of cereal he's inspecting. 'Let's go and buy you a lovely dog biscuit.'

Chapter Six

Humphrey doesn't need telling twice. He rockets out of the shop and sets off excitedly in the wrong direction. He realises his mistake and turns himself around somewhat in the manner of a giant oil tanker in the middle of the North Sea, with lots of puffing noises and manoeuvrings.

'Finally!' I say when he's facing in the right direction. 'The dog biscuits are this way. And, more importantly, the coffee.'

We walk towards The Sugarloaf Bakery. I hesitate before opening the door. It's all very well for Shirley to say they allow dogs in here, but that description seems a stretch when it comes to Humphrey.

'Excuse me,' says a voice, and I turn to see an elderly woman with a small, curly-haired dog standing behind me.

'I'm sorry,' I apologise. 'We take up a lot of space. Humphrey does, at least. Are you going in here?'

She nods, and I hold the door open for her. The small dog runs inside and jumps up at the counter.

'Now, now, Bernie!' says his owner. 'Sit down nicely, and Lily will give you a biscuit.'

I follow them inside and stand by the door, half expecting an irate staff-member to shoo us out again, sleet or no sleet.

'Hello, Humphrey!' says a pleasant-looking young woman with fair hair, who I assume is Lily. 'We haven't seen you in here for a few days.'

Relieved, I take another step inside and allow the door to close behind me. Humphrey sidles over to the counter and stares up at a basket next to the till. If anyone wanted to hide the dog biscuits, they wouldn't stand a chance with these two dogs around.

'Are you sure he's allowed in here?' I ask.

'Absolutely,' she says. 'You can sit at either of those tables near the door. We reserve those for our canine visitors, don't we, Bernie?'

The small dog, who has wedged himself under one of the two tables, looks up when he hears his name. He grins at us, and the biscuit he's been crunching falls out of his mouth. He stops grinning and makes a dart for it. That may be wise with Humphrey in the vicinity.

I sit down at the second table, hoping Humphrey knows the drill and doesn't disgrace me in front of my new acquaintances. He plumps himself down next to me and heaves an enormous sigh.

'Would you like a biscuit too?' Lily asks him. 'We have some lovely beef ones.'

She hands him a biscuit, and he disposes of it in two mouthfuls.

She laughs. 'That didn't even touch the sides, did it? Is he allowed another one?'

'I'm not sure,' I say. 'What does he usually have when he comes in here?'

'He likes the lamb and herb flavour,' says the elderly woman.

'Thank you,' I say. 'Do you know how many he eats?'

'He has two,' she informs me. 'Bernie is only allowed one, but he's a lot smaller.'

'That's an understatement,' I say, looking at Bernie, who's about one sixth Humphrey's size. 'I hope your dog isn't frightened of Humphrey. I wouldn't blame him if he was.'

'They're good friends,' she says. 'Although Humphrey can be a little overwhelming at times. Bernie's a very sensitive dog, and he prefers to play gently.'

The very sensitive dog looks up at the sound of his name. Noticing Humphrey making a start on his second biscuit, he scrambles to his feet and runs over to join him.

I instinctively tighten my grip on Humphrey's lead. He's clearly fond of his food, and I doubt he'll take kindly to being deprived of it. To my surprise, he drops the rest of the biscuit onto the floor and lets Bernie make a grab for it.

'Now, now, Bernie,' his owner chides him again. 'You know the vet said you shouldn't eat too many biscuits.'

Bernie appears sublimely unconscious of the vet having said any such thing. His expression suggests that he remembers it very differently and that the vet gave strict instructions his blood biscuit-levels should never be allowed to fall too low.

Humphrey flops down next to my chair again, narrowly missing Bernie, who's too preoccupied with the biscuit to notice he's only just escaped being squashed like a bug on a windshield.

'I'm sorry,' I tell his owner. 'Humphrey doesn't seem to realise quite how big he is. But he's very gentle. He wouldn't willingly hurt a fly.'

'We all know him,' says Lily. 'But I don't think we've seen you in here before?'

I explain who I am and what I'm doing in Honeywell. Both she and the elderly woman seem shocked when I tell them about Gran's fall and subsequent operation.

'Anyway, that's why I'm here,' I finish. 'And I'll have to stay until I find someone else to look after Humphrey. I don't suppose either of you has any suggestions?'

'I can't think of anyone right now,' says Lily. 'But I'll ask my mother tonight. She knows everyone around here and may have some ideas.'

'And I'll ask the Silver Surfers,' says the elderly woman. 'Mavis is excellent in a crisis.'

I'm not sure who the Silver Surfers are, but I'm not about to turn down any offer of help. I order a cappuccino and don't take much persuading to try one of the lemon tarts.

'Abby made them an hour ago,' says Lily. 'You're lucky my partner Isabella is out this afternoon, or there wouldn't have been any left for you.'

The elderly woman picks up her bag and prepares to leave. 'I'm Mrs Ogilvie,' she tells me. 'I'll ask around for you.'

'Thank you so much,' I say gratefully. 'I'm Lucy Hollis. Do you have my grandmother's phone number?'

'Mavis will find it. She can find anything.' She nods to Lily, and she and Bernie set off together down the high street.

I catch Lily's eye. 'Who is this Mavis person? She sounds as though she works for MI5.'

'I wouldn't be surprised,' she says. 'She runs the computer club in the village, and she's terrifyingly efficient. I hope you don't have any secrets. She'll dig them out in seconds.'

'None that I can think of,' I say. 'I should be getting home. Humphrey has his lunch at noon, and I don't want to get between him and food. He might eat me instead.'

She ruffles Humphrey's head. 'I think you're safe enough. He's the mildest-mannered dog I've ever met. But don't let Mrs Ogilvie know I said that. She's one of our best customers, and she'd never forgive me. Bernie is the light of her life, and she's convinced he's the best at everything he does.'

'That's how my grandmother feels about Humphrey,' I say, pulling on my coat and hat. 'I can't imagine how she's feeling right now. She won't care about her broken hip, but she'll be desperately worried about Humphrey. I wish I could take him to the hospital so she can see for herself he's fine. But I don't think they would appreciate that. He's a sweet-natured old thing, but even his most fervent admirers would have to admit he's clumsy.'

As if to confirm my statement, Humphrey jumps to his feet, knocking over two chairs and jogging the table so a vase of flowers falls over.

Lily picks it up. 'We all have our faults. To be fair, he's no more clumsy than my business partner. Whenever she catches sight of a fresh batch of cakes, she doesn't allow anything or anyone to get in her way. That's why we always keep plenty of spare cups and plates in stock.'

'That's very sensible,' I say. 'Humphrey kicked his bowl across the floor this morning in his rush to collect the post. I may have to buy some spares myself just in case.'

I look down at Humphrey, who stares back at me with an air of bewildered innocence.

'Let's get you out of here before you do any serious damage,' I say. 'I need to save what little money I have for Christmas presents, not paying for damaged crockery.'

I arrive at the hospital mid-afternoon. Gran is awake and looking more comfortable.

'How's Humphrey?' she asks the moment she sees me.

'Absolutely fine. He's enjoying a well-deserved nap after helping me do the grocery shopping, clean the house, and make lunch.'

I catch her eye and grin. 'When I say helping …'

Her face relaxes. 'That sounds like Humphrey. He does like to be involved with whatever's going on.'

'I expect he'll sleep all afternoon. He needs to recover his energy for this evening's walk. He didn't catch any birds last night, but he's convinced that was just bad luck.'

'I hope he isn't being too much trouble,' she says.

'Not in the slightest. I'm enjoying the break, and Humphrey is wonderful company. I didn't feel at all nervous staying in your cottage by myself last night with such a giant guard dog.'

She smiles. 'The last time he heard a noise in the middle of the night, he hid under the bed until I'd gone to check what it was. Luckily, it was only a squirrel, but he was no use at all.'

'But he looks the part. That's the main thing. If there are any burglars lurking around Honeywell, they'll take one look at him and make a note to avoid your address. By the way, I took him to the village bakery this morning. Or rather, he took me. I met one of his friends. Bernie, I think his name was.'

'I like Bernie,' she says. 'His owner spoils him dreadfully, but it doesn't seem to do him any harm. He's always delighted to see Humphrey when we bump into him on our evening walk.'

'She said she'll ask around to see whether anyone is free to care for Humphrey. And the woman who works in the bakery said she'd do the same.'

'That's so kind,' she says. 'But Humphrey doesn't settle with just anyone.'

'I promise I won't leave him with someone he doesn't love,' I tell her. 'By the way, do you remember mentioning the cookie club yesterday? You were too tired to tell me any details, but I would like to know what you were talking about.'

'It's been going since 1939,' she says proudly. 'Have I never mentioned it to you? My grandmother and her friends founded it at the start of the Second World War.'

'I hadn't heard anything about it until yesterday. It sounds fascinating.'

'There's too much to tell you now,' she says. 'But the club members will tell you all about it at your first meeting.' She closes her eyes.

'Are you alright?' I ask, concerned. 'Shall I get the nurse to bring you some more painkillers?'

'I'm just a little tired, that's all. But I'm so happy to have seen you.'

I tuck the blanket around her. 'I'll leave you to have a sleep. One more thing. You told me yesterday I needed to run this club for you.'

She opens her eyes. 'The first meeting is on Thursday evening at seven o'clock. You need to host it, and you'll need to bake four dozen cookies beforehand.'

'For the club members?' I ask. 'That's a lot of cookies. How many of them will there be?'

'They'll all bring cookies too,' she says. 'Remember, they need to be homemade. No shop-bought cookies.'

'But surely, someone else can –' I begin, but she shakes her head.

'I don't want anyone else to do it. It's a Hollis thing. And you're a Hollis. Please tell me you'll do it.'

It isn't like Gran to be so stubborn about anything. Maybe it's the drugs they're giving her.

I bend down to kiss her cheek. 'I'll do my best if it's so important.'

'It is.'

Her voice is no more than a whisper, but her jaw is set just like Mum's when she won't take no for an answer. That doesn't happen often, but when it does, we all know not to argue with her. It may be the same with Gran. Whatever's going on here is important to her. I resolve not to ask too many questions while she's so vulnerable.

'I'll host it this week,' I promise. 'And I'll feed all your guests. After that, you'll be home and able to host it for yourself.'

'I hope so. Give my love to Humphrey, and tell him to behave himself.'

'I will. Although I can't guarantee he'll take the slightest bit of notice.'

She smiles, and I leave her to sleep. With any luck, all I'll need to do on Thursday is make tea and coffee and hand out cookies, then listen politely while everyone talks about recipes and the war. Even I should be able to manage that.

Chapter Seven

I take Humphrey for a walk the next morning, then settle him into his basket for a well-deserved rest. It takes a lot of energy to chase after rats and other small mammals who heard him coming while he was still several streets away and made their escape long before he reached them.

I dig through Gran's cookery books until I find what looks like a simple recipe for oatmeal and raisin cookies. It sounds as though these club members have enormous appetites. Or maybe it's some sort of cookie-exchange thing. That would make more sense. I'm not sure why they can't eat shop-bought cookies at the meeting, but Gran was adamant, so I'd better do as she told me.

'How difficult can it be?' I ask Humphrey.

He gives me a puzzled frown that makes me laugh, then rolls over onto his back and starts to snore.

'You're no help,' I mutter, assembling my ingredients. It's not too complicated – sugar, butter, eggs, flour, baking powder, oats, and raisins. Gran doesn't appear to have any baking powder, so I improvise with cream of tartar. I can't imagine anyone will tell the difference. I can't find any raisins, but I discover what looks like a packet of currants on the top shelf.

I switch on the oven. Then, feeling rather like the little red hen, I start to mix and stir. The recipe isn't as helpful as it could be. It tells me to cream and fold but not what that means. I do my best and, somewhat to my surprise, the result looks passable. I pick up a couple of teaspoons and attempt to drop the mixture onto the greased baking sheet as the recipe instructs. But the dough isn't keen to comply. It sticks first to one spoon and then to the other. I bang one of them against the sheet, hoping to knock the dough off. Nothing happens.

I try again, then reach into the drawer for a knife and scrape the mixture off with that. Half of it ends up stuck to the knife, but I finally manage to arrange the dough into twelve irregular mounds on the tray. I can claim the size difference is intentional, to make allowance for varying-sized appetites. The oven light has gone out, which should mean it's hot enough.

I cast a quick look at Humphrey to make sure he won't dive for the oven the moment I open it. He's still flat on his back, his legs twitching at intervals. Hopefully, he'll stay that way until the cookies are safely on their cooling tray, well out of his reach.

I slide the tray into the oven, set the timer, and make myself a cup of coffee while the cookies are baking. That didn't go as badly as it might have done, even if they're not as perfectly shaped as the ones in the bakery. I expect they have some sort of machine that turns them out in a uniform size. I make a note to ask about it the next time I go in.

Anyway, I don't want my cookies to look like theirs. The whole point of making them at home is that they're … homemade. And everyone knows homemade cookies aren't all the same as each other. They're quirky and individual, which is why everyone likes them so much.

The timer pings, and I reach for the oven gloves, feeling a pang of anticipation. I open the door, lift out the tray, and inspect my creations with slight dismay. Quirky and individual is one thing, but it doesn't quite describe what I've produced. These cookies seem to have thrown a party while they were in the oven. They've spread into irregular shapes and are all stuck to each other. To make it worse, they're burned at the edges and still soggy in the middle.

I dump the tray onto the counter-top, suppressing an urge to scream. I followed the recipe to the letter, which means these cookies should look exactly like the ones in the book. That's how cooking is supposed to work. Otherwise, what's the point of having a recipe book at all? It's nothing more than a giant con.

I'll bet the person who wrote this book didn't bother to test the recipes before publishing them. It's the only possible explanation. They're aiming to make quick money from novices such as myself, while all along they have no idea how to cook either. I refuse to allow them to get away with it. I'll write to their publishers to make a formal complaint and request a refund. And a letter of apology.

I pull out my phone to find who publishes this unresearched nonsense. I don't like leaving negative reviews, but in this case I'm happy to make an exception. It serves them right. I tap the name of the so-called chef into the search bar, adding the title of the book. I frown as hundreds of results flash onto my screen. Whoever this Mary Berry person is, she seems to be fairly well known. Which makes it even more annoying that she's allowed to get away with publishing untested recipes.

I scroll through page after page of articles and reviews. No one else seems to have had the same problem. Maybe Gran's book is a misprinted edition. That would explain why the recipes don't work for me, but everyone else thinks they're fine.

I'll have to contact the publishers later, once I've decided what's going on. I have more pressing problems right now. I'm hosting this cookie club tomorrow, and I have to produce something at least partially edible before then. This cookbook isn't the answer. I'll have to find a better recipe online.

This is a more cheering thought. There are millions of free recipes out there. All I have to do is select one that's been well reviewed, and all will be well. I scroll through my phone. As I thought, there are a million and one oatmeal cookie recipes, all apparently more amazing than the last.

I see a name I recognise and click on it. Mum has always sworn by Delia Smith's recipes. She makes her Christmas cake and mince pies every year, and they're delicious. It stands to reason her oatmeal cookies will be too.

I scrape my misshapen, burned cookies into the kitchen bin. Humphrey's nose twitches, but he doesn't move. I wash out the bowl, check I still have enough ingredients, then start again from the beginning, careful not to deviate too much from the recipe. I feel more cheerful as I sift and stir and mix.

I roll the spoonfuls of dough between my hands as instructed, press them lightly with a fork, and put the tray back into the oven, feeling pleased with myself. That wasn't so difficult. The members of the cookie club are bound to be impressed when I hand these around tomorrow, especially when I casually drop into the conversation they're the first cookies I've ever baked. I don't have to mention the failed batch. It wasn't my fault the recipe was faulty.

I finish my coffee and make myself another. Humphrey is still asleep, so I pick up this morning's newspaper and make a start on the crossword. Gran won't mind. She's on powerful painkillers and won't be up to doing crosswords for a few days. I'm so engrossed in four down that I almost jump out of my seat when the timer pings. I lay down my pen and reach for the oven gloves again, giving thanks for actual competent and expert chefs.

I stare at the cookies, stifling a most unprofessional chef-like exclamation. What is wrong with these so-called famous cooks? Why are they invited to do baking shows on the television? More importantly, how are they ever invited back?

These cookies are, if anything, worse than the first batch. They look like something from a horror movie. What were supposed to have been perfectly shaped circles are now oddly shaped blobs that look like a cross between melted snowmen and the Sea of Tranquility. They don't smell right either. Maybe I shouldn't have used that cream of tartar after all, and I probably shouldn't have doubled the amount to help them rise.

These cookies belong in a museum of baking disasters, if there is such a thing. If there isn't, they should open one especially and give my cookies pride of place.

Even Humphrey wouldn't want them. Not that I'm giving him the chance. The last thing I need is to explain to a strange vet how I've managed to give my grandmother's dog severe food poisoning.

I settle down to make a third batch of cookies. This time, the recipe doesn't call for baking powder, so I don't have to make any substitutions. I also realise the packet of currants isn't all it seems. I should have noticed the label said Dried Olives. Oh, well. We live and learn.

This batch doesn't look quite as awful as the first two, so I decide to take it with me to the hospital. I've promised to visit Gran at three o'clock. She can take a look and give me some hints about what I can improve before tomorrow evening. How can making cookies be so difficult? You can't watch a holiday movie without stumbling on people merrily whipping up hundreds of batches of perfect cookies whenever they have a spare ten minutes, all iced to professional standards.

I can't let Gran down. This cookie club seems so important to her. Almost as important as Humphrey. I remind myself I'm a modern, capable woman. I can juggle several things at once. Surely, I can look after her precious dog and master the art of combining a few basic ingredients in a way that doesn't send the club members off to join her in the hospital to have their stomachs pumped.

I toy with the idea of writing a feature-length exposé of celebrity chefs. The public ought to know what's going on with these fake experts. I could challenge them to join me in the television studio kitchens and bake one of their stupid recipes, live and without special effects. We could invite real people off the street to sample the results and give their honest opinions, rather than relying on sycophantic TV show hosts to pretend everything is amazing and tastes delicious. If I were one of those hosts, I'd demand danger money before tasting anything produced on my show.

Humphrey is still fast asleep. I pick up the baking tray, cover it with a tea towel, and let myself out of the house. Thankfully, he doesn't wake up and start barking. I hate the thought of him being upset at being left by himself. But I'll be back in a couple of hours, and we can spend the evening together.

We'll go for a nice long walk to his favourite park and play fetch. By which I mean, I can stand in the cold, hurling random sticks as far as possible, while Humphrey races around, forgetting where most of them landed. We all have different ways of enjoying ourselves, and that appears to be his. Who am I to judge?

I walk carefully down the path towards the car. The remains of last night's frost still coats the flagstones, and I don't want to slip and fall. The hospital doesn't need another Hollis woman to care for. I reach out and lift the latch of the garden gate, careful not to catch my sleeve in the privet hedge. It needs a trim, but I know even less about gardening than I do about cooking, so that will have to wait until Gran is home to give me proper instructions.

I balance the tray on my left hip and reach into my pocket with my right hand. My car key is in here somewhere. Unless Humphrey has mistaken it for a dog biscuit and eaten it. I wouldn't put it past him. I find the key and step out onto the pavement.

Something catches my shoulder, spinning me around abruptly. Have I stepped on a patch of ice? A wave of pain shoots down my arm, and I gasp in horror as the tray of cookies flies out of my hands. I can only watch helplessly as they fly into the frosty air, fanning out in a graceful arc. I make a futile grab for one, but it's no good. The entire batch lands on the road in front of me and bursts like a group of shells.

I stare at them in horrified disbelief. I've spent half the day trying to make something fit for human consumption. And now they're scattered across the icy road in tiny pieces.

'I'm so sorry,' says a man's voice. 'I didn't see the gate open. Can I help you pick them up?'

Chapter Eight

It isn't often that I lose my temper. It rarely seems worth it. But I make an exception today.

I inspect the remains of my cookies and turn to glare at the man standing in front of me.

'Why can't you look where you're going?' I demand. 'I spent hours making these, and then you come along and destroy all my hard work in seconds.'

His face shows a mixture of guilt and defensiveness. 'I'm very sorry. You appeared from nowhere. By the time I saw you, the damage was done.'

'You're the one who appeared from nowhere!' I snap. 'You should have been watching where you were going.'

'I was busy looking for the footpath,' he says. 'Someone told me there was a short cut to the fields at the end of this cul-de-sac.'

'That's no excuse for stomping along without looking around you. You must have known I couldn't see around the hedge.'

Is that a look of amusement on his face? It had better not be.

'I didn't know anything of the kind,' he says. 'Mainly because I had no idea there was anyone lurking there. In future, it might be an idea to make some sort of warning noise before appearing unexpectedly – like ships sounding their foghorns in the channel.'

He sees my expression and stops smiling. 'I really am very sorry. Can I help you to … er …?'

He surveys the scattered crumbs. 'On second thoughts, perhaps not. There aren't enough pieces here to make one entire cookie.'

'I know that!' I say. 'Even if I wanted to eat cookies that had been lying in the road.'

'I'm terribly sorry,' he says again. 'Were they for a special occasion?'

'That's none of your business!' I see his lips twitch and add defensively, 'I don't know you.'

'True. But that's easily remedied.' He holds out his hand to me. 'Daniel Chapman.'

I don't take it. 'What's that thing you're holding?'

He glances down at his free hand. 'I'm not sure I should tell you. As you've pointed out, we don't know each other. I think you should tell me your name before I divulge such top-secret information.'

'I'm not interested in whatever it is,' I say, bending to pick up the cookie tray and noticing with annoyance it now has a large dent in the middle. That won't do my future baking attempts much good.

'I'm prepared to throw caution to the winds,' he says. 'I'll risk you being a top-secret spy, living here as a sleeper agent and hoping to set up as my business competitor. It's a drone.'

'I'll take your word for it. Next time you decide to take one of your toys out to play with, I suggest you look where you're going.'

I press the button on my car key, open the passenger door and dump the tray onto the seat. 'I have to go.'

I slam the door and march around to the driver's side. He moves in front of the car and stands there.

I glare at him. 'What are you doing now? I suggest you get out of my way in the next ten seconds or you and your drone will regret it.'

He doesn't move. 'Are you threatening me with the same fate as your cookies? An apt revenge.'

'I'm not threatening anything. I'm telling you I need to leave. I suggest you don't stand in the middle of the road impeding the traffic.'

'An excellent suggestion,' he says. 'We could all benefit from brushing up on the highway code now and then.'

'It's a pity you didn't brush up on it before leaving home,' I say. 'Then you might not have crashed into me.'

'That was on the pavement,' he says. 'Different rules apply there.'

'All I know is that I had a tray of cookies when I left the house. I no longer have any cookies, and this tray has a dent in it.'

'For which I apologise,' he says, sounding surprisingly sincere. 'The least I can do is buy you a new tray.'

'There's no need,' I say. 'The best thing you can do for me now is get out of my way and let me get to my appointment.'

He steps back onto the pavement. 'I didn't mean to hold you up. Can I give you a ride to wherever it is you're going?'

I wave my car keys at him. 'Why would I want a ride?'

'You might be in shock,' he says. 'I'm sure the highway code says you shouldn't drive when you're in shock.'

'I'm not in shock. I'm annoyed. Can't you tell the difference?'

'As you pointed out, I'm a stranger. I haven't had time to learn the full range of your facial expressions.'

I'd like to make a facial expression he won't be able to misinterpret, but I refrain. Gran wouldn't like me lowering the tone of the neighbourhood.

'What about the cookies?' he asks.

'What about them?'

'I assume you need them for this appointment?'

'I'll manage.'

'There's no need,' he says. 'As you say, this was mostly my fault, so I ought to replace your cookies as quickly as possible.'

'It was *all* your fault,' I say, refusing to allow him to blur the edges of the truth and attempt to share the blame. 'And they're irreplaceable.'

His eyebrows shoot up. 'That sounds interesting. Were they coated with gold leaf or just a top-secret family recipe that has now been lost forever?'

I lean against the car and survey him. I'm not sure why I'm bothering to argue. I should climb in and drive away, whether he's standing there or not. Preferably with him standing there. But there's something uniquely annoying about his attitude. He's destroyed several hours of my work, and he doesn't seem as sorry as he ought to be.

'You can make fun of me all you like,' I say. 'But I spent half the morning making those cookies. It's nowhere near as easy as you might think. Those so-called cookery writers have no idea what they're doing. I followed their recipes to the letter, and nothing came out looking anything like the photos in the book.'

'They should all be fired,' he says. 'I'll write a strong letter to the publishers if you like.'

'I'm way ahead of you. But that won't help me right now.'

'If you wait here for five minutes, I'll run up to the bakery and buy you some new ones.'

I give a frustrated sigh. 'Haven't you been listening to a word I've said? They were homemade cookies, not bakery cookies.'

'Would the person receiving them know the difference?' he asks.

'Yes, she would! And so would I. And now I'll have to start all over again and waste more perfectly good ingredients. The Christmas Cookie Club is meeting here at seven o'clock tomorrow.'

'What on earth is a cookie club?' he asks.

'I'm not entirely sure. All I know is that everyone who wants to attend has to bring home-baked cookies. And I have to make some halfway decent ones before then. It doesn't matter why. You wouldn't understand or care.'

'I do care,' he says. 'But I can't help wondering whether you're making this more difficult than it needs to be. They're only cookies.'

He peers at the crumbs lying in the street. 'By the looks of it, they were oatmeal. How difficult can it be to make a batch of oatmeal cookies?'

My temper, which was subsiding, flares up again. 'Extremely difficult! If you knew anything at all about baking, you'd know that. Why don't you try for yourself and then come and tell me how you've done? Even better, go and play with your drone and leave me to get on with my day.'

'I'm sorry to have upset you,' he says. 'Let me know if you change your mind and would like me to replace your cookies. I haven't done much baking, but I'm happy to find a recipe and have a go at making some myself.'

I give a derisive snort. 'I'd give good money to see you make better cookies than mine! It's far more difficult than you might think.'

'I'm sure you're right,' he says. 'Well, you need to get to your appointment. And I should go and … play with my drone. Maybe I'll see you around?'

I switch on the engine and slam the car into gear. 'Not if I see you first,' I mutter.

I ignore his cheerful wave and set off along the street towards the main road, taking great care to avoid the icy patches. I'm sure Daniel would be amused to watch me skid into the verge, and I've embarrassed myself quite enough for one day.

Chapter Nine

Gran is sitting up in bed when I arrive. It's good to see her with some colour in her cheeks. The last couple of times I saw her, she looked as though she could audition for the ghost of Hamlet's father.

I bend to kiss her. 'I'm pleased to see you're looking better. How are you feeling?'

'A lot more chirpy,' she says. 'The doctor saw me this morning and said I should be able to go home within a week as long as I don't do anything stupid in the meantime.'

I smile. 'There goes your plan to organise an inter-ward wheelchair race.'

I sit down next to her bed. 'I meant to bring you some cookies, but I had an … accident.'

I almost mention Daniel and his inexplicable inability to navigate an empty street without crashing into something. But I don't trust myself to describe the incident calmly and without emotion, and I'm determined to be the perfect hospital visitor. It's important not to impede Gran's recovery. Humphrey would never forgive me if I kept the pair of them apart for a moment longer than necessary.

'Do you mean you burned them?' she asks.

'I burned one batch. I'm not sure what happened with the second batch. The third one wasn't too bad. I was bringing the cookies with me so you could offer some expert advice, but I … dropped them on the way to the car.'

'What a pity,' she says. 'What kind of cookies were they?'

'They were meant to be oatmeal and raisin. I'm not great at baking, so I thought I'd start with something simple and foolproof. But they didn't turn out that way.'

'You know Humphrey mustn't eat raisins?' she asks.

'I do. I have a long list of all the things dogs shouldn't eat. Although these turned out to be dried olives, not raisins. Don't worry about Humphrey. I'm taking good care of him, and he isn't going hungry. But that's not the story he'll tell you when you get home. Promise not to listen to a word he says. He's an unreliable narrator.'

Her face relaxes. 'I won't. And I'm not questioning how well you're looking after him. I know he's in excellent hands. I can't thank you enough for dropping everything and coming down here to help out. I feel terribly guilty about it.'

'I haven't dropped anything. I'm enjoying the break. I've always loved Honeywell, so it's no hardship to stay for as long as you need me.'

Her face crumples in distress. 'You mustn't stay for long. As soon as I'm home, we'll find someone to come in and help me each day. The doctor mentioned something about the district nurse, and I'm sure we can get a carer to help me with washing and dressing.'

'There's Humphrey too,' I remind her. 'I don't think carers will be insured for walking him. I'm not sure anyone is. And you're certainly not insured for whatever he may do to them. I'm sure you'd be more comfortable with me than with strangers coming and going, and I know Humphrey would be. You know how he is with new people.'

She doesn't look convinced, but now isn't the time to argue.

'We can talk about all that another time,' I say. 'The more important thing is tomorrow evening. Do you have any special instructions for me?'

'I have a list,' she says, reaching over to the bedside table and rummaging in the drawer.

'How very organised of you. I hope it's not too long. I need to spend every minute from now until tomorrow evening perfecting a basic cookie recipe. Are you sure it wouldn't be better to ask someone else to hold the meeting at their house? The other members are sure to know what you usually do.'

Gran hands me the piece of paper. 'The meetings have always been held at Rose Cottage.'

'This club is very important to you, isn't it?' I ask.

'More than I can say.' She gives me a rueful smile. 'I can tell you think I'm being a fussy old thing, and perhaps I am. But this club has a very special history, and I'm anxious not to break it.'

I fold the paper and put it into my bag. 'How have I not heard about it before?'

'Did your mother never mention it to you?'

'I'm sure she didn't. I have an excellent memory when it comes to the subject of cookies. Eating them, that is, not baking them. I buy all my cookies at the local bakery.'

'Did you never learn to cook?' she asks.

'Mum used to let me decorate the Christmas cookies when I was small, although I usually ended up covered from head to toe in icing. And we never had anywhere nearly as much dough in the bowl as when we started. I've always been partial to raw cookie dough.'

'I remember how much you loved my cookies. I thought your mother would have taught you to bake. I'm surprised she didn't.'

'It wasn't her fault,' I defend Mum. 'I'm sure she would have taught me if I'd asked her to. But I always had my head in a book or I was out with friends. When I left home and went to university, I was living in catered halls. After I started working in London, I was too busy to learn more than the basics. I can cook baked beans and scrambled eggs, but I haven't got around to anything fancier. I wish now that I had. I don't want to poison the members of your club tomorrow. Maybe I could tell them my cookies are some kind of art installation, and you're supposed to look at them but not taste them.'

Gran doesn't comment, but I'm sure I detect a look of disapproval.

'I can do lots of other things,' I say. 'I can wire a plug and change a tyre and fix a leaking pipe.'

Her face relaxes. 'I'm not criticising you. Your mother was so keen on baking with me when she was a girl that I thought she'd have passed it on to you, that's all. But times change, and we have to change with them. No doubt she thought there were better things to teach you.'

I feel as though I'm swimming into deeper water than I'm comfortable with. And swimming is something else I'm not great at. I can manage a couple of lengths and could keep myself afloat for a few minutes if I accidentally fell into a canal. But I'm not a natural water baby. Still, we all have our strengths and weaknesses. Honeywell is several miles from the sea, so my life-saving abilities are unlikely to be called into play. There's a small river at the far end of the village, into which Humphrey has launched himself thousands of times. But, for a large dog, he's surprisingly buoyant, so I won't lose sleep over the thought of having to dive in and fish him out.

I drag my thoughts away from giant nets and flotation devices to more immediate issues, the chief of which is this cookie club. I hadn't understood at first how important it was to Gran. Now that I do, I feel the weight of responsibility settle on my shoulders. Things are bad enough for her after breaking her hip and being forced to leave her beloved Humphrey. I can't make them worse by ruining her cookie club.

'I have it all in hand,' I tell her. 'I promise you won't have any complaints, even if I have to stay up all night developing my non-existent culinary skills. And if the worst really comes to the worst, there's always the village bakery.'

Gran shakes her head. 'I told you yesterday they need to be homemade.'

I'm surprised by how definite her tone is, but I remember she isn't herself at the moment. She's had a nasty accident and is still in considerable pain. It's natural she should want to control whatever she can. And if fixating on this club takes her mind off everything else she's going through, that's fine with me.

'Homemade cookies it is,' I tell her. 'It will do me good to learn a new skill. And it makes the kitchen smell delicious, even when the finished product isn't quite what I'd hoped for.'

She sighs. 'You'll have to forgive me. You're doing so much for me, and I'm adding to your burden. I'm sorry, Lucy.'

'You're anxious for everything to go well,' I say. 'And I promise you it will. I meant to ask how this all works. Is it some sort of a cookie exchange?'

'Haven't I explained that?' she asks. 'I thought I'd told you all about it.'

'Only that it was being held on Thursday and you wanted me to host it.'

'No wonder you're confused,' she says. 'I should have explained it to you earlier.'

A hospital porter appears next to the bed. 'Mrs Hollis? I need to take you down for an x-ray before they close.'

'Could I have five minutes?' she asks. 'I need to talk to my granddaughter about something.'

'I'm afraid not. We're running a little late, and the nurse tells me they want it done today.' He pulls up the rails on Gran's bed and unlocks the wheels.

'I'll leave you to it,' I say. 'Humphrey will be ready for his evening walk. He was fast asleep when I left, which means he'll be well rested and eager to explore the muddier parts of the village the minute I get home. It's a good thing I remembered to pack my wellington boots.'

'Give him my love,' says Gran.

'I'll get him to make you a card. I can bring it in with me the next time I see you. I'll go home now and take him for a walk, then cook us both some dinner. I believe he's having steak tonight. That dog eats better than most people.'

I wave goodbye to the nurses and make my way down the now familiar corridors towards the main entrance. I pull the piece of paper out of my bag to check there's nothing important I've missed. It doesn't seem as though I have. Gran has written the time and the date of the meeting, a list of members, and a request to ask someone called Margery about anything I need to know. Her handwriting isn't as clear as usual, which isn't surprising, given what she's been through this week.

Right at the bottom of the sheet is an addendum. Gran has written it in wavering capitals and underlined it twice. It must be important. I look at it more closely and stop dead.

REMEMBER THIS IS A SECRET CLUB. DO NOT MENTION IT TO ANYONE EXCEPT THE CLUB MEMBERS!

I read it again. I'm not sure why. It's perfectly clear. I read it for a third time, hoping the letters will jiggle around before magically resolving themselves into a message saying: MAKE SURE TO SPREAD THE WORD AS FAR AND AS WIDE AS POSSIBLE!

No such luck. The words remain in their original state, their meaning impossible to mistake. Why was this not mentioned before? Everything about this cookie club is important to Gran. But, from what she's written here, the most important thing of all appears to be that it's a secret club. And the first thing I've done is tell a complete stranger all about it.

Chapter Ten

Humphrey is as delighted as ever to see me back. He wouldn't be if he knew what I'd done. Gran gave me one job, and I've spectacularly messed it up. And I've only been in the village for two days.

'Would you like your dinner before I take you for a walk or after?' I ask him.

He gives an enthusiastic bark I have no difficulty interpreting as, 'Both.'

'I only have enough steak for one meal,' I say. 'We'll have to go to the shop tomorrow. Unless I've done the sensible thing and made a run for it by then.'

I look down at Humphrey's trusting face. He gives a thump of his enormous tail. Or do I mean an enormous thump of his tail? Whichever it is, it reminds me I can't run away. He needs me to look after him. No matter what happens, I'll have to stay and face the music.

I have no idea why this club is supposed to be such a secret. It's a club for people to exchange Christmas cookies, not a top-secret summit on the latest developments in germ warfare. But who am I to argue with Gran?

According to her, the first rule of cookie club is very clear – you do not talk about cookie club. Except it's too late for that. I've blabbed the details to a complete stranger. For all I know, Daniel has already sold them to a tabloid newspaper. I may be greeted tomorrow morning by someone parading up and down outside the village shop with a sandwich board saying *Cookie Club Conspiracy Finally Crumbles.*

With my luck, the tabloid will also be the hospital's newspaper of choice, and I'll arrive to find Gran propped up on her pillows, surrounded by nurses, all of them staring reproachfully at me.

I shake off these gloomy meditations. I'll think about this problem later. I clip on Humphrey's harness, and we set off down the garden path together. I peer around the hedge in case Daniel is taking another stroll to give his drone some fresh air and exercise. But the street is empty. Of course, it is. The moment I need to talk to him, he isn't there. Typical man. I cast a quick upward glance in case a drone is hovering above my head, filming my every move.

The sky appears to be clear, so I follow Humphrey down to the field, where he spends forty minutes happily chasing the local bird life with great enthusiasm but no success. Most of the birds barely bother to move as he gallops towards them, chest heaving and tongue hanging out in the excitement of the chase.

'Come on!' I tell him at last. 'It's too dark to see any more birds.'

He reluctantly allows me to lead him back to the cottage, where I cook his steak and he demolishes it in a couple of seconds. He gives me an engaging smile, but I harden my heart.

'I've been given strict instructions about your diet, and I intend to follow them to the best of my ability.'

He gives me a mournful look and collapses into his basket. I open a tin of baked beans, drop a couple of slices of bread into the toaster, and make myself a cup of tea while I wait.

Maybe things aren't as bad as I thought. It's possible Daniel doesn't live in Honeywell. He may have been passing through the village on his way to a drone contest somewhere on the other side of the country. Possibly, his GPS malfunctioned, and he ended up staying here for an hour or two before moving on.

The toast pops up. I butter it and tip the pan of beans over it. It isn't exactly haute cuisine. But after spending such an unsuccessful morning in the kitchen, it's all I'm prepared to do. I can rise to greater culinary heights another night. I may even heat up a frozen pizza.

I dump my plate onto a tray and carry it to the living room. Humphrey follows and climbs onto the sofa next to me, where he surveys my food as though it's a long-lost bird friend and he would like nothing better than to make further acquaintance with it.

I finish my meal before he can get any more ideas about it. We share an apple, then watch University Challenge. Humphrey doesn't get any of the clues. To be fair, neither do I. But it's been a long day for both of us.

My mind drifts back to the problem of Daniel. For all I know, Gran was teasing when she told me it was important to keep the whole thing a secret. It didn't seem as though she was joking, but who knows what effect the regular administration of morphine has on elderly patients?

Assuming she was serious, I should be able to track him down tomorrow. If he lives in the village, someone is bound to know him. It would be impossible to carry drones around in a place like this without someone noticing and asking questions. I'll ask at the corner shop. Shirley seems to know most of the people in the village.

Failing that, I can try the bakery. They make excellent cakes, and it seems impossible that anyone living in the village for any length of time could resist making regular visits. And it will give me an excuse to sample another of their delicious lemon tarts.

Once I have Daniel's address, I can knock on his door and ask him to forget everything I said about the cookie club. I can appeal to his sense of chivalry, if he has one. Or I can tell him I'm suffering from severe concussion as a result of his egregious failure to look where he was going, and I'm considering contacting a lawyer unless he gives me what I want. He wasn't paying attention, so he can't know whether or not I hit my head.

If all else fails, I can contact the police. That would be a little drastic, and I hope it doesn't come to that. But there's bound to be some drone-related law he was breaking, however inadvertently.

I feel much better as I wash my plate and Humphrey's bowl, let him out for his nightly jaunt around the garden, then accompany him upstairs. I go straight to Gran's room and throw myself on her bed.

'What a comfortable bed!' I exclaim. 'I think I'll sleep in here tonight.'

Humphrey gives me a pitying look, trots down the landing, and disappears into my bedroom. I follow to find him spreadeagled across my duvet. There isn't enough room for me to climb into bed. I push hard, but nothing happens.

'You are an ungrateful hound,' I complain. 'I spend all my time cooking for you and cleaning up after you and taking you out to chase birds. The least you could do is allow me into my own bed.'

To my surprise, he rolls over. I jump in beside him before he can change his mind.

'Don't you dare roll over again during the night,' I warn him. 'It would take an entire earthquake rescue team to dig me out, and I'm not sure where the nearest one is located.'

He lays a paw on my leg, looks lovingly up into my face, and licks my hand.

'We've talked about this,' I say. 'I've told you I have a washcloth of my own. Look, but don't lick! It's an excellent motto to live by.'

He heaves a sigh and closes his eyes. Pretty soon, I follow his example. It's been a long day, and tomorrow looks as though it will be even busier.

Chapter Eleven

Humphrey and I walk to the village shop after breakfast the next day. I need to buy him some more chicken, and I've run out of flour and sugar. I'm also low on oats and butter. I try not to think about the huge amounts of ingredients I wasted yesterday in my failed attempts at baking what should have been a simple batch of cookies.

I only have this afternoon to perfect my oatmeal raisin cookies before my guests arrive to sample them. I have no idea what format the evening will take. Presumably, the participants will know. I'm providing the venue and producing refreshments. I can't be expected to do any more at such short notice.

I spend a while in the shop, filling my basket and chatting to Shirley. To my disappointment, she hasn't heard of anyone called Daniel.

'What does he look like?' she asks.

I hesitate. I've built up a picture in my mind of someone with a villainous face covered in scars. I haven't quite given him an eye patch and a wooden leg, but very nearly.

'Medium height,' I say at last. 'About my age. I think he had brown hair, but that might have been a hat.'

She looks amused. 'You'd be useless in a police lineup. They'd never catch the criminal from that description. It could be half the males in Honeywell.'

'It all happened so quickly,' I excuse myself. 'One moment, I was opening the garden gate without a care in the world. The next, my tray of cookies was flying through the air and landing in the street.'

The word flying reminds me of something. 'He was holding a drone.'

She frowns. 'One of those buzzy things?'

'That's right. Quite a large one. I have no idea why anyone would be taking a drone for a walk down the back lanes of Honeywell, but that's what he was doing.'

I remember something else. 'He was wearing red trainers.'

Her look of amusement returns. 'We could get Ivy to make us a sketch like they do on those police programmes. She's very good. She does caricatures at our Easter and summer fetes.'

I muster up the remaining shreds of my dignity. 'Thank you, but there's no need. It doesn't sound as though this man's a local. He must have been passing through.'

I pay for my groceries, ignore a couple of grinning customers who have clearly been listening in to our conversation, and shepherd Humphrey out of the shop before Shirley can make any more suggestions about identity parades.

I should go straight home. I have cookies to bake. If yesterday morning was anything to go by, it may take some time to achieve a passable result. But the lights in the bakery are alluring. I can see a group of women inside. They appear to be playing cards. It seems an odd thing to be doing in a bakery, but each to their own.

Humphrey has stopped too. He pulls me towards the door and whines piteously – the sound of a dog too exhausted to face the five-hundred metre walk home without emergency sustenance. I remember how good the coffee was yesterday and weaken.

'Ten minutes,' I tell him. 'We can't afford to be here any longer than that. And I'll need you to sleep this afternoon. I'll be busy, and I don't want you getting under my feet.'

He gives an excited wag of his tail that I decide to interpret as full agreement.

'And don't sit on that funny little brown dog if you see him,' I add, opening the door.

The bakery smells like a little slice of heaven as we enter. Humphrey makes a dive for the nearest table and curls up beneath it. At least, he would curl if the tables weren't so small and delicate and he wasn't so large. As it is, he looks like a gigantic warship trying to dock at a passenger jetty. Bits of him are sticking out in all directions. I'll have to keep an eye out to make sure no one trips over him.

Does he realise how enormous he is compared to other dogs? If need be, he could carry several small children on his back without even noticing. Not for the first time, I wonder what Gran was thinking when she chose him. According to Mum, it was love at first sight for the pair of them, and I have to admit Humphrey couldn't have hoped for a better home. He's fallen on his size-twenty paws with Gran, and he makes her very happy in return. I resolve to stop complaining about him and appreciate him for what he is rather than what he isn't.

Lily appears behind the counter. 'You're back! I thought you might be. Humphrey rarely allows Mrs Hollis to pass the bakery without popping in.'

'I'd have come in even if he was at home,' I say. 'You make the best coffee I've ever tasted.'

She looks pleased. 'A cappuccino, wasn't it? Coming right up. Would you like something to eat with it?'

I'm about to refuse on the grounds I expect to spend most of the afternoon tasting batches of oatmeal cookies. But I catch sight of some Portuguese tarts in the display and waver. If I eat one of those, I won't have to bother about lunch, which means I'll have more time for baking and tidying up before this evening.

'I'll have a Portuguese tart,' I say. 'And I expect Humphrey would like one of your dog biscuits. He enjoyed the ones he had yesterday.'

Lily hands him a bone-shaped dog biscuit and laughs as he swallows it whole. She offers him a second one. I'm pleased to see he crunches it a couple of times before gulping it down. Is it too much to hope he's learning some manners?

'My partner says we should take a course of dog first-aid classes,' she tells me. 'She's always wanted to perform the Heimlich manoeuvre on someone. None of our customers has given her the opportunity so far. I told her that was a good thing, but I'm not sure she was convinced.'

'Do you hear that?' I say, nudging Humphrey with my foot. 'You're being offered the chance to make medical history.'

He looks at me blankly, stretches out, and goes to sleep.

'I wish I could do that,' says Lily. 'I have two young children, and I'm permanently exhausted. But it still takes me ages to fall asleep each night. Even when I do, I sleep with one ear open in case one of them falls out of bed or decides to take up sleepwalking for a hobby.'

'It's the same with me,' I say. 'Not the sleepwalking bit. Humphrey barely moves when he's asleep. But I'm not sleeping half as well as usual. He's an enormous responsibility – literally! He means everything to my grandmother, and I could never live with myself if anything happened to him.'

'I'm sure it won't,' she says. 'And he obviously likes you. He wouldn't fall asleep like this if he thought there was anything to be afraid of.'

I'm not sure she's right, but I hope she is. Does Humphrey see me as his protector while Gran is in the hospital? Or does he believe he's protecting me? Anyone seeing me with such an enormous dog ought to think twice before trying anything. On the other hand, anyone seeing his uncoordinated attempts to decimate the local bird population would be forgiven for thinking they had nothing to worry about. I put all this out of my mind while I drink my coffee and eat my tart. As I expected, it's excellent.

'Please tell whoever does your baking that these are amazing,' I tell Lily as she passes my table on her way to serve a large plate of cakes to the card players.

'You can tell her yourself,' she says, pointing to a woman emerging from the kitchen carrying a tray of rolls. 'This is Abby. Abby, this is Lucy. She's Mrs Hollis' granddaughter. She's staying in her cottage and looking after Humphrey while Mrs Hollis is in the hospital.'

'I heard about that,' says Abby. 'Your mum was in this morning, Lily, and she told me about the accident. She's popping into the hospital this afternoon.'

'That's so kind of her,' I tell Lily.

'Mum keeps an eye on everyone in the village,' she says. 'It's a pretty friendly place, and most people here know everyone else.'

'Which reminds me,' I say. 'I'm trying to track down someone called Daniel. I wondered whether you might be able to help me?'

'Can you narrow it down a little?' asks Abby.

I launch into my rather less than detailed account again, refraining from adding any interesting details like a bright red beard or a skull tattoo on his forehead. If this man lives in the village, I'd like to find him as quickly as possible. A sinister description, although fun, won't speed things up.

'I can't think of anyone matching that description,' says Lily. 'Has he lived here for long?'

'He may not live here at all. But if he does, there's something I need to discuss with him.'

'Intriguing,' she says, and I flush.

'I know it sounds weird, but I can't give you any more details.'

She and Abby glance at each other, but neither of them pursues the matter.

'I'll ask my mum when I see her this evening,' says Lily. 'If this man is a resident rather than a visitor, she's bound to know all about him. Don't even think of committing a crime while you're here, Lucy. My mum would track you down in seconds.'

'I wasn't planning on any felonies while I'm here,' I say. 'And I'll do my best to ensure Humphrey remains on the right side of the law. That may not be so easy.'

He opens an eye and looks enquiringly at me.

I laugh. 'Are your ears burning? They say listeners hear no good of themselves. We should get going. We have a lot to do before tonight.'

'What's happening tonight?' asks Lily.

What is wrong with me? All I have to do is refrain from mentioning the cookie club, yet that seems to be the one thing I can't manage. Time to go before I crack and spill my guts, giving them the precise details and location of the club and ending by inviting them both to come along and bring a friend.

'I'm having a couple of my neighbours over for a cup of tea,' I say.

'That's nice,' says Lily. 'Have fun. I'll ask Mum whether she has any idea who this mystery man of yours might be.'

'He's not mine,' I say before she or Abby can get any ideas.

I'm worried she may think I see myself as the heroine of a romantic novel, who's met a complete stranger, lost her heart to him, and is now chasing all over the village to find out where he lives so she can engineer another meeting. That would be humiliating, but there's nothing I can do about it now. Better for her to think that than realise how badly I've let my grandmother down.

'Come on, Humphrey,' I say. He rises reluctantly to his feet and follows me towards the door.

'Have a lovely evening,' says Lily as we go.

'Thanks,' I say. 'You, too.'

Humphrey and I set off together down the high street. A pigeon settles on the barber shop sign and gives Humphrey a contemptuous look. He stops dead and stares up at it.

'Come on!' I say, pulling at his lead. 'I hate to break it to you, but if you're thinking about pigeon pie for lunch, you have no chance. You'll be far better off coming home with me and allowing me to cook you some chicken. It's the only bird you're likely to get anywhere near today.'

Chapter Twelve

I make three more batches of cookies before I'm happy to consider serving them to anyone. I'm not sure why this has been such a steep learning curve. It's only a case of throwing a few ingredients into a bowl and stirring them together before sticking them into the oven. But there seems to be some weird extra alchemy involved, and I haven't yet tracked it down. Maybe some people are born with the baking gene, and some aren't. If that's the case, I'm forced to admit I'm not a natural-born cookie-whisperer.

It's not that I dislike cookies. I'm as happy as the next person to get stuck into a plate of them. But I've never felt the urge to be involved in the production side of the business. My view has always been that everyone should play to their own strengths, and this clearly isn't mine. I should just appreciate them as a consumer and leave it at that.

But fate has intervened, so here I am, standing in Gran's kitchen, trying not to trip over a gigantic dog, frantically stirring and mixing and attempting to calculate the difference between the Fahrenheit temperature the recipe calls for and the centigrade dial on Gran's oven. Life is full of surprises.

Still, I've achieved my goal. Admittedly, I've set myself a low bar – to produce something edible that won't make me the laughingstock of the cookie club. But I've managed to do it without suffering more than a couple of burned fingers and several wasted batches of cookies.

The local birds have benefited from them, which is a good thing. It's been a bitterly cold week, and they must be struggling. The sudden miraculous appearance on Gran's lawn of dozens of delicious, albeit slightly scorched, cookies must have felt like a Christmas miracle to the local starlings and robins and blackbirds.

I slide the final batch onto a cooling tray. They can stay there until the club members arrive. I'm not risking anything happening to them.

I can't imagine what horrors could befall them. But I had no idea when I set out for the hospital yesterday afternoon that a strange man would materialise and send my cookies flying into the street, crushing them to powder beneath his hobnailed boots.

'Fine, he was wearing trainers,' I tell Humphrey, who has been watching my every movement. 'And he may not have stamped exactly, but the cookies were still ruined.'

He tilts his head on one side and looks up at me with soulful eyes.

'They were!' I insist. 'They burst into tiny pieces when they landed, which shows he must have knocked the tray out of my hands at a terrific speed. Cookies don't usually turn to powder the moment they hit the ground.'

I put the last cookie onto the tray. 'Sorry, Humphrey. You aren't allowed raisins. But I'll make you something nice after your walk. We'd better get going if we want to be back on time. It's all very well Gran running a secret club, but it would be taking it too far if you and I weren't here at all.'

We set off on our usual walk. I don't notice Humphrey has turned off up an unfamiliar path until it's too late. I tug at his lead, but he ignores me.

'Not today, Humphrey!' I protest. 'We're on a tight schedule. I can't afford to get lost in the middle of nowhere. We have to be home in time for me to host the club.'

He continues to ignore me and ploughs along the path at breakneck speed, with me panting along behind.

'I won't have time to make your dinner,' I warn him, but he isn't listening.

Where is he taking me? Is there a house down here I don't know about? Maybe one of Gran's friends lives there, and Humphrey is accustomed to visiting. I peer through the fading light, but there are no signs of a dwelling. Not even a house made of gingerbread with a beautifully iced roof. It's a pity. I could have broken off something unimportant, like a windowsill, and impressed the members of the cookie club with it.

Humphrey abruptly dives off the path. Has he seen a bird lurking in the undergrowth? There's no mad flapping of wings, and no sign of pheasants whirring into the air. What, then – a rat? I very much hope not. Rats are all very well in their place, but I prefer that place to be several miles away from me.

He lurches out of sight, almost tugging my arm off and causing me to drop the lead. There's a loud squelching sound, then silence. A wave of panic sweeps over me. Has he disappeared into a patch of quicksand? If so, how will I get him out again?

I crash through the undergrowth after him, trying to remember everything I've read about quicksand. I know the best thing is to stay calm and not struggle, but I'll never be able to explain that to Humphrey. All I can hope for is to find a solid patch of ground, lie down on it, and support him under his shoulders until either someone comes along or I freeze into a lump of ice. Why didn't I bring a coil of rope with me? And a megaphone. And a thermos flask. Perhaps even a small emergency tent. Those things should be basic precautions when setting off for a walk in a strange place. I can't believe I've been so woefully unprepared.

'I'm coming, Humphrey!' I shout, then stop as I see him sitting there, beaming up at me. There's no sign of the quicksand for which the New Forest may or may not be famous. But there's most definitely a massive patch of mud. And right in the centre of it is an enormous dog, coated in it from head to paw and looking delighted with himself.

'Did you know this was here?' I demand. 'Or was it a lucky coincidence?'

Humphrey scratches his ear, then collapses sideways into the mud.

'Stop it!' I tell him. 'You aren't at a spa. I wish to goodness you were. Someone else could clean you up. But I suppose it will have to be me. You're an infuriating dog!'

He flickers his eyes towards me, looking apprehensive. I remember his background and relent, kneeling down next to him and slipping my arms under his shoulders.

'I know you didn't mean to cause any trouble. Let's get you home and clean you up before anyone arrives.'

I haul him to his feet and pat his mud-coated head. I'm almost as muddy as he is, so there's no point in being stand-offish. He licks my hand, and I pick up his lead.

'There should be enough hot water for both of us to have a quick shower.'

I fix him with a stern look. 'But don't get your hopes up too much. I have no intention of giving you a seaweed wrap or an aromatherapy massage.'

Chapter Thirteen

Half an hour later, I finish rubbing Humphrey dry, check the cooling tray, and breathe a sigh of relief. These may not be the most exciting cookies in the world, but at least they're edible. And they're roughly the right shape, size, and colour. At this moment, I'll take what I can get.

I look at my watch. Half past six. I just have time for a quick shower before taking up my position by the front door, all ready to play the gracious hostess. I'm making a joke of it, but I don't want to let Gran down. This club is important to her, and she isn't here to run it herself. I'm determined to make sure it runs smoothly for her and is still in one piece when she returns.

I'm not sure what I could do in a single evening to destroy something so stable and long running, but I'm not prepared to take any risks. I've come to Honeywell to look after things for her while she's incapacitated, and look after them I will.

I check that Humphrey is dozing in his basket and not likely to leap around the house causing havoc in the few brief minutes I'm in the shower. Then I run upstairs and undress. I pull on Gran's dressing gown, snatch up my wash bag from my bedside table, and run back downstairs. It would have been more comfortable if the bathroom was upstairs instead of tacked onto the back of the house behind the kitchen, but it's better than no bathroom at all.

I should count myself lucky that, sometime between the end of the war and today, one of the owners of this cottage dug their heels in and refused to visit the outhouse at the bottom of the garden on a freezing winter's night. Humphrey still has to do that, but he doesn't seem to mind. He appears to see it as a positive thing to prance around the lawn on a bitter winter evening, leaving footprints and goodness knows what else in the frost, and checking out likely places where birds might be perching.

Still, beggars can't be choosers, and the house is warm enough this evening. I put the central heating on after lunch, and I lit the fire in the living room an hour ago. I don't know who's coming tonight, or whether they're all Gran's age. But if they are, they may feel the cold.

I switch on the shower and pull off the dressing gown, shivering in the sudden blast of chill air. Whoever built this bathroom didn't get as far as insulating it. They must have been of the tougher generation who believed in cold showers and general spartan living.

I'm from the more recent generation that is less convinced cold showers and frost on the windowsills each morning is a guarantee of mental strength in future life. What would my great-great-grandfather Simon think if he could see the coffee machine in my kitchen at home? Or, for that matter, the seat warmers in my car.

I take a deep breath, ready to demonstrate both my mental and physical toughness, when the doorbell rings. I utter an exclamation of annoyance. Who can that be? Surely, not a member of the cookie club? Their generation is always punctual – neither fashionably early nor fashionably late. Maybe it's someone here to read the meter. In which case, they're on their own. I have no idea where the meters are located. Great-great-grandfather Simon probably hid them at the far end of the garden, hoping to induce stamina and perseverance in the poor person who was sent to check them.

It can't really be a meter reader at this time of night. They'd have to pay them overtime, which is unlikely. Although it might explain the size of everyone's energy bills. I pull on the dressing gown and pad along the hallway, grumbling under my breath. If it's someone trying to sell us double glazing, I plan to give them short shrift.

I slide back the latch and tug open the door. I remember what Mum always used to say to me when I was young and pestering her to do something right *now*.

'I only have one pair of hands,' I mutter, opening the door a crack and assuming the sort of neutral expression that can be adapted into a welcoming smile or a forbidding scowl depending on who might be standing there.

'Good evening,' says a man's voice.

I push back my shower cap, which has slipped over one eye, obscuring my vision. His voice is familiar, but I can't see his face. The porch light is supposed to come on automatically when someone comes up the path. I remember Dad fitting it a couple of years ago and telling Gran the motion sensor would frighten off burglars.

'Hello?' I say cautiously.

I don't want to be rude in case he's here to tell me Gran has won a million pounds on the premium bonds, and the small print says the prize will be withdrawn if the recipient doesn't greet the messenger warmly and invite them in for coffee.

'Have I got the right house?' asks the man.

'That depends. Which house were you looking for?'

This strikes the correct tone. Not too welcoming if he's trying to sell me something, but not too repressive if he's the bearer of glad tidings.

'Can I come in?' he asks.

He's holding what looks like a tray. It's covered with a cloth, so I can't see what's on it. He can't belong to the cookie club. He's far too young. And male. He must be selling something.

'I'm afraid I'm rather busy right now,' I say. 'You'll have to come back another time.'

Why did I say that? As Mum always says, give these people an inch, and they'll take a mile.

'On second thoughts,' I add, 'I'm sure we aren't interested. I'm sorry to have wasted your time. Have a good evening.'

I start to close the door. The man sticks his foot in it, and I gasp in outrage. Who does he think he is?

'Move your foot this minute!' I say in an icy tone. 'Or I'll call the police.'

'But you invited me,' he says.

'I did no such thing! Move your foot or I'll slam the door on it, and it will be your own fault if you can't walk for months.'

'Yes, you did,' he insists. 'You invited me yesterday afternoon.'

I'm too taken aback to carry through with my foot-slamming threat. 'Yesterday afternoon?'

He shifts his foot out of the danger zone. 'That's right. You dropped your cookies, remember?'

'Of course, I remember. Some stupid passer-by was walking along without looking where he was going, and he sent them flying everywhere.'

I look at his face more closely, and he grins back at me. 'Would you call me a stupid passer-by, precisely?'

'Yes, I would. I didn't recognise you at first. Especially wearing that hat.'

'I bought it at the stupid passer-by shop,' he says. 'They like us to wear distinctive hats so people can tell at a glance we're likely to do ridiculous things like knocking people's cookies into the road.'

I feel an urge to smile but suppress it. 'So, why weren't you wearing it yesterday? Was it at the dry cleaners after you'd caused some other catastrophe?'

'I didn't know I'd need it,' he says. 'I was only walking a few hundred metres, and this street seemed deserted. I wasn't expecting someone to burst out of their front gate waving trays of cookies at me.'

'Only the one tray. And no one informed me I was supposed to give formal notice before walking down the front path to my car. What do you expect people to do – carry a bell and ring it at three second intervals?'

'That's up to you,' he says. 'A bell, a buzzer, a siren. Your choice. Any or all of them work for the members of the stupid passer-by club.'

'None of which explains what you're doing on my doorstep this evening. Are you here to apologise? If so, there's no need. It happened, and that's all there is to it. So, you can be on your way.'

He doesn't move. 'I'm not here to apologise. I did that to the best of my ability yesterday. I even offered to make reparation in the form of a fresh batch of cookies from the village bakery. But you were having none of it, so I gave up.'

'So, why are you here?' I ask. 'Whatever the reason, it's terrible timing. I have a –'

I break off, remembering I've been wanting to talk to this man. 'That thing I told you about the cookie club yesterday. It was supposed to be a huge secret. I'd be grateful if you didn't pass it on to anyone else.'

'So, the ad I took out in the free local newspaper this morning was a bad idea?' he asks.

'You didn't!' I catch his eye and see he's grinning at me. 'Very funny. But I'm serious about the club. I didn't realise when I met you yesterday that I wasn't supposed to tell anyone about it. I'm still not sure why that is, but that doesn't matter. If you want to apologise to me, the best way of doing it is to forget I ever mentioned it. And now, if you'll excuse me, I have to –'

He doesn't take the hint. 'That doesn't alter the fact you invited me to attend this top-secret event.'

'Have you been listening to a word I've said? I've told you this event is private.'

'You said secret,' he reminds me. 'They're two very different things.'

'Who cares? It's both private and a secret. Which means you're doubly not welcome here.'

He holds out his tray. 'That's not what you said yesterday. You said, "I'd love to see you do any better than I did."'

'I remember saying something of the kind. But it was a figure of speech. It didn't mean I was inviting you here tonight.'

'Then I've wasted my entire afternoon,' he complains. 'I could have been striding through the snow being a stupid passer-by. Instead, I was chained to the kitchen, perfecting my chocolate chip cookies.'

'I'm sorry you misinterpreted my words,' I say as politely as possible. 'Hopefully, you can find someone to enjoy the cookies. It shouldn't be too difficult. Most people love cookies. If yours are any good, you're bound to find some takers.'

He shakes his head. 'All my friends are gluten-intolerant.'

I don't mention how unlikely it is that no one in his entire social circle can tolerate wheat. The glint in his eye tells me that conversation wouldn't go well. He seems the sort of man who has an answer to everything. I'd usually be up for the challenge, but time is running out as fast as the warm air pouring through the open front door into the frosty garden.

'That's a shame,' I say. 'But it isn't my problem. I'm afraid you'll have to go now. You can leave your cookies here if you like. I'm sure my visitors won't suffer from the same digestive problems as your friends.'

'I can't,' he says. 'This cookie tray is a family heirloom. It's been passed down through generations of Chapmans. My father gave it to me a few years back and made me promise with his final breath never to let it out of my sight, even for a second.'

'I'm sorry your father died,' I say. 'But –'

'He didn't die,' says Daniel. 'It was after a strenuous squash game. I beat him hands down, and he bequeathed me the tray in recognition that the elder had been bested by the younger.'

Why am I continuing this ridiculous argument? I should have told him the minute he appeared on my doorstep that there had been some mistake and he would have to go.

'I get the message,' he says. 'Your invitation wasn't as clear cut as I believed. I will acknowledge defeat and leave with my tail between my legs.'

Like Humphrey, I think. As if in acknowledgment of this unspoken thought, the dog himself appears in the hall at this exact moment, probably summoned by the smell of the cookies Daniel is waving around.

Chapter Fourteen

'Hello,' says Daniel, holding out his hand to Humphrey. 'It's a pleasure to meet you. I'm the stupid passer-by who bumped into your owner yesterday and deprived you of your cookies.'

'They weren't for him,' I say. 'They were for my grandmother.'

'Then please pass on my apologies to your grandmother.'

He gives Humphrey's head a pat. 'Nice to meet you, but I have to be going.'

Humphrey stares up at him for another moment. Then, without giving me time to prepare, he slips past Daniel and charges down the garden path at top speed.

'Stop him!' I shout, but it's too late. Daniel hasn't closed the gate properly. Humphrey rushes through it and keeps going.

'Move!' I yell, shoving Daniel aside and setting off up the street as fast as I can. Humphrey is almost out of sight already and making excellent speed. I don't know where he's going, but he seems to have a plan in mind. All I can do is follow as closely as possible and hope to catch up with him before he disappears completely.

I'm not a good runner at the best of times, but I seem to be slower than usual tonight. I glance down at my feet and realise I'm still wearing my slippers. This is all Daniel's fault. He knows perfectly well I didn't invite him over this evening, yet he chose to come anyway. He seems determined to annoy me. I'm not sure why, but I don't have time to think about it now. I'm too busy concentrating on not losing my balance and ending up sprawled full-length in the frosty street in Gran's dressing gown, revealing far more than is usual in a quiet country village. That's the last time I answer the front door in anything other than full formal attire – preferably including a fur-lined coat and knee-length boots.

I hear footsteps behind me and glance over my shoulder to see Daniel racing along the street. He's gaining on me quickly, which is no surprise. He's wearing jeans and trainers, so it's hardly a fair contest.

'Which way did he go?' he gasps as he catches up with me.

I'm too winded to answer, so I point.

'I'm on it!' He increases his speed, rounds the corner, and is soon out of sight.

I slow to a painful walk, clutching my side. I could run as fast as Daniel if I were dressed for it. I'd like to see him keep up with me if I was the one wearing running shoes and he was hampered by a knee-length pink dressing gown with nothing on underneath.

I give an involuntary shiver and pull the thin wisp of material around me, wishing I'd had the presence of mind to don some sort of thick bathing costume for my shower. I've seen pictures of Victorian matrons descending from their bathing machines into the sea, swathed from head to foot in black bombazine ruffles. I've always felt sorry for those women, but I'm starting to see the benefits of it. You might not be able to swim one hundred metres in fifty seconds, but it would be far easier to sprint down the street on an icy winter's night in pursuit of the most badly-behaved dog in living memory.

People say that those who don't learn from history are doomed to repeat it. Maybe that works in reverse too. Those who refuse to repeat history are doomed to run half-clad marathons in sub-zero temperatures and die from hypothermia only metres from their own front door.

I refuse to have that happen to me tonight. There's nothing I can do about Humphrey right now. Daniel is in hot pursuit, and I'm in freezing cold non-pursuit. I should go home and get dressed before the guests arrive. I've given up any idea of getting a shower. Judging by the way this evening has gone so far, I'd step into it just as the village earthquake alarm went off, and I'd end up outside wearing even less than I am now, soaking wet, and chilled to the bone. If further calamities befall us tonight, I intend to meet them decently clad and with a hot drink in my hand, preferably laced with something alcoholic.

I turn and retrace my steps to the cottage. Presumably, Daniel won't give up the chase and return without Humphrey. I know almost nothing about him, but he doesn't seem the type to do something like that. And he must realise that, yet again, this is his fault. I was careful to latch the gate when Humphrey and I returned from our muddy walk this evening.

It isn't my fault Daniel didn't know the trick of it and left it to swing open, but he had no business being on my property at all. I seem to remember there's some legal maxim stating ignorance is no defence. If anything has happened to Humphrey, I'll sue Daniel for everything he's got.

That would be of no comfort to Gran. Humphrey is her entire world, and nothing would ever compensate her for his loss. That goes for me too. I've always been fond of Humphrey, but now that I'm responsible for his well-being, I realise it's more than that. Until Gran is home and able to take over again, Humphrey is the only thing that matters to me.

And he's running around – goodness knows where – in the pitch dark, wondering where I am. Even worse, he may be looking for Gran. As far as he's concerned, she left without saying goodbye or explaining where she was going. After which, I arrived and turned out to be an extremely poor substitute. No wonder he's set off into the night to find his real caregiver. And he hasn't the faintest chance of doing so.

A small sob escapes me as I imagine what it must be like to be Humphrey at this moment – lost and distressed and feeling abandoned by the one person in the world who truly loves him. A tear rolls down my cheek and I wipe my eyes on my dressing gown sleeve, choking back the flood of further tears that threatens to overwhelm me. I can't do this right now. Humphrey needs me to stay calm and be ready to run to his side at a moment's notice.

It occurs to me that even if Daniel catches up with him, he has no way of letting me know. We haven't got to the phone number-exchanging stage yet, and we probably never will. So far, all we've reached is the insult-exchanging stage on my side and the amused smile on his. I swallow hard and take several deep breaths. The only way to cope with an emergency is one step at a time. And step one is to get some clothes on so that I'm prepared for whatever step two turns out to be.

I'm about to open the gate when I hear a noise. Is that a bark or am I so desperate for a sign of Humphrey that my ears are shaping stray sounds into what I want them to be? I look back along the road and my heart almost falls out of my chest as I see two figures walking towards me. There's enough light from the nearest streetlamp for me to see it's Daniel and Humphrey.

I give a gasp of relief and set off back towards them, completely forgetting my exposed flesh from the knees down. Humphrey catches sight of me and gives an enormous bound, almost dragging Daniel over. He recovers his balance and breaks into a run, still holding onto Humphrey's lead. No, not his lead. That's on the table next to the front door. I squint through the gloom but can't make out what's tied to his collar. I don't care.

'Humphrey!' I gasp, flinging my arms around him and bursting into tears.

He sits back on his haunches, giving me a puzzled look. He doesn't seem like a dog who's been breaking his heart for his lost mistress and vowing never to eat or sleep again until he finds her. In fact, he looks more than usually pleased with himself.

I raise my head to look at Daniel, who grins down at me. 'Sorry you had such a fright. He's a fast runner, isn't he?'

'Where did you catch up with him?'

'At the far edge of the field. It looked as though he was carrying on down to the water meadows.'

'Humphrey!' I say. 'What did we say about staying away from wet and muddy places?'

Humphrey scratches his ear and gives me an innocent look, as if to say he doesn't remember us ever discussing the subject.

I climb stiffly to my feet, attempting to cover myself as much as possible.

'That's why I was about to have a shower when you arrived,' I explain to Daniel. 'Humphrey and I went for a walk earlier this evening.'

His eyebrows lift. 'And you thought you'd roll around in the mud for a while? Far be it from me to judge, but I'm not sure that would have been my preferred activity on a cold winter's night. Still, each to his own. It takes all kinds to make a world, and all that.'

I choke back a giggle. 'Humphrey rolled in the mud, and I got covered in it trying to haul him out. He had the first shower. I left him to dry off in his basket while I jumped into the shower and cleaned myself up. But then you rang the doorbell and –'

My grievance returns. 'You didn't even bother to check the gate was shut. This is all your fault.'

'Again?' he says.

I take Humphrey's lead from him. 'You do seem to be a bit of a disaster magnet, don't you?'

My eyes fall to the piece of fabric I'm holding. 'This isn't a lead.'

Daniel looks embarrassed. 'I had to improvise. I caught him by the collar, but I didn't trust him not to break free again. He's very strong.'

I inspect the fabric more closely. 'Is this a sock?'

'Several socks. We passed a washing line during our evening jog. I'm not sure what the laundry was doing out on a night like this, but I wasn't about to complain. I grabbed the four nearest socks and tied them together. Luckily, they were knee length or I don't know what I'd have done.'

'I hope you plan to return them before the resident realises and calls the police,' I say self-righteously.

'Of course,' he says. 'I have no wish to become known as the Honeywell Clothesline Bandit.'

We reach the garden gate, and I notice Daniel's cookies scattered along the path.

'I'm sorry about your cookies,' I say. 'I didn't mean that to happen.'

'You mean it wasn't in retaliation for what I did yesterday?'

'Of course not! That would be petty.'

'It would,' he agrees. 'I apologise for the insensitive suggestion. How can I ever make it up to you?'

'You can leave,' I suggest. 'Before you do any more damage.'

'Don't you need to shower?'

'I don't have time now. Even if I did, I don't need anyone's help with that. I've been taking showers since I was a child.'

'But surely you need someone to watch Humphrey for you while you get yourself ready?' he asks.

'Humphrey will be fine in his basket.'

'How did that work out the last time you said that?'

'He only escaped because I had to open the front door to you.'

'Exactly,' he says. 'And you've told me you're expecting a load of guests any minute now. Won't someone have to open the front door for them while you're getting dressed? Otherwise, they might all go away again.'

I waver. I want to get Daniel out of here before the club members arrive. But I also need to get dressed. And he's right. The way tonight has been going, I wouldn't put it past Humphrey to slip past one of my guests if I leave the door unlatched for them. He may end up in the next county before I've pulled on my jeans.

'You can stay for five minutes while I get ready,' I say. 'But if anyone arrives, please don't tell them who you are. Make up some story or other, then get yourself out of here as quickly as possible.'

Chapter Fifteen

Humphrey pulls himself free of my grip and sets off to the kitchen, a purposeful look in his eyes. A moment later, I hear him hurl himself against the back door.

'He needs to go outside,' I say. 'Could you let him into the back garden and stay with him while he does his business?'

'I'll watch him like a hawk,' Daniel promises. 'I assume there isn't a back gate with a broken lock?'

'The front gate doesn't have a broken lock,' I tell him. 'It just needs closing properly.'

'So you've mentioned several times. I promise to check it carefully next time.'

I want to point out that there won't be a next time. But it's getting late, and I don't want to waste precious minutes arguing about the precise mechanism of Gran's gate latch.

I unlock the back door, and Humphrey surges out into the garden.

'Do you need a torch?' I ask Daniel.

'Not if you leave the kitchen blinds open until we return. Go and get ready, and I'll keep an eye on him.'

Humphrey is scrabbling at a patch of grass and shows no sign of wanting to escape for a second time.

'Watch out for birds,' I warn Daniel as I turn to leave.

'What sort of birds?'

'Night birds,' I say nonchalantly, trying to hide the fact I have no idea. Why should I be expected to be an ornithological expert? I can just about identify robins, blackbirds, and sparrows.

He gives a snort of laughter. 'Night birds? What species is that?'

'Plenty of birds fly around at night. I thought everyone knew that. Snowy owls, for instance.'

'Snowy owls?' he asks incredulously.

'That's right. And bats. I know they aren't birds, but they flap around the garden, and Humphrey won't know the difference. He loses his head and runs after anything that flies. I'm telling you to watch him carefully.'

Daniel gives me a mock salute. 'Understood. I'll be on the alert for anything airborne. It's a good thing I don't have any drones with me today. They're surprisingly expensive. I'd hate Humphrey to mistake one for a snowy owl and launch a ground-to-air assault on it.'

'I think he prefers real things to toys,' I say. 'Anyway, it's only for a couple of minutes. I'll be back as quickly as possible. If anyone turns up, can you tell them you're the plumber?'

'The plumber?' he repeats.

'Or the dog walker or the electrician. Use your ingenuity. How hard can it be to come up with a plausible reason for you being here? The important thing is that you leave without raising suspicion.'

I don't wait for him to argue further but run up to my room, where I pull on a pair of jeans and a thick roll-neck sweater. I'd been planning to wear my one and only skirt in honour of this occasion because I have no idea how formal the club meetings may be. But a glance in the mirror shows several streaks of dried mud on my neck. There may be others I can't see in this dim light. It's best to be safe and cover as much of myself as possible. I'd prefer the story of tonight's escape to stay a secret between the three of us. It would only upset Gran if one of the club members contacted her to tell her about it.

Secrets seem to be the watchword of this club. It can't harm for me to add one more. I give my hair a quick brush and run downstairs as the doorbell rings. There's no sign of Daniel and Humphrey. They must still be hunting for owls in the garden. With any luck, I can greet whoever this is before slipping away and letting Daniel out through the back gate. No one need ever know he was here.

I compose my face into a welcoming smile – the expression of a calm and experienced hostess who has everything under control and has never heard of such a thing as a runaway dog, let alone anyone pelting along the street dressed in nothing but a flimsy dressing gown and slippers.

A woman is standing on the doorstep holding a box of what I assume must be cookies. She doesn't wait for me to greet her but steps past me into the hall and pulls off her coat.

'It's cold out there,' she says, handing it to me. 'Hello, I'm Margery Townsend.'

I glance over her shoulder before closing the door. The front gate appears to be shut. Humphrey is in the back garden, but I don't want to take any chances. Any minute now, he may break free from Daniel's inexperienced grasp, crash through the back door, and appear in the hallway, all ready for his third expedition to the local mud pit.

'I'm Lucy,' I say, looking around for somewhere to hang up the coat.

'I know you are. You're Lavender's granddaughter. She sent me a message to say you'd be hosting us tonight.'

I hope this hasn't offended her. For all I know, several members of the club have offered to hold tonight's meeting at their house, and Gran has refused. It's common knowledge what these village institutions are like, with their petty jealousies and feuds. Entire generations of families are always falling out with each other, with Shakespearean consequences. This one act of perceived nepotism on Gran's part may rend the village asunder and result in one half of it no longer speaking to the other for decades to come. Civil wars have started with less provocation.

To my relief, this woman doesn't look as though she plans to return home to fetch her pitchfork. She walks towards the kitchen as though she owns the place. It isn't surprising. If she's a long-standing member of the club, she'll have visited this house more often than I have.

'I'm not sure whether we've met before,' I say, following her into the kitchen.

She dumps her box of cookies onto the counter and turns to look at me. 'Several times. But you'd be forgiven for not remembering much about it. Your mother used to wheel you around the village in your pram when you were a baby.'

'I'm afraid I don't remember that,' I say. 'Have we met again since I was a little older?'

'Not often. I think your family usually spent Christmas in Coventry, and Lavender and Ed came to you.'

'Until she got Humphrey,' I say. 'He doesn't travel well, so Gran decided to stay here with him instead. We were going to come down last year, but my father had an accident.'

I don't elaborate. If she's one of Gran's friends, she'll know all about it, and it isn't a subject I enjoy discussing.

'I heard about that,' she says. 'A terrible business. But I hear he's going on a little better. Perhaps we'll see him down here this Christmas?'

'It isn't likely. Dad has made a better recovery than we expected when it first happened, but I don't think he'd be able to travel this far. I'm not sure what will happen this Christmas. Even if Humphrey didn't suffer from travel sickness, I doubt Gran will be going much further than the sofa.'

'I'm sure you'll work something out,' she says.

The back door opens, and Humphrey bounces in. If possible, he looks even more full of beans than usual.

Margery holds up her hand. 'Don't even think about it! I don't want mud all over my clean skirt.'

To my amazement, Humphrey abandons his evident intention of hurling himself at her. He sidles over and sits next to her, looking the picture of injured innocence.

She scratches his head. 'Good boy. You know I love you. Neither of us needs to cover each other in mud to prove it.'

She notices Daniel. 'I didn't realise you had company.'

'Not company!' I say, taking the makeshift lead from Daniel and giving him a speaking look. 'He's here to …'

I trail off, trying to remember whether Daniel and I settled on a cover story to explain his presence. Why couldn't this woman have arrived a few minutes later? I could have bundled him out of the back gate, and he would have been halfway home by now.

He holds out his hand to her. 'My name's Daniel. I'm the plumber.'

'The plumber?' she asks. 'At this time of night?'

'That's right. Lucy called me earlier this evening and asked me to stop by on my way home. It's very nice to meet you, Ms –'

He glances over at me, and I frown back at him. Why does a plumber need to know the names of all the visitors to this house? Shouldn't he be concentrating on doing the job for which he's being paid? I remember he isn't an actual plumber and bite my lip.

Margery breaks the silence. 'I'm Margery Townsend. Nice to meet you.'

'I'm afraid he has to get going,' I say. 'He mentioned earlier that he has a big event tonight. I'm sure he's looking forward to it. I'm sorry to have called you out at such short notice, Daniel, but I know my grandmother will appreciate it.'

The doorbell rings again. I hesitate, not wanting to leave Daniel alone with Margery. Goodness knows what he'll say to her while I'm gone. The one thing I'm sure of is that it will end up embarrassing me further. But neither of them moves, so I have no choice.

Three more women are standing on the doorstep, all carrying boxes. They introduce themselves as Irene Henshaw, Phyllis Meadows, and June Parker.

I take their coats and point them to the kitchen. 'Margery is here already. She's talking to the plumber, but he's about to leave.'

'The plumber?' asks Irene. 'Do you mean Steve Watley?'

'He didn't mention his full name,' I say, trying to play it safe.

Phyllis gives me a quizzical look. 'Then how did you know it was the plumber?'

'I … er … called the number, and he turned up.'

'And you didn't ask for any ID? Even I know better than that.'

She walks down the hall to the kitchen, and I follow, hoping Daniel has taken the chance to leave by the back door. What am I thinking? Of course, he hasn't. He's sitting at the kitchen table, talking to Margery. I frown at him, but he doesn't appear to notice.

'You aren't Steve Wately!' Phyllis greets him.

'You're quite correct,' he says. 'Is there any reason I should be?'

'Lucy here told me she'd called the plumber in. Who do you work for?'

'I work with someone called Marcus Turner,' he says.

'I've never heard of him. Where are you based?'

'All over the place. We go wherever we're needed.'

She looks doubtful. 'What's wrong with Steve Wately?'

'I have no idea,' says Daniel. 'This is the first time I've heard of him.'

'How can you not have heard of Steve Wately?' demands June. 'I thought all you tradespeople knew each other.'

'Not yet,' says Daniel. 'I'm new around here. But I look forward to making his acquaintance very soon.'

June glances at Margery, then at me. 'How did you get this man's number, Lucy?'

'From the local newspaper Gran has delivered each week,' I say, just as Daniel says, 'We have an online ad.'

'That's right,' I say. 'I meant to say it was an advert in the online newspaper.'

June doesn't look convinced. 'And why did you say he was here?'

I rack my brain for a plausible sounding plumbing emergency. 'I thought one of the pipes had burst. But it turned out it hadn't.'

'Interesting,' says Margery. 'This man told me he'd been called out to unblock a toilet.'

I glare at Daniel, who looks as though he's trying not to laugh.

'It was the pipe that leads to the toilet,' I say. 'I thought it was blocked.'

'You said burst,' Margery reminds me.

'That's right. I thought it had burst because it was blocked. But Daniel told me it was just frozen.'

'He told me it was one of the worst blockages he'd ever come across,' she says.

She turns to Daniel. 'I'd like you to sit right there and keep your hands on the table where we can all see them while I call the police. They'll soon find out what you're up to. Have you been doing this all around the area? I suppose you thought a place like Honeywell was the perfect place for your scam because there are so many elderly people living here. Well, you're about to find out you're mistaken. We may not be as young as we were, but we're capable of dealing with someone like you. Keep an eye on him, ladies!'

This is terrible. While I don't have any general objection to Daniel being made to leave the house, I can't let it be in the back of a police car.

'There's no need to call the police,' I say. 'Daniel isn't a plumber.'

'No kidding!' says Margery. 'I wasn't born yesterday. He clearly doesn't know one end of a waste pipe from another. He's heard your grandmother is in hospital, and he thought he'd con his way in and see whether there was anything worth stealing.'

'No, he didn't,' I say, ignoring Daniel's snort of laughter. 'I invited him in.'

'You shouldn't have done that,' says June. 'It's exactly the sort of thing our Neighbourhood Watch group is always warning us about. You ought to know better, Lucy.'

I'm tempted to agree with her that Daniel is a dangerous criminal who needs to be hauled before the local magistrates, but I get the better of myself.

'I mean I'm the reason he's here,' I explain. 'I asked him to come in and watch Humphrey for me while I got dressed.'

'You mean he's your boyfriend?' asks Phyllis.

'Absolutely not! I barely know him. At least, I know him well enough to trust him with Humphrey, but –'

I break off and glance at Daniel. 'You aren't being much help. Can you please explain who you are and what you're doing here?'

'I'm not sure I can,' he says. 'I've lost track. One moment I'm a dog sitter, and the next I'm a plumber. It's all very confusing.'

'You were lucky,' I say. 'My first idea was to tell them you were a member of the local history society, here to inspect the beams in the walls.'

'Inspect them for what?' he asks. 'Dry rot? Wouldn't you be better off calling a surveyor for that?'

'I'm not sure,' I admit. 'Carbon dating, maybe?'

'It sounds a lot more fun than being a plumber,' he says. 'Is it too late to change our story?'

'I think that ship has well and truly sailed. The best thing you can do is to come clean, tell everyone who you are, then leave before they call the police on you.'

Margery looks from me to Daniel, then back again. 'I think you'd better both sit down and tell us what's going on.'

Chapter Sixteen

I look at Daniel and see he's grinning again. This annoys me even more than everything else he does.

'I'm not sure what you find so amusing,' I tell him. 'This was your idea, so you can do the talking.'

He gives me a pained look. 'As far as I'm concerned, this is all on you. I'll admit I knocked your cookies into the street yesterday afternoon. I tried to put that right, but you wouldn't let me. It was your idea to invite me to this club. I turned up tonight, ready to do whatever I was asked, but first you threw my cookies all over the path, and then you sent me off on a muddy rescue expedition in the cold and dark with no thought for my safety.'

He glances around at the interested faces, warming to his theme. 'I co-own a drone company. We're in the area doing some work for the local council. I've only been staying in this village for a few weeks. I haven't had time to explore any of the local beauty spots or make a mental map of all the dangerous places in the area. Lucy's very lucky this didn't end up as a Hound of the Baskervilles situation, with me as the innocent entomologist meeting an untimely death in the Grimpen Mire.'

'He wasn't innocent!' I almost shout.

Humphrey looks anxious at the sound of raised voices.

Daniel leans down to stroke his ears. 'Sorry, old man. No one is angry with you. Quite the contrary. We could cast you as the lead in the next village play. You'd make a wonderful Hound of the Baskervilles.'

'Humphrey would hate that,' I say. 'He doesn't like crowds and loud noises. Crowds, in particular. I'm sure he feels there are too many people in his kitchen as it is.'

'I know a hint when I hear one,' says Daniel.

'Not so much a hint as an instruction,' I say. 'This meeting is about to start. I'm sorry you were confused and thought you'd been invited to attend, but it doesn't make any difference now. This is a cookie club, and you no longer have any cookies, so –'

'Not so fast!' says Irene. 'We've established Daniel isn't a plumber. And you've told us he isn't your boyfriend.'

'Or a member of the local historical society,' adds Phyllis.

'Should I have told them I was delivering your Christmas tree?' Daniel asks me.

'No. Everyone would have asked me where it was. And I'm tired of making up stupid stories you can't even be bothered to corroborate.'

'You could tell them the truth,' he says.

'I'm quite keen to hear the fiction,' says Margery. 'Did you consider telling us he was here to sweep your chimneys, Lucy?'

'That one didn't occur to me. But Daniel is welcome to crawl around inside the chimney if he likes.'

'I don't like,' he says.

I sigh. 'The truth is that Daniel and I bumped into each other by chance, and I told him about this club. I didn't realise it was a secret when I first heard about it. Gran only mentioned that when I visited her in the hospital later on. Anyway, one thing led to another, and Daniel somehow got the impression I'd invited him to attend this evening.'

'Lucy issued a challenge,' says Daniel. 'And honour compelled me to rise to it.'

'It wasn't a challenge!' I say. 'Daniel knocked my cookies into the street, and I told him how long it had taken me to make them. He seemed to think baking cookies was easy. I said it wasn't, and he couldn't do any better than me. The rest is unfortunately history.'

'Every time Lucy tells that story, I come out of it looking a little worse,' says Daniel. 'But I don't want to set her off again, so I'll leave it there.'

'You told him about our club?' Irene asks me.

I hang my head. 'I'm very sorry.'

'The one that's been kept a closely guarded secret for decades?' says Phyllis, looking equally horrified.

'I didn't know that when I told him about it.'

Margery frowns. 'I can't imagine what your grandmother will say when she hears about this.'

'Do you have to tell her?' I say with sudden hope. 'Could we swear Daniel to secrecy and threaten him with something awful if he ever tells anyone?'

'I'm right here,' says Daniel.

'That's the problem,' I say. 'You shouldn't be.'

'Don't put all the blame on him,' Margery tells me. 'From what you say, you were the one who told him our closely guarded secret.'

'And let the cat out of the bag,' agrees June.

This is awful. They're all looking at me as though I've committed an actual crime.

'I've already told you how sorry I am,' I plead. 'It was an honest mistake.'

'I'm surprised you're able to let yourself off the hook so easily,' says June.

'Just what I was thinking,' agrees Irene. 'It's all very well for you to brush it off like this, Lucy, but the rest of us see it as a horrible betrayal.'

I dart a look at Daniel, who's grinning again. I look from him to Margery and see her shoulders are shaking.

'Are you winding me up?' I ask her.

She gives a splutter of laughter. 'You could say that.'

'But why?'

'I'm sorry. You looked so terrified when you said you'd given away our secret.'

'I *was* terrified!' I say. 'I've been dreading you finding out what I did. Isn't it a secret after all?'

Phyllis pours herself another cup of tea. 'That's the thing. It is, and it isn't. How much do you know about the history of this club?'

'Almost nothing. Gran told me it's a village institution, and it was important I took over for her – as a Hollis woman. She didn't mention that I shouldn't tell anyone about it until it was too late. I had no idea it was a secret.'

'It started off that way,' she says. 'The club was founded by your great-grandmother Sylvia during the second world war. Honeywell took in a lot of evacuee children. Sylvia and several of her friends decided it would be a nice idea to make Christmas special for the children while they were away from their parents. So, they came up with the idea of this cookie club. They met once a week in the run-up to Christmas, and they all brought a batch of cookies. They made them into parcels and secretly delivered them to each of the households who'd taken in an evacuee.'

'Like a Secret Santa?' I ask.

'Exactly. The children would come down in the morning and find the cookies on their doorstep, and no one would know where they'd come from.'

'That's a lovely idea,' I say. 'What happened when they went back to their parents at the end of the war?'

'Sylvia and her friends kept up the tradition. They'd never told anyone who they were, and they decided it would be fun to continue like that. Each year, they baked cookies, parcelled them up, and dropped them off at various houses around the village. During rationing, they delivered the cookies to those people who were less well off. They thought it would be nice to do something to make their Christmas more fun. As time went on, those club members with daughters passed on the baton to them. Occasionally, someone else would be invited to join. By the nineteen-seventies, the club was delivering cookies to every house in the village that had children living there.'

'That's a lot of cookies,' says Daniel.

'There are around a hundred and fifty houses in Honeywell with children,' she says. 'Irene makes a spreadsheet to make sure no one gets missed out. We all bake fifty cookies each week and bring them here. We sort them into parcels of ten, and Irene tells us which houses will be getting cookies that week. It's a lot of work, but it's worth it.'

'Is it no longer a secret?' I ask.

'As I said, it is, and it isn't. The children love the tradition. They look forward to it all year. Everyone goes out of their way to make sure they don't find out who's behind it. We try to keep it a secret from the adults too. I'm sure several of them have a reasonable idea who's involved, but no one ever mentions it.'

'It's a lovely idea,' I say. 'I'm so sorry I mentioned it to Daniel.'

'Which brings us back to where we started,' says Margery.

'What are we going to do about this?' she asks the others. 'Should we retire to another room to consider our verdict?'

'There's only the living room,' I say. 'And Humphrey seems to have retired there already to get away from things. I'm not saying he won't budge up to make room for a couple of you on the sofa, but I wouldn't bet next week's salary on it.'

'He does love his home comforts,' says June.

'I don't want to hurry you,' I say. 'But time's getting on, and the rest of the members will be arriving at any moment. Would someone like to administer the oath of silence to Daniel, and then we can get on with our evening?'

'We don't have an oath of silence,' says Margery.

'If that's your only problem, I can knock one up for you in no time at all. I can even translate it into German if you like.'

She smiles. 'I don't think we need anything too formal.'

'I agree,' I say. 'Just give him a stern warning and throw him outside before it starts to snow. Hopefully, there will be a blizzard later that will hide his footsteps. No one will know he was here.'

I turn to Daniel. 'Please remember to latch the front gate properly. I don't want a repeat of this evening's performance.'

He pushes back his chair and stands. 'The people have spoken. I'll say goodbye to Humphrey and be on my way.'

'I'll show you out,' I say. 'I'd hate you to get lost in the hall and fail to find your way out.'

'Not so fast!' says Margery, and I sigh. We were so nearly there.

Daniel stops dead, and I cannon into him. 'Ouch!'

'Sorry,' he says. 'But Margery seems to have something to say. It would only be polite for us to hear her out.'

I glance at my watch. 'Fine. But it's getting late, and you're still here.'

'You have the floor,' he tells Margery.

She glances at the other three. 'The members of the Honeywell Christmas Cookie Club would like to invite Daniel to become an honorary member. For this year only,' she adds, seeing my horrified expression.

I'm not sure how that makes anything better. I'm only here this year because Gran had an accident. I'm not likely to be back here again next year. If Daniel becomes a member of the club, it may as well be permanent.

'I disagree,' I say as calmly as possible. 'For one thing, this is a women-only club, and Daniel is definitely not a woman.'

'Technically, this isn't a women-only club,' says Phyllis. 'It's always been that way because it was started by a group of women, and they passed it on to their daughters and female friends. But there's nothing in the constitution saying it has to remain that way.'

'I didn't like to say anything,' says Daniel, his face straight, but his eyes dancing. 'But it is the twenty-first century, and there are certain laws pertaining to the equality of the sexes …'

'That's irrelevant!' I say. 'This isn't a place of employment. It's a meeting that takes place in a private home. My grandmother is free to invite whomever she likes to her house.'

I turn to face the rest of the women. 'Don't let Daniel tell you that you're breaking the law if you don't admit men. It's absolute nonsense. I vote we ask him to leave at once.'

'But who are we to argue with the club members?' says Daniel. 'I'm prepared to bow to greater authority here. I'm surprised you're not.'

'This is your club,' I tell the women. 'It's up to you. I accept your ruling.'

'How delightfully formal,' murmurs Daniel. He raises his voice. 'I too accept the ruling of the court. I don't have a gavel to hand. But if I did, consider it banged.'

'That shows what you know about court proceedings,' I mutter.

'Have you two finished bickering?' asks Margery.

'Certainly, your honour,' says Daniel. 'My fellow defendant and I would like to offer our apologies for having wasted the court's time.'

She waits for a moment to see whether I'm going to speak. When she's satisfied I'm not, she picks up a teaspoon and taps it sharply on the kitchen table.

'The ruling stands. Both Lucy and Daniel are henceforth admitted to the sacred chapter of our organisation. Let the eighty-fifth annual meeting of the Honeywell Christmas Cookie Club come to order!'

Chapter Seventeen

I close the door with a sigh of relief after the final guest has left. This evening was more fun than I expected, despite the unwelcome addition of Daniel. But I'm exhausted, and I still need to clear up before I go to bed. The rest of the club members turned up shortly after Daniel and I were formally admitted, which meant an extraordinary amount of tea and coffee making.

Humphrey nudges my ankle and looks up at me with pleading eyes.

'I haven't forgotten you,' I tell him, leading the way back to the kitchen. 'But don't try to look as though you haven't eaten since yesterday. I saw you polish off that piece of shortbread that fell on the floor. You thought no one was looking, but I was. I'm learning that someone needs to have their eye on you twenty-four hours a day. That's normally Gran's job, but she isn't here right now, so you're stuck with me.'

Humphrey isn't listening. He's standing next to the larder door. I consult the list on the fridge.

'How did you know you were getting liver snaps tonight? A lucky guess, I suppose.'

I pick up his bowl and pour the pieces into it. 'Mum said I should only fill it up to the line, so don't try telling me I've got it wrong. I don't expect you have much of an appetite if you've been eating cookies.'

I'm wrong. He finishes the liver snaps in four gulps and coughs.

'Serves you right for eating too fast,' I say unsympathetically. 'Would you like to go outside while I wash the rest of these dishes?'

I unlock the door, and he catapults joyfully past me and into the garden. I check to make sure Daniel didn't attempt to open the back gate. He and Humphrey came back into the house through the kitchen, so I doubt he did. But it's as well to be sure.

I think back over the evening as I wash the dishes. How did Daniel manage to worm his way into the club? He can't have planned it all in advance. Too many unpredictable things have happened this evening for him to have done that. He might have left the front gate open on purpose, but he couldn't have predicted Humphrey would then break free and pelt down the road at top speed. Nor did he know about Humphrey's deep and unshakeable love for mud or that I would be hampered by running in my grandmother's dressing gown.

Forget Hansel and Gretel. This evening had far stronger overtones of Little Red Riding Hood. Except that my grandmother wasn't lying upstairs in bed. And Daniel, for all his annoying qualities, is hardly cut out for the part of the big, bad wolf. The most he can be accused of is clumsiness – and a propensity to appear at times and places where he's least welcome.

He certainly got what he wanted tonight. He came here with a plan to gate-crash the cookie club, and that's what he did. I'm not sure he expected to become a fully-fledged member, but that's what happened all the same. What is it with elderly women? A halfway personable man flashes them a smile and turns on the charm, and they're putty in his hands.

That's not entirely fair. I've seldom encountered a group of women less likely to do something they don't want to, or more capable of reducing those around them to stunned silence. Which must mean they knew what they were doing when they invited him to join their exclusive club, and it had nothing whatsoever to do with his smile. I'm glad because I hate to see anyone manipulated.

Objectively speaking, Daniel does have a very nice smile, but that's just a matter of genetics and no credit to him. The fact his eyes crinkle when he laughs is also irrelevant to whether he's a good person. It's the way his face is structured, and he'd better not try to use it to bamboozle people. Any hint of that at future club meetings, and I'll be forced to step in and put him in his place.

I have to admit he didn't behave too badly this evening. He let Humphrey out, but he did everything he could to rectify that mistake. He found him again, improvised a lead, and brought him safely home. And I did spoil his cookies. To my mind, that was poetic justice, and I was prepared to argue my case if Daniel complained. But he didn't, so there was no need.

Humphrey appears at the door and slinks past me, throwing himself into his basket with a gusty sigh and starting to snore.

'All finished?' I ask him. 'I see it's started snowing. I'll have to brave the cold and dark and go outside to clean up after you. I'm not digging through six feet of snow tomorrow morning to see what you've left for me.'

Humphrey's snores grow louder.

'You're faking it,' I tell him, pulling on my coat. 'You don't want to clear up after yourself, so you're pretending to be asleep.'

He rolls over and buries his face in his cushion. I sigh, open the back door, and step out into the falling snow.

I wake the following morning filled with a determination to beat Daniel at his own game. If he's so determined to be a member of this club, he can work for it. I know it's not a competition, but there's nothing to stop me competing with him privately. He doesn't even need to know about it. Nor does anyone else.

'It will just be our little secret,' I tell Humphrey. 'You want me to beat him, don't you?'

Humphrey yawns, stretches, then climbs off the bed by simply rolling sideways with his eyes shut until he crashes onto the floor. He picks himself up with a look of surprise and sidles over to the door. That's not the right word for a dog his size. It's less of a sidle and more of a crash.

He looks at the doorway with a puzzled expression, as though it's some devious obstacle I've set up during the night to confuse him. He negotiates it with care before running down the landing. I wait until the usual set of crashes and bumps tell me he's arrived downstairs, then follow at a more sedate pace. I'm too old to throw myself down the stairs and hope for the best.

My friends and I used to slide down the stairs on a tea tray when our parents were out. There must be some obscure saint dedicated to preserving small children on tea trays because none of us ever broke any of our limbs. Maybe I should give Humphrey a tea tray to use while Gran is away. I'm not sure where I'd find one big enough, but that's the beauty of the internet. There's a website for everything.

I measure out his breakfast and drop some bread into the toaster. While I'm waiting for it to brown, I leaf through the pages of Gran's baking book, hoping to find a recipe that's both simple to follow and stunning to look at. Annoyingly, the writer has forgotten to include anything matching this description, and my opinion of professional cookery writers falls even lower. How difficult would it be for them to create a gourmet recipe that only uses three ingredients and takes less than ten minutes to make?

I find Humphrey's harness and check it several times before opening the front door. We don't want a repeat of yesterday's jailbreak. I almost expect to find Daniel lurking behind the hedge as I step onto the pavement and latch the gate closed behind me. But a quick glance up and down the street shows it's refreshingly Daniel-free. Our first stop today is the bakery. Maybe I'll walk in and discover him sipping a cappuccino, but it isn't likely. According to him, he runs his own company, so he must have to work sometimes. Hopefully, this morning is one of those times.

I can't imagine what sort of things he uses his drones for. He mentioned his company was doing some work for the town council, but he didn't say what it was. Maybe they use the drones to inspect the drains. It would be a great pity if one of them got stuck and Daniel had to climb into the sewer to rescue it. If it were me, I'd be inclined to leave the drone where it was and write it off against tax.

Humphrey skips ahead of me, tugging at his lead. It's even colder than yesterday. It snowed a little in the night, but not enough for a snowball fight.

'Sorry, Humphrey, I tell him. 'Maybe tomorrow. In the meantime, you'll have to make do with a couple of dog biscuits.'

The bakery door opens, and Humphrey makes a dart for it, almost knocking over an elderly woman carrying several paper bags. She looks very like Mrs Ogilvie, except for the brightly dyed hair.

'Careful, young man!' she tells him. 'If you damage my plum slices, you'll find yourself on the wrong end of a lawsuit.'

'I'm so sorry,' I say. 'I'd like to say my dog isn't usually like this, but I was brought up to tell the truth.'

She gives a loud laugh. 'I understand. My sister and I have a badly behaved dog at home. You can't imagine how I suffer. These things are sent to try us. In fact, I wanted to change the dog's name to *Tryus*, but he refused to answer to it. It's lucky for him I have the patience of a saint.'

She gives me an amiable smile and sets off down the street at a surprisingly brisk pace.

'Did you hear that?' I ask Humphrey. 'I'm allowed to change your name if you don't behave.'

He grins up at me and thumps his tail.

'Fine,' I tell him. 'We'll go in and get your biscuits. But I need you to be on your best behaviour, or I'm changing your name to Biscuit Bandit, and there's absolutely nothing you or Gran can do about it.'

Chapter Eighteen

Humphrey and I have fallen into a routine of waking bright and early each morning. It would be nice to think the fresh country air and simple living is having a beneficial effect on me and encouraging me to embrace a more healthy and productive lifestyle. The truth is that Humphrey, despite being the size of a small to medium-sized lion, possesses one of the smallest bladders known to mankind – or dogkind.

I have to make sure he doesn't drink too much before we go to bed or my nights become a series of trips downstairs. I stand by the back door, shivering, as Humphrey gallops merrily around the garden, searching for the perfect spot in which to relieve himself. I grit my teeth as he lifts a leg and stares around before heaving an audible sigh and bounding off in search of an even more ideal location.

I have no idea what goes through his head at these times. I'm not sure I want to. Humphrey's thought processes are a mystery known only to himself. Judging by the blank expression on his face during these midnight trips, he may not even be aware of what he's doing.

But I don't intend to make a habit of standing around in the snow, however educational these nocturnal garden visits may be. Even David Attenborough would draw the line at standing shivering in his pyjamas while Humphrey makes a careful study of the local flora of south Honeywell.

I groan and roll over on Sunday morning when I feel his nose pushing into the small of my back.

'It's not even light yet,' I tell him in my sternest voice. 'You're confusing your time zones. You aren't in Asia. You're in Honeywell in December, and this isn't a time for any self-respecting dog to be awake.'

I roll away from him and close my eyes, hoping he'll take my words to heart and see the error of his ways. He nudges me again and whines.

'Half an hour?' I plead.

He yawns and waves his legs as though practising for the next canine Olympics. I'm not sure which event – possibly the heavyweight butterfly-swimming relay. He slithers off the bed and lands with a thud on the floor. Maybe he plans to take a nap there. This mattress is softer than I'd like. Humphrey may have come to the same conclusion and fears for the future health of his spine. Very sensible of him.

He heaves himself to his feet and sets off towards the bedroom door. A moment later, I hear him crash down the stairs. I sigh and swing my legs out of bed. I don't want to start my day clearing up one of Humphrey's accidents, with him staring at me as though he's wondering why I don't just kick some soil over it and wander off.

A blast of arctic air greets me the moment I open the back door. I shiver and pull my cardigan more tightly around me. Humphrey, who wears a thick woollen coat at all times, is unbothered by the cold. He dashes out, joyfully kicking up clouds of snow and barking at the top of his voice. I hope Gran's neighbour either sleeps at the front of her house or is afflicted with deafness. If she wasn't deaf when she moved in, I expect she is now.

We walk to the village after breakfast. Humphrey stops to greet everyone we pass. Most of them seem to know him by name, and they all ask me how my grandmother is doing. News travels fast in a place like this. I try to memorise all the messages people ask me to pass on to Gran when I next visit her, but it's impossible. Maybe I should carry a notebook and pen with me when I come out shopping. Or attach a small recording device to Humphrey's collar. But he'd probably try to eat it.

I pop into the bakery to pick up some cherry slices for Gran. I remember her baking them when I was small. Hopefully, the ones here will be as good.

The moment we're through the door, Humphrey flings himself under a table and closes his eyes.

'We're not staying,' I tell him. 'We're just buying something for Gran.'

He doesn't move.

'If you're playing dead, it won't work,' I say. 'I can see your ribs moving. And your leg is twitching.'

'He wouldn't win any games of musical statues, would he?' says Lily, who's watching in amusement. 'By the way, did you find that man you were looking for?'

'Not exactly looking for,' I say, keen to squash any ideas she may have got about me and Daniel.

'I thought you wanted to find out who he was.'

I give her a cool smile. 'In a sense, I suppose I did.'

She looks confused. 'In what sense?'

'In the sense of trying to ascertain his identity,' I say, sounding like a police officer giving a press conference. 'But not in the sense of being interested in him as a person.'

'A fine distinction,' she says.

'But an important one. As it happens, we did bump into each other again.'

'Is he a local, after all?'

'Temporarily. He's working down here for a few weeks.'

She waits for me to elaborate, but I don't want to mention the circumstances under which I met Daniel or tell her the reason why I needed to talk to him so urgently. I've learned my lesson about the cookie club, and I don't plan to mention it to anyone unless I know they're already a member.

'I can't stay for too long,' I say. 'I'm popping over to the hospital this afternoon.'

'How is your grandmother today?' asks Lily.

'When I called the ward this morning, they said she'd had a good night. They're hoping she'll be well enough to come home quite soon.'

'That's wonderful. She and Humphrey must be missing each other so much. Does that mean you'll be leaving us?'

'I'm not sure how long I'll be here. Gran can't stay at home by herself. She can't climb the stairs, for one thing. And she won't be able to take Humphrey for his walks. I expect I'll be around for a while longer.'

'That's nice,' she says. 'Honeywell is lovely at this time of year. Have you visited the Christmas fair yet?'

'I didn't think it was Humphrey's kind of thing. Or rather, I was worried it might be too much his kind of thing.'

'It can get crowded,' she says. 'And Humphrey is quite a large dog.'

'If he gets any bigger, he'll be a whole other species. Maybe I'll pop along one evening after Gran gets home.'

'Are you here for anything special today?' she asks.

'Apparently, I'm here to buy Humphrey some biscuits. I also wanted to pick up some cherry slices for Gran. I don't know how she's getting on with the hospital food, but it can't hurt to take her a few extras. I remember her baking them for me when I was a child.'

'Abby made a batch this morning,' she says. 'I'll pop a few into a bag for you. No charge. Tell Mrs Hollis everyone at The Sugarloaf Bakery is thinking of her.'

'That's kind of you,' I say. 'But there's no need. I can pay for them.'

She waves my offer away. 'It's only what we'd do for any of our regular customers. I'll put a couple of biscuits in for Humphrey to take his mind off being away from your Gran. Not that you aren't doing an amazing job with him.'

'I'm doing my best, but I'm a poor substitute. He'll be delighted when Gran gets back.'

Humphrey ambles over to sniff the bag. I hold it out of his reach. 'You can have one now and another if you can walk all the way home without diving into any muddy ditches.'

Gran is sitting up in bed knitting when I arrive at the hospital. She looks up and smiles when she sees me.

'I see they've put you to work,' I say, dropping the bag of cherry slices onto the bedside table.

'I've been finding it rather dull in here,' she says. 'I'm not used to sitting around doing nothing, and I've finished my book. Angela Carson says she'll drop by later and bring me the next one in the series.'

'Was it she who brought you the needles and wool?'

'Yes. She knows I enjoy knitting, and she had some spare balls of wool. I'm making Humphrey a sweater.'

'How much spare wool did she have?' I ask, and Gran laughs.

'He isn't that big. I made him one last year, and I only used three large balls.'

'Why does he need a new one? Is he fashion-conscious? Does he refuse to wear last season's styles?'

'I'm afraid last year's jumper didn't last for long,' she says. 'It was my fault. Humphrey discovered it before I could explain to him what it was. He thought it was a toy.'

'And played with it very, very gently?'

'He doesn't always know his own strength,' she defends him. 'He had a little chew, and it fell apart.'

'You mean he ate it?'

'Not all of it. Just the front half.'

I push the bag towards her. 'Your vet must have her hands full with Humphrey. What did she say when you told her what he'd done?'

'I'm not sure whether I mentioned it. Humphrey has eaten things like that before. The vet usually tells me to keep an eye on him and let her know if he's in any discomfort.'

'Or coughs up the world's largest hairball,' I say. 'It's lucky you're so patient with him.'

She helps herself to a cherry slice and offers the bag to me. 'He's an easy dog to be patient with. He's so loving and gentle.'

'He's a very friendly dog,' I agree. 'And he wouldn't hurt a fly. Although I can't say the same for birds. Luckily, he's too big to be very agile. He's like one of those cargo ships. They travel fast once they're underway, but they take a while to pick up speed. Any bird in the vicinity is long gone before he can reach them.'

'I think they just interest him,' says Gran. 'He's a naturally curious dog.'

'Poor Humphrey. It must be hard living among such standoffish birds.'

'Are you sure you don't want one of these?' she asks. 'They're delicious. Did you make them?'

'I wish! They came from The Sugarloaf Bakery, with their compliments and best wishes. And they're all for you. I thought you might be getting bored with the hospital food.'

'It's not too bad,' she says. 'Although nothing beats a nice cherry slice.'

'I remember you baking them when I was small. They were my favourites. Maybe you can teach me how to make them when you get home.'

'How did the cookie club go?' she asks.

'Very well, I think.' I clear my throat and speak in an artificially bright tone. 'We have a new member this year.'

She looks interested. 'Who's that? Did Irene bring her niece along? I know she was thinking about inviting her to join.'

'Not Irene's niece. He isn't related to Irene at all. I just meant –'

'He?' asks Gran. 'You mean a man?'

'That's right. His name is Daniel. He's staying in the village for a few weeks.'

'He's a friend of yours?'

'Not at all!' I say with unnecessary emphasis, remembering my cookies lying crushed in the street.

Gran looks even more confused. 'Then, why was he at the club? Who invited him?'

'He sort of invited himself.'

I tell her the whole story, starting with the destruction of my first batch of halfway decent cookies and ending with Daniel's admission to the club as a temporary member. I skate over Humphrey's break for freedom as quickly as possible. Gran doesn't look anywhere near as annoyed as I'd expected. I'm surprised to see she's laughing by the end of my story.

'It sounds as though you had an exciting evening,' she says. 'And don't worry about Daniel. If the members decided to invite him to join, that's good enough for me.'

'They didn't have a lot of choice,' I say. 'He'd already heard all your club secrets.'

She gives me an embarrassed smile. 'It must seem rather ridiculous to you. But the ritual and tradition of our club has been a great comfort to me, particularly after your grandfather's death.'

'Daniel has been sworn to secrecy,' I assure her. 'I'm not sure how much notice he'd have taken of me, but Margery, Phyllis and June made it clear to him he wasn't to mention it to a soul. They're scary women. I doubt he'll risk upsetting them.'

'Margery takes no nonsense from anyone,' she says. 'But she's been a good friend to me over the years. I must say I rather like the sound of this Daniel. It's about time we had some men join the club. Everyone nowadays is talking about equality, so we're keeping up with modern ideas.'

'I'm not sure men suffer from too much inequality,' I say. 'If you want to keep your club for women only, go right ahead.'

'We have to move with the times,' she chides me. 'My great-grandmother knew that. She was the first in our family to keep her own name when she married. And the rest of us have followed suit. As long as this Daniel of yours is a nice man, that's enough for me. Is he nice?'

This question takes me by surprise. I've spent most of my brief acquaintance with Daniel either shouting at him or sending him chasing off into the night in pursuit of an errant dog. I haven't had time to consider what he's like as a person.

'He seems pleasant enough,' I say. 'When he isn't hurling my cookies into the street. He was quite helpful with Humphrey.'

'Is he good looking?' she asks with a roguish smile.

'Handsome is as handsome does,' I say darkly.

She laughs. 'I look forward to meeting him and deciding for myself.'

'Aren't we supposed to assess people by their personality?' I tease her.

'Of course,' she agrees. 'But a handsome face never hurts.'

I reach for my bag. 'Your generation never ceases to shock me. I should let you get some rest. Angela Carson will be dropping by later with that book you mentioned. I don't even want to know what it's about. It will only shock me more.'

She squeezes my hand. 'Thank you for everything you've done, Lucy. Give my love to Humphrey.'

'I will. He'll be so excited to see you when you come home.'

'I can't wait to see him too. The doctor says there's a chance I may be allowed home this week if all goes well.'

'That's wonderful!' I say. 'You'll be pleased to be back in your own house after all this time.'

'I'll be delighted,' she says. 'I'm looking forward to catching up with everything I've missed since I've been away.'

She shoots me a sidelong glance. 'And I'll be most interested to meet this Daniel.'

Chapter Nineteen

I'm determined to do better at this week's meeting of the cookie club. I can't risk Daniel turning up on the doorstep bearing a plate of *langues de chat*, while all I have to show for my week is a batch of scorched shortbread.

I've finally realised where I've been going wrong. The secret is to ignore everything celebrity chefs tell me to do and use the simplest recipes I can find. I can always add my individual touches once I'm sure I've mastered the basic recipe.

With any luck, Gran will be home this week, and I may be able to withdraw gracefully from the baking part of the club. I'm only standing in for her while she's away. I'm not a proper member, which means there's no real reason I should continue to take part. I could be more usefully employed in making the tea and keeping an eye on Humphrey.

If so, will the club members suggest to Daniel that he withdraws too? They voted him in as an honorary member because they had no choice. The alternative would have been to kick him out and risk him spreading the story all over the village. He only wanted to join the club to annoy me. If I'm no longer taking part, that won't be necessary. He can go and play with his drones and forget all about baking cookies.

It's a nice thought, and I almost convince myself that's how it will play out. But I don't dare take the risk. For this week at least, I should be prepared to crush him – literally if need be. I scroll through various baking sites until I come across a recipe for cinnamon cookies. They look simple yet elegant. Maybe I could accessorise them with glitter to make them more seasonal. Do I mean accessorise? These baking terms are all so complicated. Decorate! That's the word. I can decorate them with edible glitter.

I get out the mixing bowl and prepare for action. Humphrey has been lying in his basket half asleep for the past hour, but at the first sound of me opening the larder door, he opens his eyes.

'Go back to sleep,' I tell him. 'This isn't for you. It's for the cookie club.'

I prop my phone on the counter and study the recipe. 'Take two cups of flour.' I frown at the screen. What is that supposed to mean? What sort of cups? I run an eye along the shelf above the kettle. There are several flowered teacups, two drinking glasses, and an enormous china mug saying *Best Dog Owner.*

Which one should I use? The flowered ones fit the technical definition of a cup. But the mug is much larger, so it ought to produce more cookies, which can only be a good thing. I pick up a teacup and dip it into the container of flour, then empty it out and replace it. I can't take the risk of its being the wrong size.

I read through the recipe again. One cup of butter and three quarters of a cup of sugar. This chef appears to be obsessed with the subject of cups. Perhaps their hobby is collecting rare drinking receptacles from all over the world. Fair enough, but why use them for cooking instead of keeping them in a glass display case like other obsessive collectors?

I click through the recipes again until I find one that gives actual weights. That's more like it. I measure the ingredients into the bowl and stir them together. It takes a while because the butter is almost frozen solid. I make a mental note to melt it in the microwave next time and continue mixing. My arms start to ache, but I persevere. If I keep baking, I'll develop enormous biceps and be the envy of everyone at the gym. I'd have to join one first, but it would be worth it just to see all the admiring looks.

I'm sliding the finished tray into the oven when the doorbell rings. Humphrey leaps from his basket and surges down the hall, barking loudly.

'Stop it!' I tell him without much hope. Once he starts, he takes a while to wind down, rather like a music box.

'Just a minute!' I call through the door, pulling the latch across before turning the handle. I have no intention of joining Humphrey in a brisk jog up the street today, no matter how aerobically beneficial it may be.

When I'm sure there's no chance of him escaping, I open the door a crack. If this is someone trying to sell me new guttering or persuade me to join some weird cult, they'll be sorry.

'Hello there,' says a familiar voice, and I sigh.

'What are you doing here?'

'I've come to collect Humphrey and take him round to your neighbour's house to apologise for stealing their laundry.'

'That was nothing to do with Humphrey!' I say. 'It was all your idea, and I won't have you blaming him for it. You can apologise to whomever you like, but you're not dragging Humphrey into it.'

'It was the other way around,' says Daniel. 'He was dragging me. That's why I had to improvise a makeshift lead.'

'You're wasting your time,' I tell him. 'He's staying here with me. If that's all –'

'I'm also here to see you,' he says. 'I won't stick my foot in the door again because I'm sure you'd slam it shut. But I'm hoping you'll let me in for a few minutes.'

Humphrey gives a delighted bark and scrabbles at the door.

'Traitor!' I tell him. I unlatch the door and open it a little further. 'What do you really want?'

'To see how Humphrey is after his adventure.'

'As you can see, he's fine. But I don't want him getting cold, so I'll have to close the door now.'

'And to talk to you,' he says.

I'm about to refuse when I realise this is the perfect opportunity for us to have a reasonable discussion, during which I can inform him of my resolution to withdraw from the club the minute Gran gets home and suggest he does the same.

I open the door just far enough for him to squeeze inside without Humphrey escaping. 'I'm busy right now, but you can come in for five minutes if you must. You'll have to leave any drones outside.'

He laughs. 'I don't have any with me. Do you think I take them for an afternoon walk every day?'

'That's what you were doing the first time I met you.'

'I was taking it down to the field for a test flight,' he says. 'Not showing it all the local sights.'

Once inside, he pulls off his coat and grins at me. 'Do you always welcome your neighbours with such enthusiasm and display of rural hospitality?'

'Only the annoying ones. You can hang your coat on that peg.'

He follows me down the hall to the kitchen. 'How are you?'

'Busy.'

'I won't take up too much of your valuable time,' he says.

'I'm sorry. I was making some cookies when you arrived, and I was finding the whole thing rather frustrating.'

I catch his eye and flush. 'I don't mean it's particularly difficult. But it's one more thing to do on top of everything else.'

'The first time we met, you told me baking was one of the most difficult things in the world,' he says.

'I was having a bad day. It's quite simple, really. I'm surprised you would think otherwise.'

The corners of his mouth twitch. 'I bow to your superior knowledge. Anyway, I'm not here to exchange baking tips. My landlady told me she'd heard your grandmother may be coming home this week. I wondered whether you needed any help getting the house ready for her?'

'You mean cleaning?' I ask.

'More like fitting a grab rail for her in the shower – things like that.'

I'm taken aback by this thoughtful gesture. 'That's very kind of you. I'd really appreciate that. One of the nurses mentioned she might need some adaptations. I was planning to call a handyman.'

'No need,' he says. 'I'm good at that sort of thing. And diagnosing blocked pipes just by looking at them.'

I laugh as I remember our club meeting. 'I don't think I'd trust you with anything plumbing-related. You're definitely no Steve Wately. But the shower thing would be good. Thanks, Daniel.'

'And I'm happy to stay with Humphrey whenever you go to collect your grandmother,' he says. 'It may take longer than you expect. I picked up a friend after his operation last year and had to sit in the waiting room for hours while they waited for all the right people to sign the forms and the doctors to check him over before he left. Then we had to stop by the pharmacy and pick up his meds.'

I waver. It's true that Humphrey has been fine by himself when I've visited Gran, but I've never been gone for more than an hour or two. If I end up stuck at the hospital for the entire afternoon, who knows what Humphrey might get up to all by himself? He may escape from the house somehow and end up in the mud-hole again, and I'll arrive home to find him wearing Gran's pink dressing gown.

'I could take him for a walk,' offers Daniel. 'I know where his favourite field is, and I could use a proper lead this time.'

'Would you like a cup of tea?' I ask to give myself time to think.

'I thought you'd never ask. I'll make it. I know where everything is. I've been here before, remember?'

'I'm not likely to forget.'

'I had a great time at the cookie club,' he says. 'Who would have thought there would be secret societies and goings-on in such a sleepy little village as Honeywell? It's like something out of Agatha Christie.'

'Except that no one was murdered.'

'You said that with a little too much regret. Did you mind me being there?'

I'm about to say yes, but it strikes me I'm being ridiculous. He gate-crashed a cookie club, not the secret society to promote cyber-warfare across the entire New Forest area. Technically, he didn't even gate-crash it. Our initial meeting was accidental, and I was the one who told him all about the club. If I hadn't overreacted in the way I did, he wouldn't have taken my words as some sort of ridiculous challenge and turned up at the house the following day. I only have myself to blame.

'It's fine,' I say. 'I told Gran all about it when I visited her. I thought she'd be upset, but she appeared to find the whole situation amusing.'

'I'm glad to hear it,' he says. 'I look forward to meeting her.'

Humphrey has been taking a well-earned nap in his basket. He opens one eye and looks at Daniel.

'He seems to like the idea of me looking after him for a while,' says Daniel.

'Fine, you can watch him if you want.' I hear how ungracious this sounds and add a belated, 'Thank you.'

'I'll look forward to it,' he says. 'I've often wished I could have a dog, but I move around so much it wouldn't be fair.'

'What kind of dog would you have?'

'One exactly like Humphrey.'

'There are no dogs exactly like Humphrey. He's one of a kind. I've always thought that was a good thing. I never imagined anyone would want to duplicate him.'

'I doubt I'll ever own somewhere large enough for a dog his size,' he says.

'This is a tiny cottage, but Gran seems to make it work. I'm starting to doubt your commitment to this whole dog thing.'

'He's obviously very happy here. But I may stick to a slightly smaller breed when I get a dog of my own.'

I look at Humphrey, sprawled half in and half out of his basket, his legs all going in different directions. I'm never sure how he does that. It looks as though he has several destinations in mind and can't quite decide which one to pursue first, so he's keeping all his options open.

'I'm not sure Humphrey counts as any kind of breed,' I say. 'My personal theory is that he's the original dog designed by a committee. No one could agree on the essential features, and they ended up with this.'

Daniel bends down to pat Humphrey's head. 'I think the committee did a great job. They may have gone overboard a bit on the size, but I expect that was a mixture of enthusiasm and inexperience. They got it just right with the rest of him.'

'Gran certainly thinks so. She's besotted with him. I won't say he's a substitute for my grandfather. No one could be that. But he's the perfect companion for her. She told me once he gave her a reason to get up in the morning after Grandpa Ed's death. After a while, it became a habit, and now she wakes up excited to face the day and discover what Humphrey will find for them to do.'

'No wonder he's so precious to her,' he says. 'I promise to look after him and keep him out of trouble. No more running off to search for mud.'

'And for goodness' sake use his proper harness and lead,' I warn him. 'Gran will suffer a relapse if she sees you walking him around the garden using one of her torn up sheets as a lead.'

'Why are her sheets torn up?' he asks.

'They're not.'

'Then, why …?'

'I'm talking about you tearing them up, as you very well know. And I'm telling you not to.'

He reaches into his pocket and pulls out a pen. 'Do you have a piece of paper I could use to note all this down? It's all too much for me to remember by myself.'

'How difficult is it to remember to keep Humphrey safely away from the water meadows and not to use various pieces of clothing or bedding instead of his lead?'

Daniel drops the pen back into his pocket. 'When you put it like that, it doesn't sound too bad. But I can't give you any absolute guarantees.'

Chapter Twenty

The kettle switches itself off, and he picks up the container of tea. 'How strong do you like it?'

'Medium. The milk's in the fridge.'

He reaches up to the shelf for a couple of cups and frowns. 'This one appears to have flour on it.'

'I don't think so. It's … dust.'

He inspects the cup more closely. 'It's an odd colour for dust.'

'What colour is dust supposed to be?'

'Greyish, in my experience. This is white.'

'Dust goes white when it's old,' I say, adopting an air of expertise, although why anyone would want to claim to know all the facts about dust, I have no idea. I'm not likely to appear on Mastermind any time soon. 'This is Lucy Hollis. She lives in London and works as a translator. Her special subject tonight is the history and evolution of dust – both local and foreign. Lucy, your two minutes start now!'

'That must be a countryside thing,' he says. 'In the city, it stays the same colour for years. Believe me, I know. I had a flatmate once who refused to clean his room because he was convinced that clean surfaces attract dust faster, which forces people to do more housework. His theory was that by leaving it well alone, it stops increasing and disappears entirely.'

'A self-cleaning house?' I say. 'That's the dream. Did it work?'

'Not even close. All that happened was he developed asthma and had to move out.'

'Couldn't he just have cleaned his room?' I ask.

'I suggested it several times, but he refused to accept the connection. He hinted at one point that I was in the pay of Big Cleaning.'

'Interesting,' I say. 'How do I know you aren't? You may have offered to look after Humphrey to give yourself the opportunity to snoop around the house, looking for ways to sell me your products.'

'I doubt anyone has made one to deal with persistent white dust. It's a real gap in the market.'

He pours me a cup of tea and hands me the milk. 'You don't take sugar, do you?'

'No, but there's a bowl of sugar lumps in the pantry if you do. Gran has two lumps in her tea. She doesn't like to use regular sugar. She says it makes her tea taste funny.'

'Aren't sugar lumps just compressed sugar?' he asks.

'I think so. But she insists she can tell the difference, so she continues to buy lumps. Grandpa Ed used to sneak me a few after dinner when Mum wasn't looking. We'd take them out to his shed and share them while he showed me whatever he'd been making that day. He was very good with his hands. He and Gran never threw anything away. He was always mending and repairing things.'

I point to a kitchen chair. 'I helped him fix that one. Someone had left it on the street for anyone who wanted it. Not surprisingly, no one did. It only had two legs, and the back strut was missing. Grandpa Ed and I spent a day in his shed mending it. He showed me how to use his lathe to make new legs and round them off. I remember how proud I was when it was finished and we took it in to show everyone. It must have been sat on thousands of times, even by Humphrey when he gets the chance. He likes to climb onto anything that will bear his weight – and several things that don't.'

'If you can construct something that can withstand Humphrey, you're clearly a skilled craftswoman,' he says.

'I was mostly in charge of the gluing,' I admit. 'But I finished this leg off on the lathe. That's why it's not as smooth as the others. But it does the job, and everyone kindly pretended not to notice. How about you? I suppose you must be quite technically minded if you fly drones for a living.'

'I don't build them from scratch,' he says. 'I just operate the controls.'

'That's disappointing. You're missing out on the satisfaction of creating something all by yourself – like me and that chair leg. Grandpa was right when he said all the traditional skills are dying out.'

'I'm not sure building a drone counts as a traditional skill,' he says. 'It isn't something that's been handed down through the generations by our forefathers.'

'Grandpa would have enjoyed it. He loved learning new things. The first thing he did when he and Gran bought a computer was to take it apart to see how it worked.'

'And how did that go?' he asks, taking a sip of his tea.

'Not well,' I admit. 'He had to take it in to be repaired. At first, they told him it was under warranty, and he should just return it. That was before they saw what he'd done to it. But Grandpa told me the quickest way to learn something new is to strip it down and see what's inside it.'

'I'm glad he never got his hands on one of our drones,' says Daniel. 'With high-end cameras, some of them can cost fifty thousand pounds.'

'That can't be true!' I protest. 'You could buy a car for that. Possibly, more than one.'

'I'm afraid it is. It's why it took us so long to build the business. We had to expand fairly slowly and pay off one loan at a time. But it was what we wanted to do, so it was worth it.'

'I've always wanted to translate novels,' I say. 'But that sort of thing is difficult to break into. It can be a precarious life until you build up a reputation.'

'You could do it in your spare time,' he suggests. 'Plenty of people start off a new career that way. Marcus and I used to spend hours flying drones for fun before we decided to turn it into a full-time business.'

'Maybe. But I don't have much spare time. I work long hours, and I'm permanently exhausted.'

He nods towards Humphrey, who, for some reason, is lying on his back with his legs in the air, peddling furiously. 'Looking after him must be hard work too.'

'Looking after Humphrey doesn't take much time,' I say. 'Except when he decides to visit the spa for a mud facial.'

'And you have to bake cookies for the club,' he says.

'That's simply a case of mixing the ingredients together and putting them into the oven.'

'I'd forgotten what a skilled baker you were,' he apologises.

'I'm a Hollis. It's in my genes. Don't forget my great-grandmother was the founder of this club.'

He looks interested. 'I didn't know that sort of thing was passed down the generations. I always thought genes controlled things like blue eyes or short-sightedness.'

'Talent can be passed down as well,' I assure him. 'Haven't you ever heard of someone having a natural talent for something? Where do you think that comes from?'

'Chance?' he suggests.

'Genes. Ask any scientist.'

'So, my talent for flying drones is a genetic legacy? How does that work? They only started being available commercially in the past twenty years.'

'It's the principle of the thing,' I explain. 'Maybe one of your ancestors was a fighter pilot.'

'Not that anyone has ever mentioned.'

'Then maybe you shouldn't be unleashed on the unsuspecting local citizens.'

'Speaking of unsuspecting local citizens,' he says, 'Humphrey is begging to be unleashed on them.'

I turn to look at Humphrey, who has picked up his lead and brought it over to me. He stares up at me hopefully, the lead dangling from his mouth. His meaning couldn't be any more clear.

'Just a short walk,' I tell him. 'We'll take a longer one this evening.'

'I'll come with you if you like,' says Daniel. 'Even if you don't want Humphrey to accompany me to apologise for the sock theft, you can show me exactly how you like him to be walked.'

'On his lead,' I say. 'And not in anyone else's garden. Otherwise, you'll be fine.'

He pulls on his coat. 'It wasn't snowing when I walked here, but the sky was grey, so it might start again at any moment. Does Humphrey wear a coat and little bootees? Perhaps you could shop at the same store London Zoo uses? *Giant Pets R Us* has been supplying the zoo by royal charter for more than two hundred years. You should pop in one day and ask for the baby elephant section. It's where they keep all their Dumbo-themed clothes. They should suit Humphrey very well. And you could buy him an out-sized tuxedo for special occasions.'

'I don't think he's invited to many special occasions,' I say.

'After witnessing his performance last night, I'm not surprised. However, with the right wardrobe, all that may change.'

I clip on Humphrey's harness and attach his lead, which I hand to Daniel. 'If you're planning to walk him at some point, you may as well get used to each other now.'

He takes the lead and winds it around his hand a couple of times. 'Once bitten, twice shy. You won't be getting away from me today, young man.'

'Either that or you'll end up in the emergency room with a sprained wrist,' I say.

'That would be convenient for you. You could visit me when you've finished visiting your grandmother.'

'Not a hope,' I say. 'Have you seen how much they charge for hospital parking these days? I'm in and out as quickly as possible. I don't have time for detours.'

'That's a shame. I was hoping you'd bring me some cookies while I was waiting to be assessed.'

He sniffs. 'Speaking of cookies, didn't you say you were making some before I arrived? Shouldn't they be ready by now?'

I'd forgotten about the cookies. I wonder why the timer hasn't pinged. I snatch up the oven gloves and bend down to look. To my horror, I realise that not only did I forget to set the timer, I forgot to turn the oven on. But there's no way I'm telling Daniel that.

I straighten up and drop the gloves back onto the countertop. 'They're fine.'

'You didn't open the oven door to check.'

'I didn't need to. I'd forgotten they need a couple of hours to ...' I cast around for something that sounds like a proper culinary term and remember Delia's cookbook. 'To prove!' I say triumphantly.

'Isn't that something to do with bread?' he asks.

'We generally use that term when we're talking about bread making. But it's also a technique that chefs use for certain types of cookies.'

'How fascinating,' he says. 'May I ask which type you're making today?'

I don't dare name a variety of cookie, not without knowing what the word prove means. I'd be sure to give myself away.

'I can't tell you,' I say. 'I'll be baking them for this week's cookie club, and you know they're supposed to be a surprise.'

He twists Humphrey's lead even more tightly around his hand. 'Of course. I'm sorry I asked. I look forward to trying them at the meeting if there are any extras.'

I follow him down the hall towards the front door, noticing he has no difficulty keeping Humphrey in check.

'Are you sure you don't mind me coming with you?' he asks. 'It would be good to get some practise with him and pick up some tips.'

'Not at all,' I say. 'But it will have to be a short walk. I have a lot to do today.'

'We can stay out for just as long as it takes your cookies to prove,' he says, holding open the door for me. 'I know how important timings are when you're baking. You'll want to switch the oven on at just the right moment to avoid them collapsing.'

That does it! I'm walking up to The Sugarloaf Bakery first thing tomorrow morning and asking Abby for cookery lessons.

Chapter Twenty-One

Humphrey and I walk up to the village after breakfast the following day. As usual, he stops to sniff every single blade of grass and plant on the way. He last sniffed them twelve hours ago. What does he expect to have changed in the meantime? I'd like to ask him, but there's no point. Even if he could speak, I doubt I would understand his reasons.

He and I are very different. When it's this cold, I have an overwhelming desire to stay at home next to the fire and watch the snowflakes fall from inside a warm and cosy living room. Whereas Humphrey would spend all his time outside if he could, crashing around the neighbourhood making friends with the unsuspecting local wildlife. If his genetic makeup is ever examined, I suspect he'll turn out to be equal part wolf and teddy bear.

The high street is almost deserted, which doesn't surprise me. I wouldn't be out on a day like this unless necessity demanded it.

Lily greets me with a cheerful smile when I walk into the bakery. 'Hello, Lucy. Hello, Humphrey. What can I get for you both today?'

I order a coffee and an apricot Danish while Humphrey looks up at her imploringly.

'Will he be having his usual?' she asks.

I smile down at him as he shifts from foot to foot in his anxiety to know what flavour this morning's biscuits will be. 'I'll let you choose for him.'

She brings my coffee over a few minutes later, and I ask whether Abby is working today.

'She's here until two o'clock,' she says. 'Did you want to see her?'

'I was hoping to ask her something. Maybe I could ask you instead.'

She sits down at my table. Humphrey is busy with his second biscuit and doesn't look up. She strokes his ears and smiles at me. 'How can I help you?'

'I was wondering whether Abby might be prepared to give me a couple of cookery lessons. I know she doesn't have much time, but I'm desperate.'

I hadn't intended to say that. The last thing I want is for Daniel to hear about this. I've told him how professionally I can cook, so he would be well within his rights to wonder why such an experienced chef would need any extra help.

'As a matter of fact, she does give lessons,' says Lily. 'We sometimes hold evening classes at the bakery, although not in the run up to Christmas. I don't know whether she'll have time at the moment, but we can ask her. She's due for a break soon. I'll tell her you were asking.'

Abby appears ten minutes later and comes over to my table carrying a cup of coffee. 'Lily said you wanted to talk to me.'

'Not to complain about anything,' I say before she can get the wrong idea. 'This apricot Danish is delicious.'

She looks amused. 'So, you just wanted to compliment the chef?'

'Not exactly. I wanted to ask whether you might be free sometime to give me a cookery lesson. But not if you're too busy. It was just an idea.'

'Do you want to learn anything special?' she asks.

'I need to bake some cookies.'

'Any cookies in particular?'

'Fancy cookies,' I say, and she laughs.

'Can you be more specific?'

I'd like to tell her I want to wipe the floor with Daniel, to crush him beyond hope of recovery, and to make him wish he'd never heard of the Honeywell Christmas Cookie Club. But I refrain. To an outsider, that may sound a little extreme. So, I content myself with saying, 'I'd like to bake the sort of things you might find in Harrods or Fortnum and Mason.'

She raises an eyebrow. 'Is there a specific reason why you need to become a pastry chef overnight? Do you have a YouTube channel or are you some kind of influencer?'

'Not at all. I can't even influence Humphrey not to dive into every puddle he sees. I could try to go viral with videos of him chasing birds, but I'm not sure it would catch on. I'm afraid I can't tell you exactly why I need to learn to bake, but I'd be everlastingly grateful if you could help me learn a few techniques. I have no idea what I'm doing. I can't even figure out how my grandmother's oven works.'

'I don't have a lot of spare time,' she says. 'But I could squeeze you in for an hour or two tomorrow evening. How would five thirty work for you?'

'That would be perfect!' I say. 'Thank you so much.'

'Is there anything specific you'd like to start with?' she asks.

'I'm not too sure. I was hoping you might suggest something exotic.'

She considers this. 'In my experience, making a simple recipe extremely well can be more effective than attempting something too complicated and doing it poorly.'

'I expect you're right,' I say. 'But not too simple. I need to make something eye-catching.'

'I'll think about it and try to come up with a recipe that looks good but is fairly foolproof,' she says.

'I'm sorry I can't tell you more about why I want to do this. I know how busy you must be. I wouldn't ask if it wasn't important.'

'Don't worry about it,' she says. 'I always enjoy helping people learn to bake. I often give private lessons. Sometimes, I combine them if there's more than one person wanting to learn. It keeps the price down.'

'That sounds good,' I say. 'But I'm happy to pay whatever it costs. I wasn't sure you'd have the time.'

'I never have enough time for all the things I want to do,' she says. 'But somehow, it all gets done. I like to keep busy, which is lucky working in a place like this. And now I have to get back to the kitchen. Those mince pies won't bake themselves.'

I look out of the window as I finish my coffee. A few more people have appeared on the high street, heads down against the freezing wind. It's started to snow again. The flakes swirl and eddy around their heads. From inside the cosy bakery, it's the perfect Christmas scene, although I doubt that thought has crossed the shoppers' minds.

I nudge Humphrey with my toe. 'Time to go. Don't look at me like that. I know you'd like to stay here all day eating biscuits, and so would I. But we have a lot to do before Gran comes home, and I'd like you to start by hoovering out the spare room.'

Chapter Twenty-Two

When I leave the house the following evening, Humphrey is sprawled out on the sofa and barely stirs when I say goodbye. I gave him an extra-long walk this afternoon, so I'm hoping he'll sleep until I get back from my cookery lesson. I'd like to think he'll guard the house for me, but I have to admit no security outfit would recruit him as a guard dog. He's noisy enough, but I've never met such an uncoordinated animal. Any burglars would be halfway home before he'd untangled himself enough to chase after them.

It often seems as though he's a much smaller dog trapped inside a large dog costume. His real legs have a good idea of what they want to do, but the rest of him doesn't always respond. Still, Gran didn't adopt him as a guard dog. She adopted him because she fell in love with him, and he with her. So, it isn't important that he'll never rival Kevin Costner in the bodyguard stakes.

I walk quickly up to the village. It's been a cloudy day, so it hasn't been as chilly as the last few days. But the sky has cleared now, and the temperature has dropped. It's a beautiful evening, but I hardly notice it as I pick up the pace and almost run towards the high street. The bakery is always lovely and warm and smells of cinnamon and vanilla. I wonder what Abby will teach me to bake. We may not start with cookies. She may decide to teach me something Christmassy like stollen or panettone.

'I'm afraid we're closed,' says Lily, who's busy wiping down the table nearest to the counter. She looks up and realises who it is. 'Sorry, Lucy. I'd forgotten you were coming. Abby said you should go through as soon as you arrived.'

I find Abby sitting in the kitchen drinking a cup of coffee and leafing through a binder. She jumps up when she sees me. 'Hi, Lucy. Right on time.'

'I didn't want to keep you waiting. I'm so grateful you agreed to do this at all.'

'It's fine,' she says. 'My partner is working late this evening. He's picking me up later, and we're going to the Christmas fair before meeting some friends for dinner. Have you visited it yet?'

'I haven't been anywhere except the field near the water meadows and the streets around our house. I'm not sure Humphrey would be welcome at the fair.'

'They allow dogs if they're kept on their leads,' she says.

'That's true of a lot of places. But I doubt it really applies to dogs like Humphrey. He has a large helping of carthorse in his genes.'

'I see your point,' she says. 'I know Bernie's owners always take him, but he's only small.'

'I can just imagine the scene,' I say. 'The stalls would go down like dominoes, leaving Humphrey sitting in the middle of the wreckage with that puzzled look he always wears when he's sat on something and broken it.'

The shop door jangles, and I hear the sound of voices.

'That will be my other pupil,' says Abby. 'Did Lily mention I'd found someone else who wants a cookery lesson? I hope that's alright with you. It will keep the costs down.'

'Someone else wants to learn to bake?' I ask, surprised.

'It was a bit of a coincidence, but this is the time of year for baking. He seemed very nice, and he was anxious to start at once.'

'He?' I say, a flicker of suspicion curling around my brain.

The kitchen door opens, and I turn to find my worst fears confirmed.

'Hello, Lucy,' says Daniel pleasantly. 'What a surprise to see you here today.'

'Do you know each other?' Abby asks me.

'You could say that.'

'I've always said what a small world it is,' says Daniel.

I roll my eyes. 'Everyone says that. You're not the first person to come up with the phrase. It's a massive cliché.'

Abby looks from me to Daniel. 'I hope neither of you minds me booking a double lesson. It seemed the best thing to do.'

'I'm delighted,' says Daniel. 'I'm just a little surprised. Lucy is such an accomplished cook, I didn't think she had anything more to learn.'

'Only arrogant people think they have nothing to learn,' I say.

Abby looks puzzled. 'I thought you hadn't done any baking before, Lucy?'

'I said not much,' I correct her. 'Obviously, I know the basics.'

Too late, I remember telling her I wasn't even sure how to switch the oven on.

'How about you?' I ask Daniel. 'What brings you here this evening?'

'The same as you, I imagine. It's an arrogant chef who thinks they know everything.'

'But you both seemed in such a hurry for this lesson,' says Abby. 'I thought you were complete beginners. Perhaps I should revise what I was planning to do with you today.'

'No!' Daniel and I say simultaneously.

'There's no need for that,' I add. 'It never hurts to go over the basics. There's always something new you can learn.'

'Exactly,' agrees Daniel. 'It's how all the great chefs work. Isn't that right, Abby?'

'Most people like to move on once they've mastered the basics,' she says.

'Obviously, Lucy and I approach the whole thing differently,' he says. 'She and I are perfectionists. I thought the first time we met how similar we were, and this only goes to prove it.'

'That's great,' says Abby. 'Shall we get on with the lesson?'

'Certainly,' he says. 'We can discuss our similarities another time. Perhaps over a drink at The Red Lion when we finish here?'

'I have to get home to Humphrey,' I say.

'Then, let's make a start,' says Abby. 'The recipe I've chosen combines several different techniques you may find useful.'

She points to the sink and tells us to wash our hands.

'It's like being back at school,' says Daniel. 'I remember washing my hands each day after playing in the sand pit.'

'I assume that would have been at secondary school?' I say.

'That's right. I took a GCSE in advanced sand sculpture.'

I reach for the towel and dry my hands. 'How did you do?'

'Not well, I'm afraid. I think the sand was too dry or something.'

'All set?' asks Abby. 'I thought we could start by finding out what you do and don't know.'

'Lucy knows everything there is to know about cookery,' says Daniel. 'She told me so herself the last time I saw her.'

'And Daniel is an experienced baker,' I say. 'He couldn't stop talking about it.'

'Why don't you both tell me what you're hoping to achieve in this lesson?' she asks. 'And I'll do my best to provide it.'

Daniel and I glance at each other. I'm fairly sure we're thinking the same thing. If we're not careful, either Abby will decide there's nothing she can teach us or she'll realise we've been lying to her and fail us on the spot. Is that a thing with cookery lessons or only sand sculpture examinations?

'There's no harm in refreshing the basics,' I say hoping Abby won't mention how desperate I was when I begged her to help me.

She points to a table at the far end of the kitchen. 'I've set up over there. Let's start with the basic ingredients and take it from there.'

She hands us both aprons, and we put them on.

Shall we make a start?' she asks.

'I'm ready,' I say.

Daniel smooths down his apron and gives me an irritating smile. 'Me too. Let the contest begin!'

'This is a bakery lesson, not the Hunger Games,' I say under my breath.

'I've weighed out all the ingredients to save time,' says Abby. 'I assume neither of you has any trouble with the concept of scales or weights?'

'I expect Daniel does,' I say. 'You've heard him boasting about his failed exams. I wouldn't be surprised if he had to repeat his reception year several times.'

'Miss Bright gave us an excellent grounding in weights and volume,' says Daniel. 'I was top of the class in pouring water from a large container into a smaller one and proving it couldn't be done. I was very good at fetching a cloth to wipe up afterwards too.'

'A simple yes or no will suffice,' says Abby.

'I'm sorry,' I apologise. 'I didn't mean to waste your time by talking about irrelevant things. Neither did Daniel.'

'Let's start by adding the butter and flour into the bowl and rubbing them into breadcrumbs,' she says.

I tip the cubes of butter into my bowl and add what I assume is the flour. It's a fine white powder, which means it's either flour, icing sugar, or baking powder. I'm a little hazy about the purpose of baking powder, but I don't remember any of the recipes I've made so far calling for more than a couple of teaspoons of it. I don't dare ask Abby in front of Daniel. I want to appear like someone who's very much at home in the baking arena but who recognises there's always room for improvement and isn't too proud to pick up tips from an expert.

'Mission successfully completed,' says Daniel. 'Where are the breadcrumbs?'

Abby smiles. 'I'm never sure when you're being serious.'

It seems safe for me to smile too. I'm not sure why she thinks he isn't serious, but it's always good to hedge your bets.

'You said something about breadcrumbs,' says Daniel. 'I don't seem to have any here. How about you, Lucy?'

I'm almost sure this is a trick question, but I'm not sure why. And I don't want to make a fool of myself by falling into whatever trap he's set for me.

'I'm not talking about real breadcrumbs,' says Abby. 'I'm talking about the baking technique where you rub the butter and flour between your fingertips until they combine and look like breadcrumbs.'

I'm glad I didn't say anything to incriminate myself. This way, I can maintain my pretence of culinary expertise a little longer.

'I'm surprised you've never heard of that,' I tell Daniel. 'It's a fairly basic technique.'

'Is that right?' he says. 'Would you mind demonstrating so I can get the hang of it?'

'Perhaps it would be better for Abby to do it while we both watch. I know how I usually rub the breadcrumbs into … I mean the butter … how I do it. But she may have something up her sleeve to speed up the process.'

'Not really,' says Abby. 'I'm sorry, but I've just realised the slow-rise dough is ready for kneading. It would be great to get a jump on that for tomorrow morning. Do you mind if I sort that out while you two make a start on this?'

'Not at all,' says Daniel. 'Take all the time you need. I'll watch Lucy and copy what she does.'

'Thanks. I'll only be a couple of minutes.' She walks over to a machine and switches it on.

Daniel gives me an expectant smile. 'Over to you, Lucy!'

'You don't need me to show you how to do something as simple as this,' I say. 'You heard what Abby said – you rub the breadcrumbs together until they're ready.'

'I'm not sure that's what she said, but I bow to your superior knowledge.'

He folds his arms and leans back against a pillar to watch me. There's nothing for it. Maybe if I assume an air of competence, the rest will follow.

I take a deep breath and plunge my hands into the mixing bowl. It feels revolting. The butter is cold and slimy. I move it around a bit to collect the flour, but nothing happens. I pinch my fingers together, and the butter slides through them and shoots towards the other side of the bowl.

I retrieve it and roll it in the flour again before giving it another good pinch. This time, a chunk of butter flies out of the bowl, skids across the table, and lands on the floor. I can't use it in the cookies now. It may have picked up all sorts of dirt. I'm fairly sure you aren't supposed to throw your ingredients all over the floor before returning them to your bowl and carrying on as though nothing has happened.

I drop the piece of butter into a nearby bin and return to the table.

Daniel looks from me to the mixing bowl. 'What now?'

'What do you mean?' I plunge my hands back in, trying not to shudder at the feel of the slimy paste beneath my fingers.

'Aren't you going to replace the butter you sent flying?'

'It fell on the floor, remember?'

He grins. 'Fell is rather a passive word. I'd prefer to say it flew through the air like the latest military jet plane, crash-landing three metres away from the launch site.'

'I'm still not using it in my dough,' I tell him.

'Don't you need to replace it with the same amount of butter?'

'That won't be necessary. This isn't a chemistry lesson where the exact proportions are of vital importance. Cookery is an art, not a science.'

'Fascinating,' he says. 'It's great to get an insight into a new subject from someone as qualified as you.'

I grab another chunk of butter, careful to squeeze it more gently this time. I don't want Abby to return to find all the ingredients she's carefully weighed and chopped are lying on her kitchen floor. She might slip on them and go flying. How would I explain to Lily I'd only been here for five minutes before hospitalising her pastry chef with a severe concussion?

I could blame the whole thing on Daniel. He and I are the only two witnesses, so it would be his word against mine. I glance around the kitchen but don't see any CCTV cameras. Why would there be? It's unlikely there's much risk of burglary in a village bakery. But they might be using them as a live stream for a reality TV cookery programme. If so, I'm in trouble. The entire nation will have seen me dropping the deadly butter trail into Abby's path. I'll never be able to pin the blame onto Daniel.

'Everything alright over here?' asks Abby, switching off the mixer and walking towards us.

'Mind the floor!' I say. 'I dropped some butter. If you give me a cloth, I'll wipe it up before anyone slips on it.'

'I'll do that for you,' offers Daniel. 'I'd hate to break your rhythm with the breadcrumbs. I'm learning so much.'

Abby hands him a cloth, and he kneels down to clean the floor.

'It's as though a giant, buttery snail has gone past,' he says chattily, giving it one final wipe.

'That looks almost as much fun as playing in a sandpit,' I tell him.

He straightens up and grins at me. 'You're right. I'm having a lot of fun this evening.'

I'm glad one of us is. This lesson isn't turning out as I expected. I saw myself spending an hour in a cosy kitchen with Abby, while she imparted a few little-known yet stunningly effective techniques that would enable me to knock the socks off everyone at the cookie club, and Daniel in particular.

Instead, I've ended up having to share a lesson with my arch nemesis. To add insult to injury, I'm making a complete fool of myself in front of him. Not for the first time. There are some people who bring out the worst in me for no discernible reason, and Daniel appears to be one of them. The only thing to do is stay away from them. I'd love to follow this advice, but it's a little difficult at this precise moment.

'Let's have a look how you're doing,' says Abby. She peers into my mixing bowl. To my annoyance, I see her lips twitch.

'I haven't finished,' I say. 'I was delayed by dropping that piece of butter, so I'm not quite at the breadcrumb stage yet. But I'm almost there.'

'I'm finding this entire process quite fascinating,' says Daniel. 'I can't wait for that magical moment when it all comes together and turns into breadcrumbs. It's like an experiment when you combine two chemicals and they react with each other to produce the desired result.'

He claps his hand to his forehead. 'That's a ridiculous analogy. I'd forgotten that cookery is more of an art than a science.'

'Is it?' asks Abby.

'Lucy thinks so. She was explaining the concept to me while you were busy with the dough.'

'I was simplifying it for you,' I say. 'Obviously, there's a certain amount of science in it too.'

'I would say cookery is more of a science when you're a beginner,' says Abby. 'It's important to follow the recipes until you've got the hang of basic cooking techniques and understand why they're written as they are and how the ingredients combine to produce the correct results. After that, it's fine to deviate from them in small ways and be creative. That's when cookery becomes more of an art, and a chef can start to produce signature dishes.'

'Lucy told me the proportions don't matter,' says Daniel.

'I'm afraid that's not quite true when you're making pastry,' says Abby. 'The proportions are very important.'

'That's not quite what I said,' I tell her, shooting a baleful look at Daniel. 'All I meant was that it was only a small piece of butter, and it wouldn't make much difference.'

'It was about a quarter of the butter in your bowl,' says Daniel. 'But you spilled quite a bit of flour while you were working the mixture into breadcrumbs, so I expect you thought it would all balance out.'

'You have lost a fair amount of flour,' says Abby. 'What happened?'

'I wasn't concentrating as hard as I should have been,' I say. 'Daniel was distracting me with irrelevant chatter.'

'Not to worry,' she says. 'Perhaps I'll just …'

She drops another cube of butter into my bowl, plunges in her hands, and does something mysterious for a few seconds. She tips up the bowl to show us the result. 'Breadcrumbs!'

I have no idea what she's done, but the slimy chunks of butter have disappeared, and so has the flour. In their place are tiny grains of what do actually look like breadcrumbs.

'That was going to be my next step,' I say. 'I was about to demonstrate the technique to Daniel when I lost that piece of butter.'

'You can demonstrate it with my ingredients if you like,' he offers.

'I'll bet you were the pupil always asking others to do your homework for you,' I say.

'You're quite right. I offered to pay Simon Peterson to sit my GCSE sand sculpture exams for me. Unfortunately, he was sick on the day of the final exam, which rather left me in the lurch. It's amazing how tiny things can change the course of your future forever. If it hadn't been for that, I might now have been one of the country's leading beach artisans.'

'I hate to rush you,' says Abby. 'But Chris is picking me up soon, and we haven't got as far as I'd hoped. Would you like me to finish this part for you, and then we can move on?'

'It might be best,' says Daniel. 'I can watch you and learn how to do it for next time. Lucy doesn't need to see this part. She already has her breadcrumb technique sorted.'

I don't answer but watch as Abby reaches for Daniel's bowl and deftly rubs the chunks of butter into the flour. It takes almost no time at all until she has his ingredients under control.

She hands him back his bowl. 'You see? It's very easy when you know how. The next thing is to add water to bind it together. Iced water is best. That isn't difficult at this time of year. Chris and I live in fear of the water freezing in our pipes. We live in an old flat that needs some serious re-plumbing, which we can't afford.'

She points to the jug of water on the table. 'That's nice and cold. I keep it in the fridge all day.'

Now is the time to redeem my shaky start and show I know what I'm doing. I pour a generous amount of water into my bowl, then pick up a spoon and start mixing, wondering whether there's some special technique I ought to be using – stirring anti-clockwise, for instance, or flicking my wrist to incorporate air.

'What are you doing?' Abby asks.

'Binding the pastry together,' I say, pleased to have remembered the technical term she's just used.

Daniel leans over to look. 'It's quite … runny, isn't it?'

I give it another brisk stir. 'The water soaks into the flour, and the mixture will thicken in the oven like a sauce.'

Abby is watching as though she can't believe her eyes. 'No, it won't. Have you never made pastry before?'

I stop stirring and try to look thoughtful. 'Pastry? As in pie crust?'

'As in basic pastry,' she says.

I look down at my bowl. The so-called breadcrumbs have disappeared. In their place is a sloppy, stringy mess. On the face of it, I have to admit this doesn't seem like something that might turn into a crisp golden sheet of pastry. But it hasn't been in the oven yet.

'It looks like the glue we used in primary school,' says Daniel.

I notice Abby staring at the floor, her left cheek twitching uncontrollably. Is she ill? Maybe she's angry at the waste of good ingredients. I don't know her well enough to tell.

I glance into my bowl again, hoping the flour will have performed its magic and done whatever it is that flour does – swelled, maybe – and turned into a nice, neat ball of pastry, all ready to be rolled out and formed into pastry shells. It hasn't. The contents of the bowl are as glue-like as ever. Daniel's right. It looks like the paste we used at school to stick cut-out shapes onto sugar paper.

I feel a brief flicker of hope there may be something wrong with the flour Abby gave us. That hope dies almost immediately. I've tasted some of the cakes that come out of this kitchen, and there's no way they were created using substandard ingredients. I have to face it. I'm a useless cook. I don't have a shred of natural talent, and I'm unable to follow even the simplest of instructions.

I push away the bowl and sit down at the table, burying my face in my arms.

'I give up,' I say. 'There's no point in pretending any further. I have no clue how to bake, and I doubt anyone could ever teach me.'

Chapter Twenty-Three

Neither of them speaks for a moment. I raise my head to see Daniel's lips are tightly pressed together, and his shoulders are shaking. Abby is staring at the floor. She looks up at last and meets my gaze, and I stare back at her. A small sound escapes her. Is she choking on something? It can't be my so-called pastry. It's too runny to block even the smallest windpipe.

Daniel makes a stifled noise, which seems to set her off. She starts to laugh – soundlessly at first, but increasing in volume as her entire body joins in. Her face turns red, and tears run down her cheeks.

I try to feel annoyed, but one look at the gluey mess in my bowl is enough to set me off. I laugh too, the tensions of the past week flowing out of me. It feels good. I hadn't realised how worried I've been about everything – Gran, my job, Humphrey, having to organise her beloved cookie club.

I laugh until the tears stream down my face, hardly aware of the others. I laugh until there's no energy in my body for anything else. At last, my shoulders relax, and I give a final, hiccupping sob.

Abby wipes her eyes. 'I'm sorry, Lucy. I couldn't help it. All those things you came out with about the mixture thickening in the oven were just too much. Especially when I saw what was in your bowl.'

'I'm glad to have amused you,' I say. 'I'm sorry about the wasted ingredients. I'll pay for them, of course.'

'I should pay you,' she says. 'I haven't laughed that hard in a long time.'

'I don't understand,' says Daniel. 'Are you telling me all Lucy's advice was worthless, when I've been hanging on her every word and treasuring it all up for future reference?'

'Give it up,' I advise him. 'You're not fooling anyone. It's obvious you and I have no idea what we're doing. I know why I was pretending, but I'm not sure why you were.'

'Because you're so competitive and have such a low opinion of my capabilities,' he says. 'How about you?'

Various explanations flit through my mind. But what's the point? I'm a terrible liar, and Daniel seems to read me like a book.

'Because I find you intensely annoying,' I say.

'I'd kind of picked that up. It's hard to say how. Tiny hints and vibes that would have gone over the head of a less sensitive person. No matter how hard you tried to hide it –'

'I didn't try to hide it at all.'

'That would have been why. Either way, it doesn't come as a huge surprise.'

I smile at him. 'I expect a lot of people tell you how annoying you are.'

'Daniel seems very likeable to me,' says Abby.

'That's because you don't know him,' I say. 'He can keep up the façade for a little while, but his true self always shines through in the end.'

She doesn't react in the way she should to this information. She looks more amused than horrified. 'How bad can he be?'

'How long do you have?'

'I'm right here,' says Daniel plaintively.

'You're always right there. And not in a good way, like when someone says, "I'm there for you." In your case, it's more like –' I break off, trying to think of an analogy.

'An annoying rash?' he suggests.

'Exactly. Or a mosquito.'

'In December?' asks Abby.

Daniel shakes his head. 'That's a terrible example, Lucy. You can't have been paying attention during your school biology lessons.'

'I meant in Australia,' I say. 'It's the middle of summer there.'

I'm half expecting him to look impressed at my Antipodean knowledge, but he only shakes his head again. 'Pathetic try.'

'Is that all?' asks Abby. 'Daniel is always there?'

'But it's the manner in which he's always there,' I explain. 'The first time I met him, he crashed into me because he wasn't looking where he was going, and he knocked a tray of cookies out of my hands.'

I see her eyes dart from my face to the bowl on the table. She doesn't say anything, but I'm sure I know what she's thinking.

'Today was a one-off,' I defend myself. 'The cookies Daniel destroyed were actually very good.'

'We'll never know that for sure,' says Daniel. 'For all we know, I may have done the world a favour. GPs are massively overstretched at this time of year without having to deal with cases of mass food poisoning.'

'I was taking them to my grandmother in the hospital,' I say.

'Even worse. The hospital owes me a letter of thanks. So, that's one of your objections disposed of.'

'In your opinion. But then you turned up at my house the following day.'

Abby stops smiling. 'That's not good.'

I feel a pang of guilt at having made Daniel sound like a crazed stalker. 'He kind of had a reason.'

I stop, unable to think of a convincing explanation for his presence that doesn't involve mentioning the existence of the cookie club.

'I was bringing her some replacement cookies,' says Daniel. 'As a peace offering, you might say.'

Abby's face relaxes. 'That was nice of you.'

'Wasn't it?' he agrees. 'But it was no good. Lucy hurled them all over the path.'

'That was an accident, as you very well know!' I protest.

'You told me it was. But it was difficult not to take it personally. However, being the bigger person, I rose above it and stepped in to help with your dog emergency.'

'Humphrey?' asks Abby. 'Is he alright?'

'He's fine,' I say. 'But that's another example of what I'm talking about. When Daniel arrived with his so-called replacement cookies, he left the garden gate open, and Humphrey made a break for it.'

'I rescued him,' Daniel defends himself.

'He wouldn't have needed rescuing if you hadn't let him escape. You can't cause a problem, then claim to be a hero for fixing it.'

'Hero?' says Daniel. 'That's a big word, but perhaps you're right. Let's go with that.'

'I'm so sorry,' I tell Abby. 'I can't tell you how terrible I feel about all this. I know how busy you must be at the moment. I've wasted your time after you were kind enough to offer me a lesson.'

'She's right,' says Daniel. 'I'd like to apologise too.'

Abby surveys us both. 'You'd better come with me.'

She walks towards the bakery, and we follow her. Is she about to open the door and throw us out into the snow like the little match girl? I've left my bag in the kitchen along with my phone and front door key. Daniel will have to cause a distraction while I run back to fetch it. Something tells me he won't have any trouble coming up with a hundred different ways to achieve that.

I walk over to the coat rack and reach up for my jacket.

'What are you doing?' asks Abby.

'It's snowing. I don't want to walk home without my coat.'

'We still have half an hour left of our lesson.'

'I know. I'm very sorry. Please add whatever you like to the bill.' I glance at Daniel. 'That's only fair, isn't it?'

'More than fair,' he says.

'Don't be ridiculous,' says Abby, and I'm relieved to see she's smiling. 'I haven't enjoyed myself so much for a long time.'

She opens a paper bag and picks up the tongs. 'Do you like Bakewell tarts?'

'I love them,' I say.

She drops several tarts into the bag and hands it to me.

'How about you?' she asks Daniel.

'I love them too.'

She hands him his bag. 'These are to inspire you. This is what we would have been making tonight if circumstances – by which I mean the pair of you – hadn't got in the way.'

'This is more than generous of you,' I say. 'Please add something to the bill and send it to Daniel.'

'Fine with me,' he says. 'This entire lesson ought to be on me. If it hadn't been for me distracting her, Lucy wouldn't have thrown her butter all over the floor, and none of this would have happened.'

'Some people aren't meant to become bakers,' I tell Abby. 'Obviously, I'm one of them. In the future, I'll stick to translation, and Daniel can stick to bothering the local inhabitants by zooming his cameras over their heads and invading their privacy.'

'I'm afraid I can't spare any more evenings before Christmas,' she says. 'Or I would insist you both came back until you'd learned at least some basic skills. In the meantime, I suggest you watch some YouTube videos. They're great for teaching new techniques step by step. Good luck!'

'I'll give it a go,' I say doubtfully. 'Although I can't guarantee it will work.'

'And now you can help me clean up before Chris arrives,' she says. 'That's one of the most basic kitchen skills of all – don't leave any trace behind when you finish cooking.'

She marches us back into the kitchen and hands us both a cloth.

'It's like being in the boy scouts again,' says Daniel. 'Akela taught me how to stay downwind when I was tracking animals and never to leave any indication I'd been there.'

'Are you telling me they took the cub scouts hunting?' I ask. 'That doesn't sound likely.'

He gives me a pitying look. 'It was for my photography badge. We did lots of litter picking too, which has prepared me for the task ahead of us. Cleaning up your buttery mess holds no terrors for the man who once took a picture of a fox's back leg disappearing into the undergrowth.'

'There's something I want to know,' I tell him. 'If you're as bad at baking as I am, how did you make the cookies you brought over to my house?'

He grins. 'My landlady made them for me.'

I'm about to accuse him of cheating when I remember Abby doesn't know about the cookie club and stop myself.

The shop bell jangles. A second later, the kitchen door opens, and a man puts his head around.

'How's it going in here?' he asks.

'We're finishing a little early today,' says Abby. 'Chris, this is Daniel and Lucy.'

He gives us a friendly smile. 'Nice to meet you both. How did the lesson go?'

'Abby was just saying I was tonight's star pupil,' says Daniel. 'Lucy did very well, but her heart didn't seem in it. Maybe next time.'

Chris looks around the kitchen. 'What did you make tonight? I can't smell anything.'

'That's because we haven't started the baking part of our journey,' says Daniel. 'Tonight was all about the theory. Abby insists on her pupils getting a grasp on the basics before she allows them anywhere near an actual oven. She bases her approach on the abstract rather than the practical method. It can be a little frustrating, but her pupils always thank her in the end.'

Chris glances at Abby, who shakes her head. 'I'll explain later.'

'I've only touched on the idea of her system,' says Daniel. 'Abby will explain it all to you in far more detail. It will give you something to talk about during your meal.'

Chris looks at his watch. 'We'd better get going if we want to visit the fair first.'

'Don't let us hold you up,' says Daniel. 'Lucy and I can look after ourselves. Have a lovely evening.'

'If I were you,' I tell Chris. 'I'd start by buying Abby a very large drink. And then I'd follow it up with several more.'

Abby locks up the bakery, and we watch them walk off in the direction of the Christmas fair.

'Speaking of very large drinks,' says Daniel, 'The Red Lion is just down the street. I think we should drink a toast to our successful lesson.'

'You and I have very different ideas about success,' I say. 'I really shouldn't. I can't leave Humphrey alone for too long.'

'I wasn't suggesting making an evening of it. But it feels important to mark the occasion somehow, and my landlady tells me their mulled wine is excellent. Just one glass?'

I waver. It's a bitterly cold night, and the thought of mulled wine is tempting.

'I'll walk you home afterwards and make sure you don't end up in the mud,' says Daniel.

'If your tracking skills are anything like your cookery skills, I'd be safer navigating home by myself. Fine, I'll come for one quick drink. And then I'm going home to see how Humphrey's doing.'

'Wonderful!' he says. 'It's important to celebrate the small victories in life. If you wait for the big victories, you miss out along the way. The Red Lion is down there by the crossroads. We should memorise the colour of each other's coats in case a blizzard hits and we can't see each other.'

'If a blizzard hits, I'll follow the sound of your voice,' I say. 'I can't imagine even the most violent snowstorm would stop you talking for long.'

Chapter Twenty-Four

The Red Lion is crowded when we enter. I expect it usually is. It's a lovely country pub with a welcoming atmosphere. There's a huge fire at one end with a couple of sofas next to it.

Daniel points. 'There's a table about to come free if you hurry. That couple is leaving. Why don't you grab that while I get our drinks?'

'Because I haven't yet told you whether I like mulled wine?'

'You want to argue with me while our only chance at getting a table slips away? You'd prefer to stand outside in the garden sipping your mulled wine and freezing to death?'

I consider telling him I never touch mulled wine, and all I want is a glass of mineral water. But there's no point in cutting off my nose to spite my face. I've always loved mulled wine.

'Fine,' I say. 'See you in a minute.'

He appears to read my mind. 'Text me if you really can't bear for me to be right about the best drink for a snowy night.'

I'm about to say I don't have his number when I notice a man eyeing the table Daniel pointed out. I push my way through the crowds and arrive a second before he does.

'Are you about to leave?' I ask the couple with a bright smile.

The woman finishes buttoning her coat. 'That's right. Would you like to sit here?'

'That's so kind of you,' I say, sinking into the chair she indicates and not meeting the hovering man's eye.

Daniel joins me a minute later with two glasses of steaming mulled wine.

'That was impressive,' he says, handing me a glass. 'It obviously wasn't your first attempt at snatching a seat from under a rival's nose. You did it so professionally.'

'I've had a lot of practice,' I tell him. 'Management cutbacks at work mean we're all hot-desking. We operate on a first-come, first-served basis, and the losers end up sitting on the floor. They tried to sell it to us as collaboration and space-efficiency, but it's just meanness.'

'You haven't told me much about your job,' he says. 'Until recently, I'd have hazarded a guess you worked as a professional chef, but I have to admit certain doubts have set in.'

'I'm a translator,' I say. 'I studied modern languages at university. I spent a year in Berlin after I graduated, then took a job for a cosmetics company based in London. I translate all our ad copy and brochures and promotional material into German for them.'

'You don't translate recipes in your spare time?' he asks.

'What spare time? I work for a woman who believes any of her employees who show the faintest sign of having a personal life should go on a watch list and be first in line for the next round of redundancies.'

'Aren't you working remotely at the moment?' he asks. 'How can she monitor your personal life from a distance?'

'No one in our department works remotely. Some of the other departments are more flexible, but not ours. Caroline believes that unless every one of her direct reports is physically in the office for at least ten hours a day, they'll be at home building blanket forts or writing the next great British novel.'

'Hasn't she heard of videoconferencing?'

'She has, but she doesn't approve of it. She thinks it can be nobbled to show her staff is online when they're actually creating an indoor obstacle course for their new puppy.'

'That's the sign of a bad manager,' he says. 'You have to show some faith in your staff if you want them to show faith in your company.'

'Caroline doesn't think so. Her motto is to keep your enemies close but your staff even closer.'

'I'm glad she has at least some humanity and allowed you to take emergency leave when you needed it.'

'She doesn't have any humane instincts,' I say. 'Left to herself, she would never have allowed me to come here.'

'Did you have to go to HR instead?'

'In our company, HR stands for Horrible Regulations. They're worse than Caroline.'

I take a sip of the mulled wine and feel a shot of warmth course through my veins. At this moment, Caroline feels pleasantly far away.

'I hate to be intrusive,' says Daniel. 'But I'm curious to know how you persuaded her that Humphrey was more important than their bottom line. Did you cite some little known ancient Germanic law? The Canine Companionship Act, perhaps?'

'I walked out.'

There's a brief pause.

'You walked out?' he asks. 'Literally?'

I take another sip of my wine. 'That's right. I picked up my bag when Mum called me, and I left the office.'

'And how did that go down with this Caroline woman?'

'Not well,' I confess. 'I called her as soon as I got home and told her what had happened and that I hadn't had the chance to talk to her before I left. You can imagine her reaction.'

'I'm imagining it now,' he says.

'I don't know what got into me. I was having a terrible day. I'd worked right through the weekend, and I was exhausted. People kept sending me documents and hounding me to finish them within the next hour. I hadn't eaten lunch, and then my computer packed up. The IT department only turns up if you're management, so I had no idea how long it would take to get it fixed. Then Mum called, and something inside me snapped.'

I turn back to Daniel. 'All I could think of was that my mother spends every day doing something important, even if she doesn't get much recognition for it. But I spend every day doing something I hate, simply to make money for a huge corporation. I could have asked Caroline for a few days of annual leave, but I was sure what her answer would be. I didn't want to listen to her explaining for the hundredth time that plenty of people are lining up to do my job and how important it is for us to hit our deadlines for the good of the company. For her good, she means. People at her level get huge productivity bonuses. None of which are passed on to menial employees like me, no matter how much overtime we've been forced to do.'

I pause for breath. That felt good. I haven't said that out loud to anyone before. There's no point complaining to my flatmates each night. They all have similar jobs and troubles of their own. And there's no way I'd ever mention it to Mum and Dad. They were so pleased and proud when I got this job, and they're both so anxious for me to keep it. I suspect the reason is that they don't want Dad's accident to have ruined my life too.

Daniel is different. He and I don't know the first thing about each other, or nothing personal. I know he doesn't look where he's going when he walks down the street. I know he can't bake and doesn't take anything seriously. I also know he's resourceful when it comes to fashioning a dog lead out of a couple of pairs of socks, and that he has an unexpectedly kind and thoughtful side. But that isn't the same as knowing him well. The point is, he's enough of a stranger for me to unload some of my troubles, but I'm not worried about him spreading it further.

'Good for you,' he surprises me. 'I'd have done exactly the same thing in your shoes.'

'How can you say that? I've just told you I walked out on my job with no notice during one of our busiest periods.'

'You had a good reason.'

'I did, but even I can't defend not taking it to my manager and trying to persuade her to let me take some leave rather than just walking out.'

'Any manager who needs persuading that family comes first isn't one worth working for.'

Something inside me unknots a little. I've been putting a brave face on it, but I've been worried about my actions. I called Caroline from home instead of talking to her in the office because I was sure she would refuse to give me any leave if I asked her face to face, and I might have said something I'd regret. But she has every right to be angry with me for being so unprofessional.

Daniel's reaction is comforting. It gives me hope that I've been worrying for nothing. It's Christmas, after all – the season of goodwill to all people. Maybe Caroline will not only allow me to take my leave but refuse to count it towards my annual vacation.

If Scrooge could see the error of his ways and start looking after his employees, there's still hope for me that Caroline will do the same. She may go to sleep tonight and be visited by the ghost of performance reviews past, the ghost of employee retention present, and the ghost of client satisfaction future. She'll wake tomorrow and realise how badly she's treated me and start working on plans for my immediate promotion. Hopefully, that will include a brand-new computer, a hotline to the IT department, and a company account at the nearest decent coffee shop.

Chapter Twenty-Five

The pub is filling up fast. It's a good thing we arrived when we did. People are standing at the bar chatting while they wait for a table to open up. I don't catch anyone's eye. I have no intention of moving until I'm ready. I'm exhausted after my day with Humphrey and a less than successful cookery lesson. I'd like to sit here all evening, sipping this delicious mulled wine and letting the stresses of the day flow out of me. But I can't do that because I need to get back to Humphrey. However, I can allow myself another twenty minutes before venturing out into the cold again.

'I've told you about my job,' I tell Daniel. 'But you haven't told me much about yours.'

'Yes, I have. I co-own a drone company. I've already mentioned that.'

'I wasn't sure whether to believe you. I never am.'

'That's a terrible thing to say. I'm as open and honest as a –'

'Politician at a truth-telling contest?' I suggest.

'Your words, not mine. Ask me anything you like. Nothing is off limits.'

'All I want right now is a brief history of what you do, and how you came to do it.'

'That's easy enough. I graduated from Leeds University six years ago with a degree in Environmental Science and got a job working in Urban Planning in Cardiff. I was there for two years, but I wasn't enjoying it, so I left to start my own company with my friend Marcus. We were both mad keen on drones, and we decided to use that in a positive way. We're still building the business up, but we're doing pretty well. We have more work than we can handle, so we're expanding as fast as possible.'

'You're very lucky to have found something that combines your skills and your passions,' I say. 'What sort of positive ways are you talking about?'

'It varies. At the moment, we're working for the local town council doing a roof survey. Sometimes we're hired by farmers to help with their crops. My favourite job was a couple of summers ago when a local historical society asked us to help them survey a site where they were sure there had been a Roman Villa. It was easy enough to see the changes in vegetation from the air and tell them where to excavate. You may have read about it. It was a little place in Shropshire, not far from Ludlow. They said it was one of the most important finds of the past century.'

'That sounds a lot more useful than what I do,' I say.

'Don't say that! You may be the means of improving complexions all across Europe. But only if you translate the ingredients properly. Otherwise, your company will find itself on the wrong side of a class action lawsuit.'

'I wouldn't lose much sleep over that. It might do them some good.'

'It may be none of my business,' he says. 'But why are you working there if you hate it so much?'

'Don't think I haven't asked myself the same thing a hundred times over the past year. It's complicated. Translation work can be difficult to get into when you're newly qualified. And my current job is a permanent position.'

'That makes a difference,' he agrees. 'Have you thought of moving into something else?'

'I've always wanted to be self-employed. I told you the other day that I'd love to translate novels for a living, but that wouldn't be as secure as my current job.'

'Too much of a risk?' he asks.

'Kind of.' I finish my drink and stare at the bottom of the glass.

'Can I get you another one,' he asks.

I pick up both our glasses. 'It's my turn, but this will have to be the last one. I can't leave Humphrey on his own for much longer.'

I return a few minutes later and hand him his wine. 'I should have sent you, after all. I had to fight my way to the bar, and I never learned to play rugby at school. We learned much less useful sports like tennis and badminton.'

'I was terrible at rugby,' he says. 'But I could have used my scouting skills to figure out the quickest way to the front of the queue. Thanks for this. Should we drink to something?'

I take a gulp of my wine. 'I already am – as fast as I can. I don't need a specific reason.'

'I can see that. I hope you aren't drowning your sorrows. Take it from me, that never works.'

'Not exactly,' I say. 'More like taking them for a quick swim.'

'You're welcome to talk to me any time if they bob back up to the surface.'

'That's kind of you, but I wouldn't know where to begin.'

'That sounds serious,' he says.

'Things aren't that bad. They're just more complicated than I'd like.'

He doesn't speak, which surprises me. He usually has so much to say for himself.

'It's my dad,' I say suddenly. 'He had an accident last year.'

To my surprise, I find myself telling him about the drunk driver and the weeks Dad spent in hospital when none of us knew how well he would recover. I tell him about the months of recuperation and the complete annihilation of all my parents' plans for retirement.

'I know we're luckier than a lot of people,' I finish. 'Things could have been far worse. But it's difficult to feel lucky when you see one of your favourite people in the world confined to a wheelchair and needing round-the-clock nursing care because some idiot decided to drink six pints of beer before climbing into his car and driving home.'

He nods. 'I can't imagine what you've all been through.'

'My parents more than me. My mum is amazing. She looks after him without a word of complaint. She held everything together when it first happened, and she's still doing that. She and Dad were so delighted when I got this job. They thought it would offer me some stability while I was starting out, and it would give me some great experience. I'd only been working there for a few months when Dad had his accident. I wanted to move back home to Coventry to help out, but they were both terribly upset when I suggested it. Dad said it would make things much harder for him if he thought his accident had changed my plans. I tried to tell him it was no such thing, but he and Mum were adamant. I know they feel a lot more secure knowing I'm in steady employment. It's not a boat I'm prepared to rock. Not for a while, anyway.'

'I get that,' he says. 'I hope your manager doesn't give you a hard time when she sees you again.'

'Me too. I wish I hadn't walked out like that, but I did. All I can do is hope for the best and that I get away with a written warning.'

'Meanwhile, there's no point in worrying about it,' he says. 'Are you working remotely while you're here?'

'I suggested that when I called Caroline, but she wasn't having any of it. She told me she was disappointed with my lack of professionalism and would have to think about what to do next and contact me with her decision. I haven't heard from her since.'

'It sounds as though she's the victim of her own lack of flexibility,' he says. 'I suggest you forget about her for now and concentrate on the important things in life.'

'Such as?'

'How can you ask? I'm talking about the cookie club.'

'I'm glad you're taking it so seriously,' I say. 'But it shouldn't take up too much of my time. If I do as Abby says and watch some videos, I should be able to make a passable batch of cookies for the next couple of weeks, which is all I need to do.'

'I can't believe what I'm hearing! Is that really your attitude? What happened to the woman who was so desperate to beat me that she booked herself a private lesson with a professional chef?'

'She was exposed as a fraud,' I say. 'And now she's drunk two glasses of mulled wine and doesn't care about anything at all.'

'That will pass,' he assures me. 'I'd put good money on it you'll wake up tomorrow morning and start thinking of ways to get the better of me again.'

'I'm more likely to be thinking of ways to pay my bills in the new year if I'm performance managed out of my job.'

'There's nothing you can do about that,' he says. 'But there's plenty you can do about the cookie club. I should warn you I'm in this thing to win it. If you can't be bothered to compete, it will make things much easier for me.'

'Compete in what way?'

'Any way you like. You're the one who turned this into a competition. What do you suggest?'

'You want to figure out a way to decide which of us makes the best cookies each week?' I ask.

'Exactly. You're all talk about your cookery skills. I want to see you put your money where your mouth is.'

'I don't have any money. And what little I have may need to last me a long time.'

'I don't mean literally,' he says. 'But where's your competitive spirit?'

'Why don't we ask the club members to vote each week?' I suggest.

'That wouldn't work. They'd just refuse to be a part of it. It isn't what the club was set up to do.'

'True. You come up with something then.'

He stares around at the crowd for a minute. 'Instagram!'

'What about it?' I ask.

'Do you have an account?'

'I think so. I rarely use it though.'

'Neither do I,' he says. 'But I set one up when we first started the business.'

'That's fascinating,' I say. 'Could you get to the point? Humphrey will be wanting his evening walk.'

'That is the point,' he says. 'We'll each post our cookies on Instagram and see which of us gets the most likes for them. We'll add them all up in the final week, and the person whose cookies are the most popular wins.'

I open my mouth to tell him how ridiculous this suggestion is, then close it again. I'm not sure whether it's the two glasses of wine in quick succession or something else, but this could work.

'You're on!' I say.

He holds out his hand. 'It's a deal.'

'Wait a moment. Is this a trick? Do you have ten million followers or something?'

'I doubt I even have one hundred. You?'

'About the same. It's been years since I checked.'

'There you go,' he says. 'We're both hopeless social media losers. So, we'll start on an equal footing.'

I reach over and shake his hand. 'I'm sure I'll regret this in the morning, but we have a deal. And now I have to go and see what Humphrey has been up to while I've been away. The last time I left him alone, he tried to sit on the back of the sofa. It will never be the same again. I can't imagine what Gran will say when she gets home.'

'Tell her I did it,' says Daniel.

'That's a great idea. I can say you're a social media addict, and you were posting a video for likes. She can send you the bill.'

'She won't know where to send it,' he says. He opens his wallet and pulls out a card. 'Maybe you should give her this. It has my company name on it and a number where I can be reached at any time.'

'Thanks,' I say, tucking it into my jacket pocket. 'This should be useful if she chooses to file a lawsuit. I have to go now. You know how it is – dogs to walk, world-class products to bake. I'll see you on Thursday with a box of what you believe passes for Christmas cookies.'

Chapter Twenty-Six

I spend the next morning watching cookery videos. I alternate between despair at what the amateur chefs so effortlessly produce and daydreams of the sort of thing I might produce for this week's cookie club.

I finally switch off Junior MasterChef and make us both some lunch. It snowed again during the night. I try to persuade Humphrey he doesn't really want to get his paws wet and cold by going outside, but he's having none of it. So, I stack the plates in the sink and button up my coat.

'I wonder whether they make winter coats large enough for dogs like you,' I tell Humphrey as I pull on my boots. 'You'd look lovely in a nice gilet.'

Evidently, he doesn't care about the finer points of canine fashion. He tugs impatiently at his lead until I open the front door, then sets off to the village at a brisk pace.

Lily beams at me when we walk in. 'How lovely to see you! It's been remarkably quiet in here today. I thought all our regular customers had been put off by the snow.'

I hadn't thought of myself as a regular customer until now, but I suppose I am. She leans down to pat Humphrey, and I realise she's talking about him. I'm just a temporary passer-through. I'm surprised by how much I wish that weren't the case. London isn't the friendliest place, and I've barely got to know anyone while I've been living there. It would be nice to have some local shops where everyone greeted you and knew all about you. Humphrey doesn't know how lucky he is.

'What can I get you?' asks Lily. 'Abby's been making macarons, if you like those. I can recommend the orange spice ones.'

'That sounds great,' I say. 'And a cappuccino please.'

She smiles at Humphrey. 'Would sir like his usual order?'

Again, I feel a pang at the thought of being a local and having a usual order.

'I was hoping for a quick word with Abby if she has a free moment at some point,' I say.

The corners of Lily's mouth twitch as she reaches for the cake tongs. 'Of course. May I tell her what this is with regard to?'

'I take it she's told you about last night.'

She switches on the coffee machine. 'She may have mentioned it in passing.'

'It was a bit of a disaster. Mostly due to Daniel, but a tiny bit to me.'

'I hear you didn't actually bake anything,' she says.

'I went home with some lovely Bakewell tarts. I had one for breakfast this morning.'

'I noticed several of them were missing when I came in this morning,' she says.'

'It was very kind of Abby after the shocking way Daniel behaved.'

She hands me my mug of coffee and smiles at Humphrey. 'I haven't forgotten you. Here you are.'

He grabs the biscuit she gives him and tries unsuccessfully to cram himself behind my chair while he eats it.

'There's no need to hide,' I tell him. 'Bernie isn't here this morning. He probably has more sense than to drag his owner out in this sort of weather.'

'You'd be surprised,' says Lily. 'Bernie owns an entire wardrobe of clothes. It changes every season. He has a little sunhat to keep the sun out of his eyes in hot weather. Last autumn, he appeared in a tiny Barbour jacket. None of us could keep a straight face. All he needed was a pair of cord trousers and a flat cap. And of course, he has a quilted coat and fur-lined boots for when it snows.'

'Fur-lined?' I ask. 'Aren't his legs already covered in fur?'

'Mrs Ogilvie says you can never be too careful. She told me once that a double layer of fur was safer than a single one. She was a little worried because Bernie can still get snow down his boots if he isn't careful. But he has a heated throw at home, so she wraps him in that after his walk and hopes for the best.'

'I feel as though I'm neglecting Humphrey,' I say.

She hands him his second biscuit. 'He doesn't look as though he's suffering too much. There you go, Humphrey. Try to make it last for more than a couple of seconds.'

He disposes of the biscuit in two bites, flops down, and closes his eyes.

'I promise to make my macaron last a little longer,' I say. 'It would be a shame not to appreciate all Abby's hard work.'

'Is that Lucy?' says Abby, appearing from the kitchen with a stack of cottage loaves.

'I'm afraid so. I'm not banned, am I? You didn't say anything about that last night.'

'Of course, you aren't banned.'

'You might have thought some more about the events of yesterday evening and changed your mind.'

She sits down at my table. 'Not at all. The events of yesterday evening formed a large part of our dinner conversation. Our friends were very interested to hear how the lesson went.'

I groan. 'I hope you told them it was mostly Daniel's fault.'

'I placed the blame where it was due,' she says with a grin.

I don't ask her to elaborate. As long as I don't know exactly what she said, I can imagine she told her friends that Daniel ruined her lesson while I waited patiently for him to get a grip.

'I wanted to see you this morning to apologise,' I say. 'I feel as though we wasted your time, and I'm sorry for that. It's such a busy time of year for you, and you didn't need any extra hassle.'

'I had fun,' she says. 'As I say, it gave us something to talk about over dinner.'

I'm unlikely to meet these friends of hers, so I can live with whatever they think of me. With any luck, the next time Abby has dinner with them, she can tell them how well I've learned to bake now and how the entire world agrees that my cookies throw Daniel's into the shade.

'I'm glad there are no hard feelings,' I say.

'None whatsoever. I should go now. I need to make a fresh batch of Bakewell tarts before lunch. For some reason, our stock is low.'

She gives me a friendly wave and disappears back into the kitchen.

I finish my coffee and wake Humphrey. 'You insisted on coming here, and now you have to walk home again. I refuse to carry you, although you're welcome to give me a ride if the snow gets too deep.'

He yawns and stretches but doesn't move.

'Maybe he could stay here permanently?' I suggest to Lily. 'He wouldn't be any trouble. He'd be perfectly happy lying under this table and eating the occasional dog biscuit. And he could be your guard dog each night.'

'We already have a burglar alarm,' she says.

'He would make a wonderful mascot for your bakery,' I plead.

'We already have one of those too. Bernie was awarded the title a while back.'

'I tried, Humphrey, but it's no good,' I tell him. 'You'll have to walk home in the snow, whether you like it or not. Come on, let's get it over with.'

I pull him to his feet, and he yawns again.

'Is he allowed a biscuit for the journey?' asks Lily. 'On the house.'

'That's kind of you. Your bakery will be seriously out of pocket by the time I leave. What with all those Bakewell tarts, and now a free biscuit for Humphrey. I'll have to ask him what he thinks. He may be full.'

She holds out a biscuit, and Humphrey makes a grab for it.

'Eat it slowly,' I advise him. 'You have a long journey ahead of you.'

As we reach the end of Bramble Close, I catch sight of Bernie in the distance, trotting along with his owner. As Lily said, he's wearing a tartan jacket, and his feet are encased in what I assume are his fur-lined boots. He looks very snug.

I look down at Humphrey, whose legs are soaked with melted snow. He doesn't seem to mind, even though I don't have a heated throw at home in which to tenderly wrap him until he's dried off. A thought stirs in my mind. I watch as Bernie disappears out of sight, obviously going up to the village shops with his owner.

'Stop it!' I tell Humphrey, who's attempting to drag me past the end of our road and continue on to the water meadows. 'We're going home. I don't have time to watch you racing around in the snow looking for birds that probably have more sense than to be out on a day like this. I have more important things to do.'

I call Margery and ask whether she's free to sit with Humphrey for a couple of hours so I can go into Christchurch.

'I could leave him by himself,' I say. 'But I do that whenever I visit Gran, and I know he doesn't like it.'

'No problem,' she says. 'As long as he doesn't expect me to take him out in all this snow.'

'He won't,' I promise. 'He can play in the back garden if he really wants some fresh air. Otherwise, I'll take him for his usual walk this evening.'

She arrives at three o'clock, and Humphrey greets her like a long lost relative he'd been told was stranded on a desert island and whom he had abandoned all hope of seeing again.

'That's enough, young man,' she says, pulling off her coat and scarf. 'You and I are going to spend a cosy afternoon reading my new book on the sofa, not running around the back garden building a snowman.'

'He'd prefer to chase the birds,' I say. 'But they're all safely in their trees for the afternoon.'

I make her a cup of tea, point her in the direction of the cookie jar, and slip out. Humphrey gives me a disapproving look but doesn't attempt to follow. He should be alright with Margery. As Gran said, she takes no nonsense from anyone, even Humphrey. I suspect I take rather too much nonsense from him, but I don't care. I haven't been able to explain to him why Gran isn't here, so I want to work extra hard to make sure he doesn't miss her any more than he has to.

I arrive in Christchurch twenty minutes later and park the car. The town isn't as crowded as I feared. Most people have probably had the sense to stay at home instead of inching along the icy country lanes at five miles per hour. If I'd had more time, I'd have done the same thing. But the cookie club is meeting on Thursday, and I have a lot to do to prepare.

I drive slowly back to Honeywell two hours later and unpack the car.

'You've been busy,' Margery greets me when she sees my bags. 'We haven't. Humphrey has spent the afternoon fast asleep by the window, and I've read seven chapters of my book.'

'Thank you so much,' I say. 'I hope I wasn't away for too long.'

'I have nowhere to be and nothing to do,' she says. 'An enviable position, I'm sure you'll agree.'

'I can't remember the last time I had nothing to do.'

'You'll get there when you're my age,' she says. 'For the time being, I advise you to make the most of your youth and energy.'

'Humphrey will make sure of that,' I say.

I see her off, then return to the living room to find Humphrey hasn't moved. He must be more tired than I thought. Now could be the perfect opportunity to take his measurements.

I pull a tape measure out of my shopping bag and kneel down next to him. He shifts slightly and grunts.

'Shh,' I murmur. 'You have a nice sleep while I get on with this.'

He half raises one paw, then lets it fall again. He opens one eye and looks at the tape measure.

'Don't wake up,' I say in a soothing tone.

He opens his other eye. Time to do something before he realises where he is and what I'm doing.

I take a deep breath and start to sing to the tune of twinkle, twinkle, little star.

Snuggle, snuggle, little pup,
Curl your paws and cuddle up …

To my astonishment, this seems to work. His eyelids droop, and he heaves an enormous sigh as he settles himself more comfortably on the rug.

I quickly measure him from nose to tail and across his enormous shoulders. I jot the numbers down in my phone as I go. He doesn't move, so I tiptoe out of the room with my bags and take them into the kitchen to inspect their contents. Humphrey wanders in half an hour later, still looking drowsy.

'Hi, there,' I greet him. 'Just wait until you see what I've been making for you.'

He walks over to his bowl and takes a long drink. He lifts his head at last, water still dripping from his jowls.

'Better now?' I ask him.

He shakes the water from his fur and runs over to the kitchen door. His meaning is clear.

'Hold your horses,' I say, putting down the headband I've been working on. 'Let me unlock the door rather than you crashing through it and leaving a Humphrey shaped hole.'

I let him out and watch as he romps joyfully through the snow until he finds an almost clear patch of grass. He returns a few minutes later looking delighted with himself.

'I don't suppose I could persuade you to clean up after yourself?' I ask.

He grins at me and shakes the snow off his fur.

'Wait a minute,' I say, picking up the towel I use to dry his paws after one of his muddier walks. 'That's better. Now, I need you to stand still for a few minutes while I try this on you.'

I pick up a green T shirt and slip it over his head. He gives me a startled look but doesn't try to run away.

'Good boy!' I say, slipping the arms over his front paws. Stand still for a moment while I rub some of this green powder into your fur. If you could try to look Grinch-like, that would be great.'

I take a picture of him. 'That's perfect. I see you went for puzzled rather than Grinchy, but that's ok. You're the model. It's your choice.'

He lifts his front leg and inspects it for a moment before trying to chew the fabric.

'Don't be so ungrateful!' I chide him. 'That outfit is the latest in dog fashion.'

He tries to chew the other leg. I sigh and pull the T shirt over his head. 'You aren't cut out to be a supermodel, are you? Never mind. It's early days. Now, why don't you try on this nice reindeer headband?'

I put it behind his ears before he has a chance to object, then take a couple more pictures.

'How about one with you pouting?' I ask. 'No? Well, you're the talent. I suppose you know best.'

I manage to remove the headband before he gets restless and decides to eat it.

'Prima donnas!' I complain. 'With the amount you get paid, I would have thought you'd put up with a bit more than this.'

Humphrey backs himself against the wall and prepares to resist any further attempts to turn him into a well-dressed dog about town.

'You've done very well,' I say, giving him a hug. 'Would you like a walk as a reward for all your hard work?'

Humphrey doesn't have the widest vocabulary in the world, but he knows the words dinner, biscuit, and walk. His ears prick up, and he runs to fetch his lead.

'Why couldn't Gran have broken her hip in the middle of summer?' I ask him as he drags me down the street as fast as his legs will carry him.

He ignores this and heads off in the direction of the water meadows. I don't have the energy to argue. Hopefully, his favourite patch of mud will be hidden under ten feet of snow, and he won't be able to find it.

We stay out for an hour until my toes feel as though they're about to drop off.

'Time to go, Humphrey!' I call.

He ignores me and shoots off in the opposite direction.

'Dinner time!' I shout.

He skids to a halt and pauses with his back to me. I can almost see the thought bubble hovering over his head. He turns and walks over to me.

I clip on his lead. 'I thought that would do it. You're a dog of simple tastes, aren't you? Regular walks, a warm bed to sleep in, and plenty of home-cooked food. And a wardrobe full of designer clothes.'

He snorts and shakes snow all over me.

'I'll take that for full agreement,' I say, setting off back down the path to Gran's house. 'You looked lovely in your photo shoot. That headband really brought out the colour of your eyes.'

Humphrey takes no notice. He quickens his pace as Bramble Close comes into view.

'If you pull me off my feet, we'll never get home,' I warn him. 'And then what will you do? Your personal chef will be lying in the street while you wonder where your next meal is coming from.'

He slows his pace slightly. Perhaps his vocabulary is wider than I thought. Is there a way I could capitalise on that? It would be excellent if I could get Humphrey to do the voiceovers on his own videos. Daniel could never top that.

I abandon the thought. I don't have time to train Humphrey to do anything complicated. I'll just have to rely on his natural charisma and model good looks.

Chapter Twenty-Seven

The second meeting of the cookie club is much less fraught than the last one. For one thing, thanks to a YouTube link Abby sent me, I can now make shortbread cookies that won't be mistaken for something used in the discus-throwing finals of the Honeywell sports association. For another, I don't open the door to anyone until I'm sure Humphrey is safely locked in the living room.

I'm feeling quite pleased with myself by the time the club members assemble with their boxes of cookies. Daniel is one of the first to arrive, carrying an enormous cardboard box also filled with shortbread cookies.

'What a coincidence,' says June when he opens it to show everyone. 'Lucy has made the same cookies as you have.'

'But I've iced mine,' I say, gesturing towards them. 'I went with a Christmas theme – snowmen and Christmas tree baubles.'

'Very nice,' says Daniel. 'They'll look lovely in photographs. I'm sure you've taken a few of those, haven't you, Lucy?'

'Just a couple. The same as you, I expect.'

I've taken rather more than a couple of pictures. I spent most of yesterday evening getting the light as perfect as possible while I photographed the cookies from every conceivable angle. I even took a few selfies of me pretending to bite into one of them, but the finished results made me look like Hannibal Lecter, so I deleted them.

I posted the best of them on my Instagram account, which I was delighted to see has gained several hundred followers as a result of the pictures I've been posting of Humphrey in his various outfits. I added enough hashtags to sink a small battleship and sat back to await the results.

By four o'clock this afternoon, I had more than three hundred likes for my snowman cookies. If I keep uploading photos of Humphrey, my followers will increase, and next week's cookies should get even more likes. I took a quick look at Daniel's Instagram at lunchtime and was delighted to see he only had forty followers, and he hadn't even got around to posting his cookies. He must realise there's no point, and he'll never be able to compete with me. Score one for the Hollis women.

Phyllis has brought mince pies, and someone else has made a batch of mini pizzas. People talk and laugh while they sort the cookies into boxes, all ready to deliver them around the village over the next few days.

I take advantage of the noise and chatter to speak to Daniel.

'I hope my cookies haven't made you feel inferior?'

'Not at all,' he says. 'I assumed you decided to ice them at the last moment because they weren't evenly coloured?'

'They were perfect – all golden and crisp. They didn't need covering up. I just did that to make them Christmassy.'

'You mean Instagram-worthy?'

'Have you posted yours yet?' I ask, knowing perfectly well he hasn't.

'I'll put the pictures up when I get home,' he says. 'I've been too busy today.'

'Playing with your drones?'

'That's right. And baking fifty perfect cookies. Not a crack or an imperfection in any of them, which meant there was nothing to cover up.'

'I've already told you I wasn't covering up anything. I was being festive.'

'#InstagramBaking and #TisTheSeason?' he says. 'Not very original.'

'So, you've looked at my account?'

'In passing. It gave me something to do while my emails were loading.'

I try not to look smug. 'Three hundred and four likes the last time I checked.'

'Were they for the cookies or for Humphrey?' he asks.

'For the cookies. His pictures got even more likes.'

He laughs. 'That ought to tell you something. Seriously, Lucy, don't you think that was a low trick – dressing up that poor dog for internet attention?'

I help myself to a mince pie and sink my teeth into it. 'Not at all. I would have done that this Christmas, anyway. Lily gave me the idea when she told me about Bernie's various outfits. I didn't want Humphrey to feel left out if he met Bernie on one of our walks.'

'You plan to walk Humphrey through the village dressed as a Christmas elf?' he asks.

'Maybe not. But he looked lovely in his little Santa hat, don't you think?'

'You don't want to know what I think,' he says, taking the last mince pie. 'I wonder if these were made using the little-known turning the pastry into glue technique?'

I pull out my phone and open my Instagram app. 'Three hundred and twenty likes now! You'd better up your game if you want to win this bet.'

June taps me on the shoulder. 'Do you two plan to stand here arguing all evening when there's work to be done?'

'I apologise for Lucy,' says Daniel. 'She doesn't have her head in the game. She's too busy looking at her phone.'

'Three hundred and twenty!' I mouth at him before adding, 'What can we do to help?'

'Take ten boxes of cookies each,' says June. 'Irene has printed out lists of all the houses in the village in groups of ten. Take a list of addresses and make sure all the cookies are delivered as quickly as possible.'

'But take care no one sees you,' adds Phyllis. 'It's better to wait an extra day if you need to rather than risk being caught.'

'How can we be sure we won't be caught?' asks Daniel. 'Don't some people have cameras on their doorbells nowadays? They'll see who's delivering the cookies.'

'That's up to you,' says Margery. 'We don't care how you manage it, as long as it's legal.'

'Last year, Ivy joined a group of carollers,' says June. 'She had the box of cookies under her coat and dropped it on the doorstep as they left.'

'Didn't Phyllis do something with a long stick one year?' asks Margery.

'It was a grabber,' says Phyllis. 'My granddaughter bought it for me when I had that slipped disc a few years ago. She said it was to help me pick up things I dropped. I don't think I ever used it for that, but it struck me it would work just as well for putting things down. I stayed out of range of the camera and popped the box on the doorstep using the grabber.'

'Ingenious,' says Daniel. 'Has anyone tried disabling the cameras?'

'They'd better not,' says Margery. 'We make it clear each year that everything our members do must be legal. No one will put up bail if they're caught doing something they shouldn't. Anyway, it's a test of our ingenuity.'

'Not everyone has a camera doorbell,' says June. 'The trick is to choose a time when people are busy. Or deliver the cookies in the middle of the night and hope no one is awake.'

'Humphrey would bark the place down if anyone tried something like that,' I say.

'You should find out whether there's a dog on the premises first,' says Irene. 'But don't tell them why you're asking.'

'This is far more complicated than I first thought,' says Daniel. 'I'm impressed by your level of organisation.'

'That's Lavender,' says Margery. 'She puts a lot of work into this club. It's a shame she isn't here this year.'

'She'll be home soon if all goes well,' I say.

'Please let me know if she needs anything at all,' she says. 'You too, Lucy. Will you be staying on for a while?'

'I'll be here until just after Christmas,' I say. 'My boss has finally agreed I can use my annual leave until then. I'm not sure what we'll do after that.'

Irene hands out the last of the boxes, and people start to leave. Daniel hangs around until the last person has gone.

'I'm pleased to hear your boss has had a change of heart,' he says.

'I wouldn't put it like that. Having a change of heart implies she had one to start with. She told me HR said she had to allow me to take my leave, but she wanted to make it very clear it was coming out of my holiday allowance, and I would be back in the office the minute it ran out. She's also scheduled a back-to-work meeting for me. I can imagine how that will go.'

'Maybe she'll be overcome by Christmas cheer and offer to let you work from home for the next few months,' he says.

'And maybe I'll win the lottery next week. I shouldn't complain. Caroline can't actually fire me for taking the leave I was due. And she won't find it easy to replace me even if she wanted to. Not everyone is prepared to give up their evenings and weekends at short notice for no extra pay.'

'Try not to worry about it,' he says. 'You have enough on your plate without borrowing any more trouble.'

'Speaking of plates, I must check my likes on my latest batch of cookies.'

'Please wait until I've gone!' he says. 'I'm not in the mood for your gloating.'

'Fair enough. I have to feed Humphrey and take him for a quick walk before bed anyway. You should go home and think about a strategy for delivering your boxes of cookies.'

'I have a few ideas already,' he says. 'I can be creative when I need to be.'

'Not as creative as me. See you next week, Daniel. Don't forget to latch the gate as you leave!'

'I'm never going to live that down, am I? See you around, Lucy.'

I watch him walk down the path, close the gate behind him, then check the latch with elaborate care. I laugh and close the front door.

I take Humphrey for his evening walk and give him his dinner.

'I don't know about you,' I tell him when he's finished. 'But I'm ready for bed.'

He follows me up the stairs and takes his usual flying leap onto my bed. I switch out the light and pick up my phone to set an alarm for tomorrow morning. I may as well take a quick look at Instagram to make sure the site hasn't crashed under the weight of all my likes.

It hasn't, but I'm pleased to see almost five hundred hearts under the picture of my snowmen cookies. Daniel has a lot of catching up to do.

I almost don't check to see whether he's posted his pictures yet. It feels a little mean. He accused me of gloating, and I don't want to be that person. Fine, I do want to be that person, but I don't want anyone to realise that. I intend to be gracious in victory when we finish our competition next week. I can do my gloating in private.

Maybe I'll take a look to save myself from having to log in again tomorrow. I click on his account and give a gasp of horror as I see his latest post. That can't be right! There are over six thousand hearts under the photograph of this week's cookies.

Has he found a way to hack into the system and change the number of likes? That's impossible. If anyone could do that, everyone would be doing it. Has he used some viral hashtag I've somehow overlooked? I check the post again. #MerryChristmas #ChristmasCookies #WhatDoYouThink?

His hashtag game is even worse than mine. But the fact remains that he has six thousand likes. The numbers click up as I watch. I look away when they reach six and a half thousand in case the algorithm is accidentally counting my views as likes.

I stare into the darkness, my heart beating madly. Whatever Daniel is doing is working. I have to find out what it is before his numbers reach the sort of heights I have no hope of reaching. I half close my eyes and peek at the screen again. The numbers have stopped moving, which is a relief.

I open my own account and stare at my pictures, concentrating hard. Nothing happens, which means it isn't my magic gaze that causes the numbers to climb. It's a pity because I'd be more than happy to sit here for the next couple of days doing nothing but stare at the screen. Anything to make sure Daniel doesn't win this contest.

'This makes no sense,' I tell Humphrey, but he just yawns and rolls over. Clearly, he isn't a social media buff.

I flick back to Daniel's account and see to my horror the number of likes is now over seven thousand. What is he doing to cause this? I almost call him to ask, but that would mean admitting I've looked at his account and that I care about the numbers he's getting. I have to figure this out by myself and try to do something about it.

I run my eyes down his list of followers. He only had about forty the last time I checked. He now has four hundred and eighty-five. I scan the list, although I'm not sure why. He and I aren't likely to have any mutual friends.

A name catches my eye, and I stop scanning. Cecily Montford. Why does that name feel so familiar? Maybe he and I do have a mutual friend after all. No, we don't! I stiffen in outrage when I realise why I know the name. Cecily Montford is the woman who's famous for being famous.

She's loosely related to the Royal Family, although I can't remember how. She runs a luxury travel vlog and has some sort of wellness brand. And she's some kind of activist. I saw her on the news only last week, chaining herself to the railings outside a stately home. I can't recall what she was protesting. Probably, neither can she.

She's also a terrible name dropper, although I might be too if I moved in the sort of circles she does. She posts humorous content on the 'struggles' of aristocratic life and the perils of being recognised wherever you go. I can't help thinking that if you don't want to be recognised, it might be a good idea not to turn up in some greasy spoon restaurant at three in the morning, dressed in a couture gown and accompanied by a pack of tabloid newspaper photographers. But, each to their own.

The real question is why she's following Daniel's Instagram account and liking the pictures of his boring cookies. More importantly, why isn't she following my account? If she likes Christmas cookies so much, mine are far more interesting. I've made the effort to ice them and make them look festive. All Daniel has done is put his on a plate.

It's no good. I won't sleep if I don't find out what's going on. I scroll down my contacts list and text Daniel.

Just happened to see your account as I was scrolling through Instagram. I couldn't help noticing Cecily Montford is one of your followers.

I almost switch my phone to silent so I don't have to see his reply. It might be best to let him think I'm not interested in the answer. The phone beeps while I'm trying to decide.

Just 'scrolling through Instagram' and 'just happened' to see my account? I'm not sure what your question is. Cece is an old friend of mine. I didn't realise she'd started following me.

He's the most frustrating man I've ever had the misfortune to meet. I take a deep breath before replying.

I don't suppose this has anything to do with you trying to game the system and cheat at our competition?

He doesn't reply for a minute. I'm not surprised. I've called him out, and he's realised the game is up. Did he really think I wouldn't notice what he'd done? I can't imagine how he thought it was ok to manipulate his numbers like that. Whatever happened to good, honest competition?

My phone pings again. I'd like to ignore it, but curiosity gets the better of me. I look down at the screen. Daniel hasn't written a message. He's simply sent me two emojis – a pot and a kettle, or at least a tea pot that I assume represents a kettle.

I slam my phone down on the bedside table, pull my pillow over my head, and prepare to get some sleep. I need to be well rested if I'm to come up with a plan to get the better of him. He obviously thinks he's won this round, but I'm not going down without a fight.

Chapter Twenty-Eight

My life in London feels increasingly distant the longer I spend in Honeywell. I get the occasional flash of guilt when I remember how I behaved. I'm a professional, and I shouldn't have walked out like that. But I resent being put in the position where I felt I had no other choice. It isn't as though the company has no one else to cover for the most urgent parts of my job. Marie has stepped in several times when I've been in Berlin for meetings.

I also resent the tone of the email Caroline sent to let me know I could take my leave. It was the perfect blend of condescension and annoyance. So much for employee relations. I'm not looking forward to going back to work in the new year, but it would be a shame to allow it to spoil the rest of my time here. I have a sneaking suspicion Caroline will do everything possible to make sure I don't take next year's holiday allowance at a convenient time in case I run away with the idea that the company, and she as my manager, have any of their employees' interests at heart.

I tell myself several times a day it's best not to dwell on my work frustrations. I'm sure everything will look a lot less bleak when I return. I just needed a break and a change of scenery, and that's exactly what I'm getting. People pay good money to come to a place like Honeywell.

A Hollywood producer would be delighted to shoot a Christmas movie here. It's a beautiful little village, especially blanketed with white, as it is right now. I hadn't expected the snow to last for so long, but Humphrey and I are making the most of it while it's here.

We set out together each morning, usually in the direction of the field next to the water meadows. This seems to be Humphrey's favourite walk, and I like it too. I love watching him bounding along ahead of me as though it's the first time he's ever been this way. Each new turning is a fresh adventure to him, and he greets even the most familiar landmark with wild excitement.

I wish I could be more like that with my life in London. It would be great to wake each day and eat my slice of toast as though it was the first time I'd ever come across the concept of hot, crunchy bread. I could follow it by skipping through the streets to the train station, marvelling at every flower and garden wall.

I imagine Caroline's reaction if I flew into the office each morning, exclaiming at the fact two of the chairs have been replaced, or gasping in excitement as I switch on my computer and watch the start-up routine that's exactly the same as every other day. She might be less reluctant to allow me to take my annual leave if I behaved like that.

Humphrey and I enjoy a similar walk together most afternoons and evenings, where he's equally excited and intrigued by every stone and leafless branch. I enjoy the afternoon walks the most. I'm not a morning person at the best of times, and Humphrey's exuberance at seven thirty can be exhausting. But I usually feel more energetic after lunch, and I can appreciate the way the setting sun casts a golden glow over the frozen fields. I love watching the twilight wrap around the tree trunks, causing their shadows to elongate into strips of lace before melting into the darkening snow and disappearing entirely.

I take him out a little earlier than usual on Saturday afternoon. I visited Gran this morning and stayed rather longer than I expected to. Humphrey has been restless since I got back, and I make a note not to leave him alone for more than a couple of hours again.

'I'll take you for an extra-long walk to make up for it,' I tell him. I'm not sure whether he understands the extra-long part of this, but walk is one of his favourite words, and he trots off to fetch his lead.

We crunch through the snow together. I leave a trail of footprints behind me, and Humphrey leaves a mass of scuffed up snow. He loves to run across the field, his legs pistoning wildly, snow flying in all directions and coating his fur until he looks like an overgrown snowball with a wagging tail.

I watch in amusement as he charges back and forth, making zigzags and circles and letting out excited yelps. Every now and then, he stops to shake himself off, sending a spray of white flakes everywhere. There's something so pure and joyful about Humphrey in the snow. He bounds over to me, and I reach down to ruffle his snowy fur.

'I'm glad to see you're running off some of that energy. Maybe you'll sleep well tonight and not wake me at 3 a.m. again because you think you've heard a squirrel breaking into the kitchen to steal your snacks.'

He cocks his head to one side as though considering this, then sprints off. My phone beeps, and I check to see who's messaging me while I'm busy playing with Humphrey. To be fair, whoever it is has no idea where I am or what I'm doing.

The text is from Daniel. *I've just found a recipe for Amaretti cookies. Way beyond my skills, but it should be a piece of cake for you. See what I did there?*

I roll my eyes and prepare to text back. Something about the silence around me catches my attention, and I look up in sudden alarm. There's no sign of Humphrey. He must have run down towards his favourite patch of mud. Why did I take my eye off him, even for an instant? I shout his name, my voice carrying over the snowy field so loudly that half of Honeywell could hear it. I shout again, but there's no reply except the faint echo of my own voice across the snow.

I frantically scan the field, but there's no Humphrey bounding towards me through the snowdrifts. My heart starts to slam in my chest, making me dizzy.

'Humphrey!' I yell. 'Walk! Biscuit! Dinner!'

Still nothing. I start to run, the snow crunching under my boots as I retrace our path to the road. Humphrey knows his way back to the cottage. Has he somehow grown bored and decided to return home? It's unlikely, but that would be the most positive alternative.

I scan the path frantically for paw prints. I can see the marks of my boots walking towards me and various messy areas of snow left by Humphrey's paws, but there's nothing to show he's been back this way by himself. I want to believe he has, but I somehow doubt it. Humphrey loves playing in this field and is always reluctant to leave.

I hesitate, trying to decide whether to run home and check whether he's there or stay and continue searching here. If I go home, and he isn't there, I'll have wasted valuable time that I could have spent searching around the field and water meadows. I think of all the dangers he could have encountered. Why did I ever bring him here? Having done so, why did I take my eye off him? It was just a text. It could have waited. It wasn't even an important text. Just another one of Daniel's stupid jokes.

I circle the field again, peering into the distance, hoping to catch a glimpse of brown fur. My heart sinks as I remember it won't be brown. Humphrey has been rolling around in the snow. By this time, he'll be almost as white as the ground.

Panic grips my chest as I run, calling his name at the top of my voice. The minutes pass, and there's still no sign of him. How could I have allowed this to happen? I stop at the edge of the field, gasping for breath. Should I widen the search? I could start combing the area on the far side of the hedge. But what if I do that, and Humphrey returns here? Will he have the sense to wait for me or will he think I've abandoned him and run off again, maybe for good this time?

I have to stop this. Letting my thoughts spiral won't help either of us. If only there was someone else around I could enlist to search with me. I could do with a second pair of eyes at this moment. Of course! Why didn't I think of that before? I fumble for my phone, my hands shaking, and dial Daniel's number.

His voice is amused as he answers. 'Are you calling to tell me what's wrong with the recipe I sent you?'

For a moment, I can't think what he means. What recipe? It doesn't matter right now. All that matters is finding Humphrey.

'Something's happened!' I begin.

'Lucy? Are you alright?'

A sob escapes me. 'No!'

His voice sharpens. 'What's happened? Where are you?'

'At the field. Humphrey went missing about ten minutes ago. I've searched everywhere, but he's disappeared. I desperately need some help.'

The shock of hearing the words spoken out loud, of making them real, finishes me. I start to sob uncontrollably.

'I'm on my way!' says Daniel's voice in my ear. 'Stay where you are, and keep calling for him. With any luck, he'll be back with you before I arrive.'

'No, he won't! He's gone, and it's all my fault.'

'No, it isn't,' he says. 'Just hang in there, and we'll get Humphrey back. He can't have gone far.'

He's right, but that isn't necessarily a good thing. Humphrey doesn't need to have gone far to get himself into trouble. There are probably a million hidden dangers in this field alone. I wonder why I've never realised that before. If I ever get him back, he and I will stick to sedate walks through the streets. And I'm never allowing him off his lead again.

'I'm on my way,' says Daniel again. 'I'll be with you in five minutes.'

Chapter Twenty-Nine

His car pulls up on the far side of the field a few minutes later, and I breathe a sigh of relief. I couldn't have held it together much longer all by myself. I seem to have lost the ability to think clearly.

He jumps out and runs over to me. 'No luck?'

'Not a trace of him. I can't imagine where he's gone. I've been calling and calling. He's never done anything like this before. I'd never have let him off his lead if I'd known he'd disappear.'

'You weren't to know,' he says.

'Maybe not. But if I hadn't stopped to answer your stupid text, none of this would have happened.'

I'm aware how unfair this is, but I can't help myself. Anger will keep me on my feet for a while. Thinking about my responsibility for this fiasco won't.

Daniel doesn't react. 'Did you see which way he went?'

I point. 'Over there, I think. But I'm not really sure. I wasn't watching him when he left the field. And he's been running around here so much today that I can't trace his paw prints.'

He nods. 'Let's assume for now that he took off in that direction. There's no road for miles, which is a good thing. What's between these fields and the next village?'

'I'm not sure. We've never been down there. I've mostly stuck to this area. There's some farmland nearby.'

A horrible thought strikes me. 'You don't think he's strayed onto the farmer's land, and they've shot him?'

'Absolutely not.'

'But what if he's been chasing their sheep?'

'The nearest sheep are over near Compton,' he says. 'That's in the opposite direction to here. If Humphrey has found his way into a farmer's field, the worse he'll have done is dig up the odd cabbage.'

I feel a surge of relief when I realise he's right. But that feeling is short-lived. We still have no idea what's happened to Humphrey.

'I love him so much,' I say, my voice breaking.

Daniel gives my shoulder a reassuring squeeze. 'In which case, we should get him back for you as quickly as possible. Stay here for a moment.'

He lopes off to his car and opens the boot. He fishes something out and returns a minute later carrying a drone. I stare at it, my mind racing. When I decided I needed a second pair of eyes, I meant Daniel. I didn't consider his drones, which shows what a state I'm in.

'I never thought of that!' I say.

He raises one eyebrow as he sets the drone on the ground. 'Isn't this why you called me?'

'I called because I needed help, and you were the first person I thought of.'

'Fair enough. But this is the best way I can help. Trust me, Humphrey doesn't stand a chance of hiding from this.'

He gives me a quick smile, then crouches down beside the drone. He flips a couple of switches and taps at his tablet. The drone's lights blink into life, and its propellers start to hum, a low buzzing that gradually intensifies. Daniel's eyes are focussed, his fingers moving expertly over the controls. I feel a wave of relief to realise he knows exactly what he's doing.

'Ready?' he asks, glancing up at me.

Before I can respond, the drone lifts off the ground, hovering for a few seconds just above head height. It rises higher, angling its camera to take in the entire field. I step closer, leaning in to watch the view on the screen expand into a bird's-eye perspective of the snowy landscape.

It's surreal to see the field stretch out below the drone – patches of undisturbed white, punctuated by trails and paw prints. Daniel manoeuvres it in smooth arcs, sweeping it back and forth across the field, the camera scanning everywhere.

'See anything?' he asks, his eyes glued to the controls.

I stare at the image, straining to spot any movement. 'Not yet.'

'Don't worry,' he says, steadying the drone and zooming in on a hedge at the far end of the field. 'Humphrey's quick, but this is quicker.'

The minutes tick by with agonising slowness as the drone methodically scans the area. It rises higher, then disappears over the hedge and out of sight.

'Shouldn't we follow it?' I ask.

'There's no need,' he says. 'Let the drone do the work for now. You concentrate on that screen.'

The drone flies over a small spinney and carries on.

'Shouldn't you have checked those trees?' I ask.

Daniel smiles. 'Humphrey is a gifted dog in many ways, but he hasn't yet mastered the art of climbing trees. Much to the relief of Honeywell's bird and squirrel populations.'

'I'm not talking about him climbing trees. But you didn't look on the ground beneath them.'

'I switched on the infrared as we passed over the spinney. If we don't see the runaway himself, it will pick up his body heat. Humphrey's a big dog, and he's been running around. We should be able to pick him up from a mile off.'

'Then, why haven't you?' I ask, more sharply than I intended.

He glances over at me. 'I will. I promise.'

His tone is so calm and confident that I find myself believing him. I keep my eyes fixed on the screen, willing Humphrey to appear.

Daniel stiffens. 'Is that …?'

He moves one of the controls forward, and the camera tilts steeply as it heads towards the ground.

'Gotcha!' he murmurs.

'Are you sure?'

'Absolutely sure. Look at that shape next to the building.'

I stare at the flickering orange and red blob. 'That could be anything. It could be a sheep.'

'Too large,' he says. 'And sheep don't usually dig holes in the snow.'

He switches off the infrared, and the camera straightens up again. I give a gasp of relief as I see Humphrey industriously scrabbling at a patch of snow. Daniel brings the drone down and lands it on the roof of the building.

'You found him!' I say in disbelief.

'I promised I would.'

The weight of the past half hour comes crashing down on me all at once – the terror of what might have happened to Humphrey, and the fear of never seeing him again. I can't hold it in any longer. I collapse into Daniel's arms, sobbing uncontrollably.

'It's ok, Lucy,' he murmurs against my hair.

'I was sure I'd lost him,' I choke out between sobs. 'And it was all my fault.'

'I thought it was mine for sending stupid texts.'

'I was wrong,' I say in a muffled tone into his sweater. 'I'll never say anything unkind to you again.'

'I doubt that,' he says with a laugh in his voice. 'Are you ready to collect the miscreant?'

I wipe my eyes. 'We'd better go before he decides he's had enough of digging that hole and wants to move on.'

'We'll find him if he does,' says Daniel. 'I almost dropped the controller when you lunged at me like that, but it's still in one piece. If Humphrey makes a move, we'll find him again. Let's get going before he does. He's about five hundred metres in that direction.'

I break into a run, and he follows me. When we reach the hedge at the far end of the field, I see a large gap in the branches.

'This must be where he scrambled through!' I say.

'Or he simply launched himself at the hedge,' says Daniel. 'And that hole is the result. Either way, we should go through it.'

We push through the gap and find ourselves in a second field. The snow is deeper here, and I sink up to my knees in several places. I spot the building I saw on the screen a few minutes ago.

'That's it!' I say.

'And there's the man himself,' says Daniel. 'Heading towards that fence. He must have got fed up with digging a hole in the snow and decided to move on. I'll retrieve my drone while you go and have a few words with him.'

I sprint across the field as fast as I can, shouting for Humphrey. Hearing my voice, he turns and smiles amiably, for all the world as though we've arranged to meet here, and he's wondering what took me so long.

I drop to my knees and wrap my arms around him, burying my face in his fur. He gives my arm an awkward lick.

'Never do anything like that again,' I tell him as soon as I can speak, careful to keep my tone calm and neutral. He doesn't respond well to raised voices.

Daniel appears and smiles down at the pair of us.

'For once, it's you in trouble and not me,' he tells Humphrey, who wags his tail frantically.

I pull Humphrey's lead out of my pocket and clip it to his harness. 'This is never coming off again.'

'Don't listen to her,' Daniel advises Humphrey. 'She's annoyed because she couldn't find you, and my toys could.'

I straighten up, clutching the lead. 'I'll never call them toys again. I'm more grateful to you than I can say. I don't know what I'd have done if you hadn't answered your phone.'

'You would have done exactly what you needed to,' he says. 'You'd have widened the search until you found him or he decided he'd had enough and came to find you.'

'Maybe,' I say. 'But I'm not sure I'd have stayed calm enough for that. It felt like one more thing I couldn't prevent.'

He nods but doesn't comment. I'm not sure what made me say that. The important thing is that Humphrey is safely back with us. That's enough for anyone.

We climb back through the hedge and make our way towards Daniel's car. Humphrey doesn't chase a single bird on the way. Either he's trying to show how sorry he is for his behaviour this afternoon or he's too tired after digging up half a field of snow.

'I'm sorry I can't offer you a lift,' says Daniel. 'But I barely fit into this car as it is. I can't imagine what Marcus thought he was doing hiring me a Mini Metro while I was down here. If we try to fit Humphrey in too, we'll end up looking like one of those clown cars as we pass through the village.'

'That's ok,' I say. 'Humphrey gets car sick, anyway. We're better off walking, so we can have a talk on the way. He and I need to discuss the concept of trespass.'

Daniel ruffles Humphrey's fur. 'Sucks to be you, mate! Lucy can be scary when she wants to be.'

'Not tonight,' I say. 'I'm too relieved to have him back safe and sound. I'll be cooking him an enormous piece of steak and tucking him in with a hot water bottle and a bedtime story.'

'Sounds good,' says Daniel. 'If you put some Christmas pyjamas on him and a cute little nightcap, you can post it on your Instagram account. It might get you a few more followers. And you desperately need those if you want to stand any chance of beating me when we add up our totals next week.'

Chapter Thirty

Humphrey wakes me for his walk a few days later. For once, I don't burrow under the quilt, pleading with him for another five minutes. I ignore the cold and jump out of bed, taking even him by surprise.

'Breakfast and a walk,' I tell him. 'I've decided to let you off your lead again today. But only if you behave yourself. We'll go to the field because you like it so much there, but one hint of trouble and we're leaving. After that, we need to come home and clean up. The doctor told me yesterday that Gran should be coming home today or tomorrow, and I don't want her to be disappointed with the way you and I have kept the house.

For a moment, I feel like someone telling their young child the truth about Santa. Would it have been better to have kept the news about Gran a secret and just allowed Humphrey to enjoy the surprise? I smile to myself as I remember he doesn't understand what I'm saying. I'm turning into Mrs Ogilvie and treating Humphrey like my baby. There are worse ways to approach the business of being a pet owner. Bernie is a happy little thing, and Humphrey is a happy giant thing, so all is well in both their worlds.

We eat our breakfasts, then I bundle up in as many layers as I can find to brave the icy morning.

'I don't suppose I can persuade you to put on your reindeer outfit?' I ask Humphrey. 'It would go down a storm with my followers, and it might get me some much-needed likes.'

I can't be too upset with Daniel after what he did to help me find Humphrey. But seriously, who cheats at a competition like this? I had to work hard to increase my followers, whereas all he had to do was ask his famous friend to share one of his pictures on her stories, and the rest of the sheep followed.

His cookies didn't even look that good. I put a lot of effort into mine, icing their little noses to look like carrots and tracing zigzag patterns onto the Christmas ornaments. Ok, they weren't perfect, but I did my best. And Daniel just asked some influencer woman to do it all for him.

My teachers used to tell us about the satisfaction we would feel if we did our work by ourselves without asking someone else to do it for us, even if it resulted in a lower grade. But I don't feel any particular glow as I stride along the streets of Honeywell behind Humphrey. Perhaps that's because it's so cold, and my hands and feet are already numb. Maybe I'll feel a sense of pride in my achievement once Humphrey and I are safely back in the warm.

I try not to think about the fact I'm about to lose my competition with Daniel. 'Live in the moment!' I instruct myself. I seem to tell myself that quite often these days. Not, I suspect, because I'm morphing into some Zen-like creature who's learned to take joy in the tiny things of life and is ready to write a self-help book, but because I'd prefer not to think too much about my immediate future.

Does Cecily Montford practise this same sort of Zen thinking? If so, she's bound to be twenty times better than me at it. According to her followers, there's nothing she can't do perfectly, and they hang on her every pronouncement. If she'd made outfits for Humphrey, they would have attracted millions of likes within the first few minutes of her posting them.

I catch myself. Why am I thinking negative thoughts about a woman I've never met and who's never done me any harm? All she's done is play the cards life has dealt her and built up a successful business for herself. On the surface, it may seem as though she was dealt a better hand than most people, but appearances can be deceptive. She may have had just a difficult upbringing as someone born in less affluent circumstances.

I can't help wondering how Daniel knows her. Did he perhaps meet her at some drone-flying competition? I don't follow her myself, so I have no idea about her possible hobbies. Or did they meet somewhere else and start dating? Surely not. Cecily only dates famous people – sportsmen and actors. Daniel is neither. Didn't she once date a famous chef too – that Italian guy who talks about pasta being less of a meal than a way of life? If that's the sort of man she's into, Daniel doesn't stand a chance. His last lot of cookies were adequate, but I can't imagine anyone describing them as a way of life.

We've reached the field next to the water meadows – or the ice meadows, as I suppose I should call them this morning. The frost has turned the grass into a field of silver. Humphrey tugs at his lead until I unclip it, then bounds away in his eternal quest to reduce the bird population of Honeywell to a manageable size. His breath forms little clouds in the frosty air, giving even the sleepiest bird notice of his approach.

He catches sight of a rook sitting on a low branch and lumbers towards it. It gives him a sarcastic look and flies away. Nothing daunted, he catches sight of another and changes direction. This takes him several seconds, and the second bird waits even longer before taking to the skies. It watches Humphrey with what I like to think is an amused expression before giving a leisurely flap of its wings and flying off, leaving him to chase its shadow with as much enjoyment as he chased the actual bird.

I have to admire his philosophy. If you can't get the thing you really want, pursue something else with equal enthusiasm. The joy is in the quest, not the outcome. I could learn from that. I can't entirely disregard the outcome in the way that Humphrey can. I have to eat and pay the bills. But I could certainly learn to live in the moment a little more and not sweat the small stuff.

What does it really matter if Daniel ends up with more likes than me on Instagram? The important thing is that I've learned a new skill and had fun doing it. It may take a while for my brain to catch up with this philosophy. It's still telling me it would be even better if I could both enjoy the journey and also get the outcome I want, which means crushing Daniel and showing the world how much better a baker I am than he is. Perhaps I should sign up for one of Cecily's mental wellness courses. Or Cece, as Daniel called her. I refuse to speculate why that may be. His personal life is his own business.

I come back to reality with a start. This was supposed to be a quick walk. I've promised myself to have the cottage in perfect order before Gran returns, which means doing some serious cleaning. I know how house-proud she is, and I don't want her wishing she'd remained in the hospital.

I whistle for Humphrey, who's immediately afflicted with his usual deafness. I turn away and pretend to look at the willows at the far side of the water meadows.

'What splendid specimens!' I exclaim. 'I could stand here all day studying them. I'm so glad Humphrey is busy. It gives me plenty of time to appreciate their glorious something or other.'

Humphrey ambles over to find out what I'm doing, and I grab his collar and clip on his lead.

'I thought that would do it! You're extremely predictable. And extremely contrary. Sorry about that, but we have to go. It's time for me to redeem your promise to clean the entire house for me while I lie on the sofa and watch.'

My phone rings a couple of hours later. As I expected, it's Gran.

'They've told me I'm allowed home this afternoon!' she says. 'I asked whether I could use the phone at the nurses' station. I wanted to call you before they changed their minds.'

'They won't do that,' I reassure her. 'I'm sure they're as anxious to get rid of you as you are to leave. They'll be looking forward to a little peace and quiet.'

She laughs, but her voice is anxious. 'Will you be able to come and get me? I could take a taxi, but they said they'd prefer someone to collect me.'

'Of course! I can drive over as soon as you like.'

'No rush,' she says. 'The doctor won't be doing her ward rounds until after lunch. Could you come around two o'clock?'

'I'll be there,' I promise. 'And don't worry if there's any delay. I have a babysitter all lined up for Humphrey.'

I make us both an early lunch.

'You're having Kibble,' I tell Humphrey. 'And I'm having a toasted sandwich. I'll try not to get them confused.'

I text Daniel while I wait for my sandwich to grill.

Any chance of you dog-sitting today? I'm collecting Gran from the hospital around two o'clock.

His reply comes back almost immediately.

Delighted to come over and sit on your dog. Or I could take him for a walk if you prefer. I can be there by one-thirty.

'That's a relief,' I tell Humphrey. 'I may be gone for some time, and it will be nice for you to have someone to play with. I want you to behave yourself for Daniel and promise not to mess up the house. It took me ages to clean it, and you were no help at all. What's the point of keeping you if you can't run a duster around occasionally?'

I'm glad Daniel's coming over. He can take Humphrey for a nice long walk, which should mean he's not too boisterous when Gran gets home. She'll be tired after her journey, and the last thing she needs is a giant dog landing in her lap. Knowing her, she'll make up some excuse for him, but it's best not to put it to the test.

Humphrey greets Daniel with enthusiasm when he arrives.

'He's had his lunch,' I say. 'And he's ready for his second walk. I've put his lead on for you, but there are several spare pairs of socks in the laundry basket if you need them.'

His eyes crinkle with laughter. 'Thank you for thinking of me, but I don't believe they'll be required. And we won't be walking past that house again. I went round to apologise, bearing a box of chocolates, but the man who answered the door was a little short with me.'

'You returned his socks, all nicely washed. What more did he want?'

'I'm not sure he accepted my explanation of why I'd removed them in the first place,' he says. 'If only you'd allowed me to take Humphrey with me to apologise, I might have avoided a painful scene.'

'How painful was it?'

'Let's just say I doubt I'll be receiving a Christmas card from him this year. But he took the chocolates, which was a good sign.'

'Grumpy old thing,' I say. 'I'm glad you didn't take Humphrey with you. He doesn't like loud voices, do you, sweetheart?'

Humphrey gives an enthusiastic bark, and Daniel laughs.

'I'd better get going,' I say. 'If I know Gran, she'll be sitting on the edge of her bed counting the minutes. And woe betide any junior registrar who suggests she stays for an extra night.'

'Another Hollis woman who knows her own mind?' he asks, taking Humphrey's lead from me and following me down the drive.

'I come from a long line of women who know their own minds.'

'Come on, Humphrey,' he says. 'We'd better get going before we get ourselves into any more trouble.'

Chapter Thirty-One

As I predicted, I find Gran waiting for me when I arrive at the hospital. She isn't sitting on the edge of her bed, but she's in a chair by the window.

She looks delighted when she sees me. 'They're just filling out the paperwork, and then we can go.'

'I told you they couldn't wait to get rid of you. And we can't wait to have you home. Humphrey has been preparing a special dance for you. He doesn't always remember the steps, but I'm sure you can fill in the gaps.'

'I've missed him so much,' she says. 'I can't tell you how much it's meant to me knowing you were with him.'

'I've loved every minute of it. I'll miss him when I go back to London after Christmas.'

'Did you say someone is looking after him while you're away?' she asks.

'That's right. You remember me mentioning Daniel – the man who gate-crashed our meeting?'

'Of course.' She gives me a searching look. 'He's the one looking after Humphrey today?'

'He offered ages ago. I wouldn't have asked him otherwise.'

She smiles but doesn't say anything more.

The nurse appears a few minutes later. 'All set? I've found you a wheelchair. If you'd like to hop in, I'll take you down.'

She helps Gran into the wheelchair. Hop may have been a slight exaggeration, but Gran is far more mobile than I expected. I drop off the flowers and chocolates I've brought with me at the nurses' station and thank them for everything they've done for Gran. I had considered baking them some cookies, but I decided they have enough to contend with at this time of year. I'm confident my baking is edible by now, but it's safest not to take any chances.

The nurse helps Gran into my car and issues her with last-minute care instructions. We say goodbye, and I drive slowly away.

'How does it feel to be going home?' I ask.

'Wonderful,' says Gran. 'Although I'm a little nervous in case anything goes wrong.'

'It won't,' I assure her. 'I've turned the living room into a bedroom for you. It's lucky the bathroom is downstairs. You won't need to use the stairs for a while.'

'Humphrey won't be happy,' she says, looking worried. 'He doesn't like his routine being upset.'

'I've upset his routine in every conceivable way this past fortnight,' I tell her. 'And he's handled it like a champion. Please don't worry about him.'

She doesn't look convinced. I don't say anything else but concentrate on driving as smoothly as possible. Gran isn't one to complain, but it can't be comfortable taking a journey like this on her first day out of hospital.

We chat about my week as I ease the car along the country lanes. I tell her about the last meeting of the cookie club and my attempts to deliver the cookies without being discovered.

'I don't know how Santa does it,' I say. 'I was almost caught delivering one box, whereas he has to climb down millions of chimneys without being discovered. My targets came home unexpectedly early from their evening out. Still, I managed to hide behind a bush until they were safely inside.'

'It doesn't matter too much if the adults see you,' says Gran. 'As long as the children don't. There's so little magic in the world nowadays. I like to think we can provide some at Christmas.'

She wouldn't say there was no magic in the world if she'd seen Humphrey in his elf outfit. But it may be better not to mention that. I've decided not to bother telling her about his recent costume changes.

We pull up outside Rose Cottage, and I help her out. She takes a deep breath. 'What a relief to be home.'

I open the gate and gesture for her to go through. 'Someone else will think so too.'

The minute I put the key into the door, we're greeted by an ear-splitting bark. A second later, Humphrey comes into view. Daniel has had the sense to keep him on his lead, but it's as much as he can do to hold him.

I step in front of Gran before Humphrey can send her flying. He cannons into me in his effort to get to her.

'Steady there!' says Daniel, pulling him back.

Gran bends down and puts her arms around Humphrey's neck, and I'm touched to see how gently he responds to her. It's as though he senses she needs careful handling. She buries her face in his fur for a long minute. When she raises it at last, her eyes are full of tears.

'Thank you for looking after him for me,' she tells me in a choked voice. 'I'll never forget it.'

'Not just me,' I say. 'It takes a village, remember? Everyone helped. The staff at the bakery gave him biscuits, and Margery babysat him while I went shopping. Even Daniel –'

He laughs. 'I can't wait to hear what you have to say. Any sentence that starts with *Even Daniel* is bound to end badly for me.'

I smile back at him. 'Not at all. You've been great. Just wait until you see the rail Daniel's fitted in the bathroom for you, Gran. And it was kind of him to look after Humphrey today. I didn't want us to arrive home and find he'd got into the living room and eaten your pillow.'

Humphrey gives me a shocked look that makes it clear he would have a low opinion of any dog behaving in that way.

'You haven't introduced me yet,' says Gran.

'I'm sorry,' I say. 'I'd forgotten you and Daniel haven't met. He's been such a part of my life while you've been in hospital that I feel you must already know him.'

I catch Daniel's eye and see he's smiling.

'A reluctant addition to your life,' he says. He holds out his hand to Gran. 'I'm Daniel, the newest member of your cookie club. It's a pleasure to meet you.'

'Temporary member,' I can't help saying.

'Temporary member,' he agrees.

'I'm Lavender Hollis,' says Gran. 'I've heard all about you.'

'I've barely told you anything,' I say. I don't want Daniel thinking he's formed a large part of our conversation during my hospital visits. Nothing could be further from the truth.

'Not from you,' she says. 'But I've had plenty of other visitors. They've told me about him.'

'I'll understand if you'd like me to leave at once,' says Daniel, and she laughs.

'Not at all. You must stay for a cup of tea. I want to hear everything that's happened while I've been away. Starting with Humphrey here.'

We sit at the kitchen table while I fill her in with all the news. Humphrey lays his head on her lap as I talk, and she gently scratches his head. Looking at the two of them makes me want to cry. I hadn't quite realised until now what a huge part of each other's lives they are.

'Which just about brings us up to date,' I say. 'I left Humphrey with Daniel and came to fetch you. I'm sure they had a good time together.'

'We did,' says Daniel. 'We went for the usual walk towards the water meadows. He has strong opinions on where he likes to walk, and I don't like to argue with him, although it's a little muddy there at the moment. Most of the snow has melted, and the ground is fairly squishy if you leave the path.'

'Which I have no doubt you did,' I say.

'Not by choice,' he says with a grin. 'But Humphrey saw a group of magpies, so, you know …'

'He didn't catch one?' I ask anxiously.

'I wouldn't have let him off the lead if I'd thought there was the slightest chance of that. But he got within about thirty metres of them, so he was happy enough. They moved to a higher branch to continue their conversation, so I don't think they were too bothered by him.'

'These cookies are excellent,' says Gran. 'Did one of you bake them?'

'Don't worry,' says Daniel. 'You're quite safe. Irene dropped them off while Lucy was gone. She asked me to tell you she'll pop in tomorrow morning.'

'I wasn't worried,' she says. 'Lucy tells me she's improved her baking skills no end since she arrived in Honeywell.'

'That wasn't difficult,' I say. 'I had absolutely no skills when I arrived. Even learning how to combine butter and sugar in the correct proportions was a huge step forward.'

'And keeping them in the bowl while you did it,' adds Daniel.

'The less said about that, the better,' I admit. 'But you were no more skilled than I was when we started.'

'I wasn't,' he says. 'This competition has been good for both of us.'

'Competition?' asks Gran.

'He means club,' I say quickly. 'He's saying the cookie club has been good for both of us.'

'I don't think that's quite what he meant,' says Gran. 'Was it, Daniel?'

His eyes are full of laughter as he meets my gaze. 'Help me out here, Lucy.'

'I can't. You're on your own.'

'Tell me!' says Gran.

I reluctantly tell her about our competition, with Daniel helpfully chipping in with all the more embarrassing details. I'm not sure why Gran needs to know quite how badly I performed during our cookery lesson with Abby. Especially since I'm now confident enough to tackle basic recipes. But Daniel refuses to omit a single thing.

'And that's when Lucy and I decided to make it into a competition,' he finishes. 'We knew there was no point in asking the club members to vote. They would have told us to stop wasting their time.'

'They're an efficient bunch,' I agree. 'For some reason, they all seem more focussed on the actual purpose of the meetings than telling us how wonderful our cookies are.'

'So, we decided to run a competition ourselves,' says Daniel.

I'm pleased to see Gran doesn't look annoyed. But I didn't expect her to laugh quite so hard.

'I don't quite understand the part about followers and stories,' she says. 'But do I take it you're trying to find out how popular your cookies are with the general public?'

'That's right,' says Daniel. 'So far, the general public appears to be on my side.'

'This is a happy day,' I tell him. 'So, I won't spoil it by arguing with you. Or explaining to my grandmother exactly how you've been cheating. We can leave that until another time.'

'Agreed,' he says. 'As long as we're both clear about my lead. You have as much hope of catching me as Humphrey has of bringing home a pheasant for your Christmas dinner.'

'Speaking of dinner,' I say, 'I'd better make a start on ours.'

He looks alarmed. 'Your grandmother is only just out of hospital. Are you sure it's wise to inflict a home-cooked meal on her on her first day back?'

'No need to worry,' I say. 'Angela Carson dropped a casserole round last night. Even I'm capable of heating that up without burning it, and preparing some vegetables to go with it.'

'How kind of her,' says Gran. 'Is there enough for three, Lucy?'

I want to tell her there's only enough for two. But that wouldn't be fair to Angela Carson, who's provided enough dinner for a small army. Or several people and one Humphrey.

'If you mean me,' says Daniel, 'I'm seeing friends this evening. If you mean Humphrey, the answer is no, there's never enough food for him.'

'I did mean you,' says Gran. 'Humphrey can't eat the casserole, but there's usually some steak in the freezer. Lucy can cook that for him if she doesn't mind.'

'I don't mind,' I say. 'But we don't want him getting ideas. He's supposed to be having dry food this evening.'

'It's a celebration,' says Gran. 'He and I haven't seen each other for such a long time. We must do something to mark the occasion.'

'Quite right,' says Daniel. 'Perhaps Lucy can dress him up in his spinning bow tie.'

He catches my eye and smiles. 'Yes, I saw your post last night. He looked very smart. But it won't do you any good. I have a feeling Cece is about to share my latest post on today's Instagram story.'

Chapter Thirty-Two

Gran goes to bed soon after dinner, saying she's tired. I help her with everything she needs and settle her onto the sofa bed.

'Please call if you need anything in the night,' I say. 'Daniel brought you this bell when he came over to sort out the handrail in the shower.'

'He seems like a very nice man,' she says. 'You didn't mention that when you told me about him.'

I'm annoyed to feel myself blushing. 'I barely told you anything about him.'

'I know,' she says. 'And I've wondered why. But my friends have kept me up to date. They're laying bets on how long it takes for the pair of you to get together.'

'That doesn't sound likely. You must have misunderstood what they meant. Maybe they're laying bets on which of us murders the other first.'

'I may be old, but there's nothing wrong with my memory,' she says. 'There's nothing wrong with my eyes, either. You could do a lot worse.'

'So could he!' I say, and she laughs.

'That goes without saying. I'm only teasing you, Lucy. Your love life is none of my business. For all I know, you may be seeing someone up in London.'

'Not recently. I don't have time.'

'Or he could be,' she goes on.

It's quite likely Daniel is involved with someone, although I'm a little surprised he hasn't mentioned it. He's talked about everything else. Is it really possible he and Cecily Montford are an item? Is that why she's so happy to share his posts with all her followers? I don't know him very well, but I can't imagine him getting together with someone who lives her entire life through social media and sells expensive homeopathic cold and flu cures on her website. On the other hand, she's extremely beautiful. Most men would be delighted if a woman like that showed an interest in them.

'Lucy?' says Gran.

'I'm sorry. I was thinking about Humphrey's basket,' I say, not entirely truthfully. 'Would you like him in here with you tonight? He's been sleeping on my bed while you've been away. But it's up to you.'

Humphrey answers the question by scrambling onto the sofa and flopping down next to Gran.

'You can't do that,' I say. 'Gran needs her space. I'll bring your basket.'

I fetch it from the kitchen and put it next to the sofa. 'In you get!'

I say it without much hope. To my surprise, he hops down and obligingly curls up in it.

'Wonders will never cease,' I say.

'He's very good at times like this,' says Gran. 'He's a sensitive soul, and he seems to know when people really need him to do something.'

'I needed him not to lie on my feet and cut off the circulation each night,' I say. 'But he didn't take any notice of that.'

'There's a difference between a want and a need,' she tells me. 'Haven't you learned that yet?'

'It appears Humphrey has. But if he changes his mind and causes you any bother, please ring the bell. I'll leave my bedroom door open so I'll be able to hear you.'

She settles herself more comfortably and blows me a kiss. 'Goodnight, Lucy. Sweet dreams.'

'No need for those,' I say. 'I'm getting the entire bed to myself for a change. What more could I ask for?'

I half expect to hear the bell during the night, but I don't. I tiptoe downstairs when I wake, not sure what I'll find. I put my head around the living room door to see Humphrey fast asleep in his basket. Gran is asleep too, her hand hanging down and touching his head. I smile at the picture they make. If anyone wanted to paint a portrait of unconditional love, they need look no further than this.

I switch on the kettle and return to find Gran opening her eyes.

'I don't know what was in those tablets the hospital gave me,' she says. 'But I had a wonderful sleep.'

Humphrey stirs and yawns.

'From the looks of it, so did he,' I say. 'Did he move at all after we put him to bed?'

'Not an inch. Haven't I always told you what a good dog he is?'

'You have. But I didn't fully appreciate it until now. I'm glad you slept well. I'll make us some breakfast, then take him for his walk.'

We spend the rest of the day quietly. Various people pop in to see Gran, but they don't stay for long. Apparently, Angela Carson has arranged some sort of visiting rota and encouraged everyone to stick to it.

'You're a popular woman,' I tell Gran as I help her get ready for bed that evening. 'It must be nice to live in a place like this where you know everyone, and everyone knows you. I've barely met anyone while I've been in London.'

'How about your workmates?' she asks. 'Do you get on well with them?'

I think of Caroline constantly telling me I'm failing to meet her arbitrary deadlines, and Mark undermining me at every opportunity. And Dave and his IT minions treating us as though we're the lowest possible life form if we ever dare to suggest they might pop along to fix our computers.

'They're fine,' I say at last. What else can I say? Gran has only been home from the hospital for one day. The last thing I should be doing is telling her things that are bound to worry her.

'It always takes a while to settle into a new job,' I add. 'I'm sure I'll get to know my colleagues better as time goes on.'

Gran looks distressed. 'I've taken you away from your job at the worst possible time of year.'

'Not at all,' I reassure her. 'It was about time I took some days off. I've only taken a week's leave this year. And they don't like us rolling our holiday allowance over into the following year, so I've done them a favour.'

'It's very nice of you to put it like that,' she says. 'But I know it isn't true. Maybe we can find someone to come in to help me each day, and you can go back to London. There's still almost a week until Christmas. I'm sure they'd be happy to see you.'

I'm rather less sure, but I don't want to argue with her.

'I'm enjoying the break,' I say. 'I'll return to work feeling more energetic. The nurse will be coming in for the next few days to check your stitches are healing, and you start physio next week. But you'll still need someone to cook and clean. And Humphrey can't walk himself. Please don't worry about me. I'm having a lovely time with you both. Now that I'm not so worried about leaving Humphrey by himself, I can get out and see more of the area.'

'That's true,' she says. 'Have you been to the Christmas Fair yet?'

'Humphrey gets a little over-excited when he's around too many people.'

'He's better with a few people at a time,' she says. 'And he's so large that he tends to knock things over.'

'Is the fair worth a visit?'

'Oh, yes! I'm disappointed to miss it this year. But you can tell me all about it. Tomorrow is the last meeting of the year for the cookie club, so you won't want to visit it then, but how about Friday evening? I'll ask Margery whether she'd like to pop over while you're gone. She can fill me in with everything that's happening in the village.'

I tuck her into bed and settle Humphrey into his basket.

'I thought he might wander up to visit me last night,' I say. 'But he didn't move. It's obvious who his favourite person is.'

'He's a very loyal dog,' says Gran. 'But I can see how much he likes you. You've done a wonderful job with him.'

I sit beside her. 'I've been wondering about something, but you may be too tired to talk right now.'

'Not at all,' she says. 'Is it about your work?'

'What makes you ask that?'

'Oh, I don't know. It feels as though there's something you aren't telling me.'

'It isn't about my job,' I say. 'It's about the cookie club. The other members told me all about its history. But none of them mentioned Mum. And she's never talked to me about the club. It struck me as odd, that's all. She's a Hollis woman too. Why has she never said anything about it?'

Gran is silent for a long moment, stroking Humphrey's head.

'It's my fault,' she says at last. 'Nothing to do with your mother. When she was growing up, I always thought she would stay here in Honeywell, just as I had, and my mother before me. I planned to pass the leadership of the cookie club on to her when she was old enough. But it soon became clear she planned to move away as soon as possible. She didn't want to stay in such a small place. She wanted to travel and see other places. Your grandfather encouraged her, and he wouldn't let me say a word about it.'

'Mum always told me I should leave home and find my feet in a new place,' I say. 'She said I should snatch every opportunity and try new things to discover what I wanted in life.'

'She was right,' says Gran. 'But I couldn't see that at the time. All I saw was that my daughter wanted to leave us. It took me a long time to realise how selfish I was being. And by that time, she'd already left.'

'Are you saying you and she never got past it?' I ask, and she laughs.

'Goodness, no! We made up that quarrel long ago. I saw how happy she was when she left to work in London. And then she met your father and moved to Coventry with him. She found her place, just as Ed and I had found ours.'

'So, why didn't you tell her about the cookie club then?'

'I didn't set out to keep it a secret,' she says. 'I assumed she knew I was running something of the sort. But she never mentioned it, so neither did I. It always felt to me like a symbol of everything she didn't like about living in a village – doing the same thing each year with all the same people. I was worried she might look down on it, just like she'd always looked down on her life here.'

'I don't think that's true,' I say. 'Mum has always talked fondly of her childhood in Honeywell and told me what great parents you and Grandpa Ed were. Just because she wanted to move on didn't mean she didn't appreciate what you'd given her. You gave her the confidence and self-belief to feel she could set off on her own adventure.'

'That's what Ed told me,' she says. 'You remind me a lot of him, Lucy.'

'You must miss him very much.'

'I do. But life goes on. And now I have Humphrey to look after. He gave me a new lease of life after I lost Ed.'

'It works both ways,' I say. 'You did the same for Humphrey. Look what a difference you've made to his life.'

She glances down at him with a fond smile. 'We're both very lucky. I've been meaning to ask you, Lucy. There seems to be a greenish patch of fur behind his right shoulder. Has he been rolling in the grass or something?'

Humphrey opens an enquiring eye as though interested to know what I have to say about his green fur. I wink at him.

'It's nothing to worry about,' I tell Gran. 'He's just been doing a bit of method acting while you've been away.'

Chapter Thirty-Three

I'm looking forward to spending an evening at the Christmas fair. I've done most of my shopping online this year, but it would be nice to do some in person too. This has always been one of my favourite things about Christmas – selecting the perfect gifts for people. Especially my family. My parents made it such a special time of year for me growing up, and I have so many happy Christmas memories.

I won't be seeing Mum and Dad on Christmas Day. Dad can't travel down here, and Gran isn't going anywhere for a while. Much to Humphrey's relief, I suspect. She wasn't joking about his travel sickness. I tried to take him for a walk in the forest the first week I was here, but we only got a mile down the road before he started showing unmistakable signs of nausea.

I had no wish to spend an entire day cleaning Gran's car, so I turned around and came home again. I haven't repeated the experiment, and I don't intend to. So, Gran, Humphrey and I will spend Christmas in Honeywell, while Mum and Dad celebrate in Coventry. It can't be helped. At least none of us will have such a terrible day as we did last year, when Dad was still in the hospital and no one knew what sort of recovery he would make.

I rang Mum a few days ago to update her on Gran's progress, and we promised each other that we would have a second Christmas together as soon as I can get to Coventry. I'm determined to make that happen before going back to work. Caroline has done without me so far. She can do without me for a couple of days longer.

I say goodbye to Gran and Margery as I leave for the fair. They're already deep in conversation, and I doubt they'll notice my absence. They must have a lot to catch up on. Humphrey thumps his tail as I pat him goodbye but makes no move to follow me. He's adapted very well to Gran's return home and has calmed down considerably. He seems to have adopted the role of protector and guardian and rarely leaves her side. That suits me fine. I don't want him running down the road after me, demanding to be taken out for a glass of mulled wine and a piece of Stollen.

I close the gate carefully, just in case, and look up and down Bramble Close. No dark figure emerges from behind a nearby hedge wielding a drone, which is a good start. I walk up to the village, enjoying the crisp night air and the crunch of snow beneath my feet. This feels like the perfect evening for me to visit the Christmas fair. Except for running the cookie club, I haven't yet managed to get into the spirit of the season.

My stay in Honeywell feels like a dream – a blur of dog walking, baking, and trips to the hospital. I don't feel as though I've achieved very much, but I'm oddly exhausted. Maybe that's always the way it is with holidays. It's been so long since I've taken one that I can't remember how you're supposed to feel when you get back home at the end of them.

I resolve to be far stricter about this when I return to work. I've been too quick to accept Caroline's rulings about how I'm allowed to use my free time. She's always told me the company will collapse if everything isn't done by yesterday, and I see now that isn't true. They've managed fine without me since I came down here, and they can manage fine without me the next time I need a break. If they can't, they'll have to hire more staff. It isn't up to me to run myself ragged to make up for their inadequate planning.

The Christmas fair is being held on the green at the far end of the high street. I can hear the music and laughter from quite a distance away. I was right to think Humphrey wouldn't enjoy it, but it's exactly what I need after all this time on my own. My spirits lift as I walk more quickly towards the entrance.

The smell of mulled wine and roasting chestnuts drifts through the air, mingling with the scent of pine from the decorated trees lining the path. Twinkling fairy lights are strung over most of the stalls, casting a festive glow over everything.

I make my way through the crowd, taking in the stalls selling handmade gifts, warm hats and scarves, and the boxes of glittering ornaments. It's all so wonderfully ... *Christmassy*. Exactly the kind of spirit I've been missing until now. Speaking of spirits, I notice a stall called The Snowball Saloon. It appears to be selling mulled wine and eggnog. Just what I need to start the evening. I'm wearing my thickest boots, but my feet are still cold. Not for long though.

'One glass of eggnog, please,' I tell the man.

'Make that two,' says a voice.

I turn, with a feeling of inevitability, to find Daniel standing behind me.

'What are you doing here?' I ask.

He pulls out his wallet. 'I'm in charge of the drone display.'

'Really?'

'Not really. I wouldn't trust my precious drones anywhere near this place. You've seen the sort of riff-raff the fair attracts.'

'You're here, so I see what you mean.'

'I've got these,' he tells the man.

'There's no need!' I protest, but Daniel has already handed over his card.

'I've been looking for a way to apologise,' he says, 'And this seems the perfect opportunity.'

'Apologise for what? Knocking the cookies out of my hands?'

He hands me my glass. 'I was thinking of the time I let Humphrey escape, but you're right – there are so many things I need to apologise for. One glass of this won't be enough.'

'How about you cheating in our competition and getting fifty times more likes than I did?' I ask, and he laughs.

'I have nothing to apologise for there. It isn't my fault that a friend thought my cookies were so amazing she wanted to share them with all her followers.'

'Just a coincidence, then?'

'Coincidences happen more often than people realise. On an unrelated subject, I've been admiring your pictures of Humphrey dressed in an increasingly bizarre set of outfits.'

'They're Christmas-themed,' I say. 'There's nothing bizarre about Christmas.'

'Dressing him up as the Grinch may have been Christmas-themed. And the reindeer ears were quite festive. But what about the tuxedo and bow tie?'

'People like to dress up smartly for the holidays. There's nothing wrong with that.'

'I'm not sure Humphrey agrees,' he says. 'His expression in the picture of him standing next to the tray of wine glasses was less than festive. He looked as though he'd like to throw them at someone.'

'He was hungry. He hadn't had his dinner.'

'That would account for it.'

'I'd like to see you do any better,' I say.

He raises an eyebrow. 'Isn't that what started all this – you telling me you'd like to see me do better?'

'You're right. I take it back.'

'I'm glad you did say that. If you hadn't, I wouldn't have joined your cookie club and got to know you and Humphrey better.'

There's a warmth in his eyes that makes my heart skip a beat. I'm not sure how to answer this. Do I regret accidentally inviting him to the cookie club? I thought I did at the time, but now I'm not so sure.

'Shall we look around the fair now we're here?' he asks. 'How long do you have? Is Margery staying for the entire evening?'

'How did you know Margery was visiting Gran?' I ask.

'Didn't you mention it?'

'No, I didn't. So, how did you know?'

He appears to be fishing around for some explanation, then laughs. 'Your grandmother told me.'

'Gran did? How?'

'Or rather, she sent a message to me via Margery that you would be visiting the fair this evening. She wondered whether I might enjoy it too if I hadn't already visited it.'

'Did she indeed? And had you already visited it?'

'Twice,' he says. 'But I didn't dare tell her that. And Margery didn't so much ask whether I'd like to come along as command me. You know how I am around strong women. I can't stand up to them at all. I just do as I'm told.'

'I hadn't noticed. But neither of them is here now, so there's no need for you to stay. I'll tell Gran I met you here. I won't mention that you only stayed for five minutes.'

'What if I want to stay for longer?' he asks.

I gesture towards the stalls. 'That's your call. You're a grown man, and you can do as you like.'

He smiles down at me. 'What if I'd like to stay here and spend the evening with you?'

My heart seems to have sped up. It must be the eggnog. I should ask them what they put in it.

'That's up to you,' I manage.

'And you,' he says. 'I don't intend to stalk you around the fair against your will. If you really don't want me here, I'll finish my eggnog and go home.'

My instinct is to tell him I don't want him here. It's become so much of a habit to put him in his place that I've never stopped to wonder why I'm doing it. Maybe because it's fun, and I haven't had much fun over the past year. But it occurs to me now I may be cutting off my nose to spite my face.

'Well?' he asks gently.

'You should stay,' I tell him. 'I'd enjoy spending the evening together.'

We spend the next half hour inspecting the stalls.

'It's important to take your time Christmas shopping,' says Daniel.

'I used to agree. But the last two years, it's been a struggle to buy anything at all.'

'Your father's accident?' he asks sympathetically.

'Yes. That was last December. And this year, I've been too busy at work to spare a thought for Christmas. Even down here, I've had my hands pretty full.

So, I've been ordering most of my presents online. Humphrey hasn't enjoyed that. I've had to put a note on the front door asking the delivery people not to ring or knock.'

'He's showing you what an excellent guard dog he is,' says Daniel.

'According to Gran, he's the opposite of useful in an emergency. But she took him on after some difficult circumstances, and she knew in advance there would be times when he was a bag of nerves.'

'Poor Humphrey,' he says. 'I'm sorry he had a bad start in life.'

'Me too. But his luck changed the day he met my grandmother. She loves him exactly as he is, and she puts up with all his foibles. And in return, she has a gorgeous pet to keep her company and love her back. She always tells me she has the best end of the deal.'

'They're both lucky,' he says. 'And he seems very comfortable with you.'

'He wasn't to begin with, but he's grown to trust me. Which is fortunate, seeing that he's been lumbered with me over the past two weeks.'

'Are you enjoying taking a break this evening?' he asks.

'It's nice to get out by myself for a while without having to wander around the field in the cold and dark while Humphrey eyes up the local wildlife.'

'Ornithology can be a very rewarding hobby,' he says.

'Not the way he does it. Speaking of hobbies, how's yours going?'

'I assume you're talking about my job. Fine, thanks. We've almost finished this roof survey. The council seems pleased with us. As long as they're pleased enough to pay our invoice, that's all Marcus and I care about.'

'What's next for you?'

'I haven't decided yet. We've been offered a contract in Scotland helping to survey deer populations. And another one not far from here assessing coastal erosion. Marcus and I need to decide soon. We'll have to split up and do one job each, but we haven't figured out which of us will do which.'

'I'd like to go to Scotland,' I say. 'Possibly not at this time of year. But I've always wanted to visit during the summer.'

'What's stopping you?'

'Work, I suppose. I've taken all my leave for the year, and it will be a while before I accrue more. Even when I do, there's no guarantee my boss will let me take it at a time that works for me.'

'Don't ask her,' he advises. 'Just tell her that's what you're doing.'

I feel a flash of irritation. 'Things aren't that simple.'

'Why not?' he asks.

'Because they're not. Maybe you've forgotten what it's like to work for someone else, but that's what I do. If I want to further my career and get something worthwhile on my CV, I'll have to put up with for a while longer.'

He glances over at me. 'I've annoyed you. I'm sorry.'

'You haven't annoyed me. Not really. But life is never as simple as we want it to be, and none of has as much choice as we'd like.'

'Have you finished your eggnog?' he asks. 'Would you like another?'

'Not before I finish my shopping. I don't know what they put in it, but it has quite a kick.'

'Rum,' he says. 'But we could have brandy in our next one.'

'Maybe later. I need to keep my wits about me if I don't want to end up buying a bottle of rose-scented shower gel for Dad and a skateboard repair kit for Gran. Even worse, a *World's Best Boss* mug for Caroline.'

Chapter Thirty-Four

Daniel buys us a bag of caramel almonds, and we eat them as we browse the stalls. I buy a warm scarf for Mum and a jar of chutney for Dad. We stop at a stall with the intriguing title of *A Boxful of Christmas*, where I buy a box containing a selection of scented candles and toiletries for Gran. We get everything wrapped at the charity gift wrap station.

'I'm not sure what to buy for Humphrey,' I say.

'A French maid's outfit?' suggests Daniel.

'Do they make them large enough?'

'I'm not sure. But it might gain you a lot of new followers if you post it on Instagram.'

'I'm definitely not putting that to the test,' I say. 'I've decided to quit the Instagram game. I saw what happened when you put up the pictures of this week's cookies and Celia shared them. I can't compete with that.'

'It had nothing to do with her,' says Daniel. 'People were intrigued by my baking. I wasn't surprised. It isn't often you see Christmas cookies in the shape of drones.'

'There's a reason for that. And it had everything to do with her. Even with your hashtags, no one would have had the faintest idea what those cookies were. I thought they were Lego bricks until I read the captions.'

'That's because you have no technical knowledge,' he says. 'It was clear to the most casual observer that my propellors had been accurately iced.'

'I thought they were flowers.'

'I even included the camera lenses,' he says.

'They looked like buttons. I thought you must have got them mixed up with my snowman cookies from last week.'

He shakes his head. 'Science education in the UK is seriously lacking these days. Shall I critique your last batch for you?'

'They were seasonally appropriate. Gingerbread people epitomise Christmas.'

'Drunk ones?' he asks.

'They weren't drunk! A few of their limbs may have been uneven, but they were all as sober as a judge.'

'Drunk,' he repeats. 'Several of them had eyes going in different directions, and one unfortunate gentleman had lost his nose altogether. I assume in a bar fight. They were a motley crew.'

'They were wonderful! I'm sure the children lucky enough to receive them will be delighted.'

'They'll be suffering nightmares for weeks,' he insists. 'You'd better hope word never gets out who made them or you'll have irate parents chasing you all over the village.'

'We're getting away from the point,' I say. 'I'm trying to tell you I've withdrawn from the contest. You've won. Congratulations.'

He gives a slight bow. 'That's very kind of you. I'd like to thank my parents, who gave me the courage to believe in myself, my preschool teachers, who –'

'I'll leave you to it,' I say. 'It looks as though this could take a while, and I want to see the rest of the fair before it closes.'

'You're right. I haven't had time to prepare my remarks as fully as I would wish. I'll save the rest for a more appropriate time. Perhaps I'll post the entire speech on my Instagram account under the caption *Local Man in Stunning Victory.*'

'You aren't local,' I say. 'And it would be more appropriate for the caption to read *Newcomer Cheats His Way to Undeserved Win.*'

'You're a sore loser,' he says. 'I hate to see it. Shall we put the painful subject behind us and enjoy the fair?'

'That's the plan.'

He links his arm in mine, and I don't object. It would be a pity to lose each other in the crowd and have to waste time searching.

We stop at a stall selling mince pies and sample several flavours.

'I think I like the apple and brandy best,' I say. 'But the orange and cranberry is a close contender.'

'I'm leaning towards the ginger and apricot,' he says. 'But I can't help thinking the pastry isn't as light as it could be. Maybe they forgot to toss the butter onto the floor before mixing it with the flour.'

I point to the Christmas trees. 'I wish I could buy one of those huge trees for Gran. But her living room is quite small, and I wouldn't want to scare Humphrey.'

'I like the little tree you've put up,' he says. 'I was admiring it during our last meeting. Is it real?'

'It's the one Gran uses each year. She told me where to find it in the attic. Humphrey was a little too interested in helping me with the decorations, but I got there in the end.'

'I noticed you posted it on your Instagram account,' he says. 'It didn't receive as many likes as it deserved.'

'Perhaps you could point it out to Cecily in case she missed it?'

'I'm afraid not. She told me once when we were at university together that she never mixes the personal with the professional.'

'Did you really know her at university?' I ask.

'I did. She and I didn't mix in the same circles, but we got on well whenever our paths crossed. She and Marcus dated for a few months, which is how …'

'You persuaded her to like your account?' I say.

'Cecily is a woman who recognises quality when she sees it. I wouldn't be surprised if one of her staff approaches me in the coming months to suggest a cookie collaboration for her next year's wellness promotion.'

'I'd be extremely surprised. But you won fair and square-ish, so I'll say no more about it.'

'What makes me think that may not be true?' he asks.

I laugh. 'I thought we'd declared a truce for the rest of the evening.'

'You're right,' he says. 'It's entirely in the spirit of the season. I approve.'

We stop at a small enclosure labelled *Nativity Petting Zoo.*

'Would you like me to buy you a ticket?' asks Daniel.

'Why not? I love petting zoos. It isn't often you get the chance to stroke,' – I glance at the sign – 'goats, sheep, and more.'

'It's the "more" that's worrying me,' he says, following me into the enclosure.

'No donkeys?' he asks the man running the attraction. 'I would have thought they were the obvious choice for a nativity scene.'

'We offered,' says the man. 'But the organisers thought it might be too risky in this sort of environment. Those things can kick!'

I bend down to stroke a tiny goat who's looking up at me appealingly. 'You would never kick, would you?'

'Probably not,' says the man. 'But she'll eat everything in sight, so don't let her see any food you may have bought this evening.'

He hands us both a bag of pellets. 'These are included in the entry price. They're safe for all the animals we have here.'

'Even the rabbits?' asks Daniel. 'I don't remember those being mentioned in the original nativity story.'

'Aren't they gorgeous?' I exclaim. 'Look at this one eating the pellets out of my hand!'

We spend a while inside the small hut playing with the chickens and the tortoise. To be fair, most of the playing is done by me. Daniel watches with an amused smile.

'You must be kicking yourself that you didn't bring your camera with you,' I say when the man tells us our time is up. 'You could have got your wildlife photography badge with no trouble at all. Your Akela would have been delighted with you.'

'I don't need my camera,' he says. 'I have my phone.'

Before I have time to realise what he's doing, he takes a quick picture of me lowering a guinea pig back onto the straw.

I straighten up. 'That photo had better not end up on your Instagram account. It would be humiliating if it received fewer likes than your awful cookies.'

'I'm sure it would have been equally popular,' he says. '#CutestThingEver – who knew there were #GuineaPigs at the #Nativity?'

'I'm not sure you understand how hashtags work. It ought to be something like #BunnyLove or #FamilyFun. But we'll never know how many likes the photo would have got because our competition is over. Doesn't it seem strange to you that so many people live their lives as a series of hashtags?'

'Are you talking about Cece?' he asks.

'Not particularly. She's seen an opportunity and made the most of it. Good for her. I'm speaking more generally. People reduce even the most intense experiences to a set of tags instead of enjoying them. I was looking through my Instagram feed, and there were loads of pictures of rainbows and firework displays, all hashtagged to death. It made me wonder whether they'd stopped to enjoy the moment or simply pulled out their phones and uploaded the pictures to see how many likes they would get and how quickly they would go viral.'

'Each to their own,' he says. 'I can't say I spend too much time on social media. Real life is far more fun.'

'It can be,' I agree.

He looks down at me with a smile in his eyes. 'I'm all for living in the moment.'

I stare back at him, my heart speeding up again. It can't be the eggnog this time. It's been a while since I drank that. He leans in, his hands sliding to my waist, anchoring me. The world seems to shrink until it's just the two of us, a quiet bubble suspended in time.

'Lucy?' says a voice, and I jump and pull away from him.

'I thought that was you!' says the voice, and I recognise Phyllis standing there. She claps a hand to her mouth. 'I'm so sorry. I didn't realise –'

'It's fine,' I say. 'Are you having a good time at the fair?'

'Lovely, thank you. I apologise for disturbing you.'

She gives Daniel an embarrassed smile. 'You must be wishing me anywhere but here.'

'Not at all,' he says politely. 'It's always a pleasure to see a fellow member of the cookie club.'

'Not so loud,' I tell him. 'The stalls have ears.'

'I should be going,' says Phyllis. 'Give my love to your grandmother.'

She waves and disappears into the crowd.

'That's just great,' I say. 'She'll be on the phone to Gran the minute she gets home. I wonder whether there's time for me to cut the phone lines before she gets the chance.'

'I could call Marcus to send one of our drones over to do the job,' Daniel suggests. 'But it seems a slight overreaction to a chance meeting.'

'I suppose so.'

I stare at my feet, embarrassed. The moment I let my guard down with Daniel, something like this has to happen. What will he do next? In a romantic movie, he would pull me towards him, murmuring, 'Now, where were we?' and I would melt into his arms. I find myself hoping he doesn't do anything so cringeworthy. I needn't have worried.

'Is this a hashtaggable moment?' he enquires.

'It could be. #Excruciating #WhyMe?'

'That's a negative way of looking at things,' he says. 'How about #SeizingTheMoment #TakingAChance?'

'I'm more concerned about my grandmother's friends than taking a chance,' I say.

'I'd noticed that.'

'What does that mean?'

He shrugs. 'Just that you aren't what anyone would call a risk-taker.'

'I take plenty of risks.'

'Such as?'

I struggle to come up with a concrete example. But that doesn't mean there are none. No one should be expected to think clearly under this sort of pressure.

'I'm sorry,' he says. 'Let's not spoil a great evening by arguing.'

I want to agree, to get back to where we were when Phyllis interrupted us. But I can't. I don't know why his words should have stung me so much, but they have.

'Not until you tell me what you mean,' I insist.

'I would have thought it was obvious. You're working in a city you don't like, doing a job you hate for people who treat you like dirt. Yet you won't do anything to change it. That doesn't scream madcap adventurer to me.'

My voice shakes as I answer. 'You have no idea what you're talking about. You've only just met me. How is it any of your business what I choose to do with my life?'

'Lucy, I don't –'

I feel a wave of anger rising inside me that takes me by surprise. 'My life is my business, Daniel, not yours. And I resent being lectured by someone who only knows the smallest fraction of it. I was right about you when we met. You're thoughtless, arrogant, and you think you can fix anything by being charming. It's about time you realised you can't. Other people aren't just there for your entertainment. They're real people, with real feelings, and real problems. And no amount of joking around is going to change that.'

I can't read his expression, but for once it isn't amusement. If I didn't know better, I'd say he looked stricken. But that may be how he looks when he's angry. I don't care. He can be as angry as he likes. I've said what I wanted to say, and he can deal with it.

'Lucy, you have entirely the wrong idea,' he says. 'You think that –'

My anger, which had been dying down, flares up again. 'Don't tell me what I do and don't think! I don't need any stupid mansplaining from you.'

Is that a flicker of laughter in his eyes?

'#Mansplaining?' he asks.

How dare he make fun of me? He may not understand why I'm so upset. Even I don't understand why I am. But it's typical of him to reduce everything to a joke. It's a sign he doesn't really care about other people.

'I'm going home,' I say abruptly.

'Lucy, there's no need for –'

'There's every need,' I say. 'I've been here for far too long. I have responsibilities at home. I can't hang around all night arguing with someone who will never begin to understand that.'

I turn on my heel and march away. I stop after a few steps and turn to face him. 'In case I haven't made myself clear, let me put it in terms you'll understand. #GoodbyeDaniel #DontCallMe.'

I don't wait for him to answer but run across the carpark and set off down the high street by myself.

Chapter Thirty-Five

Margery is just leaving when I arrive home.

'Did you have a good time?' she asks when I walk in.

'Fine, thanks,' I say curtly, and she and Gran exchange surprised glances.

'Just fine?' Gran asks. 'We hoped you'd be more enthusiastic than that.'

'Did you meet anyone nice there?' Margery asks with a knowing smile.

I mustn't be rude to one of Gran's guests, so I can't say any of the things that rise to my lips.

'I'm afraid not,' I say.

She looks at Gran, then back at me. 'Are you holding out on us?'

'I'm not sure what you mean. I didn't meet anyone nice this evening. But I had a good time, and I finished my Christmas shopping. I came home to take Humphrey for a walk if he's ready.'

I give them both a fake smile, grab his lead, and bundle him out into the chilly night air before either he or they can protest. Humphrey is usually the one dictating the pace, but tonight he has to run to keep up with me.

'We'll stay in the grassy area,' I tell him. 'It's too dark down by the water. I don't fancy a midnight swim in these temperatures.'

I pull out the ball I stuffed into my pocket as I left the house and throw it for him. He gives a delighted bark and runs after it. Or rather, he runs straight past it. His coordination needs work, but his enthusiasm more than makes up for it. I throw the ball for him for an hour. I prefer not to go home until my temper has cooled. None of this is Gran's fault, and I don't want to end up arguing with her as well.

When even Humphrey has tired of the game, I clip on his lead, and we walk more slowly back to Bramble Close. I find Gran preparing for bed and feel a pang of guilt that I've stayed out for so long. She doesn't seem to mind.

'You've had a lovely walk, haven't you?' she asks Humphrey as he leaps up to lick her face.

'Careful!' I warn him, but she just laughs.

'I'm a lot steadier on my feet than I was when I first came home. I think Humphrey senses that.'

I'm not convinced, but there's no point in arguing. All I want is to get the pair of them settled, then retreat to my bedroom. I'm exhausted, and not just because of my recent ball game with Humphrey.

I help Gran into bed, count out her tablets, and fetch her a glass of water.

'How did tonight really go?' she asks as I plump up her pillow.

'I've told you. It was great. I finished my shopping and had some eggnog.'

'All by yourself?' she asks.

I turn to face her. 'I know you sent a message to Daniel telling him I'd be at the fair tonight. I'm not sure why, but –'

'I thought you might enjoy some company.'

'I can find my own company if I need it.'

I see her expression and relent. 'I don't mean to be snappy. I know what you were doing, and maybe it's a grandmother's prerogative to match-make for her grandchild. But you've missed the mark with this one. Still, there's no harm done. Can I get you anything else before I go upstairs?'

She settles back on her pillow. 'Humphrey and I are fine, thank you. I'm sorry if –'

'Don't give it another thought.' I bend to kiss her cheek. 'You can't win them all. Night, Gran.'

I feel somewhat better the following morning. I'm still annoyed with Daniel, but that isn't Gran's problem. I go about my day as usual, taking Humphrey out for some exercise and stopping in at the village shop for the list of groceries Gran has given me. It isn't until mid-afternoon that she mentions the fair again.

'Phyllis called this morning.'

'Is that right?' I say, determined not to give her any help. With any luck, she'll let the subject drop.

She doesn't. 'She told me she saw you at the fair last night.'

'I may have bumped into Phyllis at some point,' I say. 'There were lots of people there.'

'You told us last night you didn't meet anyone.'

'I told you I hadn't met anyone nice,' I say. 'And I hadn't.'

'So, you and Daniel …?'

'There is no me and Daniel. I'm not sure who told you there was, but they were wrong. Perhaps you could spread that around to all your friends before they get carried away.'

'No one had to tell me,' she says. 'I have eyes in my head. It's obvious that young man likes you very much. And I thought –'

'That's wishful thinking on your part,' I say. 'Even if you were right about him, it takes two to make a successful relationship, and I'm not interested.'

'Why not?' she asks.

'I'm just not. Can we please drop the subject?'

'If you like. But I'm worried about you, Lucy.'

'Because I don't have a man in my life? Times have changed, Gran. No one needs a man to live a happy and fulfilled life.'

She smiles. 'They never did. I'm not as old-fashioned as you think. My mother told me never to settle for someone unless I was sure I couldn't live without them.'

'Like Grandpa Ed?'

'Exactly.'

'That's great,' I say. 'And I know how happy you two were. And how happy my parents have been together. But I agree with your mother. I've never met anyone I'm sure I can't live without.'

I'm hoping this will put an end to the conversation. But of course, it doesn't. This is Grandma Lavender. She's a Hollis woman, and she comes from a long line of Hollis women, all of whom are known for speaking their minds.

'You're not listening to me,' she says.

'Yes, I am. You've told me not to settle, and I don't intend to. I realise you and your friends have decided it would be fun to set me up with Daniel. But that's not your decision to make.'

'I'm aware of that,' she says. 'But you're deliberately misunderstanding what I'm saying. No one meets someone and immediately realises this is the person they want to spend the rest of their lives with. Or if that happens, it's very rare. But we meet someone we get along with, and we take a chance and see where it goes.'

'I don't get along with Daniel,' I insist.

'I'm your grandmother. I know you extremely well.' Her tone softens. 'What happened last night?'

To my horror, I feel the tears prick my eyes. 'Nothing.'

She pats the chair next to her. 'Why don't you sit down and tell me all about it?'

I sniff. 'Humphrey needs his afternoon walk.'

'Humphrey is fast asleep in his basket. You've walked him off his legs. You don't have to talk to me, Lucy, but you might feel better afterwards.'

I try to tell her yet again that she's wrong, but my voice cracks, and the tears start to my eyes. Gran doesn't look perturbed. She pours me a cup of tea and waits.

'We had an argument,' I say at last.

'About what?'

I try to remember. 'Daniel was being his usual obnoxious self.'

She smiles. 'He's never struck me as particularly obnoxious.'

'That's because you don't know him.'

She takes a sip of her tea. 'What did you argue about?'

'My job.'

She considers this. 'That doesn't sound like a contentious subject.'

'He implied that I hate it, but that I'm too cowardly to change it.'

'Why does he think you should change it?'

'Because he's an interfering know-it-all.'

I catch her amused smile and add, 'It's true! He's known me for a couple of weeks, and he thinks he knows everything there is to know about my life.'

'Is he wrong about your job?' she asks.

'No, but that isn't the point.'

She hands me the plate of cookies. 'Are you sure? You haven't seemed happy for a while. I've been worried about you.'

I select the largest cookie. 'You're allowed to be worried about me. He isn't.'

Her eyes dance. 'I suppose you told him that?'

'I told him I never wanted to see him again and not to call me.'

'I realise I'm old,' she says, 'and your generation sees things differently to mine. But that strikes me as rather an overreaction. From what I can tell, he was just expressing concern for you.'

'I didn't ask for his opinion,' I say. 'Maybe it was an overreaction. But he hit a nerve.'

'I thought so. Out of interest, why have you stayed at that job for so long when you hate it so much? Is it because of your father?'

There's never any point in trying to hide things from Gran. She always puts her finger straight on the point, whether or not I want her to.

'I can't bear to let my parents down,' I say. 'They were so upset at the thought of Dad's accident affecting my life too. I tried to tell them several times that I'd made a mistake in taking that job, but they thought I was trying to make them feel better about the idea of me leaving it and coming home to help. In the end, I gave up. It won't hurt me to stay there for a while to gain experience. And it will stop them worrying. They have enough on their plates without that.'

Gran is silent for a while. She looks up at last and meets my gaze. 'Why didn't you tell Daniel all that? I'm sure he would have understood.'

'Because he made me so angry,' I admit. 'I don't know why. I'm not usually an angry person, but these past few months have felt different. Everything makes me snappy. It's as much as I can do to be polite to people sometimes. Maybe I need a proper holiday.'

'I think you do,' she says. 'But it isn't just that, is it? Have you ever talked to anyone about your father's accident – not just the facts of it?'

'Not really. There's not a lot to say. He was almost killed. We thought he might never walk again. He's had a year of painful physiotherapy and still doesn't know how well he'll recover. The man who did it will be out of prison soon and free to go about his business with no consequences, while Mum and Dad serve a possible life sentence for what he did.'

'I doubt that young man's life will be entirely consequence-free,' she says.

I feel the familiar flare of anger. 'That's what Mum said the last time I talked to her about it. It made me angry, but there was nothing I could say. She and Dad have been so positive about this whole thing. It would be wrong for me to bring them down. They have the right to handle it in any way they like.'

Gran's eyes are full of understanding. 'You have the right to your own feelings too, Lucy. Don't let them get lost in all this.'

Tears prick my eyes again. 'What's the point? All the anger in the world won't turn the clock back to last December and the decision that man made.'

'It won't,' she says. 'But pretending you don't feel anything won't make it magically disappear either. I was angry when your grandfather died. No amount of reminding myself we'd had more than fifty happy years together stopped me feeling that way.'

'What did?' I ask.

'Talking to my friends about it. Telling them how I felt and how confused and guilty I was. And hearing the ones who had gone through the same thing say they'd experienced similar emotions, and I wasn't a bad person for feeling what I felt.'

'I don't know anyone whose father's life has been upended by a drunk driver,' I say.

'But you know people who have felt grief and anger and pain and come through it. It doesn't have to be exactly the same situation for someone to understand what you're going through.'

'You're right,' I admit. 'But I don't have many close friends. We all went our separate ways after university, and I haven't made any new ones in London. I thought Daniel was becoming a friend, but he turned out not to be. He's just like everyone else. He'll never understand how I feel. He showed me that last night.'

'He won't understand if you don't let him,' she says. 'Why not give him a chance?'

'It's too late for that now. And frankly, I don't have the energy.'

'So, talk to someone else,' she says.

'You mean a therapist?'

'Or me, if you prefer. I promise not to tell you how you feel, and I make an excellent cup of tea. We could add a little something to it if that helps. Just to keep the cold out, you understand. The bottle is in the larder.'

This makes me laugh. I wipe my eyes. 'Thanks, Gran. I have to walk Humphrey soon, and I don't want to get lost, so I'll stick to regular tea. But I think it might help to talk to someone.'

She pushes the plate of cookies towards me again. 'There's no time like the present. Humphrey won't be awake for a while.'

I pick up another cookie and take a bite without tasting it. Then, leaning back in my chair, I start to talk.

Chapter Thirty-Six

I wake the following morning feeling lighter than I have for months. I'm not sure why talking to Gran made such a difference, but it did. I told her all the things I've been pushing down inside me for an entire year, and she wasn't shocked or horrified. She just listened.

It took quite a while. When I finally finished, she gave me a hug and told me I'd done wonderfully well, and that Mum and Dad were lucky to have a daughter like me, which made me cry again. Then she asked me to peel the potatoes for supper and check whether Humphrey had enough dried food left to last for the Christmas week.

I did as she asked. After that, I took him for his walk and helped Gran make a shepherd's pie for dinner. We watched a murder mystery together while we ate it. It was lovely to have a normal, uncomplicated evening. I was worried that if I opened the lid of that box, it would be impossible to nail it shut again. But, to my relief, it doesn't seem to work like that. I was able to tell Gran how I've been feeling, then go about my regular life without collapsing in a broken heap. Not for the first time, I'm glad to have someone like her in my life.

We spend the next few days quietly. I'm too tired to make more than the most basic preparations for Christmas, and Gran assures me she prefers not to make a fuss this year. She seems to mean it, which is a relief. I'm distinctly lacking in enthusiasm for the festive season. I wonder whether I'll ever recover it. Maybe I'll end up like Scrooge after all – before the ghosts visited him. I wouldn't blame them for taking one look at me and deciding to give the whole thing a miss and move on to a more receptive target.

Gran and I haven't talked about Daniel since the night of the Christmas Fair. I'm grateful to her for respecting my privacy. I don't intend to think about him again if I can help it. I'm not sure what happened between us, or didn't happen.

But I don't have the capacity to do anything about it. He may be on his way to Scotland by now, if he isn't there already, and that's a good thing for both of us.

I have a sudden vision of him driving up the motorway in his hired car, closely pursued by a flock of drones in close formation. I remember my resolve not to think about him and force myself to resume my regular routine with Gran and Humphrey.

It's a shock when I wake on Tuesday to realise it's Christmas Eve. I feel completely unprepared for tomorrow's festivities, but Gran doesn't seem worried.

'There's plenty of time for any last-minute touches,' she tells me over breakfast. 'When I was a child, we didn't even decorate the tree until Christmas Eve.'

'I know you don't want a fuss, but I had visions of you coming home from the hospital to a beautifully decorated house with carols playing in the background and the smell of mince pies baking. I'm not good at this Christmas thing.'

'Lucy, you looked after Humphrey for me. That was all I cared about – not some Hallmark version of Christmas. Besides, we have the whole of today. We can get a lot done in a day if we want to.'

'I won't have you climbing up ladders to hang mistletoe,' I warn her. 'Humphrey wouldn't cope with you disappearing off to the hospital again. But I'd be grateful for a few hints.'

'Isn't it time for Humphrey's walk?' she asks. 'We can talk about everything else when you get home. He's been especially frisky this morning, so I'd appreciate it if you could give him an extra-long run.'

I grab his harness and open the front door. Gran is right. It may be almost Christmas, but that's no excuse for neglecting Humphrey's exercise regime. He has no idea today is Christmas Eve. I try to suppress the thought that I'd prefer not to know either. The idea of spending a week on a remote island in the Caribbean and ignoring the entire holiday season is appealing.

'Don't be such a Scrooge,' I chide myself. 'You'll be posting *Bah, Humbug!* memes on Instagram soon. Or you would if you hadn't deleted your account after your crushing defeat.'

I know that wasn't very sporting of me, but I don't care. There's a good reason I stay away from social media. I should never have allowed myself to be sucked into using it for our ridiculous competition. I have no idea what got into me to make me agree to such a thing. A treacherous little voice tells me it was fun, but I tell it to pipe down. It was a stupid thing to get involved with, and deleting my account ensures I won't be tempted to do anything like that ever again.

I stay out for as long as possible, watching Humphrey charge around the field. There aren't many birds about today. Possibly, word has spread. But he manages to flush a pheasant from the undergrowth. It rises into the air with a whirr of its wings and a look of utter contempt on its face.

'Poor you,' I console him, fixing his lead back on. 'You can't catch a break, can you? Never mind – you shall have some turkey tomorrow.'

He pricks up his ears and gives me a considering look.

'Don't worry,' I say. 'No one will expect you to dress up as Santa or one of his reindeer. I'm done with all that. We'll have a lovely, quiet day with Gran. You can open your stocking in the morning when you wake up. And if there's enough snow, I'll take you outside for a snowball fight. You'll enjoy that.'

He sets off happily towards home. I envy his life. It's so simple and predictable. I don't want to live exactly as he does – too many walks, for one thing – but I find myself wishing things could be as uncomplicated for me.

He prances up the garden path, then stops at the front door, looking up at me with a worried expression.

'What's wrong?' I ask him. 'Can you hear something? Or do you think another delivery driver has been here while we were away? There's nothing for you to worry about. I know you don't like them, but they've been useful this year.'

He stiffens his legs and refuses to move. I bend to stroke his head.

'It's alright, Humphrey. Shall I go in first and check the coast is clear? If it's a delivery driver, they won't have stayed around. They're far too busy at this time of year – almost as busy as Santa.'

I put my key in the door and push it open, to be greeted by a wave of noise and laughter. Is Gran having a party? Does she do that each time I leave the house? She was quite insistent on me taking Humphrey out for a long walk. Maybe she keeps a selection of friends in the garden shed, bringing them out whenever she manages to get rid of me.

'Lucy!' calls a voice, and I see it's Irene. 'Come on in. Everyone's here!'

Everyone who? I keep a tight hold on Humphrey's lead as I step inside.

'Did you have a pleasant walk?' asks another voice. It takes me a moment to place where it's coming from. I catch sight of Phyllis, precariously balanced on a step ladder, fixing a piece of tinsel around the hall window.

'What's happening here?' I ask.

'A special meeting of the cookie club,' says Margery, bustling out of the kitchen with a tray of glasses.

'But we've delivered all the cookies,' I say, confused. 'I saw the final list. We didn't miss a single house.'

'We're not here to deliver cookies,' she says. 'We're here to decorate your Gran's cottage for Christmas.'

I look around, stunned, trying to take in the transformation. The once-plain hallway has been draped with garlands of evergreen. Glittering silver tinsel catches the light and sends it shimmering across the stairwell. Someone has twined a string of fairy lights up the banisters, casting a warm glow across the hall below. And a sweet, spicy scent fills the air.

June opens the front door to hang a wreath above the door handle. I instinctively tighten my hold on Humphrey, but he doesn't make a dash for freedom. He sits on the mat and looks around him with interest. Someone has fixed sprigs of mistletoe and holly to the ceiling. The red and white berries reflect the shine of the fairy lights.

Several more garlands have been strung above the kitchen door, and there are paper snowflakes along the walls and windows.

'You did all this while we were gone?' I say.

'Of course,' says Margery. 'It doesn't take long when you're all working together.'

'Where's Gran?' I ask, and she points.

Humphrey and I walk into the living room, and the sight takes my breath away. The Christmas tree has been transformed. Gran's old decorations have disappeared, and it's now adorned with shimmering glass baubles and tiny silver ornaments. Gold tinsel twists through the branches. Someone has removed the tired-looking angel from the top of the tree. In its place is a delicate silver star that flashes and glows in time with the lights twinkling beneath it. It looks as though someone has stretched out a hand and picked it straight from the night sky.

There's a red velvet tree skirt draped around the base of the tree, embroidered with little snowflakes and reindeer. I feel as though I've landed in the middle of one of Hans Christian Andersen's fairy tales. Several brightly wrapped packages are lying on the velvet cloth.

'We'll have to move those before Humphrey sees them,' says June. 'But we wanted you to see the effect.'

'It's amazing,' I say.

Gran smiles up at me from the sofa. She's wrapped in a red checked shawl I haven't seen before. 'I told you not to worry about Christmas.'

I sit next to her, still holding Humphrey's lead. 'You did, but I had no idea what you meant. Did you know they were coming over to do this?'

'Of course, she did,' says Phyllis. 'She called the moment you left the house and told us the coast was clear. We'd hoped to finish it all before you came home, but Vera spilled a box of glitter, and it took a while to clear it up.'

'I wouldn't have spilled it if you hadn't left those cups and plates for me to trip over,' Vera defends herself.

'Please don't quarrel on my account,' I say. 'You've done an incredible job. And it's my fault for coming home early. Gran asked me to give Humphrey an extra-long walk, but my feet were so cold I was worried I might be developing frostbite, and I was hungry.'

'We have just the thing for that,' says June.

She points to the coffee table next to the window, where I see a tray of mince pies dusted with powdered sugar, looking as though a light snow has fallen on them. There's also a plate of gingerbread people, all perfectly iced. Their limbs are going in the correct direction, and every button and bow tie is in place. They clearly haven't been at the eggnog, as mine had.

'Spiced cider?' asks Margery.

'Is that what I could smell when I walked past the kitchen?' I say.

'That's right. But don't think I'll telling you what's in it. It's an old family recipe, and I'm sworn to secrecy.'

'I'd love some,' I say. 'And I promise not to ask any inconvenient questions.'

She disappears, returning a minute later with two large glasses, each with a stick of cinnamon sticking out of the top. She hands one to Gran and the other to me.

'I still can't believe you've done this,' I say, taking a sip and feeling the warmth make its way straight to my toes. Maybe they won't develop frostbite and drop off after all.

I take another gulp. It's delicious – full of warmth and spice, with a hint of something fruity. I'm sure I can taste honey too. There's something else I can't quite identify, although I recognise the comforting blend of cinnamon and cloves that always says Christmas to me.

'It's like drinking a warm hug,' I say.

'It's supposed to be,' says Margery. 'I remember my grandmother making this cider for us each Christmas. She left out the secret alcoholic ingredient when I was small and would never tell me what it was. But it still tasted wonderful. Of course, it tasted even more wonderful when I was old enough to drink the real thing.'

I glance around the room. 'I can't believe the entire cookie club is here.'

'Except for the other temporary member,' says June, and Gran shoots her a warning look.

I pretend not to notice. I'm not sure how I'd have felt if Daniel had been here today. My brain feels like my best friend from university's almost permanent Facebook status – It's complicated.

'I bumped into him at the shops recently,' says Irene. 'He was telling me about the new contract he's been offered. Somewhere in Scotland, he said. I can't remember where.'

No one looks at me. I clear my throat and hand my glass back to Margery. 'I'd better see about Humphrey's lunch.'

'No need,' she says. 'We brought him a beautiful piece of steamed salmon. It doesn't seem fair for him to miss out on all the Christmas fun.'

'He'll love that,' says Gran. 'Aren't you a lucky boy, Humphrey?'

He licks her hand and allows Margery to lead him to the kitchen.

'Are you alright, Lucy?' Gran asks me in a low voice.

'Of course. Why wouldn't I be? I'm just stunned by everything your friends have done for you today.'

'We're a team,' she says. 'We look out for each other. We always have. This is much more than a cookie club. It's a family.'

'That's right,' says Phyllis, reeling past holding a large glass of cider. By the looks of it, this isn't her first, or even her second. But who cares? These women have just performed a miracle, and they deserve to party.

'We're like the three musketeers,' says June. 'All for one, and one for all.'

'Except there are ten of us,' says Gran. 'But the principle is the same.'

I look around at the laughing, chattering women. This Christmas may not be exactly what I was expecting. But that's no reason for me to wish it was cancelled. It's like most things in life – it promises one thing and delivers another. Sometimes better, sometimes worse. All you can do is go with the flow and meet it cheerfully.

This must be what my parents decided to do after the accident. No one could have predicted what would happen to Dad, but it happened all the same. They had the choice to allow it to crush them and take away all their hopes and dreams or to adapt and make the most of what they still had. I wish I'd talked to them about it more. It might have helped me let go of some of my bitterness and anger.

Gran has done a lot to help me. And so has this party. I doubt any of the women here has led a completely trouble-free life. But they've made the most of it and kept going and supported each other through everything. They're an inspiration.

The party continues for most of the afternoon. Humphrey grows bored around three o'clock and takes himself upstairs to nap on my bed. As well as the mince pies and cookies, the club members have brought sausage rolls and quiches and tiny sandwiches cut into festive shapes. There's an enormous platter of cheese and crackers with tiny sprigs of rosemary tucked alongside them. June produces a bowl of spiced pecans and walnuts, which disappear in minutes.

Margery wanders around the room, topping up our glasses, while the members share stories of past meetings, each more hilarious than the last. At one point, a conga line forms in the hallway, led by Phyllis.

No one mentions Daniel again, which is good. I don't want to think about him for a while. I'm glad he's going to Scotland. It means I won't bump into him around the village this week. He's probably left already. He's completed his contract for the town council, so there's nothing to keep him here. And no reason for me to think of him ever again.

The afternoon slips by far too quickly. The sound of carols plays softly in the background, blending with the crackling of the fire and the occasional bursts of laughter. I wish it would never end.

But, like everything else, it does. June looks out of the window at five o'clock and sighs. 'It's dark already. We should be going. Don't worry, Lucy. We won't leave you a huge mess to clear up. We'll take it all with us when we go. You'll never know we were here.'

'But I want to know you were here,' I say. 'This has been one of the best afternoons of my life. I never want to forget it.'

'You have plenty more afternoons like this to look forward to,' she says.

'I hope so. But it will take a lot to top this. Thank you all so much. I wasn't in the Christmas mood when I started, but I am now.'

They're as good as their word. They gather up the paper plates and cups and put them into a large garbage bag. Margery wipes down the kitchen counters, while Irene stacks the empty boxes next to the front door.

'Get to bed early,' she advises me and Gran. 'Remember, Santa only visits when you're asleep.'

'I doubt he visits here,' I say. 'Humphrey would wake the entire village.'

'You never know,' she says. 'Christmas Eve is full of surprises. I've always enjoyed it more than Christmas Day. There's still so much to look forward to.'

Humphrey comes downstairs to see them off. Or, as June suggests, to make sure all the unwanted visitors have departed.

'That was quite the afternoon,' I say when they've gone.

Gran smiles. 'Whatever you do in life, Lucy, make sure you find a group of friends who will do what these women did today, and you won't go far wrong.'

'I'll do my best. But you must be exhausted after all that partying. Can I make you a cup of tea?'

'I'm not tired at all,' she says, glancing at her watch. 'Goodness! It's nearly six o'clock.'

'Are you counting how many hours until Santa arrives?' I ask.

'Something like that. I'm almost sure I heard his sleigh outside. Could you just check for me?'

I laugh. 'How many glasses of cider did you drink?'

I'm surprised to see she isn't smiling.

'I'm sure I heard a noise out the front,' she says. 'Take a look for me, would you, Lucy?'

'Of course.' I walk down the hallway and look through the peephole. 'I can't see anyone.'

'I know I heard something,' she insists.

'I'll go and check. Keep a hold of Humphrey, would you? It's snowing, and I don't want him to disappear.'

I open the door a crack and peer down the driveway. An unfamiliar blue van has drawn up outside. Is this another Christmas parcel? I'm surprised they're still delivering at this time on Christmas Eve.

'I'll see who it is,' I tell Gran. 'I don't want anyone leaving the gate unlatched.'

Just as I reach the gate, the driver's door opens, and Mum climbs out. She catches sight of me and beams. 'Lucy! I'm so glad to see you.'

I stop dead, staring at the van. 'What are you doing here? Whose van is this? And where's Dad?'

The passenger window rolls down, and Dad leans out. 'Hi, sweetheart. Happy Christmas!'

Chapter Thirty-Seven

I wake early on Christmas morning and lie in bed, thinking back over the extraordinary events of yesterday evening. I used to stay awake for hours waiting for Santa's sleigh, but the arrival of that blue van was even more magical.

There's no sound from downstairs, but I'm not worried. Humphrey will let me know when he and Gran are awake. I lie back on my pillows, feeling more relaxed than I've done for a long time. I hadn't been looking forward to Christmas very much. Last year was enough to make me wonder whether I ever would again.

And then the cookie club arrived and turned the cottage into a Christmas wonderland. Not only that, they helped me to understand what's really important in life. Mum and Dad's arrival was the icing on the cake – the best Christmas delivery in the history of Christmas deliveries. Whatever Santa may have loaded onto his sleigh this year can't top that.

I should get up. Mum and Dad are staying in a bungalow a few miles away so they don't have to worry about the stairs. I have no idea what time they'll arrive this morning. And Humphrey will soon want his walk. I tiptoe downstairs and take a shower. There's still no sound from the living room. That's good. It was an exciting evening for Humphrey and Gran too, and they need their sleep.

It was sweet to see how pleased Humphrey was to see Mum and Dad last night. He saw Mum a couple of weeks ago, but he hadn't seen Dad in over a year. He sat by Dad's chair all evening, looking up at him with huge, soulful eyes. None of us could understand it until Dad admitted he'd filled his pockets with dog treats before leaving home.

I dry myself off and return to my bedroom as quietly as possible to put on some warm clothes. A glance outside tells me it's been snowing in the night. By the look of the sky, it won't be long until it starts again. Humphrey and I may be making that snowman after all.

I pull back the curtains more fully, and something catches my eye. It's a large bird flying slowly across the patch of grass beyond Gran's back fence. I'm not great at identifying birds, but it's nothing like the crows and jackdaws whose acquaintance Humphrey is always attempting to make. Is it a heron or a stork? Do we even have those in this country? Perhaps they make a special appearance on Christmas Day.

It rises higher, hovering like a bird of prey. I rub my eyes and look more closely. It's not a bird at all. It's a drone. It slowly rises into the air and flies over the fence and into our garden, where it hovers about ten feet away from my bedroom window and starts to play music. Is that Jingle Bells?

This has to be one of Daniel's drones. Doesn't he know I'd be within my rights to shoot it down as an enemy aircraft? I'm not up to date on the finer points of British aviation law, but I'm sure I'm at least allowed to throw my hairbrush at it.

A banner has been fixed to its struts. The letters are large and slightly crooked, clearly painted by hand. I squint to make out the words.

'*Permission to enter hostile airspace?*' the banner reads.

A laugh bubbles up inside me. I step closer to the window, watching the drone as it drifts back and forth. How am I supposed to communicate with it? I remember the drone Daniel used to locate Humphrey. It had a small camera at the front and underneath.

I raise a hand and wave. The drone waggles its wings in acknowledgement, then turns and disappears over the back fence. I watch it go, baffled. Why has Daniel sent a drone to my window, only to recall it a minute later? Just to show he can violate enemy airspace at will? I've been watching too many World War Two movies with Dad.

As I stare into the garden, trying to make sense of this, the drone reappears. This time it's carrying something, although I can't be sure what. It's wrapped in green and red Christmas paper, with a silver ribbon that sparkles in the morning sun. It hovers next to my window for a few seconds, then flies over the roof of the cottage.

I pull on a thick sweater and run downstairs. I open the front door and peer outside, unsure what to expect. I spot the drone hovering next to the hedge. As I watch, Daniel appears at the gate. He isn't holding a remote control. How is he doing this? Has he programmed it in advance and set it on autopilot?

Apparently not. Just as he's closing the gate, the drone gives a violent wobble, the claws open, and the package crashes to the ground, narrowly missing the privet hedge.

'That wasn't supposed to happen,' he says.

I walk down the path to meet him. 'What are you doing here? And why is half your drone stock flying over my house with cryptic messages?'

'Not cryptic,' he says. 'It's basic drone etiquette when flying over potentially hostile territory. Always obtain the landowner's permission first.'

'I'm not the landowner,' I object, and he grins.

'Shall we call your grandmother to sign a waiver?'

'She's still asleep. But Humphrey may wake up at any moment and decide it's a rogue magpie that needs taking down.'

'Too late,' he says, waving to the drone, which turns and drifts away over the hedge.

'How are you doing that?' I ask.

'I'm not. Marcus is. And I'll be having strong words with him later about his delivery technique.'

'I don't understand,' I say. 'I thought you'd gone to Scotland.'

'Who told you that?'

'Irene mentioned she'd met you in the village. She said you'd finished your work here and were off to Scotland for your next contract.'

'I said I might be. I told you we'd been offered two contracts – one in Scotland, and one locally. Marcus and I haven't yet decided which one of us should take on the Scottish contract.'

I stare at my feet. 'How will you decide?'

He takes a step towards me. 'I thought I'd leave that up to you.'

My breath catches as he puts his hands on my shoulders and looks down at me. There's a slight smile playing around the corners of his mouth, but there's an unfamiliar look of anxiety in his eyes.

'Up to me?' I ask, my voice barely above a whisper.

He nods, his gaze steady. 'If you'd rather I stayed around for a while, I will. If not, I'll take a train to Scotland tomorrow and spend the next few months wishing things had turned out differently between us.'

I can't speak for a moment. I thought I would never see him again. After my behaviour towards him at the fair, I didn't think he would ever want to see me. Yet here he is, telling me he wants to make this work. The question is, do I?

I look into his familiar brown eyes and realise this isn't even a question. I nod.

'Just to confirm,' he says, leaning a little closer. 'That's a yes to me staying?'

I can't speak, so I nod again. He pulls me into his arms, and his lips meet mine, soft and warm in the cold morning air, snowflakes drifting down around us. It feels as though we're the only two people in the world as I kiss him back. When he finally draws away, I look up at him and smile.

'I didn't think I'd ever see you again.'

'I was worried I'd never see you again,' he says. 'You and I had unfinished business. I wanted to find out what it would be like to kiss you without being interrupted by Phyllis.'

I flush as I remember the Christmas fair. 'I'm sorry I was so awful to you that night. It's a complicated situation, but I shouldn't have taken it out on you.'

'I was the one to blame. I had no right to tell you what you should do with your life. I'm sorry, Lucy. I won't do that again.'

'I may have overreacted slightly,' I say. 'I've done that quite a bit over the last year.'

His eyes soften. 'I can imagine. You told me what had happened to you and your family. I should have been more understanding.'

'I didn't give you the chance. I've been holding people at arm's length all year and refusing to allow anyone to help me deal with it. Gran helped me to see that. I didn't understand it at first. But then all her friends turned up yesterday to make sure she and I had a wonderful Christmas. And I realised what a difference it makes if you let people help instead of shutting them out.'

'I heard about the emergency meeting of the Honeywell Christmas Cookie Club,' he says.

'I'm sorry you weren't invited,' I say, conscience-stricken.

'I was. Irene told me all about it and suggested I come along.'

'No one mentioned that to me.'

'That's because I told her I'd prefer to sit this one out and wait until I'd talked to you alone. It didn't seem fair to land on your doorstep without giving you the chance to decide whether you even wanted to see me.'

'I could have thrown you out if I didn't,' I say. 'Or got Humphrey to do it for me.'

He laughs. 'I was worried about that too.'

'It would have been publicly humiliating. I understand why you might have wanted to avoid that.'

'I have my dignity,' he says.

'I've watched you trying to bake. No, you don't.'

'No, I don't,' he agrees. 'But I still wanted to see you alone.'

I move closer to him. 'We're alone right now, and there don't seem to be any more drones around.'

'So we are,' he says, his arms tightening around me. 'I think we should make the most of it.'

He leans down, his lips brushing against mine. His kiss is gentle at first, but when I respond, nestling closer to him, it deepens. His hands find their way to my waist, and I wrap my arms around his neck, pulling him in as though the world outside has disappeared, and he and I are the only two people left.

I barely notice the noise of an engine coming up the street or the sound of it pulling it up to the kerb.

'Oh, my goodness!' says a voice, making us both jump.

I turn my head to see Mum standing by the garden gate, looking at us with a stunned expression on her face.

Chapter Thirty-Eight

I try to take a step away from Daniel, but it's too late. She's already seen us standing there wrapped in each other's arms. And what excuse can I make – Daniel was testing the fabric of my hoodie to check it's properly waterproof?

'Hi, Mum,' I say in a carefully casual tone. 'This is Daniel.'

Her face lights up. 'I've heard so much about you!'

'No, you haven't,' I say. 'I've never mentioned him in any of my calls.'

'But your grandmother has. She's mentioned him several times.'

'Lovely to meet you,' she tells Daniel. 'I'd give you a hug, but you seem a little … tied up at the moment.'

'Just a temporary state of affairs,' he says. 'It's lovely to meet you too, Mrs Hollis.'

'You can call me Liz,' she says. 'I have a feeling we're going to be seeing more of each other.'

'I hope so,' he says. 'Does your husband need help getting out of the van?'

Mum claps her hand to her mouth. 'I'd forgotten about Robert!'

'Poor Dad,' I say. 'First you drag him all the way down here, and then you abandon him in the freezing cold.'

'It's lovely and warm in there,' she says. 'I told you the insurance came through last month. There was enough left for us to buy a properly adapted van. And I made sure it had an excellent heater. I hate having cold toes when I drive.'

'You can tell us more about your temperature preferences later,' I say, freeing myself from Daniel's arms and walking over to hug her. 'Meanwhile, Daniel can make himself useful and do whatever needs doing.'

'I'm happy to,' he says. 'While I'm doing that, maybe you could pick up the parcel over there?'

'Why is it lying in the snow?' asks Mum. 'Did the postman throw it over the hedge? He ought to be more careful.'

'Don't blame the postman,' I say. 'There are no deliveries on Christmas Day. This arrived by … other means.'

I try to catch Daniel's eye, but he's already walking towards the van.

'I'll tell you later,' I say to Mum. 'Or Daniel can.'

'Is he coming in for a while? I do hope so. Your father and I have been looking forward to meeting him.'

'I haven't asked him,' I say. 'But I'm sure the answer is yes. Daniel has a habit of turning up when he's least expected and finding any excuse to stay.'

She only smiles and returns to the van. I retrieve the parcel from the snow. I give it a gentle shake and hear a slight rattling noise. I hope it isn't something fragile like wine glasses. Even Daniel should know better than that. I carry it into the house and put it on the hall table.

'Is that you, Lucy?' calls Gran's voice from the kitchen.

'Happy Christmas!' I say, giving her a hug. 'And to you, Humphrey. Has Santa visited?'

'He has,' she says. 'I noticed Humphrey's stocking had been filled when we woke up this morning. Santa must have been extremely quiet. Humphrey didn't bark at all.'

'Perhaps Santa waited until you were both asleep,' I suggest.

'Is that your parents I heard outside?'

'They arrived a few minutes ago.'

'I thought I heard a noise in the back garden earlier,' she says. 'I must have been mistaken.'

'That was Daniel. More precisely, it was one of his drones.'

She looks pleased. 'Did he accompany it?'

I smile back at her. 'He did. He and I have decided to … we thought that …'

'I'm delighted to hear it,' she says. 'Several members of the cookie club stand to make a fair bit of money from the news – including me.'

'I'll pretend I didn't hear that.'

The front door opens again, and Dad comes in. He's leaning heavily on his sticks, but he's walking by himself. Mum has obviously been keeping secrets from me, just as I have from her.

'I've met Daniel,' he says as I help him off with his coat. 'He seems like a pleasant lad. He's been telling me about his drone company.'

Daniel appears in the doorway behind him. 'Don't get your daughter started on the subject of drones. She has a low opinion of them.'

'Not always,' I say, remembering the night Humphrey got lost. 'But I wouldn't recommend you sinking all your money into starting a delivery business. Look what happened to that parcel.'

'It's fine,' he says, handing it to me. 'I wrapped it in several layers of paper.'

I tear open the package to find a smaller box inside containing a whisk, a spatula, a Christmas apron, and a tiny rolling pin.

'It's beautiful,' I say. 'But I didn't get you anything. I wasn't expecting to see you today.'

'You didn't throw me out on my ear the moment you saw me,' says Daniel. 'That's more than enough for me.'

'Don't stand in the hallway getting cold,' says Gran. 'Come through to the living room. I've lit the fire.'

I hold out my hand to Daniel. 'No need to ask whether you're joining us.'

'I don't want to intrude,' he says. 'I can come back another time.'

'Don't even think about it,' says Mum. 'There's plenty of room for us all.'

This isn't quite true, particularly when Humphrey joins us. But we all squash in. Dad sits in the armchair by the window, while Mum and Gran sit together on the sofa with Humphrey between them. I hand Gran Humphrey's stocking, and Daniel and I sit on the rug by the fire to watch him open it.

Gran dips her hand in, pulls out the first parcel, and holds it out to Humphrey, who stares at it thoughtfully.

'He may need a little help,' I say.

She unwraps it and hands him a large rubber bone. He snatches it from her and sinks his teeth into it. It makes a loud squeaking noise, and he drops it at once.

'It takes a bit of getting used to,' I reassure him. 'Why don't you see what else you have?'

Five minutes later, there's a small pile of gifts in front of him. As well as the bone, Santa has brought him a teddy bear with triple reinforced seams, a bag of treats, a warm blanket, a large rubber ball, and some fur-lined boots.

'You're a lucky dog,' Gran tells him, but he's too busy with his treats to respond.

'I should put the turkey on,' says Mum. 'I saw it defrosting last night. It looked big enough for the entire village.'

'I should go,' says Daniel. 'I had no intention of gate-crashing your Christmas meal. Marcus's parents don't live too far away, and they've invited me to join them if I don't have any other plans.'

'Don't bother arguing,' I advise him. 'You'll be staying for Christmas dinner if Mum has to lock the doors to prevent you from leaving. You've already told me you can't say no to the Hollis women. My advice is to give in gracefully and do as you're told.'

'I wouldn't dream of locking the door,' says Mum. 'But we'd love it if you would stay. Isn't that right, Lucy?'

'It wouldn't be the worst thing,' I say, and Daniel laughs.

'I'm keen to hear more about this cookie club,' says Dad.

Daniel turns to me. 'Would you like to tell them or shall I?'

I smile at Gran. 'I think this is your story, don't you?'

Mum and Dad listen while Gran tells them the history of the cookie club and brings them up to date with the goings on this year.

'I'm sorry I didn't tell you all this before,' she says to Mum. 'I've been regretting that for a while now.'

Mum slips an arm around her and gives her a hug. 'I can see why you didn't. I was a horrible teenager. I didn't value what I had here until I'd lost it. And why shouldn't you have something of your own? From what you've told me, it sounds like a pretty special club.'

'Not that special,' says Daniel. 'They made me a temporary member.'

'If you're still around next year, we'll consider making it permanent,' says Gran. 'Lucy too.'

'Are you coming down from London next December?' Mum asks me. 'How lovely.'

I hadn't meant to talk to her about my future until later, but the opportunity is too good to pass up.

'I won't be in London next year,' I say. 'I've given in my notice. I emailed Caroline yesterday and told her. I may have to go back and work out my notice, but I suspect she'll be only too happy to get rid of me.'

Mum opens her mouth to speak, and I hurry on. 'I've hated every minute I've spent there. I tried to make it work, but it isn't for me. I've decided to do what I've always wanted to do and set up for myself, translating novels into German. I've registered with a couple of sites, and I'm going to give it a chance. I know you and Dad were keen me to spread my wings, but I don't want to do it like this.'

I take a deep breath and turn to Gran. 'I was wondering whether I might stay with you for a while? I'd pay rent, of course. But it struck me this could be the perfect solution to both our problems. I'll need somewhere to live while I try to make things work with my career, and you'll need someone to help look after you and Humphrey while you recover.'

Gran's face lights up. 'Oh, Lucy. That would be lovely.'

'I think it's a fantastic idea,' says Dad.

'You do?' I ask.

'Of course, we do,' says Mum. 'I had no idea you hated your job so much. This would be perfect for you.'

'Even though it means living in Honeywell?'

'What's wrong with Honeywell?' she asks.

'I thought you'd see it as a backward step. I'll be returning to the place you were so desperate to leave.'

'But that was me,' she says. 'I never wanted you to follow my dreams. I wanted you to find your own and follow those. And if that turns out to be here in Honeywell, that's wonderful.'

'I'm glad that's sorted,' says Dad. 'And now I want to hear more about this drone company. Did Lucy say something about you using them to deliver parcels, Daniel?'

'Not so much deliver them as hurl them from a great height,' I say. 'We're lucky I'm not lying in hospital at this very moment suffering from a severe concussion.'

'We haven't perfected our delivery system yet,' admits Daniel. 'That's why I didn't attempt to deliver you a cup of a coffee or a bottle of wine.'

'I thought at first it might be some kind of bomb,' I tell him. 'Cunningly disguised as a Christmas gift.'

'It was more like a peace treaty,' he says. 'Although it wasn't one I was sure you'd accept.'

'At least you dropped the parcel in the front garden. For one terrible moment, it seemed as though you planned to drop it onto the roof, and I'd have to risk life and limb climbing up to retrieve it.'

'It's an intriguing idea,' says Dad. 'Not the part about you scrambling over the roof in the snow. But the idea of replacing Santa with drones. It would give the reindeer a well-deserved rest.'

'That's very true,' says Daniel. 'In a way, you could say Santa was the first prototype drone delivery system. It shouldn't be a surprise. He originated from Germany, and they've always been at the cutting edge of technology.'

'When I first saw it hovering over the back garden, I thought it was a Christmas Eagle,' I tell him.

'Is there such a thing?' asks Mum.

'Humphrey would like to think so.'

'I've brought him something too,' says Daniel, reaching into his pocket and producing a small parcel. 'I'm afraid I don't have anything for the rest of you. I didn't expect to get any further than the garden gate this morning. But I'm excellent at washing up, so that can be my gift to you all.'

'Don't be ridiculous,' says Mum. 'We're delighted you're able to be here with us today.'

'Are you about to tell him his presence is present enough?' I say. 'Please don't. It's bad for his ego. What did you get for Humphrey, Daniel?'

He hands the parcel to me, and I pull out an envelope containing a large sticker saying *Beware of the fierce guard dog!*

'It's for your front door,' he explains. 'To stop unwanted people knocking and upsetting him.'

'That's very thoughtful of you,' says Gran. 'Humphrey will appreciate that.'

'If that doesn't do the trick,' he says, 'I've found an online store selling doorbells that make a loud growling sound whenever someone presses them. Humphrey will never be bothered by visitors again.'

'I must make a start on the meal,' says Mum. 'Lucy, would you and Daniel like to give me a hand?'

'We should drink a toast first,' says Gran. 'It's been a while since we've had three generations of the Hollis women together in the same room. That's surely something to celebrate. There's a bottle of sherry and some glasses on that shelf.'

Daniel fills five glasses, and I hand them around.

'What are we drinking to?' asks Dad.

'You being here today,' I say, smiling affectionately at him.

'And to Lucy moving to Honeywell,' says Gran.

'And to Daniel's almost successful package delivery business,' I add. 'And to Mum and Gran for teaching me how to follow my dreams.'

'Such a lot of things to drink to,' says Daniel. 'I hope I'm up to the task.'

He slips his arm around me, and I rest my head on his shoulder.

'#TakeTwo #WorthTheWait,' he murmurs into my ear.

'There's one more thing we should drink to,' says Dad.

'Are you sure?' I ask. 'We don't want to run out of sherry.'

'We can't miss out on this toast,' he says, raising his glass and smiling around at us. 'To the Honeywell Christmas Cookie Club. May it never run short of ingredients!'

Thank you for reading!

Join my mailing list to be the first to be notified about my upcoming books.

rosemarywhittaker.com/signup

The Sugarloaf Bakery Series

Available now in paperback and Kindle ebook

A Year Away

Available now in paperback and Kindle ebook

Printed in Dunstable, United Kingdom

65817528R00281